*About women who have
lived too long alone—
and men who have stayed
too long at war . . .*

Destiny's Women

Willo Davis Roberts

FAWCETT POPULAR LIBRARY • NEW YORK

DESTINY'S WOMEN

Published by Fawcett Popular Library, a unit of CBS Publications,
the Consumer Publishing Division of CBS Inc.

Copyright © 1980 by Willo Davis Roberts
All Rights Reserved

ISBN: 0-445-04531-0

Printed in the United States of America

First Fawcett Popular Library printing: March 1980

10 9 8 7 6 5 4 3 2 1

Prologue

Red Georgia dust rose in puffs around his horse's hooves as Patrick Ryan rode toward home. He was tired and hungry and his leg ached where he'd taken a Yankee bayonet three weeks earlier.

His place wasn't much by Southern standards, only forty acres, but the land was his, and the need to see it again, to stand on his own fields, was strong. The gelding, too, realized where they were, for the horse nickered and quickened the pace of its own accord, and Ryan spoke softly.

"Me, too, boy. Me, too."

Yet when they topped the ridge and his own small brick and clapboard house appeared, Patrick Ryan cast only a glance at it. He reined in briefly, looking down the slope in another direction toward the stand of live oaks that lined the white shell drive—shells brought all the way from Savannah—at the big house.

Mallows.

Something Ryan could not have put into words twisted in his gut. Mallows, with its white pillars and broad piazza and what looked like the same small black boy tending sheep to clip the lawn. From here the house looked the same as it always had in the old days, when it had been painted a gleam-

5

ing white every other year and had seemed a palace to a scrawny sharecropper's son.

His blue eyes shifted to his own chimney, to the faint thread of smoke indicating that someone waited for him. And then he returned his gaze to the big house, to Mallows, his mind made up. He kneed the horse, and plunged down the slope toward the twin rows of live oaks, turning his back on those who waited. He'd stop at Mallows first.

The original house at Mallows had been built by Ellen Mallow Stanton's great-grandfather for his bride in 1752. In graceful Georgian style, it was not the largest house in Georgia, nor even in Tattnall County, but it was well known for its pleasing proportions, and the decorative plaster work on the main floor was said to be the finest south of Virginia. That house had burned to the ground in 1838 and was replaced with a considerably larger Greek Revival structure with a grand row of Corinthian columns rising from its curved piazza.

The plantation of Mallows was Ellen Stanton's life. She loved it with a passion far beyond anything she had ever felt for her husband. In fact, she felt far more affection for Roger now that he was dead than she had while he was living, although no one except Roger's mother suspected that.

The second house at Mallows was built of native Georgia woods. Locally quarried marble columns soared sixty feet to the overhanging roof from the level of the piazza that encircled three sides of the house. There were four slaves who did nothing but tend the lawns and flowers that surrounded it, during the years when Ellen was growing up.

The ground floor was entered either at the main front door which faced west or from French doors at the north or south sides, the front one opening into a spacious foyer, the side ones into broad halls that intersected. There was also a door at the back that led onto a shaded brick terrace, and one from the winter kitchen.

The rooms were generously proportioned, with high ceilings that helped to keep them cool during the long summers. Double drawing rooms that could be opened into one another for entertaining on a large scale were to the right of the foyer, while a study, a library, and the huge formal dining room occupied the opposite half of the front section. Behind these rooms were the winter kitchen, the smaller dining area

6

where the family ate when they were alone, and an office where the affairs of the plantation were carried out.

A wide, magnificently constructed stairway rose from the center of the foyer, branching at the landing to form two arms that attained the second floor. There were seven bedrooms and a sitting room there, and another narrow stairway rose to two tiny rooms kept for house servants. A broader stairway from the same level led to the ballroom on the top floor, a room where two hundred people had often assembled for dances and weddings, in the days when such things were still of primary importance.

Ellen's childhood could not have been happier. There was plenty of money to maintain Mallows in the style intended by its builder. There were houseparties and balls that often brought neighbors from as far away as Savannah and sometimes even from Atlanta and Augusta.

Ellen's four brothers were all older than she; she was cosseted, petted, spoiled, yet, for all that, remained a sweet-natured child. Her brother Harry had once teased her that she had no reason for ill temper, since she was never thwarted.

She loved Mallows. She loved the old live oak trees, which spread their dark branches as much as fifty feet to each side of the thick trunks, along which an agile child could run almost as fast as if she were on the ground. She was the only one of the family of five children who had never broken a bone in falling from one of the oaks; the temptation was strong to scurry along the upper branches as well as the lower ones, sometimes with disastrous results. She, too, had taken her share of tumbles; these never discouraged her from further climbing. The trees continued to enchant her, as they had enchanted all the children who came before her.

She loved walking with her mother through the slave quarters, dispensing advice and medications and kind words. She enjoyed sitting before her father when he rode out to see to his fields, where the blacks worked in the cotton and the corn, and she loved hearing their melodic voices lifted in song.

Ellen knew every tree, every rock along the bank of the creek that separated Mallows from the adjoining plantation. She had played there with her brothers, wading in the cool water on hot summer days, helping to pole a raft across the clear brown stream.

7

She loved Mallows. She had no desire ever to live anywhere else, although Harry made it clear that he intended, as the oldest, to take over the estate eventually.

"You'll have to leave when you marry, silly," he told her when she was ten.

"Then I'll never marry," Ellen said softly, and disregarded his laughter.

Harry died when she was twelve, the victim of an untamed horse. She was the one who found him, who cradled his bloody head in the lap of her pink dimity while one of the servants ran for help. He lived for three days, and during those days Ellen talked to him, softly and prayerfully, about the plantation they both loved, thinking *that*, if anything, would bring him out of his comatose state.

It didn't, of course. She missed him, though he was, after all, ten years older and they had not been really close. It was not until she was fifteen, the year that the three remaining brothers drowned in a foolish, tragic escapade on the Ohoopee River, that the tenor of her life changed.

Ellen's parents grieved to the point that they seemed to forget they had one remaining child. They were no longer interested in entertaining, and gradually old friends stopped issuing invitations. Dorothy Mallow withdrew not only from the world but from her family, refusing to share her sorrow even with her husband.

Ellen took over the running of the great house, and then moved into her mother's place in the slave quarters as well.

There were nearly four hundred blacks at Mallows in those days. Edwin Mallow was a good and a just master. He provided adequate quarters for his people, and they were well fed and clothed. He took an interest in their families, and saw to it that none were neglected. Before her sixteenth birthday, Ellen was attending to the sick and the birthings of the babies.

The first time she was nearly sick herself. The sight of a sweating, writhing black woman, straining to bring forth her child, made her sway dizzily in the heat of the cabin. If it hadn't been for the other Negro women, the mother would have had no assistance at all.

But Ellen stayed, conquered her nausea, and watched. When the pale-skinned squalling infant was wrapped and handed to her, she felt a responsive maternal tug within her.

She stayed, and she learned what to do. She was always

8

soft-spoken and kind, and the women loved her. She herself entertained no thoughts of marriage. To begin with, she had no intention of ever leaving her beloved Mallows. And on top of that, her initiation into the mysteries of birth—and her speculations about how this "miracle" came about—aroused no interest, only aversion.

Even when Roger Stanton came to the plantation to purchase slaves for his own holdings, Ellen was not sufficiently drawn to him to think of him in terms of marriage. He was the only young man who had visited Mallows in two years, and he found both the girl and the plantation much to his liking. His persistent wooing would have failed—indeed, she did not at first realize that she was being wooed—had not her father finally rallied from his depression.

"He's a good man, Ellen. And you need a husband."

"I have Mallows," Ellen answered serenely.

"But you can't run Mallows alone. I won't be here forever, the boys are gone—" For a moment he was lost in bitter thoughts. "You need a man to run it. Roger Stanton could do that."

In the end, that was the argument that won her over, although Roger never knew it. She needed a man to run Mallows.

They were married before she was seventeen, after a two-month courtship which consisted of four visits on his part, and none too soon. Edwin Mallow died less than six months later, leaving Roger in charge.

Roger had taken his responsibility seriously, and Mallows prospered. If he had cause for disappointment in his wife's performance in bed, no one knew of it. Ellen dutifully produced five children, two of whom died in infancy. She tried to teach the remaining three to love Mallows as she loved it.

Book I

One

Valerie Stanton was tall and slim, with her mother's coloring: rich auburn hair and hazel eyes. She might possibly be thought a beauty, if there were any males about to consider the matter. If she'd been born ten years earlier, if it hadn't been for this damnable war, she'd have had her balls and houseparties and entertainments, and by now she'd be a respectable matron instead of a nineteen-year-old spinster.

Suddenly she leaned forward, peering more closely into her mirror. Was that a freckle, on her left cheek? No. She sighed, relieved. It was only a flyspeck on the glass. She had what Georgians called a "peaches and cream" complexion, and it had a tendency to freckle if she allowed the sun to reach it.

She turned away from the mirror with a wry smile. What a silly thing to worry about, a freckle when there was no one to see her, anyway. And men did sometimes marry girls who had freckles, her cousin Sally Ann had hundreds of them, and she'd married a very nice boy, hadn't she?

The smile faded away. Yes, Ward was a nice boy, and he'd gone away to war the same as her own brother Evan, and her father . . .

Almost a year had passed, yet the pain of it still caught her in moments such as this, moments when the memories came back sharp and clear, of Roger Stanton, smiling and handsome and indulgent of his wife and his daughters.

Valerie swallowed hard. Would there be any men left when the war was over? Her father had died on the banks of the aptly named Chickamauga, the Cherokee word for "river of death," where his blood had mingled with that of more than thirty thousand Confederate and Union soldiers, last September. Patrick Ryan had brought his body back, slung over a mule as if it were a sack of flour rather than the remains of her beloved father.

No. She brought herself sharply under control. She would not think about it, she wouldn't go downstairs with reddened eyes and trembling lips for the others to see. Not that anyone would ask what was the matter, of course. It was only that when one of them gave way, it made it harder for the others, the five women living together in this great house that had once been full of people.

She looked down at her faded blue dress. It was starched and ironed, fresh and clean; that was all one could say about it. No hoops, no ruffles or furbelows, simple faded blue percale. The sort of thing the servants used to wear. Would there ever be pretty things again? Skirts eight yards around, real lace, materials that clung to a bosom and swished just off the floor?

She closed the door to her room behind her and walked toward the head of the stairs. From the second-floor sitting room she could hear her two grandmothers in one of their customary exchanges, and she smiled.

They were in frequent abrasive contact, though neither of them ever seemed to wear the other down. Grandma Dolly was as soft and seemingly pliant as a rag doll, yet as sturdy, too, for she did not break. Grandma Lacy reminded Valerie of a cocky little banty rooster, with her halo of white hair and her snapping dark eyes and her darting pecks at the other woman.

Lacy's voice carried to her now, so vigorous that a stranger would never have guessed she was seventy-two years old.

"Why in heaven's name don't you open up a few windows and get a breeze through here? It's stifling!"

"At my age," Dolly's softer tones stated, "one chills easily. I cannot bear drafts."

"Your age is precisely eight years younger than mine," Lacy said with asperity. "And you don't see me wrapping up in shawls and closing windows to keep out the drafts in weather like this!"

Valerie paused, one hand on the balustrade, to hear Dolly's response to that.

"You have always been blessed with excellent health, Lacy. While my constitution has always been delicate."

That, apparently, was more than Lacy could bear. She made a snorting noise and emerged into the upper hallway under full steam. She was a tiny person, a wisp of a thing in her black silk, yet she'd been known to back off strong men by her very presence.

Her dark eyes raked over her granddaughter.

"Eavesdropping again?"

"It's hard not to," Valerie told her mildly, "when voices are raised."

"I didn't want to put you to the trouble of pressing your ear to the door," Lacy said. "Delicate constitution! That woman has the constitution of a horse, and she'll outlive the lot of us! The only reason she became 'delicate' was to avoid going to bed with Edward Mallow." She considered briefly as they started down the stairs together. "Come to think of it, maybe she had a point, at that. However, since he's been dead for years, you'd think she could rejoin the human race."

Valerie laughed. "I always understood that Grandpa Mallow was very nice."

"Oh, he was. If you like that sort. Ineffectual, indecisive. Now your Grandfather Stanton, there was a *man*."

"Yes. I liked him, too." A wistful note came into Valerie's voice. "I wonder if I'll ever find anyone the like of either of them, or of Papa. Will there be anyone left for me and Julie, when this damned war is over?"

Lacy was the only one she could have spoken to in that way. The swearing came more easily to her these days, although she was careful not to speak it aloud in front of her mother or Grandma Dolly. The Stantons might live in genteel poverty, they might worry themselves sick over where Evan was and how he was, they might wake at night in a cold sweat wondering what would happen if the damned Yankees won this cursed war, but ladies didn't swear. Not at Mallows, they didn't.

Lacy now cast her a thoughtful glance. "With your looks, there'll be someone. For you and Julie both. You're stunning, even in the rags you have to wear these days. Someday we'll

15

be able to go back to my house in Savannah, and there will be silks and velvets and laces again, and you'll see. You'll see."

They walked down the stairs together, side by side, the tall slim girl and the white-haired old lady, each of them remembering.

Three years earlier Lacy Stanton had rented out her home in Savannah, the place she loved best in all the world, because it became impractical for an old woman to stay alone. She had come to Mallows, to live with her son and his family.

"You'll all take care of each other while I'm away," Roger Stanton had told her.

He'd made it sound as if she did them a favor, to come. Lacy appreciated that, that he hadn't made her feel an unwanted guest, because she knew she'd had little choice. There simply was no money any longer, not enough to keep up a big house. No money for servants—not even to keep them fed. There had been four house servants, besides the old man who'd cared for the horses, and she'd had to sell them all. They had wept, and Lacy had wept; she'd had them for years and was as devoted to them as they were to her.

The lovely old house just off Reynolds Square, in which Lacy had lived since the day of her marriage to Charles Stanton, was rented out. Her own beautiful furnishings, the heavy velvet and damask draperies and the fine imported rugs, were rolled with tobacco in them to keep out the insects, and stored in the attics. She had taken her cherrywood desk and her own favorite rocker and her massive four-poster bed with her to Mallows; everything else had had to be left behind for strangers. Sometimes she ached with the longing to return to Savannah.

Valerie remembered the house, too, although with different memories. She had visited it as a small child, the handsome gray brick with its elaborate wrought-iron balconies and railings and shutters. There was a walled garden in the back, with bricked walks and a fish pond where goldfish gleamed brightly in the sun, a garden shaded by flowering crape myrtle and redbud, mimosa and dogwood, and one towering magnolia with its glossy leaves and creamy fragrant blossoms. Through the wrought-iron gates that opened onto Bryan Street Valerie and her little sister could watch the traffic go by, the carriages with handsomely dressed ladies and gentlemen, the matrons strolling with their children, faces shaded by parasols that matched their gowns.

Valerie had especially enjoyed walking the few blocks with her Grandpa Stanton to his office on Factor's Row; it was exciting to observe the activity of busy clerks and hear the men talking business—the price of cotton was the important thing—to look out over the river and the docks where the great bales were stacked and loaded for shipment to factories in the north. The riverboats brought things in, too, and Grandpa Stanton was always lavish with his gifts, including everything from a dress length of shot silk to bananas and oranges and pineapples.

To children brought up on a remote plantation, however much they might love their home, Savannah was a fairyland city. In addition to being spoiled by doting grandparents, they enjoyed walking the bricked streets, playing in the numerous small squares where moss-draped oaks shaded walks and benches, and flowers bloomed in profusion a good part of the year. They loved dressing up and attending Christ Church on Johnson Square, so they could watch the elegant ladies and gentlemen and hear the fiery sermons and the organ music.

One of Valerie's favorite places, although Julie found it macabre, was the Colonial Park Cemetery facing Ogelthorpe Avenue, where the soldiers from the Revolutionary War were buried, along with some of Valerie's own ancestors. The cemetery was laid out much like a park, with walkways and carefully tended grassy expanses; the tombs themselves were like small, round-topped houses, some of them containing three or more members of the same family. Julie shuddered and ran away, but Valerie would walk about, reading the inscriptions and imagining the people who had died nearly a hundred years earlier.

She did the same thing strolling the streets close to the Stanton house, looking at the residences of the well-to-do cotton merchants and bankers and lawyers. If the servant with whom she walked did not move quickly to intercept her with a sharp reprimand, Valerie would press her face against the iron bars that kept her from the private gardens, admiring other people's wisteria and azaleas and oleanders, perhaps reaching small fingers between the bars to pluck a blossom from a Cherokee rose or a camellia to put into her hair. The servant would scowl at her and speak crossly. Yet since the flower was already torn from its bush there was little point in dropping it into the street; she was usually allowed to keep it.

Savannah was a fragrant city as well as a beautiful one, alive with blooming trees and shrubs from early spring until late fall, and it was cooler than at Mallows, too. On the hottest days they could go down into the cellar, where ice shipped from the north was covered in sawdust and housed in the tabby foundations; every spring the compartment was filled and sealed; the oyster shell, lime, and sand cement was thick enough to keep in the cold until the ice was gone. They were allowed to chip off bits of ice to suck on, and sometimes the servants were instructed to make ice cream—delicious confection!—and there was plenty of ice to cool lemonade or limeade.

The ice was one of the things Valerie missed most now, sometimes even more than she missed the pretty clothes. Ice, on a hot summer day, clinking delicately in tall frosty glasses.

As they reached the foot of the stairs, Pansy came running through the doorway from their right. She nearly collided with Miss Lacy, who dodged her with a snort of mingled annoyance and tolerance and went on toward the back of the house.

Pansy was fourteen and nearly as black as the kettle her mother used to cook in. Her voice was as thin as her flat-chested body, rising now on a note of excitement.

"They's somebody comin' up the road!" she announced. "A horseman. He's wearin' gray, and he's ridin' right this way, Miss Val!"

Gray? A horseman?

Hope leapt in Valerie's breast. Could it be Evan?

They hadn't heard anything of her brother since the disastrous battle at Resaca, except that he'd survived it. *Oh, please God, let it be Evan!*

Aaron, tall and moving silently, materialized out of one of the shadowy rooms to answer the door. There was no bell or knocker at Mallows; there had never been a need for them, not with servants constantly watching for the approach of any visitor.

Aaron was much lighter-skinned than Pansy, although he was obviously of negroid descent. He wore the same shabby uniform he had worn for the last four of his twenty-five years, and he'd grown some; the sleeves were short enough to

18

show powerful wrists and the material strained across his shoulders.

He gave Pansy a quelling look. It was his job, not hers, to greet visitors.

Valerie, however, could not wait for the newcomer to climb the steps before Aaron threw open the front door. She ran to it herself, then stopped, eyes stinging in disappointment.

Two

It was not Evan.

She knew at once, looking out across the veranda toward the approaching figure, that it was not her brother. This man was bigger, both taller and wider through the chest and shoulders.

He rode straight up the drive between the double row of live oaks where no breeze stirred the draped Spanish moss that hung from the spreading limbs.

Valerie was conscious of the perspiration on her own body, the limp fabric of the old gown that hadn't so much as a hoop to redeem it, of her hair that was carelessly pinned in a knot instead of being elegantly coiffed.

She squinted in an effort to make out more about the approaching rider, then recognized him at once when he pulled off his hat and held it in his hand as he rode slowly toward her.

Patrick Ryan. Disappointment made her throat ache. Nobody else in the world had hair that color, flaming red where the sun hit it. Well, maybe he had news, anyway. He might have seen or heard something of Evan.

Valerie waited, watching him come, red hair gleaming like a helmet. She'd known Patrick Ryan all her life, and for the last six years before the war he'd been overseer at Mallows. Her father had thought a lot of Patrick, and trusted him with heavy responsibilities from the time he was little more than a boy.

Patrick had his own house, out of sight beyond the trees, on his own small acreage. That had been part of his demand of Roger Stanton in return for his services: that he be paid not just his three hundred dollars a month, but in land as well. Ellen had at first strongly resisted this, any whittling away at the edge of Mallows; she had eventually given in because Ryan had been adamant about the matter, and Roger wanted Ryan.

It was only a little land, of small value compared with Mallows. Still, Ryan had come a long way from the ragged boy Valerie remembered from her own childhood.

Her cousin, Sally Ann, thought Patrick Ryan incredibly attractive. Val herself couldn't see it. He was too big, too tough, with a chiseled tanned face that seldom revealed the thoughts behind it. And he didn't waste any of his precious words making compliments to ladies, not even the daughters of his employer. In fact, he'd always treated both the Stanton girls as if they were nuisances. Although he'd never been openly disrespectful, Valerie guessed that if he spoke his thoughts, she'd probably have had occasion to slap his face.

Anyone would think twice about slapping Patrick Ryan, however. Man or woman, they'd probably be slapped back.

He didn't bother to lift a hand in greeting, nor to speak until he'd dismounted and handed over the reins to the little boy herding the sheep that kept the lawn clipped.

His voice was as deep and intimidating as she remembered it. He looked lean and tired, but the vigor was still there in his words.

"Morning, Miss Valerie."

"Good morning, Mr. Ryan." Her mouth was dry and there was a tremor in her lower limbs. It had been Ryan who brought the news of her father's death after the bloody battle at Chickamauga; she prayed that he did not come again with such news. There was no body draped across a following mule this time. She blotted that image out of her mind and spoke steadily. "Have you news?"

He came up the shallow marble steps, between two of the eight white pillars that supported the roof far overhead. His mouth twisted in a wry amusement.

"There was a time when a caller at Mallows was invited in for a cooling drink before he was interrogated," he said.

Valerie felt the blood suffusing her neck and face. Damn the man, anyway! Why did he always contrive to make her feel gauche or ill-bred? Interrogated, indeed! Not for the first time, she wondered at her father's wisdom in seeing that he learned to read and write, as Ryan certainly could not have done without Roger Stanton's aid. The man was insolent, arrogant, in a way he had not been as a boy.

"Of course. Come in," she said, stepping backward so that he could enter the coolness of the vast entry hall. Aaron appeared behind her to relieve Ryan of his hat. "What would you prefer, sir? We can offer you coffee that's no more than half chicory, tea, or some of Papa's fine brandy." That last, intended as a small jibe, didn't ruffle him.

"The coffee will be fine. If it's less than one hundred per cent chicory, it'll be better than what I've been getting." The smile he had not produced for Valerie touched his mouth as he released his hat into Aaron's hand. "How are you, Aaron?"

"Fine, Mr. Ryan," Aaron said softly, respectfully.

Ryan was too close to her. Valerie fought the impulse to step back quickly, not away from the smell of horse and sweat and tobacco but from the size of him, the maleness; he made her uncomfortable, though she couldn't have said exactly why. It wasn't the odors, which were common enough to any man; something about Ryan himself always put her on the defensive.

"Mornin', Mr. Ryan," Pansy said. Her white teeth gleamed in the black face, genuinely welcoming.

"Morning, Pansy. You're looking spritely. How's your grandma?"

"Oh, she's tolerable, Mr. Ryan." Pansy's smile widened. "I'll tell her you asked after her, sir."

He always remembered them all by name, every slave on the place, even when there were over three hundred of them. There weren't that many to keep track of any more, especially among the men, since most of them had run off to join the Union Army.

Ryan followed Valerie toward the back of the house, moving an exact three paces behind her, into the breakfast room. They still called it that, although it had long served them as dining room, as well. When they were a household of only

22

five women, it seemed silly to be served around a table that could accommodate twenty people even before they put the leaves in it.

Lacy had preceded her, and both she and Ellen stood to greet the newcomer. The sunlight filtering through the leaves of the sycamores behind the house gave a pleasant greenish cast to the room. Valerie was suddenly conscious that the panoramic wallpaper—handpainted in France before the war—was coming loose in a few places, and that the woodwork needed repainting—and it was painful that anyone, even Patrick Ryan, should see the house in this condition.

Ellen Stanton experienced much the same sensations as her daughter: hope, and fear. She could not force a smile, not until she knew with what news he came; she did stretch out a hand to him in a way she would never have done while he was overseer here.

She did not have Valerie's stunning beauty, but she did have a quieter, sweeter beauty of her own. Her thick auburn hair showed a few threads of gray, and her hands revealed the fact that she now did chores she would never have done in the old days. She remained the gracious hostess of Mallows, however.

She gestured toward the table where places had been set for four.

"Mr. Ryan! Please, join us. Pansy, bring Mr. Ryan a plate."

"Only coffee, thank you." Patrick eased onto one of the chairs around the oval table. "Miss Lacy," he acknowledged, nodding at the older woman, who waited, blue-veined hands unconsciously curled around a fragile china cup, for whatever was to come.

"Mr. Ryan." The dread was there in Lacy's dark eyes, mute, appealing.

"I've brought you some letters." Ryan pulled the crumpled missives from inside his coat and slid them across the polished surface of the table toward Ellen. "And I won't keep you in suspense. I haven't seen Evan, nor had any news of him. I'm sorry."

There was a small exhalation of breath around the table. No good news, but no bad news, either; it might have been worse.

Ellen plucked at the worn fabric of Ryan's sleeve. "You've been wounded yourself, Mr. Ryan."

He looked down at the bloodstains Valerie had not noticed. "Only a scratch." He didn't mention the bayonet wound. "John Douglas wasn't as lucky. He was killed at Vicksburg in early July, in case you hadn't heard. I rode with Paul Amhurst, who's stopped off at Cedars to tell them."

The silence was palpable, the women's hands stilled on their cups. The report of a death was hardly unusual any more, yet they never got used to it. Valerie felt a twinge of something that combined regret and relief: regret about their neighbor's son, relief that the sorrow was not their own.

Cedars, the Douglas plantation, was only six miles away. The Douglases had been their closest neighbors and friends all Valerie's life. John was considerably older, and she had always found him to be rather annoyingly arrogant. Yet his sisters were as close as any friends she had.

Ellen bit her lip. "Poor Frances. First Tom, and now John. I suppose I'd better ride over and see her."

"That's one reason I stopped," Patrick said. He thanked Pansy for the steaming cup she brought, sipping at it before he explained. "It isn't safe for you to travel away from home any more." His blue eyes fastened upon Valerie with almost physical impact. "Especially for Miss Valerie and Miss Julie. Stay at home, and prepare to bar your doors. That won't keep out a major band of marauders, or stop them from molesting you, but maybe it will discourage the stragglers. And if the Union forces come, why, my best advice is to open your door, greet them as guests, and try to stay together for mutual protection."

Valerie wasn't the only one who went pale. Ellen's lips trembled as she leaned toward him to put her question. "You think they'll come here? To Mallows?"

He looked at her with a sad compassion, this woman who was a relic from another era, whose way of life was gone forever, whether she knew it or not. He'd always liked Miss Ellen; she'd been kind to him when he was a boy, the son of a sharecropper who couldn't always keep his family fed. He remembered wishing that his own mother had smelled the way she did, and had such soft, pretty hands.

"They'll come here, ma'am. Our own men are deserting, heading for home, foraging as they go. And the way things are going it won't be long before the Yankees get here. Sherman's determined to crush Georgia under his heel, and he's in a fair way to doing it. Don't let his heavy losses at Kennesaw Mountain fool you. He outnumbers us probably two to one, and he's cutting off our supply lines. He tears up the railroads faster than we can fix them. President Davis has sent General Hood out to take Johnston's place after we were defeated at Dalton and Resaca and New Hope Church, but how the hell—pardon, ma'am—we're going to hold out against Sherman is beyond me, no matter who's directing us."

He paused to drink and Valerie locked her hands in her lap to keep them from shaking. Distress made her voice unsteady. "But we saw a copy of the Atlanta *Intelligencer*, printed in early July. They spoke quite confidently, saying that the Yankee forces would disappear from Atlanta before the end of August." She looked toward her mother in an appeal for verification of this.

Ryan shook his head. "Blind optimism, I'm afraid. The man's going to take Atlanta. One way or another. And once he does, he'll come on here, on his way to Savannah. Maybe the main body of the army will pass north of us, but it'll be a miracle if some of them don't show up here, even if it's only to scavenge for food. He has to feed sixty thousand men, and his own supply trains can't keep up with him. If you've any foodstuffs that can be hidden, do it. They'll be like locusts, same as they've been other places; they won't leave you a crumb if they know where it is."

Valerie sat in a state of shock. True, her father had died in September of 1863, almost a year ago. There had been various reports of other deaths among friends and relatives. But until now Georgia, her own part of Georgia, had remained relatively quiet. Except for minor thefts, probably by runaway slaves, and the occasional small band of Confederate soldiers who had been fed from time to time, the people at Mallows had seen none of the actual participants in the war.

Ellen's lips were bloodless except where she had bitten through the soft flesh. "What will they do to us, the Yankees, if they come?"

Ryan sipped again at the chicory-coffee. "It's not *if* they come, I'm afraid. It's *when*. As I say, they'll be looking for food. They'll take anything else they see that they want, as well. I assume you've already hidden the silver, any cash you have, that sort of thing."

He glanced over at Lacy, whose eyes showed more acceptance than did either Ellen's or Valerie's. "I'd remove my jewelry, Miss Lacy, and hide it in a secure place. I've heard of

25

them cutting off fingers to get a ring like that, with a diamond in it."

Lacy's voice was whisper-quiet. "I haven't taken this ring off my finger in nearly fifty years." She didn't add that it was the only thing of value she had left in the world.

"Now's the time to do it. For the sake of both the ring and the finger. Besides the things they can steal," he went on, his tone roughened as he turned his attention to Valerie, "they may be interested in women. They've been away from home a long time, most of them."

The heat warmed her face once more. "Surely they won't bother decent women!"

His rusty eyebrows rose fractionally as he appraised her. Judging by his expression, he found her lacking, at least mentally. "There aren't enough of the other kind to go around, I'm afraid. If you'll heed my advice, you'll stay out of their way. Out of their sight, as far as it's possible. And stay together. They're less likely to attack a group of women than a lone female."

"Are you saying they'll probably rape us?"

All heads turned toward the door to face Julie Stanton, who had come up behind Ryan, unheard.

There was a strong facial resemblance between Julie and Valerie; they would have been recognized anywhere as sisters. In coloring, however, they were completely different. Where Val had inherited her mother's rich auburn hair and greenish-brown eyes, Julie was Roger Stanton's daughter. Her hair was nearly black and curled naturally; her eyes were wide and brown and thick-lashed, gazing now at Patrick Ryan with quiet apprehension.

"I hope not, Miss Julie. Only it's happened before, and it could happen again. Being prepared may make the difference."

There was another small silence as each of them digested the unpalatable idea; perhaps there was even some resentment against Ryan, for forcing them to think of such a thing.

Julie was wearing pink, a faded pink and white checked gingham, and she had tied her hair back with a matching ribbon. Patrick's mouth stretched in an unwilling smile as he looked at her.

"Anyone looking at you would know you're a lady of quality, Miss Julie. Just be careful. I'll be around for a few days, if there's anything I can do. Then I'll see if I can help delay

Sherman by an hour or two." There was bitterness in his words as he pushed back his chair and stood up. "Thank you for the coffee, Miss Ellen."

Valerie heard her own voice, sounding too sharp. "If the situation is so desperate, sir, may I ask you why you're here instead of with General Hood?"

He gave her a measuring look. "Even in times of war, a man may request leave between the battles to attend to matters at home, ma'am. My grandmother's very ill and my sister sent word to come if I could. I'm on my way there now."

They thanked him profusely, everyone except Valerie, who stood apart as he left. Why did he always put her on the defensive, or make her feel like attacking him? He never smiled at her the way he had just done at Julie, as if he liked her. Well, that was all right. She didn't particularly like him, either. There was too much of the physical animal about him.

Ellen walked him to the door. The others sat silently awaiting her return. Julie poured herself a cup of coffee, not drinking it. Pansy hovered, the whites of her eyes showing that she, too, had been frightened by Mr. Ryan's words.

Yankees, here at Mallows. It was what they had dreaded—thought they had become accustomed to dreading—for such a long time. And now, according to Ryan, it was going to happen. The fear was a fresh, new thing in each of them, tearing as a woman is torn during childbirth.

Valerie thought her turbulent emotions remained her own, until her mother returned to the breakfast room. Ellen looked tired and upset. She picked up her cup, long gone cold, and drained it, grimacing. "I wonder if we'll even enjoy real coffee again? Well, it was nice of him to drop by and tell us what he knew, wasn't it? Why do you always antagonize him, Valerie?"

Her words were quiet, as they usually were, yet they showed the strain that Ellen was under. "We're a household of women, with your father gone and Evan God knows where. We're not paying Mr. Ryan any more, and he owes us nothing, really, except good will. I'd like to keep that. No matter what happens in this dreadful war, we're going to need the help of some man to keep Mallows going. Someone stronger than I am, to keep the field hands in line, to bring production back up to where it should be."

"Evan will be back," Julie said quickly. "Won't he? Evan will run Mallows, with or without an overseer."

"Yes, of course. He'll need help, though, and I hope that Patrick Ryan will return to the duties he always did so well. I don't need to tell you what Mallows means to me, how much I want it to return to the way it was, all the years I was growing up and then living here with your father."

No, they didn't need to be told. There was an uncomfortable silence, with Ellen reluctant to discuss further disaster, yet unwillingly impressed by Ryan's words.

"If they do come . . . the Yankees . . . we must none of us do anything that would . . . incite them to violence. They must not harm Mallows."

The murmur of agreement rippled around the table. And then Valerie reached out to touch the letters Ryan had brought. Not Evan's handwriting, she could tell at once. 'Who are they from?" she asked.

The mail system in the South had deteriorated to the point where getting a letter was a major event; newspapers, which they read so avidly during the early days of the war, were equally hard to come upon, at least for those who lived away from the railroad lines and the towns.

Ellen unfolded the first of the papers with fingers not quite steady. "This one's from Betty Abernathy." Her eyes skimmed the written words from her old friend; the others watched, interpreting the tightening of her mouth correctly as more bad news. When she had finished, she pushed the page toward her mother-in-law, then made a partial explanation to her daughters.

"She wrote this on her way back to Macon. She's been at her mother's in Savannah for a month, and she drove past Miss Lacy's house there. She was . . . distressed, by the condition of the house and gardens." She always referred to her mother-in-law as *Miss Lacy*, and even after more than twenty-five years she could not think or speak of her in less than a formal way. "Prices are impossible. She had to pay six dollars for a new pair of spectacles; her sight has grown so poor that she cannot read at all without them now. Gingham is five dollars a yard; each of the servants has had one new outfit, and she doesn't know how she'll manage new ones for winter, at those rates. Beef is three dollars a pound in Savannah."

They sat, silent; rising prices they were used to. Cash money had long since become a thing of the past; Mallows was as self-sufficient as it was possible to be, and the things
28

like coffee and sugar and manufactured goods they had enjoyed in the old days were simply things they now did without.

Lacy looked at the written pages before her, only the twitch at the corner of her mouth revealing the pain it caused her to know that her beloved house was neglected. "Butter at ten dollars a pound! Who can afford such an absurdity as that!"

They all looked guiltily at the bowl of chilled butter in the middle of the table, ready to melt on Mamie's hot biscuits or cornbread. They still had one cow producing enough to provide them with butter at least for breakfast most of the time.

Good God, Valerie thought. *Ten dollars a pound!*

Ellen was already perusing the second letter, and her small involuntary murmur brought all attention back to her.

Her voice was thin. "It's from Grace." Grace was her cousin, who lived in Atlanta. "Listen to this: 'Dear ones all—I pray that things are better at Mallows than they are here. The Yankees are making it nearly impossible to get any supplies in, and for the first time, we are actually hungry. We try to make a garden in our little back yard, but our own neighbors steal from it as soon as there is anything big enough to be worth cooking! I am sorely concerned for Sally Ann; her confinement is only a few months off, and she looks so poorly. Part of it is the heat, of course, but more, I'm afraid, is due to a diet of rice and beans, most of the time without even a bit of fat pork to flavor it. And now it appears that that horrid man may move into the very city. I despair of what will happen to us if he does! Dear Ellen, could you see it in your heart to take in two more strays? I know your own supplies must be strained, but they cannot possibly be as short as ours here! My own health continues poorly, and I do not know how I shall manage when Sally Ann takes to her bed. Can you imagine, caring for an infant at my age? Kelsey, wretched ingrate that she was, simply took my second-best dress and disappeared during the night, won away by the false promises of those Yankee dogs. So we are left with only one servant, old Hattie, who is more trouble than she's worth since her knees are too stiff to allow her to stand for more than a few hours at a time. The way she carries on, you would think she was the first person ever to have rheumatism. Dear Ellen, I know that getting a message

29

back to me may be quite impossible. So I must rely on your kind generosity and pray that you will take us in in our hour of need, can we but find a way to reach you. The train would be far more comfortable for poor Sally Ann, but they are completely unreliable now. General Sherman is determined that the trains shall bring us no supplies. So if we can find a ride in someone's wagon, we will try to reach you. Pray for us, as we do for you. Love, Grace.' "

This time the silence around the table was a stricken one.

Julie was the first to find her tongue, trying for a ray of hope. "Perhaps we'd all be safer, if there were more of us here when . . . when *they* come."

"Three more mouths to feed." Ellen stared, unseeing, at the page beneath her hand. "Dear God! They'll bring Hattie, no doubt, and she'll be of no use whatever. And I doubt the Yankees will treat seven females any more gently than they would five."

"At least no one's robbing our garden, so far," Lacy pointed out, setting aside her personal griefs in the face of a coming ordeal. "Our diet may be boring, but we haven't yet gone hungry."

Uncharacteristically, Ellen spoke with a caustic pessimism. "That may very well change, if Mr. Ryan is correct about the Yankees." It was several minutes before she managed to gather her own inner resources and to say in a more normal tone, "I suppose I'd better go and see Frances Douglas. Poor soul, both her sons gone now, as well as her husband. There'll be no one to return to Cedars. Would anyone care to go with me?"

Valerie checked the instinctive refusal that sprang to her lips. The last thing she wanted today was to sit during a long condolence call. "They won't expect all of us," she pointed out, "and Julie's much better at that sort of thing than I am. If Aunt Grace and Sally Ann are coming, maybe I should open up rooms for them, and see about linens. Are there any decent sheets left?"

"If not, they'll have to make do with patched ones, the same as the rest of us." Ellen rubbed absently at her temple, as if it ached. "How foolish that sounds! As if we haven't all been making do, for years now. Well, all right, open up the back bedrooms. I don't suppose anyone's dusted in there for ages, and there's no telling when they'll show up."

She glanced down at the letter to verify the date. "This was written almost three weeks ago. If they found a ride at once, they could arrive anytime. Will you come with me, then, Julie?"

Julie, who had sat silent through this exchange, sighed softly. She had no more liking for condolence calls than her sister. It was always Valerie who thought up the first excuse for not doing something she didn't want to do. And Julie *did* feel sorry for the Douglases, and guilty because she couldn't help being glad it wasn't Evan whose death had been reported. "Yes, I'll go," she said.

They had forgotten about breakfast. Only Lacy remained at the table when Pansy timidly poked her head around the edge of the doorway to inquire who would have mush.

Lacy stopped twisting the ring on her finger. "Yes, I'll have mush," she agreed. Mush, she thought without enthusiasm. No doubt they should be grateful there was plenty of *that;* Ellen had kept the Negroes tilling the corn patch, even if there weren't enough of them left to do much of anything about raising cotton.

For a moment she remembered the breakfasts she had had for years in the lovely old house on Abercorn Street in Savannah: slices of tangy, smoke-cured ham, eggs fresh from the country, chunks of fresh pineapple, or sliced peaches, or perhaps strawberries dipped in sugar. And real coffee, all she wanted of it.

When the girl brought the mush, Lacy ate it, reflecting that it put no strain upon one's teeth, at any rate. She listened to the sounds of departure and she, too, was glad that the condolence call was someone else's responsibility, not her own.

Three

Ellen found it difficult to credit the reality of war, even after Mr. Ryan's words, when there was no sign of it. No sound of cannons, no marching soldiers. Only the fields where the remaining hands listlessly chopped cotton, slowly, more slowly than they had ever done when there was an overseer keeping track of them. It was such a small field of cotton she wondered if it was worth the effort it took to try to keep the hands moving.

She stood for a few minutes at the open window, listening to the familiar voices, then turned to her mother, who sat knitting a stocking as she rocked.

"I'm going to ride over to see Frances Douglas, now," Ellen said. "It's the least I can do. A husband, a grandchild, and now the second of her two sons. Life is unbearably cruel these days."

Dolly Mallow was a small, well-rounded woman; she had a softness in contrast to Lacy's wiry strength, softness in her flesh and in her voice and in an almost complete lack of physical energy. She looked up with her subdued request.

"Hand me those scissors, will you? There, on the table. I thought Mr. Ryan said it wasn't safe to leave the house."

"I don't think he meant *now*, today. The Yankees are still

32

the other side of Atlanta, or were the last he knew. There wouldn't be any stragglers within two hundred miles of us. Poor Frances! If Mr. Ryan is right and the war is nearly at an end, how bitter a dose to lose a son *now!*"

"Give her my condolences," Dolly said, snipping at a bit of yarn, then going on with her knitting. In truth, she was wrapped in her own little world that included only the members of her own household. The death of her husband had not shaken her as deeply as the loss of three sons, all at one time; Edwin's passing was scarcely noticed, so insulated had she been in the cocoon of misery she had wrapped about herself.

She did not care to be strongly involved with her daughter or grandchildren, although she had lived with them all their lives. Involvement, to Dolly Mallow, meant pain. If not immediate pain, then eventual pain, to be contemplated with both foresight (and thereby avoided) and hindsight that would last for years.

Had she been thrust into closer contact with Lacy Stanton (closer than living in the same house, as close as maintaining constant day-long, daily contact in a confined area) she might well have been jolted out of that protective shell, for Lacy was one person who had the power to disturb, to unsettle. Lacy's personality was an abrasive one, as far as Dolly was concerned. Dolly preferred never to be in the same room with her, which was one reason she took most of her meals in the second-floor sitting room rather than with the family, even though Lacy had pointed out that this made it harder on the shrinking staff of servants.

"Oh," she said now, "when you go downstairs, dear, will you ask Mamie to send me up some tea? With lemon, please, if there is any lemon."

"Certainly, Mother." Dolly had taken her tea with lemon for fifty years, yet she never failed to specify it. "We'll be gone for the rest of the day. If there's anything else you'll want, it would help if you could think of it now. There's no one to run up and down stairs to wait on you. Pansy will bring your lunch, of course."

"If you're gone, Lallie won't be busy, will she? Lallie might look in on me," Dolly suggested.

Lallie, who had been Ellen's personal maid for eight years, resisted Dolly's effort to encroach upon her time. And, truly,

33

since neither of the girls had personal maids any more, Lallie did not have any time to spare, in serving the three of them.

"Lallie will be busy, I'm afraid. She'll have to help Valerie see to rooms for Grace and Sally Ann."

The older woman rested her knitting in her lap. "Poor things. I suppose it is terrible in Atlanta, as they say. Yet it won't be convenient to have them here, either."

"No," Ellen agreed. "It will mean three more people to feed." Her mouth flattened, thinking of it.

"I won't have to give up my eggs, will I?" Dolly looked up with faded, anxious eyes.

"The way things are going, there won't be eggs much longer. If the Yankees come they'll take chickens and all, more than likely. I'm leaving now, Mother. If you need something, ring for Pansy, but don't bring the girl upstairs unless you have to; she has a great many other things to do."

For a long time after her daughter had gone, Dolly Mallow sat with pursed lips, reflecting on the cruelty inflicted upon her. Nobody cared about her. Nobody at all. She could sit up here and die, and no one would ever know, she thought, and wondered what was taking Mamie so long with her tea.

Patrick Ryan saw them go, riding up over the ridge that was visible from his own front porch.

He swore, not bothering to lower his voice, and his sister Ruth came to stand behind him in the open doorway. She was a younger, plumper version of Patrick, toned down in coloring. Her hair was more brown than red, her eyes a less arresting blue. She had been very pretty as a girl; now, at nearly thirty, she was still an attractive woman except that she looked worn and tired.

"What's the matter? Oh, the Stantons. I suppose they're paying a condolence call on Mrs. Douglas."

"Stupid damned women. I told them to stay home, that women aren't safe moving around."

"They probably thought you meant from the Yankees. They're not an immediate danger, are they?"

"Who the hell knows? Sherman's two hundred miles away, or was the last I knew, but there's no telling about his men. Do you think he isn't sending out advance scouts, maybe even disguised in Confederate uniforms?"

34

Ruth Ryan Gerald moistened her lips. "They'd be shot for spies, surely."

"If they're caught, yes. We've all run the risk, for more than three years, of being shot. You get used to it. You can't run scared to death forever. After a while it gets easier to take the little additional risks, if they're for something important. Or even if they aren't so important."

He stood, one booted foot resting on the white painted railing of the porch, staring after the women as their buggy vanished over the top of the grassy ridge, between the trees. "Why do I continue to feel responsible for the women of Mallows? I don't work for them any more. I don't owe them anything."

Ruth's full lips quirked in a smile. "It's the kind of man you are, Patrick Ryan, and thank God for you." The smile vanished. "Gram's dying, isn't she, Pat?"

His hesitation was scarcely perceptible. "Yes. I doubt if there's anything a doctor could do for her even if we had one. And less that I can do. I can't wait here with you until it happens, Ruthie. My leg's pretty well healed, and I'll have to go back."

"I know," Ruth agreed softly. "I'll stay with her."

"It might be months, though my guess is it's more likely to be only days. Either way, you'll have to handle it alone."

She watched him staring broodingly out over the familiar landscape, and wondered how much of his reluctance to return to duty was due to concern for the old woman in the house behind them, and how much was for those women in the big house over at Mallows.

The house at Cedars, the home of Frances Douglas and her surviving children, was a graciously proportioned one of red brick, with white shutters and white pillars. From a distance it was imposing and impressive; as the buggy rolled to a stop before the front steps, however, it was clear to even the casual eye that little or no maintenance had been done for some time. Weeds grew between the stones of the path, and the paint was flaking on both posts and shutters.

The old man who opened the front door (also peeling) to the Stanton females had been weeping. His black face was controlled, however, and he greeted them as hospitably as ever.

"Miss Ellen! And Missy Julie! How good of you to come!

35

Miss Frances be most pleased to see you. She taken bad, poor soul."

Ellen pulled off her gloves, looking up into the dimness of the entry hall. "Is she upstairs, Timothy?"

"Aye, that she is, Miss Ellen. Done took to her bed, she has, ever since she got the news about Mr. John. You want to go on up, she be glad to see a friend." Timothy wiped a tear from the corner of his eye, unself-consciously.

"Thank you, Timothy. Are the girls up there with her?"

"No, ma'am. Miss Henriette and Miss Charlotte, they out on the side porch. You want me to tell 'em you here, Miss Julie?"

"No, I'll find them." Julie was only too glad that she wouldn't have to face Mrs. Douglas in her grief. Seeing John's sisters would be painful enough.

She had been in the house many times, and she needed no one to show her the way. The Douglas sisters had heard the buggy and turned expectant faces. It was Henriette who stood up and came to Julie for a quick embrace.

The Douglas girls were both slim, pretty brunettes; Henriette was seventeen, the same age as Julie, and Charlotte was a year older. Both had been weeping, also, but were not hysterical as Julie had half-feared they might be. God knew they had something to be hysterical about, with a crumbling house and a plantation with an inadequate number of Negroes to work the fields, and no man ever coming home from the war to take care of them again.

"I've sent for some lemonade," Henriette said. "No ice to put in it, I'm afraid, but the water's fresh from the well. Take off your hat, Julie, and sit down."

Her eyes were red and swollen, yet she managed a smile. Julie complied, grateful that the visit would not be as bad as she had feared.

It was not until late in the afternoon that Ellen emerged from her friend's chamber for a consultation with her daughter. Julie was summoned into the drawing room where they had once had such gay parties, and where Tom Douglas had given Julie her first kiss. Julie had never fancied herself in love with Tom, yet she had felt a special sadness upon hearing of his death, a sadness that brought a renewed tightness to her throat in view of this latest tragedy.

She refused to dwell on the memories in this handsome, elegant room. "Are you ready to go, Mama?"

Ellen pressed her fingertips to her temple, unaware that she was beginning to make a habit of the gesture. "She begs me not to go, and it's clear she needs someone here besides the girls. I brought some laudanum with me, but I'm afraid to leave it here for fear she'll take it all at once. She's in such a state she feels there is nothing left worth living for."

"There's Henriette, and Charlotte, and Cedars," Julie pointed out. "Are you going to stay with her tonight, then?"

"I think I'd better. She's hardly rational right now. Do you want to stay, too? I can send Rudy on back to tell them, at home."

"Rudy has to ride home anyway, so I might as well go with him." In truth, Julie had no wish to remain in this house of mourning. Though torn by guilt, she felt an urgent need to escape. "If we leave right away, we'll be home for supper. Shall I send Rudy back for you tomorrow afternoon?"

This was agreed upon, and the two took leave of one another. Neither of them seriously considered Patrick Ryan's warning as a notice of immediate danger. They had ridden over peacefully enough, fording the creek and making their way through the quiet countryside, along the red dirt road that connected Mallows and Cedars, as they had done so many times over the years. Broad-brimmed hats shaded their faces from the sun; the pine trees gave off their familiar pleasant scent, and the birds were silent in the heat of the day. There was nothing alarming about the ride. They saw no one, heard nothing out of the ordinary.

It was the same, only a bit cooler, when Julie set off on the return journey with Rudy handling the reins. Nobody knew exactly how old Rudy was. Probably over eighty; he had retired from the fields several years ago and now enjoyed the special privilege of driving the Stanton ladies on their infrequent excursions away from Mallows.

The sun was dropping toward the trees to the west as they approached the creek again. The horse whinnied, and Rudy turned a grizzled head to speak to his passenger.

"He lookin' for a drink, Miss Julie. Maybe I better let him have a few swallows, and we go slower the rest o' the way. It sure hot today."

Julie wished the creek was cleaner; she could have used a drink herself. The lemonade had long since evaporated out of her system. "All right, stop a minute. Mind he doesn't get too much, though."

Old Rudy chuckled. "I been handlin' horses since before you was born, Miss Julie. I ain't never let one eat or drink too much, at the wrong time."

"We don't want to dally for long. I've no wish to be out after dark, even if the Yankees are still a long way off." It suddenly occurred to her that an unarmed old man would be of little use to her if they were accosted. She would never have given it any thought if it hadn't been for Patrick Ryan's words earlier in the day.

"Plenty time," Rudy said, and gave the horse its head. The animal nickered and headed for the stand of willows along the bank of the small, sluggish stream. The trailing branches were low enough to prevent them from seeing, until they had ridden to the water's edge, that there was someone there ahead of them.

Four men, in ragged Confederate uniforms, were surprised in the act of refreshing themselves. Two of them, one with a bandaged leg, were cooling their feet in the water. A third knelt by a small, nearly smokeless fire, tending a pair of skinned rabbits on a stick. The fourth turned an unshaven, gap-toothed smile in her direction.

"Why, hello, there! Just in time for supper, miss!"

Julie knew, even before he reached for the bridle, that they were in trouble.

Four

Valerie and Lallie had personally cleaned two bedrooms in preparation for the expected guests, with Pansy doing the running up and down stairs to spare their legs. They had dusted and swept and made up the beds with clean sheets and made sure the netting that hung from the canopies wasn't so rotten it would let in mosquitoes.

"In the old days," Val observed when they had finished, "we'd have had flowers, too, three or four vases of them."

"Nobody has time for arrangin' flowers any more," Lallie responded, giving a final punch to a pillow with an embroidered starched white case turned so as to hide a mended spot. "It's all we can do to put enough to eat on the table, and that's more important." She hesitated, then asked a question that might have been considered insolent. "These cousins, they bringin' anything to eat, Miss Val?"

"Not likely. That's the reason they're coming here, besides to get out of Atlanta before Sherman comes into it. They think we country cousins have more to eat than they do. Well, I guess that will do it, Lallie. You'd better see if Mamie needs any help in the kitchen now."

Lallie was twenty-two years old, and for ten of these years she had worked here in the big house. If it was a choice between hoeing cotton and waiting on Miss Ellen, she preferred the latter. Yet when she looked into a mirror, at her own light-colored skin and fine features, Lallie knew that she was far more white than black, and knew as well that if she could get away to the North she might very well pass as white. Life would be infinitely easier, if her black blood could be completely forgotten.

She, too, had heard Mr. Ryan's news this morning, and her reaction to it was different from that of the others around her. She, too, was afraid of the Yankees. Yet there was a thread of excitement running through the fear, for if the rumors were true, the Yankees would free the slaves. *Free* meant she would no longer belong to Miss Ellen, that she would never again have to do what a white woman said, never have to worry that a white master would force her into his bed, or himself into hers.

Lallie had been very glad when Mr. Roger went away to war; at almost nineteen Lallie had developed a lushly rounded figure and she did not like the way Mr. Roger looked at her when she was helping Miss Ellen with her hair or her clothes. Lallie had learned quickly to watch her step, to avoid being where Mr. Roger might catch her alone. She knew that Miss Ellen would never tolerate either seduction or mistreatment of her maid. But there were lots of things that went on at Mallows that Miss Ellen didn't hear about, at least not until after they'd happened, and what good would that do anybody?

They had worked together all day, the young mistress and the slave. They were both tired. Only now Lallie had to go down to the kitchen and help in the preparation of the evening meal, while Miss Val would refresh herself with a sponge bath, change her dress, and sit with her feet up until suppertime.

No resentment of this was revealed on Lallie's pretty countenance. And Valerie, having grown up in a household where she was expected to do nothing for herself, gave no thought to Lallie when the other girl went on down the stairs.

Valerie did, indeed, sponge herself in the tepid water from her night table, and put on a freshly ironed green voile. Green was her color, her father had always said; it brightened her eyes and set off the reddish highlights in her hair.

The heat remained in the house, although Pansy had

opened the louvered shutters that had been closed during the heat of the day; it was growing cooler outside and there was a faint breeze. It was still too warm to appreciate her hair touching her neck. Valerie caught it up with a ribbon that matched her dress and experimented, lifting the hair high on her head, then settling for a knot on top as the easiest. She felt a fleeting regret that Amanda had run off with a lover; Amanda had been very clever at dressing Valerie's hair and arranging it in precise curls at each side of her face. She had been Valerie's maid since both were twelve years old.

Valerie did indeed intend to sit with her feet up until suppertime. To her surprise she found both grandmothers in the library that now served as an informal sitting room on the ground floor, for they seldom sought one another's company. It was at once apparent that Dolly had come down because she missed the attention she usually commanded; with Ellen gone, and no one else caring to check on her oftener than every few hours, Dolly had decided that even Lacy Stanton was better than blank walls.

"When is your mother coming home?" Dolly asked. "It's getting rather late."

"Soon, I'm sure." Valerie hesitated over a bowl of ripe peaches, selecting the largest one and preparing for the juice of it with a large napkin from the stack provided beside the bowl. She bit into it, enjoying its sweetness. "Ummm, these are good. Anyone else want one?"

They did not. Dolly had brought her knitting; Lacy was engrossed in a book. Valerie chose a romantic novel in the hope of losing herself in it, and curled up on the red damask-covered sofa.

It was not until Mamie, the cook, appeared in the doorway that they all looked up, torn out of their private worlds. "How'm I s'posed to know what to do about supper?" she demanded crossly, "when people don't come home like they say they goin' to?"

Valerie licked at a finger sticky with peach juice. "Maybe Mrs. Douglas is taking it very badly, and Mama decided to stay overnight."

"And don't send no message?" Mamie asked scornfully. Mamie was Pansy's mother, a woman of massive proportions and skin so dark that her teeth and the whites of her eyes provided startling contrast to it. She had been ruling over the

Stanton kitchens for more years than she could remember, a privileged position, and she was not awed by any member of the family. "Your mama never do that. She knows we all worry if she don't come home for supper. Maybe you oughtta ride out and see is they comin', Miss Val."

Valerie cleaned another finger of the sticky juice. "They'll be here before long. Go ahead and fix supper. What are we having?"

Mamie regarded her as if Valerie were personally responsible for the lack of supplies. "What you think we havin', oysters and lobsters? We havin' yams and salad greens, does that lazy Pansy get out there and pick some for me." For a moment her dark glance slid sideways to rest upon her offspring, hovering in the doorway. "If them Yankees is comin', the way Mr. Ryan says, maybe we might just as well go ahead and eat the rest of the ham, afore *they* gets it. Ain't no way you can bury a ham, the way you do the silver. Might as well eat it."

"All right. Cook us some ham, too. Don't worry, Mama and Julie will be here when you're ready to put it on the table."

The afternoon waned, however, and there was no sign of Ellen and Julie. She wouldn't have thought anything of it, Valerie reflected, if it hadn't been for Patrick Ryan's warning. Damn the man, why did he always have to be the bearer of bad tidings? Less than a year ago he'd brought Roger Stanton's body home . . .

The familiar stab of agony was still surprisingly sharp; Valerie wrenched her thoughts away from that memory and put aside her book after Mamie had gone.

"Maybe she's right. Maybe I should walk to the top of the ridge and see if they're coming," she said reluctantly.

Her maternal grandmother looked up from one of the interminable socks she was always knitting. "Put on your hat, dear. You freckle so badly."

"The sun will have dropped behind the trees before I get to the top of the hill," Valerie observed.

"With skin like yours, it's wiser not to take chances. Men don't like freckles," Dolly said smoothly. "Hand me that ball of yarn, will you, dear? It's rolled beyond my reach."

With a sigh, Valerie retrieved the yarn and handed it over. "All right. I'll wear a hat. Although if there are any men

42

around to notice my freckles, or lack of them, they're staying well hidden."

"The war cannot go on forever. When things are back to normal, you'll see."

"Will things ever be back to normal?" Valerie asked. Her gaze met Lacy's, and she saw her own concerns mirrored in her grandmother's face. Dolly, however, remained complacent.

"Of course. There have always been wars, and things always eventually return to normal."

"I pray to God you're right," Valerie said, wishing Patrick Ryan and his bad news had not spoiled what otherwise might have been a reasonably enjoyable day.

Her naturally good spirits rose, however, when she started out across the lawn. It was summer. There were bees buzzing around the roses that had once been so carefully tended and now straggled in wild profusion up the latticework on the side porch, and though supper would be simple, there would be plenty of it. Valerie was young, and healthy, and possessed of enough imagination to make up an episode of gaiety to compensate for the lack of actual events at the present time. When the war was over, and Mallows was restored to its former elegance, they would have a ball, and people would come from all over the county and beyond. She would have a new gown, a peach-colored silk—she could not wear the pinks that were so becoming to Julie, but peach color, yes, that would be striking with her hair and eyes. Eight or nine yards of material, just for the skirt, it would take, and she would have it cut daringly low on her bosom, and she would borrow Grandma Lacy's pearls—no, came the dampening recollection, those had been sold last winter. Well, by the time the dream came true, no doubt there would be other jewels. Diamonds, why not diamonds? As long as she was dreaming, she might as well have whatever she liked.

Valerie grinned, making her way along the path that skirted the nearest of the fields. Dolly had been right about the sun; it had not yet dropped behind the trees and Valerie adjusted the brim of her hat so as to keep the warmth off her face.

"Evenin', Miss Val!" A chorus of voices greeted her as the workers paused, leaning on their hoes, to watch her pass. Their garments were sweat-soaked and stained, their black bodies sagging with fatigue at the end of their day, yet they all had smiles for her.

Except one. Valerie met his gaze, and the boy's did not drop, nor did he smile.

"Good evening, Chad." She would force him to speak, she thought, amused.

But he did not speak. He only nodded, barely escaping insolence, and even that was not missing from his attitude.

She managed to keep her own smile intact long enough to pass by him; even after he was out of sight, his image remained in her memory. Tall, thin, but with a broadening set of shoulders, Chad left a disturbing impression.

He was only fourteen, yet nearly a man in size and strength. A few months ago, though his expression might have been guarded, he would not have dared behave as he had today, refusing to verbally acknowledge Valerie's greeting. No doubt he had heard the news that Ryan brought, and though he hadn't run off to join the Yankees like so many of the young males, it seemed likely that he welcomed their approach. Mr. Lincoln had said the Negroes would be free, and Chad was waiting for the Federal troops to come. Had it not been for a deformed leg, crippled in an accident when he was a small child, he probably would have gone with the others, months ago.

A small ripple of uneasiness ran through her as Valerie trudged on along the dusty road toward the ridge. What would happen if all the Negroes left? If the Yankees did set them "free" and there was no one to work the fields? Poor disillusioned people, she thought, a touch of compassion blending with her uneasiness. Would they know what to do with their "freedom" when it was attained? Did the Yankees have any idea how simple these people were, how totally unequipped to care for themselves?

She left the red clay road and started up the grassy bank of the ridge, a shorter route to the top where she could view the road to Cedars, seeing when it was too late to change her course that Patrick Ryan was ahead of her. He'd taken off his coat and draped it over a stump, and was kneeling a distance away, doing something she couldn't make out.

She had no desire to speak to Patrick Ryan, but he'd looked up and seen her, now, was rising to his feet, and she wouldn't give him the satisfaction of knowing he'd discomfited her by changing her direction. Valerie continued to climb.

She was halfway up the ridge when she heard her sister scream.

Five

She had no doubt at all that it was Julie. She'd heard Julie scream before, when she was small and Evan had put a toad or a snake in her bed or her dresser drawer, and more recently when the chandelier in the breakfast room had torn loose from its moorings and dropped just short of the middle of one of Mamie's bowls of excellent stew.

Valerie ran without being aware that she ran, lifting her long skirts in both hands, lungs laboring with the exertion of the uphill climb. Ryan reached the top before she did, and she would have run past him had he not put out a hand to stop her.

Together they stared at the tableau below them. The road was a red ribbon stretching off across the small valley and into the woods beyond, the road toward Cedars. The buggy, however, was not on the road; Rudy, in a panic, had taken to the fields in an attempt to escape from their pursuers, and the vehicle had just lost a wheel that, even as they watched, rolled a few more yards and toppled flat into the grass.

Julie had been catapulted forward and clung to the back of the seat where the old slave had been sitting; he, in turn, had been spilled onto the ground and was making a valiant effort to control the horse.

For a moment, pressing her hand to a stitch in her side, Valerie watched the horsemen galloping after the still-moving buggy without comprehension. There were four men, the trailing pair mounted double on the same horse, men in Confederate uniforms that, for a moment, reassured her.

And then, as the first rider reached the disabled conveyance and leaped down to calm the frightened horse, the second rider dismounted and hauled Julie roughly upright. They heard old Rudy bellow a protest, and heard as well the sickening sound as the first man turned and hit the old man with the stock of his rifle.

Rudy folded forward into a heap, and Julie screamed again.

Beside Valerie, Patrick Ryan swore, an epithet he would not normally have voiced in front of a woman.

Valerie choked out a bewildered cry. "But they're our own soldiers!"

"They're *men*," Ryan said. "Damn it to hell, I told you to stay at home!"

Under other circumstances, she would have resented intensely such a remark from the former overseer. Now, however, her concern was for her sister, for Julie struggled in the grasp of one of the soldiers even as the other two reached them, and involuntarily Valerie started down the other side of the ridge.

This time when Ryan grabbed her, his hand was hard and hurting. "Where the hell do you think you're going?"

"To help my sister, of course! If you were any sort of a man, you'd be down there already—"

She tried to pull away, and the fingers bit painfully into her flesh. "Shut up, and get down, before they see us! You want them to rape you, too?"

"My God, are you going to stand here and let them do it?" She opened her mouth to yell, although later she could not imagine what she had expected to accomplish by shouting at four armed men.

"Maybe you haven't noticed," Ryan said through his teeth. "They're all carrying guns, and I'm not. My pistol is with my coat, back there on the stump. Go and get it, and hurry!"

She could not move without tearing a piece out of her arm. She heard Julie cry out again, in pain and despair, and Valerie's own breath came harshly.

"And what will you be doing?"

"Starting down that hill." Dislike was strong in his face and his voice. "Now stop acting like the spoiled brat that you are and maybe we can keep them from seriously hurting her. Get me my gun and my coat and cover me. The holster's come apart, don't pick it up by that. If you have to shoot, you'd damned well better shoot straight—hit one of them, not me. And don't try to maim, shoot to kill."

When he let go of her, Valerie staggered back and almost fell.

"I'm starting down now, and if they don't see me before that, I'll yell when I'm halfway down the hill. You'd better be back up here with that pistol by then or we may all end up dead. Hurry up!"

He didn't wait to see if she intended to comply with his orders. He plunged off the top of the ridge, moving rapidly; Valerie had only time for a glance at the struggling figures below, and then, fighting terror, she ran.

Once she fell and for a moment she thought she'd broken her ankle, but when she stepped on it the pain was bearable, and she closed her hand over the jacket a moment later. The pistol was there, and she resisted the urge to cock it at once. Not until she reached the top of the ridge, she thought. *Don't panic, it won't help Julie to panic.*

The stitch in her side was a scalding pain and her chest ached with the effort of breathing as she hurried back up the slope.

She reached the top and fell to her knees just as Ryan shouted.

"Here, you, let the girl go!"

Oh, God. She was exhausted, trembling, yet she had to steady the pistol, to shoot if necessary. She was too tired to get up, the pain in her side and her chest made it almost impossible to think. She *had* to think, she had to cock the pistol.

Valerie lay sprawled on her stomach in the waving grass, smelling her own rank perspiration, feeling the faint breeze blowing the tendrils of hair about her face. She blinked to clear her vision and held the pistol in both hands, arms outstretched, remembering what her brother had taught her. And then, what Ryan had said: *Shoot to kill.*

Julie lay in a limp heap beside the tilted buggy. Valerie could see only a mound of pink and white gingham from here, and the stillness of it made her mouth dry and quick-

48

ened her already pounding heart. Everything had happened so quickly. Surely they hadn't had time . . . ?

The men had all paused, lifting their heads in Ryan's direction. One of them knelt beside—over?—the pink mound. Another stood beside him, and the other two had been securing the horses.

The sun was a blazing orange ball just above the silhouetted cedars beyond the road. The light would soon be gone, but right now it hurt her eyes, as it must be hurting Patrick Ryan's.

"Get up, get on your horses and ride off, and that'll be the end of it," Ryan called now. He was still striding toward them, angling slightly to the left, and Valerie cursed under her breath. *Not that way, you fool, give me a clear shot—*

She squirmed, ignoring a stick that poked into her stomach, until Ryan was out of the line of fire. That one, she decided, the big one standing just beyond Julie's still form, was the leader. He'd be the one to shoot.

Sure enough, he was the one who responded to Ryan's command, only not before bending easily to scoop up his rifle.

"Who you to be givin' orders, mister? We got here first, so mind your own business."

Ryan barked out his name, rank, and division. It would undoubtedly have been more impressive if he'd worn his full uniform. The note of authority was there, however. A corner of Valerie's mind noted that he was a sergeant; she hadn't known that.

"Put down the gun," Ryan said, in the manner of one accustomed to being obeyed.

The obscene reply scarcely registered with the girl lying in the grass at the top of the ridge. She was going to have to shoot him, she thought, and willed her hands to be steady. Though she was a fair shot, she'd never fired at a man before.

"Convince him, Val," Ryan called, without turning his head.

The leader of the quartet laughed. "Been a long time since anybody bluffed me, mister—"

Valerie took a deep breath, exhaled, and squeezed the trigger.

She never knew whether her own tension threw off the shot, or whether she was simply incapable of shooting to kill.

The report deafened her, and she watched as if with someone else's eyes; the man staggered back, the rifle sliding from his hand as he was spun halfway around.

Ryan yelled a warning; Valerie had already seen the movement of the man nearest the horses and squeezed again. This time the target screamed and fell, thrashing, so that the tethered animals reared and screamed their own fear. The man flopped and lay still, the unfired rifle rendered harmless.

Valerie shifted position to bring her weapon into line against the third man, who stood motionless. Although she could not see that he had a gun, the only safe assumption was that he was armed.

"Raise your hands, both of you," Ryan directed, and ever so slowly both remaining men did so. And then, without turning his head, Ryan called, "Come on down, Val."

He had never before addressed her except as *Miss Valerie*. In spite of her shock, that registered. Valerie scrambled to her feet, hoping she wouldn't disgrace herself now by fainting; her laces were too tight for this sort of thing, and she felt unable to get enough air into her lungs.

She made her way down the slope, bits of grass clinging to both dress and hair. The stitch was still there in her side, though not as intensely painful as it had been a few minutes earlier.

Ryan was at the foot of the hill by this time, no more than a dozen yards from the second man she had shot. Valerie peered fearfully in that direction, fighting the queasiness that threatened to empty her stomach. Had she killed him?

She must have said the words aloud, for Patrick Ryan, turning to take the pistol from her limp hand, walked to prod the fallen soldier with one booted foot.

"Nice shot. He won't give anyone else any trouble."

The nausea rose, uncontrollable, and Valerie turned away, retching. When she faced him again, wiping at her mouth, she said, "I didn't really mean to kill him."

"Damned good thing you did," Ryan replied coolly. "He'd drawn a bead on me, and at that range he could hardly have missed. The other one's only wounded. See to Miss Julie."

The tremors that shook her were so strong she had to concentrate on keeping her footing. "What are you going to do?" she asked fearfully, for he still held the pistol in a businesslike manner. His casual dismissal of the dead man led her to expect that he might, with equal deliberation, shoot the two remaining ruffians.

"Get rid of this trash."

Her heart leaped, but it was at once obvious that he did not intend to shoot the others.

"Gather up your buddies, get on those horses, and go back to wherever you came from. You probably deserve to be shot as deserters, but I have too much on my mind right now to deal with that, and the goddamned war is going to be over before we could bring you to trial, anyway. With a little luck, maybe Sherman's men will find you." Ryan spat into the grass.

The survivors wasted no time in following orders. Ryan did not allow them to retrieve their rifles—as Valerie had assumed, there were four of them—and she heard the first one she'd shot groan when they hoisted him to the back of a horse. Not dead, then. He was bleeding badly, though, from a shoulder wound; the blood seeped down the sweating flank of his horse, and Valerie turned her head away.

She had to pass the old slave to reach her sister. Rudy lay as he had fallen, and she didn't pause to see if he was still breathing. Her thoughts were all for Julie, who had not moved or spoken.

The reason for this was apparent at once. A dark bruise spread over her jaw and cheek, where she'd been struck with something that had rendered her unconscious. Not dead, Valerie saw at once, for her sister's bosom rose and fell rhythmically under the pink and white gingham. There was a faint trickle of blood at one corner of her mouth, but otherwise there were no visible injuries.

The intent of her attackers, had there been any doubt about it, was as obvious as it could have been. The billowing skirts had been wadded up around the girl's waist, and her undergarments removed. Valerie hastily covered Julie's nakedness, feeling the heat of shame and anger. Not only the strangers but Patrick Ryan had seen Julie so exposed. For a moment she felt a fierce exultation that she'd killed one of them and wounded the other, and then her compassion for Julie washed over her in a wave that made it hard to hold back her tears.

"Julie?" She knelt beside her sister, touching her gently, bending close to speak to the familiar, quiet figure.

51

Julie didn't react in any way, and Valerie lifted a desperate face to Patrick Ryan. "She's unconscious!"

He stared for a few seconds more after the departing Confederate deserters, then came to kneel beside Julie. His big hand went out to touch the bruise, then on to explore the flaccid body in an expert sort of way. It occurred to Valerie that Ryan had had some practice in dealing with victims of violence.

"Maybe it's just as well," he said slowly. "Maybe she won't remember much of this. Old Rudy hasn't come around yet, either, but he's still breathing. Maybe we should have killed the other two bastards, too." This was said with a lack of passion that was more chilling than fury would have been. "Well, we'll have to get both of them back to Mallows. The buggy won't go anywhere, and one horse can't carry everybody. I'll stay here with them, and you go to the top of the ridge and get someone to help. Somebody should have heard the shots and be coming this way, anyhow."

That was not necessary, however, for the shots had, indeed, been heard. Though frightened half out of their wits, two of the fieldhands had crept cautiously up the far side of the ridge to ascertain what was happening. When Ryan yelled and gestured, they were quick to obey, and half an hour later the farm wagon bearing Julie and old Rudy jolted up to the front steps of Mallows.

For once both old ladies moved and spoke in accord, standing on the veranda, exclaiming softly as Patrick Ryan lifted Julie and carried her up the broad steps. Valerie hurried ahead, opening doors, leading the way to Julie's own room.

If carrying the girl was a strain, Ryan didn't reveal it, except that he seemed to favor his right leg. Valerie gave it no thought; she was desperate for Julie to wake up and tell them she was all right, and she was beginning to wonder if her mother was safely ensconced at Cedars for the night or if she, too, was a victim of this assault. True, there had been nothing belonging to Ellen in the buggy, which seemed to suggest that Ellen had not been there at all, yet the niggling worry remained.

Ryan strode up the wide stairs across the polished oak flooring to the door Valerie held open. He seemed overlarge and completely out of place in the feminine-oriented bed-chamber; he deposited his burden on the bed as Lallie and Valerie parted the netting for him.

"How long will she be like this?" Valerie asked hoarsely. "Why doesn't she wake up? Do you think she's more seriously injured than just being knocked out?"

"I don't think so, but I'm no doctor." Ryan straightened and stood for a moment looking down at her. "Might be a good idea to send someone for Miss Ellen; she's as good as a doctor would be. Give Chad a horse; nobody's likely to bother him, if there are any more stragglers in the neighborhood." His wide mouth went flat as he turned to face Valerie. "This wouldn't have happened if you'd all done what I told you, stayed home. It was stupid for Miss Julie to be riding around alone with only an old man for protection."

Warmth crept up Valerie's throat and flooded her face. She knew that what he said was true, although the decision had not been her own. Her anger rose to meet his, anyway.

"And you *weren't* stupid, of course, taking off your coat and leaving it and your pistol on a stump, so it wasn't handy when you needed it. One warning shot would probably have stopped them if you'd had the gun when we first saw them." Her remark was at least partially unfair. She knew he had put the weapon down because the holster had broken. Yet she was too angry and upset to care about being fair.

A muscle jerked in the tanned cheek. *"Touché,* ma'am. Two stupidities don't help Miss Julie or old Rudy, though, do they?"

With that he turned and stalked out of the room; she heard his boots on the stairs, quick, savage steps that conveyed his mood precisely.

It was not until the sounds had died away that Valerie realized she hadn't even thanked him. Regardless of what she'd said, she knew perfectly well that if Patrick Ryan hadn't been there, if he hadn't had a gun even if it was some distance away, Julie would have been raped and possibly even killed. And if she herself had run heedlessly down that slope, her own fate would have been the same.

Well, they could thank him later. The important thing now was Julie. Valerie bent over the bed, speaking softly, urgently. "Julie, do you hear me? Julie!"

When the girl on the bed stirred and moaned, Valerie sank onto the stool beside the bed, the strength gone from her own limbs as relief turned her bones to water.

Lallie stood beside her, tongue snaking over her lips. "We goin' to send for Miss Ellen, Miss Val?"

"I don't know." For just a moment Valerie rested her head against the edge of the bed. Maybe Patrick Ryan was used to this sort of thing and could take it in stride; she wasn't, and couldn't. "I can't decide what to do right now. Is someone looking after Rudy?"

"The men took him to his own cabin." Lallie hesitated. "Was she raped, Miss Val?"

"No. But it was a near thing." For a moment the memory of Julie's exposed body sent a wave of sickness through her again. "I wish we had some ice. Her face and jaw are swelling, where they hit her. Maybe a cold cloth would help some. Have Pansy draw some fresh water from the well, Lallie. I think she's coming around. We'll decide when she does whether or not to send Chad for Mama."

Lallie murmured compliance and withdrew from the room, and Valerie bent again over her sister, speaking persuasively until Julie opened her eyes.

Six

The soft involuntary protest made it clear that Julie knew at once what had happened to her. She put up a hand to her face, flinched, and turned her dark eyes toward Valerie.

"It's all right," Val said quickly. "We heard you, and Mr. Ryan made them stop."

Julie winced again, rising onto one elbow, looking down at her disheveled clothing. Valerie had replaced her undergarments before the men arrived with the wagon, but Julie knew they'd been removed. Her small face was hot and miserable.

"Oh, God, it was terrible! We tried to outrun them, but the wheel came off the buggy, and they dragged me out and said such dreadful things, they put their hands on me and . . ."

"You don't have to tell me." Valerie covered her sister's hand with her own, patting at her awkwardly. "Try not to think about it."

It was as if the younger girl had not heard. "The big one was missing some of his teeth, and he smelled awful! They held me down on the ground and they . . ."

"Julie, don't. You're all right, you're safely home. Do you want me to send Chad over to Cedars to bring Mama back tonight?"

A shudder ran through Julie's body. "No. No, don't send

for anyone. Val, I want a bath. I want to throw these clothes away and never see them again. Tell Pansy to bring the tub so I can bathe . . ."

Relieved to be talking about bathing rather than the attack, Valerie rose quickly and reached for the pull rope that would summon one of the house servants. She needed a bath herself, and would have one as soon as Julie was finished. A glimpse of herself in the full-length mirror confirmed the fact that she looked almost as bad as if it had been she who was attacked, with bits of debris still clinging to her skirts, her hair a complete mess, and sweat stains under her arms.

Good heavens! Patrick Ryan had seen her this way, and those other men . . . That was a mistake, to think about the other men. She had killed one, actually killed one, and wounded another.

She looked at her hands, as if she expected there would be blood upon them.

"Yes, ma'am?" Pansy, panting, met her at the top of the stairs. "I brung the cold water, miss."

"I'll take it. Fetch the tub, and then bring up hot water for a bath. I'll want one, too, as soon as Miss Julie has finished."

Pansy's face registered dismay. When she just stood there, Valerie spoke sharply. "Go on, get the tub and some hot water!"

"It'll take me a while, Miss Val, to haul all that water by myself."

"Well, get Lallie to help you."

"Lallie went out to see 'bout old Rudy." There was a sullen note in the girl's voice, a note that would never have been tolerated in a Mallows servant only a year ago. Valerie checked the reprimand that would ordinarily have resulted from such insubordination, too distraught herself to take the time to deal with it.

"Then call in someone from outside to help. For heaven's sake, Pansy, you have a brain! Use it! I don't care who carries the water, just see that we get it!"

"Yes, ma'am," Pansy muttered, and fled back down the stairs, determined that someone else should do *that* job.

Exasperation fading simply because she was too weary to maintain it, Valerie, holding the basin of cold water in both hands, backed against the bedroom door to open it.

And stopped, throat closing on the words she had intended to say.

56

For Julie had stripped off her clothes and stood before the tall gilt-framed mirror, staring at the purplish bruises on her thighs: the marks left by a man's thumbs and fingers on the white flesh. Unaware that she was observed, Julie turned, collapsing into a chair, and buried her face in her hands, weeping.

Seven

The morning was hot and muggy, promising a rain that would be more than welcome. It was late when Valerie woke, and for a few seconds she didn't remember why she had slept so badly.

Then it came sweeping back in full recall and she groaned and rolled over, wondering why Lallie hadn't come up with her coffee yet. Judging by the angle of the sun through the eastern window (where the louvered shutters had not yet been closed, either) it was far past her customary hour of rising.

She felt horrid. Not only had she tossed and turned restlessly for hours, but she'd dreamed when she finally slept. Dreams of men with missing teeth and unshaven faces and rough hands, and blood running down the heaving, sweating sides of a horse, and of the high shrill scream of man and animal when she fired and the man went down.

Valerie pushed back damp strands of hair and sat up, parting the netting. The house was still, and not even a bird chirped outside. She'd had to give Julie a sleeping draught last night, so she might well still be sleeping, but what about everyone else?

She walked across the room and peered at her own face in

58

the mirror over her dressing table. Except for smudges under her eyes, it looked the same as it always had. Amazing, she thought, that I could shoot two men, and kill one of them, and look no different than before.

At least she wasn't shaking this morning. She poured tepid water from the pitcher into the basin for a quick sponge bath, reflecting on the matter. It wasn't as if the man hadn't deserved to die, so why had it been so upsetting? Was it like that on the battlefield? Did a man get sick when he'd shot off an opponent's head, or run him through with a bayonet? Or were they too busy just staying alive themselves to think about it?

Patrick Ryan had been calm enough. Of course he hadn't done the shooting, but she had no doubt that he would have, had he had the pistol on him instead of sending her to fetch it. He'd probably killed many times, she thought. Only wouldn't it be different, a soldier shooting an enemy soldier?

She wished to God he *had* had the pistol himself. At least he'd admitted, more or less, that he'd been stupid in leaving it with his coat. *Touché,* he had said, when she charged him with the matter.

An odd word on the tongue of a sharecropper's son, even if he had risen to overseer on a sizable plantation. She doubted that any other overseer she'd ever encountered would have known the meaning of the word, let alone used it.

She reached for fresh undergarments and began to dress. Should she ring for Lallie to help with her stays or simply leave them off? Heaven knew she was thin enough so she didn't have all that much to hold in. Her mother would be outraged if she didn't wear any such garment, but the temptation was strong, and there was the excuse that no one had come to help her. She couldn't possibly lace the damnable things properly by herself.

In the end, with a mental note to change before her mother came home for supper, Valerie put on pantalettes and petticoats and another of her well-worn dresses, this one of a soft pale green dimity, sprigged with tiny pink and white flowers. Her mind wasn't on the clothes. Oddly, she thought of Patrick Ryan.

He had handled her rather roughly yesterday, not caring if his grip was painful. Perhaps he could be excused on the grounds that he, too, had been under strong emotion, but she suspected he'd rather enjoyed using that small measure of physical force upon her.

Patrick had not been intimidating as a boy. Her first memory of him was as a skinny, carroty-headed, barefoot youth of perhaps sixteen when she was only three. He had stood watching from the shadow of one of the live oaks when she had a birthday party on the front lawn. Odd, that she recalled that, since there was little else about the day that she remembered except for the cake and the candles and the pony her Grandpa Stanton had bought her. Only Patrick, peering from around the thick-trunked old tree, a strand of swaying Spanish moss concealing, then revealing, his presence where he had no business to be.

Patrick Ryan was always around while Valerie and Julie were growing up. For some obscure reason, Roger Stanton had taken a liking to him.

From time to time her father had related, with amusement, how the boy had approached him, at the age of ten, in search of employment.

"But I have four hundred blacks to work for me," Roger told Ryan. "Why should I want an uneducated white boy, who would expect to be paid, when I am already supporting four hundred slaves?"

"Because," Ryan had replied at once, although his freckled face was pale with his own audacity, "can't none of them read and write."

Roger had smiled at that. "And can you read and write, boy?"

"No, sir. But it ain't illegal to teach me."

At that Roger had thrown back his head and laughed aloud, for the boy *was* audacious, indeed. Encouraged, Patrick Ryan pressed his advantage.

"You going to need somebody can read and write," he stated. "And when I'm grown up, I'll be overseer on this plantation for you, Mr. Stanton."

"By God," Roger told his family later, "I had to admire his spunk. And it's true, I can't legally teach any of the blacks to read and write, and it would be a hell of a big help to have someone besides myself to keep the accounts. Old Landry is getting so he makes mistakes, and he's not worth what I pay him any more. So I think I'll see how this boy works out."

Patrick Ryan had learned to read and to write. Not only that, but, to Ellen's initial disapproval, he was given access to the Mallows library, which he devoured with a hunger as strong as his need for food. Ellen's fears about having a dirty urchin in her house soon vanished, for the boy was clean and always wiped his bare feet before entering and never left footprints on her rugs or polished floors. After the spurt of boldness that saw him through the first job request, he was not at all objectionable in any way. He was courteous to the ladies, absorbing manners as he observed them in the adults around him; he was never what Dolly called "pushy," and after a time Ellen stopped worrying about the possibility that he would filch a piece of silver from the sideboard if he were left unobserved for a moment or two.

Patrick Ryan became a fixture about Mallows, much as the blacks were fixtures. Conversations were carried on before him, as before them, as if he were no more than a wooden post, without ears.

Well, Valerie reflected at this time many years later, he had obviously learned a great deal. *Touché,* indeed.

She turned to leave the room, then paused to scoop up her discarded nightshift. Only Dolly Mallow, of all women in the house, had not learned to pick up after herself (at least part of the time) since there were no longer enough servants to do everything that had been done in the old days.

No servants, a diminishing food supply, no cash to buy even what few items as were available, none of the luxuries everyone had taken for granted for so many years. And no men. That last one might be the most difficult of all to bear, Valerie thought, descending the stairs with a hand trailing the balustrade that needed polishing.

In the library, along with more "important" books, were novels, romantic novels, and she had read every one of them many times. The books stirred something in her, something that, even as it stirred, was clearly yet almost dormant, undeveloped, and she longed to know fully what this relationship was between a man and a woman.

In spite of her late rising, she found Lacy and Julie still in the small dining room, finishing mush and chicory-coffee. They looked up at her without their usual good spirits. It was easy to see that Julie, especially, had shared the restless night. The bruises on her face were darker than they had been, and she held her lips steady with an effort as she murmured a greeting.

Valerie slid into her chair, nodding as Pansy moved forward to pour coffee into the cup set for her.

"You want mush, Miss Val?" the servant asked.

Valerie grimaced. "Mush. Lord, how I'd like to have eggs again, and bacon, and ham, and soufflés and omelettes . . ."

"Don't," Julie said softly.

"Well, I'm sick of mush. No, Pansy, I'll just have some sliced peaches. There are plenty of those, aren't there?"

"Plenty peaches," Pansy agreed. "No sugar."

Valerie shrugged, and Pansy moved off toward the kitchen. "Pansy, are there ever any eggs any more? This morning?"

"Two. Miss Dolly have 'em."

Of course. Miss Dolly was delicate; her stomach wasn't up to daily mush, which meant that if there were eggs, she usually ate them.

As if reading her thoughts, Lacy said dryly, "Once in a while I hanker for a delicate stomach, myself. Ah, well. Julie, love, there's a basket of mending; would you like to join me with it?"

Julie started, nervously fingering the edge of the tablecloth. "What? Oh, the mending." Her dark eyes filled with tears. "I'm sorry. I feel as if I'm about to fly apart, in all directions. I can't help thinking, what if Mr. Ryan's right, and the Yankee soldiers come here? I think I'd rather die than go through anything like that again!"

Valerie went very still, but Lacy spoke briskly. "Nonsense! Dying is very final, my dear! Granted, it's most unpleasant to be abused by a disgusting group of soldiers, but you were not actually violated. You will forget about it when you take up your ordinary tasks."

Julie's mouth quirked unhappily. "I *feel* as if I'd been violated. I feel so dirty, and so ashamed. Everyone will know, won't they, what happened? Everyone at Mallows already knows!"

"Where is the shame in being attacked by ruffians? Would you feel ashamed if you'd been forced to give up your purse? Or if they'd simply beaten you? Pull yourself together, child, and take the sensible view. It was an unfortunate incident, but due to your sister and to Mr. Ryan, you escaped the worst. We'll deal with the Yankees when they come; don't borrow trouble before that. We are all sorry that it happened, yet we will not make overmuch of it, and you shouldn't, either."

Seeing that her granddaughter was unmoved by this, Lacy added with calm deliberation, "While most painful, being raped is not the end of the world. Thousands of women, including myself, have survived it without visible scars. And I assure you, I have had many good and happy years since the event. I am heartily glad I did not elect to kill myself, although I considered that option at the time."

They both stared at her in amazement, this tiny, peppery old lady with her halo of rather untidy hair and her black silk. Lacy, raped?

Julie had at least momentarily forgotten her own plight, yet it was Valerie who spoke.

"It happened when you were a young girl?"

"It happened on my wedding night." And then, at the change in their expressions, Lacy added with asperity, "Don't think that made it any less traumatic, that it was my husband rather than a stranger! He *was* a stranger, or as good as! The which over three hundred people from the best families were when I was a girl. I was sixteen years old, and I had never lived on a plantation like this, had never treated the sick or helped with the birthings of the slaves, the way your mother did. I was an only child, and I knew nothing. Nothing! I read novels, and I dreamed silly romantic dreams, and I knew nothing. I was excited about a big wedding, a reception to which over three hundred people from the best families were invited, the wedding gifts, the house I was going to move into. I thought it would probably be pleasant to be kissed by a handsome man, which Charles certainly was. I hadn't the slightest idea what would happen once the bedroom door had been closed behind me."

Lallie had come to the doorway behind the old lady. Valerie saw her, but she did not want this to be interrupted, and so ignored her. Lallie did not withdraw; she stood listening, her pretty face revealing nothing of her own thoughts on the matter.

"Charles was drunk," Lacy went on. "We were married at two in the afternoon. He'd been at the champagne steadily all day, and then fortified himself with an additional glass of brandy before we retired. Of course, he was far more used to it than I, who had only sipped at the champagne, because it made me feel peculiar. He wasn't so drunk that he didn't intend to demand a husband's rights on our bridal night."

If Ellen had been there, Lacy would not have talked this

way. Never for a moment would Ellen have countenanced such a subject at her table, or anywhere else in her household, if she could have prevented it. Neither of the girls, however, even thought of changing the direction of the monologue.

"We retired late, after an evening of dancing following everything else," Lacy said. "And we'd hardly closed the door when Charles began to tear at my clothes. At first I was so astonished I couldn't even protest! And then when he threw me down on the bed and fell across me, crushing me, hurting me, I cried out. I didn't consider that anyone might overhear us, I only wanted him to stop hurting me. Only he was much stronger, of course, and he went on hurting me. I can remember, yet, how dreadfully it hurt, and I fought with him. It didn't do any good; he forced himself upon me, and I learned that night about the marital relationship from a man no more loving or considerate than your soldiers, my dear. Legally, a man cannot rape his wife. But in actual fact, if one is forced by a man, what difference does it make if one is married to him? True, except for the brandy he did not smell bad, and he was clean, but that was the least of my considerations at the time. So you see, dear, I know whereof I speak."

Looking stunned, Julie said, "I always thought you and Grandpa Stanton were very happy together!"

"And so we were, once I'd established my own position." Lacy smiled, remembering. "He fell asleep, snoring in what I considered a disgusting manner, and left me to take my bloody self off for a bath for which I carried the water myself because I did not want the servants to know what had happened. Once I'd bathed, I locked myself in the room across the hall and lay awake for most of the night, alternately sobbing and gnashing my teeth in anger. I must have been a charming sight when Charles kicked in the door the following morning and demanded to know what in the hell was the matter with me."

Valerie felt her jaw go slack. Grandpa Stanton, who had held her hand going through the streets of Savannah, who had put her up on her first pony, who had always been a soft touch for a little girl who wanted an ice cream or a new frock? Her shock was mirrored on her sister's face across the table; only Lallie remained impassive, unsurprised.

"What did you do?" Valerie whispered.

"You might not believe it now," Lacy said, "but in those

days I had a bit of spirit. Came of being spoiled, I suppose; Papa and Mama seldom failed to give in to whatever I wanted. Anyway, I was still furious. I suppose that was why I didn't carry through on the thought of killing myself. I wanted to kill Charles more! It was all I could do to keep from leaping on him and scratching his eyes out. He was astonished; he didn't even remember most of it! We had a long intense discussion of the matter—all in delicately couched terms, of course—and I informed him that I was prepared to be his wife but not his slave, and we came to an understanding. It was some time before I came to have the feelings for him that one calls 'love,' and even longer to learn to enjoy lovemaking, but, oh, yes, Charles and I had a long and good life together." She twisted the diamond ring on her finger, thoughtfully. "I, too, thought I would rather die, Julie, than to endure another night such as that first one. It would have been a dreadful mistake."

It was not Julie who responded to that.

"You did come to enjoy loving a man," Valerie said. "I suppose it's what every woman dreams of."

Lacy, with a fleeting thought for her daughter-in-law, qualified that. "Well, not *every* woman, but most of us. Life without a man and children is a poor life. And there will be men for you, I'm sure of it, when this dreadful war is over."

Julie shuddered. "I don't care if there aren't. I don't care if no man ever touches me again."

And Valerie, who *did* care, wondered how, considering all the thousands of Confederate soldiers who had died, her grandmother could be right.

It was early afternoon when Aaron paused in the doorway of the library, where Valerie, Julie, and Lacy all sat mending and darning, discussing everything except the matters that were uppermost in their minds.

"Buggy coming," Aaron said. "From Cedars. Miss Ellen, I think."

They had not been able to send for her as arranged, since the only vehicle they owned outside of a farm wagon had been disabled the previous day. Valerie had sent two of the fieldhands out to inspect the buggy and, she hoped, repair it;

they had returned with hunched shoulders and shuffling feet to report that they didn't know how to do it, ma'am.

Frustration was something they lived with more and more. Valerie was quite certain that any reasonably intelligent male, even a slave, could figure out how to replace the wheel on the buggy. She was equally hopeless in knowing how to handle the situation when they pretended innocence and ignorance and stuck to them through entreaties and sharp demands.

They had, at least, to get a message to Ellen, she decided, and had therefore given orders that the boy, Chad, go first thing in the morning to Cedars to see if the Douglases could spare their buggy and a man to drive it.

They had both looked forward to, and dreaded, Ellen's return. Julie composed a note for Chad to carry, informing her mother in the simplest terms of the previous day's mishap. With an unsteady hand, Julie assured her that there was nothing to worry about, that she was perfectly safe, and that old Rudy was being nursed by his wife, Sheba.

All hands stilled in their laps at Aaron's words, and their chatter died; in the silence, they heard the sound of wheels on the white shell drive.

Aaron was at the door, opening it, at the precise moment that Ellen reached the top step and started across the shaded piazza.

"Welcome home, Miss Ellen," he said in the soft, educated speech that set him apart from most of the other Negroes. For, quite contrary to a law that was harshly enforced, Aaron had also been allowed to learn to read and write. And he, too, availed himself of the library, although not so openly as Patrick Ryan had been able to do.

Ellen had not approved such a course—everyone knew it was dangerous to allow blacks to have book learning that would give them ideas above their station in life—and had protested so vehemently that her husband had apparently given in on the matter.

From that time on, Aaron was given chores that kept him near the schoolroom. Ellen conveniently failed to notice that he was an observant boy, or that he picked up the speech patterns taught by the governess, little Miss Abigail Tatterson. And she quite truly did not know that the handsome house servant borrowed, one at a time, the same books that had so enthralled a sharecropper's son in earlier years, that he kept these volumes carefully hidden during the daytime so no one

66

would come across them. All that impinged upon Ellen's consciousness was the fact that Aaron was prettily spoken, the source of envy among her friends, and a perfect servant.

He accepted now the broad-brimmed hat she handed him with her murmured greeting. "Where is everyone, Aaron?"

"Miss Dolly upstairs, ma'am. Everyone else in the library." There were times when Aaron remembered to try to sound like what he was, a black slave. That this variance of speech patterns might make an observer wonder did not bother him; there was seldom anyone at Mallows any more who might put two and two together, and the family gave him no thought at all as long as he did what he was supposed to do for their convenience and comfort.

True to form, Ellen did not look directly at him, turning instead to her left, where she met the rest of her family. Even her mother was there, Dolly having come downstairs unnoticed a moment earlier because she had heard the buggy approaching.

"Mama," Julie said, moving to her for a quick embrace.

She wished, now, that she'd written more detail of yesterday's terrible ordeal, because then she wouldn't have to explain it in person. Except for her father's death, nothing in Juile's life had ever provided such a shattering experience, and she knew she couldn't talk about it calmly, the way Valerie was able to speak of killing a man.

Ellen, however, gave her only a perfunctory kiss and a greeting to the others. Her mind was on something else altogether.

"I met a wagon on the way home," she said. She spoke softly as she usually did, yet the tension was there for an intimate to read. "They're perhaps half an hour behind me, and I'm sure I don't know how we're going to manage. Grace is ill, she could hardly sit up to talk to me. And Sally Ann's had her baby, a month early, and is still bleeding—the child was born yesterday and a poorly looking little mite he is, too— and in addition to that worthless Hattie they've picked up another stray—I didn't get the sense of it—some cheap-looking young woman who's apparently attached herself to them permanently and they're all taking it for granted they're welcome here at Mallows!"

She was greeted with a dismayed silence until Valerie found her tongue. "Four of them, besides Hattie? And everyone but the stranger is ill?"

"They do look half-starved, poor things," Ellen went on, peeling off her gloves and handing them to Lallie, who had materialized behind her. "Miss Lacy, if I might presume upon your assistance, would you convey to Mamie that there will be four more to feed at dinner, and they'll no doubt appreciate something cold to drink when they get here. Both Grace and Sally Ann are so weak I can't think they'll want more than a good rich broth to begin with, at least, and perhaps some fruit."

She withdrew a handkerchief from her purse and patted at the moisture on her face, already pulling herself together now that she was home, taking charge as she had always done.

"I'd hoped we could put Sally Ann in one of the small servants' rooms on the third floor," she said, unnoticing of the flickering of Lallie's gaze. For Lallie had long occupied one of those rooms, the only servant still allowed to sleep inside the house. After Roger's death almost a year ago, Ellen had decided that it was "too much bother" to have the others inside, when there was so little help to keep the place clean; not even to herself had she openly admitted that, with Roger gone and so many of the people having run off and some of the others showing traces of rebellion that her husband would quickly have put an end to, she was afraid to have anyone but Lallie locked inside with the family at night.

"Now, having seen her," she went on, "I can only conclude that would be impossible; the girl's going to be an invalid for weeks, if indeed she ever regains her health, and having her in such an inconvenient place is unthinkable. So we'll put her and the baby in the corner bedroom, and this other girl they've picked up can go upstairs, and Grace can have the back bedroom—it isn't quite as pleasant and light, but I think Sally Ann and the baby have more need of the larger room—and Hattie will have to sleep in the quarters. Valerie, see to sheets for that bedroom across from Lallie's, and Julie, get Aaron to go up into the attic and fetch down the cradle. I thought we'd have weeks yet before that was needed, and it will have to be cleaned, and made up—"

Ellen paused for breath. "Good heavens, are they coming already? I thought for certain they'd be farther behind than this!"

"No, ma'am, it ain't a wagon," Lallie said, peering out the window. "I think it's that Mrs. Gerald, Mr. Ryan's sister. She riding that old piebald horse o' his."

"Ruth Ryan?" Ellen bit her lip. "Of all the inconvenient times—whatever can she want? Valerie, see if you can get rid of her—the rest of you, please, help me prepare for this invasion. The cradle, especially, is an immediate need. Oh, and see if there's anyone to wet-nurse the child, too, Julie. Is Callie still nursing? Or Opal?"

Valerie left them discussing wet nurses and cradles. Aaron, who never missed knowing that anyone was approaching, apparently did not consider Ruth Ryan important enough to bring him to the front door. Indeed, he probably expected that she would go around to the back.

She did not. She rode straight up to the front porch and dismounted with the aid of the projecting marble block that had served several generations of females in getting off and on their horses.

Valerie had never actually spoken to the woman, although she had occasionally observed her at a distance. Unlike her brother, Ruth had never approached anyone at Mallows, and had married and moved away when Valerie was only about ten years old.

What did she want now? Valerie could not stifle a sensation of apprehension as she opened the door.

Eight

"Miss Stanton," Patrick Ryan's sister greeted her. She looked older than the age she ought to be, Valerie thought, and then as she drew closer she decided that it was not age but extreme fatigue and worry. "I'm sorry to bother you. Would it be possible to speak to Mrs. Stanton?"

"She's very busy," Valerie told her. "We're expecting relatives from Atlanta at any moment, and two of them are ill; we weren't prepared for them, so there's a great deal to do. Could I help you?"

Unlike her brother, Ruth didn't suggest that she be invited inside and offered a drink before she stated her business. Her reddish brown hair was carelessly dressed, and the sleepless nights had left their traces on a once-pretty face. Her bosom rose and fell under her striped cotton bodice in a heavy sigh.

"I'm sorry to have come at an inconvenient time. My grandmother is dying, Miss Stanton, and she's in pain. I've nothing to give her to ease it. I thought perhaps Mrs. Stanton might be able to help—she's always been so good to your own people, I know, and is an experienced nurse. But if she has all these problems of her own—"

Something about the older woman's quiet resignation tugged at Valerie's emotions, and she spoke impulsively.

70

"Please sit down there in the shade, and I'll find Mama and speak to her. Perhaps she can give you something."

Ruth's mouth relaxed in a half-smile, the best she could summon under the present circumstances. "Thank you. I'd be most appreciative."

Valerie left her there in one of the rattan chairs near the rose trellis, pausing long enough to intercept Pansy as the girl fairly flew through the entry hall on some assigned errand.

"Pansy, Mr. Ryan's sister is on the piazza. See that she has a cool drink, will you? And do you know where my mother is?"

"Miss Ellen in the kitchen. Miss Val, I ain't got time to bring no cool drink for nobody, I s'posed to git some rags to clean a cradle, and Miss Julie said . . ."

"The cradle will wait five minutes while the woman has a drink." Valerie's tone brooked no argument. She turned away, taking it for granted that Pansy would obey orders, hers first, and then Julie's. The infant was newborn and could safely be left in the middle of the big bed while the cradle was readied, surely.

She found Ellen in the summer kitchen, a detached white-washed brick building set apart from the main house and connected to it by a roofed gallery. Cooking in the main house was limited to the cooler months of the year, since the fires would have contributed to the already stifling heat during the summer. There was also a safety factor in doing the cooking at a distance, since a fire there would not be likely to burn the house as well.

Valerie heard Ellen's voice before she saw her, a voice abnormally sharp.

"Mamie, this is going to be inconvenient for all of us, but we have no choice. Please do as I say."

Valerie stood at the doorway, looking into the familiar room which also served Mamie as a sleeping room. There was a fire in the fireplace, as well as one in the big black iron stove, and the aroma of freshly baked bread. The golden-topped loaves sat to cool on a scoured block table in the middle of the room, and beyond it Mamie, her black face scowling and beaded with perspiration, stood with hands on her ample hips.

"I gettin' old, Miss Ellen. I ain't got what it takes to cook for no four more people, and them sickly. What I s'posed to do, be a nursemaid, too? Them people don't mean nothin' to

71

me, poor white trash, they is, and that Hattie, she one lazy nigger! I remember, when she been here before! She don't do nothin' but act like she white lady, needin' to be waited on."

Ellen's teeth closed with an audible click. "Mamie, I will listen to no more of this. You're no older than I am, and you will do the same as I do, continue to meet your responsibilities until you are physically unable to do the chores any longer. My cousin and her daughter will need a nourishing soup, and send one of the boys to pick some more peaches."

"There ain't no sugar for 'em," Mamie pointed out. "And what I goin' to make a nourishin' soup out of, less'n I kill them hens what lays your mama's breakfas' eggs?"

"Then make it without chicken. There are plenty of vegetables left. From the look of them, they haven't had anything fit for human consumption in months; they're skin and bones. And Mamie—" Ellen spoke more quietly, with a force Valerie had seldom heard, "I will not be spoken to, about my relatives, in that way. Do you understand? You will prepare the necessary meals, and I will hear no more of this kind of talk."

She did not give Mamie a chance to reply, and if her legs were shaking as she walked out of the kitchen, nearly colliding with Valerie in the process, no one knew it but Ellen herself.

"Mama," Valerie said, "Ruth Gerald is here, Mr. Ryan's sister. Her grandmother is dying, and she has nothing to give her for the pain. She was hoping you could help her."

For a moment Ellen hesitated, massaging her temple, resting her eyes by closing them against the responsibilities that continued to pile up on her.

"The laudanum is locked in my cabinet." She fumbled at the ring of keys in her apron pocket and handed them over. "Give her a small vial. And tell her I'm sorry."

Valerie rested a hand on her mother's shoulder, feeling the tremor she had known instinctively would be running through Ellen's body. "It'll be all right, Mama. We'll manage."

Ellen summoned a watery smile. "Yes. Of course we will; we always have, haven't we?"

But after Val had gone it was a moment before Ellen followed, and she wondered with an ache in her throat how much longer she could go on managing alone. Because, for all that there was a houseful of people, she *was* alone, insofar

72

as making the decisions were concerned. And now the pressures would be greater than ever before.

If only Roger would be coming back, if only she knew that eventually someone would lift this load from her. Evan, she clung to the memories of him, this only surviving son, who, though he had not so far evinced any desire to step into his father's shoes, would surely do so now that there was no one else.

For a few moments she was comforted by the thought of Evan. Like all her children, he was handsome and healthy, for which she daily thanked God. Tall, and slim, and looking quite a bit like his father with dark hair and eyes; merry eyes, that always saw the humor in everything, even when the joke was on himself.

It didn't matter that he'd been more interested in gaming and partying than in growing cotton; he'd been only a boy, and boys always sowed their wild oats. He had been gone from home for two years, and during those long months she had only seen him three times. There had also been four letters, scrawled by firelight in a hand shaking with fatigue; once there had been bloodstains, unexplained, across the corner of the page. Those, and an occasional message sent by an acquaintance to tell her he had survived yet another battle, were all she'd had of Evan.

Pray God he would come safely home. Ellen inhaled deeply, squaring her shoulders for the next assault the world would make upon her, and wondered what she was going to do about servants who were increasingly uncooperative, even surly and openly rebellious. In the old days any slave who had spoken to a white person in such a fashion as Mamie had done a few minutes ago would have been severely punished.

The trouble was, Ellen thought wearily, she no longer had the power to punish them, and they knew it. They had always been good people, and were always well treated. Yet now that the Yankees were coming, their resentments were surfacing in a way she felt incapable of coping with. That boy, Chad, who had come to Cedars for her . . . He had not actually said or done anything that she could put a finger on. Something was there in his eyes, however, something that frightened her. Imagine, frightened by a fourteen-year-old black boy!

Ellen trotted along the bricked walkway to the main house,

wondering how long it would be before she could lie down in her darkened room with a cool cloth over her eyes, to wait for her headache to go away.

The wagon jolted into the yard and rolled to a stop. The travelers were almost too weary to realize they had arrived, with the exception of the girl handling the mules.

She was about twenty, Valerie guessed as she descended the steps to meet them with her mother and Julie close behind. A blond girl with blue eyes and rather prominent teeth that somehow did not detract at all from her prettiness. She wore a plain blue cotton frock that had been laundered so many times that it had lost most of its color, and when she lifted her skirts preparatory to climbing down from the seat, Valerie saw that her shoes were in shreds, literally disintegrating on the girl's feet.

"Oh, laws, am I glad to get here!" the girl said wearily. "You-all are the Stantons, I hope, and this is Mallows?"

"I'm Valerie Stanton." Val extended a hand to help her. "This is my mother, and my sister Julie."

"I'm Blossom Curtis." The girl smiled, and exposed front teeth that were not only prominent but overlapped slightly. "Lord, ain't it hot? We kept hopin' it would rain, but maybe it's better it didn't, what with Miss Sally Ann lyin' there with a new baby and all. Would it be too much to ask for something to drink, ma'am? I swear my throat's so dry I can't hardly talk."

"Of course. Mamie's fixing some lemonade right now," Ellen said, stepping forward with as hospitable a smile as she could manage. "Grace, how are you? Can you get down by yourself? I don't know where Aaron's got to . . ."

Grace Havers lifted a head gone astonishingly gray in the three years since Ellen had seen her cousin. She was only ten years older than Ellen, still two years shy of fifty, yet she looked as old as Dolly Mallow. She had once been a heavy woman; now, deprivation had wasted away her flesh, leaving the skin hanging in sagging folds at her neck and upper arms. She licked at her lips and spoke with an effort.

"I think I can walk if someone will support me. Oh, Ellen, you don't know how grateful we are that you'll take us in—it was terrible in Atlanta, terrible! That dreadful General Sherman . . . Hattie," she spoke to the black woman dangling her feet from the back of the wagon, "bring my little satchel with my medicine in it."

Hattie stared at her with enigmatic eyes. "Yes'm," she said, and eased her bulk to the ground, groaning loudly as she did so.

"Lemonade!" the girl called Blossom exclaimed. "We ain't had no lemons in Atlanta for a while, I can tell you! Nor much of anything else, comes to that. Shall I help Miz Havers on this side, and one of you on t'other, and we'll get her inside? I don't think Miss Sally Ann can walk at all, poor thing."

Valerie had stepped close to the wagon and looked over its edge into the straw. Sally Ann lay with her eyes closed, her freckled face shaded by a straw bonnet held limply in one hand. Beside her, a bundle of toweling moved slightly and emitted a faint cry.

"I reckon he's hungry," Blossom said, reaching up over the wagon gate to ease the older woman down into her own and Ellen's waiting arms. "I don't guess his mama's got much for him to eat. She's hopin' you got someone can wet-nurse him."

Ellen took her cousin's weight—which was still considerable—with a small involuntary grunt. "We don't have a soul who's still nursing, I'm afraid. Maybe it's only that he came early. If Sally Ann suckles him herself, perhaps the milk will come. Otherwise," she grunted again as Grace's bulk shifted toward her more heavily, "we'll have to give him a rag to suck. We don't have much milk, but there's enough for one small baby, I should hope."

Sally Ann hadn't moved. She did not stir even when Valerie reached in and lifted the infant in its makeshift wrappings from her side. Indeed, at close range Sally Ann's normally pale skin was almost bluish-white; Ellen had not overstated the case in saying that Grace's daughter was in a sorry state.

The baby moved against her hands, and Valerie felt something totally unexpected stir within her. She peeled back the edge of the toweling and saw the tiny face, the mouth opened for another of the thin cries.

Why, it looked more like a monkey than a human baby, she thought, except that it had almost nothing in the way of hair. Poor ugly little thing! Compassion washed over her in a way she had not envisioned.

"I'll take him upstairs, Sally Ann," she said, bending over

75

her cousin. "We fixed up a cradle for him. We'll get some help, and get you out, too, right away."

"I'll stay here with her while you get Aaron," Julie offered, bending to peer at the infant, her startled expression revealing that she, too, found Sally Ann's baby less than handsome.

Aaron was found to be bringing a tray of drinks into the foyer, on his way to the front drawing room. Valerie, cuddling the child against her breast, both excited and alarmed by its small movements because they seemed so feeble, paused to speak to him.

"Leave the lemonade there, Aaron, and let people take what they want as they pass through. None of them is in any condition to go sit in the parlor. Julie's out there with my cousin, who will have to be carried upstairs, I think. To the corner room where we put the cradle."

"Yes, Miss Val," Aaron said. "I'll see to it."

"Oh, my, what a beautiful house! I never seen such a chandelier!" Blossom exclaimed, looking up at the crystal confection high overhead. "It must really be somethin' when all the candles are lit!"

Her blue eyes swept around her, evaluating the French wallpaper, the family portraits, the polished hardwood floors with the scattered Persian rugs in muted, beautiful colors, her mouth half-open in admiration.

"I think," Ellen said mildly, "that the sooner we get my cousin into bed, the better."

Grace sagged between them, murmuring, "Please. Let me sit for a moment before those stairs."

Valerie, carrying the infant, left them there, resting and taking their cold drinks. Already, when the newcomers were not yet all into the house, it was plain to see what a change would be made at Mallows. Invalids and infants, and Blossom Curtis. She felt a moment's curiosity about Blossom, who was quite beyond Valerie's experience. How had she attached herself to the party? Did she intend to remain here, too, even though she was a complete stranger?

At the top of the stairs she met her grandmother. "Look," she said, offering the infant for Dolly's inspection, "this is Sally Ann's little boy. Do all new babies look so much like monkeys? White babies? I never saw a white baby before, not this small. He's an ugly little thing, isn't he?"

Dolly did not pretend an interest she did not feel. Her own babies, boy babies, were long since cold in the ground, and

76

she had no intention of becoming attached to another one. A glance was sufficient to assure her that she would have no difficulty in controlling any dormant maternal urges, since, as Valerie had pointed out, the child was not a pretty one.

"You're going to put it and its mother in the room next to mine, Julie says."

"Yes. It has the most windows, and is the bigger room." Correctly guessing her grandmother's concern, Valerie added, "He shouldn't bother you, Grandma Dolly. He's so weak I doubt if you could hear him cry from across the room."

Dolly sniffed. "I hope not. My health has never been good, and I have difficulty sleeping, you know. It upsets me terribly when my sleep is interrupted."

Fascinated by the scrawny and incredibly tiny arm that had just emerged from the toweling, Valerie didn't reply. She walked away, oblivious of the pinched expression on Dolly's face, into the big sunny bedroom at the southeast corner of the second floor. It had been made ready for its occupants, although no one had time to pick any flowers for a welcoming note. The cradle, the one Valerie and Julie and Evan had all slept in, and Ellen before them, stood beside the high tester bed, swathed in mosquito netting that had been parted, ready for the newest infant.

Valerie lowered him into it, peeling away the layers of material to examine him more fully.

Clearly Sally Ann had not been prepared for an immediate birth. An old chemise had been torn up to fashion the diaper he wore, and when his little body was exposed he moved matchstick arms and legs in an aimlessly protesting way. He was so small that he could have rested easily in the palm of a large man's hand.

Why did that make her think of Patrick Ryan? For a moment she was distracted by the recollection of Ryan's sister, and her gratitude—there had been tears in her eyes—for the laudanum for her grandmother.

Ah, well, she was sorry about the old woman who had taken over the Ryan brood when her daughter had died. Valerie knew her only by sight, from a distance; she had often been seen in her faded calico out in the garden patch behind Ryan's house, scratching with a hoe. Her life was coming to an end, and this one, this tiny fellow whose entire body could be covered by her own hand, he was only beginning.

If they could keep him fed, if he did indeed live.

Valerie spoke to him very softly, bending over the cradle as she rocked it gently with one foot on the lower bar. "You have to live, little man. The South needs new sons to replace the ones who've died. Be a fighter, and survive!"

The baby stopped moving; it seemed that his eyes focused momentarily on her face, as if he understood.

And then she heard the others coming, and turned to help when Aaron carried Sally Ann over to the bed.

Whatever the next few weeks were going to be like, Valerie guessed they would not be dull.

Nine

It was not dull. Julie welcomed the increased activity, and the fact that there were only four house servants where there had once been a dozen meant additional chores for everyone, and diverted her from the memory uppermost in her mind.

She had wondered, the night after it happened, whether she would ever sleep soundly again. The face of the man with the missing teeth, his bristly unshaven cheek pressed upon hers, the fetid odor of his breath, remained with her even in sleep so that she woke, struggling and gasping. After a day of running up and down stairs waiting on invalids, however, she was tired enough to sleep without dreaming at all. Unlike Dolly, she didn't even hear the baby cry during the night.

Sally Ann continued to bleed and Ellen divided her time between Grace Havers and the new mother, caring for her and the baby, who was also sickly. A wet nurse had been brought from Cedars, a fat, lazy, stupid girl of twelve who professed not to know how she had come to have the healthy brown-skinned child of her own. She had had to bring him with her, of course, since she must feed both her own Rastus and the new infant, who went nameless for the first week of his life.

Another mouth to feed was the last thing Ellen felt the

need of, yet it was clear to everyone that Sally Ann could not produce enough milk for her baby. Ordinarily she would not even have tried, since nursing an infant was a nuisance and extremely confining; no woman of any station nursed her own child. These were not ordinary times, however, and if the tiny boy was to live, some source of food must be produced for him.

The wet nurse was called Gilly. She was a cheerful compulsive talker; more than ten minutes of her company was enough to send either Ellen or Dolly into nervous prostration. Julie found her amusing, and she selected one of the huts in the quarters for Gilly and her child and old Hattie, who could watch Rastus when Gilly must be at the house to feed the white baby.

Hattie, who had been a house servant all her fifty years, was openly resentful of being placed in the quarters. She stood in the middle of the small room, staring with contempt at the bare walls from which the chinking had fallen loose, leaving cracks between the boards. She kicked at the dirt floor. "I ain't never had to live in no place like this," she said, her tone sullen.

Julie kept her voice level and light. "I'm afraid it's the best we can manage," she said. "This big house is quite full, Hattie. If you were up to nursing Miss Grace, she might want you to put a cot in her room."

"I'se gettin' old," Hattie said sourly. "I can't run up and down all them stairs, fetchin' and carryin' for no sick person. I sick my own self. My knees so stiff in the mornin' I can't hardly get out o' bed. Every bone I got ache like a toothache, most all the time——"

"Well," Julie interrupted, thinking Hattie and Grandma Dolly had quite a bit in common, aside from the color of their skins, "everyone at Mallows does what he can to help out, and it seems the most help you can provide right now is to be here with Gilly and to see to her baby when she's gone."

"I ain't nobody to watch no baby," Hattie said. "I too old for babies."

"Nevertheless," Julie replied in her mother's best no-nonsense tone, "that is what you will do, for the time being. I think there's everything here you'll need, Gilly. Because you'll be working in the house, you can eat in the kitchen with Mamie and the other house servants, so you won't need to cook."

"That's good. I can't cook nothin'," Gilly said cheerfully. "This a pretty quilt, ma'am. I reckon Rastus like playing on that pretty quilt. Mind you don't let him roll off," she cautioned Hattie. "He pretty big for fo' months, ain't he? He roll off on his head, once, and Miz Douglas say I got to be more careful. He too valuable to mess up his brains, she say."

She pressed a hand to the breasts straining against her simple cotton garment. "It 'bout time to feed somebody, ma'am. You want I should feed the white lady's baby first, afore Rastus?"

Rastus, as smiley as his mother, did not appear in urgent need of feeding.

"Yes, that might be best. You are to wash yourself, you know, before you feed the baby each time. With soap and water. It will be there in Miss Sally Ann's room."

Astonishment washed the smile from Gilly's face. "Wash myself? Every *time?*"

"Every time. Come along now. I'm sure Hattie will see to Rastus."

The old black woman muttered under her breath when they left her there. Julie walked briskly, so that Gilly had to trot to keep up. The child—she was no more than that— looked around at the long line of wooden houses where the black people lived, then up at the big house.

"This a nice place. Be a pity that man burns it," she observed.

"Burns it?" Julie broke stride to look into the round black face beside her. "What are you talking about?"

"That Gen'l Sherman, he comin', sure as God. They say he gonna burn things up so nobody can use anythin' any more. You think when they come, ma'am, they'll rape black women same as white ones?"

Julie's throat constricted painfully. "Why do you say such a thing? There's no reason to think they'll rape anyone."

"Miz Douglas think they might. She tryin' to think where to send Miss Charlotte and Miss Henriette, to keep the Yankees from gettin' 'em. Trouble is, she ain't got nobody to send 'em to where she be sure the Yankees won't come."

For a moment a wave of nausea swept over her and Julie clamped down, hard, on the emotions that threatened. "There is no sense in talking about rape, Gilly. The Yankees may not come anywhere near us."

Gilly bounced a little as she walked, half-skipping. "Them ladies from Atlanta, they think the Yankees comin', don't they?"

"They came here to get away from the Yankees," Julie reminded.

"Then if the Yankees don't come, that mean we don't get freed?" Gilly asked. "Or is everybody goin' to be free, even if they don't see the Yankees?"

"Well, you aren't free yet," Julie said with a trace of tartness, looking down at the stains appearing on the front of Gilly's dress, "and if you don't hurry up and get to the baby there won't be anything left for him."

"Oh, they's plenty," Gilly assured her. "When I get free, will I still have to suckle white folks' babies, I wonder? I gonna get me a new dress when I free. A red one. I never had me a red dress."

Julie watched her go up the back stairs with mingled feelings. If the Yankees did free all the slaves, what would happen to them here at Mallows, and at Cedars, and on all the other plantations, all through the South? It was bad enough now, with so many of the blacks running off by ones and twos, slipping away from the fields at dusk so that they could be far away in the woods before anyone knew they were missing. When Patrick Ryan was overseer, there had been nighttime checks to make sure everyone returned to quarters after the day's work. No one did it any more, not since Evan had left and Ryan had joined the Army. What good would it do? What could they, a household of women, do about it if the workers ran off? Mrs. Douglas had posted a reward for the return of a pair of valuable runaways, who had subsequently been brought back, paid for, and run off again, and she was out the money she now desperately needed to keep her household going.

Dear God, Julie thought, *bring us through this. Help us. And keep Evan safe. Oh, God, keep him safe!*

She walked through the winter kitchen, empty now since all cooking was done in the white brick building at the back of the house, and through the dining room. It was magnificently proportioned, as were all the rooms at Mallows. There had been a time when there had been lavish dinners by candlelight under the sparkling chandelier, the mahogany table gleaming with silver and crystal and fine china and flowers in low bowls.

Someday, Julie promised herself, *someday we'll have those dinners again, and Mama will sit there*—for a moment the thought wavered, and then she mentally placed her brother in her father's chair—*Mama in her pearls and her diamond eardrops, and she will wear a gown of heavy turquoise satin. I will wear pink, with a hoop so wide I have to turn to come through the door, and there will be young men, and music, and dancing . . .*

She blinked, and looked down at the table. When she touched it, her fingers left faint traces in the dust. That Pansy, she was supposed to keep it dusted and polished . . .

As if knowing she was thought of, Pansy spoke complainingly behind her; she and her mother had followed Julie into the house.

"My legs about run off," Pansy whined. "Them ladies say fetch this and carry that, and they even give me a whole stack of dirty linens to wash out! I ain't got time to do no washin', and them lazy women s'posed to do it, they holler like *they* bosses! Seems like ever'body's a boss but me!"

"Well, you think you got problems," Mamie's deeper voice drifted in from the kitchen, "you ought to try cookin' for a bunch of sick people. 'Specially when there ain't nothing much to cook *with.* I tell you, I hope them Yankees *does* come, and puts a end to all this!"

Julie turned and saw her mother standing in the open doorway from the front entryway. For a moment she was frightened by something about Ellen, who was very still, very quiet.

And then Ellen was herself again. She moved past Julie and stepped to the kitchen door, where she spoke quietly and firmly.

"You'd better pray the Yankees don't come, because right now you have a home, a safe place to sleep, and food as good as anyone in Georgia has been getting these past few years. There won't be anybody to provide those things for you when the Yankees come; *they* can't keep their own soldiers supplied without stealing from us, and they certainly aren't going to worry about feeding *you.*"

Julie shifted position so that she could look over her mother's shoulder. Mamie's face remained stubbornly sullen. "But I be free, then."

"Free?" Ellen struggled to keep the shrillness from her words. "Free for what, Mamie? Free to find your own food, your own house? Free to take care of yourself when you're sick? Or when you're too old to work any more? What are you doing in here? I thought you were making something for our guests to eat?"

"I come to git some herbs in here. Ain't got no more bay leaf in the summer kitchen. Got no meat for broth. I got to put in somethin' to give that water some flavor, or I might as well give 'em hot water."

"Get it, then," Ellen said. "And finish the soup."

She stood quite motionless until they had both gone, Mamie to the kitchen and Pansy with more water to be carried upstairs for yet another bath.

Ellen turned with a sigh and saw Julie's face. She tried, unsuccessfully, to smile. "They'd never dare to speak to me that way if your father were here. Or even if he were coming home again. Sometimes I think I'm losing control, that I've already lost it, and I don't know how to get it back."

It was a shocking admission, revelatory of how weary Ellen was. Julie put out a hand to touch her arm. "Evan will come home, Mama. And they're only talking. They'll do what you say."

"Yes. For the moment, yes, if I say it firmly enough and often enough. I didn't use to have to say it more than once. And I pray you're right, that Evan will come home and make things right again."

"He will," Julie said, "I know he will."

"Yes. Well, right now we need something done about clothes for that poor little mite upstairs. Lallie's tearing cloth to make diapers, but he'd ought to have more than that. Would you mind going up in the attic, near where the cradle was, and see if you can find a box of baby clothes? They're old, but there may be something salvageable."

"How's Sally Ann? Is she still bleeding?"

"Yes. I've done everything I know to stop it. Perhaps it isn't as bad as it was. We'll have to tear up some more old sheets to use . . . what was that?"

"Thunder. It's only thunder, Mama." She, too, however, had for a fractional moment feared it was cannon fire. "It couldn't be General Sherman, he couldn't have come this far so fast even if he's captured Atlanta."

"No. You're right. Imagine, jumping at the sound of thun-

der. Good, it will cool things off. The heat's making everything worse." She didn't spell out what *everything* was. "How
did Hattie take to being asked to share quarters with that girl
Frances Douglas sent over?"

Julie's amusement surfaced briefly. "About as well as could
be expected."

"Nora's baby is due within a few weeks. When she can
feed Sally Ann's baby, we'll send this one home." She didn't
add *if he's still alive*, though both of them knew she was
thinking it. "Julie, I'm so *tired*. I really feel I must rest for a
short time. I think everything's running smoothly at the moment, so keep an eye on everyone and call me in half an
hour, will you?"

"Of course. Why don't you make it an hour? We'll manage, Mama."

After Ellen had gone, however, Julie spent a moment with
her eyes closed, praying.

Valerie, too, found the visitors a distraction, and a welcome one. The baby required frequent attention and, ugly
though he was, was enchanting in his own way. After
watching Gilly with him for one changing, Valerie knew that
the girl could not be trusted to do anything more than feed
him, and took upon herself a good many of the chores surrounding him.

When Sally Ann opened her eyes and murmured her first
words of concern for him, Valerie was able to smile at her
reassuringly.

"Well, he isn't very big, but he ate quite well and he's
sleeping now. How do you feel, cousin?"

"I thought I was going to die," Sally Ann said truthfully,
and as if it didn't matter very much. She was skeletally thin;
her too-white skin provided a strong contrast with freckles
and carroty hair. "Am I, Val?"

"I shouldn't think so. Mama says the bleeding has slowed
somewhat. Can you eat something? Pansy brought up some
of Mamie's good soup."

Sally Ann was too weak to feed herself, so Valerie fed her,
spoon by careful spoonful. She and Lallie had bathed Sally
Ann when she was put to bed—nearly three weeks on the
road in an open wagon, with no bathing facilities except the
streams they passed, had left all the travelers much in need of

soap and water. Now Valerie brought a basin and a cloth and sponged her cousin again, simply because it was hot and it would make her more comfortable.

Thunder rumbled in the distance and Valerie paused to listen, then smiled down at the girl on the bed. Sally Ann was only a year older than she herself; today she looked thirty.

"It's going to rain. That'll clear the air and make us all feel better. Here, I've brought a fresh gown. I think that's enough activity for a while, now we'll let you sleep."

Sally Ann moved her face in a grimace meant to be a smile. "You are good to me, Val. Thank you. I'm sorry to be so much trouble. It was so terrible at home—you couldn't believe how terrible it was." Tears slid out of the corners of her eyes, and Valerie patted them away with an end of the towel.

"Don't think about it. Just rest, and get strong. You're safe here now, and we'll take care of the baby. Had you thought of a name for him?"

Valerie waited, but her cousin's eyes had gone shut, the stubby reddish lashes against bloodless cheeks. Valerie dropped the netting into place about the bed and retreated. There were many things she longed to know; clearly Sally Ann was in no condition to convey anything, though.

On the second-floor landing, which actually formed a sizable room in the center of the house, she found someone who could convey quite a bit. Blossom Curtis stood in admiring contemplation of a portrait of a handsome young man with dark hair who leaned casually against a black marble fireplace, smiling.

She turned to Valerie, lips parted in a quick smile. "Lord, he's a good-looking one, isn't he?"

"He's my brother, Evan. Grandma Lacy says he could be taken for Papa when he was that age. The last we heard he was with General Johnston at Resaca. We haven't had a letter from him since then."

"You have a handsome family," Blossom observed. "And such a beautiful home! Before she took sick, Miss Sally Ann talked about it like Mallows was heaven, and she's not far from wrong, is she?"

"I guess it is, for us. Sally Ann used to come here as a child, and we had good times together."

"She kept saying everything would be all right, once we got to Mallows. Like it was a magic place, you know? As if nothing could go wrong, once we got here. I'm most grateful for the bed, ma'am. I surely am, and the food, too. I ain't been full in so long I can't remember what it felt like, until this morning."

"We still have plenty of meal for mush, I guess." Valerie gave in to her own curiosity. "My cousin is sleeping, and I'd like to stay where I can hear the baby if he cries. Come into the sitting room and we'll sit and talk. I haven't heard yet how you came to meet my aunt and my cousin."

She led the way. Dolly was there, looking up with a pinched expression at this invasion of her privacy; Valerie murmured a greeting, and indicated a chair for the other girl.

Blossom gazed around her, as she had done elsewhere in the house, with obvious awe. The sitting room had its own balcony at the front of the house, overlooking the oyster shell drive with its shading live oaks, and when Valerie opened the French doors onto it, to let in the breeze, Dolly ostentatiously gathered her shawl about her shoulders.

"It's stifling," Valerie announced. "This will give us a little cross-ventilation. Here, take this chair, Miss Curtis."

Blossom reverently touched the flowered chintz of the proffered chair and glanced down at the soft patterned rug beneath her feet. "What a pretty room. Like spring flowers, all those pinks and blues and greens and yellows. And you can see way out over the countryside." She smiled, sinking into the chair. "After ridin' in that wagon all those miles, my bottom sure enough appreciates this chair, ma'am."

Dolly gave her a quick, shocked look, then returned her attention to her knitting, grimly intent upon the gray wool.

"Tell me how you came to meet up with my aunt and my cousin," Valerie invited, taking the opposite chair placed so that the faint breeze blew across her face. "You lived in Atlanta, too, did you? Have you family there?"

"I got no family anyplace." Blossom idly stroked the chintz-covered chair arm. "I was orphaned when I was twelve, and the Mastersons took me in. Not charity, you know, I worked for my keep. Mrs. Masterson was an invalid, or said she was, though when the house caught fire she ran as fast as anybody else. Always talkin' about her aches and pains, always needin' to be waited on hand and foot."

Valerie sneaked a glance at her listening grandmother, concealing her own amusement at Dolly's compressed lips.

"It got worse and worse in Atlanta," Blossom went on, oblivious. "That Yankee general, he didn't hardly let anything in for us to eat, you know. And when anybody did get in with supplies, they was so high-priced couldn't nobody afford to buy anything. Everybody that could has gone, sent out their families, and the ones that're left are scared to death what he's going to do when he takes the city. Even now the shells are reachin' into town, you know. One big fine house on Ponder Street got the whole back end blown out of it, and the Federals ain't even close, yet. You got to be careful, walkin' out to market or anythin', and be ready to dive into a gopher hole when they commence firin'. Not many people gettin' killed, but it's a scary thing."

It was true, then, what Patrick Ryan had said, that the fall of Atlanta was inevitable. Valerie had accepted his declaration in that regard, yet confirmation of it was a blow, nevertheless.

"Old Mr. Masterson got desperate, and went outside of town to try to get food. He never came back, and that was more'n a month ago, now. Closer onto five weeks, I guess. The old lady fussed a whole lot, but there wasn't nothin' I could do, was there? We was down to nothin' but some dried meat she couldn't chew less'n I soaked it all day, and then she said it didn't taste like nothin'. I sure got tired, listenin' to that old lady complain, I call tell you."

Blossom shifted to a more comfortable position in the big chair. "And then one mornin' I went in to see why she wasn't bellowin' as usual for her tea, and she was dead. So maybe she was sick, after all," the girl added with a naivity that was quite unconscious.

"So you decided to leave Atlanta?"

"Well, there wasn't nothin' for me there. The house was bone-empty of anythin' to eat 'cept a little cornmeal, and not much of that. I was afraid of that General Sherman, too. There was still some people gettin' out of the city to the southeast, so I decided to try it. I packed up my stuff, what I could carry, and started out."

"You didn't have the wagon, then?"

"No. I was walkin'. Near walked the shoes right off my feet." She lifted one foot to demonstrate the truth of the statement. "Don't know how I'm going to get me another pair, come cold weather. I ain't got a cent to my name. Anyways, didn't nobody stop me walking out of Atlanta. I slept the first night under some bushes. It was kinda scary because there was two soldiers on the other side of them, didn't know

I was there, and I thank God for that, I do. Way they was talkin', I'd of been a goner if they'd found me, I reckon. All they could think about was somethin' to eat besides horse meat with maggots in it, and women. They wanted a woman, and they wasn't particular who it was, either. I kept real still, and they went away in the morning, but I didn't sleep too good.

"I didn't have no breakfast the next day, and I kept on walkin'. I carried my shoes so they wouldn't wear out any faster, and I kept goin' 'till I came to a wagon standin' alongside the road. I was going to ask the man in it if he had anythin' to eat—I was so hungry by that time I'd of done about anythin' to get somethin' to eat—only there wasn't no use to say anythin' to him. He was dead."

"Dead?" Valerie echoed. Unbidden, the image arose, of the man she had shot. "What had happened to him?"

"He been shot. Didn't you notice the blood on the wagon seat? I didn't see who shot him. He was an old man, anyway," she dismissed him, winning her another sharply scandalized glare from Dolly, which she did not notice. "I reckon maybe he was carryin' supplies to Atlanta, or maybe just goin' home. Anyhow, there wasn't much left in the wagon 'cept some sugar and a bag o' cornmeal they missed, under the seat. So I figured, no sense in the wagon just standin' there while I'm wearin' out my shoe leather walkin'. I could get farther away from them Yankees in a wagon than on foot, so I pushed him off," she said with an innocent lack of concern, "and turned them mules around and headed away from town. I hadn't gone but a couple of miles when I met Miss Grace and Miss Sally Ann."

It was impossible not to put herself in Blossom's place. What would she have done under similar circumstances? Probably not too differently from what Blossom had done, Valerie thought.

"I could see at once they was quality. I mean, they had good clothes and good shoes. They'd had a horse and trap, but the trap busted down, the axle broke, and the horse got away from 'em. I don't reckon he went very far; these days, anybody wants a horse takes him, even if it's to eat. Well, there was that skinny little Miss Sally Ann with her belly stickin' out a mile, and she'd sat down alongside the road, said she had to rest. Miss Grace was feeling poorly, too, with a inflammation of the bowels, and they was pretty sad, I can tell you. They called out to me, and offered to pay me a bit for a ride.

"I would give 'em a ride, anyway. Two females, and sick at that, you know. We couldn't hardly get Miss Sally Ann into the back of the wagon. She laid down and closed her eyes like she didn't care what we did with her, long as she didn't have to walk no more. It was easier than walkin', but I guess it wasn't good for her, joltin' along with no springs that way. Miss Grace asked me where I was goin', and I told her I didn't know, just away from Atlanta and the Yankees, and she said they was comin' here. To Mallows. She said her cousin would take 'em in, and me, too, if I'd take 'em there."

Indignation flickered in Dolly's face. She concentrated on beginning to turn the heel of the sock she was making, bending forward over the work in her lap.

"They had a little money," Blossom continued, "and we found a farmer sold us some vegetables. We didn't have no way to cook anythin', of course, so we ate them raw. They ain't bad, turnips and such, if you're hungry enough. We rode about two weeks, it was, when Miss Sally Ann started into have cramping pains. They said it wasn't her time, yet, but I guess sometimes that don't matter. She kept it up for two days, and then wasn't no doubt she was goin' to have that baby, time or not."

Blossom looked at Valerie. "You ever help deliver a baby, ma'am?"

"No. I never did." Ellen had never wanted her daughters to become involved in such matters, though she herself had done so at an early age.

"Messy business, it is. I don't think she'd of had such a time of it if she hadn't gone so long without somethin' decent to eat, maybe. She was so weak, you see. It took a long time, even if he was so little. I had to do everythin' mostly by myself; her mama was cryin' and carryin' on, and wasn't all that much help. I tell you, ma'am, I was sure enough glad when it was over, even if Miss Sally Ann did lay there like she was dead. At least she wasn't hurtin' no more, and the baby wasn't much trouble 'cept we worried about feedin' him. His poor mama didn't have no more milk than a billy goat. He'll be all right now, I reckon, that he's got a wet nurse. Your mama's a fine lady, Miss Valerie, she's the kind don't get beside herself and let somebody else do everythin'."

"Mama's had the full responsibility for Mallows for quite a

while, now. Well, that's a rather harrowing tale." And although Grace had perhaps overstepped herself somewhat in assuring the girl of a welcome at Mallows, might Valerie herself not have done the same thing under identical circumstances? She didn't doubt in the slightest that Sally Ann would have died if Blossom hadn't rescued them with her "found" wagon. "Well, while we can't meet the standards of old times, Miss Curtis, if there's food at all, you're welcome to share it, I guess."

She remembered how her mother's shoulders had sagged, how drawn her face had been, a few hours earlier. If this girl was going to stay here, she might as well make herself useful.

"As you can see, we're very short of household help. With Aunt Grace ill, Sally Ann in bed for weeks yet, probably, and an infant to care for, we'll need any assistance we can get. I take it you're used to working in the kitchen."

"Well, I ain't no *cook*," Blossom said. "But I'll be glad to help where I can, ma'am. I can wash dishes, and iron clothes, and dust down some o' that pretty furniture."

"Good. That will help a great deal. I'll tell Mamie you'll help her in the kitchen, and maybe you can tackle the mountain of linens that need washing, from the sickrooms."

"Miss Val! Oh, Miss Val!"

They turned to see Pansy, panting from the exertion of running up the stairs, holding a hand pressed to her flat chest.

"What's the matter?" Valerie asked, rising from her chair, for there was something about the girl that carried conviction of disaster.

"They's soldiers comin', Miss Val! Confederate soldiers! Aaron seen 'em!"

Ten

Neither of the soldiers was Evan Stanton. How many times would they be so let down before Evan came home?

It was all Valerie could do to concentrate on what the man said, so overwhelming was the disappointment.

They were gaunt and ragged, and not until they gave their names did Valerie realize she had met them both several years previously at some forgotten social engagement. They were friends of Evan's, and they had brought news of him at last.

"He said to stop and tell you he's still alive, and you'd see we got something to eat on our way home." They had come to the back door and been invited into the kitchen. "We're too dirty to sit in anyone's parlor," Hal Wilkins said. "And we got fleas, besides. But we're sure as God hungry, and if you can spare anything, anything at all . . ."

"Of course," Ellen assured them, and gestured to Mamie to serve them some of the soup that had been simmering for the invalids. Mamie gave her an outraged glance, for what was she to feed the family in place of it? even as she dished up steaming bowls.

It wasn't until they'd finished eating that Ellen put the question that had been trembling on her lips from the moment they had mentioned Evan's name. "How is my son? How does he look?"

No one missed the significance of the exchanged glance. "Well," Hal said, "he's hurt. Took a shot in the foot. But as he said, maybe he'll be better off it takes him out of the fighting."

"Where is he? Why doesn't he come home, if he's injured?"

"He's not up to walking, Mrs. Stanton," John Uttley told her. "And there isn't much available in the way of transport."

"We've a farm wagon here. We'll go and get him," Ellen said. "Just tell us where to find him."

Both men, this time, studiously avoided eye contact. "It's like this, ma'am. He doesn't want you to try that. It's too dangerous. Sherman's men are all over the place, and there's no way we can hold against them. There's two of them to every one of us, at least. Evan said to tell you not to worry. They turned the Atlanta Medical College, you know, there on Butler and Jenkins streets, into a hospital. They'll see to him."

They had to be content with that, crumb that it was. They said the reassuring words to one another, in hopeful tones overlying a deep-seated dread. Was the injury worse than Evan's friends reported? Was there something else they hadn't been told? Else why, if he was not too far away, had he not managed to find a way to get home?

Valerie looked at the two men and wondered why, with battles still to be fought, they were obviously on their way home. Deserters? Memory of the other deserters sent a tremor through her, a vivid image blinding her to present surroundings. She would remember until her dying day how it had felt, lying in the grass with a stick poking her in the stomach, steadying that pistol and squeezing the trigger with a man as a target.

"Will you be going back? Rejoining your company?" Ellen asked as the men were leaving. "Will you be seeing Evan again?"

Again there was evasion. "I doubt it, ma'am, although if we do see him, we'll sure tell him you all look fine, and you still have food. We're much obliged for the soup, ma'am, we surely are."

Valerie could bear it no longer. Against all training, she put the rude question. "You're going home to stay, now?"

Uttley's gaze slid across her face and away. "Well, it's harvesttime. They need help at home. If the war's still going on when we've finished . . ."

Wilkins seemed to feel compelled to justify their actions. "We have families, ma'am, that need us. A man has to think of his own."

Valerie, who would certainly have welcomed that one remaining male in *their* family, could not bring herself to reply to that. Ellen's lips moved stiffly, however, in a conventional reply. "Of course. Thank you for stopping, gentlemen. We're grateful for your news."

The men went on their way, and the women returned to their tasks. There was plenty to keep them busy with their hands, and there wasn't a one of them whose legs didn't ache at times from running up and down stairs. And the same thoughts hovered in all their minds; the menacing cloud of Sherman's army hung over them in a funereal pall.

It was midafternoon when Ellen, glancing out from the upstairs windows, realized that there were fewer workers in the field than there should have been. A query put to Aaron resulted in more disquieting news.

"I expect they just slipped off into the woods, Miss Ellen. Four of them, this time."

Four of them. Fieldhands worth from five hundred to a thousand dollars apiece, vanished into the forest. And the others, no doubt, considering the matter. Whispering while they worked, plotting, planning.

Her mouth was dry and her heartbeat was audible in her ears. "Did you know they were going, Aaron?"

It would have been easy for him to deny it. Instead, adding to her disquietude, Aaron said nothing at all. He looked into her face, his own visage impassive, saying nothing whatever.

Perhaps it was only that she already felt so pressured and since the arrival of the two soldiers her stomach was knotted with renewed anxiety over her son; at any rate, Aaron's refusal to answer her was a shattering thing. She had thought Aaron, the only male house servant remaining, was loyal to her. She had thought she could trust him. And now his silence told her that she could count neither on his loyalty nor on his open honesty.

For a moment Ellen felt dizzy and fragmented, as if different parts of her were being drawn out and away from her body, toward all the people who depended upon her, so that there was nothing left to sustain her own inner self.

94

She turned away from Aaron without further speech, plunging once more into the routine details of running a household containing two invalids and a sickly baby.

The defection of four more fieldhands had, it seemed, a perceptible effect on those blacks remaining. While there was no open insolence from them, as there had been from Mamie in the kitchen, Ellen was convinced they moved more slowly in obeying orders, that there were secret thoughts of rebellion behind the seemingly guileless dark countenances. Her fears grew.

It was Pansy who brought the news that Patrick Ryan's grandmother had died.

"Oh? Did you talk to Mr. Ryan's sister?" Ellen asked.

"No, ma'am. I just heard it, the old lady died."

It was fruitless to ask how Pansy had come by this information. A shrug was the usual response to such a query. They just knew, that was all. Sometimes Ellen wondered if there was some primitive sixth sense in these people, for they did actually seem to know some things—particularly on matters pertaining to life and death—without being informed in the more usual ways.

She sighed now, looking at her daughters over the stack of laundry they were folding on the dining room table. "I suppose we ought to go over there. They are, after all, neighbors, too. And Mr. Ryan has continued to be helpful to us even though we no longer employ him. I don't want to leave the house, though, while Sally Ann is still so low. Valerie, why don't you go?"

Taken aback, Valerie emitted a small protesting sound. "Alone?"

"No, of course not. Take Blossom with you. I can't imagine how she earned her way doing housework for those people she lived with; she's virtually no use here. She can't even dust properly. Take her, and ask if there's anything we can do to be of help." She sighed again. "God knows what it would be, since we haven't much more than they have. We could send Chad and Thomas to dig a grave, at least, and perhaps make the coffin, if Ruth Gerald is there by herself."

It was not a task Valerie relished, yet it was fair that she take her turn with the condolence calls. Julie and Ellen had gone to Cedars. At least there was small likelihood of encountering anyone like the four deserters between home and Ryan's place.

Still, she wasn't so sure of that that she wanted to risk it. Saying nothing to her mother, she went to the cabinet in the study, off the library, and removed one of her father's pistols from the glass-fronted case.

Her fingers were unsteady as she loaded it and then hid it under the wagon seat, praying to God she would have no occasion to use it. For all her grandmother's insistence that being raped was not the end of the world, she had no intention of finding out for sure, firsthand.

Blossom was delighted to have an outing, even such a one as this. "I heard about Mr. Ryan. The overseer, wasn't he? Good-looking man, I understand."

Valerie's lips were wooden. "If you like the big physical type."

"Why, certainly, honey! That's the kind I like best," Blossom assured her, laughing. "I had me a friend, big, handsome man. I guess maybe we'd got married, if he hadn't got himself killed." Her amusement faded. "Looks like there ain't going to be no men left, by the time this war is over."

Well, they had that belief in common, Valerie thought wryly. She called Thomas from the fields to drive the wagon, not an elegant way to go calling, yet better than walking.

Thomas was a year older than Chad, fifteen, a more willing, obedient boy. Today he seemed to have nothing to say, however. This was not as noticeable as it would ordinarily have been because Blossom chattered incessantly.

"This is sure a pretty part of the country, ain't it? All them nice trees. I love live oaks, don't you? I didn't know they'd grow so good, this far inland. They're kinda spoky at night, in the moonlight, all that moss stirrin' like ghosts. In the daytime, though, they're sure pretty. I hear they got a lot of 'em in Savannah. I never been to Savannah, have you, Miss Val?"

"My grandparents lived there. We often went to their house when we were children."

"Did you? I don't remember my grandparents. I always thought it would be nice to have a dotin' grandpa to buy me things. I guess my grandpas never had no money, anyway, so it don't matter I don't remember 'em. My, that's a wonderful garden! All them things to eat! I'm sure glad you saw fit to take us all in, ma'am, or I guess I'd starved by now. I hope you won't be ashamed of me, ma'am, with these raggedy old
96

clothes and the shoes fallin' off my feet. I don't suppose you got any old shoes would fit me, have you?"

Valerie stretched out a leg so that her foot was side by side with Blossom's. "I don't think they'd fit, even if I had any. We've none of us bought shoes in two years, I guess."

Blossom regarded the unmatched feet. "I reckon mine is a lot bigger, ain't it? Well, dainty feet is nice, attracts the men, I guess. But I never had any trouble attractin' men, if there was any around. You got a beau, Miss Val?"

"No," Valerie said quietly.

"You have one? One that went off and got himself killed?"

"No." What opportunity had there been to meet anyone, with all the men going off to fight, and social gatherings all but forgotten?

"Pity. Pretty girl like you. Your sister, too. You're about the prettiest things I ever saw. Miss Sally Ann, she's quality, but she ain't pretty. All them freckles, and she's so skinny. Course, maybe she wasn't skinny when she got enough to eat. And she got herself a husband, didn't she? Her mama don't seem to be any better, does she? Poor thing."

Valerie listened to this with half an ear, the other (and her eyes) alert for trouble.

There was none, however. The threatened rain held off, and there was no breeze to stir the mossy swags on the live oaks. The shells crunched under the wagon wheels, covering any small sounds that might have warned of danger.

They left the crushed oyster shell drive and turned onto the dusty red road, parasols held to protect them from the afternoon sun. Blossom, undaunted by monosyllabic responses, exclaimed over Ryan's place as soon as it was visible through the pines, twirling her borrowed parasol.

"My, it's pretty too, ain't it? Not grand, like Mallows, but real nice. Will he be there, do you think? Mr. Ryan?"

"I don't know. Quite possibly he's gone back to rejoin his company." Valerie hoped he had. She didn't want to see Patrick Ryan; he made her uncomfortable, and he was a reminder of that terrible episode she never wanted to think of again.

Although she had ridden or driven past it many times, she had never been inside Patrick Ryan's house. Her curiosity was almost as strong as Blossom's when the wagon rolled to a stop in the side yard and they climbed awkwardly down. Getting out of a wagon was not nearly as gracefully accomplished as descending from a buggy, and she hoped no one observed the descent.

Ryan's house was sturdily built of red brick topped by white-painted clapboard, the lower floor sunk to the bottoms of the windows in the earth, so that one had to climb a steep set of steps to reach the front door. There was a vine-shaded front porch with a white railing, and if it was not perfectly kept up, why, in that it didn't differ from the other houses in the South which hadn't been painted in nearly four years.

Valerie walked past the rocking chair and tapped lightly on the door. It was opened by Patrick himself, in his shirt sleeves and his stocking feet.

He was not nearly so disconcerted as Valerie was. She had to clear her throat to speak. "Good afternoon. We heard your grandmother had died, and Mama sent me over to see if there was anything we could do."

For a moment Patrick simply stood there, staring down at her. Then the gaze shifted to Blossom, lingered briefly, and came back to Valerie. He stepped backward to allow them to enter, running a hand through his rusty hair.

"Well, that's very kind of you, Miss Valerie." He didn't sound as if he really thought so. She saw that his belongings were laid out as if he prepared to leave, including the pistol atop a pair of freshly ironed shirts, and that except for those things the place was neat and everything in its place. Somehow she hadn't expected it to be that way, so attractive. "Ruth's down in the kitchen. I'm sure she'll appreciate your coming. Please tell Miss Ellen we're both grateful to her for letting us have the landanum. Go on down and talk to Ruthie, right down those stairs. You'll excuse me if I don't go with you; I'm late getting away, and I'm in a hurry."

"Yes, of course." Without appearing to, Valerie glanced around at the wide polished pine floors, the brick fireplace, the pair of comfortable chairs. This living room took up the entire front of the top floor. On each side of the descending stairs at the back was a bedroom; through the doorways she could see the poster beds, made up with colorful quilts. There were even several shelves of books, although she didn't know why that should have surprised her. Patrick Ryan had been forever borrowing from the library at Mallows when he was a boy.

"Oh, you go ahead, Miss Val," Blossom said. "I think I'll

just sit here a minute, if it don't bother Mr. Ryan. I think I got a stone in my shoe."

Valerie had almost forgotten Blossom. How she'd gotten a stone in her shoe when she was riding in a wagon was a mystery, until Valerie turned and saw the other girl's face.

Coquettish, smiling, showing the prominent teeth that overlapped, Blossom was looking up at Patrick Ryan. A ripple of something she refused to acknowledge as jealousy surged through Valerie; she kept it out of her matter-of-fact tone, however, "Oh, I'm sorry, I didn't introduce you. Mr. Patrick Ryan, Miss Blossom Curtis. Miss Curtis is our guest."

"Happy to know you, Miss Blossom." Infuriatingly, Patrick smiled. "By all means, sit down and take the stone out of your shoe. Go right on downstairs, Miss Valerie."

She went, wondering why she was so annoyed with both Blossom and Ryan. It was, after all, none of her business what either of them did. And probably they were well suited to each other.

Her heels sounded on the wooden stairs, and she emerged at the bottom into a spacious brick-walled kitchen. It was a warm and homey room, with a small polished table and four chairs at one end and a fireplace and iron cookstove at the other; there were white muslin curtains and a pair of oval rag rugs in muted colors on the brick floor. Had the house belonged to anyone but Patrick Ryan, she would have thought it charming in its simple way.

Ruth Gerald turned from the fireplace with a skillet in her hands, speaking before she realized it was not her brother who had come down. "Eat this now, and I'll fix you a lunch to carry . . . why, Miss Valerie! I'm sorry, I thought it was Patrick. Please, excuse me, Pat's getting ready to go, and I'm trying . . ."

"I'm sorry if I interrupt you. We had word that your grandmother had died, and wondered if there was anything we could do to help. Mama will send over several of the boys to make the coffin, if you like, or help in digging a grave . . ."

Ruth smiled in obvious gratitude. "Why, that's very kind of her. We don't need anything, though. Patrick made the coffin several days ago; we knew she couldn't last long. And dug the grave, too, because he knew I'd be alone here after he'd gone. Tell your mother that she died peacefully, thanks to the

99

laudanum. You can't know how much that meant to us, that she didn't continue to suffer right to the last."

Valerie noted the tear-reddened eyes and shifted her weight uncomfortably, wondering if she would control herself as well in a similar situation. "I'll tell Mama. Are you sure there's nothing else you need, now?"

Ruth shook her head, lowering the skillet onto a trivet on the sideboard. "Thank you. She's buried now, just an hour ago. Patrick's leaving as soon as he's eaten, if I can get him to stay that long, and in the morning I'll go, too. Back to my family in Midway Church."

It hadn't occurred to Valerie that Ruth had a family, except for a husband. "Have you children?" She thought of Sally Ann's tiny baby, and guessed that Ruth Gerald's infants would be stronger, healthier, prettier.

"Oh, yes. Four. Three boys and a girl." Ruth smiled, thinking about them. "All redheads."

"You must have missed them very much, while you were here."

"Yes, I have. And Earl, too."

"Your husband is there, with the children?"

"Yes. He lost an arm in Chancellorsville," Ruth said quietly.

Pain, a physical thing, touched her. Valerie swallowed. "How terrible for you, and for him."

"It was hard," Ruth admitted. "But I'd rather have him with one arm than not have him at all." She indicated one of the chairs at the shining little table. "Won't you sit down, and have a cup of coffee? Well, it's part coffee."

"No, thank you. If you don't need anything, I'd better go back. We have a houseful of people, and two of them are ill."

She didn't remember quite what was said after that. Later, she recalled many details about Ryan's small house, and she was grateful that the old woman had been buried and that she hadn't had to view the body. Most of all she remembered coming quietly up those stairs and seeing Blossom and Patrick Ryan together, and hearing their subdued laughter.

She had paused, watching as Patrick did something to the girl's shoe and then put it back on her foot. Blossom lifted her foot to rest it against his knee as he knelt before her.

Blossom looked up and saw her, her face glowing a rosy pink. "Ah, see, Miss Val, he's fixed my shoe!"

Ryan stood up, his mouth quirking. "Should last for another three or four days, if you're lucky. After that, well, it'll be warm enough to go barefoot for a few months yet."

Blossom rose to go, reaching out to shake his hand. "Thank you. And good luck to you, Mr. Ryan. I hope you get through the rest of this awful war safe, and all."

"I'll try," Patrick said, with more amusement than Valerie had ever seen him display. It vanished when he looked at *her*. "Take care of things over there, Miss Val. And remember, when the Yankees come, don't get any foolish ideas about holding them off. Hide what you can, let them take what you can't hide, and you'll survive."

"Thank you for the advice," Valerie said stiffly. She wanted, like Blossom, to tell him she hoped he'd survive, as well, but the words would not form. "Good afternoon, Mr. Ryan."

On the way back to Mallows, she listened in silence to Blossom's prattle. Blossom thought Patrick Ryan was quite the most interesting man she'd met in a long time. "Them eyes," she said, rolling her own and giggling. "The kind looks right through a girl's clothes!"

"I hope not through *mine*," Valerie retorted, and felt uncomfortable when Blossom laughed again.

They were halfway home when the rain that had been threatening came without further warning. There was no thunder this time, simply a wall of water washing over them, soaking garments and hair and making them gasp for breath.

Thomas drew the wagon up before the broad marble steps and the girls raced for the house. Lacy met them at the front door, and at the sight of her face, Valerie braced herself for the next catastrophe.

Eleven

"She died half an hour ago," Lacy said. "We haven't told Sally Ann yet; your mother doesn't think she's strong enough, and her mother hasn't been visiting her, anyway, so maybe she won't realize it for a while, that Grace is gone. Maybe she'll be feeling better by then."

"Poor lady," Blossom said. Her cheeks still glowed with the pleasure of her ten-minute talk with Patrick Ryan. "I reckoned she might not live if she kept on with the diarrhea that way. A body can only go on so long. Was that what killed her, ma'am?"

Lacy, who had never particularly liked Grace Havers (she was on the Mallow side of the family, not the Stanton side), gave Blossom a level look. "We're none of us doctors, but it would seem so. She's been bleeding from the bowels ever since she got here, and God knows for how long before that. Valerie, your mother needs all the help she can get right now. Julie's with her, and she asked that you come up as soon as possible."

They said that death came in threes. These days, Valerie reflected as she stripped off her wet dress and petticoats a few minutes later, death came in bunches. And God knew how

102

many more there would be before they came to the end of them.

Grace was buried the following day. The rain had cooled the air, and the damp earth sent up wisps of steam. Ellen read from the Bible, very briefly, and they all trooped back to the house.

They had not wanted to leave Sally Ann and the baby alone, so Julie had remained with them, secretly glad not to have to stand at the graveside.

With the exception of Ellen, who had done a major share of the nursing, no one had realized that Grace was critically ill. They were a subdued and somber group who returned to take up their customary duties.

Life fell into a pattern of work-filled days that left them more than ready for sleep when night came. Ellen tried bringing in some of the outside workers to assist, with notable lack of success. Either the women were incredibly stupid, or they pretended to be; she suspected the latter. With no overseer directing them, they could get by with less physical effort if they stayed in the fields.

Working directly under Miss Ellen's supervision was no longer a coveted position.

And so the burden of running the household, nursing Sally Ann, and caring for a sickly infant continued to fall primarily on Ellen, Valerie, and Julie. Blossom was not much more use than Gilly. Lacy, without being asked, took on the small mountains of mending, an important task when everything was wearing out and there was no money to replace any of it. Dolly, of course, simply pretended to be unaware of any need and contented herself with knitting quantities of socks as she waited for someone to bring her tea.

The baby, who was finally given the name of Hugh Alexander, suckled eagerly at Gilly's black breast and thrived as Gilly's own child thrived. It was a pleasure to see the flesh appear on the tiny limbs and to see the face fill out so that he looked like a human child rather than a monkey. Lacy took upon herself the chore of providing him with garments, too, to supplement the old ones that had been brought down from the attic.

They worked, and they waited. During the early days of
103

September, six more of the fieldhands slipped quietly away into the surrounding woods. The weeds grew thicker in the cotton, as there were less hands to chop them out, and vegetables were harvested from the garden and put away against the coming winter by those who remained.

Old Rudy recovered from his head injury in time to supervise the fall butchering. Hickory fires in the smokehouse sent out tantalizing aromas, and Blossom was put to work helping Mamie and two other young girls, salting down pork and rendering lard.

Though every effort went into preparing for it, no one mentioned the winter to come. All of them dreaded it. There was not only the matter of food, which would be more scarce than it had been the previous year; the dwindling cotton crop promised less cash for the things they could not produce themselves. There was the matter of warm clothing, for the remaining one hundred and thirty-seven slaves as well as for the family. If the cotton brought a reasonable price, Ellen estimated that she might exchange it for enough yardage to make a garment apiece. If she could get the cotton harvested at all, with only women, a few old men, and rebellious boys like Chad to do it.

On September 2, General William T. Sherman and his forces marched victorious through the streets of Atlanta.

It took more than two weeks for the news to filter through to Mallows, nearly two hundred miles away.

While General Hood remained in the field, the South reeled under the loss of Atlanta. The Confederacy was broken. Its men began to melt away, those who were left; many of them returned to their homes and families and farms. It was from one of those that they heard the news they had been braced for, and it was more devastating than any of them had thought it would be.

Until now, there had remained a faint spark of hope that some miracle might prevail, that prayers might be answered.

With the fall of Atlanta, they knew.

The hated Yankees had won. No one any longer doubted that the war was virtually over. There remained only the matter of the final degradation of the South, as Sherman proceeded to crush Georgia beneath his heel.

There was not much at Mallows that hadn't already been either sold or hidden. What little was left—Ellen's plain gold wedding band, the everyday silver—was buried. She had to do it herself, with the aid of no one, because there was no Negro she could any longer trust, and if the girls and the old women did not know, why, then, they could not be forced to divulge its whereabouts. The thought that anything might happen to her, leaving the valuables forever lost, did not occur to her. She had borne a heavy burden for nearly four years, and she expected to go on bearing it until the bitter end.

Sally Ann had gradually recovered to the point where she could sit for a few hours a day in a chair, looking out over the deceptively peaceful countryside, and hold little Hugh Alexander. If she grieved over her mother, she did so quietly. Perhaps, Valerie thought, she was relieved that at least one of them was finally at rest, at peace. It might be easier to be dead than to continue to struggle to survive.

Not that Valerie had any idea of giving up the fight. The end of the war was in sight. The things they heard of Sherman painted him as a brutal man—Southern newspapers referred to him as "Attila of the West"—but he was only a man, and eventually all this would end. Things would return to some semblance of normal.

They heard nothing from Evan. Although no one voiced the fear, they all shared it, that he had been taken prisoner because he was unable to move fast enough to escape Sherman's voracious armies. Those who had been in a Yankee prison, or a Yankee hospital, described both as matching the pits of hell. Surely, they prayed, the Federals would not bother with men in the Confederate Hospital, men who offered them no opposition.

In October Ellen rallied her flagging strength to direct the remaining fieldhands in harvesting the cotton. It went slowly, and the crop was a poor one, yet it was the only hope of cash money that she had. In the end, every available pair of hands was pressed into service, including even those of the house servants and Blossom, Valerie, and Julie.

Blossom fared reasonably well, for she had done manual labor before. Valerie, Julie, and Lallie were less sturdy, and the work was backbreaking. None of them could do it for very long at a time.

They wore long sleeves and gloves and broad-brimmed hats to protect against the sun. Even so, it was impossible to keep complexions and the skin of their hands in decent condition. For the first time, Julie and Valerie knew what it was like to be too exhausted to sleep, the weariness a physical ache that sometimes took hours to dissipate enough so that rest was possible.

Aaron, impressed into service along with the others, worked with them for three days. At the end of the third day he straightened, refrained from putting a hand to his aching back, and spoke quietly to Valerie, who was closest to him.

"I won't do any more of this, Miss Val. I'm not a field nigger, and I won't pick cotton any more."

Valerie, massaging her own sore muscles without thinking much about it, was too taken aback to think of an immediate reply. She hated it, too, but she realized the necessity of getting whatever money they could out of the cotton.

"I'm afraid Mama would be very upset to hear you say that, Aaron."

"I'm sorry to upset your mama," Aaron said, and walked away without another word, leaving Valerie deeply disturbed and not knowing anything to do about it.

It was late the same night when, unable to sleep for aching body and limbs, Valerie descended to the kitchen for a drink of something colder than the tepid water in her bedroom pitcher. She found Lallie, fully dressed at nearly 1 A.M., ahead of her.

Lallie's hands stilled, then after a moment resumed what they'd been doing: cutting thick squares of cornbread and wrapping them in packets of old napkins.

Valerie stared at her. She was very tired and she wondered if her brain played tricks on her; it seemed to resist her command that it function on the most elementary level.

"Lallie? What are you doing?" It was a foolish question; it was quite obvious that the girl was packing food to be carried away. Lallie, running away? It was unthinkable!

Valerie stood there, literally swaying on her feet in fatigue. Should she call her mother, or could she dissuade the girl herself? Any words of persuasion refused to form on her tongue, however, and she was still standing there watching Lallie when the back door opened and Aaron slipped silently inside.

It was not hot, but Valerie felt clammy with perspiration. Her throat closed so that she could not speak, and Aaron did not immediately see her standing there in the shadowed doorway.

"Is it ready?" He spoke crisply. "I want to be well away from here by dawn."

Lallie replied as if she, too, were unaware of the listener. "What will I tell Miss Ellen?"

Aaron's black face was strongly outlined in the light from Lallie's candelabrum, borrowed from the dining room because it held three tall candles. His voice held only the slightest undercurrent of tension, and no indecision whatever. "Tell her I've gone. That's all."

Valerie moved then, out of the shadow, reaching for him. Her fingers closed over his forearm; she felt the taut muscles, the complete resistance, yet was compelled to speak anyway.

"Aaron, you can't go."

The planes of his face did not soften. "I mean to go, Miss Val. They say there are hundreds of Negroes following General Sherman's army, taking their freedom. I'm going to join them."

"Why? You've remained loyal through so much, and we need you . . ."

He moved, pulling away from her hand, and began to put the packets of food into a larger bundle.

"The slaves are freed, Miss Val. Haven't you heard? You can't own us like cattle any more. We're free to do as we please. If I leave a day or two ahead of them, why, that can't matter to you very much." He tied the bundle and slung it over his shoulder. For the first time she noted that he was wearing a workshirt such as the fieldhands wore, and old trousers, instead of the garments he had always worn as a house servant. Only his shoes had been retained.

It made him seem a different person. Or perhaps the change was not in his garments but in his bearing, in his voice, which was quietly assured. "I'm sorry about Miss Ellen, but she'll make out. She always has. She's a strong lady, your mama is."

Oh, God, give me the wit to say the right thing! I cannot let him go, we need him too badly. "Aaron, you can't have thought this out. It's true, Mr. Lincoln freed the slaves, only it's not as simple as that! Most of them are ignorant and untrained for anything except working in the fields, and where will they all go? Who will look after them? Aaron, you'll be better off to remain here! Wait until we see what happens . . ."

"I've waited," Aaron said, and even the dropping of the

107

polite form of address he had always employed was a measure of his newfound determination. "Through this whole war, I've waited. And now it's time to go, to see what I can find for myself. I'm not an ignorant field nigger. I can read and write, and I think there will be something I can do to fend for myself."

"Haven't we always been good to you?" Valerie asked, helplessness washing over her. She didn't know how to deal with him. An aggressive approach might have worked with some servants; she knew instinctively that such a thing would be absurd with Aaron.

"Good to me?" For a moment sardonic amusement was reflected in the black face. "Oh, certainly, by your own lights you have been good to me, Miss Val." The courtesy title was back, only said with an intonation that made it seem insolent, mocking. "As you would have been good to a little dog, except that I was not allowed to sleep on the foot of your bed. I have even been locked out of the house at night for the past two years because I was black, and you are afraid of black people these days. You can't trust us, can you?"

When she made no response to this, Aaron tucked a knife into a homemade sheath at his belt, and turned to go. At the last moment, however, he paused to look back at her.

"A young lady never been out of the state of Georgia is maybe bound to think the way you do, Miss Val. I s'pose you can't help it, looking on niggers like they're your pets or your mules, to do the work. I don't know about the rest of them, running away to a place they know nothing about, with no skills except picking cotton. What I do know is that inside of *me* there is a *man* struggling to get out. Not a slave, not a servant, but a human being type *man*." His attention shifted to Lallie, who had stood quite still and silent through this exchange. "I'll be back for you," he said, and then he was gone, slipping out the back door into the night as noiselessly as he had come.

For a moment neither of the remaining pair said anything. Lallie began to brush at the crumbs, gathering them in her hand.

"You, too. You're deserting, also." Valerie couldn't keep the bitterness from her voice.

"When the time comes," Lallie said flatly. "There's no point in tryin' to explain it to you. Aaron was right about

108

that. Anybody with a drop of black blood will never be a human being to you, will they? Yet even a fieldhand yearns to be somethin' more than a beast of burden, Miss Val. To be *free*."

Valerie stared at her in frustration at her own inability to convey the truth. "*We're* free," she said at last. "I'm free, Mama's free. You've seen what being free had done for my mother. She's worn out with the responsibility for us, and for all of you as well. Is that what you want, to be free to find your own food and to secure your own roof over your head? You've been cared for at Mallows, nursed when you're sick as if you were a member of the family."

"But I'm *not* a member of the family, am I?" Lallie asked. For a moment there was almost compassion on the face that was little darker than Valerie's own. "I'm nearly as white as you are, but I'll always be a *nigger* in Georgia. And in this house, I'll always take orders. Do this, Lallie. Do that. Don't matter if I'm so tired I could drop, if somebody says Lallie, run up the stairs, Lallie runs. If I want to lay down and die, somebody says Lallie get up, and I get up." She paused to lick at the crumbs in her hand. "When Aaron comes back for me, I'm goin'. So, you want to lock me out of the house at night, too? Just in case you can't trust me, either?"

Feeling sick, forgetting what she had come down here for, Valerie gave up, defeated. Maybe she should have called her mother before Aaron left, maybe *she* could have talked some sense into him. "Are you in love with Aaron, then? Will you marry him? Mama would have let you marry him, if you'd told her . . ."

Lallie made a ladylike sniffing sound. "Would she? White folks don't have to be *allowed* to fall in love and get married, do they? They just do it. No, Miss Valerie, I ain't in love with Aaron. He's just a smart nigger, and he'll help me. Once I get up north, I might just forget there's any nigger blood in *me*, and marry me a white man, and make white babies instead of black ones." She began to put out the candles. "You want me to sleep outside from now on?"

Valerie turned away without answering. She wanted to cry, yet for some reason the tears would not come. She lay awake for a long time, listening to the night sounds, hearing Gilly when she came to feed tiny Hugh Alexander, and was still awake when her mother rose at dawn to begin a new day.

Aaron's defection was a worse blow than Ellen would have admitted. She had counted on him so heavily for so many things, and now he was gone. Except for the infant Hugh, Mallows was truly a household of women.

They were gathered in the upstairs sitting room when Pansy again was the announcer of news. They all sat darning and mending and knitting. Only Sally Ann was not busy with these tasks; though up and about, she was still feeling weak, and sat rocking the cradle with one foot and admiring her son.

Pansy had just brought up tea, and they had taken a welcome pause; Dolly asked querulously to have the windows onto the balcony closed, although the others were perfectly contented to have the breeze on a fine autumn day.

Pansy, one hand on the French door, made a peculiar, strangling sound. Valerie, who was the closest, thought the girl might be suffering a seizure, for when she turned, Pansy's eyes were rolled back, showing the whites, and her free hand reached for the support of a chair-back.

"What's the matter?" Ellen asked.

Valerie rose and reached for Pansy, though by the time she touched her she didn't need to be told.

Far down the white oyster shell drive two figures rode slowly between the live oaks toward the house.

A sinking sensation made her head swim, so that for a moment she saw them through a blur.

Valerie forced her lips to move. "They're here," she said. "The Yankees are here."

Twelve

Major Otis Quinn was a man of fifty, not large, ramrod-straight in the saddle. His hair was going gray, the same color as his eyes, which ought to have made him a colorless man, which he was not. There was something about him that sometimes made perfect strangers step aside for him in the streets.

His companion was younger and he, too, attracted attention, though for a different reason. Captain Jack Ferris was thirty, with dark hair and eyes and a lean gracefulness that would have drawn feminine eyes even if he hadn't been quite extraordinarily good-looking.

Most of the time he was well aware of this impression he made; today, however, after twelve straight hours in the saddle with scarcely more than a pause to relieve himself, and nothing to eat since before dawn, his interest was all on the house ahead.

Beside him, his commanding officer spoke dryly in his clipped New England accent.

"By God, they do themselves well, these Southerners."

"It's quite a house," Ferris agreed.

"It is, indeed. I think it will do for our purposes, wouldn't you say, Captain?"

"We have yet to see the inside. But yes, sir, I would guess it would serve adequately."

Quinn shot him a steely glance. "I forget, you're used to elegant houses, aren't you, Ferris?"

A tired grin split the tanned face. "New York houses don't match this one."

They rode the rest of the way without speaking, both absorbed in the façade that Mallows presented to the afternoon sun. A big house, beautifully proportioned, with those elegant marble pillars and the spacious, welcoming porch that surrounded it on three sides. Yes, it should serve admirably.

When the girl appeared on an upper balcony, to be joined a few seconds later by a second girl, Jack Ferris muttered only half-audibly. "The Southern belles appear all that we've heard they were."

Major Quinn wasted no more than a glance at the females. It was the house that interested him. Jack Ferris was still looking upward, however, when they reached the front steps.

Fear held them all rigid as the blue-uniformed men advanced.

Valerie's fingers curled around the railing so hard that they cramped there. Beside her, she heard Julie's rapid breathing, the little choked sound as her sister fought for self-control.

"Remember what Mr. Ryan told us," Ellen said from behind them. "Receive them as our guests. Do nothing to antagonize them. And stay together, at least in pairs."

Lacy, who had moved up behind her granddaughters, spoke with grim deliberation. "They're officers. Which probably means that even though there are only two of them, there are plenty more coming behind them. Look, isn't that smoke?"

All eyes shifted from the approaching horsemen to the blot on the sky beyond them, a blot that grew as they watched to a roiling column above the treetops.

"Cedars," Ellen breathed. She was deathly pale, yet she spoke with the surface calm of a general directing a battle. "They're burning something at Cedars. They must not burn anything here. Does everyone understand? We will give them anything they ask for, do nothing to provoke them, and perhaps they will simply take what they want and go away."

Valerie's eyes were fixed on the column of smoke. She

thought she could even smell it, now. Only the house itself, surely, would give rise to such a quantity of smoke. She was icy cold, yet perspiring; she could feel the cold wetness on her body.

Julie, close beside her, was visibly trembling. The other men, the Confederate deserters, had nearly succeeded in raping her. Would these men, the hated Yankees, make the same attempt? Only it wouldn't be an attempt, of course, since there would be nothing to stop them this time.

She thought of the pistol she had hidden beneath the cushion in Dolly's chair of this room. In spite of her grandmother's story, she was not convinced that being raped was preferable to being killed. Those fingerprints on her thighs had taken days to fade away, days in which they had been a hateful reminder of the thing to which she'd been subjected. And now there were more men, enemies of the Confederacy and of Georgians, riding up to their front door with all the assurance of conquerors.

Pansy gave a squeal of terror, and Ellen spoke sharply to her.

"Stop that. There will be no hysterics. Nothing to arouse in them any desire to punish us, not even a look, do you understand? We will go downstairs—not all of us, only Pansy to open the door, and Valerie will come with me. The rest of you, stay up here."

Valerie hesitated for a final look downward, and found her gaze locking with that of the younger of the Union officers.

A shock ran through her, as if he'd touched her, though he gave no sign, and neither did she. And then, as the men stopped and began to dismount, Valerie turned away, following her mother.

The stairway had never seemed so long. Pansy, whimpering, turned to her mistress in appeal.

"I can't open the door, Miss Ellen! Not to them Yankees!"

"Of course you can open the door. Don't be foolish." The recollection of that ominous cloud of smoke was enough to put steel into Ellen's voice. "You don't have to say anything, or do anything else. Simply open the door."

And so, as had always been the case with visitors to Mallows, there was no need for the Yankee officers to hammer upon the door. As they came up the marble steps between two of the great pillars that were even more impressive at

113

close range than they had been from the far end of the drive, the front door of the mansion swung inward.

Pansy, quaking, bobbed her head at them, retreating with the door.

Ellen, with Valerie standing slightly behind her and to her right, stood in the middle of the entry hall. She would have preferred greeting even such unwelcome guests as these in something other than a worn dimity gown, looking like one of her own servants. In truth, no one in the world would have taken her for a servant. Her manner, her bearing, the tilt of her head would all have convinced anyone that she was a lady of quality, regardless of what she wore.

The officers came through the wide doorway, hesitating just inside as their eyes adjusted to the dimness. The day was a warm one, and both men showed sweat stains under their arms, though this did nothing to make them seem more human.

"Madam," the older officer said. "What place is this?"

Ellen replied with a quiet dignity. "The plantation is called Mallows, and I am Mrs. Stanton."

The older man, who had drawn off his gloves and was slapping them gently against one hand, made an open appraisal of what he could see of the house. "Admirable. A pity, a real pity."

Hidden in the folds of her skirt, Ellen's hands curled into fists. "A pity, sir? I do not take your meaning."

A wintery smile touched his lips without softening them. "That such a way of life must be at an end." Then, as if he had wasted enough time on amenities, he spoke crisply to his subordinate. "I suggest you familiarize yourself with the place, Captain Ferris, and report back to me at once. We have no time to spare."

"Yes, sir." The younger officer was just as businesslike, except in the way that he appraised the two women as well as the house. He strode off, peering into doorways and around corners, then bounding up the stairs.

They waited in silence. What was he looking for? There was no sound from the second floor, where the rest of the household waited. It was so still that they all listened to one another's breathing, though after a few minutes Major Quinn strolled across the polished flooring to peer at some of the ancestral paintings hung beside the library door.

Captain Ferris did not spend overlong on the second floor.

His heels clicked smartly on the stairs as he descended, and Quinn turned to await his report.

"Seven bedrooms up there, sir. A sitting room. A stair going to the third floor." He turned a questioning look on the women, and Ellen told him, "There is a ballroom on the top floor."

"A ballroom! Extraordinary!" Quinn muttered. "A pity it's up two long flights of stairs, and therefore useless for our purposes. It meets with your approval, does it, Ferris?"

"Yes, sir."

"Very well." Major Quinn slapped his gloves again against his palm. "We will require some of the bedrooms upstairs, madam, and the use of the study, the library, and the main dining room, as well as those two rooms over there." He indicated the drawing rooms that could be opened into each other. "The rest of the house can be kept for your own use."

Ellen's jaw sagged before she remembered what that must look like. "The bedrooms! Sir, you do not understand that we are a full household! There are seven women here, and an infant, plus our servants."

"I'm sure you'll find a place for each of them. Which rooms will we require of those upstairs, Ferris?"

"The sitting room and all but the three rooms on the east side of the house," Ferris said promptly.

"Very good. You may retain the back three rooms for your own use," Major Quinn informed them. "The other rooms are to be vacated by the time we return, which I estimate will be about midday tomorrow. My officers will take their meals in the dining room. I trust you have a cook who will provide us with dinner tomorrow night? We will provide for ourselves until that time."

Speechless, Ellen struggled to control the tremors that weakened her lower limbs. Whatever she had expected, it had not been this, that the Yankees would move in and take over her house!

"Good day, ladies," Quinn said, turning on his heel and leaving them there, ignoring Pansy, who still peeked from behind the opened door.

Captain Ferris, too, turned to go, to be stopped when Valerie cleared her throat. She didn't know where the courage came from; she only knew that the suspense of wondering about the fate of Cedars was unendurable.

"If you please, sir—"

"Yes?" Ferris stopped, waiting.

"Could you tell us—what's happened at Cedars? The last house you must have passed, if you came from—from Atlanta? We saw . . . smoke."

"I believe they set it afire," Jack Ferris said.

Beside her, Ellen swayed, and Valerie put a supporting arm around her mother's waist.

"What about the people—the Douglases?"

"I couldn't tell you, ma'am. I wasn't with the men who stopped there. Excuse me, ma'am." He touched his hat brim in what seemed a parody of good manners, and strode after Major Quinn.

For a moment, after the men had gone, neither of them had the strength to move. Pansy slowly closed the door, her eyes enormous.

"Oh, Miss Ellen, you think they burned up that whole family? Everybody at Cedars?"

"Of course not," Ellen said. However, there was a lack of conviction in her voice, and a hint of tears. "Dear God, what are we going to do? Three bedrooms, for the lot of us! And the house full of Yankees for God knows how long!"

"If the house is full of them, at least they won't burn it," Valerie pointed out slowly.

Ellen blinked, brushing a hand across her eyes. "Of course. You're right. We must be grateful for small blessings. Tomorrow midday, he said."

It was not until the sound of the horses had died away on the shell drive that anxious faces appeared at the top of the stairs. "Have they gone for good?" Lacy demanded.

"I'm afraid not," Ellen explained. "I can see no choices but to do as they say. How are we going to fit the lot of us into three bedrooms?"

"They didn't notice the two little bedrooms," Julie offered, clinging to the banister as she peered down at them. "Lallie and Blossom have those, and the rest of us will have to share."

"Lallie and Blossom," Ellen decreed with returning strength, "may have to share one of those rooms. Julie, they want all but the back three rooms. You can sleep with Valerie, so the two of you can begin to move what you'll need. Mama—" she hesitated, anticipating her mother's reaction to being forcibly ejected from the room she'd had for so many years.

116

The obvious thing, had one not been aware of the antagonism between them, would have been to put the two old ladies in the same room. However, that was unthinkable.

Ellen sighed. "Mama and I will move into the room that Grace had. Miss Lacy, you may have the other little room, if Blossom moves into Lallie's room, or share with Sally Ann. Neither ideal choices, of course, since one involves another flight of stairs and the other sharing a room with an infant."

Lacy, gratified that the suggestion hadn't been made that she sleep in the same bed with Dolly Mallow, spoke matter-of-factly. "I'll share with Sally Ann and young Hugh."

"Good. Then everyone set to, moving belongings. There's no telling how long they will occupy our house, so take everything you might need over a few weeks. Lallie and Pansy, help wherever you can. Miss Lacy and Miss Dolly will probably require the most assistance; carry whatever they tell you."

There was surprisingly little dissent, even from Dolly, although her mouth was more flatly compressed than usual and she did almost none of the actual work. She kept Pansy and Lallie hopping, telling them what to carry while she supervised. Apprehension ran high, however, and not least among their uncertainties was the matter of being unable to lock doors. No interior door at Mallows had ever been locked in many years, and if there had ever been keys, no one now living knew what had become of them.

"Perhaps," Julie suggested nervously, "one of the men could improvise a system of bolts, at least on the rooms we'll be using."

"Even a bolt couldn't keep them out, if they're determined to enter." Ellen rubbed again at her temple, where the throbbing ache was an almost constant companion these days. "No, I think that might antagonize them. It would be obvious they'd just been added, bars, I mean. It might give them ideas they didn't already have. I think it might be best to act as if we consider them to be honorable gentlemen. People often live up to what is expected of them."

No one disputed that, although no one was particularly reassured, either. Still less was anyone calmed when they heard, a few hours later, what had happened at Cedars.

Thirteen

It was Lallie who found them, crying and whimpering as they staggered through the woods along the edge of the cornfield. She had gone down to the quarters to remind Gilly that young Hugh must be fed, for Gilly had a way of forgetting the time, or at least avoiding the big house when it appeared there might be other chores for her to do. In truth, Gilly was of so little use that for the most part no one felt it worth the effort to try to get her to do anything beyond feeding the baby.

Lallie, who was tired from an afternoon and evening spent hauling someone else's clothing and personal belongings from one room to another, had no fewer apprehensions than any of the others. If anything, she thought, she had a right to more fears. For although Mr. Lincoln had issued a proclamation stating that slavery was abolished, there had been precious little evidence as yet of that supposed new freedom.

She could have run off with the others (though Aaron had not encouraged her to go with him, not before determining what he had run away *to*), yet she remained at Mallows for the present, because it seemed safer than leaving it. For all that she had said to Valerie about freedom, Lallie was not stupid. She had never been mistreated at Mallows; she'd always had plenty to eat and decent clothes to wear, and a private room in the big house that was far more luxurious than anything in the quarters. She had no assurance that if she left the plantation she would continue to have those things.

Lallie harbored the same fears as the white women. She had been raped once, when she was fifteen, by a visitor to Mallows, an older man who was a friend of Roger Stanton's. She had never revealed this to anyone except Mamie, who had told her what to do for herself and made her understand that reporting to Miss Ellen would be foolish.

"Nothin' anybody can do about it now," Mamie pointed out. "Can't nobody make you a virgin again. And if you ain't a virgin, they looks down on you, even if you black and you been took against your will. They thinks less of you. If you told, Mr. Roger have to be angry with his friend, and he don't want to be angry. So that make him angry at *you,* girl. So you wash yourself up and forget it."

She had not forgotten it, of course. And there had been times when she'd been afraid of Mr. Roger himself, so that she had learned to avoid him, to protect herself by staying close to Miss Ellen.

Now, with the Yankees swarming all over Tattnall County, every female would be vulnerable. And the black ones, as usual, would be more vulnerable than the white ones. Nobody thought anything of throwing a black wench down in the nearest haystack, or wagon-bed, or invading her own cabin. Lallie was grateful that she slept in the house and took it for granted that Miss Ellen would try to protect her as she would try to protect her own family, although if the soldiers were quartered in the house there was no telling what would happen. The man who had raped her came from Boston; the men from the North were no different from those in the South. None of them could be trusted.

Lallie was not very happy about being sent out for Gilly. It was not quite dark and there was nothing to suggest that danger lurked in the lengthening shadows, yet she could not control her fears that one of the blue bellies would suddenly appear and leap upon her.

When the sounds came from the edge of the woods, Lallie felt the hair rise on the back of her neck. She spun and started to run before a voice called after her, a feminine voice.

"Lallie! Wait, help me, it's Henriette Douglas!"

Lallie stopped, peering to make sure it really was the young lady from the neighboring plantation. Cedars had been burned, they said. Hours ago, before the Yankees had come to Mallows.

"Miss Henriette?"

"Oh, please, Lallie, help me! I don't think Charlotte can go any farther, and she's bleeding terribly! Help me!"

Henriette's pretty face was dirty and tear-streaked, her clothing considerably the worse for wear after the long walk through the woods. Her sister, however, was in much more shocking condition.

Lallie sucked in a disbelieving breath, looking down at the figure sprawled exhaustedly between two large trees. This demented creature clawed at the earth, making animal noises when Lallie bent to touch her shoulder; she bore no resemblance to the fashionably smart young lady Lallie remembered.

"My God! What happened to her? Here, here, missy. I ain't going to hurt you!" Lallie's eyes met Henriette's over the other girl's heaving shoulders. "Was it the Yankees?"

Henriette caught her breath on a sob. "Please, help me get her to the house! Miss Ellen will help us."

Lallie wasted no more time on questions, questions that Henriette was clearly unable to answer. "You take that side, miss, and I'll take this side," she said. She had forgotten Gilly.

Julie took one look at her friend and turned away, sick to her stomach and sick at heart. When she had emptied her supper into the nearest chamber pot, however, she returned to the room where they had taken Charlotte Douglas.

Ellen, grimly competent, handed the bloodied garments to Pansy. "Burn them. They're beyond repair. Wait a minute, you might as well take the rest of them. Valerie, bring the brandy. It might help, if we can get some of it down her. Charlotte, do you hear me? It's Miss Ellen!"

"The swine," Valerie muttered. "The damnable swine!" She herself had gone so white that her hair seemed a vivid halo around her face. Except for the fact that Cedars was on the main road, while the road to Mallows went nowhere in particular, it might have been *here* that the foraging soldiers came. And the Yankees were coming back; they would be here at midday tomorrow. The surge of fury that swept over her was so strong that had any of the enemy soldiers appeared at that moment she would have shot them, and the consequences be damned. Anyone who would do what had been done to this girl was a wild animal and deserved to be killed as one would destroy a rabid fox.

She stood helplessly by as Charlotte choked on the brandy, then held the basin as Ellen bathed the trembling limbs, sponging blood from Charlotte's abdomen and legs.

Throughout the entire proceeding. Charlotte continued to shake and whimper. "No, please, don't!" It did not seem that she spoke to them, rather to the men who had done this to her. She did not know where she was, nor whose hands tried to soothe her. It was a relief to them all when Charlotte lay back amidst the pillows and sank into a stupor.

"Now," Ellen said, "tell us what happened, Henriette."

It was not a pretty story, nor quickly told. Henriette sipped of the brandy, too, as the others encircled her in the upstairs sitting room. Lallie had lighted candles, and the flickering flames illuminated pale, frightened faces.

Frances Douglas had not recovered from the death of her sole remaining son. While she dragged herself about and gave perfunctory orders about the household, she had taken no true interest in it or anything else, Henriette related.

They had talked of fleeing Cedars when the news came that Sherman had entered Atlanta. It was a foregone conclusion that he and his men, sixty thousand strong, would move from there to Savannah, and undoubtedly pass through Tattnall County. General Hood, still hovering in the background, was helplessly ineffectual against the Union forces.

The trouble was that the Douglases really had no place to go. There were relatives in Milledgeville, which was also in the path of the expected march. Frances had a brother in New Orleans, which was much too far away. In a buggy or a wagon, traveling by themselves, they had little hope of reaching that refuge.

So they stayed at Cedars, and the Yankees came.

No one heard them come. Frances was lying down with a headache, a cool cloth over her eyes. Henriette was upstairs, also, mending a dress that could not be replaced and so must be repaired.

Charlotte was in the dining room, arranging the last of the fall flowers in a vase for the table. It was a gesture of normalcy in a world that disintegrated around her from day to day, almost from hour to hour, as her mother withdrew more and more into herself.

There was a thunderous banging on the front door, and then, even before old Timothy could open it, it was kicked in.

Three men forced their way past him, covering his protests with loud voices. "Who lives here, old man? Eh, speak up! What place is this? Who lives here?"

Beyond the intruders Timothy saw that the lawn was overrun with blue-uniformed Federal soldiers. They swarmed up the front steps and into the house. When the frail old slave tried to block their way into the dining room where Charlotte stood, he was shoved aside with a jocular remark. "What's the matter, old man? Don't you know the niggers are free? What you protecting back there, eh?"

The soldier stopped in the doorway, his eyes narrowing. "Well, well! Look what we got! A pretty little Southern belle, damned if it ain't! What's your name, sweetheart?"

Charlotte backed away, still holding a gold chrysanthemum against her breast, her eyes wide with alarm. The man reached her in four strides, crushing the flower between them as he drew her in for a long kiss.

She struggled against him, gagging when he forced her teeth apart, trying to cry out for help. There was no help, of course. The kitchen servants fled through the back of the house, only to encounter more soldiers in the surrounding yard, soldiers interested in food supplies, not slaves.

Henriette frequently faltered as she told the story. Julie, leaning against her mother's side, felt that she would faint with the horror of it. Grandma Lacy was wrong: It wasn't worth going through such unspeakable things as this, just to survive. And tomorrow the Yankees had promised to return to Mallows!

"They swarmed over everything," Henriette said, her words heavy with tears. "They wiped the kitchen clean in a matter of minutes, even the crumbs. The servants were terrified, although a few of them tried to protest when they took everything. They didn't hurt any of the servants, they only jeered at them and asked them why they were staying there, things like that. But Charlotte—"

Henriette choked. It was several seconds, during which

122

their eyes stung and Julie and Ellen gripped each other's hands, before she could continue.

Charlotte had been raped the first time there in the dining room. Her screams brought Frances Douglas from her darkened bedroom, the wet cloth still in one hand. When she saw her house full of Union soldiers and heard her daughter's cries, she rushed back into her room for the pistol.

These soldiers, or others just like them, had killed her beloved husband and both her sons. Reason fell before rage and the agony of grief; Frances stood at the top of the stairway and shot the next two men who came through the front doorway before they brought her down.

"They shot her right here." Henriette, whispering, touched a finger to the center of her forehead. "She fell halfway down the stairs, and the men didn't even bother to walk around her when they ran up to the second floor. One of them did pause long enough to pull the rings off her fingers."

Henriette had sprung up in alarm at her sister's first outcry. Had she not tripped and fallen over the dress she had forgotten she carried, she would have been at her mother's side when Frances was shot. As it was, she had hit her head and lay for a moment, half-stunned. She had emerged onto the upper landing in time to see Frances fire the second shot and see her fall.

Somehow, instinctively, Henriette had had sense enough not to go rushing out to meet the same fate. She could hear Charlotte screaming, but the sound told her the front hall was full of men; she darted the other way, down the back stairs, and came out in a lower passageway near the kitchen.

There were men there, too. She could hear the rough voices and booted feet, the exultation when they discovered a ham that had been brought into the house for the evening meal.

"By God," one of them said clearly, "they're even cooking it for us!"

Where could she go? What could she do?

Henriette was soaked in her own sweat, and she could scarcely breathe for sheer terror. Charlotte had stopped screaming, which she recognized as ominous rather than otherwise, but how could she help Charlotte?

"I couldn't," she told the silent circle of listeners, and the candlelight was reflected in the tears that rolled down her

123

pale cheeks. "I couldn't do anything for her. There were so many of them."

She didn't remember how she had gotten out of the house, although it had to have been through the window in the pantry, only seconds before the scavengers found that storehouse of supplies. Not that there had been a great deal; no one in the whole of the South had a full larder these days. The men had fallen hungrily upon what there was—the cornmeal, the dried fruit, the pathetic remains of the salt pork that had once been considered fit only for the slaves to eat.

Henriette had been rescued, at least temporarily, by those slaves. Of one accord, they closed in around her, shielding her from the rapacious army. One of them, more quick-witted than most, stripped off the kerchief knotted around her own head and covered Henriette's hair, which would have given her away even from the back. Black hands guided her, hurried her, away from the house, and beyond the summer kitchen.

"In the root cellar," someone muttered, and a wiser head protested.

"No, no, that one of the first places they look. They lookin' for food!"

Had the soldiers not been so intent upon that task, they would surely have noticed the girl being led across the yard toward the slave quarters. There was, however, no such thing as a Northern supply train; Sherman himself had said, as he began the invasion of Georgia, "Convey to Jeff Davis my personal and official thanks for abolishing cotton and substituting corn and sweet potatoes in the South. These facilitate our military plans much, for food and forage are abundant." The soldiers were expected to shift for themselves, to eat from the rich farmlands, and they did. If that left the natives with nothing, why, those were the fortunes of war.

Henriette was hidden beneath a heap of coarse garments in one of the slave huts. She had huddled there for hours, expecting any moment to be discovered and brutally abused. She knew her mother, with a bullet hole in the center of her forehead, was dead. Charlotte's fate she did not learn until the soldiers had gone, leaving nothing of value behind them.

She was too tightly laced and had no way of getting out of the constricting garment by herself; between that and her fear, it was almost impossible to breathe. She would have welcomed swooning, which she felt very close to, except that she feared being unconscious, and that much more defenseless, even more.

When voices were raised in the distance, Henriette's trembling increased. Were they coming this way? Would they find her, in spite of the efforts of the servants to hide her?

Charlotte, dear Charlotte, she cried, the tears mingling with the dirt from the earthen floor beneath her. *I'm sorry, I'm sorry. I would have helped you if I could have.*

The voices grew louder, and Henriette dared to lift her head, listening. It was then that she smelled the smoke.

They were burning Cedars.

She scrambled out from under the smelly rags and staggered to the doorway, looking out toward the house. The roof was fully engulfed in flames. The structure itself was brick, but the interior was flammable; she could see the draperies blazing behind the windows. Every remaining Negro on the place, it seemed, stood there watching. There was no way to stop it, nothing except to let it burn itself out.

Charlotte! Dear God, was Charlotte still in there? Alive, or dead? Henriette ran, tripping and stumbling on legs unwilling, after the cramped hours of crouching, to hold her up. The soldiers had gone, leaving destruction in their wake. They had trampled the lawn and the flowers, and there was a bloody cross on the white-painted door. Whose blood? she wondered. Where was Charlotte?

She screamed her sister's name, and the slaves parted for her to move between them. No one touched her this time, nor spoke. The only sound was the voracious crackle of the fire that consumed everything left that had ever meant anything to her.

Charlotte lay sprawled between the main house and the summer kitchen. For a moment Henriette could not credit the fact that this poor limp, bloody, violated thing was her sister. Someone had at least pulled down the skirts over the defiled body to cover it. Henriette dropped to her knees, reeling under the shock of what she saw, desperate to find some trace of life.

"Charlotte! Charlotte, speak to me!"

"They knock her out, Miss Henriette. She don't hear you, and that better, poor thing."

Henriette felt the hand on her shoulder and recognized the voice of Dulcie, who had been her mother's maid for a dozen years.

"She's not dead?"

"No, but she hurt pretty bad. Them Yankees, they treat her pretty bad."

Henriette did not ask how many of them had used her sister. She did not want to know, even if the servants could have told her.

"We have to do something," Henriette said desperately. "We can't let her lie here."

A few yards away, glass exploded out of the house, sending a shower of splinters over those who stood too close.

"Help me, Dulcie."

"Come on." The new voice was deep, masculine, angry. "We leavin', Dulcie. We don't belong to the white folks no more. You comin' with me, it gonna be now."

The pressure on Henriette's shoulder tightened for a moment, and then the hand was removed. "I got to go, Miss Henriette. Colby, he leavin'. There ain't nothin' left here for us. Them Yankees didn't leave nothin' to eat, so we got to go."

And leave her here alone with this? Her eyes glazed, Henriette looked up in appeal. How could they leave her? What would she do? She glanced uncertainly toward the house as something crashed within. "My mother—"

"She dead, child," the black woman said, not unkindly. "She don't feel nothin' any more. I got to go, or Colby'll leave me."

They were all going, melting away, some of them not even bothering to return to their cabins for their personal belongings. Only a few paused long enough to offer their awkward, inarticulate sympathy.

Oh, yes, they were sorry. But they were going to leave her alone, and she didn't know what to do. Henriette knelt for a long time beside her sister, wracked by silent sobs before she thought of going to Mallows. It was six miles by road, and there were neither horses nor mules to get them there, and Charlotte did not stir. Finally Henriette began to shake her. "Wake up, Charlotte. We have to get away from here, before any more of them come. Wake up, you're going to have to walk, because there's no other way to get there!"

She would never, to her dying day, forget Charlotte's eyes when she began to respond to the shaking. Her eyes, and the strangled plea. "Don't hurt me any more," Charlotte begged. "Please don't hurt me."

And hardening her heart, Henriette forced her to sit up, and then to stand, and finally to walk. It took them nearly five hours to reach Mallows.

The house was quiet, but no one slept. Not even Dolly, who had been frightened in spite of her efforts to remain apart from what went on around her, could escape from the day's events. The burning of Cedars, the condition of the Douglas sisters, and anticipation of the return of the Yankee officers, for whatever purpose, on the morrow: All combined to keep them from sleep in spite of near exhaustion. That, added to the fact that they were sharing beds where each was used to sleeping alone, made for restless discomfort.

The evening was a warm one for so late in the fall. Julie and Valerie, sharing Valerie's bed, lay covered only with a sheet. Had she been alone, Valerie might well have stripped off her nightshift and dropped it on the floor, as well as foregoing the sheet. Modesty, however, had been drummed into her since birth. She squirmed into a different position, trying not to disturb Julie in case she had fallen asleep.

Julie sighed audibly. "Val?"

"Can't you sleep, either? Why don't you go down and play the piano for a while? It always relaxes you."

Beside her, Julie shuddered. "It would seem . . . almost sacrilegious . . . to play now. Besides . . ."

"Besides, what?"

"I'm afraid to go downstairs alone," Julie confessed in a whisper. "I feel as if there are eyes watching me, and I'm afraid. Val, if the Yankees come back here and do the things they did at Cedars . . ."

"They won't," Valerie said quickly. "They came here to look the place over for some specific purpose. If they want to use it, they won't destroy it."

"Not the house, maybe. What about us? What if they—oh, dear God, I couldn't go through what Charlotte did, or Henriette! I couldn't, Val!"

"You won't have to," Valerie assured her, hoping she was right about that. "Try not to think about it."

"I have tried, do you think I want to think about it? How can I stop?" There was anguish in the whisper.

Valerie had no answer for that. Instead, she speculated aloud on the matter of the Yankee officers. "I wonder what they intend to do here? If that Major Quinn uses Mallows as his headquarters, it should protect us from roving bands of scavengers like those who went to Cedars. As long as he's here, he'll keep them off."

"Do you think so? Do you think that's it?" Julie was willing to clutch at straws, however flimsy. "They won't stay long, if that's the case, will they? If they're all moving toward Savannah?"

"Remember how beautiful Savannah is?" Valerie murmured. "Remember how we used to walk along Bay Street, and down along the river, with Grandpa Stanton? Remember how he'd buy us bananas right off the boats, and ripe pineapples? Remember how good chilled pineapple tastes?"

"I wonder if things will ever be that way again," Julie said. "When we can buy things, and visit other plantations, and Grandma Lacy can move back into her Savannah house. I do hope they haven't damaged her house."

Some of the tension had gone from Julie's voice. Valerie lay, listening to the night noises, as her sister's breathing gradually slowed and became regular. Julie had knelt beside the bed, bowing her head in prayer before she climbed into the four-poster. Valerie wished sadly that she felt it would be of any use to add her own prayers.

God was up there, all right, as they'd been taught He was. She no longer had a very strong faith that He was listening, however. He'd allowed this dreadful war to go on and on, allowed thousands of men to die, and now He'd calmly overlooked what had happened at Cedars today. Where was there any reason why He'd be watching over the women at Mallows when the Yankees came again?

Something stirred in the darkness beyond her door, someone moved on the landing at the head of the stairs. Her mother, making a final check on the household? On impulse, Valerie slipped out of bed without disturbing Julie and made her way toward the doorway. Her mother was working so hard, and taking practically all of the responsibility for everything and everyone. If only there was something she could do—maybe just talking would help her, if Ellen couldn't sleep, either.

Valerie paused in the hallway, listening. Downstairs, had the figure gone down the front stairs? No. She spun in the direction of the room that had been Julie's before Julie had moved out to make way for the Yankee officers. It was to that room that they had taken Charlotte, and Ellen had called for a cot to be set up there for Henriette, as well; Henriette had begged to be allowed to stay there, too, at least for tonight.

"Charlotte?" Henriette's voice, low and urgent, carried to the girl in the hallway. "Charlotte?"

"What's the matter?" Valerie asked quietly, moving toward the candlelight that suddenly bloomed there, throwing great shadows that moved with the approach of light.

Henriette's face was sharply etched in lines of fear beyond the candle flame. She had let down her hair and had not bothered to braid it for the night; it spread down her back, looking dark in the subdued light.

"She's gone. Did you see her?"

"I think I heard her. Wait, she's in the sitting room, she's lighted a candle there."

Valerie's calm seemed to have a soothing effect. Together, Henriette carrying the candle, they padded on bare feet toward the dim rectangle of candlelight across the landing. She did not hear them coming. For a moment, seeing Charlotte bent over the chair where Dolly usually sat, Valerie did not correctly interpret the girl's actions. Not until she saw the pistol. How had Charlotte known it was there, how had she been so observant when she had seemed unaware of anything around her?

Her face was white and still, except for a tic at one corner of her mouth. Charlotte checked the weapon to make sure that it was loaded, then lifted its muzzle to her temple. Almost too late, Valerie realized what her friend intended. She threw herself forward, hearing Henriette cry out a protest, and knocked the pistol aside even as Charlotte pulled the trigger.

The explosion rang in their ears, deafening them, but the only damage was to the ornamental frieze overhead, which sent down a shower of plaster over a small rosewood table.

"Give it to me, Charlotte." Valerie wrenched the gun from Charlotte's now nerveless hand, breathing heavily.

Charlotte looked at her with glazed, hurting eyes. "You should have let me do it," she whispered.

"No. No," Valerie said gently. "Come back to bed, dear. Everything will seem better tomorrow. You'll be all right."

"Nothing will ever be all right again," Charlotte said with a conviction that was as chilling as her attempted suicide had been.

Yet she allowed herself to be led back to bed; the women in the other rooms were assured that the gun had been discharged accidentally, and that they were secure for the night.

And after the night, what? Valerie wondered bitterly. And wondered, too, if she should have let Charlotte do what she had intended to do.

Fourteen

Everything that could be hidden had been hidden. There was no point in trying to conceal their foodstuffs, Ellen decided, since the Yankee officer had indicated that he expected Mamie to cook for his men. He expected to eat from Mallows supplies, and they must continue to feed themselves as well.

Before they were invaded by the enemy, she spoke to those who sat around the breakfast room table with their morning mush and chicory-coffee. Only Charlotte was not there, and Henriette; Charlotte had fallen into a sleep so deep she might have been drugged, and Pansy had taken Henriette's breakfast to her there in the bedroom, because Henriette was afraid to leave.

"What happened at Cedars," Ellen said with a surface calm that deceived no one, "must not happen here. Whatever the cost, Mallows must not be burned. We will do whatever the Yankees want, and when they are finished with us, they'll go away. If we have the house, and the land, we'll have something to begin over with, when the time comes."

"Will it ever come again?" Julie's voice was wistful. "A time when we have a choice, when the Yankees are gone?"

"Soon," Ellen said firmly. "Remember: Do nothing to antagonize them, whatever you can do to appease them. Cover

131

your hatred, and if you can, conceal your fear. We are ladies of quality," she included even Blossom in her sweeping glance, "and we will behave as such. And we will pray that they will leave us as they find us."

So little they could do, to prepare for the men who were to come. The demand for four bedrooms seemed to indicate that the party would consist of at least four officers who would be quartered within the house. How many more might shift for themselves outside, they could only guess.

Mamie, upon being informed that she would be expected to serve dinner that evening to at least four Yankee officers, allowed her ample bosom to swell to greater proportions as indignation registered on her black face.

"I got to cook for Yankees?"

"Cook for them, and hold your tongue. Remain civil. Feed them as well as we can. In return for that, there is a good chance they'll leave Mallows intact when they move on."

"Yankees!" Mamie spat upon the floor she had only recently scrubbed. "I never thought I have to cook for scum like that! And what I s'posed to feed 'em? Mush and greens? This year's meat still in the smokehouse."

"There is still a ham, I believe. And vegetables from the garden. And the scuppernongs are ripening; the girls can pick some for the table. Biscuits or cornbread. That should be adequate."

"Ain't no butter," Mamie said. "That poor ole cow don't hardly give no cream, any more. Be more use if we butchered her and ate her."

"It's not beyond belief that that is just what may happen to her," Ellen admitted. "And if there is no butter, we'll do without. Have the boys taken the rest of the sheep and the pigs out into the woods?"

"They took 'em, but the Yankees got noses like bloodhounds, I reckon. They find somethin' to eat, no matter where you hide it."

No one doubted the truth of that. They could only try to save as much as they could for themselves, after the Yankees had gone. That became the phrase of the day, and of the days to follow: *after the Yankees have gone*.

While there was no directive on the matter from Ellen, every woman there chose to meet the Yankees looking her best. No one came down to breakfast that morning in her old rags, except that Blossom did not have anything to compare with
132

those of the others and wore an old gingham dress that revealed more than was necessary of her ankles. The bodice, too, was snug. Blossom laughed, patting her bosom. "Everything I got is shrunk so it squeezes me," she said.

The Douglas girls, of course, did not have any clothes and would have to be supplied from the wardrobes of Mallows. This meant Julie's things, because she was nearer their size; Valerie was several inches taller and more alterations would be necessary to convert her garments for the smaller girls.

All were ready for the Yankees, or as ready as they could be, long before there was any sign of them. They had taken pains with their hair, too, assisting one another in achieving fashionable coiffures; it was as if these small things gave them the armor against the enemy that they could not find in guns. To resort to guns would mean only that Mallows would be destroyed, like Cedars, and all of them subjected to similar abuses such as the Douglases had endured.

It was absurd, Valerie considered, that Ellen should have them all running around at the last minute with dust rags. Who cared what the housekeeping was like, when they might be molested or killed at any time? Yet, like the others, she ran a cloth over the tops of tables and desks, and made no comment when Julie arranged a vase of late-blooming Cherokee roses, as if they were expecting guests.

At midday, when there was no sign of the Yankees, they ate. No one was hungry, they were all too nervous for that. Charlotte, after her nocturnal excursion, had sunk into an apathetic state, lying in silence, eyes unfocused, and failing to respond to anything that was said to her.

Henriette was afraid to leave her alone, and so once more ate her meager meal in the upstairs bedroom. Henriette suffered her own guilts, although the others had all assured her that rushing to her sister's aid would only have resulted in being abused herself. She knew, intellectually, that nothing she could have done would have made any difference in what happened to Charlotte. Yet the guilt persisted, perhaps in part because, in a secret corner of her mind, she knew that she was glad it had not happened to *her*.

It had been decided that the officers, when they returned, would be greeted only by Ellen and one of the servants. Ellen longed with a desperate intensity for the comforting presence of Aaron; the pain of his defection was a deep ache within her.

She looked between Pansy and Lallie for the servant to attend her, then. Both of them quailed before the glance, each praying that she would choose the other.

Lallie gave an inward sigh of relief when she was excused, with the others, from greeting the Yankees. If they would so treat that poor little Miss Charlotte, what would they do with a slave girl who looked, except on the closest of scrutiny, to be white? She had always taken pride in knowing that she was pretty; for the first time, beauty was clearly of no asset to any woman, while the Yankees roamed the countryside.

It was, therefore, a visibly trembling Pansy, her small dark face unable to conceal her panic, who stood with Ellen in the entry hall and opened the door to the Yankee officers.

It was Blossom who saw them coming, from her vantage point in the upstairs sitting room. Her emotions were more mixed than those of any of the others. They were Yankees, the enemy, but they were also men.

Blossom knew and liked men.

The South, the Old South, had offered little to a girl of Blossom's class. All her life she had been one of those who stood on the outside, viewing the festivities and the luxuries within. The home of the old couple in Atlanta had been superior to anything she had known before, and it seemed to her now that the slaves at Mallows had things better than the Mastersons had had. There was a lot of loose talk about freedom for the slaves, but if the truth were known, those slaves on a plantation such as this had things a lot better than ordinary people did. They were fed and housed and cared for with more concern than had ever been shown for her.

Well, nobody knew what was going to happen now. Some thought the Yankees would take over everything and run things to suit themselves. A few anticipated grabbing the holdings of the former plantation owners, thinking that as the rich were leveled, the poor would rise to that level, and the wealth would be more equitably distributed. Blossom knew only that she had to shift for herself. She was passably pretty, though she was no beauty like the Stanton girls. Even in one of those fancy gowns, she recognized that she could never compete with Valerie Stanton, for style. There was something about Valerie that marked her as a lady, no matter what she wore.

And so, as she watched the blue-coated soldiers riding slowly up the white oyster shell drive, the sun glinting on an occasional sword or perhaps a burnished button, Blossom speculated about the invaders.

She, too, feared what had happened to Charlotte. Wasn't it possible, however, that a romantic liaison with one of these officers—all men who had long been away from home, wives, and sweethearts—could lead to a better life for herself? That a relationship with one man might be the protection she needed from the *other* men?

Heart pounding, she turned from the windows and spoke clearly to those waiting behind her.

"Here they come," she said.

Unlike the soldiers who had ransacked and burned Cedars, these men were not on foot. They rode horses, and there were mules pulling wagons. It was not until the wagons drew up before the house that Ellen realized what they carried.

Not supplies, but men. Wounded men.

Mallows was to become a hospital.

They moved into the house, wearily efficient. Major Quinn and an aide established an office in the study. The library, adjoining it, would provide a sitting room for the officers. The twin drawing rooms with their elegant gold satin chairs and settees, the gold velvet draperies tied back with gold cords, the muted pale yellow carpets with encircling pastel flowers, were to be cleared of furniture so that the injured men could be carried inside.

Had Ellen had any inkling of what was planned, she would have rolled up the rugs and had them hauled to the attics. As it was, she was given no choice. Her quick suggestion, once the Yankee plans were made clear, were brushed aside.

"There is no time for that, madam," Quinn told her flatly. "These men are in urgent need of rest, out of the sun and the weather. Besides since we have no beds for them, they will be more comfortable on the rugs."

The chairs and sofas and tables were carried out the side door, clearing the rooms. Ellen regarded them with dismay, knowing that everything would be totally ruined if allowed to remain outside.

"Pansy. Run to the quarters—no one is working today, anyway, from the look of it—and round up everyone capable of carrying these things. We'll store them in the empty cabins, the ones on this end of the row. Hurry." There were plenty of empty cabins, at any rate, since so many of the Negroes had deserted her; she must take her satisfaction in such limited fashions as she found them.

Pansy ran. Bug-eyed, she regaled the open mouth Negroes with her own version of the invasion.

"All over the place," she said. "And they's wounded men in all them wagons, bleedin' all over theirselves! They gonna put 'em right on Miss Ellen's Persian carpets!"

Valerie remained upstairs no more than half an hour after the arrival of the enemy. "I'm going down," she announced, when there had been no summons by then. "Whatever they're doing down there, it sounds as if the place is being dismantled. Does anyone want to come with me?"

Julie did not really want to confront the Yankees; her skin crawled in revulsion at the idea. Yet if the men were in the house, and to stay for an indeterminate period of time, she knew she would have to confront them eventually. Better to go now, with Val and Blossom, who had also risen, than to face them by herself later.

They descended the stairs three abreast, slowly, gracefully, quite unconsciously regal in bearing. Even Blossom maintained a certain dignity.

Jack Ferris, directing the removal of the furniture from the drawing room, turned and saw them coming. *Well,* he thought. *This might prove interesting. Three of them, and all very attractive.*

It was the tall one, the redhead, who caught and held his interest. He had thought her pretty before; today she was stunning in a pale green gown with a very full skirt and a neckline and bodice that, while modest, revealed a perfect bosom and throat. No jewelry, no doubt she had sold or hidden that, but a girl who looked like this one didn't need the adornment of jewels.

He left the men to their task and stood waiting for the young women at the foot of the stairs.

"Good afternoon," he greeted them.

"Captain Ferris," Valerie responded, as if he were any gentleman guest in the house. "May we know what is happening here?"

"Your home is being transformed into a Federal hospital. Everything will be removed from the drawing rooms to accommodate the patients. I don't think we can get the piano out of there, though, unless we let it sit on the veranda. It
136

looks a fine instrument; it would be a shame to ruin it in the weather. Do you play, Miss Stanton?"

"My sister is the polished performer, although I can pick out a tune," Valerie told him. The admiration was readable in his face, which did nothing to reassure her. Not when the man was in a position to take what he wanted by force, if he so chose.

"May I know who these young ladies are?"

She introduced them, again as if they were meeting socially. Was there a prayer of a hope that Ellen was right, that if they treated these men as if they expected them to behave as gentlemen, they would respond in kind?

"Maybe we can move the piano out here into the foyer," Captain Ferris suggested. "If it isn't in our way, you could still use it, and it wouldn't be so likely to be damaged."

It took six men to do the moving, after Ferris had given an offhand order. "If you'll excuse me, now," he said then, "I'll see to my patients."

Valerie's unspoken query was there on her face, and he paused for one more brief exchange. "Yes, ma'am. A sawbones, at your service. Here, Lofton, bring those cases in here. Right through that door."

He was gone. They retreated from the gaze of the men who moved about the hall. It was impossible not to remember what had happened at Cedars. Perhaps it had been partly because there were no officers with those soldiers that they had not settled for simply looting. Mallows was being utilized for the Yankees' own purposes now, yet there was no guarantee that the soldiers had no designs on a group of helpless women.

The wounded men were lifted from the wagons and carried either into the drawing rooms, the doors thrown open between them, or laid upon the broad piazza. There were no pallets for them, no niceties of any sort.

The odors were the advance notice, to anyone coming down the stairs or into the foyer from the back of the house, of the condition of those injured men. None of the inhabitants of Mallows, except for Ellen, had any experience with gangrene, the putrefaction of the flesh that inevitably resulted in death unless the afflicted limb was surgically removed. None of them was ever to forget the odor of it, an odor that caused them to turn and flee, to vomit into the shrubbery or to gasp for fresher air.

137

Now they knew the smell of death.

Ellen, walking out across the piazza to find Major Quinn in order to determine how many men she was expected to feed, and when, stopped in bone-melting horror. A young man, a boy, really, lay at her feet. His blood-soaked jacket was missing a sleeve, as he was missing the arm that should have been in the sleeve. The stump had been hastily dressed, but his life's fluids continued to soak through the bandaging.

He lay staring up at her with pain-glazed eyes, around which the flies crawled with impunity because he was too weak to brush them away with his remaining hand.

Aversion mingled with compassion as she stood rooted, unable to step over the boy, or beyond him. Sweet God, she thought, was Evan like this, somewhere? Helpless, in pain?

The boy's lips moved in a soundless plea that did not carry to her. Ellen looked about and saw the men lifting another comrade from the nearest of the wagons, a comrade who moaned when they touched him and screamed as they carried him up the steps.

When the newest arrival had been lowered unceremoniously onto the piazza floor, the two soldiers would have walked past Ellen again without speaking if she had not reached out and tugged at the nearest sleeve.

"Please, this boy is in dreadful shape. Is anyone doing anything for him? Shouldn't he be carried inside?"

One of the men looked at her without expression. "He's dying, ma'am. No use to carry him inside. We got orders to take the ones in there that got a chance."

She forgot that the wounded were Yankees. They were simply human beings who were terribly hurt, and there were already half a dozen others within hearing range, on the porch, who must have overheard the matter-of-fact statement.

The speaker pulled away, plunging down the steps and back to his grisly task.

If Evan were in like condition . . . no, she would not allow herself to think of Evan. She glanced down again, and the boy's lips moved once more. In an instinctive reaction, Ellen knelt and lowered her head over the boy's, brushing at the flies that rose in a small cloud and settled again as soon as the motion was ended.

"Water," the boy said, almost inaudibly.

"Yes, of course." For a few seconds she pressed a hand

138

into the boy's good shoulder, then stood and moved swiftly into the house. "Pansy! Pansy, where are you?"

The frightened black face appeared from behind the door, where Pansy had been huddling ever since she had opened it.

"Fetch a bucket of water and a dipper. Hurry! These men must have been traveling for hours."

"Yes'm," Pansy said, and fled, praying that Miss Ellen would not expect *her* to go out among all those near-corpses.

That was just what Miss Ellen did expect. Pansy carried the bucket, while Ellen knelt, heedless of her skirts, and held the dipper to the mouths of men unable to hold it for themselves.

The boy drank greedily, spilling some of the water down his chest, then whispered a *thank you* and closed his eyes, and Ellen went on to the next of them.

There were thirty-seven injured men, four privates to do the dirty work, two corporals, and a sergeant, as well as a Lieutenant Hoskins and a Lieutenant Froedecker, in addition to the two officers they had already met. There were no moderately wounded men. Anyone who was ambulatory, or had friends to carry him off, had found his own way to deal with injury. Those remaining were left to the mercies, tender or otherwise, of the officers in charge.

Major Otis Quinn seemed an odd choice for an officer to take responsibility for a hospital. He was a stern man at the best of times, and walked through the dying men on the piazza with no more obvious concern than if they were slaughtered sheep. It was not long before everyone in the household was aware that the assignment had not been Quinn's choice, that he resented being where he was when he might have been sweeping gloriously with the victors toward the sea.

His subordinates were courteous and respectful, though no affection was noted in the attitude of any of them. In fact, Valerie surprised naked hatred in the eyes of Lieutenant Hoskins after Major Quinn had given him a sharp order and walked away, leaving the younger man fighting not to clench his fists.

The women of Mallows met the officers at the dinner table that evening. Mamie, for all her ill-tempered protests, had done a credible job of putting together a meal with the ham and sweet potatoes and a gumbo from a recipe her mammy had brought from New Orleans.

Valerie felt that it was all unreal, a parody of the dinners

139

that had so often taken place in a festive way around this beautiful old table. The women were well dressed, the men in uniform, and for the first time in nearly two years the chandelier was ablaze with candles. It was, perhaps, a foolish gesture for the supply of candles ran low, and unless they managed to keep the rest of the hogs hidden until they were ready for butchering, there might not be enough to replenish the supply. Without the lard, there would be no candles. Ellen had given the order, however, and the candles were lighted. Lallie and Pansy were pressed into service both in the kitchen and to serve in the dining room.

Major Quinn was reserved and coldly correct in his behavior. His officers, all considerably younger, were less formal, though restraining themselves under his eye. Captain Ferris they had already met. It was he who seemed the most at ease in the present setting. Clearly he was not awed by the house, its occupants, or the service. He was used to linen napkins— at some time in his past, if not in the field of war—and good wine with his meals. His dark eyes roved casually over the faces and figures of the women, including the servants. The two lieutenants were in their middle twenties, Valerie guessed. Both were ordinary young men, pleasant-faced, and clearly out of their element in a grand house such as this one. Robert Hoskins was dark and serious, watching carefully to see how Captain Ferris handled his forks. Fritz Froedecker, tow-headed and efficient of movement, paid more attention to the women than he did to the table service.

None of the men, except for an amused Jack Ferris, had ever previously encountered okra. Major Quinn, examining the contents of the spoon lifted from his bowl of gumbo, inquired as to the peculiar vegetable.

"Okra," Ellen informed him. "It's a favorite in the South."

Quinn grunted a noncommittal acknowledgment of the information, and continued to eat. Lieutenant Froedecker gave Ellen a broad smile. He had a lean, tanned face, and surprisingly vivid blue eyes.

"An excellent meal, ma'am. Even the okra's an improvement over army cooking."

"Thank you, Lieutenant." If it was difficult for her to see these enemy soldiers—whose counterparts had slain her husband, her neighbors, her friends—seated around her own table, no one would have known it. She was the gracious hostess in brown silk, her elaborately coiffed red hair scarcely

140

faded, presiding as such women have presided over the ages at festive tables.

This meal was not festive, of course, yet it was not as uncomfortable as it might have been. At least not during the early part of the evening. They learned that Captain Ferris was a native of New York City, and that he had a home there and an interest in a family manufacturing plant. Major Quinn was from Boston. While nothing was said of the matter, Valerie guessed that his family, though respectable, was not the social equal of Ferris's, or perhaps the difference in standing was purely financial.

Lieutenant Hoskins, clearly middle-class, came from up-state New York, a small village of no particular significance. He was married and had a young daughter, whose pictures he was to show them numerous times over the weeks he spent at Mallows.

Fritz Froedecker said little of his own family and background except that he had grown up on a farm in New Jersey. He ate steadily, the blue eyes following the progress of Lallie as she moved silently between dining room and kitchen. His attention was also caught by Blossom, who sat opposite him in her very best dress. While the gown was in no way comparable to those of the other women, she knew it was attractive, and that the particular shade of light blue was becoming to her own fair hair and deepened the blue of her eyes.

When her gaze met his, Blossom smiled, ever so tentatively. For a fraction of a second, Fritz forgot to chew. And then he resumed mastication, allowing his own smile to widen encouragingly.

Ellen saw the small exchange and one more area of uneasiness was added to those already crowding her mind. Still, she thought, if Blossom was discreet, she might relieve the pressures on the rest of the women in the household. Yes, now that she thought about it, a romantic liaison between Blossom and the Yankee officers might be a good thing, as long as her own daughters didn't realize what was going on. Was it worth her time to speak to Blossom about the need for circumspection? No, she decided. Better to pretend not to notice, and let the matters take their course.

Ellen turned to Major Quinn and replied, civilly if not cordially, to a question he had put.

Mallows would survive this invasion by Yankee soldiers as

Georgia would survive the rape by Sherman. She hardened her resolve in this matter, determined to ignore the quaking jelly of fear deep inside herself.

Mallows *must* survive.

Fifteen

The first meal with the Yankees in the house lulled them, briefly, into a false sense of security. The officers were appreciative of the food and except for Major Quinn, who remained aloof, entered into the sort of social conversation which all of the women had missed.

Sally Ann contributed little or nothing to that conversation. Her wide eyes shifted from one to the other of the men, however; following their words, she tried to read the intent behind them, and at last spoke falteringly to Lieutenant Froedecker as they had all risen to leave the table.

Her words were so low that, had not all other conversational flow happened to cease at that point, she would not have been heard by anyone but the young officer to whom the query was addressed. As it was, everyone heard her, and movement as well as talk came to a halt.

"You mentioned coming through Atlanta, sir," she said. "Could you tell us—how bad things are there?"

For a few seconds Lieutenant Froedecker hesitated. "Bad, ma'am," he told her, and clearly would have liked to leave it at that.

Sally Ann's face was even whiter than it usually was. Her

143

pale fingers curled over the back of the chair for the physical support that she needed. "The houses, are they still standing? Most of them?" She licked colorless lips. "Our house was at Collins and Ellis streets, a two-story white house with green shutters, and a big yard. There are three large chestnut trees."

Froedecker glanced uncertainly at his superiors, then evaded. "Atlanta's a sizable place, ma'am. And we only came through it. We weren't there long enough to learn our way around by the street names, except for a few of them. The railroad depot was destroyed, what did they call it? The Car Shed, near Peachtree Street? Mostly the things they put the torch to were business buildings. Factories and the like, the woolen mill at Roswell, a cotton mill, that sort of thing. Lots of the houses are still standing, ma'am."

And lots of them weren't. Valerie moved closer to her cousin, touching her shoulder with what little support she could give her. Even if the fires had only been set in commercial places, they would have spread to private residences simply because they were unchecked. There had been no reassurance for Sally Ann that her home remained for her to return to.

Behind Valerie, Ellen cleared her throat. Since the subject had come up, and the tension and dismay were already uppermost in everyone's minds, she might as well put her own pressing question.

"My son is in the hospital at the Atlanta Medical College," she said, more firmly than Sally Ann had done. "We do not know the extent of his injuries. Since you are medical personnel, perhaps you would know something of the general state of affairs there. Not of any particular patient, of course, but the hospital itself—we heard that many buildings were heavily damaged by the shelling. Do you know about the Medical College—?"

Lieutenant Froedecker ran a finger over his sandy mustache, clearly uncomfortable. "I couldn't say, ma'am. The only hospital I got near was one in a private house. St. Paul's Way, I believe it was."

"The Grant home," Captain Ferris interjected quietly. "And yes, the Medical College was undamaged, as far as I know."

It wasn't much, but it was something. Ellen and Valerie and Julie began to breathe again.

Yet as they all passed out of the dining room and returned to their own activities, the women upstairs and the men remaining below, no one relaxed very much. Understated though the story had been, they all knew that Atlanta had suffered hideously in that ruthless siege. That, and their more personal knowledge of what had happened at Cedars, would send them all to bed in their own besieged state. Ellen, although she did not admit it, now wondered at the wisdom of deciding against bars on their bedroom doors. Certainly none of these men had so far indicated that they would be aggressive in such a manner, and it was still true that since they occupied the house it would be impossible to keep them out of any room they desired to enter; yet she would have felt better had there been something to slow them down, at least.

Good God. She had forgotten to inform them that one of the rooms they had demanded for their own use was now occupied by the Douglas sisters.

Ellen turned away from her mother, who was already complainingly beginning to undress, and without explanation left to seek out one of the officers. It wouldn't do to have them open the bedroom door and send poor Charlotte completely out of her mind, if that hadn't already happened. It was difficult to judge the matter, since Charlotte refused to respond to anything that was said or done.

Ellen hesitated at the head of the stairs. There was no light in the entry hall below. A pale rectangle reached out from the library door, however. She heard the clink of glasses and low laughter. Bitterness surged through her and for a moment she wondered if she would not have better followed Frances Douglas's example; if she'd met the Yankees with a pistol, they'd have killed her at once, and perhaps she'd be the better off for it.

The impulse lasted only a moment. No, she would never give in to them. She'd fight to survive, and to protect her beloved Mallows, and someday—God, how distant a day?—life would return to normal. Things would be good again.

For all her resolution, however, she could not seem to force herself to take that first step down the stairs. To beard the Federals in her own library. They'd had half an hour or so to drink, by now, in addition to the wine they'd had with their supper. Heaven knew what condition they were in.

An uproarious burst of laughter from the lighted room

145

strengthened the supposition that inroads had been made into Roger's brandy. Unfortunately, there was plenty of it left; the cellars had been well stocked when he went away to war, and the women had scarcely touched the brandy except for medicinal use.

She must go down. She must not let them surprise Charlotte and Henriette. Would they make her move the girls out, or would they agree to allow them to remain where they were?

Steeling herself, Ellen began the descent of the stairway she had trod so many times. She had nearly reached the bottom when Captain Ferris emerged from the library. He had divested himself of his tunic, which he carried over one arm; he paused to light a slim cigar, and only when he'd taken his first puff on it did he see her, standing there in semidarkness.

"Mrs. Stanton. I'm sorry if we're disturbing you."

She was glad it was this one, rather than the major. And this one, after all, was a physician.

"I'd forgotten to mention something, Captain. You had asked for four bedrooms, and we've had to put one of those to use. Our neighbors, the Douglases, were burned out yesterday. Mrs. Douglas was shot and killed by . . . by your soldiers. The two daughters are here, and one of them is in poor condition. We had to give them shelter, and there was nowhere else to put them."

Ferris hesitated, then puffed once more before asking, "Poor condition? Was she shot, too?"

"No, sir." Ellen willed her voice not to tremble. "She was raped, repeatedly, by Union soldiers. I hope that her physical hurts have been taken care of; I can say nothing for her mental state. She hasn't spoken all day, and I fear for what might happen if any man, let alone one in a Federal uniform, should open her bedroom door."

"What's going on?"

Ferris turned to see a rather disheveled Lieutenant Froedecker in the lighted doorway. Ellen could smell the brandy fumes from a dozen feet away.

"Something wrong, Captain?"

"Not at all," Ferris said lazily. "Only a slight change in plan. You'll have to bunk with Hoskins rather than having a room to yourself. Which room is occupied, ma'am?"

"The middle room on the north side of the house, sir."

"Very good. You and Hoskins will take the one on the northwest corner, then, Fritz."

Froedecker made a sound of disgust. "He snores to wake the dead! You hear that, old horse? We're roommates again." He turned back into the library, and there was a clink of glass on glass as more of the brandy was poured.

Ellen had not moved from her position near the foot of the stairs, although her business was concluded. Ferris looked down on her, his dark eyes unreadable in the dimness.

"My regrets over the fate of your friends would be of little comfort, Mrs. Stanton. May I quote General Sherman on the matter: *War, like the thunderbolt, follows its laws and turns not aside even if the beautiful, the virtuous, and the charitable stand in its path.* And, on the same subject, *You might as well appeal against the thuderstorm as against these terrible hardships of war.* Even so, ma'am, I am sorry that these things were necessary."

"Necessary?" For a moment she forgot her own admonition that nothing was to be said to antagonize the Yankees. "Necessary, to burn a home, shoot a woman half-crazed with grief over the deaths of her husband and two sons, and to violate a young girl in as brutal a manner as could be managed? Necessary to what, sir?"

"Necessary, perhaps, to bring the South to its knees. War has always been a brutal thing, and sometimes the women as well as the men must suffer. No orders were given for these acts, you understand. It is simply that men not under control of their officers will take matters into their own hands."

The rage and frustration were too strong to be contained.

"And the men here, Captain. Are they under control of their officers? Are the officers themselves under control? Or can we expect to be violated, too?"

She was sorry the minute she'd said it. It was, almost, an invitation to further violence.

Captain Ferris looked at her in silence, until at last she turned and moved quickly up the stairs.

She closed the bedroom door behind her, breathing heavily. He had not, she thought in despair, given her an answer.

Valerie and Julie lay side by side, not talking, listening to the occasional bursts of hilarity from the ground floor. Drinking, undoubtedly the Federals were drinking. How dangerous

147

would they be when their revels had ended and they came up the stairs to their beds?

There were some Southern houses in which a door was locked between the quarters where the women slept and those provided for the men. There was a stairway on each side of the door (which would be secured as soon as the women withdrew after dinner) for each group to reach their sleeping rooms. By the time the gentlemen had been at the bottle for a few hours, they would not have to restrain any baser impulses with their own willpower; with that locked door between, they could not possibly reach the females of the household until morning and sobriety had set in.

There was no such device as a divided stair and a locked door at Mallows. If the women found it difficult to go to sleep, it was no wonder.

Julie's nightmares returned with the arrival of the Yankees; she had dozed off and wakened in terror, so that Valerie put a hand over her mouth and shook her awake.

"It's all right, you're only dreaming."

Julie gasped and clutched the sheet under her chin. "They won't come, will they? They won't bother us?"

"No, no," Valerie soothed. "Go back to sleep."

It was good advice, although Valerie herself could not follow it. She heard the stealthy footsteps long after her sister slept, realizing almost at once that they descended from the level where the two servants' rooms were rather than rose from the ground floor. Not the soldiers, then.

Lallie, or Blossom?

She couldn't tell. Valerie breathed deeply and willed herself to relax.

Blossom did not own a dressing gown, and her only nightshift was a poor affair, long since worn threadbare. She had, therefore, while helping to carry clothes from one room to another the previous afternoon, seen fit to appropriate a garment from Dolly Mallow's belongings.

It was a wrapper of pink silk, lavishly ruffled and laced, and though it was dusty, it was one of the prettiest things in Dolly's chifforobe. Since the old lady kept mostly to herself, and Blossom expected to wear the wrapper only after Dolly had retired, she didn't think any issue would be made of the matter. Every woman in the house had twenty garments to

148

every one of Blossom's. It wasn't quite fair, and she felt no compunction about borrowing a few things to make up for her own lack.

Lallie, too, was restless, it seemed. Blossom waited a long time for the sounds to cease in Lallie's room. Then she rose, shrugged into the pink wrapper, and made her way silently down the narrow stairway to the second-floor landing.

She did not carry a candle (the coal oil for lamps had long since run out at Mallows, and there was no cash to buy more) but the man she met on the stairs did. Blossom had already marked Captain Ferris as the one with whom a liaison would be most advantageous; instinctively, she tightened the sash of the borrowed wrapper so that her full breasts were provocatively displayed, and allowed a tentative smile to reveal the crooked teeth.

Ferris scrutinized her thoroughly as she descended toward him. He didn't pause, however, merely greeting her as courtesy dictated, with a nod and her murmured name. He didn't ask where she was going or if there was anything he could do for her. He didn't act any different than if she'd been Lallie or, even, Gilly, that silly little black child.

Ferris passed her and went on up the stairs. Blossom's smile slipped momentarily. Oh, well, she'd known Captain Ferris had class. No doubt his interests were on a higher level. She'd noticed that he looked at Valerie more often than at any of the rest of them. Blossom said a farmyard word to herself. It would be uphill work to compete with Miss Valerie. Still, Captain Ferris wasn't the only man in the place. It was a pity Patrick Ryan had ridden off to rejoin his regiment; Patrick Ryan was worth half a dozen of any of the rest of them if she was any judge.

She didn't want to meet Major Quinn. Blossom had never known a man like Quinn, yet some intuition told her that he was dangerous. She was glad she didn't see him at all.

The next man who came out of the lighted library below was reeling from the effects of the excellent brandy from Mallows' cellars. He wasn't too drunk to appreciate a female apparition in pink silk, however.

It took him only a few seconds to recall her name. "Miss Blossom. Evening, ma'am."

That was better. He spoke respectfully, yet with admiration.

"Good evenin', Lieutenant. Warm, ain't it?"

Fritz Froedecker had to consider that. "Yeah. Yeah, it is."

"The water in my pitcher is like soup. I thought I'd go to the well for some cool, only I don't know if I'm brave enough to go out there by my ownself." Blossom waited for this to work through his thickened brain.

"Why, I'd be glad to walk out to the well with you, ma'am. Won't anybody bother you if I'm with you."

Blossom's smile grew. "Makes a difference to a girl, havin' a strong man around. Thank you, Lieutenant."

It took him a few seconds to get turned around in the opposite direction. Blossom tucked her hand into the crook of his arm and steered him toward the back of the house.

By the time they reached the well, out beyond the summer kitchen, both of them had forgotten the water they'd presumably come for.

Valerie, looking down from her bedroom window, could not tell which of the men it was down there with Blossom. She was sure it was Blossom; the figure wore something pale and flowing and quite unlike anything Lallie owned, and that meant it had to be the other girl. She saw the two figures hesitate, then meld into one shape amidst the shadows.

She stood there for some time, waiting for them to return to the house. They did not. They had simply vanished between the trees, into the darkness.

Valerie rubbed at her bare arms. Well, that hadn't taken long. She felt alone, and as lonely as she had ever been in her life. What would it be like, to be taken into a man's arms, to know his strength and his tenderness?

Which of them was it, out there with the girl from Atlanta? Not Quinn, she couldn't imagine him making love to Blossom or anyone else. Captain Ferris, maybe, or one of the lieutenants. Lieutenant Hoskins was married; would that make a difference? Either to him or to Blossom?

She turned at last away from the window, slipping into the bed beside her sister's still figure. Tears prickled behind her eyelids, tears for something she could not have put into words. She had no desire to establish any sort of relationship with the men in the house, the Yankees. They were the same as those men who had killed her father, and the Douglas boys, and wounded Evan.

150

She lay awake for more than an hour before she heard Blossom return, creeping quietly up the stairs. Valerie turned, burying her face in the pillow, wishing she had not heard anything at all.

Sixteen

No one commanded, or even suggested, that the women of the household concern themselves with the sick and injured men. It was simply impossible, during the following days when the house was seldom totally silent because of the moans of suffering men, to ignore the misery. They were Yankee soldiers. Yet, when their uniforms were cut away, there was nothing to distinguish between a Yankee and a Confederate except his accent, if he spoke.

They were so young. Younger than Evan, some of them. And considering the severity of their wounds, most of them made surprisingly little complaint. They lay on Ellen's pale yellow rugs in the drawing rooms, their eyes following any of the females who appeared within their line of vision, the mute appeal there in blue eyes, or gray, or brown. The appeal for a touch of kindness, of sympathy, of humanity.

In each of the young faces, Ellen saw Evan. In the hospital in Atlanta her son lay, possibly with injuries as severe as these, and she prayed that someone there cared for him. That someone carried water and spooned soup for him, if he wasn't strong enough to do it for himself.

Sally Ann was not strong, yet she was able to care for herself. She spent many hours resting in the big bedroom she now shared with Lacy; Gilly came to feed the infant Hugh Alexander at two-to-three-hour intervals.

"If you need anything, ring the bell," Ellen told her. "I'm going to help with those boys downstairs, but I'll come if you need me."

Sally Ann seldom called for assistance, and Ellen's days grew longer than ever. She moved among the men on the piazza and in the drawing rooms, Pansy following with a bucket of water and a dipper. She knelt beside man after man with bowls of the savory soup that Mamie kept simmering at all times in the black iron kettle.

They ate better, since the Yankees had come. No one asked where the two corporals had come by the chickens they brought back. Pansy plucked them and Mamie stewed them—"Too tough to fry," was her verdict—and the nourishing broth was dispensed to those too ill to eat heavier food.

The Yankees brought white flour, wheat flour that had not been seen at Mallows in over a year. There was plenty of rice flour, yet the treat of fresh bread made with wheat flour was a luxury long denied, and they relished it. Wandering cattle, "deserted" according to the men who brought them in, were butchered for Major Quinn's table, a welcome addition to their own pork.

There was sugar again, and Mamie baked her feather-light cakes, even at the expense of depriving Dolly of her morning eggs. Cake, after so long without, was a rare treat. If Dolly's stomach became a bit more delicate when forced to share the mush of the others, why, no one had time to listen to a litany of lamentation. They left her more and more alone, and Ellen had the temerity to deliver to her (in the room she and Ellen now shared, since the upstairs sitting room had been taken over by the Yankees) a basket of mending, with the request that she do it as soon as possible. Dolly, outraged, had stared at her daughter in disbelief. Ellen, however, scarcely noticed. She was engrossed in more important matters.

Gradually every woman in the house, with the exception of Dolly and Sally Ann, was drawn into full involvement with the hospital patients. Mamie was kept busy from dawn until dusk, cooking. This task was supposed to fall to one of the corporals, a taciturn little man by the name of Trenton. Trenton, however, had no knowledge of cooking. When Mamie tasted the soup he had simmered up in a kettle in the yard, she spat it out in disgust.

"Ain't fit for hogs, let alone sick mens," she announced. "I tell you, soldier. You bring me chickens and what I needs to fill the pot. Do what I tells you, and we give them sick ones somethin' fit to eat."

Trenton had had no previous experience of slaves, except to know that they were black. He was astonished to find himself taking orders from this woman who outweighed him by a hundred pounds, and might have resented it to the point of mutiny had it not been for the truth of Mamie's allegations regarding his cooking ability.

From that point on, the diet of everyone at Mallows improved. Since he stole what he brought back, Trenton didn't care if Mamie deftly transferred part of his loot to the table inside the house. He, as well as the patients, became adequately fed for the first time in months.

Things such as chicken and roast goose and butter reappeared on the menu. The population in the hen house mysteriously increased so that there were occasionally eggs to go with the breakfast ham. A scrawny cow was driven in from the woods, and after she'd given birth to a pair of twin heifers, she produced milk that was rich with thick cream.

"It a pity," Mamie said wistfully, "you-all can't bring us some shrimps. And oysters. Ain't had any oyster stew in a long time."

The Union Army, Corporal Trenton pointed out, was moving toward the sea, not away from it. There was no way he could get seafood. "We get to Savannah," he promised the black woman, "we'll get you whatever you want."

Pansy, who would have much preferred helping in the kitchen to looking at those near-corpses, was pressed into service in the hospital. If not carrying the water bucket for Miss Ellen, she might be given a stack of soiled linen dressings to be burned. The stench of them sometimes made her throw up. Nobody, she thought, could survive wounds that smelled the way these did.

By the second day, Valerie and Blossom and Lacy worked along with Ellen. They spent hours feeding and cleaning the men; this last task was reserved for Ellen and Lacy, since the unmarried women were deemed too innocent to perform it.

Julie could not bring herself to stand by, as Valerie learned to do, while dressings were changed by one of the lieutenants. She did spend hours making bandages of whatever materials came to hand, great stacks of them. When she trailed a hand

154

over the piano keys one afternoon, and one of the men called out to her with a feeble request that she play, she became their entertainer. Neither Major Quinn nor Captain Ferris had any objection if she sat for hours at a time at the keyboard, playing the old familiar tunes.

After one such session Julie paused in the doorway, searching for her sister, and looked down on a soldier near her feet. Tears spilled over his stubbled cheeks as he whispered, "Thank you, ma'am. My mother used to play for us, and read the Bible. Ain't nobody read me the Bible in a long time." He paused to clear his throat before adding, "I'd like to hear it once more before I die."

Shocked, Julie spoke without thought. "You aren't dying, sir!"

He wiped the back of one hand across his face. "Oh, I think so, ma'am." He reached down and opened his unbuttoned tunic, exposing a thick pad of torn sheeting, soaked in blood. "They can't do nothing about this hole in my side. Ma'am—ma'am, would you be so kind as to do somethin' for me? Would you write me a letter home? So they know where I died, you know? So they don't go on wonderin'?"

That was the first letter, penned in Julie's neat script. And letter writing was added to her tasks, letters that carried traces of her own tears from time to time. In addition to the letter writing, a reading of any kind, from the Bible to any scrap of newspaper that came to hand, held a hushed audience. Some of them would never again see the sweet faces they remembered; dying was a little less lonely with this lovely dark-haired girl's voice soft in their ears.

Ellen observed, and approved. She had been much concerned about Julie's reaction to the attack by the soldiers earlier; she knew that the girl needed to put men back into perspective, as human beings rather than predators, in order to deal with her own inner turmoil. Certainly none of them, after that first night, had much difficulty in sleeping. They were all so exhausted by the time they went to bed that sleep was likely to cut short the prayers of those who chose to say them lying down rather than on their knees.

Valerie wasn't sure how she became Captain Ferris's unofficial assistant. She had had no such intention; indeed, she was drawn unwillingly into direct contact with these injured enemy soldiers. She would have preferred making bandages, as Julie did, or chopping vegetables for their soup, or doing anything that didn't involve looking at and speaking to the Yankees. Their injuries, after all, had been inflicted by Confederate troops defending their homeland from the invaders. The Yankees undoubtedly deserved what they had gotten. Yet it was impossible, when staring at the exposed stump of a severed arm, to think of the torn flesh as *enemy*. A scream of agony left her as drenched in perspiration as the man who twisted under the restricting hands of the two corporals while his rotting foot was cut away.

It made her sick, and she was so filled with revulsion that she would gladly have avoided the hospital patients entirely had it been possible. Yet she was there on the piazza when Jack Ferris, stripped to a pair of bloodstained trousers, performed that operation.

She had been out to the slave quarters, to check on the pregnant Nora; Pansy reported that Nora was going into labor, and calling for Miss Ellen. Knowing her mother was busy, Valerie went herself and was returning, relieved not to have to take the responsibility for Nora herself, to report. She didn't realize there was a surgery in progress until the man screamed.

Valerie stopped in dismay, there on the steps; she saw blood spurt out across Captain Ferris's hands, heard him swear as his assistants fought to hold the patient down. And she moved, to her own astonishment, in compliance with Ferris's snapped order.

"Give us a hand, hold his head!"

She did, sinking onto her knees to grip the man's head as tightly as she could manage. Shaking as she was, it was a miracle she had the strength for it, although that was needed for only a few minutes. The victim of the surgeon's knife went limp.

"Good, he's fainted. Miss Valerie, bring me one of those pads." Ferris nodded to indicate the stack of dressings Julie had prepared earlier, a basketful of them.

Legs unsteady, she moved to obey; he accepted the linen and pressed it firmly against the new wound he had created. Her mind ordered escape; instead, Valerie sank onto the porch steps and rested her head on her knees, swallowing hard against nausea. When she finally conquered it and looked up, Jack Ferris was watching her while he splashed his hands and arms in the basin of water beside her.

He grinned.

156

"Not bad, for your first operation."

Her voice wavered. "Do you always do it that way? Just . . . just hold them down, and . . . start *cutting?*"

He shook off the red-tinted water and reached for a towel. "If the damned supply trains ever catch up with us, maybe there'll be something to make it easier."

He scrubbed at his hairy chest with the towel, then at lean, muscular arms. His torso was as tanned as his hands and face; obviously he worked in this half-nude fashion all the time. "I don't like it any better than they do, this way, but it's better than letting them die with gangrene. Having trouble breathing, were you? Leave off your stays so you can get some air into you, and you won't feel faint next time."

Outraged at such a suggestion, Valerie opened her mouth to tell him that she didn't expect to be around again. Before she could speak, however, Corporal Lofton called across the piazza.

"We got the next one ready, Captain."

The blood drained from Valerie's already chalky face. "You're going to cut off another foot?"

"Not this time. It's a couple of mangled fingers." He tossed the towel to one side.

"Wait! Wait, Captain, surely there's something . . . Whiskey. Wouldn't whiskey help, or brandy?"

His dark eyes were perceptive. "Is there some? Besides the 'last bottle' your mama produced after dinner last night?"

It was a waste of time to feel embarrassed about such an understandable lie. "There's a whole cellar full of it."

"Is there, by God. Suppose you rustle some of it up for us, Miss Valerie, and we'll let the next operation wait a bit until it takes effect."

And so she brought the whiskey, and the soldier was aided into a drunken stupor before his fingers were removed. And somehow Valerie stood there through the entire thing, handing over bandages when they were needed.

At the end of the proceeding, Jack Ferris grinned again. "Very good, Miss Valerie. And remember, next time leave your stays off. You'll find it easier to breathe, as well as a hell of a lot more comfortable."

She made no reply to that, walking into the house to wash her hands and face, although none of the blood had spattered onto her. She wondered how Captain Ferris ever managed to feel clean, no matter how much he washed.

Ellen was coming down the stairs, a faint frown marring her customary composure. "Valerie, have you seen Gilly? That baby has been screaming his head off for a quarter of an hour."

"She's out with Nora, I think," Valerie remembered. "Nora's gone into labor, Mama. The women with her said it would probably be a few hours, and Gilly said she'd never watched a baby birthed."

Ellen stifled her exasperation. "Well, she isn't going to watch this one. She has a baby to feed, and when the time comes Nora won't need anyone around her who can't be of assistance." She noticed, belatedly, that Valerie did not look quite normal. "Are you all right? Have you been out in the sun?"

"No. I've been watching Captain Ferris remove a foot and two fingers." Strangely enough, she felt much steadier already. "Shall I go with you out to see to Nora?"

Ellen's glance was discerning. She had always deliberately kept her daughters away from sickness and birthings. She had protected them against the more unpleasant facets of life. Yet Valerie, for all that she was pale, had come through what was surely a trial by fire, and appeared little the worse for it. It occurred to Ellen that it would be a great relief to share the responsibility of caring for the sick.

"Yes," she decided. "Come along."

They did not cross the veranda, where Captain Ferris and his men were probably pouring more whiskey down some poor boy, preparatory to another surgery. They went out through the kitchen and along the bricked walk, hearing Mamie singing to herself as she worked, then on to the unpainted wooden cabin, where a cluster of women around the doorway marked Nora's quarters.

They moved aside as the mistress approached, and Ellen spoke to them sharply. "What are you doing here? You all have chores to be done. Marliss, why aren't you doing the laundry? Gilly, you're needed at the house. That baby has been crying long enough, and you don't belong here. Get along with you."

Gilly reluctantly emerged from the dim interior. "I never seen no baby born, ma'am. When Rufus came, I couldn't see nothin'."

Ellen wasted no more words on her, instead pushing the girl with a firm hand. Gilly, disappointment clearly written on her good-natured face, began to plod toward the big house as Valerie ducked her head and followed Ellen into the cabin.

It was a duplicate of all the others in the long double row of dwellings that had housed Mallows slaves for a hundred years. About half the size of one of the bedchambers in the main house, it contained a double bed and a table and chairs; there was a line of pegs along one wall for the inhabitant's garments, and a few rough shelves formed a cupboard. Cooking was done in the fireplace, which now was fortunately cold.

Fortunately, because the room was stifling. There were seven women there, besides the newcomers and the woman on the bed. Ellen moved to her side as the others parted to let her through.

"How are you doing, Nora?"

Nora was a small, fine-boned young woman, about to give birth to her first child. Her husband was one of those who had slipped off during the night; because of her condition she had not dared to go with him.

Her face was shiny with sweat. She smiled broadly. "I goin' to have me a fine big boy pretty soon, Miss Ellen."

Valerie stood at the foot of the bed, holding her breath against the overpowering odors that thickened the air. She watched her mother bend over and place a hand on the distended belly, holding it there until it went into a spasm that left Nora gasping. When it had subsided, Nora's smile was not quite so broad.

"They gettin' harder, Miss Ellen."

Ellen waited, judging the time between the contractions, before she spoke reassuringly to the girl and then withdrew. Like a silent black curtain, the women moved aside for her passage, then came together again around the bed.

The fresh air outside was more than welcome, and Valerie inhaled deeply, expelling the fetid air that had nearly choked her. "Is she all right?"

Ellen pressed a hand to her temple in that familiar massaging action. "I hope so. She's rather small, and Clay was such a big man. If the baby is very large, she may have a difficult time of it. It won't be soon, I think, not for a few hours. Maybe we'll get to eat dinner, first."

We, she had said, including Valerie. Valerie wasn't certain; was she pleased about that, or uneasy? But if she could watch the brutal surgery of removing a man's foot, she could learn about birthing babies, which was a far more normal procedure.

She didn't want to go back into the house yet; she didn't want to take a chance on being again pressed into service in the alfresco surgery.

"The scuppernongs are ripe," she observed. "I think I'll get a basket and pick some for the table."

Ellen nodded, her mind on something else. "Very well. Good heavens, is that wretched child still hanging about? Poor little Hugh will have died of starvation by this time, or at least lost his voice from screaming!"

Gilly, hovering at the corner of the house, turned wide-eyed toward the approaching ladies. It had belatedly occurred to her that, though she knew she had belonged to Miz Douglas at Cedars, this could no longer be the case. Cedars was burned, they said, and Miz Douglas was dead, shot by the Yankee soldiers.

"Where I belong now, Miz Ellen?" she asked.

"You belong upstairs feeding Miss Sally Ann's baby," Ellen told her firmly. "Why are you still out here?"

"I don't want to walk through all them soldiers to get inside," Gilly pointed out. "I scared of people what are dyin'."

"Don't be silly. They're only ordinary people who have been injured, and they can't possibly harm you. Besides, there's no need to cross the piazza; you can go in the back door and up the back stairs from the kitchen if you want to avoid the soldiers."

"Yes'm. Only there's a soldier in the kitchen, too, and he done tole me to get the hell out." Gilly's grin flashed briefly. "He takin' a bath."

"In the kitchen?"

"Yes'm. In a washtub Pansy brung in for him. It that Corporal Trenton. I guess he need a bath, all right. He been helpin' that doctor one cuttin' off people's parts. I don't got to help wash up them bloody clothes, do I, Miz Ellen? Blood make me sick, and it ain't good for me to feed them babies when I feel sick."

Ellen had had enough. "Go in through the little dining room. Surely there is no one taking a bath in there. And you can reach the main stairs without passing anyone either dying or bathing. Hurry up, that child is starved half to death."

Gilly went, singing a little song to herself, which she made up as she went along. She still didn't know where she belonged, but she was sure enough glad she hadn't been at Cedars when the Yankees came. Glad what happened to poor Miss Charlotte hadn't happened to her. She paused to think about that. Did she belong to Miss Charlotte and Miss Henriette now? Neither of them would come anywhere near the Yankees, wouldn't come downstairs since they'd been here.

She let herself in the door at the rear of the house. There was no one in the breakfast room. She hesitated at the inner doorway. Sure enough, there was still splashing sounds from the adjoining kitchen. Gilly looked around to make sure she was not observed. That baby waited all this time, a minute more wouldn't matter. She applied her eye to the keyhole in time to see Corporal Trenton emerge from the tub and reach for his towel.

Seventeen

Valerie came toward the house with her basketful of the fruit she had just picked. She was tired, yet pleasantly so. Now that she was away from the injured men, she took a certain amount of satisfaction in knowing she had been of some use. If only she didn't think of her brother every time she passed through the hospital; if only she didn't have to keep on worrying about Evan.

"Miss Valerie. That looks heavy; can I carry it for you?"

She hadn't seen him, resting there in the shade of the rose arbor. He'd cleaned up and was in full uniform. When he came toward her, Jack Ferris was smiling the way a man does when he admires a woman.

He lifted the basket from her, then peered down at it. "Brown grapes?"

"Scuppernongs," Valerie explained. "Don't you have them in New York?"

"Grapes are purple where I come from. Are these ripe?"

"The brownest ones are the ripest." Valerie felt a peculiar sort of ambivalence about this man. He was attractive, there was no denying that. And he was a physician, a healer, a benefactor to mankind. Yet he was also a dreaded, hated

162

Yankee, and he had invaded her home without so much as a by-your-leave.

His hand, lifting a bunch of the scuppernongs and bringing them to his mouth, was tanned and clean, yet she remembered it covered with blood. She couldn't suppress a small shiver of revulsion, remembering the blood.

Captain Ferris savored the fruit, nodding. "Delicious. Scuppernongs, eh? Hell of a name for a grape." He began to walk toward the house. "You offer some of these to Major Quinn. They might be enough to put him in a better mood for the evening."

"Why, is he in a bad mood?" She didn't really care about Quinn; she was trying to sort out feelings about this man strolling beside her. What would it have been like, if she'd met him before the war? Or if there had been no war? How would they have reacted to one another?

"Haven't you noticed?" Ferris sucked open another scuppernong with obvious relish. "He's usually in a bad mood, because he doesn't want to be here in charge of this insignificant small operation; he wants to be riding with Sherman, sweeping through Georgia like a cutlass. Only Sherman despises him, so he was given this demeaning command in spite of the fact that he has powerful connections back home. And today he is bogged down with paperwork, which he hates. Offer him a bowlful of these."

Again, almost against her will, Valerie's attention was drawn to his hands. Why did it make her feel so oddly unsettled to look at them? She moistened her lips. "Doesn't it bother you, to—to do what you do? Amputating limbs and things?"

His expression grew quizzical. "Are you one of those people who don't believe in doing a thing, if it bothers them?"

She didn't meet his gaze, instead plucking a small leaf from the basket he carried as if it were important to remove it. "I don't know. I suppose I've been sheltered; I haven't been bothered by very many things, until recently. Deserting soldiers, and . . . and attacking innocent girls. Surgery is different, of course. It's not . . . destructive, in the usual sense. Yet it is very . . . brutal."

"Brutal, and necessary. They'll die if I don't do it, you know."

She remembered Ruth's statement about her husband.

163

"And they're better off without a limb than dying." She didn't sound sure of it.

"They don't always think so, at the time the surgery is necessary. But it's like anything else; they adjust to it. They can still, most of them, be husbands and fathers. Ask their women if they wouldn't prefer them maimed rather than not at all."

Troubled, Valerie made no response to that. They had reached the summer kitchen and Captain Ferris rested the basket on the edge of the bricked outdoor sink where vegetables were cleaned.

"Are you waiting for someone to come back, Miss Valerie?"

His words were soft and unexpected. Valerie lifted her head to face him, her heart suddenly and unaccountably racing.

"Only a brother. My father died at Chickamauga."

"No lover."

"No lover," she repeated.

What did she read in his face? How did he react to that? Was it a casual question, or a personal one? She couldn't tell. Jack Ferris had schooled his own reactions, as was only to be expected in one who had chosen to be a physician and a surgeon.

"Captain! Captain, we got a man bleedin' real bad!"

They turned, then, to see Corporal Lofton running toward them across the grass. "It's Major Babcock, sir. I think he just went berserk all of a sudden. He's torn off his bandages and started running and my God, the blood is spoutin' everywhere!"

"Well, damn it, hold him down, and put pressure on it," Ferris said irritably. Before he left, he helped himself to another bunch of scuppernongs, striding briskly away from her without a farewell. Valerie watched him go, disturbed and stirred at the same time. What *would* she feel, if he weren't a Yankee?

Blossom, much to her chagrin, found that the morning after what she had considered a very satisfactory interlude with Lieutenant Froedecker, he did not even remember it. He had told her how pretty she was, and he'd made love to her, only slightly inhibited by the amount of brandy he'd drunk. And then, the following day, when she greeted him with a wide

164

smile heavy with meaning, the lieutenant had responded with no more than a perfunctory nod.

She thought at first that it was only that he was busy, absorbed in whatever tasks were his lot that day. When she offered a few tentative reminders of that episode, however, Froedecker flushed.

"I guess I was pretty drunk last night," he confessed. "I'm sorry if I did or said anything offensive, miss. I surely didn't mean to."

Didn't mean to! Her outrage grew as the day progressed. All those things he'd said, and he hadn't meant them?

Angry humiliation sent her looking in another direction. She would show him he wasn't the only man on the place. Her tentative overtures to Lieutenant Hoskins brought only further frustration, however. When she engaged him in conversation, he pulled out the likeness of his wife and his daughter, eager to show them to someone, to talk about them.

Any one of the privates would have been grateful for her attentions; they all made that clear. Still stinging, however, at what she looked upon as rejection by the officers, Blossom was not ready to settle for a private whose total resources were no more than nineteen dollars a month, when he got paid at all.

The corporals were not much better paid, and were low on the pecking order, too. Blossom decided to cast her bread upon different waters, and made it a point to carry a cup of coffee—real coffee, rounded up somewhere by Corporal Trenton—out to Sergeant Alvin Gates, whose job it was to oversee the routine matters of caring for the injured when the expertise of the medical officers was not called for. Alvin Gates was twenty-five years old, rather too skinny for Blossom's taste, and with an Adam's apple that was distracting. But he looked healthy, and he had thick reddish blond hair and direct blue eyes that openly reflected admiration for this girl and her thoughtfulness.

"Thank you, ma'am. Most welcome, I'll tell you." He was not sure of Blossom's status in this household; an impoverished cousin, was his guess. "Been a long time since a pretty girl done me any favors."

Was there an invitation in that? Not wanting to risk another rebuff, Blossom worded her response carefully.

"I reckon, you been in Georgia, you ain't done many favors for any girls to return to you."

Alvin Gates laughed. "You got a point there, miss. Well, I'll be watching for an opportunity to do you a favor, and I'll look right kindly on any return of 'em." He hesitated, gauging her reaction. "I'd be right pleased, Miss Blossom, if you'd walk out with me this evenin'. Man gets tired of sittin' around the campfire listenin' to a bunch of soldiers jawing about the same old things. How they wish they had something better to eat or to drink, and how much they miss their mamas or their wives or their sweethearts."

Taking that opening, Blossom asked off-handedly, "You got a wife, Sergeant Gates? Or a sweetheart?"

"Nary a one. Had me a girl," Gates allowed, "but I heard she married up with a farmer after I went off to war. Can't blame her, I s'pose; he had a nice tidy forty acres and a house. More'n I could have offered her, even if I was there. When my pa dies, though, I'll have a nice little farm, too. Then maybe I can find myself another girl."

Blossom knew enough about farm life to aspire to higher things. Still, the way things looked in the South, if all the slaves went away, these women wouldn't be much better off than they were now. And farmers always had enough to eat, didn't they?

"I guess there wouldn't be nothing wrong with that," Blossom said, sounding prim. "To walk out with you in the evenin'. Before dark, of course."

"Sure," Gates said. "Before dark."

Blossom smiled, walking away from him back to the chores that Miss Ellen had assigned her in the house. If he couldn't make the walk last until it was dark, Sergeant Gates was a poorer man than she thought he was.

Henriette Douglas was quite willing to do anything she could to be helpful, as long as it didn't involve contact with the Yankees. Either the healthy ones or the injured ones. It wasn't difficult to understand her point of view; it *did* add to the problems of running a household. Except for mending and sewing, there wasn't much she could do in the room she shared with her sister. And Charlotte was hardly fit company for anyone, twenty-four hours a day, no matter how sympathetic one might be for her condition.

Charlotte occasionally spoke in a normal, rational way.

That was rare, however. For the most part, she didn't speak at all. And when she did, it was likely to be on some topic far removed from the conversation around her.

Julie, who also chose to avoid the Union officers when she could, identified closely with her friend. Had it not been for the grace of God and the intervention of Patrick Ryan and Valerie, she herself would have been as badly treated as Charlotte had been. Feeling guilty that she had escaped, while Charlotte had not, Julie at first made an effort to spend some time in the room that had previously been her own. She tried to engage Charlotte in conversation, feeling that anything was better than allowing the memories to fester like the wounds of the men out there on the piazza.

Yet it was disconcerting when Charlotte said things like, "Ask Mama to bring me up some milk, will you, Henriette?"

Her sister was quick to reply in some soothing way. Julie, however, could not cope for long with a reversion to childhood, with Charlotte's references to her parents and dead brothers as if they were still alive, as if they would appear at any moment to do whatever she asked.

Troubled, Julie asked Valerie's opinion. "Do you think she'll ever get better?"

Valerie hunched her shoulders in a helpless shrug. "Who knows? I suppose it's that she can't bear to think of all the terrible things, so to keep from going crazy, she pretends she's a little girl again, and that everything is all right."

"Will she keep from going crazy?" Julie persisted softly. "Or is it already too late?"

"I think she knows the truth, really." Valerie had continued to brush at her thick auburn hair. "I've seen the look on her face, once or twice, when one of the officers has come upstairs and she's glimpsed him. There's hatred, livid hatred, and terror. I think she'd kill them all if she had the means."

They left it at that. Gradually their concern shifted to Henriette, for Charlotte, in withdrawing from reality, had solved her own problem, at least temporarily. Henriette had not.

At Ellen's suggestion, Henriette was brought into more contact with Sally Ann and the infant Hugh Alexander. The baby required a good deal of attention, and Sally Ann remained poorly, in spite of the increased quality and quantity of food. After at first resisting anything that took her away from her sister—guilt lay heavily upon Henriette, and she felt

167

that she ought to spend every waking moment making up to Charlotte, somehow, for the fact that she and not Henriette had been ravished—Henriette accepted her new duties with enthusiasm.

For one thing, it was more cheerful to talk to Sally Ann. Sally Ann had little to be optimistic about except that as she had not been informed of her husband's death, there was still the possibility that he might come home one of these days, and her soft-voiced chatter was more appealing than Charlotte's silence and irrational outbursts. Mostly, though, it was Hugh Alexander who took Henriette out of herself. Who could fail to be enchanted by the little fellow who suckled so eagerly at Gilly's breast, who grew fat and learned to smile at those who hung over the cradle and cooed at him?

With several members of the household refusing to descend to the ground floor where they must encounter the Yankees, someone, then, must run up and down stairs fetching and carrying for them. There were meals to be carried up, and water for washing and drinking, and of course extra clothes to be hauled to and from the washhouse out beyond the summer kitchen. Lallie and Pansy were the chief beasts of burden, and they were joined by two other young black women from the quarters who were no longer needed in the fields now that the cotton had been harvested.

Ellen spoke to Major Quinn about the cotton.

"It is imperative that I get the cotton to market," she told him in her most regal manner. "It's the only hope we have of any cash to keep us going through the winter."

Major Quinn regarded her from behind the highly polished desk in the study, now spread with his own papers. A bottle of Roger Stanton's best brandy stood at his elbow, half-empty.

"There is no market, Mrs. Stanton. General Sherman is moving toward Savannah, and any cotton that is there when he arrives will be burned. It's unlikely that anyone will care to pay you for it, under those circumstances. You'll be better advised to simply store it where it is until matters are settled. I'm afraid those are the fortunes of war."

With another man, she might have resorted to pleading. With Quinn, she decided it was no use. The man didn't care whether Mallows made it through the winter or not, once he'd gone. She longed to ask when that would be, and dared

168

not. And she prayed that he was wrong about the cotton market at Savannah.

Valerie had just started to undress, in the flickering light of a single candle, when the tap came on her door.

Julie, already in bed, sat up instantly, her eyes wide. "Who is it?"

"No one knocking the door down," Valerie pointed out, and moved swiftly to open it.

It was Lallie. "They needin' someone in the quarters, Miss Val. Nora, she havin' trouble. Miss Ellen down there an hour ago and say it goin' to be all night and she goin' to rest. I looked in on her just now, and Miss Ellen sound asleep, plumb wore out. I thought maybe you better come."

A peculiar sensation stirred within her. It was one thing to go down there with her mother, quite another to go on her own. Still, Valerie knew that Ellen was exhausted; she looked more worn down by the hour.

"All right. I'll go," Valerie said quietly.

"Do you want me to go with you?" Julie's tone revealed how little the idea appealed to her.

"No, of course not. I probably won't be gone long. If she's having a serious problem, I'll have to call Mama, anyway."

"Pansy says it's a very messy business." Julie clutched the sheet between her knees. "And it hurts a great deal."

"What does Pansy know about it? She's never had a baby, nor seen one delivered, either. Go on to sleep. I'll try not to wake you when I come back."

She spoke calmly, as she had heard her mother do so many times when called to a sickbed. Yet it was with quickened pulse that she made her way down the back stairway that emerged into the winter kitchen. It was dark now, and silent; from the front part of the house, in the library, she heard men's voices and the clink of glasses. Valerie moved through the darkened room; she had not brought a candle because she had to accustom her eyes to the night before she went outside, anyway.

The path was familiar enough; she'd been walking it all of her nineteen years. There was the smell of woodsmoke in the air, and the tang of ripening grapes blended with the fragrance of the surrounding pines. She loved it here, Valerie thought unexpectedly. They had sometimes teased her mother, when they were all children, about her passion for a

169

piece of ground and a house. But Mallows *was* special, and perhaps it was as important to her as it was to Ellen.

There was a low fire burning in front of the cabin where Nora lay in labor, and dark figures moving slowly about. They turned toward her as she approached, parting to let her through the doorway as if she had been doing this for years.

The odors in the cabin hit her with the impact of a physical blow. Someone had lighted a fire in the fireplace, against the slight chill of the evening, and it was too hot. Again, the room was full of women, who shifted position to allow Valerie's approach.

She stepped to the foot of the bed and drew in a quick, sharp breath. Only a few hours ago, Nora had been confidently looking forward to the birth of her son. How could she have changed so much in such a short time? The young black woman looked up to her with pleading, frightened eyes. She seemed years older, her scalp soaked in a pungent sweat that was overpowering at close range. As another of the contractions hardened her belly, Nora gasped and cried out, "Oh, God, help me! Help me!"

Valerie didn't move. Usually the women had their children with little difficulty; by the following morning, when she had sometimes gone to visit them and examine the new infant, she had always found the mothers rested and smiling and proud of their accomplishments. What was she supposed to do if the baby didn't come?

The women had stepped aside to allow her access to the side of the bed. Hesitantly, Valerie eased forward. She put out a hand to lay it on the bulging abdomen as she had seen Ellen do, and found it rock-hard. Nora's cry became a scream of anguish, which ended when the contraction faded, leaving her limp and slippery and panting. When she could speak, she clutched at Val's hand.

"They somethin' wrong, Miss Val. It ain't comin' the way it s'posed to."

Valerie allowed her gaze to drift around the circle of faces, reading affirmation on all of them. She resisted the impulse to lick her lips, not wanting them to read her own uncertainty, although they all knew she had never assisted at a birth before.

"How long has she been like this? Having severe pains?"

The women consulted under their breaths. "She been in
170

bed two days," one of them finally offered. "Been hurtin' bad since the middle of the day. Miss Ellen say it a big baby."

Yes. Nora's Clay was a big, powerful man, and he'd throw a large baby. What did you do when the baby was too big?

No one had ever died in childbirth at Mallows, not in Valerie's recollection. Yet it seemed possible, as Nora felt another of the contractions coming and gripped the side of the bed and gritted her teeth for it, that a woman could easily die in the effort to force the child from her body. Nora's scream tore at her own vitals, until she felt as if she herself lay there on the bed, straining to accomplish what might be impossible.

"I think we'd better call my mother," she said, hating to admit to defeat yet totally helpless against the torture that Nora suffered. "Marliss, you go. The kitchen door is unlocked. Go in, upstairs. Mama's sleeping in her chair. Go in and shake her awake, and tell her Nora needs her."

The minutes passed slowly. Valerie forgot the odors and the heat; she forgot everything except the woman on the bed, writhing and screaming, then unable to hold back tears between pains as she waited for the next one.

Marliss did not return, and Valerie's impatience grew. Where was the woman? Had she stopped to dally with one of the men, or what? Why didn't someone come to help?

"Here she come," someone said at last from the doorway. "But Miss Ellen ain't with her."

Marliss had not dallied; she'd run both ways. "I can't wake her up, Miss Val! Miss Lacy say her head hurtin' bad and Miss Ellen took a little laudanum to ease the pain. She must taken more than she thought, 'cause we couldn't make her wake up!"

In spite of the heat of the cabin, Valerie felt a chill. Dear God, her mother couldn't leave her alone with a woman like this! She knew nothing, absolutely nothing! She turned her head away from the rising hysteria in Nora's face, to speak to the woman beside her, a woman who had had seven children of her own.

"What should I do, Vera? What can I do to help Nora?"

Vera moved uncomfortably. "I don't know, Miss Val. All my babies come quick and easy, like slippin' a sausage out of its skin. I seen a few slow birthings, but they don't take as long as this."

Fear flickered along her nerves. "Babies sometimes do take

171

a long time, though, don't they? As long as this, and still come all right?"

Vera rubbed work-worn hands together. "Long time, Miss Val. And she mighty little for a big baby."

Why in the name of God had she waited so long to learn something? Why hadn't she insisted on joining her mother in caring for the sick, years ago? Ellen seldom talked about those excursions except to say that so-and-so had had her baby, or was feeling better, or, occasionally, had died. The latter cases were mostly old people, and once in a while the victim of some savage accident. She knew that there had been times when she came down to breakfast in the morning to learn that Ellen had been out in the quarters all night, or most of it, with some needful soul; why hadn't she pressed for details? Asked what happened, and what to do when things went wrong?

Well, she hadn't done any of those things, and now she stood here in total ignorance while Nora twisted and screamed as the pain tore her body again.

The truth of the matter was that she'd been selfish. She didn't want to know about pain and blood and suffering, because it would have disturbed her own tranquillity.

What had Captain Ferris said to her? *Are you one of those people who don't believe in doing a thing, if it bothers them?*

Yes. Yes, that was exactly what she was. It would have bothered her to watch the bleeding and the suffering, so she had simply pretended it wasn't happening. So here she was, and more to the point here was poor Nora, depending upon her.

Beside her, Nora moaned and whimpered, too weak now to do anything except collapse between contractions. Valerie fought the panic that choked her. Surely, it had been long enough for the baby to deliver, if it was going to. Surely it was time for drastic measures if Nora and the infant were to be saved.

Yet what measures? What was she supposed to do?

Eighteen

An hour later, Valerie made her way through the darkness toward the house. She was almost as drenched in perspiration as the woman who struggled to give birth. Marliss had been sent again to see if Ellen could be roused, and when she could not, Lacy had been awakened.

Lacy had not attended a birthing in a good many years. She had never, she informed Valerie in low tones, been present at one which was complicated in any way.

They had stepped outside, to suck greedily at the cool night air, and to speak privately. Valerie was trembling with fatigue and the strain of being in charge of a situation she was in no way equipped to handle. No wonder her mother so often looked worn out, if she went through this sort of thing.

"Is she going to die?" Valerie asked.

"Probably, if someone doesn't do something to help her." Lacy, too, revealed tension in her voice.

"But what? What can anybody do?" There was no telling how much of the laudanum Ellen had taken; it might be well into the following morning before she woke to be of assistance, and no assurance that even she would be able to save Nora.

Lacy spoke with reluctance. "I've heard of them removing

173

the child surgically. I never heard anyone who lived through it, though, although the child may well live."

A great sickness swept through her; Valerie swallowed hard, remembering how the young soldier had screamed when they cut off his foot. "Cut into her belly? While she's *conscious?*"

"I suspect she would faint before it was very far along. Valerie, child, have you considered consulting Captain Ferris? He's a doctor, isn't he?"

Captain Ferris? For a moment she had a vision of him, stripped to the waist and splattered with blood. Yet his patients still lived after he'd cut them, and although they were in pain they didn't scream with it, most of the time. He knew about amputating limbs and tending gunshot wounds. Did he know anything about delivering babies? A few hours earlier, she would have resisted the idea of calling him. No man had ever attended birthings at Mallows; no woman would have allowed it. Perhaps her mother would not countenance it now, if the decision were hers to make. It was up to Valerie, however. And Valerie had had all she could take; she felt as close to the limit of her endurance as Nora must be.

"Stay here with her," she said now, feeling numb. "I'll go and speak to him."

It was all she could do to climb the stairs, clinging to the rail for the stability she didn't have in her legs. She tapped on Captain Ferris's door and waited, a wordless prayer running through her mind without her actually being aware of it.

"Yes?" He pulled open the door, bulking large in the opening, a thicker dark figure in the surrounding darkness. "What is it?"

"Captain Ferris, do you know anything about babies? Birthing them, I mean? One of our women has been in labor for two days, and she's in terrible pain. My mother—" Valerie faltered, fighting tears. "She had a headache and took something for it, and we can't wake her. And I don't know what to do."

"Babies." He swore. "Well, I haven't had much experience with babies, but I'll come take a look. Wait'll I get my pants on. Why are you running around in the dark? Here, I'll light a candle, and you can go downstairs and get my instrument case. You know where it is, in the drawing room?"

174

"Yes." Relief that someone was going to share the responsibility almost caused the tears to overflow. "I'll get it."

"I'll meet you at the back door as soon as I'm dressed," he said, and closed the door.

She was there ahead of him, handing over the small case, then trotting to keep up with his longer strides as they set out toward the dying fire that marked their destination.

There was a subdued murmuring as the black women again parted ranks. Some of them had gone off to their own beds; most remained, and these Ferris immediately ordered outside, except for one of them. "You," he said to Vera, "you stay. The rest of you get the hell out. Christ, it's a wonder the woman hasn't died of suffocation." He looked around for a place to put down the instrument case and lowered it onto the plain wooden table. "Isn't there any way to get more light in here? No," as Vera turned toward the fireplace, "don't build that up any more. Candles, get some more candles."

One of the onlookers at the door was dispatched for those. Captain Ferris didn't wait for them, however. "Here," he said, putting the single lighted taper in Valerie's hand, "hold that for me."

That meant, of course, that she must stand close beside him, and close to Nora, too. Valerie willed her arm to be steady as she obeyed orders.

Ferris peeled back the coarse cotton gown and put a hand on the swollen abdomen. Nora scarcely seemed to realize that anyone was there; her eyes were half-closed and the animal noises were weaker than they had been.

Ferris removed his hand from her belly and felt for the pulse in one outflung wrist. "This is her first baby?"

"Yes. And her husband is a very large man," Valerie said. The additional candle had arrived; Lacy lighted them at the fire and held two of them at the foot of the bed.

It did not seem that Captain Ferris needed the light, however; he moved to examine the exhausted woman with his hands. It was Vera who put the question Valerie dreaded to speak.

"You goin' to have to cut her open, Cap'n?"

He made a sound that might have been disgust. "I've heard of a Caesarean section, but I've never done one nor seen one done. Besides that, practically all the women die of them, either of blood loss or subsequent infection. No, I don't think that's the answer. Under these conditions, hell, I couldn't

175

even see what I was doing. No, I think there's a chance the infant is simply turned wrong. I don't know if we can save it, but there's at least a chance we can help it along through the regular process."

Sweat dripped off the end of his nose and his own body scent was added to the ones already present. Valerie was conscious of that, and then she forgot everything except what the man did with his hands.

He gave a grunt of satisfaction. "Just as I thought. It's trying to come feet first, rather than head-on, and without that skull for a battering ram, it's just stuck there. And she's too tired to push the way she ought to, by now. Listen, girl, you hear me? I'm going to cut you to make the opening bigger, so your baby can pass through. You understand? It won't hurt nearly as much as what you've already gone through. You try to rest between pains, and when I tell you, you get ready to push. You push as hard as you can, because we've got to get the baby out. You understand? When I tell you, you hang onto somebody's hands, and you yell if you want to, and you push like your life depends on it."

Which, Valerie thought, it did, of course. Vera moved to take Nora's hand on one side; Valerie put down her own free hand to Nora's other side, and immediately wished she'd called someone else in to do that part of the job. Nora's grip was bone-crunching, and it was too late now to do anything else. At least from this new position, Valerie didn't have to watch the actual cutting, and there was no spurting blood. She wanted to close her eyes, to pretend she was somewhere else, only Ferris's sharp, "Hold the light steady!" ruled out that luxury.

"Now," Ferris said, "push, girl! Push like hell!"

Nora did, and screamed, and Valerie thought every bone must be broken in her hand.

"All right, that's good. I've got hold of his foot. Rest a minute, then we'll try it again—Push! Push, damn you, push!"

And a moment later he lifted his hands holding the infant, a grin spreading across his face, and Nora's grip relaxed.

"You have your boy, and he looks fine," Ferris said, handing the infant to Vera, who had moved forward with the birthing blanket. A moment later the child gave a piping cry to add credulity to the statement.

176

Nora was still breathing heavily, but she opened her eyes. "I ain't goin' to die?"

"Not tonight, you're not." He glanced at Lacy, who was regarding him with more calm than Valerie felt. "Thank you, ma'am. No reason for you to stay any longer. Miss Valerie can help me with the rest of this, and I'll see her back to the house. Here, bring the light down here so I can put a few sutures in. This is going to sting, girl, but you hold still, all right? The worst is over."

This time, Valerie could hold the light and close her eyes so as not to watch what he did. There was no way she could control the trembling, and he didn't complain about that.

"All right. The baby doing well?" he asked, turning at last from the bed to the table, where Vera was washing the child.

Vera's dark face split in a delighted grin. "He's fine, Cap'n. He a big, handsome boy!"

"Good. You'll take care of him, now?"

"I take care of him," Vera assured him. "Looky there, he tryin' to eat his han' already! I bet he ready to suck, too!"

Jack Ferris put a hand on Valerie's shoulder and steered her toward the opening of the cabin. "Good. We'll check on her in the morning; until then, they're both in your hands."

"I take care of 'em both," Vera agreed cheerfully.

Valerie stumbled across the threshold and out onto the grass, gulping in the cool night air as if it were the finest champagne, and beside her Jack Ferris put a steadying hand under her elbow.

"Oh, God, thank you! I didn't know what to do, and I thought she was going to die . . ."

The tears that had threatened for so long began to spill over, now that it no longer mattered. She stopped, feeling as if she could not go a step farther.

Life and death matters were routine to Ferris. "Hey, don't fall apart now. As the resident physician, I prescribe a good stiff shot of brandy. For both of us."

She didn't resist when he guided her through the darkened house into the library, where she stood uselessly as he lighted the candelabra on the mantel.

"Here." He sloshed the amber liquid into a glass and pressed it into her hand. "It'll make you feel better."

Surprisingly, it did, although she choked over getting it down. He drained his own glass and stood watching her, grinning.

177

"You did very well, Miss Valerie. You'll make a fine assistant with a little more practice."

She shuddered, whether from the brandy or the idea wasn't certain. "I felt so helpless."

The grin faded away. "We all feel helpless, from time to time. In a war, on a battlefield, we're all helpless. The important thing is not to give up."

He took the glass from her hand and replaced it beside the brandy bottle on the table. "You haven't had time to learn it yet, but I think you're a lady with intestinal fortitude, Miss Valerie."

He was standing very close to her. Both were tired and could have done with baths, and in only a few hours he'd be shaving; the bristles stood out darkly on the lower part of his face. Nothing very attractive about either of them, Valerie thought. Her own hair had long since come loose from its pins and straggled over her neck and around her face. Yet there was something about Jack Ferris that made her heartbeat quicken, something quite apart from what he'd just done for Nora, and when he reached for her she did not even think of resisting.

His mouth was firm and warm over her own, his arms hard around her as he drew her close. Valerie's lips parted to receive him as she sank into a series of pleasurable sensations she had never before experienced. Oh, she'd been kissed, by casual friends of her brother's, at those almost forgotten parties; stolen kisses between children, she thought now. Jack Ferris was no child. And the leaping response in her own body told her, if she had not already guessed, that neither was she. She was a woman, and the spark Jack Ferris had ignited spread through her, liquid flame that touched off all the emotions she only imagined before tonight.

When at last they drew apart, he was smiling again. "You are a lovely, lovely lady, Miss Valerie. Is it too much to hope that we don't have to remain enemies? We've been through a lot together tonight. Can we be friends from this point on?"

She'd forgotten he was a Yankee. She'd forgotten her gratitude for saving Nora. She'd forgotten everything except the lean male body pressed against her own, the demanding mouth. The taste of him, the smell of him, the feel of him. She couldn't answer. Not because she didn't know that never again would she feel quite the same about him as a Yankee, but because he had opened a door for her into a world she

178

was more than ready to enter. The world of a woman capable of responding to a man.

Perhaps he saw that speech was beyond her. The smile returned, a softer smile, and he bent to brush his lips lightly across hers, this time with no hint of passion. Then he turned her about to face the door.

"Let's go back to bed, before it's time to get up again," he said. They climbed the stairs side by side, not touching, not speaking until they parted on the second-floor landing.

"Good night, Miss Valerie," Ferris said quietly, and her own response was quieter yet.

"Good night, Captain Ferris."

She hesitated just inside the door to her room, listening to Julie's soft breathing. She put a hand to her face, beside her mouth, where Ferris's beard had scratched the tender skin.

Then, with a tremulous exhalation of breath, she made her way toward the commode and poured water carefully into the basin for a sponge bath. Her body felt different, she realized, as the garments slid to the floor around her feet. Her breasts were firm yet soft as she sponged them, the nipples taut and erect. She was aware of every curve of hip and thigh as she had never been before. And her mouth—her mouth continued to tingle as if she could still feel the pressure of that other mouth, still know the taste of it.

She washed herself there in the dark and then, shivering, pulled her nightshift over her head and slid into bed. Her sister stirred and murmured.

"Everything's all right," Valerie told her softly, and Julie subsided into sleep.

Tonight, Valerie thought, tonight, Valerie Stanton had become a woman. She didn't realize that her lips curled into a smile as she, too, sank into slumber.

Nineteen

In spite of the long, stressful night, Valerie woke early, at the usual hour. She felt full of energy, eager to dress and meet the new day. She stared at herself in the mirror, amazed that there was no change in the familiar features. Tousled auburn hair, dark-lashed hazel eyes, the clear fair skin were all the same as they usually were. But wasn't there a difference, too? Wasn't there something softer, fuller, about her mouth? Could a woman look different simply because she'd been kissed?

"Val?"

She turned to look at the bed. "Good morning."

"It's a horrid morning. It's raining," Julie pointed out.

"Oh? I hadn't noticed. Anyway, it's a good morning for me. Nora finally had her baby, with Captain Ferris's help, and for a few hours I didn't think that was going to happen."

Julie's dark eyes widened. "Were you there? When the baby was born?"

"Yes. Holding a candle in one hand and having Nora crush my other one when the pains were bad." She wiggled her fingers and discovered that they were, indeed, tender.

Julie sat up, brushing back a black curl, which immediately fell forward again. "Was it horrid? Messy, and disgusting?"

180

"Disgusting? No," Valerie decided. "It was—once he was born, it was wonderful. The baby was turned wrong, upside down to what he should have been, so it took a long time. I suppose," she said, trying to be truthful, "it was messy. There was a lot of bloody-looking fluid. But no, I don't think it was disgusting."

Julie regarded her with a slight air of puzzlement. "You look—different, somehow. As if you've—fleshed out, overnight. Isn't that silly?"

"Very silly," Valerie agreed, and laughed. Yet she *felt* fleshed out, her lips more full, her breasts more rounded and pushing more firmly against the fabric of her chemise. And there was a vitality in her veins that had not been there before.

She pawed through her clothes, choosing at last a yellow sprigged dimity that she'd always considered becoming. It was almost too cool for it, and the dress was not appropriate for assisting in amputations; she hoped none were scheduled for today.

Leaving Julie to her own more leisurely dressing, Valerie let herself out of the bedroom and ran down the stairs, suddenly ravenous. The fragrance of bacon wafted to her as she turned toward the family breakfast room. That was one meal that they did not share with the Yankee soldiers, although judging by the aromas they did share the improved food.

Ellen was there, looking drawn and tired in spite of her long drugged sleep, sipping at real coffee with no more enthusiasm than she'd shown for chicory. Lacy, none the worse for her nocturnal excursion, looked up with a good-humored greeting.

"Bacon and eggs this morning, believe it or not! Having the Yankees in the house isn't all bad. And baking powder biscuits with butter!"

Valerie slid into her chair and nodded in Pansy's direction as the girl peeked around the edge of the door from the kitchen. "Yes, please! As much as I can have of everything!"

"Been so long since I ate bacon and eggs, I don't remember," Blossom said.

Valerie glanced toward the other girl and felt something catch in her chest. For Blossom, too, looked different. There was a rich satisfaction in her smile, and surely she was wearing a new dress? Not one of the pitiful collection she'd brought when she escaped from Atlanta? Who? Valerie wondered. Which one of them had brought Blossom the dress, and where had it come from? Which looted, plundered home? Not Cedars, of course. There had been nothing left at Cedars. Still, it bothered her to think that Blossom wore a gown stolen from some other unfortunate woman. No one else had noticed, apparently. They had other things on their minds. Ellen turned with a wan smile.

"I understand you took over for me last night, and very efficiently. I've been down to see Nora; she and the baby are both doing very well."

"Captain Ferris is responsible for that, not me." Valerie accepted the cup her mother pushed toward her and drank cautiously of the scalding brew. Did the color flow into her face, at the mention of Ferris? She decided to change the subject. "You're looking very pretty today, Blossom. Isn't that a new dress?"

The other girl beamed with pleasure, touching her fingertips to the front of the rose-colored silk as if she caressed her own breast. There was nothing particularly sensual about the gesture, yet Valerie had a sudden vivid knowledge of how exciting it would be to be touched, there, by a man. By Jack Ferris. Damnation, why couldn't she think of something that wouldn't make her blush?

"It is pretty, ain't it?" Blossom agreed. "Sergeant Gates brung it for me. It fits real good, except it's snug across the top. I guess I'm just shaped that way; everything is tight there on me." She laughed, enjoying that.

What had she had to do to get it?

It was there, an ugly intrusion in Valerie's unexpected thoughts. Why was she so sure Blossom had done anything? Yet she was, and she had a strong suspicion what that something had been. The most disturbing thing was that Valerie wasn't as shocked as she ought to have been. *That* was what was shocking.

Valerie ate from the plate that Pansy brought her, two fried eggs and two strips of bacon and four biscuits with butter. When had food ever tasted any better?

They were all still sitting there, having a second cup of the precious coffee while Julie ate her breakfast, when Sergeant Gates came to the doorway.

"Excuse me, ladies."

With her newly developed perceptiveness, Valerie decided

he looked too possessive when he smiled in Blossom's direction to be innocent. It was to Valerie that he spoke, however.

"Cap'n Ferris, he says would you join him, please, ma'am."

She drained her cup and pushed back her chair. "Yes, of course. Thank you, Sergeant."

She was eager, yet half-afraid, to see him again. How would he look upon her after that shared middle-of-the night kiss? Would he think less of her for having allowed it? Or would there be some special magic between them now? Would Jack Ferris, too, have this fine tremor in his limbs, the joyous sense of anticipation?

When she found him in the drawing room, however, Captain Ferris merely smiled and said good-morning, and put his flatly stated request. "Will you assist in changing dressings this morning? You've a much lighter touch than either Hoskins or Froedecker."

Disconcerted—it was impossible that the interlude had meant *nothing* to him, wasn't it?—Valerie murmured compliance, feeling flattened.

And then he turned to look more directly at her and grinned. "You're prettier, too."

And it was there. In the eyes that usually gave away nothing: the recognition that there was something exciting between them.

"I should hope so," she said, with a commendable appearance of composure, and he laughed aloud.

Changing dressings was a nasty business, not a task Valerie would ordinarily have welcomed. This morning, however, though she often averted her eyes from the wounds revealed when bandages were peeled off, it did not depress her. In fact, she admitted to herself, it would have taken more than a rainy day and an unpleasant job to depress her, because Jack Ferris excited her.

And the next time it was necessary to do surgery and she saw blood gush over Captain Ferris's hand, she did not have quite the same feeling of revulsion. She had seen those same hands, gentle on a black woman's distended belly, quick and firm in drawing forth the newborn child.

The Yankees had been there for two weeks, and seven of the original patients had died, when a wagon came with a dozen more.

"Why?" Valerie asked. "Surely there is not continued fighting? General Sherman moved through Georgia virtually unopposed?"

A little news filtered through to them now, with straggling soldiers of both armies, with supply wagons, and in the newspapers that once again issued from the city of Atlanta. General Hood, unable to cut off Sherman's supply lines, had settled on a last-ditch gamble: He turned his back on the Federal troops at Atlanta and moved into northern Alabama, and from there he turned his army toward Tennessee, in the hope that Sherman would feel compelled to come after him. In the meantime, Joe Wheeler, with Hood's cavalry, remained in Georgia to harass the Yankees in whatever way he could. General Sherman paid about as much attention to these tactics as he would have to a gnat.

No one knew exactly where General Sherman was; rumor had it that he and his sixty thousand men moved steadily toward the seaport of Savannah. No doubt there were scattered skirmishes, but the Confederates were simply not in a position to threaten the enemy to any great extent. There were no major battles.

Where, then, did the wounded men come from?

Captain Ferris gazed out at the wagon. "Well, let's find out, shall we?"

Some of the newcomers had been injured in the battle of Atlanta, and were recuperating from those injuries, or, in several cases, were succumbing to them. By now Valerie knew the putrid smell of gangrene. She knew without being told that more amputations were in order, since there was no other way to deal with the otherwise fatal affliction. In addition to those whose wounds were weeks old, there were accident victims. In war, as in peacetime, there were those who through carelessness or the whims of the gods suffered various mishaps. In the long run, it didn't matter whether their injuries were inflicted with intent or by chance; the results were the same.

"Is there communication with the people in Atlanta?" Valerie pressed. "Can you do anything to find out about my brother? Evan Stanton, who was last heard from at the Atlanta Medical College Hospital?"

"Your mother sent off a letter," Ferris reminded. "But I'll see what I can find out."

The days at Mallows settled into a sameness as the weather

moved through autumn into early winter. The leaves had turned color and fallen, the rains were more frequent and colder, so that fires must be lighted in the fireplaces.

Firewood grew around them in abundance, if there had been anyone to cut it. The only "men" left of the Mallows slaves were the elderly and the infirm, or the fourteen- and fifteen-year-olds like Chad and Tom. These boys might have been of some use had they so chosen; they did not, and there was no longer any pretense that they did the chores they were asked to do. Asked, no longer told, Ellen thought with the weariness of despair. Had it not been for the Yankee privates, who rode around the countryside with the wagons, appropriating wood where they found it, no one would have had any fires.

Heating the upper floors of the main house was impossible. The breakfast room on the ground level became the family meeting place; it was small enough to be kept habitable with the least amount of fuel. Major Quinn, of course, was enabled to sit in comfort in the study or the library, and an effort was made to warm the dining room morning and night. Quinn grew increasingly restless, and one day, after a messenger had ridden in with orders, Valerie saw him literally gnash his teeth and tear up the papers and kick them into the fire. An hour later he rode out, with Lieutenant Hoskins in attendance.

"Where's he going?" she asked, as much to herself as to the man at whose elbow she worked.

Captain Ferris glanced after the retreating figures. "He didn't bother to tell me. My guess, though, is that Sherman is nearby, and he's hoping to get his orders changed. He wants to get out of this stinking hospital and back to what he considers a more regular soldier's job."

"Why don't they let him go? He isn't really serving any valuable purpose here, is he?" Major Quinn had nothing whatever to do with the injured men, she knew.

The grin flashed briefly as Ferris bent over a young boy with hideous open sores over his face and neck. "His purpose here, I suspect, is simply to keep him away from Sherman. The major made the mistake of expressing an opinion in the general's hearing, and since it didn't agree with Sherman's, why, this is how generals deal with underlings they don't like."

185

"And you?" Valerie asked. "Are you being punished, too, with this duty?"

"No. I'm a physician, and if it weren't duty here, it would be the same job somewhere else. It doesn't matter to me." He straightened, rubbing absently at his back. "I'll admit I'm beginning to think with longing of home, though. And an end to this stink, and the blood, and the dying. I thought it might get easier, seeing them die, but it never does. The only good thing that's come out of this vile war," he said, looking directly at her across the sick youth, "was meeting you. You are a flower on a dung heap, Miss Valerie, and I thank God for you."

There had been no more kisses, although if he had made any overtures in that direction Valerie knew she would have responded. In fact, working beside him for long hours every day, she knew the torment of longing for some physical contact between them, and it did not come.

Blossom, on the other hand, was quite obviously enjoying herself; not only with Sergeant Gates but with Corporal Trenton and two of the privates, as well. If Valerie read the signs right, and she could not doubt that she did, the girl juggled them all quite handily for someone with no previous admitted experience, and grew more open about leaving the house to "walk" with one or the other of them.

The soldiers, who had pitched tents on the lawn to begin with, now had a choice of remaining in those in colder weather or moving into some of the vacated cabins. To begin with, they had resisted the cabins, protesting the smells. After a time, however, when tents became more and more uncomfortable, Valerie noted that they were put away altogether, and smoke rose from the chimneys of more of the cabins. She was convinced that the black women who had helped clean out the cabins now comforted those men at night, and wondered if Blossom minded sharing with the slaves.

At first, shocked at what was going on and what nobody especially bothered to conceal, Valerie had expected her mother to explode into action, protesting immorality between a girl living in her household and these soldiers, and on the part of her slaves. Ellen, however, did not seem aware of anything out of line. She continued to work indefatigably, directed Mamie in the preparation of meals, and fell into bed at night, insensible almost before the candle was put out.

If Ellen worried about what would happen when the

Yankees had gone, she did not share her worries. If she sometimes helped herself to some of the Yankee supplies, hiding them in various places unlikely to be discovered by the invaders, no one knew but Mamie, and Mamie did not tell anyone. After the first bout of indignation, Mamie had rallied to her old standards. It was, after all, far more satisfying to cook for gentlemen than for ladies alone, since they had such hearty appetites. And the provisions that Corporal Trenton brought in made it possible to cook almost in the old ways.

Major Quinn came back from his excursion—if indeed it was Sherman he went to see, the mission was obviously a failure—in a foul humor; he remained closed in the study much of the time, except that he sometimes wandered about the house, examining everything. He asked many questions of Ellen regarding the origins of things like chandeliers and wallpapers, paintings and china. He knew, of course, that the valuables of Mallows had been hidden from the Yankees. He would say, "What was your silver like, Mrs. Stanton?" and she would describe it for him in detail, since she seemed to take considerable satisfaction in knowing these things, even to the pattern on the good china and which piece of missing furniture had stood in what place. He had a perceptive eye; he knew instinctively when something was out of place, or missing.

"A very gracious house," he said more than once, nodding agreement with himself.

He was interested in the running of a great plantation, too. How many blacks did it take to plant, to chop, to pick a certain number of acres of cotton? Of corn? How many servants to keep a house of this size in proper order? How much food and of what types to keep the plantation going through the winter?

Most of these questions were asked at the dinner table. The rest of the time, Major Quinn shunned the company of the inhabitants of Mallows, as he also habitually avoided his own staff. He hated the stink of the infirmary: If he felt any sympathy for the sick and the injured who were at least technically under his care, he managed to conceal it admirably. When it was necessary to choose a burial site for those who had died, he consulted with Ellen over the matter, deferring to her judgment that it would be best to keep the Yankee soldiers separate from the family graves. It was one of his few consultations, however; Major Otis Quinn made his own decisions, for the most part, without regard to what anyone else thought.

The news, when it came, made them glad they had a protective small force of enemy soldiers quartered at Mallows. For Sherman was on the march with an army of sixty thousand men, who moved like locusts through the Georgia countryside. They ate, confiscated, or destroyed everything in their path. "I can make Georgia howl," William Sherman had said, and proceeded to prove it. The march was unhurried, and the army fanned out in a sixty-mile-wide wave, rolling inexorably toward the sea. There was no rush; the Georgians had done their best to prepare for the winter, and there were plentiful supplies of beef and ham and sweet potatoes and corn. What they could not eat, or feed to their animals, or haul in their wagons, the Yankees burned.

If there was any serious effort to control the Union Army forces, no one knew of it. The marauders did as they pleased, and what they pleased was to satisfy their own wants to the fullest extent. If that included the destruction of homes, the violation of Southern women, why, who was to deny them this gratification after their long years of struggle? When taxed with the matter, Sherman easily justified his own position. His intent was to get his army to the sea, and he had not enough officers to keep the common soldiers tightly in hand, nor had he the means or the inclination to protect the people of Georgia from the roving bands. Georgia had chosen to fight against the Union: Now Georgia must suffer the consequences.

Nearly four years earlier Sherman had addressed a statement to the South; those at Mallows had read it in the newspapers and prayed that he was wrong. Now they saw that he had not been. "The North can make a steam engine," Sherman said, "a locomotive, or railway car; hardly a yard of cloth or a pair of shoes can you make. You are rushing into war with one of the most powerful, ingeniously mechanical and determined people on earth—right at your doors. You are bound to fail." The bitter truth of this was forced upon them in earnest now. Not only had the Confederacy failed, they were to be stripped of all pride and possessions. They would truly be made to crawl before the victors.

Yet as long as Mallows remained a Yankee hospital, it was unlikely that any damage would be done to it, or so they prayed.

As to the effect that the Yankee occupation had upon those who lived at Mallows, that was a different matter. Knowing she could not control the immorality, Ellen saw no choice but to pretend to be unaware of it. Unlike Valerie, who had at least a limited understanding of Blossom's position, Ellen regarded her as a slut, little better than a woman of the streets. That Blossom had to do what she could to ensure her own survival was not a matter of consideration to Ellen. She herself had never had any desires of the flesh; she quite honestly did not believe that any decent woman took pleasure in such things. Procreation was necessary, of course, and she had dutifully submitted to Roger Stanton's physical demands: she had not enjoyed it and had felt only relief when she did not have to think about it any more.

To have this girl in her house now galled Ellen in the extreme. That Blossom was of the lower class was obvious the moment she had opened her mouth; no, even before that. One could tell simply by looking at her. And that she was now engaged in relationships with more than one man was also obvious. Blossom did not flaunt this—indeed, she thought she was being circumspect—but she was as devious as a child, and as transparent. She exuded an aura of earthy sexuality as unconscious as it was genuine.

Ellen had tried, once, to meet the problem from the opposite direction, by speaking to Captain Ferris about it in carefully couched terms. Blossom was obviously visiting the privates and one or both of the corporals in their quarters; was it not incumbent upon their superior officers to maintain discipline?

Captain Ferris gave her a long, level look. "Miss Ellen, I appreciate the sensitivity of your feelings. However, the girl serves a very worthwhile purpose. The men are more content, and discipline better maintained, if their human needs are met." And then, seeing the hot angry color staining her cheeks, he added the clinching argument. "Has it occurred to you, ma'am, that if the men are satisfied with Blossom, they won't think of molesting your own daughters?"

Somehow, since nothing untoward had happened so far, Ellen had taken it for granted that no harm would come to her daughters, or to the other young women in her charge. She had convinced herself that the Yankees, enemies though they were, were gentlemen who would observe certain standards of behavior.

Some of what she felt showed on her face. Jack Ferris gave her a considered bit of advice. "I suggest you leave well enough alone, ma'am. And hope for the best."

Was that a subtle threat, that if the men did not have Blossom they would prey upon the others? Ellen wasn't sure, but she understood what he'd told her, all right. Leave Blossom alone.

And in spite of Blossom's apparent availability, Ellen knew with a bitter certainty that after the Yankees had gone there would be a crop of light-skinned babies out there in the quarters. Promiscuity was something that had never been condoned at Mallows; the people were guided into proper marriages, when the time came, and those who deviated from the accepted pattern had been punished. Now it was beyond Ellen's ability to punish anyone. When she allowed herself to think ahead, beyond the time when the Yankees were here, she was terrified. There were not enough people left to work the land; she had so little money that it could not hope to provide for them through the winter, and she had no idea what would happen when that money, and perhaps the rest of the slaves, had gone.

Her compromise, and her link to sanity, was to live each day as it came along. She rose early and worked late, supervising food preparation and the running of the big house, and working in such ways as she could among the hospital patients. If she was perturbed because Valerie spent so much time with the physician, seeing dreadful sights and being exposed to constant contact with the Yankees, she kept it to herself. Captain Ferris's warning had been explicit enough to frighten Ellen very badly.

It was a wet night in early November when word finally came from Evan. Julie, always with less stamina than her sister, had gone early to bed, and Valerie undressed by candlelight to join her.

She moved slowly and sensuously, as she had come to do with this new awareness of her own body. With the garments in a heap around her ankles, she turned to view her reflection, taking pleasure in what she saw. Would that slender body with the high rounded breasts be attractive to a man? She knew it would, and there was no shame in the knowledge. Men and women were meant to mate, were they not? To be attractive to one another?

190

In the past few days, since the medical duties had been less pressing, there had been a few occasions when there was time to sit, to talk, to look at each other. And it was surely not her imagination that Jack Ferris made excuses to touch her: to brush her hand as they exchanged instruments or dressings, to move with her through a doorway so that they must press together, shoulders, arms, thighs, for a few seconds.

If he asked her to go with him, when he left Georgia, would she go? The idea had been in her head for days. The thought of leaving Mallows was one she did not allow herself to dwell upon, since she did not want to think of leaving it, certainly not forever. But Captain Ferris came from a well-to-do family in New York; there was a manufacturing plant that made machinery of some sort, and therefore plenty of money. Indeed, the war had expanded the business so that, Jack said cheerfully, he might even discover he'd grown rich while he was away at war.

He didn't ask her to go home with him when he went; he did tell her about New York, which was a great city and, to hear him tell it, the hub of the universe. He knew nothing about farming, and it did not appear that he was interested in learning. Still, if he had the money, and Mallows provided a beautiful home for one who could afford to maintain it, might he not be persuaded to return here? Someone else was running his factory now; could he not continue to do so, if the owner decided to live in Georgia? There were so many plantations run by men who did not do any of the work themselves; they hired overseers, like Patrick Ryan.

She hadn't thought of Patrick Ryan in weeks. She didn't even know if he still lived; he might have been killed in the battle of Atlanta. It was uncomfortable, thinking about Patrick Ryan while she stood here nude before the mirror. She felt almost as if he could see her. Why should that cause this tingling sensation, the sudden erection of her nipples? She knew now that *that* happened when she was excited by Jack Ferris; it seemed that it also occurred at the thought of any other man. Well, it was a peculiarity unexplainable, but of no consequence. She had no intention of ever being seen naked by Patrick Ryan.

Something struck the window behind her, and Valerie spun, reaching swiftly for the petticoats at her feet to cover herself. Which was absurd, of course. The window was forty feet off the ground, and there were no balconies on that side

191

of the house. Yet it had not been rain, surely; the wind had to blow with some force to drive the water under the eaves enough to hit the windows.

It came again, and she knew at once what it was, that time. A rock, aimed from below with precision. Valerie glanced toward the bed, where Julie lay curled in sleep, facing away from the middle of the room. Valerie reached quickly for the wrapper that lay across the nearest chair, knotting the sash around her as she moved quickly to the window and threw it open.

It was too dark to see anything. The air was cool and fresh on her face as she leaned outward, trying to penetrate the blackness. Captain Ferris? Was he trying to summon her outside for a rendezvous?

Before she could react to that stimulating idea, however, she heard a familiar voice, though it was not one she expected.

"Miss Val, you better come down," it said.

"Aaron? Aaron, is that you?"

"I got Mr. Evan," Aaron said. "He's in bad shape, Miss Val. You better hurry."

Twenty

She pulled on the most essential of the garments she had discarded only minutes ago, leaving off stays and petticoats. Evan, and in bad shape! *Oh, God, please!*

She fairly raced down the back stairs. The kitchen was warm and there was a yeasty smell. Valerie paused long enough to catch up one of the capes hanging on a peg inside the outer door; with it held over her head, she slid back the bolt and peered out.

"Aaron? Are you there?"

He materialized out of the gloom, his black face thinner than she remembered. "I thought I better look around before I brought him in, and it's a good thing I did. Place is overrun with Yankees. Even some of 'em sleeping on the piazza in the cold. What's going on?"

"This is a Yankee hospital." She kept her voice pitched low, to match his. "Where's Evan? How is he?"

"He pretty bad. I stole a wagon to bring him in, he can't walk. He feels mighty hot, to me, too. He needs to be inside, where somebody take care of him."

"I thought he was in a hospital, in Atlanta." Valerie clutched the cloak tightly around her face and tried to keep it from billowing out around her; there *was* a wind, once they got away from the shelter of the house, and it was colder than she'd expected.

"He was," Aaron said, setting the pace, which was a strenuous one for her shorter legs. "But they didn't have anything to do with—no medicines, not much food. He said bring him home to die. I didn't want to come back, to tell you the truth, but Mr. Evan always good to me. I owe him something. So I stole the wagon."

"You went to see him there? In the hospital?"

They worked their way toward the front of the house, staying in the shelter of the trees, although there was little likelihood anyone could see them from the house. There were lights in Major Quinn's room, and in Captain Ferris's, too. Everything else was dark.

Aaron was getting ahead of her, and Valerie reached for his sleeve to slow him down. "Aaron, tell me. Is he dying? Or is he only frightened and sick?"

"I'm no doctor, Miss Val. He looks pretty bad to me. No, I didn't go to visit him. I got caught up in a mob fighting over something to eat, and somebody hit me over the head with an ax. Didn't split my skull, I aimed a kick in the right place to send it to the side, but I had a good cut. I had to have it sewed up, and while I was at that place I saw him. Mr. Evan. Didn't hardly know him at first."

Valerie tripped on some unseen branch and would have fallen if he hadn't steadied her. "So you just took him out? To bring him home?"

"Well, not right that minute. I saw him, and I spoke to him, and the look that came over his face, seeing someone from home—He begged me to get him out of there. Said he was starving, and his foot wasn't getting any better. The hospital was so poor even the Yankees didn't want it."

The truth of that would seem to be borne out by the fact that Major Quinn and his men were here. An improvised surgery and infirmary were preferable to the established Confederate hospitals, which were undermanned, overcrowded, and had no ready source of supplies. And Evan had lain there, helpless, for months!

Valerie put down the memory of those rotting amputated limbs she had seen; every wound wasn't necessarily fatal. In the past week two of the men whose injuries had been severe had improved enough so that they were now walking around, doing what they could for their fellow patients. It might be that all Evan needed was good food, loving care.

"I could see it was true. The men were dying all around him," Aaron said. They had skirted the front of the house and now made their way along the drive; once they were a short distance from the house there was little danger of being heard by anyone but the unfortunates who slept on the piazza, rolled in their blankets. Few of them were ambulatory and none curious on a wet, dark night.

"Looks like the house is full of soldiers," Aaron observed. Now that they were on the drive, she didn't need to touch him to be able to tell where he was, and it was easier to keep up when she didn't have to worry about tripping over things. "What you want me to do with Mr. Evan, Miss Val? No way to smuggle him inside, is there?"

"The only place we could possibly take him is to the ballroom, and I'm afraid if they stay here much longer they'll try to get their own wounded men up there. They ought to be inside tonight; half of them will have pneumonia," she predicted.

"The house would have been best, but not if it's full of Yankees. We'll have to take him to the quarters, then."

"No!" It was an explosive protest as she thought of the men out there, and the nighttime traffic as Blossom conducted her various intrigues; getting back and forth to care for Evan there would be virtually impossible.

"Where, then? He gonna die if we don't get him out of that wagon pretty soon, and take care of him proper."

He was right, of course. Yet the quarters and the house remained severely impractical.

"Ryan's house," she said suddenly. "We'll take him to Ryan's house."

"That's a long walk from Mallows," Aaron said.

"Which should make it safer from the Yankees. I don't think any of them have been there, except when they first came, and then it was only to make sure it was empty and of no particular value to them. It's too small and not luxurious enough for their officers. And we can drive the wagon right there, without anyone knowing. Yes, we'll take Evan to Ryan's house."

When they reached him, however, Valerie wondered if he'd live long enough for them to take him anywhere.

Evan lay under the dubious shelter of a piece of canvas

195

stretched over the wagon bed. He muttered when she spoke his name, not rousing completely even when she grasped his shoulder and shook it.

"Evan, it's me, Valerie! Do you hear me? You're home, you're at Mallows!"

His response was obscene; for a moment she drew back, then reached for him again. This time she touched bare flesh, and found it burning hot.

"My God! He has a terrible fever! It will have to be Ryan's, Aaron. Hurry!"

She scrambled up into the wagon bed, burrowing under the canvas to lie close to her brother. Her brother who was quite suddenly a stranger. Her thought had been to keep him warm, but he was already so feverish that the heat of his body came through his damp garments.

The wagon started with a jerk, and she prayed the wheels would not become mired in the heavy soil as sometimes happened during the rain. Her mind darted this way and that, like the tiny goldfish she remembered from the pool behind the house in Savannah, trying to work out a rational plan to care for Evan, to keep him safe. Would it matter to the Yankees that he was a Confederate soldier, considering his condition? He surely posed no threat to anyone in his present state. Maybe she could sound them out; maybe it would be perfectly safe to bring him home, where he belonged. Not to die. She hadn't forgotten what Aaron had said, that Evan wanted to be brought home to die. She wouldn't let him die; she had to keep him alive, and help him to be well, because they all needed him so badly. Mallows needed him.

When the wagon stopped she was afraid to speak until Aaron said her name, for fear they'd halted because they'd encountered some of the Yankees. The ones at Mallows weren't the only ones abroad, and the scavengers appropriated anything they found, from wagons to mules to women.

"He all right?" Aaron asked, throwing back the canvas to expose them to the rain. "I had to break open the kitchen door, round in back. I'll have to carry him, same as I put him in there."

He reached up to grasp Evan under his arms, and pulled.

Evan cried out. "Stop it, you black bastard, you're hurting me!"

"I got to get you out, Mr. Evan. Got to get you into the

house. You draw the curtains, Miss Val, and it'll be safe to build a fire, I think. Have a light, so we can see what we're doing."

She left him to the task of hauling a man as large as himself out of the wagon and into the house. Since the kitchen level was belowground, that meant down steps, rather than up, which made it a bit easier. She remembered how spotless the brick floor had been, the day she'd been here when Ryan's grandmother died. Well there was no help for it; they'd have to track in mud tonight. Why hadn't she thought to bring matches? Where would they keep them? She felt her way across the room, collided with a table edge, and got her bearings. The fireplace was over there. Would there be matches on the mantel? Pray God there would, and pray also that there was something to build a fire.

There were not only matches, there were candles. Gratefully, Valerie lighted one, and then two, and saw that there were both kindling and firewood in the box beside the door. She busied herself with building a fire while Aaron brought Evan in and more or less dragged him into the nearest of the two bedrooms on that level. By the time she carried her candle in to help, Aaron had pulled off Evan's outer clothes and covered him with one of Ryan's colorful quilts.

Valerie's hand trembled as she held the candle over her brother, who had sunk back into his stupor. Evan? This unshaven, stinking skeleton of a man?

Her eyes met those of the black man on the other side of the bed. "I told you," Aaron said. "I didn't know him, at first."

Carefully, Valerie lowered the candle to the small chest beside the bed. Then she bent deliberately over him and unbuttoned his shirt. The exposed chest was pathetically thin; the ribs stood out prominently. Here, also, his skin was hot and dry. Without speaking, she moved to the foot of the bed and forced herself to a surface calm as she plucked carefully at the soiled dressing on his left foot. There was no smell of gangrene, although the odor was putrid enough; the suppurating wound was open, unhealed, draining. Stifling nausea, Valerie replaced the dressings.

"I don't know if there's anything in the house to eat. Probably not, Ruth would have taken most of it with her when she left. Still, it's worth a look."

She turned away from the bed, so blinded by sudden tears

197

that she could not see where she was going and ran into the door frame. She rubbed at the place where the corner had struck her shoulder, although in truth she scarcely felt it; the inner pain was so much greater than that.

She found a kettle to heat water, and hung it over the open fire. There was tea, too, a little, and that was all. The tea would do for a start. She'd have to go back to Mallows for something more nourishing. If only it weren't so far to walk! It would be much easier to move on foot without attracting attention, impossible to go in and out with a wagon or a horse. She brewed the tea and carried the cup into the bedroom. Behind her, Aaron watched with a quizzical expression, then helped himself to a cup. He sipped at it thoughtfully as Valerie began to try to spoon the fluid between Evan Stanton's parched lips.

"What are we going to do?" Valerie asked half an hour later as she leaned her elbows on Ryan's table and stared across it into the fire.

"We?" Aaron repeated.

His tone brought her head around in a questioning way. He had only been gone from Mallows for a short time, but the changes in him were notable. Though thinner, and with none of the elegance he had had when greeting visitors at the front door, Aaron looked older, taller, and something else. Confident. There was nothing subservient about him, in stance, manner, or choice of words. Her brother's condition had shaken her badly. What she saw in Aaron's face shook her further.

"You won't stay and help with him?" she asked slowly, when he did not speak.

"I got to go, Miss Val. Georgia is no place for a free nigger. There are hundreds of black men, and right now most of them are running around laughing and stealing what they want to eat and planning how they're going to take what the white folks have. You know, and I know, that isn't going to happen. The Yankees may have set us free, but they don't like us very much. You know that, Miss Val? They don't really like us at all. They invite slaves to join them, but you know what happens to a black man who shows up to join their army? He gets put to doing the kind of work that means nothing. Peeling potatoes. Chopping wood, driving a wagon

198

with some white soldiers to tell him just how to do it. They don't like the way we look, or talk, or smell."

The room had grown warm and moisture made a sheen on the dark forehead. She could see the puckered scar above his left eyebrow. "People in Georgia always looked down on a black man. They don't want to think he's got a mind, or a soul, or the right to call his body his own and to do what he wants with it. A black man is an animal, and they even made a law you couldn't teach him to read and write, to make damn sure he don't get no ideas above his station in life."

He lapsed into an exaggerated parody of a slave accent. "Everybody knows a nigger ain't smart enough to learn nothin'. Ain't that so? Ain't nobody in Georgia goin' to give a black boy a job doin' anythin' that don't break his back, because everybody knows he ain't got no *brain* to work with. Ain't that so?"

Stunned, Valerie could make no response. She did not know this man, this Aaron who had lived at Mallows since childhood, who had always spoken to her softly, respectfully, even affectionately. There were none of those things in his words now.

"They say it's different, up north. Maybe they don't *like* niggers, but they ain't convinced they too stupid to earn a living. Niggers up there, in the big Northern cities, they have jobs, get married, raise families, without somebody tellin' them what, and to who, and how. And I got to go and see for myself. I woulda been gone a long time, now, if it hadn't been for Mr. Evan. I'd be halfway to that New York City, or Chicago, or maybe Boston. I stayed to see Mr. Evan got home, 'cause I could see he was dyin', and he begged me to help him die at Mallows. I never had no place I cared that much about, and I don't figure on dyin' for a long time yet. So now I got Mr. Evan here, I reckon I'll be on my way north."

Aaron bent to pick up the blanket he'd had wrapped around Evan. "I guess you won't mind if I take this with me. I'll give you a ride back to the end of the drive, if you want. And then I got to find me something to eat." A brief spasm of amusement twisted his full lips. "I guess I got to steal it, just like the rest of the niggers. If the Yankees left anything to steal."

Valerie felt drained, empty, bereft. She had taken it for granted that Aaron would stay here with Evan, care for him,

199

while she would make a secret trip here each day with provisions. She hadn't thought any further than that, not about whom she would tell, or what help she would try to get for Evan.

"There's plenty of food at Mallows," she said finally, pushing back her chair to stand up. "You might as well take some of it; at least you won't be hanged for stealing, as you might be if you got caught."

"Plenty? The Yankees treatin' you all right, then?"

"Treating themselves all right, and we benefit because we're there." She turned back to the doorway of the bedroom and stood for a moment, looking at the sleeping man. "He doesn't even know he's home, does he?"

"He knows. Deep inside, he knows." Aaron's voice softened. "I'm sorry, Miss Val, but I got to go."

"Yes. I understand." Curiously, she did, though she did not think her mother would. She threw another log on the fire, which should be safe enough to leave in this brick-walled room, and blew out the candle. "Let's go."

She sat beside Aaron on the seat of the wagon, exposed to the chilling rain, saying nothing during the entire short journey.

Aaron drew up beside the road and helped her down when they reached the end of the drive. The oyster shells made a pale straight ribbon between the shadowy live oaks, barely visible.

"They ask you about the wagon, you don't know nothin'," Aaron suggested as they walked briskly toward the house.

"Aren't you going to take it?" She looked toward him, seeing nothing, only sensing the bulk of him. "Can't you get farther, faster, with the wagon than on foot?"

Aaron chuckled, a sound of genuine amusement. "Sure. And the first white man comes along says, 'Hey, there, boy, where'd you steal that wagon?' and he holds a gun on me until I get down off it and hand it over to him, mules and all. I could have got here in a fraction of the time if I'd dared to drive in daylight, and on the main roads. I had to travel at night, and stick to the back country, and try to find a place to hole up where nobody'd find us, days, or hear Mr. Evan yelling and swearing. I couldn't make him understand they'd likely shoot us both if they caught us. Blue bellies, and Confederate deserters, and just plain thieves everywhere. And none of 'em going to admit a black boy could have any legitimate right to a wagon and a pair of mules, even if he got a
200

wounded Confederate officer ridin' in it. No, ma'am, I ain't goin' to try to take that wagon north. Maybe I'll ride it until dawn, though, leave it up the road a ways. That way won't nobody suspect you had anything to do with it."

She couldn't reconcile the change in manner of speech, and the ideas, to the Aaron she knew. Nor could she really recognize that sick man there at Ryan's as her brother Evan. Nothing was the same, the world had taken a nightmare turn, and it was spinning out of control. For a moment she had the fleeting thought that it would be nice to fly off into the sky and never have to worry about anything again. It was a luxury she couldn't afford, even if she'd known how to manage it.

Again, they skirted the piazza, where the soldiers were sleeping to the drumming of the rain, and made their way to the back of the house. Aaron stood just inside the door, dripping, while Valerie filled his pack with cold meat and bread and, a last-minute inspiration, a packet of sugar and another of the Yankees' real coffee.

Aaron's teeth gleamed in the candlelight as he watched. He accepted the pack and turned toward the door, then paused for a final word.

"You're a real lady, Miss Val. One high-quality white Georgia lady."

He was gone, vanishing before he'd gone two yards into the night, and she stood there, eyes stinging, for long moments before she closed the door.

Now what was she going to do?

Twenty-One

She ached in every limb, and she wanted nothing more than to crawl into bed and take warmth from Julie's body, and sleep for hours.

She could do nothing of the sort.

Valerie inhaled and turned back to the scrubbed wooden block table. She hoped Mamie would think the Yankees had been stricken with nocturnal hunger pangs and raided the kitchen. They did, sometimes. It was the reason Mamie hadn't moved in here to sleep on a pallet before the fire when she returned to the winter kitchen; she didn't like being disturbed by drunken officers who either wanted food, or a bath, or to relieve themselves out the back door.

She made up another packet, this one more carefully chosen. Tea, and coffee, and bread, and cold meat, and soup. Some of Mamie's chicken soup was probably the best thing for Evan. Sugar, for the tea and the coffee. Eggs—there were half a dozen of them. Mamie would scream for certain when she found them missing, so maybe, Valerie thought, she'd better warn her. It wouldn't do to have Mamie raise a ruckus and get the Yankees wondering who, if not themselves, had raided the kitchen tonight. But eggs would be so good for

Evan. Eggs, and milk, and a little ham, maybe. If he got enough better, he'd welcome the ham.

When she'd assembled the supplies, she looked at them with a sinking heart. She couldn't carry them herself, not all that way. And what was she to do about Evan? He couldn't be left alone until tomorrow night, without care. Someone had to feed him, to keep him clean, and the house warm. Or did she dare to keep a fire there, during the day? What if anyone spotted the smoke? Would the Yankees go to investigate? They knew there had been no one there when they came. Yet if she didn't keep a fire, how bad would it be for Evan? In spite of the fever, she knew he should be kept warm.

Should she tell her mother? Ellen had a right to know, of course. As did Julie. But would they be able to keep his presence a secret from the Yankees? Julie, especially, was not schooled at covering her emotion. And until Valerie knew how the Yankees would react to a wounded Confederate soldier in their midst, she dared not let *them* know. If she told Julie and her mother, what then? Drag them out of bed and through the rain to that little house, to a sight that could hardly be more distressing than if the Yankees had cruelly planned it for their benefit? None of them could stay there tomorrow; they'd be missed.

Who was there who wouldn't be missed? Whose presence, or lack of it, would cause no interest or comment among the Yankee officers?

She sifted through them, one by one. Henriette seldom came downstairs, and so might do, if she could be persuaded to leave Charlotte. She knew little or nothing about nursing, however, and the mere mention of a wound such as Evan's had been known to make her turn away with a hand over her mouth. That had happened more than once when Valerie spoke of the things that kept her busy during the long days. And if Henriette did agree to go, what about Charlotte? Charlotte did nothing for herself, and they couldn't have her roaming the house. There was no telling what she'd do if she came face to face with one of the uniformed Federal soldiers.

Lacy would go in a minute, but her absence would be noted. She not only took her meals downstairs, she was up and down on various errands every day, with the energy of a much younger person. The same was true of Lallie. Any prolonged absence was certain to be noted.

Dolly was dismissed with no serious consideration. She was deeply immersed in her own personal problems; she had long since made it plain she had no time for anyone else's.

And Sally Ann was still frail; she couldn't be expected to leave her baby, nor to take him with her to Ryan's house to care for a very sick man. She probably didn't have the stamina for such a demanding task, anyway.

One of the black women, then. Not one of the ones who were carrying on with the Yankees, not one who would be missed if she disappeared for a few days, or a matter of weeks.

Hattie? The woman whined and complained and was most unhappy because she'd been sent, for the first time since childhood, to live in the slave's quarters. Yet she had once been a competent servant in Grace's Atlanta household.

As if in response to these thoughts, the door opened behind her and Gilly walked in. She had wrapped herself against the weather and began to peel off layers of clothing, not at all surprised to find Miss Valerie in the kitchen so late at night.

"I seen the light," she said, flashing a grin. "Usually I got to wait for somebody to come down and let me in, when that baby kicks up a ruckus and got to be fed. I glad I didn't have to stand out there, waitin', tonight."

"Close the door, Gilly," Valerie suggested. She moved to shield the provisions she had set out, although Gilly gave no indication that she noticed the foodstuffs, nor that she attached any significance to them.

"Yas'm. I sure gonna be glad when that baby decide he don't need to eat in the middle of the night. My Rastus, he ain't woke up in the night for a long time." A note of maternal pride crept into her voice as she hung her dripping clothes on a hook beside the door. "Rastus, he a fine, big baby. He ain't no trouble at all, hardly. Even old Hattie don't complain too much 'bout lookin' after Rastus, he so good."

Valerie moved a little farther so that her body completely blocked Gilly's view of the table. "Is Hattie still sickly? The way she was when she came?"

Gilly shook her head. "You ask me, ma'am, there ain't nothin' the matter with Hattie, 'cept she lazy. She one of the laziest niggers I ever saw, so it a good thing Rastus don't make no work, much. She all out of temper 'cause she can't live in the big house, like she used to. She say she ain't no fieldhand nigger, used to dirt floors." She cocked her head,
204

listening. "I hear that baby? I better go; Miss Lacy, she don't like him to scream enough to wake her up 'fore I get there to feed him."

"Yes," Valerie told her. "Run along and feed him."

She made the foodstuffs into several bundles as soon as the girl had gone, hauling them outside to sit in the shelter of the covered walkway, and once more wrapped in the soggy garments, she headed for the slave quarters.

Gilly and Hattie and the baby Rastus had been given one of the cabins at the far end of the double row. There was no sign of life from any of the cabins in between except one: from that issued low-pitched laughter, and a man's good-natured voice, a voice with a Yankee accent detectable through the soft sounds of the rain.

Valerie was too weary and too anxious about Evan to feel indignation about the goings-on between the black women and the soldiers. She hoped she'd be able to keep going until her brother was cared for, and although she would have preferred someone more able than Hattie, she saw no better choice for the moment. Tomorrow would be a different matter, when she could share the burden of knowledge and responsibility with her mother.

She pushed on the door of the last of the cabins, poking her head inside to a faint, welcome warmth. The fire had died down to no more than glowing coals, not enough to enable her to find her way about.

"Hattie? Hattie, wake up."

Valerie groped for the table and the candle, then lighted it at one of the embers, throwing the room into relief.

Hattie raised up in bed, her eyes wide and rolling. "What the matter? Who there?"

"Miss Valerie. Get up and get dressed, Hattie, I need you."

"Need me?" Hattie heaved her bulk toward the edge of the bed, pulling the quilts off the sleeping child beside her. "What for? Miss Sally Ann been took bad?"

"No. It's something else. Something I can't tell you about until we're away from here."

"Away?" Hattie echoed the word in rising anxiety. "Where we all goin'? You ain't sendin' old Hattie away, in the middle of the night?"

"I need your help. Hurry up, put on your clothes." Valerie stepped to one side while the woman stumbled about, gathering up her belongings, muttering under her breath. Valerie stood beside the bed, reaching out to draw the covers over the sturdy child, who slept on, undisturbed. "Who's next door to you? Rudy and Sheba, isn't it?"

"Old folks," Hattie confirmed. "It rainin' out there, ain't it? Why we got to go out in the rain?"

"You won't melt," Valerie assured her, knowing that if she did not remain firm, she could easily lose control of Hattie, as she'd watched her mother lose control with so many of the others. "I'll be back in a minute, and you be ready to come with me."

She took only a moment to speak to Sheba. "Gilly's at the house, and Hattie's been taken sick," she told old Rudy's wife. "If you hear the baby cry, look after him until Gilly comes back."

Sheba spoke out of the darkness. "That one don't wake up before dawn, more'n likely. But I listen for him," she agreed.

It wasn't easy, getting Hattie to move beyond a snail's pace. She complained about the rain, and the darkness, and the cold. And when she found she was expected to carry provisions, she nearly rebelled.

"You outta your mind, Miss Val! We can't go runnin' around in the dark carryin' all this stuff! Why for you gone crazy?"

"We only have to carry it a little way, and then we'll use the buggy." Thank God the soldiers had rescued and repaired it for their own use; Corporal Trenton often took it on his excursions around the countryside, looking for provender. It didn't carry as much as a wagon; Valerie suspected he felt more elegant in a buggy than in a farm wagon, and a horse was more to his liking than a pair of recalcitrant mules.

She wasn't used to hitching up by herself, but she was afraid to call anyone to do it for her. She didn't trust Chad, who was the nearest at hand, not to give her away to the Yankees. Her hands were cold, her fingers clumsy, yet she managed it; she loaded the materials she'd gathered, and old Hattie, into the buggy, praying that by now everyone was so sound asleep that no notice would be taken of a horse and buggy leaving the grounds. It would have been safer to walk, for it wasn't as far over the field as it was around by the road and the route would not have taken them past the house. She was too tired, however, and there was too much to carry, and Hattie wouldn't have lasted halfway there.

Hattie hunched beside her on the seat, clutching a cloak

around her head. "When you gonna tell me what this all about?" she demanded.

They were well away from the house, now. Valerie urged the mare to a trot along the shell drive. "You're sick, Hattie. You're going to leave the quarters and live inside for a few days, while you get better."

"I ain't sick!" Hattie protested, astonished. "You is crazy!"

"We're going to tell people you're sick, in case anyone asks. And you will be inside, you'll like it better in a nice cozy house. You're going to take care of my brother, Hattie. He's very ill, and I can't stay with him without the Yankees knowing about it, so you'll have to nurse him. I know you can do it; Aunt Grace said you were a good nurse."

That statement had been made years ago. Yet Hattie became more calm, sitting with some dignity on the buggy seat. "I allus was a good nurse. I nursed Miss Grace through that diphtheria, when everybody thought she was goin' to die. And when Miss Sally Ann a little girl, and she had that whoopin' cough so we scared every breath gonna be her last, old Hattie sit up every night and hold her, and she don't die."

"Good. Now you do the same thing for Evan," Valerie said, and prayed that Hattie would once again produce a miracle.

It seemed to her that she had been gone for many hours. Yet the house was still warm; the fire needed only a little more wood to be good until dawn, probably, which could not be far away.

Evan slept, restless, troubled. Valerie inspected him briefly, then returned to the brick-walled kitchen to issue orders to Hattie. "You can sleep in that other bedroom," she said, pointing. "I'll unpack these things, and we'll make some sassafras tea; it's healing, and good for fever. Try to spoon it into him, as often as you can get him to take it, and mind it isn't too hot so that it burns him."

Hattie, after a gratified look into the bedroom, gave her an indignant look. "I been takin' care of invalids since before you born. I know about sassafras tea. He be needin' somethin' more than that, come mornin'. You bring any of that chicken soup Mamie have for supper? Chicken soup got more good in it than sassafras, once the fever break."

A little of the tension went out of Valerie's body. Hattie

207

did sound as if she'd make a fair try at nursing. Maybe this wouldn't be a disaster, after all.

She wished she dared crawl into bed here, herself; she wasn't sure she could get the buggy back to Mallows, and the horse unhitched, without falling flat on her face. She'd have to pretend to be ill, and spend the next day in bed. Except, of course, that she had to tell her mother about Evan, and probably would have to come back here with her, as well.

She spoke calmly, competently, giving Hattie her orders. And then she went back out into the rainy night and headed, for the last time that night, for home.

Twenty-Two

She didn't have to pretend to illness.

Valerie awoke with a sore throat, a cough, and a throbbing head. Her brow, when she laid the back of her hand against it, felt hot, too. She made a sound of distress, and Julie turned from the mirror, where she was tying her hair up with a ribbon to match her dark blue dress. The morning was chilly, and it was a winter dress of fine light wool.

"I'm sorry. Did I wake you up? I know you came to bed late last night. Was there some trouble? Someone sick?"

Valerie's hesitation was minimal. "Evan's here. I mean, he's at Ryan's house. Aaron brought him home."

For a matter of seconds, Julie didn't move, although her color receded. Then she flew across the room, joy and anxiety warring in her lovely face.

"Evan! Val, how is he? Is he all right?"

"No. No, he's very ill." Valerie watched the delight fade, wishing desperately that she didn't have to be the bearer of such tidings. "I haven't told anyone yet, except Hattie. I took her over there to care for him until we know if it's safe to bring him home."

"Mama doesn't know?"

"Not yet. Julie, listen to me. It's important that the Yankees don't know, at least for now."

"Yes, of course. At Ryan's. That's so far, if we have to walk . . ."

"Yes, but it seemed the safest. Look, I hardly slept at all, and I feel dreadful. I think you'd better call Mama in here, and we'll tell everyone I'm ill. No doubt she'll want to go to Evan, we'll have to think of some excuse—is it still raining?"

"No, it's beautiful. Bright and sunny. Val, how . . . how bad is he?"

"He's running a fever, and he didn't know where he was, nor recognize me. His foot . . . is smashed, and it looks very bad."

Julie's eyes were wide and dark in a chalky oval face. She'd seen enough in the past few weeks, as she knew Valerie had done, to take this seriously. The time had passed when either of them could deny the actuality of death, could believe that it wouldn't touch them, personally. Death was all around them, every day.

Mercifully, Julie didn't ask if Valerie thought Evan would live. She withdrew from the bed, bringing herself under control. "I'll call Mama," she said.

Telling Ellen about her only son was perhaps the most difficult thing Valerie had ever had to do. Yet Ellen did not crumble, did not give way to hysteria or panic.

"We must get the things to him that he needs," she said.

"I took what I could last night. Hattie's done nursing; she'll take care of him. The important thing is that no one knows he's there."

"Captain Ferris is a doctor," Julie interjected. "Surely he'd take care of him? Evan can't pose any threat to the Yankees now, they'd have no reason to . . . to do anything to him."

Tales of the Yankee atrocities had continued to filter through to Mallows. Furious at the way Federal soldiers had been starved in the Confederate Libby Prison near Richmond and at Andersonville, in Georgia, the Yankees had little pity for captured Confederate soldiers. It didn't matter that the Confederates had had no choice, that their own soldiers were often no better fed. The rumor circulated that Union soldiers had bayoneted their injured enemies rather than be forced to feed them.

Ellen swallowed and assumed command, as she had always done. "For the moment, we'll tell no one. Valerie's managed it nicely. If anyone asks about Hattie, which they probably won't, we'll simply say she's been moved into the house because she's ill. Julie, I know you want to see Evan as much as I do, but it will be safest if you don't go at once. Stay here to answer the door if anyone should come to it, and tell them Valerie is ill. Say she's sleeping, or doesn't feel like seeing anyone. Anything, so long as you keep them out. I'll let it be known that there's illness in the quarters, too, and that I intend to be working out there today. The serious cases downstairs are fewer, now; the Yankees can manage on their own if they have to. With the change in the weather, no one will be surprised if there is increased illness."

Valerie, after only a few hours' sleep, would have liked nothing better than to crawl back between the sheets. Her concern for Evan, however, drove her to sit up and look listlessly toward her clothes. "Maybe you should mention to Captain Ferris that I'm ill, and I'll stay here until he comes up to see me. That way he won't do it later on, if I say I just want to stay in bed and sleep."

Ellen's fingers crept toward her temple, pressing, stroking. "Yes. That's a good idea. Maybe while he's up here I could get a few things from his supplies. Laudanum, for one thing. I haven't much left. And iodine. I've no iodine. They want eight dollars a vial for it. And brandy with cloves, to sponge Evan with; I have those in our own supplies. Have the Yankees any quinine?"

"Yes." Quinine had been a staple in Southern dispensaries for years, until the price of fifteen dollars an ounce prevented the purchase of it for many people. "And glycerine, get some glycerine. That and the iodine might make a difference to his infection. And for fevers Captain Ferris prescribes tartar water with oranges, and Seidlitz powders."

Ellen nodded. "There are oranges, Corporal Trenton brought some back day before yesterday. With that cough, you could do with some, yourself."

"How are we going to get to Evan without anyone knowing about it?" So readily, Valerie relinquished the responsibility for making decisions.

"I'll signal to you from the trees beyond the winter kitchen when it's safe to come down. Use the back stairs, the Yankees never use them, and be careful moving through the kitchen itself. Wear old clothes, cover your head so no one can see your hair. We'll go out behind the quarters and take to the woods. If we're caught, why, we'll say we took you down to consult old Sheba, to get some of her herbs," Ellen improvised.

Valerie perked up a bit, improvising on her own. "It would be a good idea if we could account for smoke from Ryan's place, if it's visible from here. Could we say Hattie's come to open up the place for Ryan? They won't know she's from Mallows; I've heard them all, at one time or another, say the Negroes all look alike to them. That way, if they go there, maybe she can put them off without letting them get inside."

Ellen nodded. "All right. She'll have to keep a fire going. I'll go down, now. Julie, get something to eat while I ask Captain Ferris to look in on Valerie, and then you can stay here."

When they had gone Valerie glanced down at the ragged gown she had worn to bed. In spite of her concern about Evan, she couldn't help a surge of anticipation at the thought of Jack Ferris visiting her here in her room. Only not in *this*.

She sprang out of bed and hurried to the chiffonier, tossing garments helter-skelter as she searched for the one she wanted. There, *that* one. She stripped off the nightshift she wore and quickly pulled on the newer one. Though it was old, too, it was in good condition, and had lace and pale blue ribbons woven through an eyelet trim at sleeves and throat.

She looked heavy-eyed and pasty; she had lifted her fingers to her cheeks to pinch some color into them when she remembered. She was supposed to be sick. It wouldn't do to look too healthy.

When the time came, she had no difficulty whatever in convincing Captain Ferris that she was unwell. He sat on the edge of the bed and held her hand—did he notice the quickening pulse?—and touched her forehead. Valerie went into a coughing spasm that led to an examination of her throat, his face close to hers so that she could see a tiny patch of stubble under her chin that he'd missed when shaving this morning.

"Well, if your throat is sore, I'd suggest gargling with hot salt water. I have some balsam of wild cherry and wood naptha that will make it feel better. I'll tell Mamie to slice a couple of those oranges of Trenton's with sugar on them for you to suck, too. You probably aren't especially hungry, but some soup would be a good idea later on. You feel a little warm; if the fever goes up, let me know and I'll bring up some Seidlitz powders, but it doesn't taste good, so you won't want it unless it's necessary."

He had finished with his professional advice and sat looking down at her, still holding her hand, in a way that made something tighten in her groin, tighten and then spread with a frightening, yet not unpleasant, warmth.

"You're taking a day off at a hell of a time, you know," he told her. "I've got three cases of near-pneumonia among the men sleeping on the veranda. I'm going to have to move them inside today; another cold wet night out there and all the work we've done will be for nothing. It will make for a lot more work, but I've decided to move the ones who won't fit into the drawing rooms up into the ballroom. I'm pulling everyone, even Trenton, off all other duty to do it; they'll have to be carried, and getting a stretcher up that last bit of stairs without standing them on end will be strenuous work."

Her heart lurched at the thought that she had considered, no matter how briefly, trying to hide Evan on the third floor.

"It will be a lot more work," she agreed, hoping he would attribute the sudden additional acceleration of pulse to his own nearness rather than to fear.

She could tell by the change in his face that he was no longer thinking about his patients, before his words confirmed it. "You're most fetching in a nightgown, I must say. Maybe it's worth it to have you sick, if not *too* sick. As long as it's only for a day or so."

His thumb stroked her upturned palm, and then he ran his hand up her arm and bent forward to kiss her. Valerie felt suffocated, yet willing to be so disposed of, when his mouth covered hers, roamed from the corner of her lips to the bottom of her ear, then slid downward to the hollow at the base of her throat.

When he drew away, leaving her far more weak and shaken than her infirmity could account for, there was laughter in the dark eyes. "Get well, my dear. I'll look in on you again later."

She struggled back to sanity, remembering what she must do today. "No, don't come until evening. I slept so badly last night, what with coughing so much, that I really want to make up for it by sleeping all day."

"All right. I hope we don't disturb you, getting our men up those damned stairs. A pity they didn't make them the width of the main stairs to this floor; we could manage *those* with a horse and buggy, if we had to."

He grinned at her, made a mock salute, and was gone.

Valerie moved quickly out of bed, tossing the nightgown across the footpost and reaching for the clothes she would put on. She hesitated, however, to stare at her reflection in the great gilt-framed mirror that showed everything but her feet. Her breasts swelled with the indrawn breath, the nipples taut as she had known they would be from the moment Jack Ferris touched her. She brushed one with experimental fingers, knowing it would not be the same, if the fingers belonged to Jack. And then she let her hand slide downward, across the flat belly to the triangular patch of hair that covered the area where she still felt the tingling warmth.

"Val?"

She jerked convulsively, averting her face from the doorway, snatching up the undergarments. Today she would take Captain Ferris's advice, she would forget about stays; if her mother noticed she wasn't wearing them, she could say Julie hadn't come back until she was dressed, and there was no one to help draw the strings tight.

"Is everything all set?" she asked, unable to face her sister.

"I guess so. Mama went out to make sure the coast was clear. It should be easier if they're going to be moving the men from the piazza, as long as no one looks out the ballroom windows at a crucial moment. I'll let you know for sure that the way is clear to the back stairs, shall I?"

"Yes, do," Valerie agreed, still unable to meet Julie's eyes, although obviously her sister had noticed nothing.

Logic, against all former teaching, told her there was nothing to be ashamed of in touching her own body. When she married, her husband would be privileged to caress any part of her in the most intimate way; she would be expected to submit to that, even castigated by the Church if she did not. How, then, could it be truly wrong to touch herself in the same ways? Why should she not have the freedom to do whatever she liked with her own body?

Instinct, however, told her not to try explaining that point of view to her sister, nor to her mother. Had Ellen ever longed for caressing fingers, for a warm, compelling mouth? Had she ever felt this dark, sweet stirring of desire? For the first time, it occurred to Valerie to wonder seriously about the relationship between her parents. She had never seen them

214

display more than superficial gestures of affection, mostly verbal. What had they done in the long black nights, in that big bed across the landing? Somehow it was impossible to imagine her parents in a sweating tangle of arms and legs, whispering passionate words; easier to imagine herself, with Jack Ferris.

"Val? Your face is so red! If you have a severe fever, maybe you'd better stay in bed, really, and I'll go with Mama."

"No, no." She pressed hands to fiery cheeks. "I'll be all right. Just tell anyone who comes around that I'm sleeping. Oh, and cough once in a while, just to convince anyone passing by the door."

She grabbed up her shawl and fled before Julie could speculate any further on the blush Valerie had been unable to control, almost forgetting, until she reached the bottom of the back stairs, the need for caution.

Later, she thought. Later, there would be time to think about Captain Jack Ferris. For now, she had to do what could be done to save her brother's life.

They found Evan resting more comfortably, although he still burned with fever. Ellen bent over the bed, touching cool lips to his forehead, caressing his cheek gently with her fingertips.

"Evan? Evan, do you hear me?"

With an effort, the heavy lids opened, the cracked lips moved. "Mama."

"Yes, darling. You're home."

Evan made the effort to open his eyes wider, to gaze around the brick-walled room with its heavy overhead beams, at the polished chest and the thick warm quilt spread over him. "Not Mallows," he said.

"No, dear, you're at Ryan's. Mallows is full of Yankees; they've made it a hospital, ironically enough. You'll be safe here. Ah, here's Hattie with some soup. Do you remember Hattie? At Aunt Grace's, in Atlanta?"

Evan made no response to that. When his mother sank onto a stool beside the bed, he obediently opened his mouth for the spoon. It wasn't until the chore was accomplished that Ellen inspected Evan's injured foot.

Shock held her in a painful grip; Valerie saw her fingers

215

whiten as she clutched at the footpost. Her throat worked, although she kept her tone level as she spoke.

"Your leg is in very bad shape, Evan. Didn't they do anything for you, in Atlanta?"

His speech was thickened by fever, pain, and weakness. "The bastards wanted to cut it off."

Ellen moistened her lips, fighting for control. "We can try iodine and glycerine on it. And I brought garlic, for Hattie to put in the soup. Garlic sometimes helps with infections."

Valerie, looking down at the same macerated extremity, wondered if anything on earth could help with this one. The smell of it permeated the room when the dressing was lifted off from it.

"Came home to die, Mama," Evan said into the stillness.

Beyond the bed, the fire crackled on the kitchen hearth and Hattie's slippers slapped on the brick floor as she moved from kettle to table. Valerie's throat closed; she could not look at either of them, could only endeavor to hide the emotion that threatened to tear her apart.

Ellen, except for touching her tongue to her lips, controlled herself with the greater ease of longer practice. She put a hand over Evan's atop the quilt. "You've come home to get well, son."

The corner of his mouth twitched. "Whatever you say, Mama. Just as long as you don't get any ideas about sawing my leg off."

Ellen made no reply to that. While Valerie stood by, holding the basin for soiled dressings, then preparing the fresh ones, Ellen cleaned the injury as best she could. When she applied the iodine and glycerine combination, Evan gritted his teeth and his fists knotted on the quilt; perspiration stood in globules on his face, and Valerie gently wiped them away.

They were nearly as exhausted as he was by the time they had finished. The covers were peeled back and his nightshirt (borrowed from Patrick Ryan) laid open so that he could be sponged with the brandy and cloves to bring down his fever. Valerie was sent out of the room, to preserve her innocence and Evan's modesty, during this last procedure. Though she protested that she had been assisting with the Yankee patients for weeks, and that she could assist with her brother as well, Ellen was adamant.

Valerie, for all her weariness, could not sink into one of the cushioned rockers before the fire and rest. She moved

216

about the room, examining the furnishings with as much interest as she could have mustered in anything at that time. There were not many items of furniture; what there were, were of fine quality. Surprisingly good taste, with simple lines, solid construction, and highly polished surfaces.

She wondered if Ryan had chosen them himself, or if his sister had done so, or possibly his grandmother. There was a cross-stitched sampler on one wall, with the Lord's Prayer in gold-colored thread, against a pastoral scene. A daguerreotype of a middle-aged couple stood atop an oak cabinet, beside a bowl that would hold fruit in season; Valerie recognized the couple as Patrick Ryan's parents, who had both died when she was a little girl.

She ought not to have been impressed by the number of books in the house, but she was. She had known Patrick haunted the library at Mallows for years and she had noticed the shelf of books upstairs. But at the end of the kitchen away from the stove and the fireplace, there were hundreds more, in shelves of gleaming yellow oak against one of the brick walls. She found the titles a curious mixture of history, novels, science, and philosophy, all of them dog-eared from many readings. She wondered how much good his self-educating would do him; one did not need book learning to be an overseer, and he could hardly hope to rise above that level.

That reminded her of Aaron. Aaron, who also loved to read, although the law clearly stated that no black man could be taught to read and write, and she wondered where he was, and how well he was doing.

The door opened and Valerie whirled to face Ellen as she emerged from the bedroom. Her mother's ravaged face revealed her inner anguish; seeing Evan's skeletal body and his mangled foot had hit her harder than anything else so far in this unspeakable war. She had not looked this stricken when her husband was killed. She spoke with her customary common sense, however, giving orders to Hattie about the amount of laudanum to administer so that Evan could sleep at night, and about sponging him and feeding him.

"We'll be back tomorrow to change his dressing and bathe him." Ellen glanced around at the room, dusted and gleaming with recent care. "Are you managing all right, Hattie?"

"Oh, yes'm. Massa Evan, he sleep mostly, 'cept when I feed him. He don't sleep *good*, he hurt a lot, and he cry out. But he ain't so much trouble I can't take care of him. And I

217

feel better, myself, being inside a real house where it warm. Them quarters ain't warm enough for a old woman like me. Makes my joints ache. Inside, where my joints don't hurt so much, I can still work."

Ellen accepted that message without resentment against the giver. "All right, Hattie. We'll see that you sleep inside from now on."

"Thank you, Miss Ellen. I be much obliged," Hattie told her.

They walked home through the woods, not saying much, each lost in her own thoughts. It was only as the roofs of Mallows came into sight that Valerie put the worst of those thoughts into words.

"The foot should come off, shouldn't it?"

Ellen didn't look at her. "Yes. If it heals it will be a miracle."

They'd had precious few miracles lately, Valerie thought. And yet, maybe they had had one, in a sense. The Yankees did not destroy what they had a use for, which might well be the only reason Mallows had not gone the way of Cedars, up in smoke.

They did not say any more. Ellen went ahead to make sure the way was clear for Valerie to slip back into the house; Valerie went upstairs and fell into bed before she had completely undressed, asleep before she could draw the covers over her.

The days had been long and tiring; now they became complicated, as well, as they juggled to avoid revealing Evan's hiding place to the Yankees while going over at least once a day to care for him. Twice Ellen left the big house as soon as it was dusk, after announcing her early retirement, and spent the night at Ryan's house with her son, returning shortly before dawn.

Julie went when she could do so without neglecting the duties she had assumed under Captain Ferris's command. The sight of her brother, looking worse than most of the men in serious condition in the improvised hospital at Mallows, unnerved her so that she returned to her tasks in a state that left her unprepared for death, any death.

When she walked into the drawing room with her paper and pen to write a letter she'd been requested to send to a

218

mother in Boston, she discovered that the young soldier who'd asked for it was dead. He had died peacefully enough, in his sleep, and the lines of pain were gone from his face. For a moment Julie didn't realize why he looked different, until she put a hand on his shoulder and he toppled toward her, his cheek resting against her knee.

She had seen others die before this. Yet having come directly from Evan, torn by fears for him, she could not bear it. Julie folded over the boy, holding his outflung hand, forgetting he was a Yankee, forgetting that his compatriots were responsible for her brother's injuries, as the tears slid down her face. She was shaken with sobs she could not stifle; grief for this boy, and for Evan, and her mother and Valerie and herself, for she was convinced that Evan, too, was going to die. And then they would be truly alone, no man coming home to them ever, and what would they do?

Lieutenant Froedecker found her there, collapsed in a small heap beside the dead soldier.

"Miss Julie—"

He lifted her away from the still figure, and Julie sagged against him, scarcely aware of his identity, knowing only that he was strong and warm and alive, and that she needed that contact even though she could not reach out for it. Fritz Froedecker spoke to her soothingly, and led her to the library, which was the nearest place where he could sit her down and get her a drink of brandy, the only thing he knew to do.

The dam of control once broken, Julie cried for them all: the Douglases, Aunt Grace, her father, and Evan as well as for the enemy soldier. Froedecker did not know about any of them, except for the boy from Boston. He marveled at her compassion for an enemy, and he held her until the sobbing quieted, as he would have held his sister under similar circumstances.

By the time the last hiccup had been swallowed, and Julie was using his large handkerchief to wipe at her sopping face, Fritz Froedecker had begun to feel something else, something not at all brotherly. He had admired Julie from a distance ever since the first moment he'd seen her, never with any thought of touching her. There were other women available to a man who needed one, and he'd enjoyed an occasional tumble with both Blossom Curtis and one of the more attractive young mulattoes down at the quarters.

The fact that Julie Stanton was an enemy, and the knowledge that he could probably have taken her with no official reprimand (let alone punishment), had not led him to do anything foolish. This girl was a lady of refinement, and while he had no compunction about taking what was offered in other quarters, he was not of a mind to use force on any woman. Many of his fellow officers had no such qualms, indeed, felt that using a woman was one of the privileges of the victors. It had nothing to do with their own supposed Christianity and the morals it was incumbent upon them to practice in their home towns. Certainly the army made no serious protests when the Southern women were violated, so it couldn't be all that seriously wrong, could it?

Fritz Froedecker sat beside the forlorn figure as long as she stayed there, and wondered what Julie would do if he did make an overture, knowing he would not.

Twenty-Three

Valerie did sleep through the afternoon, deeply and soundly, while the wounded soldiers were transferred from the piazza to the third-floor ballroom. When she did not feel up to joining the others for dinner, Captain Ferris brought her a tray.

He grinned at her surprise. "I offered to save Pansy a climb. Besides, you're my patient and I wanted to see how you were doing."

"Horrible," Valerie said, and the word was a hoarse croak. "I'm afraid you're going to have to wait another day for my help, if I don't feel better in the morning."

"I missed you today," he admitted freely. "Here, Mamie's sent you chicken soup with plenty of garlic in it. You can't beat that for the last word in medical therapy."

It did taste good, and felt good in her sore throat. Sitting up to eat it tired her, though, so that she was glad to slide back down under the covers when he lifted the tray away.

"Thank you," she told him, and Ferris made a mock bow. "Anytime. Your servant, ma'am."

It was only after he'd gone that she wondered how she could approach him about Evan. Did her brother have any remote chance of survival if the foot was not removed? And was there any likelihood that Evan would allow him to do it?

She remembered what Patrick Ryan's sister had said about her husband, that she preferred him minus an arm to losing him altogether. She didn't know how Ruth's husband felt about it, of course, if it made his previous way of life impossible to him now.

Evan had always been active. He loved to ride a horse, and swim, and dance, and hunt, and fish. An active man, an outdoor man. The library at Mallows was an attraction only on a day when it was impossible to do anything outside. Evan had also been popular with the ladies. How many of them would rally around a man who was missing a foot, or a leg? He'd already expressed himself on the subject. He'd begged Aaron to take him out of the hospital in Atlanta to prevent the doctors there from sawing off his foot, and he'd tried to extract that same promise from Ellen.

Valerie knew, deep within her, that amputation was Evan's best chance. Jack Ferris was qualified to do it. Only what rights did she and her mother have, when balanced against what Evan wanted? If they allowed the limb to be amputated against his will, would he eventually adjust to the physical limitation and learn to lead a productive and satisfying life? Or would bitterness turn him away from all of them, away from everything and everyone he'd ever loved?

She knew instinctively that, though Evan loved Mallows as his home, he did not share his mother's passion, which amounted almost to obsession, about the plantation. He enjoyed living in the great house, enjoyed the good things the plantation had made possible to him, but would he place the welfare of Mallows ahead of his own personal needs? Could he ever be content to direct the machinations of the place from an office, giving orders to an overseer rather than riding the fields himself?

Valerie had come to no conclusions when she slipped once more into sleep that was troubled, this time, by dreams that made her moan and whimper and try to push away from whatever they involved.

She woke into darkness, except for a faint outline of light around a door that stood ajar onto the second-floor landing. She could not remember any of the dreams, although she knew they had been disturbing. She felt, she realized with a sense of wonder, much better, except for a slight remaining sore throat. That, and an overpowering hunger.

It was dark, but it could not be late. Julie had not come to bed, and from the room across the landing she could hear voices. The family had gathered in Sally Ann's room; she heard the baby cry, and a soothing voice, and Lacy's laugh. Past suppertime, then, but not yet bedtime. Would she continue to feel as well as this if she got up? She did, only a little weakened from her day in bed, and that mostly from starvation, she decided. Chicken soup was fine as far as it went; now she needed something more substantial.

She wouldn't have bothered to dress if there hadn't been all those men in the house. As it was, she would dispense with everything but the essentials of pantalettes, one petticoat, and the dress she'd worn earlier. She made a halfhearted attempt to secure her hair, not looking at the final results in the mirror; she intended to go down the back stairs and would see no one, so it would be wasted effort.

The door to Sally Ann's room was open, and the voices came more clearly. Including Henriette's—she'd left her sister for an evening of badly needed companionship across the hall. Valerie didn't want to talk to any of them. Now that her head was clearing, she wanted to think. Think about Jack Ferris, and the way he'd kissed her. Probably he was with his fellow officers in the upstairs sitting room; although the door there was closed, there was a ribbon of light beneath it, and the subdued murmur of masculine voices. She knew they played cards there in the evenings, accompanied by a bottle of Roger Stanton's best brandy.

Valerie walked quietly so as to attract no attention, down the narrow back stairs and into the lingering warmth of the winter kitchen. The aromas of suppertime lingered, as well, and she poked about for whatever would best satisfy her hunger. There was a bowl of oranges on the table, but she'd had enough oranges for one day. There was a cold joint and she whittled off a slice of the meat, nibbling on it as she searched out cornbread to go with it.

Something crashed in the front part of the house.

Valerie stood for a moment, listening. The sound was not repeated. Curious, she lifted the candle and moved through the dining room and out into the front hallway. From there she could hear the voices upstairs. One of the men sleeping in the drawing room coughed. There was nothing else, no illumination on the ground floor except for the taper she carried.

She turned back, assuming that one of the injured men had

223

caused the earlier sound, then paused. As long as she was down here, she would get something to read in case she decided to stay in bed any part of tomorrow. She pushed open the library door and stepped confidently into the room. It had been reserved for the Yankees since their arrival, but since there was no light she didn't expect it to be occupied.

The man kneeling on the hearth, groping amidst shards of broken glass, turned before she could retreat, and she saw that it was Jack Ferris.

"Dropped the bottle, and then I couldn't find the candle," he said. His words were somewhat slurred, and the smell of brandy wasn't entirely from the broken bottle. The candles were right where they should have been, on the mantel above him, and there was enough left of a dying fire to have lighted them if he failed to locate the matches.

He stood up, kicking the remaining glass into the front edge of the fireplace where it wouldn't be stepped on. "Don't walk over here until it's been swept. Why are you running around barefooted? You'll take a chill."

"You've cut yourself," Valerie said, stepping toward him.

Ferris laughed and took the candle out of her hand, reaching around to put it down on a low table. "Don't set us both afire with that thing. Yes, I think I ran a splinter into my thumb. Take a look, can you see anything?"

They stood, bending toward the light, heads together as they examined the bloody thumb. He produced a handkerchief to wipe the blood away and grunted. "There, I think that wiped it out." He pressed experimentally upon the spot with the opposite thumb. "It doesn't stick any more."

He straightened, looking down on her. Valerie was suddenly conscious of her old gown, her lack of proper undergarments, the disheveled state of her hair.

"I—I woke up hungry, and came down for something to eat."

"Nothing to eat in here," Jack said. "Plenty to drink, though. Your father had excellent taste in both brandy and whiskey. Let me pour you some."

"No," Valerie said, though he was already moving to do it. "I never drink it."

"For medicinal purposes only," he told her. "Does wonders to hold off a cold, or a chill. Here, try it."

It was true that the ladies at Mallows seldom drank anything more than a glass of wine with meals. Ellen had strong

224

opinions on women who drank hard liquor. This, however, was apricot brandy, and Valerie did like the taste of it; she accepted the glass he put into her hand.

"That's far too much," she said, looking at it.

"Who's the doctor around here, you or me?" He poured a second glass for himself, touched it with a faint *clink* against hers, and then did not drink after all. "You know, either I've had too much to drink, or I'm falling in love with you."

Warmth rushed through her in an overpowering flood. She felt giddy, and he did not appear at all drunk, now, only pleasantly relaxed.

Not knowing what to say, she said nothing. Jack touched glasses again, and sipped at his, smiling. "Drink it. It'll warm you from the inside out."

She didn't need more warming, not after what he'd said. Yet she sipped at it obediently. It went down with smoothness, generating heat only after it had reached her stomach, a warmth that eased her nervousness.

"Come on, sit down, be comfortable. I'll throw another log on the fire." He gestured toward the nearest of the brocaded sofas, then came to sit beside her after he'd stirred up the fire. "It was lonely down here by myself," he said, sipping again from the glass, draining it. "Will you have some more?"

Meeting his smile with her own, Valerie shook her head. He was right; it made her feel better almost at once. "This is more than I've ever had at one time before. It makes me feel as if . . . as if my bones are going all soft."

He laughed and moved closer to her, so that their knees were touching, although he seemed unaware of that. He rested an arm along the back of the sofa. "Good. I like a female with soft bones. Soft everything. How soft are you, Valerie Stanton?"

He didn't wait for an answer to that, but bent to brush her lips with his, almost making her spill her brandy.

"Here, get rid of that," he muttered, and removed the glass from her hand, reaching to set it on the table before them. Valerie was glad enough for that; already she realized that she'd had all she should on an empty stomach, and her hand felt too relaxed to hold it. She watched, mesmerized, as Jack pinched out the flame of the candle, leaving only the flickering flames on the hearth in the darkened room.

This time, when his mouth claimed hers, when his arms

225

came around her, liquid fire, more potent than the brandy, coursed through her. At some far distant point in her mind, she realized that this was dangerous ground, yet she was incapable of resisting. She didn't want to resist. She was melting like the butter on Mamie's hot cornbread, melting, fusing her lips with his lips, her body with his.

Shocked into renewed awareness when his fingers worked expertly at her buttons, Valerie gasped and tried to sit up. When had she been eased back against the cushions, how had her skirts become disarranged, how had she allowed him to expose her bosom, her thighs?

She tried to protest, mildly alarmed now, but his weight bore her downward on the sofa, and his mouth was both firm and soft. Incongruously, he chuckled into her ear. "I told you you'd be more comfortable without those damned stays! I'm glad you followed my advice."

The brandy, or was it Jack himself, caused an incapacitating lethargy; it no longer seemed to matter what anyone else would think about what she did, she only knew that she wanted him. Touching her own body had been no more than an insignificant foreshadowing of what she felt now; his hands and his mouth roused her to heights she had never dreamed of, and it was too late to stop him. Too late, too late—the words echoed in her head, like distant bells, having nothing to do with her own response to this man.

His breath quickened in tempo with hers, his voice rasping in her ear. "Oh God, you're wonderful! Beautiful, beautiful girl!"

The brandy might have slowed her mental processes; it did nothing to quell the sensations that lifted her, carried her beyond any volition of her own, allowed her to drift with him, willing to do whatever he wanted to do. When he came to her in a final urgent passion, she cried out once, then locked him in her own embrace until it was over. They both lay, breathing audibly, spent and content, in one another's arms.

"You're fantastic," Jack whispered, shifting to a more comfortable position. "Everything I dreamed you'd be."

He had dreamed of her, too. Valerie smiled in the semi-darkness, reaching to run a finger along the line of his jaw and to the corner of his smiling mouth. He reached to press her fingertips against his lips for a kiss, then drew her face close to his. She allowed her lips to part under the pressure,

226

ready to sink again into that exquisite river of pleasure, when they heard the first shot.

Private Samuel Waynerose had been ambulatory for almost a week. The wound that had felled him in the first place had healed, and he'd have been out of this place several weeks sooner—luxurious though it was, compared to what he was accustomed to, Mallows remained a hospital, with all that implied—if he hadn't contracted some sort of respiratory ailment. That left him in a weakened condition that he deliberately prolonged, because he didn't want to be returned to limited duty. That, in this situation, would have meant emptying chamber pots and going up and down stairs with trays for those unable to carry their own.

The previous day, he had sat for a time downstairs, observing the activity, and listening to the latest rumors. Sherman was sweeping toward the sea, the South was done for, the war was nearly over and they'd all be going home by Christmas. He hoped to God they were right. He was sick of the war, sick of the South, sick of unfamiliar trees and flowers and people. He wanted to go home.

But not, he decided, without tasting some of the fruits of the conquered land. His own wife was fat and unattractive, her chief virtue being that she had brought with her to the marriage a small farm in northern Illinois, free and unencumbered. The girl with the taffy-colored hair and the warm smile stirred something in Private Waynerose that had been dormant since he'd taken a Confederate rifle bullet in the chest at the battle of New Hope Church.

"Morning," Blossom greeted him. "Anythin' I can do for you, sir?"

She meant in the way of food and drink, which she was dispensing to those patients housed on the ground floor. Private Waynerose chose to interpret her words differently, however. Hell, he'd heard she'd do it with some of the others; why not with him?

"I think you could do a lot for me," he told her boldly, after checking to make sure there were none of the officers around to overhear. "In a more private place than this. You just tell me where your room is, and I'll come along after dark. We'll talk about it."

As he'd hoped, Blossom took no offense at this brash approach. She laughed. "Well, you won't have no trouble findin' me, I reckon. All you got to do is walk down the stairs from the third floor and turn left. That nigger gal is across from my room, though, and she don't go to sleep 'til after nine."

Private Waynerose grinned, showing gaps in his teeth. "What do we care about her? We ain't aimin' to ask her to join us, are we?"

Blossom made a prim mouth. "You got to remember I'm a guest in this here house. I got to be discreet."

In truth, none of her liaisons had so far taken place under the roof of the big house; she feared Ellen's reaction if she were caught. On the other hand, this man didn't have one of the cabins in the quarters, and it was too cold in the evening to enjoy an alfresco romantic interlude. She had heard that word once, years ago, and upon learning its meaning had dropped it into various conversations since then.

She did not, therefore, want Lallie to be aware of what went on in the next room, just in case Lallie should take it into her head to drop a word to her mistress.

"Oh, Blossom, would you fetch the rest of those dishes back to the kitchen, so Pansy can wash them?"

Ellen's voice behind her had brought her heart into her throat, and Blossom turned away from the soldier, trusting that the other woman had heard nothing.

And Private Waynerose sat there, feeling his juices rise in happy anticipation. After nine, he thought. It was going to be a hell of a long day.

It would also be his last.

Twenty-Four

Henriette would subsequently berate herself for having left her sister alone. Yet most of the time it did not seem that Charlotte knew whether she was there or not. And Henriette craved the company of those who at least made a pretense that things were normal, that life would eventually be resumed, that the horror of war was not a constant threat. The voices of the other women, the quickly shushed cry of tiny Hugh Alexander, even an occasional low laugh issuing from the room across the landing, drew her like a magnet. Charlotte was asleep, or at least lay on the bed with her eyes closed, and did not respond when spoken to. Surely there was no harm in joining the others for an hour or so.

Henriette left the door ajar so that she might hear Charlotte if she called out. The Yankees were at their card game in the sitting room, and if her fear of them had not dissolved completely, it was considerably abated; they had menaced no one since their entry into the house. She had no reason to think her sister was in any more danger from them, alone, than she would have been with Henriette in the same room.

And thus it was that when Private Samuel Waynerose came cautiously down the stairway from the third floor in an advanced state of excitement, his eye was caught at once by the half-opened door, beckoning, it seemed to him, an invitation.

Down the stairs, and turn to the left, Blossom had said. And there it was, the half-open door. Blossom, however, had neglected to mention that turning left involved using the little narrow stairway that led to the two servants' rooms, tucked away between floors, so to speak. The door to *that* was not ajar; Private Waynerose did not even notice it.

Charlotte did not hear him coming. She was not actually asleep, as she so often pretended to be. Paradoxically, she both resented being left alone by her sister, and welcomed the freedom from solicitude that Henriette continually offered.

Charlotte wished, quite sincerely, that she was dead. She had endured the unspeakable at the hands of the Yankee soldiers, and there were more of them in this house. She had made up her mind, weeks ago, that never again would she submit to such violation. Her parents were dead, her brothers were dead; there was only Henriette left, and Henriette had not suffered the things *she* had suffered. Had she been able to work up her courage to do it, Charlotte would have killed herself. She knew she was a coward, she cringed and trembled yet, when she woke from the dreams that left her bathed in sweat, reliving that dreadful afternoon.

If she could have gotten her hands on the laudanum, it would have been a simple matter to take too much of it and just go to sleep. Both the Yankee doctor and Miss Ellen kept the drug under lock and key, however, except when they were dispensing it. She had no access to it.

She did have the means to take her own life. Valerie had taken the pistol away from her, that other time; since then, Charlotte had located two more. One she had found in Ellen's bedroom, tucked beneath neat stacks of undergarments in the chiffonier. There was no spare ammunition for it, but it was loaded. The other pistol she had stolen, during a nocturnal wandering, from one of the Yankee officers. She had known they were downstairs in the library—they laughed so boisterously that it was easy to keep track of them—and she had removed the weapon from the holster that hung over the back of a chair. He must have noticed that it was missing by now, yet no alarm had been raised. Perhaps he was afraid of the consequences if he reported the theft to his superiors. At any rate, Charlotte had the pistol beneath her pillow, and she took care that Henriette was not allowed to make the bed and therefore find it.

She had two pistols, but so far she hadn't mustered the courage to use either of them. Sometimes, when Henriette was safely out of the way on duties elsewhere, Charlotte would take one of them out and hold it against her temple, or her heart. Her pulses would pound until she was deafened with the rushing of blood in her ears, and her mouth would go dry; she would will her finger to become steady on the trigger, but she could not make herself squeeze it. And when Henriette returned to their room, Charlotte would be lying motionless on the bed, pale-faced, with tears glistening on her lashes.

Tonight, she felt rather than heard the arrival of the Yankee soldier. He wore no shoes, and he moved with caution, yet she suddenly knew that someone was there. Charlotte opened her eyes and saw the bulk of a male figure blocking the light from the room across the hall. She did not know who he was; it didn't matter.

"Miss Blossom?" Private Waynerose whispered.

She didn't hear him. The thundering blood suffused her head, rendering her deaf, blind, dumb. Her hand groped under the pillow; the pistol was so heavy she could hardly lift it with both hands. For that reason, trying to steady it, she allowed the intruder to come to the foot of the bed before she fired.

The explosions—three of them in rapid succession—echoed and re-echoed throughout the house. For a matter of seconds, no one moved at all. And then doors were thrown open, candles snatched up, and they came.

They found Charlotte sitting bolt upright in the tester bed, the pistol resting against her upraised knees. She did not seem aware of any of them. Private Waynerose lay sprawled in a widening lake of his own blood, blood that gushed from the hole in his chest. Except for an expression of surprise, and a bullet hole in the middle of his forehead, he looked as the others had seen him earlier in the day.

Major Quinn, who had not been a member of the card-playing group but had, instead, been writing a letter in his room, was one of the first on the scene. His immediate reaction was one of rage. Why had this happened to him now, when this tour of duty was nearly over? It would mean more damnable reports, explanations, and perhaps reprimands! His hate-filled glare would have terrorized Charlotte, had she been aware of it. He wanted to throttle her with his bare hands. Instead he stood quietly, the toe of his boot in the dark viscous fluid that continued to leak out of Waynerose's body, only the bulging veins at his temples revealing his stress.

"Where did she get the gun?" he demanded.

The officers behind him were silent, shocked. They had left the war behind when they came to this place; they had expected neither to kill nor to be killed while on hospital duty at a remote plantation while the war rushed to a conclusion, elsewhere, without them.

Lieutenant Hoskins cleared his throat. "It—it may be mine, sir."

Major Quinn turned, leaving a red smear on the polished floor. "*May* be, Hoskins? *May* be?"

Poor Hoskins was breathing quickly through his mouth, his face mottled red and white. "Mine . . . mine is missing, sir."

"Missing?" The words hissed from between Quinn's lips. "Have you reported it missing, Lieutenant?"

Hoskins started to lick his lips and thought better of it. "No, sir. Not yet."

"Not yet. And when did you notice that it was missing, Lieutenant?"

The irony in his superior's tone was not lost on Hoskins. He swallowed hard and straightened his spine.

"Sev—several days ago, sir. I—I thought I would find it."

The veins pulsed and throbbed at Quinn's temples; it wouldn't have surprised any of those present if Quinn had suddenly frothed at the mouth and fallen into a fatal fit.

He did not, however. He barked into the circle of white faces outside the doorway. "Where is Captain Ferris?"

"Right here, sir. What happened?"

Jack Ferris, who had perhaps clothed himself more quickly than he had ever done before in his life, was still buttoning his tunic as he moved quickly from the top of the stairs.

"What's happened is that stupid bitch has killed one of your patients. Who is he?"

Ferris stepped past his two lieutenants and stared down at the man on the floor. "His name's Waynerose, sir. Samuel Waynerose."

There were no questions about what the soldier had been

doing inside Charlotte's bedroom. That seemed evident enough to everyone.

"There's nothing to be done for him, sir. Not with a hole in his chest like that," Ferris observed.

"I'm aware of that, Captain. I have seen dead bodies before." Quinn allowed his gaze to settle on the girl in the bed, the girl who did not appear aware of any of them, who still held the pistol that might well have several remaining shells. "Get that gun away from her."

Ferris stepped over the victim and took the pistol from Charlotte's unresisting hands. He didn't ask where the gun had come from; he didn't want to know, although no doubt he would be told when Quinn chose to do it.

"I'll have someone clean up this mess," Ferris stated, as he would have done if a patient had vomited. The others backed away to let him pass through their ranks, and Quinn turned to Lieutenant Froedecker.

"Place this woman under house arrest until such time as she can be taken to prison," he said.

The minute rustlings of movement on the landing ceased. It was Ellen who first found her voice, and the courage to protest.

"Major Quinn, the girl was only protecting her virtue, surely that is obvious! And she is the one who was so brutally ravished by your troops, she has been severely disturbed, mentally, ever since! You cannot hold her responsible for shooting a man under those conditions!"

The major's mouth was a flat line. "She has killed a Union soldier. She must be held responsible for it; her fate is not up to me, it will be decided in a federal court. The rest of you, clear out of here. See that this door is locked, or put a guard on it. The woman is not to leave this room."

Henriette emitted a small sound of distress: When Major Quinn swung his glacial gaze in her direction she was not quelled by it, but rather driven to desperate speech.

"Please, sir! She cannot care for herself, she is—she is not of sound mind! You cannot lock her up alone, with no one to do for her!"

"You are mistaken," Quinn said. He turned his back on the scene of carnage, issuing his final order on the matter in the general direction of Lieutenant Froedecker. "See to it that the woman is kept in that room, and that no one goes in or out without my permission."

Private Waynerose must first, of course, be removed. A stretcher was hastily brought from the piazza, and a sheet to cover him. This latter was of little value in making the removal less distressing, because the blood immediately soaked through the sheeting in a grotesque crimson splotch.

Julie, numb with horror, nevertheless rallied enough to put her arm around Henriette and lead her back to the room where the baby was screaming at the top of his lungs.

"What will they do to her? It's not fair, it's inhuman to torment her any further!" Henriette whimpered. "They won't hurt her, will they?"

Julie had no answers.

Valerie had not dared to run up the front stairs with Captain Ferris; whatever had happened up there, whoever had fired three shots, she could take no chances; it must not be obvious that she and the Yankee officer had been together when it happened.

Her euphoric haze was gone, dissipated like a thread of mist in a strong wind. The brandy, which had made her feel so warm and comfortable, deserted her, now when she needed it. She shook so that she could hardly get the candle relit; already she could hear Ferris's feet on the stairs, and excited voices, and she prayed that she could join the others as if she'd come from her own room, not from the ground floor. Her mother, at least, was bound to wonder if both Valerie and Ferris showed up from the same place, both in a state of disarray.

Valerie sped through the dining room and the kitchen, and up the back stairs. Dread was an icy trickle through her veins. Who had fired the pistol? Who, if anyone, had been shot? She arrived at the top of the stairs breathing heavily, legs trembling, and eased open the door.

Everyone was there, clustered around the room that had been given over to the Douglas sisters. No one noticed her as Valerie closed the door behind her and joined the others in time to hear Major Quinn's final words before he stalked to his own room. She stepped back so that Julie and Henriette could pass; neither of them took any notice of her. It was Ellen who turned and saw her, moving quickly to Valerie's side.

"Don't go any closer, it's horrible. Come away, there is nothing we can do for the moment, although we must try to think of something to persuade Major Quinn of the injustice

, and when they turned out to be one and the sa[me] it was only sensible to prevaricate to whatever deg[ree] necessary to extricate oneself from the mess. [As] far as the Yankees were concerned, the matter w[as] [close]d.

[T]here was guilt, though not as much as she might have ex[pec]ted. When the appalling evening was over, when Henriett[e] [had] been sedated and put to bed in Blossom's room (much t[o] [Blo]ssom's dismay) and all the others had gone to bed as well [Va]lerie lay in darkness. Julie had elected to sleep up there [wi]th Henriette, in case she wakened in spite of the drug Cap[ta]in Ferris had given her. Blossom had, quite unceremoni[ou]sly she thought, been told to take a few things over into [L]allie's room.

It didn't matter that Lallie's skin was light enough so that a [s]tranger would never have guessed at her Negro blood. Lallie was a slave, and they'd simply taken it for granted that Blossom would move in with her, when the room she had been occupying was needed for someone else. It had been taken for granted that Henriette could not be expected to sleep in the room where her sister and a Yankee soldier had just died. Even Blossom admitted she would not have cared to sleep there, either. Yet why didn't they send Lallie out to the quarters with the rest of the slaves, and let Henriette take *that* room?

Valerie, of them all, was the only one who slept in a room by herself that night. She was grateful for that, because she had a great many things to think about. For a time, when she had put out the candle and lay looking up into blackness, she had, like the others, been overwhelmed by the events of the evening. Two deaths, at a time when they were beginning to believe the deaths were done with, for the most part. Two violent deaths, but they could not completely take away what Valerie had had, for a brief time, down there in the library with Jack Ferris.

Maybe she ought to feel ashamed to be thinking about him, at a time like this. *But I'm alive,* Valerie told herself. *I have waited all my life to be loved by a man, and tonight it happened, and I can't put down the happiness over that. I don't want to put it down; I want to think about loving a man.*

Gradually the horrors of the day faded away, and there re-

of what he does. Quite aside from the fact that poor Charlotte is not responsible, any female should have the right to protect herself against men like that."

No questions were asked. When they assembled in the big room where Sally Ann and Lacy and the baby now slept, Valerie realized at once that everyone took it for granted that she'd been in bed, asleep, when the shooting took place. Hugh Alexander, nuzzling contentedly against his mother's shoulder, for once drew no other attention than that. The women's faces were chalky in the candlelight, and if there was guilt mixed with shock on Valerie's countenance, no one noticed it.

She sat on the little gold brocaded sofa between Lacy and Ellen, contributing nothing to the conversation, picking up details from what the others said. She was as horrified as the rest of them, yet she did not want to talk about Charlotte and the man she had killed. She didn't even want to listen to the rest of them talking about it. She wanted to withdraw to complete privacy and think about herself.

Herself and Jack Ferris.

Henriette turned a tear-stained face toward the trio on the sofa. "What are we going to do? How can we save Charlotte?" she begged.

None of them had any answer to that.

Blossom was the only one who guessed what had actually happened. Had the stupid fool mistaken her directions? Had he gone to that poor crazy girl instead of to *her?* She didn't say anything. This was no time to draw attention to herself; she knew perfectly well that she risked being thrown out in the cold, with nothing but the clothes on her back, if Ellen Stanton knew she had had any assignation in Ellen's own house. There was no risk now, however; if she simply kept her mouth shut, there was no way anyone could know that Private Waynerose had been on his way to Blossom's room and mistaken the way. Yet, she, too, was shaken. She would be more careful in the future, Blossom decided.

While the others sat debating Charlotte's future, planning ways to prevent her being tried and possibly sent to jail, Charlotte took matters into her own hands. When the man appeared in the doorway, she had not hesitated for a moment. And she had had no trouble at all in pulling the trigger to stop him.

She sat, apparently unseeing, as two of the orderlies cleaned up the evidence of the man's death at the foot of her bed. "Looked right at us, she did, but like she was blind, didn't see nothing at all," as one of them later said. "It was creepy as hell." They gathered up their stained rags, and closed the door. There was no way to lock it; a man would have to be left on guard in the hallway outside Charlotte's room.

As soon as the men had gone, Charlotte rose from the bed and padded across the room to the chiffonier. Her groping fingers closed around the mother-of-pearl handle of the dueling pistol Ellen had had hidden in her own belongings, and not yet missed. This time her hands did not shake. There was no need to work up her courage. Charlotte stuck the barrel of the pistol into her mouth and squeezed the trigger.

Major Otis Quinn addressed his subalterns in a voice with fury. "My official report will state that the woman Waynerose, with the pistol that she had managed to con in her room, and then *immediately* turned the same wea upon herself. Captain Ferris, you will add your signature mine. And if the matter is ever questioned, you will each you," he raked their faces with the icy glare, "tell the san story. Both of them are dead, and there is nothing to b gained by going into explanations of how one of my officer allowed his weapon to be stolen, and did not report it until i had been used to kill one of my own men. Is everyone clear on this matter?"

It would have taken a brave man to dispute Quinn's version of the affair. Certainly Robert Hoskins had no desire to do so. He felt nothing but relief that he was apparently not going to be court-martialed, although he had no illusions about the major's attitude toward him. Thank God the war was nearly over, and once he'd been mustered out he'd never need to see any of these people again as long as he lived.

Captain Ferris signed his name in a bold hand, testifying to the veracity of the report, with no qualms whatever. There was such a thing as truth, and there was such a thing as stu-

mained the blissful euphoria of reliving Jack Ferris's embrace, his kiss, his lovemaking. How quickly the inhibitions, drilled into her over her entire lifetime, had vanished! The reality of flesh and blood swept away Ellen's teachings as debris was carried by the creek in spring flood.

Oh, guilt was there, in some small measure. A properly brought-up young woman did not give herself to a man before marriage; she knew that, and agreed with it, on principle. Yet this was different; she was in love with Jack, and he with her, and these were perilous times, for all that the end of the war was in sight.

They must be circumspect in future meetings; she was well aware that it would not do to be caught in the act. She wondered how her mother had produced her children; impossible to imagine Ellen making love or giving birth to a baby. As impossible as imagining, now, *not* making love with Jack Ferris again; already, after a single brief, ecstatic episode, impossible to bear the thought of being deprived of that tender kiss, the skillful wooing. If there had been a few moments of pain, why, that was wiped out, and more, by the joy of soaring sensations that even yet, hours later, had the power to set her nerve-ends tingling.

Would she have to leave Mallows and live in New York? New York was a city, and she knew little of cities except for Savannah and Atlanta, the latter visited only twice and the former far different from the big city in the north.

The speculations about the future were over before she knew it, as Valerie slid into the depths of slumber.

Twenty-Six

Except for Captain Ferris and Lieutenant Froedecker, none of the Yankees was in attendance at the cemetery when Charlotte was buried. Chad and Thomas had made the coffin, and Lallie had lined it with blue silk from an old dress of Ellen's, artfully draped to conceal the few small tears.

It was Ellen and Lallie who laid out the body; even if Charlotte had not died in such a way as to leave mutilated remains, Henriette was totally incapable of participating in that final operation. It was all she could do, supported by Valerie on one side and Julie on the other, to stand while Ellen read from the Bible, concluding with "From henceforth blessed are the dead who die in the Lord; even so saith the Spirit; for they rest from their labours." Comforting words, yet there was no comfort for Henriette, and very little for anyone else. Ellen's face was weary, and calm, and she did not falter in the readings that she knew so well.

The task of covering the grave was left to Chad and Tom. The others walked back through the brisk, sunny morning, silent except for Henriette's quiet sobbing. When she stumbled and went nearly to her knees, Jack Ferris stepped forward and scooped her up as if she'd been a child, to carry her the rest of the way.

240

And Julie, blinded by her own tears, reached out for Valerie—the reassurance of a warm hand was imperative at that moment—and found, as well, that Lieutenant Froedecker was at her other side. She made no protest when he put a firm hand under her elbow, not releasing her until they'd reached the piazza steps. It was there that he stopped, glancing over his shoulder with a puzzled expression.

"Is that smoke?"

Valerie, heart suddenly pounding, followed his gaze. "Yes, it's from Ryan's place. He must have sent word that he's coming home; probably old Hattie's come to ready the house for him."

"Ryan, that was the overseer, wasn't it? He in the army?"

"Yes. Or maybe his sister's come back. She lives at Midway Church." Valerie improvised with what wit she could muster. "Maybe I should ride over and see. If Mr. Ryan is returning, it may be because he's been wounded. Or Hattie may be in need of something; there is no one there during the summer to keep a garden. Do you think someone would have time to hitch up the buggy for me?"

Ferris had gone on into the house with Henriette; Fritz Froedecker still stared at the telltale wisp of smoke above the trees.

"Oh, sure. Maybe I'll go—"

"Lieutenant," Julie said, before he could finish the sentence, "would you help me? After you've asked someone to hitch up the buggy for Valerie? Some of the furniture we had to put out in the quarters is showing signs of damage—the cabins are unheated, of course, with no one living in them. Mama thought it might help to wrap them, and the servants are so clumsy about such things unless they're supervised every minute. Maybe having something to do will take my mind off—off everything else."

The young officer forgot about the smoke. "Why, certainly, Miss Julie. I'd be glad to help you."

"I'll change my clothes and meet you back here, then, in a few minutes?"

A smile transformed his face, and he tugged at one end of the sandy mustache. "I'll see about that buggy, and come right back."

The sisters stared at each other after he'd gone, both of them breathing through open mouths. They exchanged no words. They had, for the moment, distracted attention from

Ryan's place. If they could successfully establish that a servant had returned to reopen the house, perhaps they could keep the Yankees away from it indefinitely.

"Tell Mama where I've gone," Valerie said when Froedecker returned leading the horse and buggy. "If you wouldn't mind."

His thoughts on Julie, the lieutenant agreed at once. "Certainly, ma'am."

It wasn't quite as good as having Ellen to go with her; it was better than having to walk, and it would have made too much of the matter if Ellen had been invited to go, too. There were too many things to be done at home to make it appear logical that the mistress of Mallows would run about on behalf of the servant of a mere overseer. If they believed there was a servant at Ryan's, would it be trusting too much to luck to attempt to convince the Yankees that Hattie was in need of more frequent visits of assistance? Would they take Valerie's word for it, if she said Hattie was lame, or crippled, or ill? Anything that would give her an excuse to take the buggy out? Otherwise, she had to walk, and surreptitiously, at that.

She found Evan sleeping; that was the only good sign. His fever raged, in spite of the Seidlitz powders and the sassafras tea.

"I been spongin' him," Hattie told her, "but he don't get no cooler, Miss Val. I sure wish we had us some ice."

If wishes were horses, beggars might ride. The old phrase from a childhood book flashed through her mind. As well wish for a miracle, as for ice. The brandy and cloves were the best they had.

Her mother was not there to object, and so Valerie, with Hattie's help, stripped Evan down for further sponging. She had seen him partially unclothed before; it did not prepare her for the shocking thinness of his body, and she stared in dismay at the leg above the injured foot.

"It's worse, isn't it, Hattie?" Her gaze beseeched repudiation of what her own eyes told her. "The redness is higher than it was, and the swelling?"

"I 'fraid so, ma'am. What you reckon to do?"

Her lips were so stiff she could scarcely form the words. "There's only one thing that can be done." She would have to talk to Jack Ferris. He wouldn't betray Evan now, not under

242

these conditions. Surely he would not! And he was her brother's only hope.

"No." The word was quiet, intense, issuing from lips that barely moved. "I won't let them cut it off, Val."

His eyes were open, fever-glazed yet lucid. The intelligence and the pain in them made her speak more plainly than she would otherwise have done, that and the knowledge that there was no time to waste.

"There's a surgeon at Mallows, Evan. And you're going to die if he doesn't amputate."

Evan spat a curse, weak but no less vehement for the weakness. "I'm going to die no matter what happens. The poison is all through me, I'm burning up with it. Better to die a whole man, than to live half of one."

It tired him to speak, yet she did not try to stop him; he needed to say these things that even the fever could not quell. Valerie took the thin hot hand in her own, bending over the bed.

"Evan, listen to me. Captain Ferris says that most of the men fight the idea of amputation, but afterward, they adjust. They can still be husbands and fathers, still have useful lives—"

This time he didn't bother to swear. "No. No, Val. I'll never forgive you if you let them take it off. I won't be a cripple, not ever."

"Evan, listen. It's because you're so sick, that you can't handle the thought. Ruth Ryan told me about her husband, he lost an arm at Chancellorsville, but he's all right now! He's learning to do things with the other arm, and she said she'd rather have him that way—"

"Val. Don't."

The quiet voice stopped her where a raised one might not have. With an effort that made veins stand out at his temples and perspiration bathe his body, Evan lifted himself on his elbows to look down at his exposed lower extremities. A brief look was enough. He sank back, exhausted, and Hattie hurried to him with a glass, spooning the fluid into him.

Valerie was shaking. Should Evan be allowed to make this decision for himself? Or was it up to her? Would he accept, as Ruth's husband had done? Or would he truly never forgive her if she let them take off his leg?

Evan opened his eyes once more and spoke so quietly that she had to bend over him to hear.

"Take me home to die, Val. Take me home."

The ache in her throat almost made speech impossible; she pressed his hand, and brushed a kiss across his forehead. "All right, Evan. I'll take you home," she promised.

There was no way she could get him into the buggy, not she and Hattie together; although he was skeletally thin, he was still a full-grown man and beyond their strength to lift. She would have to get some help from Mallows.

It was a good thing the horse knew the way home; her vision was so blurred by tears that she did not realize when they had reached the beginning of the drive and must make the turn. The piazza at Mallows seemed strangely naked, without the injured soldiers lying about it. Valerie crossed it blindly, not knowing whether she wanted to encounter her mother, first, or not. She could, of course, hand the problem over to her mother, and thus feel less of the responsibility herself. Yet she'd promised Evan she would bring him home; how could she renege on that, regardless of what Ellen thought of the dangers of exposing him to the Yankees?

She didn't meet Ellen. She met Jack Ferris, coming out of the library at a purposeful pace which he interrupted when he saw her.

"Valerie, what's wrong?" He saw at once that it was more than the funeral they had attended a few hours earlier, and he reached out for her, oblivious of any possible observers. "What is it? What's happened?"

For a brief moment she leaned against him, letting the tears spill over, and then she drew back. "It's my brother. Evan. He's at Ryan's place, and he's . . ."

She couldn't say the rest of it. She didn't have to. Jack stared down at her for only seconds. "Do I need help?"

Valerie gulped hard against the painful lump in her throat, nodding.

"All right. Fritz, bring my kit and come with us." He was already moving toward the door when Valerie touched his sleeve.

"My mother—"

"Yes, call her. She's in there." He gestured toward the drawing rooms, not pausing to wait for her.

Ellen was feeding soup to a listless boy from New Jersey. She stood at once when Valerie spoke her name, handing the

244

bowl and the spoon to Pansy. "Here, you finish this. What is it, Valerie?"

Valerie's throat worked in the effort to say it.

"Evan? Is it Evan?"

"Yes. I've told Captain Ferris. Evan—wants to come home to die, Mama."

Ellen had been braced for this, yet it was a blow, all the same. She wasted no time in following Valerie out to the buggy, the only sign of agitation the whiteness of her knuckles as she gripped the edge of the seat.

Hattie let them in, her black face frightened.

"All that talkin', it too much for him, Miss Val. He sunken so bad I can't get no spoon in his mouth, and he don't answer me."

"I've brought the doctor," Valerie said, and led the way into the house.

Ellen followed the men into the bedroom; Valerie stood in the kitchen warming herself at the fire, wishing the warmth could reach inside to where the chill was freezing her. She'd forgotten she no longer believed that God was listening and would answer; she prayed earnestly, desperately, for Evan's life.

She heard Jack's soft oath and braced herself when he stepped back to the doorway.

"It should have come off, weeks ago. There was never any chance that he'd ever be able to walk on that foot again; it's too badly mangled. Where the hell has he been?"

Valerie stood with a hand pressed to her bosom, pressing against the sharp pain there. "He was in the hospital in Atlanta. A servant found him and brought him here. He—he refuses to have it amputated."

Jack's words were quiet, yet harsh. "Well, he's past making that decision for himself. And whatever you two decide," he included Ellen in the statement, "had better be quick. Now. I'm not sure I can save him even if the leg comes off. And he'll sure as hell die if it doesn't."

They had known it, of course. From the very first, they had known it was that bad. That didn't ease the anguish of hearing it from Captain Ferris. What was the right thing to do? How could she know? What if it really was better to let Evan die than to be surgically crippled?

If it were me, I'd rather be mutilated and live, Valerie thought. Yet was that valid for Evan?

And in the end, coward that she was, she said nothing and let her mother, as usual, make the decision.

Her face white, her head high, Ellen spoke with only the faintest of tremors. "Then take the leg off, Captain."

Two tables were brought together in the brick-walled kitchen to serve as an operating table. It was a bright, sunny day; little additional light was needed, and Valerie wasn't expected to provide that this time. Indeed, Jack Ferris ordered them out of the room after Lieutenant Froedecker had been sent back to Mallows for Lieutenant Hoskins and one of the corporals.

"There's time enough to get all the help we need," Jack said. "I'll start trying to get as much of this brandy into him as he can take. You two either go upstairs, or outside. Or return to Mallows, if you like."

They elected to stay in Patrick Ryan's sitting room, upstairs. It was impossible to sit, and talking only made things worse. They moved about, looking at Patrick's books, gazing out the windows across the fields, listening for any small sound from below. They saw Fritz Froedecker return, with the wagon as well as the buggy, heard the door close downstairs, the murmur of voices. They could make out none of the words.

Valerie turned from the oak sideboard at one end of the pleasant room, lifting the bottle that stood there. "I'm going to have a drink of this, and I think you'd better have one, too, Mama."

They did, choking over the strong whiskey, forcing it down in spite of the tears it brought to their eyes, the fiery burning as the liquor went down. It was nothing like the apricot brandy Valerie had drunk in the library, the night Jack had made love to her. That had been smooth and delicious in flavor; this was so harsh it was all she could do to swallow it.

The scream of agony sent them into each other's arms. They stood close together, hearts pounding, unable to control their tears, clinging together for a long, long time.

They carried Evan home and upstairs, putting him into the room that Charlotte and Henriette had shared. He was flaccid and white, and there was a heartbreaking new configuration

246

of the sheets drawn over him. Jack Ferris had taken the leg off at mid-thigh.

Julie tiptoed in to look at him, her face nearly as pale as Evan's. "He'll never be able to ride again, will he?"

"He's alive," Ellen said.

Yes, he was alive. Valerie sat beside him, waiting for him to regain consciousness, dreading it, dreading the realization that would be there in the dark eyes. Would it be enough, to be alive?

It was early evening, and Valerie had just stood to light the stubby candles in the candelabrum beside the bed when Evan moved, ever so slightly. Senses quickening, her body going stiff with apprehension even before he moaned, Valerie turned and looked into her brother's open eyes.

Twenty-Seven

It did not come then, the storm she expected, because Evan awakened to suffering so great that it was all-enveloping, blotting out coherent thought. He groaned and tried to move, and Ellen was beside him at once, pressing him back against the pillow.

"Lie still, darling. It's all right. I'll call the doctor, I'll tell him you're awake. He'll give you something for the pain."

She gave Valerie a quick glance, a warning? and then rushed away. What warning? Not to tell him? But he would know, Valerie thought. As soon as he fully recovered his senses, perhaps even before that, he would know.

Evan threw his head to one side, breathing through his mouth, gasping. "Oh, God! Oh, God, stop it! Stop it!"

She put aside the candles and held his shoulders, leaning her head close so as to put her cheek to his. "Lie still, Evan. Please, try to lie still."

Jack came more quickly than she would have expected, and she stepped aside at once.

"He's in terrible pain. Can you give him something for it?"

Jack was already moving, dispensing the opiate that had not been available for the earliest patients, that was blessedly

248

available now, courtesy of the Federal supply wagon that had finally caught up with the Yankee hospital troop.

"Don't let him move around," Jack told her. "He can't afford any more blood loss. Hold him down, if you have to, until that takes effect."

And so they held him, until Evan slid once more into unconsciousness; the women were both wet with sweat and trembling with emotion and fatigue when at last his body stopped straining against their hands.

Valerie looked at her mother across the wide bed.

"Mama, go and rest. I'll stay here with him, while you sleep. Have Lallie close the shutters and bring your supper to you in bed, and then get a good night's rest." Seeing the protest forming on Ellen's face, she added the clinching argument. "You'll be no good to Evan unless you manage to stay well, yourself. Please, Mama."

"You'll call me if he needs me?"

"Yes, of course." It had been a long, terrible day, and Valerie would have liked to sleep, herself, yet she dared not. She had to be the one who was there when Evan woke up, undrugged, and realized that his leg had been amputated.

Pansy brought her a tray shortly after Ellen had retired, and Valerie ate without knowing what it was. She was sick with exhaustion and guilt over her part in what they'd done to Evan. Never to ride again, or dance, or do anything of the things he'd always enjoyed. Jack had said that most amputees could become husbands and fathers, yet how many women would seek out a man so handicapped? How would she herself feel about marrying a man with only one leg?

If it were Jack? Yes, she thought in a rush of warmth, she'd marry him with one leg, or one arm. She was already in love with him, though, and that made a difference. Would Evan allow any woman to come close enough to him, now, to learn to love him? He was bound to be bitter, and he'd never gone through anything to prepare him for this. He was spoiled, had always been spoiled, as all the Stanton children had been spoiled before the war. Whatever Evan had wanted, he'd only to mention it, and it was his. He'd been denied nothing, deprived of nothing, and therefore he had always expected everything. Wealth, health, property, admiration; he'd had it all.

Valerie put aside the tray and sank back into the chair

she'd drawn up to Evan's bedside. She didn't intend to sleep, and was not aware when Julie, and later Jack Ferris, looked in on her.

It was late when she woke. She knew that considerable time had passed because the candles had burned out and there was the gray tint of dawn in the windows across the room. She was stiff and her neck ached; Valerie put up a hand to rub at the sore place and froze in that position.

Evan's eyes were open and he was watching her. Watching her with an expression she had never expected to see on her brother's face. Watching her with hatred.

"Evan—" She breathed his name, and his lips curled back in a snarl that revealed his teeth.

"You bitch," he said clearly. "You let them saw it off."

Appalled, she could not speak.

"I could kill you," Evan said. "I could kill you for letting them do it."

There was such venom in his voice that she was sick, sick enough to feel the vomit rise in her throat, and she struggled against it, pressing her hand over her mouth.

"No! No, Evan, don't say such a terrible thing!"

Ellen stood there in the doorway in her nightclothes, steadying herself with a hand outstretched to each side. Her breast rose and fell too quickly beneath the lawn and lace, her lips trembled. "Don't blame Valerie; it was I who made the decision. I had no choice, Evan, believe me! You would have died!"

"You should have let me die. Who the hell are you, to decide that I'm better off living than dying? I told you," Evan said, his final burst of strength already failing in spite of his determination to speak. "I told you, Val, not to let them do it. I said I'd never forgive you, and you didn't even try to keep them from doing it."

Valerie sat, cold and still, unable to refute what he said. Had she been wrong? Should she have let him die, should she have insisted to Jack and to her mother that no amputation be done?

Ellen saw her stricken face and moved closer to the bed, reaching out to touch Evan's hand. He jerked it away from her, wincing with the pain the movement brought, but she captured it anyway.

"Evan. Darling, you're in no shape now to think through all these things. Only don't blame your sister. It was I who
250

made the decision to take off your leg, because you mean so much to me that I could not let you die. So if you must blame someone, blame me."

"No," Valerie whispered. "No, he's right. It's my fault, because he did tell me. Only I thought that when it was over, he'd—he'd accept it, and we'd—we'd still have him. Evan—"

He ignored the suffering in her voice, turning his face away. "Leave me alone, both of you," he said distinctly, and closed his eyes.

Ellen, her own hurt visible in her eyes, turned from Evan to Valerie. "Come along. I'll send Lallie to sit with him until Hattie comes upstairs." Not until they had passed beyond Evan's hearing did she add, "He will accept, in time. He must, because Mallows needs him."

Valerie made no response to that. For once, she was desperately afraid that her mother was wrong.

The horseman rode into the yard in mid-morning of the following day, carrying dispatch papers for Major Quinn. Pansy ushered him into the entry hall and timidly knocked upon the study door.

"Yes, who is it?"

Pansy opened the door a small crack. "They a soldier here to see you, sir."

"Well, bring him in here," Quinn said, pushing back his chair. "Who is he? What's he want?"

No sooner had Pansy seen the young man closeted with Quinn than she went flying to the kitchen. "He brung papers of some kind! You reckon he got orders? You reckon the Yankees goin' to leave?"

"Praise God, if they do," Mamie said. "You hang around and listen, so you can tell Miss Ellen the good news!"

Pansy did not have to spy to learn what the dispatches contained, however. She was just in time to observe the encounter when Major Quinn and the messenger emerged into the front hallway to confront Captain Ferris.

"Captain, our orders have come. We're to move on to Savannah at once," Quinn told him, in a voice heavy with satisfaction. "How soon can you have your men ready to roll?"

Ferris stared down at his superior officer from the advantage of some eight inches. "Move, sir? A good many of

251

my patients are in no condition to be moved all that way in a wagon."

Astonishment held Quinn silent for only a matter of seconds. "I don't think you heard me, Ferris. The orders say I am to report to Savannah at once."

"The men will die if I move them. Jouncing all that distance in a wagon will reopen wounds that haven't healed. Four of them have pneumonia; exposure to the elements for even a day's traveling could well kill them, too. I respectfully submit, sir, that moving all of these men at this time would be gross neglect. May I suggest, Major Quinn, that you go on ahead with those who are well enough to travel, leaving me enough men to take care of the remaining patients, until they can safely be transferred to Savannah."

Pansy, frightened off at that point by the expression on the major's face, spread the word quickly. The Yankees were leaving.

Valerie was on her way out, having requested the buggy for a trip back to Patrick Ryan's house. They had left supplies there, and had not done more than a quick clean-up; she did not want Ryan to return home to find blood on his tables and floors, his beds slept in and unmade. She had considered having one of the women go with her to do the heavier chores. Yet she wanted nothing less than the company of anyone else at the moment. She had just come from her brother's room and the sickness within her increased when Evan turned his face away from her. He would not respond in any way, and after a few minutes, Valerie left.

She had slept poorly the previous night, sitting in the chair beside Evan's bed. After leaving him, she'd washed and crawled into bed for a few hours, waking when Julie arose at the usual hour. She felt tired and slow, yet returning to bed throughout the day was impossible. What she really wanted, she thought, was to go off by herself and cry.

Pansy's news, blurted out to Ellen and Valerie as they both stood on the covered walkway waiting for the buggy to be brought around, did nothing to elevate Valerie's spirits.

Ellen murmured a "Thank God," but Valerie bit her lip.

"We were safe while they were here," she said. They were leaving. Jack was leaving. Dear Lord, how many blows was she expected to absorb at one time? "What will happen when

252

they've gone? We'll be at the mercy of casual marauders again."

"All that will soon be over," Ellen told her. "Things will be getting back to normal, soon. There's your buggy, dear. Are you sure you don't want one of the women to go along and help you?"

Valerie shook her head, and accepted the reins when Thomas handed them over. Now, more than ever, she wanted to be alone.

She had been working in Patrick Ryan's house for well over an hour when she heard the horse's hooves on the hard-packed earth. Not more bad news, Valerie protested inwardly. She couldn't bear any more bad news today. She glanced around the room, which had been restored to its previous immaculate condition. She had bundled sheets to take them back to Mallows for laundering, having made up the beds with fresh ones from the chest beneath the stairs. If Patrick came home, he would never guess to what use his house had been put.

There was no expected knock on the door; instead it swung inward and Jack Ferris stood there. Something swelled within her chest, a pressure that was almost unendurable.

"Valerie. They told me where you were. Major Quinn has orders to go after Sherman, with as many men as are able to travel."

She stood there facing him, unable to move; he reached her in four quick strides and drew her into his arms.

"Pansy said she told you. But *I* wanted to tell you the rest of it; I'm not going, not until all of the men can safely be transported that distance without harm. I'll be here for a few weeks more, at least."

The pressure burst, leaving her limp with relief. Jack's arms tightened as his mouth sought hers in a passionate kiss that left them both shaken.

"Valerie, I love you. I didn't know how much until that damned messenger came this morning, with orders to evacuate Mallows. It isn't only the patients, it's you. I can't bear to leave you."

All morning she had felt like crying. Now the joy that rushed through her was almost as disabling; she sagged against him, clinging to him, and made no resistance when he scooped her off her feet and carried her toward the nearest of the open bedroom doors.

Jack's lovemaking was expert and tender. Valerie forgot everything except that she loved him, and he loved her, and that he was not leaving Mallows immediately, after all. Knowing those things, she could bear the other, less happy, circumstances.

Three wagonloads of Yankee wounded left Mallows early the following morning. Major Quinn was eager to be gone, taking with him as many men as Jack Ferris had not insisted upon keeping to care for the remaining patients.

"Get some of those lazy niggers in here to do the menial chores," he suggested. "How many patients do you have left, not counting that Rebel with the private room? A dozen?"

"Fourteen," Jack Ferris reported. "Reduced in numbers enough so that they can all be fitted easily into the drawing rooms. It'll make it easier to care for them, certainly, with no stairs to slow things down. I'd like to keep Lieutenant Froedecker, sir, and Corporal Trenton; we'll still need someone to forage for supplies, and he's become an expert at it. Those two, and two of the privates, and we should be able to make out."

"One of the privates," Quinn compromised. "Use the blacks who are already here."

Jack would have agreed to the loss of both privates and Corporal Trenton, to be rid of Major Quinn. The Southerners were not the only ones who were glad to see the procession head out.

Valerie, watching from the upstairs windows, felt her spirits soar. The worst of the Yankees were gone, Jack Ferris remained, and Patrick Ryan's small, neat house offered a trysting place that was both safe and comfortable.

For the moment, it was enough.

Twenty-Eight

The atmosphere at Mallows changed immediately and perceptibly when the main body of Yankee soldiers had gone.

With fewer patients, the work load was lightened to a considerable extent, even though those remaining were the more critically ill. Two of the pneumonia patients died the first week, and were buried with their fellows in the red Georgia clay.

Jack Ferris and Lieutenant Froedecker worked to keep the others alive, including Evan Stanton, who refused to communicate or cooperate with any of them in any way. In spite of the intensive care needed for the remaining dozen patients, there was substantially more free time for everyone, and they made the best possible use of it.

Froedecker, who wanted Julie Stanton very much, was in constant attendance upon her in small ways. He had, by this time, learned of the episode with the Confederate deserters, and he knew that to rush her would be to frighten her off permanently. He could, of course, have simply taken her as part of the victor's spoils, but that was not what he wanted. He knew he had nothing to offer the daughter of this distinguished family, yet irrational hope flickered within him, a hope strong enough to make him shy away from Blossom Curtis when her "regulars" went off with Major Quinn. He knew instinctively that, were Julie to learn of any relationship with Blossom, his hopes of anything between himself and Julie would be at an end. When the need for a woman was too strong, he found relief elsewhere, away from Mallows; and he waited.

For her part, Julie was unaware of Fritz Froedecker's growing regard. She was elated that most of the Yankees had left; she did not particularly fear those who remained, and since she was the one member of the family Evan was not furious with, she spent a good deal of her time with him. Hattie had moved into the house and continued to do much of the actual nursing; Julie saw to Evan's comfort, insofar as that was possible, and spent long hours reading to him, trying to get him to talk, or simply in sitting beside her brother's bed in case he wanted anything.

Valerie lived for the stolen moments at Ryan's house. As the days went by—few of them without the opportunity to slip off through the woods on a walk that now seemed easily accomplished—she felt a bittersweet happiness. The loving was sweet, but the knowledge of what must come was bitter, for eventually, and not long from now, Jack, too, must leave Mallows. She waited for him to speak of it, to say that he would return, or that he would send for her. When he did not, although he told her daily how much he loved her, Valerie could not resist bringing up the matter herself.

"What will happen, when you leave?" she asked one afternoon as they lay close together on Patrick Ryan's bed. "Will you have to stay in the army, or will you be allowed to go home?"

"Not home, not for a while." Jack traced the curve of her cheek with a thumb, then bent his head to kiss her fully on the mouth. "The war isn't over yet, you know. They're still fighting. If I get this batch ready to muster out, they'll send me somewhere else, until it's completely over, and even then there may be extended duty until the wounded are *all* ready to send home. I can't make plans at this stage, sweet; it's all up to the army."

She had to be content with that. Having Jack made the loss of Evan's friendship a little less difficult to bear. And there were plenty of jobs to keep her busy, when she wasn't sneaking off to meet Jack. There had been no new garments at Mallows in a matter of years; they were reduced to handing over curtains and sheets to be cut up for the servants, and their own wardrobes needed mending at virtually every wearing.

Ellen, relieved of some of her duties among the sick, also spent a good deal of time with her son. She ignored his resentments and spoke to him of Mallows, of the things that had been done and needed to be done, asking his advice in an offhand way.

One day Evan turned on her savagely, the pain from his stump unendurable, the frustration more than he could bear. "Don't talk to me of Mallows!" he bellowed in a voice heard clearly by Sally Ann on the other side of the landing, behind a closed door. "I don't give a damn what you do with it! There's nothing *I* can ever do with it again, so leave me alone!"

Ellen shriveled inside, yet held her ground. "I'm sorry, Evan. It isn't true, you know; you can run Mallows from the house, if you have to; it's *you* who are important to us, not your physical body. But if it bothers you, I'll try not to annoy you with mundane matters."

In truth, there were few mundane matters. Everything now was a matter of survival. The weather had grown cold, and in early December it snowed more than an inch, leaving the landscape strange and beautiful. So peaceful, it looked. If only things could be as peaceful as it looked that morning.

Yet there were still Confederates fighting, farther north, and no one knew exactly where Sherman and his hordes were, and Corporal Trenton had stopped foraging for food. He knew the Federals would be at Mallows for very little longer; there was plenty to last. It was easier to sit in the kitchen, soaking up the warmth of the fire, than to travel the countryside looking for food stores that had already been stolen or destroyed.

Ellen, with the instincts of a squirrel, stole and hid away whatever she could from the dwindling supplies. She didn't know if the Yankees would take the remaining stores with them when they left; she knew only that she had one hundred and twelve slaves left to feed, besides those living in the big house, and it would be a long time until next year's harvest. If, indeed, there would be any harvest, or anyone to plant, cultivate, and gather whatever would grow.

She kept herself going on prayer and hope, and on determination that Mallows would once more, someday, be the showplace and producing plantation that it had been. Evan was suffering greatly in a physical way; when his stump had healed, he would see things differently. He would realize that he could still function in many ways, and realize as well how badly she needed him.

Blossom, to her chagrin and anger, was kissed goodbye by each of her paramours with nothing more than fleeting regret. There was no hint from any of them, not from Sergeant Gates or any of the others, that she might eventually follow them back to their Northern farms.

Where was she to go, if Miss Ellen threw her out? With less people about now, less activity, it would be harder to carry on continuing affairs with the remaining Yankees. It would not be so easy to be lost in all that bustling around: The house was locked up at night as if it were a vault instead of an impoverished mansion; getting in and out for a rendez-vous was a risky business. And in the daytime, they kept her too busy. Blossom had never dreamed there would be such quantities of linens to be washed and ironed, furniture to dust, floors to be swept and scrubbed.

Oddly enough, Blossom was one of the few people in the house that Evan seemed to relate to. When she cleaned his room, her artlessly naive remarks evoked more response than anything his mother and sisters said to him. Blossom was not concerned with what happened to Mallows, in the long run; she did not dwell upon it as the center of the universe, as his mother did. Evan, when the pain subsided for a few minutes as it sometimes did, took an interest in this girl who was quite different from any of the girls he had previously known. He spoke to her, and when the pain was great, he tolerated her in the room when he would tolerate no one else.

Ellen observed this, and made her judgment. Evan would never be seriously attracted to a girl of Blossom's class. If, therefore, the girl lightened his days at no danger to Evan, Ellen would close her eyes to it.

She was not, as Valerie thought, totally unaware of the at-traction between her older daughter and Captain Ferris. No one could have watched them without seeing that they were drawn to one another. This match, too, was totally un-suitable, and caused Ellen more concern. She looked forward to the day when Captain Ferris would be gone. He would rehim for some assurance that the parting would be no more than temporary. He had no assurances to give her. The following morning, at dawn, the last of the Yankees rode away from Mallows.

turn to his wealthy family in New York, and Valerie would get over him.

Ellen did not, however, suspect that the relationship had gone beyond one of languishing looks. Any young woman dreams of romance—herself excepted—and Valerie would naturally be attracted to a good-looking young man, especially one who had tried to do so much for her brother. When Ferris had gone, the matter would be at an end. Valerie was well brought up and intelligent; Ellen totally discounted the hot blood of youth, because she had never felt it and had observed it primarily in the lower classes.

She observed, as well, the way that Lieutenant Froedecker looked at Julie. This was of no concern at all, since Julie was clearly oblivious of it, which was as it should be. Lieutenant Froedecker, also, would soon be gone forever.

Sally Ann received word in early December that her Ward had expired of pneumonia and deprivation in a Yankee prison. She took the news as quietly as she had taken everything else; she was no more than a frail wraith, moving about the house more freely now that some of the enemy soldiers were gone, saying little, eating less. Had it not been for Hugh Alexander, Ellen suspected she would have wasted away to nothing.

As it was, the baby continued to thrive and grow on Gilly's rich milk. He was a happy child, much fussed over by the household of women. One day Blossom brought him in to show him to Evan, who had commented on his crying. Evan, with no hope of ever fathering a child of his own, did not want to look at him, nor talk about him. Blossom did not bring him again.

Lacy continued to share the room with Sally Ann and the baby. It was Dolly who regained the privacy of a separate room when Major Quinn vacated his. And they all regained the upper sitting room; if the remaining officers sometimes joined them there, why, no one was any longer frightened by this. For the most part, Dolly had it to herself, where she sat and rocked and knitted for as long as the worsted held out to work with.

Lallie waited to hear from Aaron. She was worn out from working so hard, and like the other young women, she longed for a better, easier life, and romance. Not the animal coupling of a slave expected to produce another valuable slave, but the affectionate loving that was as possible between a man and a woman of color as between whites. She did not love Aaron, but she depended upon him to get her away from here, to some distant city where she might find love and security and freedom.

Christmas drew near. The holiday had always been a festive one, and even last year, with war raging and nothing to do with, they had managed a celebration of sorts. In December of 1864, they again made an effort. For the baby's sake, they ought to do something, Ellen said. Even if he didn't remember his first Christmas, they should be able to tell him about it.

Gifts were, of necessity, handmade. Embroidered handkerchiefs, stockings, aprons. Small things of no value except for the sentiment behind them. All lavished their maternal instincts upon Hugh Alexander; he was presented with booties and sweaters and a lap robe and bonnets, until Sally Ann had to smile, a little.

Firewood became as precious as food. The snow melted after one day, but the cold remained. The Yankees had made no effort to put in a supply of fuel beyond what would be required for their own needs. Chad and Thomas were set to work felling and chopping trees at the edge of the forest; the pine was quickly burned and did not put out as much heat as hard woods would have done, yet it came more easily to hand.

A few days before Christmas, although the inhabitants of Mallows did not know it, Sherman's forces entered Savannah.

The small Confederate force remaining in the city, under the command of General William J. Hardee, could do nothing to hold the city against the invasion, and prudently withdrew across the Savannah River rather than surrender. This left the city open for the taking.

Its citizens, well aware of the fate of Atlanta, met to consider how they might spare their own city such a holocaust. If Sherman burned the forty thousand bales of cotton sitting in their warehouses, as he could be expected to do, a good part of the rest of the city would go up in flames as well. And so they devised an unorthodox and clever plan. They would greet General Sherman as a guest, offer him Southern hospitality, and make him a gift of the cotton.

What man would burn his own cotton?

The general was offered, as well, the house of Charles

Green, on Macon Street, to use as his headquarters f long as he had need of it. Here, too, the Savannah merc and cotton factors saved face as well as avoiding invitin hated officer into their own homes. For although the h was one of the finest in the city, its owner was a British ject, not a Georgian. Mr. Green gave a party for the Fed officers, and with so many of the military present it was too obvious that few members of local society attended.

Sherman was made welcome, and he would have bee churlish dog, indeed, if he had rewarded Savannah by sett it to the torch. He did not, and the city was one of the few the South to escape the ravages of war.

The news of the occupation of Savannah did not rea Mallows until New Year's. By then their pitiful celebrati was over and forgotten; they had resumed the grim struggl Only Valerie, of them all, found any reason for happines and that was tempered by the knowledge that it must soon end.

The patients in the dwindling infirmary either died or recovered. And the day came at the end of January 1865 when Jack Ferris met Valerie for the final tryst at Ryan's place. He didn't tell her until they lay, warm and sated with their mutual loving, beneath the colorful quilt, late one afternoon. The sunlight streamed through the muslin curtains at the window, and there was the promise of a shared cup of tea from the water simmering over the fire in the kitchen.

Valerie stretched lazily, languorously, turning to him for one last kiss before she left his side to brew the tea, when he drew her close with unexpected violence, burying his face her auburn hair.

"What is it? Why are you . . . Jack? Jack?"

"We leave tomorrow," he said into her hair. "Fritz seeing to the loading of the wagons right now. I can't d any longer, there's no medical reason why the survivors travel."

She pushed him away so that she could see his face mentarily stupefied. "Tomorrow! But you didn't tell me .

"I didn't want to spoil it any sooner than I had to. D you don't think I want to go, do you? I'm a soldier, I take orders, and my orders were to follow after Q soon as my patients could be moved. I've already several days longer than I should have, because of you

Valerie clung to him, willing herself not to cry, r

Book II

Valerie walked through the house with Ellen and Julie, assessing the damage, adjusting to the freedom, for the first time in months, of having the place to themselves. The atmosphere of Mallows had altered at once, when the Yankees were gone. Voices sounded different in empty rooms. Feminine voices, only feminine voices.

In a way, Valerie was as glad as the others to be rid of them, except for Jack. He hadn't even kissed her goodbye, not really. He couldn't have done so at dawn, in front of everybody, of course. He might have sought her out last night, though, for a private moment. He had not.

She had stood with the others on the piazza to watch them off, biting her tongue to keep from begging him to write to her. She had not dared to do that in front of anyone else, either, and now she was sorry. He had told her he loved her, he'd made passionate love to her, and she knew that he cared. He would surely write to her, or come back, when he could. Reason told her to leave it at that, not to press for promises he might not be able to keep.

Yet now, trailing after the others into the big drawing rooms that opened into one another so emptily, Valerie wished with all her heart that she'd been brave enough to say

265

something to Jack, to win the assurance that this parting was not permanent.

Blossom, appearing from the kitchen end of the house carrying a cup of coffee in one hand (a practice frowned upon by Ellen, for fear of spills), looked down at the drawing room carpets.

"It's a shame, ma'am, what they done to your rugs. You think you can ever get those stains out?"

"I don't know. We'll have to try. We certainly can't replace the carpets, not before harvest next fall." Ellen paused to run a hand over a deep scratch mark on the door frame. "It will take years, when we have the money again, to set things to rights. The floors are in terrible shape, what with all those men running in and out. They'll have to be completely refinished by experts."

She looked up at the tall windows where the pale gold draperies were beginning to show splits in the fabric; the lower part of the hangings, where they had come in contact with the men who had lain on the floor, were soiled, perhaps beyond repair.

"Well, we'll have the men bring the furniture back inside. We can't heat this part of the house, and we won't attempt to use it before summer, but the furniture may be safer here than in the quarters. Perhaps it would be best, for now, to leave the piano in the entry hall, where it is. We can't exactly heat that, either, but we'll be going in and out of heated rooms, opening doors, so it should be drier there than back in the drawing room."

That first morning after the enemy soldiers had gone, that was all Ellen did. Walk through her beloved home, and touch gentle fingers to scratches, gouges, and stains. Few things were actually broken so as to need replacement, but virtually every floor and wall had sustained damage. Not because there had been deliberate vandalism, for the Yankees had not been like the crew that burned Cedars. They were men, however, with a casual disregard for the property of anyone else; and the care of desperately wounded men had taken priority over any concern with house or furnishings. Only in the study, which had been Major Quinn's private domain, was there no damage to be found at all.

If Ellen wept at what had happened to her house, she did it in private. The others, knowing the suffering over it was greater for her than for them, watched in understanding silence and admiration.

For Ellen drew herself visibly together at the end of the inspection tour, and once again took charge. Orders went out for the return of the stored furniture, and the closing off of such rooms as could be left unheated. The Yankees had left them less than a week's supply of firewood, and that was an immediate concern. Some of the old men, who were all who remained except for a few young boys like Thomas and Chad, were also put to work sawing and chopping. The women who lived alone in the quarters would be expected to chop what they needed for their own cabins. Small children could be put to work carrying the wood once it had been cut into the proper lengths for burning.

The library, the study, the big dining room, as well as the double drawing rooms, were all closed off. Fires would be kept in the kitchen, and in the breakfast room that served them all as a dining area, and in the upstairs sitting room. Everything else must stay unheated until spring, even Evan's bedroom.

If anyone found solace in the fact that Mallows had survived relatively untouched, compared to Cedars and other homes of their neighbors, no mention was made of it.

Life without the Yankees became infinitely more difficult.

Without Corporal Trenton to forage for the kitchen, supplies rapidly sank to the pre-Yankee level, except for a few staples Mamie and Ellen had managed to hide. Behind them were the comparatively lavish meals Mamie had been able to produce with the corporal's assistance.

Egg production among the "borrowed" chickens had fallen off to no more than a few eggs a day. Ham and egg breakfasts were only a pleasant memory. It was Valerie who spoke out boldly about the remaining eggs, before Dolly's delicate stomach could again come into the picture.

"If there are only a few eggs, it seems to me they should be shared," she told Ellen bluntly. "Grandma Lacy's older than Grandma Dolly, and though she doesn't complain as much about her health, it doesn't mean she's any more sturdy. Let's save the eggs until there are enough for each of us, or for an omelette to be shared, or put them into custards or cakes, as long as the sugar holds out. I don't think we ought to go back to old bad habits just because we once gave all the eggs to Grandma Dolly."

Ellen said nothing; when Julie added her own quiet opinion, echoing her sister, Ellen turned and walked away. Mamie, however, nodded her head.

"You right. It ain't fair, one person should git all the eggs. If they's invalids in this house, it be Mr. Evan and Miss Sally Ann."

Neither of the invalids named made any special demands. Indeed, Sally Ann did not seem to care whether she ate or not, and Evan picked at his food, too.

They watched Evan closely for signs of infection. The wound created by his amputation was a terrible one; it was usually Ellen and Hattie who changed the dressings, and Ellen prayed earnestly that it would heal properly. If Captain Ferris had not taken all the diseased tissue, there would be no one to do anything about it now. Evan would die, as they had watched other men die, of gangrene.

It seemed to Valerie that she was constantly cold. Her outer garments were threadbare; they allowed the wind and the chill to go right to her bones. Her shoes were so thin she could feel every stone, every ridge of shell, when she walked out along the drive.

Yet the cold she felt on the surface was nothing to what she felt within. How had they borne it, all those women whose men had gone off to war? How could they give them up, even in a righteous cause? Had her mother felt this way, when Roger Stanton rode off to fight? And Frances Douglas, about her husband? Both of them had gone off, never to return, and there were thousands more like them whose widows knew the bottomless pit of grief that could surely never be assuaged.

With all that agony, the air should be full of it, Valerie thought. She felt as if she could reach out and touch it, the sharp, cutting edge of the pain of loss. Yet Jack Ferris was not dead. He had only gone on with his duties of caring for the wounded and the sick. The chances were that he would survive what remained of the war, and that he would come back for her. Although he hadn't said so, she had to believe it, to warm her cold body with the hope that Jack would return.

With the bedrooms emptied of Yankees, sleeping arrangements were adjusted. Lacy moved out of Sally Ann's room into her old room at the northwest corner of the house. Ellen and Dolly returned to the rooms they had occupied for years.

Henriette settled into the center bedroom on the east side of the house, the least desirable room available, yet far superior to the tiny room from which Blossom had been temporarily evacuated on the level between floors.

That left Julie and Valerie together in Valerie's own room.

It was, no doubt, the logical distribution of the bedrooms. Evan was in Julie's old room, so she could not return to that. Yet Valerie chafed under the company she did not want. She wanted to be free to throw herself across the bed and cry without being asked why. She yearned to be allowed to sit in her own chair, looking out over the wintry landscape, dreaming about Jack Ferris and the life they would someday have together, without interruption.

And Valerie lay at night beside her sleeping sister, so acutely aware of the needs of her newly awakened body that this, in itself, was a deep, intense ache she could not put aside.

Once, as she ran her fingers lightly over her own breasts and then down her flanks, imagining Jack's caress, Julie stirred and asked, "Val? What're you doing? You keep moving!"

"I'm sorry. I'm just restless tonight," Valerie said, heart thudding.

She did not continue to move her stroking fingers until Julie's breathing took on the regular rhythm of sleep. Resentment surged through her, that she had not the privacy of her own bed, the freedom of her own thoughts in this way. She knew, too, that there was no one she could talk to about this.

Ellen, Valerie was convinced, had never known these powerful emotions, these strong sensual stirrings that would not be denied. Ellen, despite the evidence of three living children, remained cool, aloof, untouched by animal desires. She not only would have no understanding of what her daughter was experiencing, she would have refused to listen to a mention of it, and condemned the wicked thoughts.

Julie, though less frequently visited by nightmares of being raped, would not understand, either. She had no longing to be held by a man, to be made love to; her idea of "romance" was a chaste kiss, or perhaps a mere touching of hands. She would be stunned to know that her sister had not only made love, she had wildly, joyously sought each lovemaking.

Sally Ann? Sally Ann had known the love of a man. She continued to grieve for her Ward in silence. Sally Ann, perhaps, would know how she felt, had perhaps suffered in the same way herself. (Did one lose the overwhelming desire, during pregnancy? Valerie didn't know, but she doubted it. It was too wonderful, drowning willingly in those marvelous sensations, and surely carrying a child did not change that!) Yet Sally Ann had lost her husband, and could not expect ever to know his lovemaking again—perhaps not with any other man, either—and it would be unspeakable cruelty to remind her of that.

Of them all, the women in the household, only Blossom was likely to remain unshocked at the mention of raw emotions. Blossom, too, knew and reveled in the things a man could do with a woman. Blossom as a confidante, however, did not tempt Valerie. Blossom was as earthy as a barnyard animal; there was not one man in her life, but half a dozen or more, and she didn't love any of them. Certainly not the way Valerie loved Jack Ferris. There was nothing in common between herself and Blossom except that both enjoyed making love.

With all of the men now gone, except the few blacks who remained in the quarters, Blossom was, indeed, feeling the lack. The only male on the premises, the only white male, was Evan Stanton.

That he was not an immediate candidate for sexual liaisons was obvious. His pain seldom left him; and his disposition improved little through the long cold days of January. Ellen suggested that he might, with help, get to the sitting room, where there was a fire, and company. His surly reply dismissed the company, though he would have welcomed the fire. His unheated bedroom defied comfort; he must keep himself piled with quilts and comforters, and since he could bear nothing touching the stump of his leg—even the dressings felt weighty—Hattie had rigged a frame to keep the pressure of the covers off from it. This had the effect that he constantly felt cold, as he would not have done with the blankets tucked more closely around his limbs.

The worst of it, for Evan, was that he still felt the amputated foot. Several times he actually threw back the covers and stared at the point where the foot should have been. How could it be, when the damned thing was missing, that he could feel the pain in it? In the foot, and in the leg, the pain that made him clench his teeth to keep from screaming?

Captain Ferris had left laudanum to supplement Ellen's

vanishing supply; a dose of it sometimes got him through the eternity of night with a reasonable amount of sleep. On Ferris's orders, however, Ellen was reducing the dosage, and refused to give it to him at all during the day. He might have hauled himself out of bed, and dragged himself across the floor, to reach Ellen's supply of the opiate, if he hadn't known she kept it locked up.

Blossom did not seem to mind his outbursts of bad temper. She had tended old Mrs. Masterson long enough to know how crotchety invalids were; and this patient had far more in the way of looks and potential charm than Mrs. Masterson. If he threw something at her—a glass that shattered—Blossom picked up the pieces without comment. Evan would not apologize in so many words. Some of the fury would go out of his speech, however, and they would go along as if nothing had happened.

One day when she was passing by his open doorway, Evan called out to her. "Blossom, come in and talk to me!"

"Yes, sir," she agreed. "What do you want to talk about?"

He stared at her in exasperation. "Can't you think of a subject on your own?"

"No, sir. I ain't had much reason to think up things to talk to a gentleman about."

"Well, what do you talk to non-gentlemen about? You must have encountered ordinary men somewhere along the way. Anybody who looks like you do is bound to have met men. What do you talk to them about?"

Blossom evaluated this and decided it would be better not to be entirely truthful. "Nothin' interestin'," she evaded. "They mostly likes to talk about themselves."

"And they're not interesting?"

Blossom shrugged. "They're soldiers, or farmers. They talk about battles, or guns, or breedin' pigs. No, they ain't very interestin'."

"What do you like to read, then? Tell me the last thing you read, what it was about."

Blossom eased inside the room, standing at the foot of the bed to face him. His dark brows nearly met at the bridge of his nose; his brown eyes were penetrating enough to be disconcerting.

"I never read nothin'," she told him. "I don't know how to read."

"You never learned?"

"No. That old woman I worked for didn't want me to go to school. She said she needed me to work all day, every day, waitin' on her. I can sign my name—B. Curtis—and that's all." She didn't feel inferior because of this lack of ability; she knew more people who couldn't read and write than ones who could.

"How'd you like to learn?" Evan asked.

"Sir?"

"I said, how'd you like to learn? To read and write?"

She considered that, scratching absently at her head through the thick fair hair. "Be a lot of work, wouldn't it? And I don't know what use it would be."

"You could read to me," Evan suggested. Once the idea had taken root, his enthusiasm grew, an enthusiasm long dormant. "There are hundreds of books downstairs, you could read them to me."

"Miss Julie reads to you," Blossom pointed out. "And your mama."

"Pap," Evan dismissed it. "You could read me whatever I wanted to hear, not that drivel they think appropriate for an invalid. Bring me a book, Blossom, and I'll teach you to read."

Usually she did exactly as he told her. This time, however, she hesitated. "I don't think I want to learn to read, Mr. Evan."

"Damn it! I said bring me a book!"

She hesitated a moment longer, then turned away, only to be stopped by the bellow that followed her onto the landing.

"And not the Bible, you understand? Bring me something that doesn't mouth platitudes!"

Blossom had no idea what a platitude was. She was reluctant to be pushed into this astonishing new project, because it sounded like work. On the other hand, Miss Ellen seemed pleased when she did anything that kept Mr. Evan contented, if you could call not yelling at people being contented. And maybe learning to read would be easier than going out and chopping wood in the cold, with old socks over her hands because she had no mittens.

It occurred to her, going down the broad stairway carefully so that the ragged soles of her shoes wouldn't make her trip, that it might not be a bad idea, after all, to learn to read. Mr. Evan was going to be in that bed for a long time yet. And when he got up, he was still going to be confined to the house. If he liked her, and wanted to spend time with her, maybe he'd want to do more than teach her to read.

Excitement kindled a warmth that grew and spread within her. Sure, why not? Most women weren't going to want a man with only one leg—given a choice, Blossom herself would have preferred someone like Patrick Ryan, with two good legs and everything else a woman admires in a man— but marrying a man like Evan would have its advantages. He was going to inherit Mallows, wasn't he? Of course, Miss Ellen wasn't all that old, and she'd probably stay mistress as long as she was alive, but that was all right. Let her run things, tell the servants what to do, and plan the meals. Blossom didn't care about those things.

As for the physical side of marriage, why, she'd learned enough to know that there were other positions in which to make love than the one that was most customary. Having only one leg needn't prevent Evan from making love. It made her feel peculiar, to think of doing it with a man who had only a stump for a leg. Yet no doubt she'd get used to it, after a while, and it would be worth it, wouldn't it? To be married to the man who owned Mallows? The idea grew more stimulating, the longer she thought about it. It was going to be hard for Mr. Evan to meet any young women; she'd have the inside track, there, from the start. And if knowing how to read and write would make her more acceptable as a wife, why, it would be worth the effort.

She had seldom been in the library. It was very cold in there, the hearth giving off nothing but an acrid odor, and she didn't linger. She reached for the book that came most easily to hand; she knew it wasn't the Bible. That was a big thick book with a black cover that was not on the shelves at all but lay open on its own table in the corner. This one had a red cover with gold printing, an elegant volume, and not too thick. She closed the library door behind her and raced back up the stairs as fast as her flapping shoe soles would allow.

"Here. I brung this one," Blossom said, handing it over to Evan. "Is it all right?"

Evan read the title aloud. *"The Scarlet Letter.* Well, my mother might not think so, but it'll do," he said, and laughed.

Blossom had never heard him laugh before. There was a

273

peculiar quality to it that made her uneasy, and she didn't understand what was funny.

She drew up a chair beside the bed, as Evan directed, and stared with grave misgivings at the meaningless marks on the opened page.

Two

If they had thought to see the last of the Yankees, they were soon disillusioned about their new security from abuse.

The blue-coated soldiers swarmed into the yard and onto the piazza, the thick red mud tracking across the marble steps and the white-paneled planking. They did not wait for the front door to be opened for them; four men pushed through it into the entry hall to be confronted by Ellen at her most regal at the top of the stairs.

"What do you want?" She regarded them with no outward sign of her inward quaking.

"What you-all got?" one of them asked, with an exaggerated imitation of a Southern accent. "We'll take just about anything, ma'am."

She saw at once that there were no officers among them. How many, all together? A dozen?

"I have a letter," she said clearly, "signed by Captain Jack Ferris, stating that this household is not to be disturbed by Union soldiers."

"Have you, now?" The first speaker turned to his nearest comrade. "You know a Captain Jack Ferris, Jake?"

"Never heard of him. I can't read nohow, so what difference does it make?"

Ellen began to descend the stairs, slowly, gracefully. "I suggest that you wait until one of you who can read, does so, before you touch a thing in my house. We have performed a service for the Union Army, in having a hospital in our house and in assisting in the care of injured Union soldiers; in return, we were promised immunity from depredation by your men."

They hesitated, slowed both by her note of authority and by her words. "What's depredation?" one of them muttered.

"I think it means wrecking their place. OK, lady, let's see your letter," the leader agreed.

When Jack suggested writing the letter, Ellen had thought it unlikely they'd have need of it, for had not Sherman's troops already passed through Tattnall County?

It seemed not all of them had. From the unkempt, almost slovenly appearance of these men, it was easy to guess that they were stragglers, under no particular command, and therefore perhaps not answerable to anyone for their actions. Indeed, without knowing who they were, it would be impossible to report them with any expectation that they would receive even a reprimand, no matter how much damage they did. Certainly General Sherman had so far shown no concern for the people of Georgia.

She came down the stairs, walked between the men into the study, and came back with the letter Captain Ferris had signed. He had a bold, strong hand, clearly legible; the leader of the Yankees read it haltingly.

"Well, that's what it says, all right. We ain't supposed to burn the place down. Shame," he added, glancing around him. "This'd sure make a pretty bonfire."

Dear God, Ellen prayed. *Not now. Not when it's nearly over. Don't let them burn anything.*

"It don't say nothin' about gettin' ourselves somethin' to eat, does it?"

"I don't care about no damned letter," one of the men said. "I'm hungry, and I'm takin' what I find. Come on, where's the pantry in this place?"

Everyone except Ellen and Mamie remained upstairs, out of sight. They could hear the booted feet, the raised voices as the men found things they took a fancy to. Pictures were removed from the walls. Books were tumbled out of their shelves and kicked about, pages torn out and footprints left on them. The candles in evidence were confiscated.

276

The worst damage was done in the kitchen and the pantry. They filled their pockets and their knapsacks and whatever containers they could find with the riches of the Mallows storerooms.

"Thank God some of it was still hidden." Ellen's inspection tour, when the men had gone without doing any more damage, was disheartening, yet not totally a matter of despair. "From now on, we'll keep food hidden, except for a few days' supply at a time. What did they do outside?"

"They try to start the corncrib afire," Pansy reported. "Only they didn't stay long enough to see if it going to burn. The boys put it out. They don't even look in the cotton shed; I reckon they thought that already been stole or burned."

They had gotten off better than most of their neighbors.

The Gundersons, from just beyond what was left of Cedars, came to say goodbye. They were a decent, sober family whose pre-war holdings had been on a small scale compared to Mallows. There was nothing left, Calvin Gunderson told them.

Ellen had invited the family of parents and four young children in for a farewell cup of what remained of the Yankee coffee. The day was a fine one, with a few scattered clouds in a bright sky; the Gundersons left a wagon piled high with belongings to trudge through the echoing entryway to the welcome heat of the breakfast room.

"We just wanted to tell you, case anyone comes looking for us," Calvin Gunderson said. "We don't know what's happened to Rosemary's people; there might be some of them left, over around Augusta. If they come, tell them we're heading west."

"West," Ellen repeated. "To anywhere in particular?"

"No. But I hear there's good land out there, free for the taking, if a man wants to start from scratch. I reckon that's what we're going to do. Head west, until we come to a good stopping place."

"You've done so much with your own place," Ellen said slowly. "You have a nice house and a good barn, and . . ."

"Had," Gunderson said. His mouth was grim. "They burned the barn and what was left of my cotton. Burned the hay and the corn. Stole just about everything else."

"Not your house, they didn't burn the house—?"

"Might as well have." Rosemary Gunderson was a small, quiet woman of thirty-two. Ellen had never heard her speak

277

with such bitterness. "That rabble that came through here yesterday destroyed everything but the outside walls. What they couldn't carry away with them, they smashed."

"You have the land—"

"What's it going to be worth, with nobody to work it? We got but one slave left, Abraham, and he's decided to go along with us, west. The rest of them all ran off, and from now on it'll depend on hired labor. I don't have any cash to pay anybody. The boys are getting big enough to help, so we'll take our chances out west. I have a notion the Yankees are going to hold this war against us for a long time, Mrs. Stanton. It's not going to be easy or pleasant to live here, the way it's going to be. I'm not a stiff-necked man, but I'll be damned if I'll bow down and lick the boots of those blue bellies, begging your pardon, ma'am, for the frank words. And that's what they'll expect us to do."

His words troubled Ellen long after the Gundersons had gone. Was he right? Was it going to be impossible to work a plantation unless one had cash to pay wages? How could she raise cash to get next summer's crop in, and worked, and harvested?

There was the silver that had been in her family for more than a hundred years. When things began to settle down she could dig that up and sell it, although in a way it would be like selling a child. There was also a small quantity of paper money hidden away, though not enough to cover more than a few basic supplies. Shoes were an immediate need, for the servants in particular, since none of them had had spares to begin with and now were, some of them, wrapping their feet in rags when they had to be outside.

The women in the big house were a little better off. They had all had fragile things intended for use in the house and at parties. When they were forced to work in the cotton, those shoes quickly wore out and fell apart, until now the inhabitants of Mallows were a ludicrous lot, with Dolly reduced to house slippers (which didn't matter quite so much as the predicament of the others) and Valerie and Julie in footwear designed to be worn with elegant bouffant gowns instead of simple cotton dresses.

Henriette had written to her relatives in New Orleans and Milledgeville; she was doing everything she knew to contact some family connection who would offer her a refuge. There had so far been no response, and Ellen never considered saying anything to make the girl feel unwelcome. If Henriette's position had been reversed, and it had been Ellen's daughters who were left homeless, she knew the Douglases would have taken them in with sympathy and affection. Yet every mouth at Mallows was another to be fed on the dwindling provisions, another body to be clad and shod.

Ellen regarded Blossom Curtis in quite a different light from that in which Henriette Douglas stood. She owed Blossom thanks for having rescued Grace and Sally Ann and the baby. Yet how much did that entail? Was she, for the sake of a wagon ride months ago, to continue to look after the girl indefinitely?

Ellen quite frankly did not like Blossom. She found her earthy frankness embarrassing; her bulging bodice distasteful; and even though the Yankees had gone and there could no longer be any liaisons there (Ellen did not know for certain how many men had been involved, so suspected the worst), there was still Evan.

She would have chosen almost anyone except Blossom to spend time with Evan. Since he did not want anyone else, however, and their time together was limited by the slowness of Evan's progress in recovering both from the amputation and from months of malnutrition, Ellen hesitated to interfere. Evan had some absurd idea about teaching the girl to read and write, which ranked in Ellen's mind on a par with such teaching for Negroes; it might give the silly chit ideas above her station in life, ideas that could never translate to any elevation in status and would, therefore, be more harmful than otherwise.

The lesson sessions were not very long; Evan was in considerable pain, and short of temper. Through the open doorway, he could often be heard berating Blossom for her stupidity in grasping what he sought to convey. Once or twice he threw the book across the room; Blossom became quiet on those occasions, retrieving the book and smoothing the crumpled pages.

"Get out!" Evan would bellow, and Blossom would leave the room, apparently realizing that the frustration was as much from pain as from disgust with his pupil. The following day, the lessons would be picked up once more.

Ellen would have been considerably more disturbed about Blossom and Evan than she was if she'd guessed Blossom's thoughts about marrying the crippled heir to Mallows. As it

279

was, the idea that Blossom would aspire to such heights never occurred to her. Her own belief in Evan's good sense and good taste would have caused her to reject the notion had anyone brought it to her attention.

Ellen's confidence in Evan's sense and taste, however, extended only to the matter of choosing a proper wife. It was not marriage that concerned her, it was whatever relationship might develop between her son and this girl when he was well enough to think about such things. She was not completely blinded to the fact that men, even her precious son, had an earthy sexuality (although the word was not one she would ever have thought, let alone spoken). For the present, Evan could not possibly do anything but lie in bed. She doubted that he was within months of feeling well enough to do so much as think about pinching a well-rounded bottom as it passed; it would only be when his suffering receded that she need take the move to get Blossom away from him.

Had the girl had anyone to take her in, any relative or friend, Ellen would have had little compunction about encouraging Blossom to go. As it was, knowing Blossom was completely alone in the world, untrained for anything but house service in an area where domestic services were almost entirely the province of black women, it was difficult to see what could be done about her. She was, in a sense, no more than a child, and a responsible person did not turn a child out of house and home.

Ellen's concern about Blossom and Evan was tempered by her relief that Jack Ferris was out of the house. That there had been a growing attachment for him on Valerie's part could not have escaped her notice; if the girl moped now that he was gone, why, Valerie would get over it. And eventually there would be someone suitable, both for Valerie and for Julie.

Newspapers were once more being distributed from Atlanta, and once in a while one found its devious way to Mallows, so they had some idea what was going on around them. President Lincoln had been re-elected, a fact that promised little for the tottering South. The war, virtually over in Georgia except for the roving guerrilla bands who preyed upon whomever they encountered, without regard for politics, had moved north. Hood, who might have harassed Sherman's forces, chose instead to strike out for Nashville, a disastrous
280

move in a series of disasters that brought the war closer to its end.

Though postal service had not been fully resumed, a few letters began to trickle through, to be eagerly pounced upon by those anxious for news of their loved ones and friends. Ellen, who had no relatives other than distant cousins except for those under her own roof, was pleased to learn of the survival of at least part of them. Valerie, so tense that she was nearly sick to her stomach whenever a letter appeared, in anticipation of a letter from Jack Ferris, had to go off by herself to conquer her disappointment when there was nothing.

It was in anticipation of news that she hurried into the entry hall one afternoon when Pansy's screech notified the household of the impending arrival of a visitor.

With Aaron no longer a watchdog, strangers now sometimes had put a foot to the front steps before alerting those within. Pansy reached the door only split seconds before the new arrival and was breathing heavily when she opened the door to him.

"Good afternoon, sir," she said, her apprehension easing as she saw that he wore the remnants of a Confederate uniform and that he carried himself like a gentleman, hat in hand.

"Good afternoon. May I speak to the mistress of this place?"

His voice was soft, well educated, and quite without aggression. Valerie, listening from the dining room, stepped forward to invite him in.

"I'm Valerie Stanton, sir. My mother is not in the house at the moment, I think, but I'll send someone to the quarters for her."

He was tall and very thin; he had been, and would be again, an extraordinarily good-looking young man; she guessed his age at no more than mid-twenties, although it was hard to tell with any degree of accuracy, when a man had been inadequately fed for a period of time.

Pansy reached for his hat, and he handed it over like one used to such small services, at least in the distant past.

"Galen Battersby, ma'am." His lean face revealed anxiety. "From Milledgeville, and on my way there now. I recently had word from my mother there with a request that I inquire about her cousins in Tattnall County when I passed through. Mrs. Frances Douglas. I've just come from the burned-out re-

281

mains of their house, and am in hopes that you've better news for me than that leads me to expect."

Valerie caught her breath. "Mr. Battersby—please come in. There's a fire back here, and Pansy will bring us something hot to drink." And then, capitulating to the worry in his eyes, "I'm afraid my news is not good, sir. Your cousins were the victims of a band of marauding Yankees some months ago. Mrs. Douglas . . ."

She could not quite speak the words, and Galen Battersby's mouth tightened.

"All of them? All dead?"

"All but Henriette," Valerie admitted. She wished she did not have to see the effect of this. "She's here, in the breakfast room, I think. We'd just been having tea."

"All of them but Henriette." He repeated her phrase softly. "That is bitter news, indeed, to take to my mother."

Henriette, hearing voices, had risen to her feet and appeared now in the doorway before them. For a moment she did not react except with curiosity. And then, as recognition of this emaciated figure seeped through her, she gave a small cry and flung herself into his arms.

"Galen! Galen, it *is* you! You're safe, you're alive!"

He held her awkwardly, looking over her head at Valerie as Henriette collapsed in a paroxysm of weeping.

"She's been through a great deal," Valerie said, in a classic understatement. "Up to now, she hasn't given way like this; perhaps it's what she needs, distressing though it is to the rest of us."

Henriette, gasping, accepted the linen square that Valerie produced and mopped at her wet face. "I'm sorry, I am distressing you, aren't I? I'm sorry. But they're all gone—Mama and Daddy and the boys and Charlotte—and I hadn't heard anything from anyone, I didn't know if I had a blood relative left anywhere in the world—"

She made a valiant effort to bring herself under control, even attempting a pathetic watery smile as she led Galen Battersby into the heated room so that the door could be closed against the chill of the rest of the house.

"Galen was one of my favorite cousins, when we were children and we all went to Grandma Douglas's house outside of Milledgeville," she told Valerie. Tears continued to stream from her dark eyes and she dabbed at them with the already
282

sodden handkerchief. "I haven't seen him in—oh, it must be nearly four years! You're so thin, Galen!"

His mouth twisted briefly in wry amusement. "I've done better than most, at that. At least I escaped injury, during a summer when men were dying of gangrene because of infected mosquito bites as well as gunshot wounds. I think as many died of sickness as of injuries, this past year, and we'd no more to eat than was necessary to keep us alive."

"Please, Mr. Battersby, sit down close to the fire," Valerie urged. "Pansy, bring our guest some tea, and then tell Mamie he'll need something to eat, as well. It won't be elaborate, I'm afraid, sir, but at least we haven't yet gone actually hungry."

"Then you're luckier than most." He took the indicated chair, turning it from the table so as to stretch out his long legs toward the open hearth. "I don't want to deprive you of your own rations, Miss Stanton. Tea would be sufficient in itself."

"There's no nourishment in tea, and we've plenty of plain fare," Valerie assured him. Now that he was seated and she looked at him more fully, she wondered if he were ill. His hand trembled as he accepted the teacup.

Henriette had drawn up a chair to face him, close enough so that her knees nearly touched his thigh, and reached out a hand to grasp his. She barely restrained herself from recoiling from it.

"You're burning up! You have a fever!"

"I'm all right," Galen Battersby said. And then he put the lie to this statement by a violent burst of uncontrollable shaking so that he had to put the teacup down or drop it.

"He's ill!" Henriette lifted a pleading countenance toward Valerie. "He can't go on toward home like this!"

"No, of course he can't." Valerie turned toward Pansy, who was just coming through the doorway with a plate of cold cornbread and slices of the previous night's ham. "I think perhaps soup would be more appropriate for our guest, Pansy. And then run for my mother. I think we should offer Mr. Battersby a bed until he's feeling better."

"I'll be fine, I can't put you to any such inconvenience," Galen said through chattering teeth. "It will stop in a moment, it usually does."

"It's happened before, then! Valerie's right, you should be put to bed and dosed with something—Mrs. Stanton is an excellent nurse, almost as good as a doctor, really! She'll help you, won't she, Val?"

"Yes, of course."

She kept her misgivings to herself, as to how Ellen would look on having yet another mouth to feed, another invalid to care for. If it were Evan, she'd want someone to care for him. She would do it for this young man, too. Yet Valerie couldn't help thinking of the shrinking food supplies, and wondering how long they could go on taking in strays without going hungry themselves.

Three

Ellen had gone down to the quarters in the crisp, bright morning, shawl wrapped securely around her against the cold wind, feeling the chill of the ground through the thin soles of her slippers. Mamie had greeted her with news only half an hour ago that caused a chill as real as that of the winter earth.

"They ain't no eggs this mornin', Miss Ellen. And won't be no more, nor chicken, neither. Some thievin' varmint cleaned out the henhouse right down to the feathers. Two nights ago they got away with a pig. We ain't goin' to have no stock to carry on with, somethin' ain't done to stop that riffraff. Can't hide them critters from the Yankees and the deserters all the time, day and night. Pretty soon we won't be eatin', ourselves, lessen we go out and steal, too."

Ellen took this blow as she'd taken so many before: It staggered her, yet she rallied. "I doubt there's any place to steal from, any more. We haven't a neighbor less than eight miles away that still has anything left to steal, now that the Gundersons have gone. We'll have to put a guard over the remaining stock, I suppose."

"Better do somethin'," Mamie muttered. "We ain't got much left worth stealin'."

285

Ellen sought out the younger occupants of the slave quarters, pursing her lips when she found them playing some sort of gambling game on the floor of one of the cabins. She said nothing about the game, however, although they might all have been profitably employed in chopping wood.

There were six of them, ranging in age from twelve to fifteen. Thomas, the oldest, at least looked disconcerted at having been caught in this fashion. Chad, a year younger but the bigger and sturdier of the two, rose to his feet and leaned negligently against a post that supported his bed. The expression on his face made her want to hit him; she was surprised and a little frightened at the intensity of the compulsion.

"We've lost another pig and all the chickens," she informed them, controlling the chastising words that would be better not spoken. "We're going to have to do a better job of keeping track of the stock, or we'll all go hungry."

The black faces regarded her unhelpfully. The two younger ones looked instinctively to Chad, as the leader. He was a more forceful personality than Thomas, and Ellen had recognized for some time that he was potentially dangerous. Yet what choices did she have? It was either these young boys, who were strong and healthy, or old men like Rudy, who were neither.

She kept her voice level and pleasant. "I'd like to have you boys take turns, patrolling at night around the quarters and the smokehouse. You can take it in shifts, and see that one of you is out there at all times. The thieves are stragglers, they may well be frightened off if you raise an alarm. I suggest you carry a stick and a pan, to make a racket if you see or hear anyone. If that happens, the rest of you can create a commotion, too, so they'll think they're facing enough trouble to make it not worthwhile to try to steal any more from us."

Again the boys allowed their glances to slide to Chad, and then back to her. It was he who replied. Not respectfully, but with insolence in both tone and words.

"You goin' to give us guns to shoot them thieves, ma'am?"

"Guns?" Did she sound as hollow as she felt?

"Be more use," Chad told her, "than sticks and pans. A man hungry, he ain't goin' to be scared off by no sticks and pans. They mostly soldiers, goin' home. They got guns. I don't aim to get myself shot by a soldier wants a rooster for his supper. Not without I got a gun to shoot back."

286

The idea of a weapon in the hands of this hostile, man-sized boy made her faintly ill.

"I don't think that will be necessary. They may be soldiers, some of them. They're out of the army, now, and won't have ammunition. And they'll steal where it's the easiest, where no one is standing guard. You'll begin tonight. You can stand watch in pairs, if you like; yes, that might be best."

"We stand guard at night, when we get to sleep?" Chad wanted to know.

"You'll only have to do it a few hours at a time, and then you can call in the next two boys."

"I don't reckon I gonna feel much like choppin' wood in the mornin', I be up watchin' for thieves in the night."

In spite of her best intentions, Ellen's control slipped slightly. "If you want to eat, you'll do as you're told. Unless we can stop the thefts, there won't be anything left to cook a meal out of."

Chad reached up to scratch his ear. "I don't reckon I gonna miss them eggs and chickens. Don't recollect they ever got cooked in my cookin' pot, anyway. Mamie come out to kill a chicken, it wind up at the big house, seems like."

For a moment there was only the crackle of the fire in the open fireplace and Ellen's own breathing. The latter was too loud, revealing her perturbation. Chad would one day be a prime fieldhand, a valuable one. Yet she wished he'd been one of those who ran off in the night, heading for the imagined better life in the north. He was a troublemaker, the kind that Roger or Patrick Ryan would have handled with ease; Ellen feared that she could not handle him at all.

"Whether it's chicken, meat from the smokehouse, or corn from the crib," she said slowly, "everything that's taken means that much less for those of us who are left." She shifted her attention to Thomas. "You choose a partner and take the first shift, as soon as it's dark," she told him, and was relieved to see his head nod.

"Yes'm, Miss Ellen."

"Naturally I don't expect you to risk your lives against armed men," she added. "But here at Mallows, off the beaten track, we're not likely to see many of those. They'll be mostly strays who don't want real trouble."

None of them spoke until she'd stepped out through the cabin doorway; as she pulled the door closed behind her, she heard Chad's voice. Deep, like a man's.

"Oh, sure. That right, boys. They don't want any trouble. But Miss Ellen don't offer us no guns to protect ourselves in case she wrong. You s'pose she afraid of black boys with guns?"

She was meant to hear it. They meant to frighten her, and they had succeeded. Ellen hurried up the slight slope toward the house, fingers clutching the shawl so tightly that they cramped. If only Evan would get well, if he'd take over things like this for her! It would be different, for them to take orders from a man. Evan's stump was healing as well as could be expected; now if only his mind would heal, as well.

Ahead of her, two young black girls stood facing each other, deep in conversation. No one, it seemed, was working around here today.

Pansy and Gilly shivered in the sunshine, their breaths making vapor in the cold air. Ellen readied her lips for a reprimand—Gilly was undoubtedly on her way to the house to feed Hugh Alexander, and Pansy had probably been sent on some errand—when she noticed something about the smaller girl's figure that sent the mild scolding right out of her mind.

"Gilly?"

The girls turned guiltily. "I goin', Miss Ellen, I goin' right now!"

"They's a visitor," Pansy said, recalling the message she was to deliver. "Miss Val say—"

Ellen waved a hand to silence her, then, upon reaching them, put out the same hand to Gilly's belly. "Gilly, have you been—?"

"I been what, ma'am?" Gilly's face was innocent, good-natured. "I on my way to feed that baby, ma'am."

Ellen's eyes narrowed as she pressed the calico print skirt tight against what was certainly a more rounded abdomen than one would expect on a young girl.

"Gilly, have you been messing around with one of the young men?" She deliberately used the coarse term the girl would understand, or at least Ellen hoped she would.

Gilly looked down at her shapely outlined belly. "You mean I done got that way again, ma'am? Like I was, afore Rastus was borned?"

There was little question about it; the girl was almost certainly pregnant. Worry and angry frustration added a shrill
288

note to Ellen's voice. "Who is the man? Who dared to touch a child like you?"

"I ain't no child, ma'am. I gonna be thirteen years old in the spring. Pretty soon, now. I gonna have another baby, ma'am?"

A few pertinent questions—which obviously meant nothing to Gilly, who answered unhesitatingly—confirmed Ellen's supposition. Another baby, and her with one just beginning to crawl!

"Didn't Mrs. Douglas tell you it was wrong to lie with a man, before you were married to him? Without permission from your mistress?"

Gilly assumed an injured air. "I didn't do nothin' wrong, ma'am. Not as I know of."

"You've gone to bed with a man," Ellen said, blunt at last. "Otherwise you couldn't be pregnant. Who is the man? Which of them did you allow to do this to you?"

"Gone to bed? I ain't gone to bed with nobody, ma'am, 'ceptin' old Hattie, afore she got to move onto the cot in the kitchen."

"You have certainly done something with a man." Ellen's face flamed in mingled anger and embarrassment at the necessity for this conversation. Could the girl really be as stupid as she seemed? "If not in bed, then in a haystack, or out under a tree. It doesn't matter where it happened. The thing is that if you allow a man to—to do things to you, you're going to wind up like this, with another baby in your belly."

Gilly met her gaze without shame or agitation. "Is that so? What kind of thing a man have to do to me, to get a baby?"

The heat in Ellen's face was scalding, but before she could be pressed into a more clinical explanation, Pansy took over. She leaned forward and whispered into Gilly's ear, a few short words, then drew back, eyeing Miss Ellen with mild apprehension in case her ire should spill over onto Pansy, too.

Comprehension washed over Gilly, and then she broke into a smile. "Is *that* what does it? Nobody ever told me that. But it feels so *good*, ma'am—"

"Who?" Ellen interrupted, not wanting to listen to Gilly's opinion on that matter. "Who is the man? Or have there been several of them?"

"No, ma'am, ain't but one feller ever done it. Except for when I was at Cedars, when Rastus growed inside me. I ain't suppose to let nobody do it, ma'am?" Gilly's pleasure at finally grasping what Miss Ellen was getting at faded as this new understanding filtered through her head. "I can't do it no more?"

"You can't do it any more. It's wrong, it's wicked," Ellen told her.

Obviously Gilly did not see the logic of this. How could something that gave a person such pleasure be wicked? And besides, her face brightened as the idea occurred to her, since there was already a baby inside her, wouldn't that make a difference?

"But he won't plant no more babies, will he, while this one growin'? So can't nobody tell if he do it any more, 'til after the baby be borned."

"Who is the man?" Ellen said through clenched teeth, resisting the overpowering urge to reach out and shake the girl until her teeth rattled.

"Why, it that Chad boy. He told me—"

Chad. She might have known. Good grief, neither of them old enough to be parents even if they'd had any sense, which of course they hadn't. "I don't want to know what he told you, Gilly. I only want you to promise me that you won't do it again. That you won't allow Chad to touch you any more."

Promise? Gilly's vocabulary was not large, yet she knew the meaning of that word. Promise not to indulge in the only pleasurable pastime that had ever come her way, in a life where she was expected constantly to consider the needs and pleasures of white folks all around her? It didn't seem fair.

And then she thought of a way out.

"That Chad, he mighty coaxin' in his ways, ma'am. And he much stronger than I am."

"If he attempts to force you, scream," Ellen told her. "And report it at once to me."

Gilly, spared the necessity of making a promise she did not want to make, nodded. "I do that, ma'am." It didn't seem likely that she would be forced to scream. And if she didn't scream, why, then, she wouldn't have to tell Miss Ellen, would she?

"Remember what I've said," Ellen told her, and moved on toward the house, pushing Pansy ahead of her. She didn't want Pansy and Gilly talking about the situation; she didn't want Pansy to get any similar ideas. "What did you say about a visitor, Pansy?"

"Young man as is Miss Henriette's cousin," Pansy supplied. "Name of Mr. Battersby, and he sick. Miss Val say they going to put him to bed."

To bed? Ellen's lips closed in a grim, flat line. Where? What empty bed?

When would it end, dear God? When?

Lacy was agreeable to having Henriette share her own room, to make a place for Henriette's cousin in the room she vacated. Galen Battersby protested against this intrusion on their household, but even Ellen could see that he was in no shape to send on his way. She drew upon her medical stores, and dosed him with quinine for the fever. She would have ordered up chicken soup, if there had been any chicken to make it from; as it was, Mamie must make soup out of what remained of the vegetables in the root cellar.

She had, over the last few weeks the Yankees had been in the house, become reasonably proficient at pilfering. It was amazing how easily it came to her, she who had never before taken so much as a pin that belonged to anyone else, this adroitness at slipping small quantities of needed goods away to be hidden for future emergencies.

There had been food, of course, and that was the easiest, because there was no guard on the kitchen supplies, and she'd had Mamie's connivance. Food had not been the only important need, however. After years of poverty, Ellen's supply of medicinal aids was very low. The Yankees had not been lavishly supplied, either, but their stores were better than her own. She had no compunction about stealing whatever she thought she could get away with, against the uncertainties of the coming months.

It appeared that she would have the opportunity to use them all, before the nightmare ended. They brought a nightshirt of Evan's for Galen Battersby, and again Ellen deplored the lack of a man servant in the house. She had considered, very briefly, bringing Thomas inside and attempting to train him to follow in Aaron's footsteps. She was afraid, however, that Thomas was too much under the influence of Chad, whom she did not trust at all. No, it wasn't safe to bring any of them inside. Yet it was very difficult when there were sick men; she felt she could delegate none of the intimate care to the younger women.

Her mother would have been immeasurably shocked had Ellen suggested that *she*, as a once-married woman, was an appropriate alternate nurse to herself. Shocked, and refusing. Dolly Mallow would not nurse her own grandson; she certainly would not do any more for a perfect stranger.

There was Lacy, of course. Lacy, who would perhaps make a better nurse than Dolly, although she had had no more experience at it than her counterpart, but would by her own nature have taken on a necessary task without undue fuss. Ellen could not, however, bring herself to ask Lacy for help. They had been antagonists, of a sort, over all the years of Ellen's marriage; never allies. Though Lacy had never said so, Ellen knew that her mother-in-law looked upon her with a sort of amused contempt. She found herself wishing that Lacy would offer to take on part of the burden of nursing two young men. She could accept it, if Lacy offered. Yet she could not ask for that help. Pride made it impossible even when she was so tired she wanted to drop in her tracks.

Not that Galen Battersby took the intensive kind of nursing that Evan required. He was not totally bedridden, though it was clear that in addition to the fever he suffered from exhaustion and malnutrition. So the girls could attend to some of his needs; they could bring up water so that he could bathe himself, they could see that he was fed, they could clean his room and change his bedding while he wrapped up in a dressing gown of Roger Stanton's—now riddled with moth holes—and sat in a chair.

Henriette eagerly took on such tasks as she could do. She was almost fanatically attached to this cousin, now that her immediate family was dead.

Valerie watched her fall in love. Very quickly, and just as deeply, as she herself had fallen. It was there, for anyone with perception to see, in the touch of color that came to Henriette's face, the way her mouth took an upturn at the corners, in the way her dark eyes fastened upon Galen Battersby's face when he spoke, in the way her complete attention centered upon him whenever they were together. Henriette sat for hours beside his bed, reading to him or talking of old times. Good times, when they were children, and all was right in their world, when war and hunger and illness were as remote as the moon.

Valerie watched, and her own pain increased. Where was Jack Ferris? Did he think about her? Had he tried to write to her? Was there a letter, somewhere, misdirected, lying undelivered? If she had known where to address it, she would

292

have written a letter to him, whether he wrote first or not.

The Union soldiers, of course, were moving (the stragglers who remained) toward Savannah, not away from it. They wouldn't be available to carry return messages even if she dared take the risk of Ellen learning of an attempt to contact him. It would mean so much to hear, to have the briefest of scribbled notes, to know that he was alright and that he missed her.

Henriette's romance held more promise than her own. A second cousin, of respectable family, a Southerner: Galen Battersby was eminently eligible, if such things mattered any more. Certainly Ellen smiled upon this romance, when she recognized it as such. That it was two-sided became obvious within a few days, as soon as Galen began to feel somewhat better.

He came to Ellen, in the absence of any male head of the household, to seek her counsel before speaking to Henriette. He was weak from days of fever. Once it had passed, however, and his mind was functioning again, he began to plan. Henriette was at the center of those plans.

He found Ellen sitting, for once, alone in her room, mending the hem of a dress which should actually have been discarded; it was so worn that repairing it was almost a waste of time. Yet she bent her head over the task, noting how her hands had become reddened and roughened so that she wondered if she would ever be able to bring back their softness.

"Miss Ellen," Galen said, and waited in the doorway for her to lift her head. "I wonder if I might speak with you on a matter of importance."

She was glad to put away the depressing chore for the moment. "Of course. Come in, Mr. Battersby, and sit down."

The day was past—at least temporarily—when a lady might not entertain a gentleman in her own chamber, when there were few other choices. It was a fine day, and the afternoon sun had warmed the room so that it was not too miserably cold, although Ellen was warmly dressed and kept a shawl about her shoulders.

Galen took the offered chair, sitting on the edge of it and resting his elbows on his knees as he leaned toward her. "First, I want to thank you for your hospitality, and your care, during that bout of fever."

"I could do no less for any man who fought, as my husband and son and my neighbors fought, for our Southland," Ellen told him quietly.

"My own family could not have been more solicitous." Amusement touched Galen's thin face. "No doubt my mama will write to you, appropriately, when she knows about it. And not only in thanks for taking me in, but in what you've done for her cousin's family."

"There was little I could do for them. For Frances, almost nothing."

"You did what you could, and that's what counts, isn't it, ma'am? You took Charlotte and Henriette in when they had nowhere to go, no family to turn to, and brought Henriette through everything that happened later. Without someone like yourself, she might well have taken her sister's way out. I thank God she did not."

Ellen waited, knowing already what was on his mind, although he seemed to be sorting it out himself as he spoke.

"You've taken the responsibility for Henriette for some months, in addition to the considerable burdens of your own household. You've taken the place of her own mother, insofar as you could. It seems to me now that . . ."

Galen paused, taking on a faint color. "It cannot have escaped your notice, I think, that my cousin and I have developed an—an attachment for one another. I believe that, eventually, I will ask Henriette to be my wife. It would be premature to speak to her now. It is too soon after the tragedy she has suffered, and I don't know what my own future will be. Like your family, ma'am, mine has operated a plantation, with the use of slaves. They are all gone, now, I believe, except for a few old family retainers. How we are to go on from here I don't yet know."

Ellen nodded. "I fear the whole of the South faces such problems."

"Yes. The thing is, I'm sure I'll be well enough to go on my way toward home within a few days. I have only one horse, but if I go slowly I think he might bear the two of us. If you agree, ma'am, I think the best thing would be to take Henriette home to Milledgeville with me, to what remains of her family. And if, in time, she agrees to marry me, why, that will make me a very happy man. In the meantime, I think she should be with us, at my parents' home, not depending further upon you, Miss Ellen."

He waited anxiously for her reaction to this, for if she

294

thought it improper for him to take Henriette away, he would have to return later. He saw no opposition in Ellen's face, however, and his smile widened when she nodded.

"Yes. Yes, Mr. Battersby, I think that would be best for Henriette," she agreed.

"Have I your permission, then, to ask her if she would like to leave with me?"

"Yes, of course. I'm certain she will want to go."

Ellen sat for several minutes after he had gone, listening to the low murmur of voices across the landing as he spoke with Henriette. She could not distinguish the words; she didn't have to.

One less to care for, then. Now if only she could think what to do about the rest of them, about Mallows, she thought, and picked up the old dress to continue her mending.

Four

When Henriette and her cousin had gone, the household was expanded again, ever so slightly. The back bedroom was empty. Lacy had her own room to herself. And Valerie wished urgently that Julie, without being asked to do so, would move into the vacated chamber.

It did not seem to occur to Julie that her sister craved privacy. She herself had grown used to sleeping with Valerie, and did not mind it at all, especially during these cold nights. The bed coverings, like everything else, had suffered; quilts and comforters grew worn and thin, and there was no way to replace them. A warm body to curl up to was a welcome thing.

If her own room had been empty, Julie might have thought of returning to it, since many of her belongings still filled the chifforobe. Evan, however, continued to occupy that room.

And so Valerie often lay, feigning relaxation, until Julie had fallen asleep. If she could not have Jack Ferris beside her, except in imagination, then she would put aside any feelings of guilt and imagine to her heart's content. Imagine Jack's mouth, warm and hard on hers, imagine that it was his hands, rather than her own, that stroked the firm breasts and touched gently between her thighs. And if Julie stirred and

296

murmured, "Valerie? What are you doing?" she would say, "Nothing. I'm just restless."

It was late in February when the letter finally came.

It was carried by a distant neighbor who had ridden off the main road to deliver it, along with several others, to the grand house at Mallows. It was a fine day, with a welcome hint of spring, and Valerie had been out walking simply because she could no longer bear to be cooped up inside.

It was she who met the neighbor and accepted the letters, not daring to look them over too eagerly at once, not while the man's gaze was upon her.

"If you care to ride to the house," she told him, "my mother will be happy to provide refreshments for you."

"No, thanks." He was a middle-aged farmer, and weary from a long ride. "Another time, perhaps. My wife is ill, and I rode to town to see if I could get calomel and an anodyne for her inflammation of the kidneys. Had to pay the earth for them, but I guess I was lucky to get anything that might help, and I'll be on my way back as fast as I can go. Those blue-bellied devils are still roaming around, and there's only my youngest son at home with his mother. What can a twelve-year-old boy do against them?" He hesitated, then asked. "Have you heard what they've done at Midway Church, that Kilpatrick and his damnable cavalry?"

Midway Church, Valerie thought, that was where Ruth Ryan Gerald and her husband and children lived. Her lips moved woodenly. "No. What?"

"They camped there for weeks, penned their cattle and their horses in the cemetery, with a total lack of respect for the dead. That's not the worst of it, though. They've used the church as a slaughterhouse, cutting meat on the melodeon, and why God doesn't strike them dead is beyond me. They've stripped the villagers of everything worth having; and a sorry lot those poor people are, too. At least we in the country, in isolated areas, had some small chance of growing a mouthful that we've been able to hide."

Valerie pulled her shawl tighter about her shoulders, although the chill could hardly be alleviated by the warmth of it.

"We thought, since the main body of the Union Army went on to Savannah so long ago, that it was nearly over. Are they going to continue to ravage the country forever?"

"It would seem that way. There are still a fair number of

them about, wandering in twos and threes, without any sort of supervision. Apparently anything they do is all right with their corrupt leaders. I had to leave the road several times, to avoid them; they will confiscate anything a traveler may be carrying, if they have a hankering for it. And I don't think, ma'am, that it's safe to walk about alone. A female is fair game to many of them."

"I see." She clutched the precious letters against her breast, unable to keep herself from glancing along the road. There was no one, of course, yet it was easy to imagine them, the hated Yankees, concealing themselves within the edge of the trees. "Well, I thank you, sir, for taking the extra time to deliver our mail. We are most grateful," she told him sincerely.

"You're welcome, miss." He touched the brim of his battered hat and wheeled his horse, heading back in the direction from which he'd come.

Valerie's hands trembled as she examined the letters he'd left her. They had been roughly handled; they were crumpled and dirtied, yet legible. Two for her mother—that one was from a friend in Savannah, the other from a distant cousin in Augusta. And the third—

The third was in a bold slashing hand she had learned to know while Jack Ferris was at Mallows.

Something in her chest swelled painfully, impeding her breathing, then burst like a soap bubble blown by a child. She stood quite still in the middle of the oyster shell drive, fingers almost too awkward to open it.

It was dated some two weeks earlier.

"My dearest Valerie: There is much to do here, and this is the first opportunity I've had to write. There are fewer injuries to care for, at least in Savannah, but much illness. There is more disease than one would expect at this time of year; no doubt the men are more susceptible to various illnesses because of their general lowered state of health. I've been called upon to attend a few civilians and their families, as well as serving among the military. It is not about sickness that I would speak to you, of course. Darling girl, while my days are too busy to think of anything save what I must do to alleviate suffering, my nights are filled with thoughts of you. When I am too tired to sleep, I don't care, because I bring to mind your sweet face. At the present time there is little hope of gaining leave. General Sherman and his men have left Savannah, and I feel lucky not to have followed the war into the Carolinas; there are plenty of sick to be taken care of here, though no doubt I will eventually be ordered after the main body of the army. However, I have hope that should that happen there will be enough warning so that I may obtain a short furlough that will enable me to see you once more before I travel north. A better possibility, perhaps, would be for you to travel to Savannah, perhaps to inspect your grandmother's property here? In that hope, I will seek it out and check in upon it periodically, in the event that you can leave a message for me there, and that we might have a few precious hours together."

It was signed, in the familiar confident scrawl, simply with his name.

Valerie read it again, through a blur of tears that she resolutely blinked away. Travel to Savannah? Was there any hope of such a thing? She didn't think so, but the very idea acted upon her electrically; she felt charged with excitement.

She had forgotten the possibility of roving soldiers. She hurried back toward the house, the oyster shells crunching under her feet; she had forgotten the state of her shoes, also, until a sharp fragment of shell penetrated the sole of one of them. She stopped to withdraw it, wincing, then continued at the same quick pace.

Gilly walked out across the piazza as she approached, her movements languid, and as she turned to descend the side steps Valerie saw, quite clearly, the way the girl's skirt outlined a rounded, swelling belly.

Poor silly child, who hadn't even known how babies were made in spite of having made one, who had now begun another. Ellen had reported the news, disgust heavy in her voice, and hopelessness.

What if *she* had gotten herself with child?

Gilly went out across the grass toward the quarters, unaware of her observer. Valerie continued toward the house, slowing her step, considering the matter.

In truth, she had given no thought to the danger of pregnancy, that first time. All she had been aware of was the new and marvelous sensations Jack Ferris had evoked in her body. And later, when it did occur to her that such a disgraceful thing as pregnancy might happen, she had simply put the idea aside. She had no idea how likely it was to happen; certainly, conception did not take place each and every time one made love. And Jack was a physician; surely he knew about such things and would have protected her in some way, if it had been necessary.

In some ways, she was as ignorant as Gilly. And though Ellen did not understand how Gilly could have succumbed to Chad's importunings, Valerie did. No doubt, she thought, deliberately allowing herself to picture the scene, Chad had put his hands on the girl, and poor little Gilly had melted under them, as Valerie had done with Jack.

Was it the same, for a black girl as for a white one? Was there any difference in the emotions and sensations it was possible to feel?

She knew, with a certainty as strong as any she'd ever had over anything, that if it were possible to go to Jack, she would not hold back from lovemaking because of fear that she would conceive his child. Being in his arms, even for an hour, was worth some risk. Yet the risk was strong, and she knew that Ellen's dismay about Gilly's behavior was nothing compared to what it would be over her own. Gilly was an ignorant black girl; Valerie had been properly reared and taught, and knew perfectly well that, before marriage, she should have allowed no man to touch her.

If it ever came down to that, to pregnancy, what *would* Ellen do?

It was easy to imagine her mother's horror and repugnance. Ellen would feel personally disgraced. She had scolded Gilly, and attempted to extract a promise that Gilly would sin no more. (Could Gilly keep such a promise, even if she wanted to? If Chad came up behind her in the dusk, and put his hands on her breasts, breathing into the hair at the back of her neck, pulling her against his own hard, muscular body, could Gilly fail to melt against him, to give in to his demands?)

Of course, Valerie told herself, their situations were not at all the same. Gilly was a child, and Chad was no more than a boy for all his size. And they were not free to marry; they could not do so without Ellen's permission, which she was unlikely to give. It was impossible to say what they might legally do, once this God-awful conflict was over; but Chad had no way of supporting a family, and he probably didn't want to. All he wanted was that soft female flesh beneath him when the desire rose in his veins. She couldn't imagine Chad actually *loving* the girl.

While Valerie, of course, was in love with a man who

300

might well, when the end of the war freed him to a regained control over his own life, ask her to marry him.

Would her mother understand that, if she tried to explain? Comprehend that she and Jack loved each other, and wanted to be together forever, when such things were possible again? Would that, in Ellen's mind, ameliorate the so-called wrong-doing?

Valerie did not feel that what she and Jack did together was wrong; not when they loved each other so. Yet she knew instinctively that her mother would not view it that way. Nor would Julie. Grandma Lacy might, she thought wistfully, and knew that she did not dare speak plainly to her, either.

"Valerie? Letters?"

Valerie started. She had been so absorbed in her own thoughts that she hadn't even seen her mother standing there in the shadow of the roofed piazza.

"Yes. Yes, one from Cousin Alice and another from Mrs. Haines, in Savannah, I think." She held the three letters together against her breast, heart hammering. What on earth had possessed her, to walk in without concealing Jack's letter? In this household, there was no such thing as a "private" letter; messages were too hard to come by, and so scarce, that naturally everyone's curiosity was piqued by the casual note as well as by long family chronicles. The very thought of anyone else's eyes reading the words Jack had written for her was enough to send a wave of panic through her.

"Come on back where it's warm," she temporized, not handing over the letters as Ellen obviously expected, ignoring her mother's outstretched hand.

She led the way, hurrying, and managed to stuff the top letter into the front of her dress before she opened the breakfast room door, praying that it would not give her away by crackling or making an odd shape under the sheer brown wool.

Julie and Lacy were at the table, warming their hands around their teacups, and Dolly as well, blocking the direct heat from the fireplace by standing before it. Sally Ann, juggling the baby on her shoulder, turned with less anticipation than the others; there was no one from whom she expected any news, good or bad. Her husband was dead, her mother was dead, and her friends from Atlanta might well be the same.

"Letters," Ellen said brightly, waving them as she sank

onto her own chair. "From Alice and from Mary Haines. Who brought them, Valerie?"

"Mr. Haystock. He'd been out for medicine for his wife; she had an inflammation of the kidneys." She told them of the desecration of the church at Midway Church; anything to keep Ellen from focusing attention on the matter of why she hadn't handed over the mail directly, instead of rushing in here with it. Surely Jack's letter was safe, though; Ellen would have mentioned it at once if she'd noted anything amiss in Valerie's actions.

The letters were spread out on the table and read aloud, with comment from everyone a part of the reading. Valerie sat, acutely aware of the missive inside her bodice; it was impossible not to imagine how they would react to such a reading of Jack's letter. *My dearest Valerie. Darling girl, my nights are filled with thoughts of you. When I am too tired to sleep, I don't care, because I bring to mind your sweet face.*

The memory of those written words warmed her in a way the open fire could not have done, even if Dolly hadn't been cutting it off from the rest of the room. *Darling girl.*

Jack loved her, as she loved him.

She suddenly realized that Ellen had paused in her reading, that the encircling faces had that familiar expression of sorrow. Death? Whose? She hadn't heard what her mother read.

"Poor Alice," Ellen said. "It's true Aunt Winnie was very old, yet it's hard to lose one's mother, I'm sure, even at the age of eighty-two. At least the boys were still safe, the last she'd heard." She went on reading aloud. " 'James was slightly injured when his own weapon misfired; it was enough to send him home to recover, and now it seems there is little likelihood he will ever return to duty. The reports we hear of our own troops are greatly saddening; it does not seem that they can triumph over the superior forces of the Union Army. As a mother, I cannot but be glad that my oldest son is here, and that when the time comes to think about planting another crop, I will not this year have to manage alone. Very few of our people are left, and those are the old and infirm, and the women with young children. I cannot but think they are misled by the Yankees into running off; will the enemy see that they are fed and clothed? The Good Lord knows that such things have become a terrible burden to us, yet how we are to plant and harvest crops without fieldhands, I do not know.' "

302

This was depressingly close to home, and there was more.

" 'Yard goods have become so dear, and we are all in rags. Who can afford sixteen dollars a yard for wide calicoes? What little cash we have been able to hold together has gone mostly for firewood, at eighty-five dollars a cord. We live in the kitchen these days, because at that price it can be used only for cooking, not for comfort heating.' "

They looked guiltily at one another; at Mallows there was plenty of wood, for those with the energy to cut it. Eighty-five dollars a cord!

" 'Even the pleasure of a cup of tea is lessened, with the price at sixty cents a pound. Yet for all that, we are mostly healthy, except for Grandpa Morrison, who continues to suffer badly from the rheumatism so that many days he cannot leave his bed. And having James at home again makes up for a great deal. I long for spring, and the warm weather, and pray that before the cold weather comes again things may improve considerably. There are those who still hope for a Confederate victory, but from the things James has told me, I cannot believe there is any chance of it. I want only, now, for it to be over, even if our gallant boys are defeated. Surely the Yankees will eventually go home and leave us in peace, though how we are to manage without Negroes is a bitter question.

" 'Dear cousin, we pray daily for your safety at Mallows, and that your Evan will return to you as James has to us, whole and strong, to pick up whatever pieces the Yankees leave us.' "

Ellen's voice broke. No one spoke while she drew herself together, and finished the reading, folding the pages neatly together before taking up the second letter.

This one, from Ellen's friend in Savannah, was in much the same tone. There was an attempt at hopefulness, and Savannah had, it seemed, suffered considerably less than Atlanta and many of the other places. Due to the cunning of the Savannah merchants and cotton factors, General Sherman had been kept from burning the city. Prices were exorbitant, as they were everywhere, but the city continued to function, and there was little property damage.

Mary Haines had walked past Lacy's house at Abercorn and Bryan streets, and deplored the way it had been treated. The garden was overgrown and neglected, there were broken windows which had been boarded over because there was no glass to repair them, and the tenants hung their laundry, including ladies' undergarments, in plain sight of passersby.

Ellen finished the letter, filled with references to old acquaintances; they rejoiced in what good news there was of them, and observed in small silences the announcements of still more illnesses and deaths.

Valerie had fastened onto the image of the house off Reynolds Square. Jack knew where it was, and he'd go there when he could in the hope that she'd have managed to leave him a message. She felt sick with the desire to be with him again, and helpless to know how to bring up the subject of going to Savannah without giving herself away.

Ellen folded the letters again with nervous fingers, then pushed them out into the center of the table. "Well. I suppose I should write to all of them, and tell them how things are here. I'm going to have to go into the county seat to transact some business, perhaps the first of next week, and we could mail letters off then. Although I gather there is no regular postal service, there are some kind people who are willing, like Mr. Haystock, to carry letters along."

Ellen had not left Mallows, except to visit at Cedars, in so long that no one could remember the event; her announcement caught them all by surprise.

"You're going to Reidsville?" Julie echoed. Her own thought was of the disastrous results the last time *she* had left home; the very idea of leaving the comparative safety of Mallows was frightening, and nothing in the letters that had been delivered today gave her any reason to think that the countryside was any safer than it had been when the soldiers tried to attack her.

"Yes. There are some things we must have—our salt supply was almost exhausted when the butchering and curing was done. Mamie says we'll be out completely within a few weeks. I don't know if it's possible to obtain any more laudanum, but I think I must try. I have very little of that, either, and Evan cannot sleep without it. In fact, he begs for it during the day." She rubbed at her temple, unaware of the lines of strain that were becoming a permanent part of her face. "There is so little cash left. It can't possibly stretch until next year's harvest, if there is one."

She had admitted, out loud, that there might not be a harvest. The silence around the room was absolute except for the mewing of Hugh Alexander as he squirmed against his

304

mother's breast. Ellen did not notice the troubled faces as she pressed harder at the pain in front of her right ear.

"I think I'll have to try to arrange for a loan," she said. "Perhaps . . ." She paused, and then said the words with great reluctance. "Perhaps I can arrange to borrow money, against Mallows."

For once, Dolly Mallow reacted to something the same as the others around her. She took the necessary steps forward to lean with both hands on the edge of the table, staring at her daughter in disbelief.

"*Mortgage Mallows?* You've lost your senses!"

Ellen looked up at her, wondering where her mother had been for the past four years, how she could be so blind, so stupid. The thought shocked her, yet she saw that it was true. Maybe some of it was even her own fault, for she had allowed her mother to slide into a reasonably comfortable cocoon of selfishness that isolated her from what was happening to anyone else. Yes, maybe even so small a thing as allowing her to have all the eggs, when the others were just as hungry for them, had contributed to what Dolly had become. Ellen stared at her sole remaining parent, and for once she was neither conciliatory nor protective.

"What do you suggest I do, instead? To see that we're not all barefooted and hungry? I can't plant so much as a single row of cotton without money, and there is none. Do you have any jewelry you've hidden away? Anything you want to donate to the cause, anything that can be sold to pay for the things we need?"

Dolly did not mistake the tone of her daughter's voice. She flushed in mingled anger and chagrin. "You know that I have nothing of value. There is nothing left but the land, and this house."

"Precisely. Which is why I have no choice but to mortgage the place. I am speaking of survival, Mama. Literal survival."

"There has never been a mortgage against Mallows," Dolly said feebly.

"There has never been such a war before. I have never lost my husband before, and watched my only son come home—crippled." That last word was a first, too; she had not previously voiced it, had not even allowed herself to think it. Yet now Dolly's opposition against what seemed to Ellen her only course drove her to harsh words, and a harsher tone. "If anyone has any better ideas, I am certainly open to them, would

305

welcome any alternative with prayers of thanksgiving! I've spent months lying awake at night, trying to figure a way out of our predicament, and there is only one. I must borrow against Mallows."

Valerie sat with her hands clenched in her lap, the letter from Jack forgotten. Her own horror was little less than her grandmother's. That Ellen could make such a suggestion revealed fully the depths of her own despair; she would never otherwise have considered putting her beloved plantation in jeopardy in any way.

That a mortgage could jeopardize Mallows was obvious even to the relatively uninitiated. To borrow meant that eventually the money must be paid back; and if that was not possible, the lender would claim the property that had been put up as security for the loan.

Across the table, Lacy Stanton cleared her throat.

"There is one alternative," she said slowly.

All eyes turned in her direction, and they waited.

"I could sell the house in Savannah," she said.

And with the rush of pain that seared her heart, Valerie also felt a leap of joy.

Because selling Lacy's house would mean that someone must go to Savannah.

Five

Ellen sat, stupefied, considering the old lady's proposition. She knew, better than anyone, how much the Savannah house meant to her mother-in-law. To sell it? Even to save Mallows?

Julie's hand crept out to cover Lacy's in a wordless gesture, conveying her understanding of the magnitude of the sacrifice. Valerie wanted to walk around the table and hug her grandmother. This was not entirely, nor even primarily, because of the selfish surge of delight at the idea that it might, after all, be possible to go to Savannah herself. She, too, loved the house on Abercorn Street. Many of her happiest childhood days had been spent there.

Lacy had dropped her hands into her lap so that no one could see how they trembled. "I'm too old to go back and start over," she said quietly. "You are all the family I have left, here at Mallows. So I shall stay here. There is no money to run my household, any more, and it couldn't be done without servants. So the sensible thing is to sell the house, and turn the money over to Ellen to keep Mallows going. I think," she said, pushing back her chair, "that I'll go upstairs now, and write the letters, so that you can mail them in Reidsville. One to the tenants, to tell them that I am coming to inspect the property, and that I will be putting it up for sale. And another to my lawyer, to ask him to look for a buyer."

Lacy stood up, her legs trembling as they had not done when the Yankees came. When she walked around the table, Ellen reached out and touched her hand, the first time she had ever deliberately done so.

"Thank you, Miss Lacy. God bless you."

Lacy could make no reply. She was afraid her voice would crack. Well, she thought, climbing the stairs like the old woman that she was, God *had* blessed her, hadn't He? After an inauspicious beginning, she'd had a good marriage with Charles Stanton, an exciting and satisfying marriage. Only one of her children had survived to adulthood, but Roger had been a good son, loving and dutiful. If he had chosen to marry a big-eyed slip of a girl who was probably as cold in bed as a dead bass, why, that was Roger's affair. He had never complained of his wife to his mother, and if he had taken his pleasures elsewhere, he had been discreet about those affairs; he was so like his father that she could not but believe him hot-blooded, yet Lacy had not heard of any specific women in Roger's life.

And he had given her three beautiful grandchildren. She loved them as she had loved Roger himself, knowing their shortcomings and their weaknesses, and loving them in spite of them. It was not for Ellen's sake, but for theirs, that she had offered to sell the Savannah house. Her grandchildren, and herself. For it was true. When one is past seventy, and without personal funds, one must make the best of things. And for Lacy, the best of things were here, in the bosom of her remaining family.

She reached the top of the stairs and turned toward her room, moving more slowly and more heavily than usual. Behind her, that Blossom girl called out something to her; Lacy pretended not to hear.

She closed her bedroom door behind her, and crossed to the cherrywood desk she had brought with her to Mallows. She sat down on the chair with the red velvet seat. She took out paper and a pen and ink, and then those things dissolved before her in a mist she could not blink away.

Lacy leaned her head forward into her hands and wept.

"I'll still have to go to the county seat," Ellen told them.

"If you'll make a list of your needs, I'll bring back what I can."

"You're not going alone, are you?" Valerie asked. "Can't we all go? You, and Julie, and me?"

"I don't want to go," Julie said quickly. "You go, Val. She's right, Mama, you can't go by yourself."

"I had no intention of going by myself. I'd thought I would take Lallie with me. But there's no reason why Valerie can't go, as well. We'll leave early Monday morning. I'll speak to Rudy about having the buggy ready."

Julie, remembering how much use poor old Rudy had been before, was unable to stifle a protest. "Take one of the younger men with you, Mama. And carry a pistol. There are still so many ruffians roaming about."

"Younger men? There are none, unless you count Thomas and Chad. I wouldn't trust Chad, even without the pistol, and I'm not sure about Thomas, any more, either. He's fallen too much under Chad's influence, I'm afraid. No, my dear, let's face it. We aren't guaranteed safety no matter who goes with us. We'll just have to be careful."

Valerie listened to the plans being made, without joining in. She would go to Reidsville, and then, when the time came, she'd accompany her grandmother to Savannah. Julie was even less likely to want to go there, a much longer journey, and Lacy must have a companion. Valerie did not believe that her mother would leave Mallows long enough to travel that far, and Sally Ann had the baby to care for. She herself was the logical companion for her grandmother.

And Jack Ferris was in Savannah.

Evan healed, physically, but there was no lessening of his anger against his family, no end to his depression. His tongue was caustic, and Blossom, not the best of pupils under ideal circumstances, was on more than one occasion tempted to take the hated book and throw it in his face.

Only when he had drunk deeply of the whiskey that he persuaded her to bring up to him could Evan treat her as if she were a human being. What would he be like, as a husband? When he was stronger, when the pain eased, she determined to find out. *Before* accepting the proposal she now confidently expected, not afterward. Not for her a man who was brutal in bed and disagreeable out of it. Mallows was a fine mansion, and she looked forward to being mistress of it

309

once Valerie and Julie had married and gone. The mansion would not be worth it, if she must continue, forever, to put up with Evan's vile temper.

Also, she had been here long enough now to see that the entire place, elegant and beautiful as it was, was deteriorating from lack of funds to keep it up. Blossom dreamed of silks and velvets such as the Stanton women had; close inspection proved those, too, to be rotting and falling apart.

It would be best to know exactly what she was getting into, before she was committed to a lifetime of sharing whatever was to be had at Mallows.

Ellen could not have failed to be aware of the inroads being made into the whiskey supply. The Yankees had helped themselves, liberally, to Roger's potables. They had preferred the brandy, which was of excellent quality, and had taken away with them as much as their wagons could conveniently carry. What remained was a considerably diminished supply, and it was easy to see—for one as practiced as Ellen at inventorying her stocks of all things—when another bottle, and yet another, were removed from the cellar shelves.

It was one more thing Ellen chose to overlook. Evan needed something to make life bearable; she allowed him the laudanum when he could not sleep at night, and the whiskey seemed to help him during the day. so she pretended to be unaware of Blossom's delivery of the bottles to his room.

She hated the thought of leaving him for the journey to Reidsville. She did not like the idea of Evan, manipulated by that chit of a girl, being without her own influence for so much as two days, which she had decided would be the extent of the trip. There was no way of reaching friends at the county seat to assure that there would be a place for them to spend the night; they would simply have to chance it. The Yankees jeeringly spoke of "Southern hospitality"; they had no concept of the depth of it, the sincerity with which it was offered. If anyone she knew still had a roof over their heads, Ellen knew she would be welcomed.

To say that a tremendous burden had been lifted from Ellen by Lacy's announcement of her willingness to sell her own house would have been the most gross of understatements. New vistas opened before her. She could buy seed, she could replenish her supply of the things that Mallows could not produce, such as sugar and salt, and perhaps there would even be enough to see that everyone had a pair of shoes. It

310

was probably too much to hope that she'd dare to purchase dress materials, but that would come, once Mallows was producing again.

She still had last fall's scanty crop of cotton; she would send it to Savannah as soon as she could ascertain that it was safe to do so, that she would be paid for it rather than having it confiscated by the Yankees. That might provide for clothing, when she could be paid for it.

While Ellen had never liked Lacy Stanton (in the way that she had liked Frances Douglas, for instance), she had actively worked at *not disliking* her. She could not have said precisely why she felt that Lacy had never fully approved her as a daughter-in-law. Perhaps it was the reserve in Lacy's manner, on any subject on which they did not agree; when under Ellen's roof, Lacy did not challenge her. At the same time, the older woman managed to convey her feelings with nothing more than silence. And Ellen had sometimes noted an expression on Lacy's face, an expression that left no doubt that she found her daughter-in-law lacking in some way.

Without ever stating it in words, Lacy had subtly put across her feeling that Roger might have done far better, in choosing a wife, than little Ellen Mallow. Lacy had mentioned the young women he had known, stressing Roger's attractiveness, his intelligence, all without emphasizing Ellen's shortcomings. And at the end of it, Ellen felt diminished, somehow, by the very lack of attention from Lacy.

She had not seriously minded, since she had, of course, her beloved Mallows. During the years of her marriage to Roger, Lacy had lived in Savannah, and there was not that much social intercourse between the two families. Ellen was uncomfortable at Lacy's Savannah home; on her own turf, she was mistress, and she knew it. When Lacy came to live with them, at Roger's insistence, it was Lacy who was the guest. Ellen went through the motions of making her comfortable, and was scrupulously fair (except in the matter of breakfast eggs) in dealing with Lacy and her own mother. She did not, in fact, spend much time thinking about Lacy at all, and did not honestly care that there was no warm affection between them.

Now, since Lacy's astonishing offer, Ellen found an undercurrent of shame below the level of surface joy. She knew perfectly well that never, for anything or anyone, would she have sacrificed Mallows. That Lacy had given up *her* hopes

311

of return to her Abercorn Street house was almost beyond comprehension. For a day or so, Ellen feared that Lacy might change her mind. She had, after all, spoken impulsively. But the morning that she brought her letters to Ellen for mailing, Ellen allowed herself to believe that it would happen, that the sale of the Savannah house would save Mallows.

For the first time since Jack's departure—excepting upon the arrival of his letter—Valerie was charged with excitement. The trip to Reidsville would have been a treat in itself, simply because it had been so long since she'd been anywhere. More importantly, however, it would give her the opportunity to send a letter to Jack.

She could not be certain of the exact address, but his rank and his position in caring for the wounded would surely simplify matters. She wrote out an impassioned letter, hid it when Julie came into the room, and re-read it later in private and decided that something more decorous would be wiser and safer. She did not write for her mother's eyes, but if by any mischance the letter fell into Ellen's hands, it must not reveal the depth of Valerie's relationship with the Yankee officer. She rewrote it, informing him that she hoped to be in Savannah within a few weeks, and expressing the additional hope that they would be privileged to meet while she was there. Jack would understand the necessity of understating her own feelings.

Though it was only a business trip, Valerie prepared for it carefully. If the weather was good, they would leave on Monday morning. There was little point in wearing one's best dress to drive over a road that would cover them with red dust, so on the journey itself she would settle for a severely simple brown wool. She would also take one of the better of her winter dresses in a dark green wool, and then, just in case the weather turned warmer as it well might do in early March, a lighter-weight, paler green silk. She would have loved wearing hoops, although she'd heard rumors that they were going out of fashion, probably because it was so difficult to get enough material for the enormously full skirts.

Ellen, however, ruled out hoops for anything but ball gowns. To attempt to manage them in a buggy was the height of absurdity. Ellen herself was content to take the dress in the best repair, a gray merino with white collar and cuffs;

she, too, would wear an older brown wool for the trip, since it would show the dust less than anything else.

"With these shoes," she pointed out ruefully, "it would be impossible to look elegant even if we wore pearls and diamonds. Besides, we aren't going to be admired."

This was true enough. Yet what young woman, still shy of twenty, could fail to hope that an approving masculine eye would be cast in her direction? The fact that one's affections are already engaged elsewhere does little to diminish that most feminine of traits, and Valerie was no exception.

Ellen issued orders to everyone remaining behind as if she expected to be gone for weeks. Julie would make sure that Evan was kept as comfortable as he could be; under no circumstances was he to be left entirely in Blossom's hands. "See to it that his door is left open at all times, when that girl is about," Ellen instructed.

Julie was also advised to keep Gilly as busy as possible, to keep her out of trouble. There was little Ellen could suggest in regard to the young boys supposedly patrolling the grounds at night. There had been no more raids by scavengers since the patrolling had begun; whether that was due to the fact that the boys scared thieves off, or because there was so little left to steal that no one bothered, was uncertain.

For once, Ellen didn't make elaborate arrangements for the comfort of her mother while she was away. Dolly would have to take her chances, the same as everyone else, and eat the same fare they did. The lemons were gone, the sugar was nearly so, and eggs were no more than a distant memory. If the others survived on mush, so could Dolly.

Sally Ann came downstairs on the morning they were to leave, carrying letters to be mailed, also. "To my second cousin Aureila, in Augusta, and to my great-aunt Laura in Valdosta. It may be that neither of them is still alive. If they are, however, they might have need of my services, and could offer me a home. I can't impose on your hospitality forever, generous as it has been."

Ellen paused in the act of pulling on her worn gloves, to give the girl a spontaneous hug. "Don't be silly! You're welcome for as long as you need a home. Aren't you my own cousin's only child? And that Hugh Alexander of yours has won all our hearts. We should be sorry to see him go, you know that. Besides, you aren't well enough yet to travel any such distance as to Valdosta, nor to work for an old lady, either."

Sally Ann's pale freckled face colored. "I'm not much use, I know. But I think I am getting stronger, really I do, and when it's summer, and the warm weather comes, surely I'll improve more quickly."

"I'm sure you will," Ellen agreed, accepting the letters. "You'll want to know how these relatives are faring, at any rate. We'll see that they're sent."

Valerie, impatient to be off, had to endure one more round of orders and cautionary statements for those remaining behind. She went out onto the piazza, looking up at a brilliant sky with only a few clouds, and those not threatening. It would be a beautiful day for the drive; a day for adventure. Not of the sort that Julie had encountered, she amended, but *fun*.

Ellen came through the doorway, calling over her shoulder. "Goodbye, take care, and Julie, be sure the house is securely locked up so that you can't be surprised by wandering scavengers."

"Yes, Mama," Julie said obediently, wishing they would go, and the warnings be at an end. She was somewhat nervous about being left more or less in charge; while Evan was in the house, he was in no condition to make decisions on any emergency that might arise. Indeed, he refused to listen to any discussion of either problems or solutions, and thereby became one of the problems.

Ellen allowed Thomas to assist her into the buggy; she was quite capable of managing the reins herself, but thought it better to allow old Rudy to do it. He was quite recovered from his ordeal last fall, and showed no apprehension about leaving the plantation.

"This old nigger got a hard head, Miss Ellen," he told her, smiling. "Take more than one crack to split it open."

The old man clucked to the horse, slapping the reins across its rump, and the buggy rolled down the drive, between the live oaks.

It was spring, Valerie thought. The leaves were tiny pale green flecks against the sky, and white dogwood blossoms appeared here and there amidst the greenery. Soon it would be summer, and for a few months, at least, they wouldn't have to worry about firewood, and food. Mallows' gardens had always produced all they could eat.

Rudy set a steady, sedate pace. Neither of the women spoke, although both braced themselves for the sight of Cedars as they approached the main road. Valerie would have liked not to look at it at all; she did not want to be reminded of past horrors. Yet looking at the ruined house was as strong a compulsion as putting one's tongue into a hole in one's tooth, or scratching an itch.

The walls still stood, the red brick darkened where smoke had issued from doors and windows. The roof was entirely gone; twin chimneys emerged from the gaping opening, starkly etched against the sky. Even from the road, they could detect the acrid odor of burned wood. The lawn was overgrown, and the redbud was an incongruous splash of color. Frances Douglas had once prided herself on the lawns and shrubs and flowers at Cedars; neither Ellen nor Valerie could help thinking how easily it might have been their own house that stood, deserted, gutted by fire, a sad reminder of a once beautiful family home.

Cedars was not the only obvious casualty of the Yankee invasion. Truly it was possible to see how lucky they themselves had been. As they rode along the main road, there was evidence everywhere of the passage of the enemy. Scarcely a house or a barn remained intact. In some instances the Yankees had not stayed to see that their set fires did the job completely and only part of a structure had been destroyed. In those cases, the inhabitants had done such repairs as they could manage, without regard to appearance. They saw many boarded-over windows, and few farm animals, and widespread neglect of everything from lawns and fences to houses and outbuildings.

Mamie had packed them a basket, and they stopped in late morning to eat cold cornbread with slices of ham. Had it not been for the Yankees (who, although they ate freely of Mallows' stores, had added to them as well), they might easily have had neither the meat nor the cornmeal. Major Quinn had taken what he wanted when he headed for Savannah; Jack Ferris, a few weeks later, had been more generous in what he left behind, and from the look of things Ellen guessed that Mallows was one of the few places where the cotton crop had not been maliciously destroyed.

They reached Varner Hall in mid-afternoon.

The Varners had been friends of the Stantons for many years, although they had not seen each other more than a few

315

times since the outbreak of the war. The house was set well back off the main road, hidden by a thick stand of trees, and they approached it tensely, fearing to find a duplication of the ruins at Cedars.

The house sat peacefully in the sunshine, however; except for the need of paint, it looked much as it always had, a gracious house with a broad veranda across the front and a gallery beneath the overhanging roof that extended across both sides as well at the second-floor level. Two huge magnolia trees flanked the walkway, and a small Negro boy ran out to hold the horses when Rudy brought them to a stop.

The white-haired woman who appeared in the open doorway peered anxiously, then gave a cry of delight.

"Ellen! Ellen, my dear, what a wonderful sruprise! Come in, come in!"

There was much laughing and tearful kissing, and as Della Varner led the way inside, they poured out their questions, and their news. Valerie, eager to go on the last mile or so to the county seat, forced herself to patience through these necessary exchanges. At least in this household, there were no recent deaths. Both Varner sons had come through the war unscathed, and had already returned home to their wives and young children.

Malcolm Varner, nearing sixty, walked with a cane and was losing his vision so that he had to come very close to identify them. He was cheerful, however, and vigorous in both speech and mental activity. Refreshments were brought, and they were assured again of their welcome. Beds would be made ready for them, and dinner would be served when they returned from their errands in town.

"And then," Della cried, "we'll sit up half the night, not letting you sleep, while you tell us everything that has happened to you! We have often wondered how you are faring, and wished that the mails made it possible to find out."

Valerie listened to their voices, only half taking in their meaning, and looked about the drawing room. It was in better shape than the ones at Mallows, not having been used as a hospital; yet here, too, were the signs of wear and neglect and a clear lack of money to remedy the situation.

She wished they'd get past this first burst of chatter so that she could get on with the matter of mailing the letters. She had to be allowed to do it herself, while Ellen did something else, in order to post the one to Jack. Valerie accepted the tea

316

a servant brought, and sipped at it, wondering how quickly they could get away and go on into town.

There was something about Ellen—a new liveliness, a vivacity—that had not been a part of her for a long time. Valerie, her own senses more keen simply because of what she felt for Jack, what she looked forward to with him, watched her mother thoughtfully. Ellen had needed this trip, too, had needed the contact with old friends.

She listened to the outpouring of news, trivial and momentous, and realized for the first time that her mother had no one to talk to in this way, at Mallows. Grandma Dolly did not want to be bothered with anything that did not directly touch upon her own personal comfort. Lacy and Ellen had never meshed, somehow, although Valerie found her paternal grandmother easy to be with and to talk to. Ellen had been, ever since Roger Stanton went away to war, very much alone, for all that she lived in a houseful of people. Only now, with her own need to share the thoughts and emotions uppermost in her mind, did Valerie realize how strong the need could be for a trusted confidante.

Ellen turned her head and found Valerie's gaze upon her. She drained her cup and sprang to her feet. "The rest will have to wait; we do have things to do in town. I'm not sure how soon, we'll be back, Della—"

"Don't worry. The way we eat these days, nothing elaborate, the meal can be held back until you're ready for it. I wonder if I should have Malcolm go with you. I don't like the thought of it, just the two of you traveling alone, with only that old colored man."

"I intended to bring Lallie," Ellen said, pulling on her gloves. "Only when Valerie said she wanted to come, why I thought it would be best if she stayed home to help wait on the rest of them. Has there been trouble, then? Do we run a risk, going into Reidsville?"

Della Varner sighed. "These days, everything's a risk, isn't it? Including going to bed in your own house. There have been a few unpleasant episodes, nothing as serious as it might have been. The main body of the Yankee forces passed through weeks ago, but there continue to be stragglers and some Confederate deserters, even. Mostly things are quiet, though."

Ellen forced a smile. "It sounds as if the best thing is to

go, and take care of our business, and get back here before dark."

Della followed them out onto the wide veranda, standing there to wave them off. Ellen's smile was genuine when she looked back and waved.

"It's good to have friends," she said. "Good to know they're there, whether you can visit with them or not."

They encountered only a few farm wagons and two men on horseback, approaching the county seat. All of the men nodded and touched their hats. The main street showed little activity, and no sign of marauders. Ellen touched Rudy on the shoulder to direct him to the general store.

"Stop here, Rudy, please. I'll see about the household supplies first, and then we'll cross over to the pharmacy. I suppose Mr. Nevins is still the one who'll take the mail."

"I can do that, while you're in the store," Valerie offered. She had prepared for this moment, and kept any eagerness out of her voice, any suggestion of urgency.

"No, dear, that isn't necessary. I'll feel better if we stay together. This is fine, Rudy. Pull up right here, at Codder's."

Vexed, Valerie descended and lifted a hand to aid her mother out of the buggy. They hadn't taken time to do more than minimal freshening up at Varner Hall; she still wore the brown wool with only part of the red dust beaten out of it, and she felt grubby and unattractive. If she made an issue of the matter of the mail, Ellen's suspicions might be aroused; yet Valerie *had* to be the one to take it.

"I wait right here, Miss Ellen," Rudy assured her, getting down to stretch his legs.

They climbed the steps and entered the store, where there were several other customers. Ellen brought out her list and approached the counter at the side of the store, while Valerie lingered to look at an assortment of shoes on display. They were sturdy and practical rather than stylish, and the prices ranged from $4.75 to $6.00. Valerie bit her lip; at those prices, they wouldn't be taking shoes home with them today.

A young woman moved past her, cradling an infant in one arm and holding to a small child with her other hand; her shoes were no better than Valerie's, which might have made her feel less conspicuous, but didn't.

"Mrs. Stanton! It's been a long time since we've seen you," the proprietor greeted the newcomers. "How can I help you?"

Ellen handed over her list. "Good afternoon, Mr. Codder.

318

I haven't bought anything for so long, I don't know what the prices are any more. I hope I have enough cash to pay for the basic things, at least." She opened her handbag and drew out a sheaf of bills.

The man's smile vanished and he cleared his throat. "That's Confederate money, Mrs. Stanton."

"Certainly it's Confederate money," Ellen agreed. "What else would I have?"

He licked his lips. "You haven't any gold, or silver coin?"

"No." Alarm coursed through her. "It's good, isn't it? This money?"

The store owner was definitely uncomfortable now. "Well, it's like this, ma'am. They say it isn't going to be worth anything at all, once the Yankees are fully in control, so to speak. When the peace is signed. There won't be any Confederate government, and the paper money they printed is going to be worthless. If I take it, I'll have to take a loss on it, sooner or later. So I'm asking for Federal money, or gold or silver."

Blood suffused her face, the heat of shame and humiliation and frustration. Ellen glanced toward Valerie, who was running a finger over the toe of a lady's boot.

For the first time in her life, Ellen was going to have to beg for credit. She couldn't bear to share that humiliation with her daughter. She reached into her handbag and drew out the letters and the small quantity of coins that were all she had.

"Maybe you're right, Valerie. It would be best for you to mail the letters while I finish up here. Come straight back, though, won't you?"

Valerie spun, smile widening, including the proprietor. "Yes, of course. Don't worry, I'll be here when you've finished."

She did not notice the apologetic air of the storekeeper. She didn't realize that her mother was fighting desperately for self-control. She only knew that the way had opened for her, and she could mail the letter to Jack.

Valerie took the letters and went out the door and down the steps, heart suddenly soaring.

Six

The delicious taste of freedom from parental supervision was like wine in her blood. Such a simple thing as walking down the street in this small county seat, free for a moment to do what she would, was a foretaste of what would happen when she accompanied Lacy to Savannah. Her grandmother, she thought, would be easier to deceive than her mother would be. Lacy retired early, as befitting a woman in her early seventies. It should not be all that difficult to arrange a meeting with Jack, once she'd made contact with him. If he knew she was coming, he would make plans accordingly.

She wouldn't need apricot brandy to make her drunk; sheer joy of living was enough, when you were young and in love, and were loved in return.

The letters were handed over to Mr. Nevins, who assured her that while there was no regular mail route at present, there were plenty of people traveling about who were willing to carry them to their destination.

"They say Atlanta's getting back to normal," he observed. "Under the Federal flag, of course, but maybe that's better than existing in this no-man's-land, the way we still do here. It'll be months before the trains are all running again; those Yankees took to bending the tracks they've torn up so they

320

can't be straightened and can't ever be reused, unless they melt them down and start over again. But one of these days, everything will be back to normal, I reckon."

Normal? What was normal? Valerie wondered, letting herself out of the small shop. Did anyone remember? She wasn't sure she did.

She stood irresolutely on the edge of the street. Her errand had taken only a few moments; Ellen wouldn't have concluded her business this soon. Dared she step around the corner and peek into the tiny millinery and dress shop there? She wouldn't go in, she had no funds to make that worthwhile, but it would be a treat to see something pretty, something fashionable.

Valerie glanced along the street to where the horse and buggy stood. Rudy was bent over, examining a wheel or perhaps something in the roadway. What harm could it do, after all, to indulge herself with at least a glimpse of something she could go home and dream about? If Miss Emmonds hadn't been driven out of business, that was.

Valerie walked briskly, rounding the corner, seeing the familiar sign. She stopped abruptly, drawing in a deep breath.

There was no garment in the window, only a bolt of material partly unfolded and gracefully draped for the inspection of a possible customer. Apricot velvet, thick and smooth, the very shade she had envisioned upon herself. In a full skirt, with a bodice that molded her waist and breasts, it would be stunning, with or without jewelry. It was a shade she could wear, that would complement her hair and skin and eyes. Apricot velvet. The hunger in her was a physical thing. It had been so long since she'd had anything nice, anything new. Her brown wool was not only dusty, it was dowdy, ugly.

Without conscious thought, Valerie opened the door and walked in. She had to see it close up, to touch it, to fix the reality of it in her mind.

"Why, Miss Stanton! How nice to see you!" Miss Emmonds was a little woman of middle years, with graying hair drawn severely back to an untidy knot at the back of her neck. Valerie had never seen her in anything but the black delaine she now wore, or a twin to it. "What can I do for you?"

"Nothing, I'm afraid. I haven't any money," Valerie said,

apologetic. "But I had to touch that piece of goods in your window."

"Exquisite, isn't it? I never would have dared to buy it, in these troubled days. My brother won it, gambling with a Yankee officer. I suppose *he* stole it, or took it from a blockade runner. I didn't ask. I'm told a velvet like that sells for sixty dollars a yard in Savannah."

Sixty dollars a yard! Shock held her rigid, and then Valerie put out a reverent hand to stroke it. "I've never seen anything half so lovely."

"I always thought green was your color," Miss Emmonds said. She reached to lift the end of the material and drape it across Valerie's bosom. "But this is charming on you. Charming!"

She turned Valerie gently to face the mirror arranged so that ladies could see into it when trying on new bonnets. Valerie brushed her fingertips over the velvet, examining her own image.

Her hair was a rich deep auburn, her skin clear and unblemished, her hazel eyes thickly lashed. And the velvet, the rich apricot velvet—

"I think," she said slowly, "I'd give my soul, for a dress made from this."

Miss Emmonds did not find that a melodramatic statement. She smiled. "You are the one who should wear it. I would love to make it up for you—cut rather low, to reveal your bosom, no?" Her smile faded and she sighed, withdrawing the material and rearranging it in the window for display.

"I doubt that there is anyone in Tattnall County who can afford such a dress, at present. Yet it draws women to my shop, for the things they *can* afford. Everyone wants to look at it up close, to touch it."

It was a disturbing thought, that the other women coveted it, as she did. Valerie was reluctant to have it taken away from her. "Don't sell it," she said. "One of these days, I'll be back for it."

Miss Emmonds smiled again. "I hope that it will be here, waiting for you, when that day comes."

Valerie was both elated and depressed as she stepped back out into the street. Elation was uppermost, because the velvet proved that there still were things of beauty to be had in this world, if one had the means. How she would like to wear a dress of velvet, to meet Jack!

322

One day, she thought, one day, when she was a young matron with an elegant home of her own, she would come sweeping down a broad stairway such as the one at Mallows, to meet her handsome husband and the admiring guests below, wearing a dress of that fabulous velvet.

"Well! I thought those damned Southerners were keeping all their pretty ladies locked up, but they've let one of them loose!"

She had been so absorbed in her own thoughts she had not noticed the men until they were almost upon her. Four of them. Union soldiers, unshaven and reeking of whiskey, which probably meant that they were on their own, not under the control of their officers. They were between her and the main street. Valerie looked back over her shoulder, fear rising in a paralyzing wave. Miss Emmonds had just drawn the blind, closing her shop. No help there.

Where, then?

The men were coming toward her at an unhurried pace, grinning. One of them staggered and nearly went down, well the worse for drink; his companions shoved him goodnaturedly back onto his feet.

This was how Julie had felt. Cold, icy fear coursing through her. Their eyes were fixed on her, bold glances raking her face, assessing her figure. One of them called out a lewd invitation.

An outraged bellow made her turn toward the big man trotting across the street.

"There you are, you thieving bitch! Did you think I wouldn't catch up with you?"

Valerie stopped. There was nowhere to go. The soldiers had hesitated, too, staring uncertainly at the tall redheaded man in garments so worn that it was impossible to tell whether they had originally been part of a Confederate uniform or not.

Patrick Ryan! The sweet flood of relief was cut short when he reached her, slamming her against the wall of the nearest building with a force that knocked the wind out of her.

"I'll teach you to steal from a sleeping man, you she-devil," he said savagely. He fumbled for the neck of her dress and caught it, tearing it so that her chemise was exposed, and triumphantly brandished a small pouch. "There! There's my money, what little there is left of it!" He glared around at the Yankees, who stood openmouthed. "Let me buy her drinks

323

until dawn, then made off with everything I own when I passed out! If she wasn't diseased, I'd take her right here in the alley, to show her a thing or two!"

He stepped back a pace, and Valerie, in a state of shocked bewilderment, clutched at her torn bodice.

"Damned good thing somebody told me about her," Ryan observed sourly, opening the purse to count its contents. "Or I'd have gone to bed with her, as well as buying her a drink. You're welcome to her, if you want her."

He stuck the pouch inside the front of his shirt.

He was insane. Totally insane, Valerie decided.

And then she saw their faces, the Yankee soldiers.

"Diseased, is she?" one of them asked. "I don't reckon we're that hard up, are we, boys?"

"Might be worth it," another countered. "She's about the prettiest thing I've seen in the whole damned stinking state of Georgia."

"You take what she's got home to your wife," the first soldier suggested, "and you'll wish you'd got killed in the war, instead of at home."

There was general laughter, and the men moved on, jostling each other, making humorous remarks. Valerie, feeling so weak in the knees that it was a wonder she didn't slide down the wall onto the ground, stared into Patrick Ryan's face.

"I'm sorry about the dress," he said, not sounding particularly apologetic. "I had to do something fairly drastic. I wouldn't have got far, challenging four of them."

"Diseased," Valerie said, her voice faint.

He laughed, throwing back his head. "That was an inspiration, wasn't it?"

"You took a chance, telling them they were welcome to me."

Patrick shrugged. "It's all a chance, isn't it? They might have shot me, before they raped you. There are enough women around, why should they risk picking up a disease to take home with them, if they've managed to stay clean thus far?"

He'd indicated to them that she was a whore. That was only now fully penetrating her bemused brain. And they had believed him.

"You don't ever learn, do you?" Patrick bent to pick up

324

the small purse she had dropped, handing it over to her. "What are you doing running around here, alone?"

"I stepped over to look into Miss Emmonds' shop window," she said, sounding as if her voice came from the bottom of an empty barrel. "Mama's back there, at the store, and I thought it was safe enough, in broad daylight. We hadn't seen a sign of a Yankee soldier."

His expression altered perceptibly, and for a moment she thought he was going to lecture her, as he always seemed to be doing. It was not at Valerie that he looked, however, but over her shoulder.

"Well, there are plenty of them around, including three more coming from that direction. No, don't turn around. We're going to play act some more, Miss Valerie, and if you're clever enough when I give you the cues, maybe you can get out of this place without getting any closer to being raped than you were a minute ago."

She heard them coming and stiffened, clutching the tapestry bag against her breast, where her heart seemed to be trying to break through her rib cage. There was not time to build again to full terror, however; the Yankees were coming quickly, and Valerie realized in some still functioning section of her mind why so few people were on the streets. The Yankees were everywhere, and it was a rare citizen who dared to defy them.

"Faint," Patrick Ryan ordered tersely, "and make it look good."

For a matter of seconds, she did not take his meaning. And then she did, and between suffocating stays and agitated breathing, it wouldn't have been too difficult to make the faint genuine. As it was, Valerie swayed and let her knees buckle, trusting to Ryan to catch her.

He did, swooping her up in his arms and turning immediately to face the oncoming soldiers. Valerie willed her body to go limp against the man, who held her as easily as if she'd been a child.

Ryan didn't wait for the Yankees to take the offensive. He spoke to them in a voice conveying urgency.

"Please, is there a doctor? Does anybody know if there's a doctor? I think my wife has diphtheria!"

The men, who had been looking for a bit of sport with the much overrated Southern belles, came to an abrupt halt.

"Do any of you know anything to do for her? See, look,

325

she has a yellowish coating on her tongue, and she's been complaining of a sore throat, and now she's collapsed!"

"Don't bring her any closer to us, you damned fool. Go on, get away from us!"

"But she needs a doctor," Patrick insisted, taking yet another step toward them. "Do any of you know anything about diphtheria? Can you look at her? Can you tell me?"

They broke, stepping aside, moving around him, shouting back obscene suggestions. Patrick made no reply, but carried her in long strides along the walk toward where Rudy stood beside the buggy.

The old man turned and saw them, his eyes bulging.

"Mr. Ryan! What happen to Miss Valerie?"

"Nothing, no thanks to her idiocy in wandering around by herself. We're pretending she's sick, Rudy, until we can get her out of town. Hold that damned horse while I get her into the buggy."

"Yes, sir, Mr. Ryan."

Valerie stirred against the broad chest and Patrick snapped in her ear. "Stay unconscious. We're not out of the woods yet."

It was not easy, to feign limpness when she was literally rigid with fear, and it was an awkward business getting her onto the back seat of the buggy. She hit an elbow, painfully, on something, and moaned.

"If you could throw up, or bleed, it might help," Patrick said without a trace of sympathy.

He had saved her from the Yankees, not once but twice, and it didn't help to know that he was right about the foolishness of wandering about alone. Yet she wanted to strike him.

And then, unexpectedly, Patrick Ryan was with her in the buggy, cradling her against him as he might have done had her illness been genuine. He bent over her, resting his head on her breast like a husband stricken with grief.

Surely he carried it too far? Were they still being observed by the enemy soldiers? His head was heavy; the thick red hair lay against her chin and cheek and smelled of woodsmoke, and she was suddenly aware of him as a man. Aware of the lean muscularity of arms and thighs, of the rasp of a whiskered chin as he moved his head, burying his face against the exposed flesh above the chemise.

He murmured into the softness. "Not bad, Miss Valerie. I

think you could have held still and let them examine your tongue for diphtheria, if they'd had the courage to do it."

He was laughing, and she pushed against him, only to find that it was too late for that. Patrick Ryan's head lifted long enough to allow him to look down at her, and she to gaze up into the familiar, yet now strangely unknown face.

She had known Patrick Ryan all her life. She had never before been this close to him. He'd grown a mustache since she'd seen him, a luxuriant growth the same color as his hair. There was a tiny scar at one corner of his mouth, running through his upper lip and disappearing under the red brush above it. His eyes were a vivid, hard blue. And as she looked into them, something shifted and changed there, almost in synchronization with her suddenly accelerated pulses.

For a matter of seconds they looked into each other's eyes, only inches apart. And then, quite deliberately, Patrick Ryan lowered his mouth to hers. It was different from Jack Ferris's kiss. She could not have said exactly how this was so, only that it was. The scent of him was different, and the brush of the mustache, and the taste of him. It was not a show kiss to convince the casual observer of anything. It was a kiss for the benefit of Patrick Ryan, because he wanted it.

Her instinct was to protest, and be damned to any watching Yankee, but his arms were a vise immobilizing her. And as the liquid fire exploded and spread throughout her body, Valerie was astonished that anyone other than Jack Ferris could so kindle the heat of desire. Desire, yes, for a space of seconds, she knew desire, with an urgency that surely must have matched that of the man who held her.

And then she heard her mother's voice, sharp and angry, and the desire died, leaving Valerie boneless and shaken.

Seven

The Stantons, and the Mallow family before them, had traded with Codder's General Store for as far back as Ellen could remember. To the best of her knowledge, no member of either family had ever had to humiliate himself, begging for credit for a few paltry supplies.

Mr. Codder shifted his weight and looked uncomfortable when Ellen put her request. "You know it ain't that I don't think highly of you as a customer, Mrs. Stanton. It's just that I got to pay for my supplies, and I can't afford to carry anybody any length of time. I do, and I'll be out of business, and that won't help anybody."

"It wouldn't be for long," Ellen said, cheeks burning, wondering if the other customers in the establishment could make out her words. "My husband's mother, Mrs. Lacy Stanton, is putting her Savannah house up for sale. It's a fine place, a beautiful one, in a most desirable location, right off Reynolds Square. I could clear the bill as soon as the money is paid over on that. A few weeks, surely no more than a month."

Her distress and desperation were evident, and Mr. Codder liked her. His wife didn't; she'd always thought Ellen Mallow Stanton stuck up and unfriendly, but he knew it was just that she was a lady. She had quality, Mrs. Stanton did.

She saw the indecision in his face, and twisted at the ring on her left hand, pulling it free. "Here. My wedding ring, I'll leave it for security."

The present scene was not a new one for Mr. Codder. These days everybody had troubles, and no one had any cash money, including himself. His wife wouldn't like it, if she knew he'd given Ellen Stanton credit. On the other hand, he kept the books himself, and the poor woman wasn't asking for a great deal. Sugar, salt, molasses, a few staples.

He pushed the narrow gold bank back toward her. "I don't want your ring, Mrs. Stanton. If you say you'll pay in a month, I'll take your word for it. I'll get these things together for you in a moment."

Relief left her weak and she thanked him unsteadily. "I have an errand at the pharmacy, too," she said. "Will you put the things in my buggy, please?"

"Yes, of course," Mr. Codder said, and hoped she'd have driven away with them before his wife came along and saw whose buggy it was.

It was amazing to Ellen that she could walk down the steps and across the street, that she could speak so calmly to the pharmacist. She'd had a bit of practice, though; this time she didn't bring out her pitiful sheaf of Confederate bills. She told him instead about the sale of Lacy's house, and asked with commendable surface confidence if he might let her have the few drugs she needed, to be paid for within a month's time.

To her overwhelming gratitude, she did not have to offer her ring as security, nor reduce herself to groveling. She had known, crossing the dusty street, that she would grovel, if she had to. Evan needed the medication for pain, and there would be other suffering to be alleviated by whatever means came to hand. If necessary, she'd beg for it on her knees.

She came out of the pharmacy and hesitated, for there were soldiers, Yankees, out there. She waited in the doorway until they had passed, then stepped off the walk into the street. She didn't realize, until she was right alongside the buggy, that Valerie was in the seat of the buggy, and that there was a man with her. Patrick Ryan, it could only be Patrick Ryan with hair that color. He was, incredibly, kissing Valerie as she lay sprawled across the seat.

"Valerie! Mr. Ryan, I will thank you to remove yourself from my conveyance at once!"

Ryan lifted his head and sat up straight, not at all disconcerted. "Miss Ellen. I'm glad to see *you*, at least, haven't been molested. I'm sorry the two of you didn't pay any attention to my warning about roaming around the countryside."

Ellen was too furious to defend her journey to the county seat. "I asked you to vacate my buggy, sir."

"Certainly. I hope you've a safe place to spend the night? That you aren't going to be on the road? Early morning's the best time to avoid the marauders; most of them are sleeping off the previous night's drink then."

He descended to the ground, leaving Valerie feeling, for more reasons than one, as if she'd suddenly been set down on a heap of eggshells poised over a deep abyss.

"Mama, you don't understand," she said quickly. "Mr. Ryan rescued me, twice, from the Yankees. We had to pretend that we were man and wife, and that I was ill—" It seemed best to pretend, as well, that it was the only impression they had given; she could imagine her mother's reaction to Patrick's remark about Valerie's *disease*. "He was most inventive in outwitting them, when they most certainly intended me considerable harm."

Patrick grinned, looking back up at her. "I didn't read all those books from the Mallows library for nothing, you know. I've never taken up playacting before, except in a few tight places during the war, but I find it rather to my liking."

"And this exhibition you were putting on, in broad daylight, in front of the citizens of Reidsville?" Ellen demanded, unappeased. "Kissing my daughter? If you saved Valerie from something disagreeable, then I must of course be grateful. Yet I hardly see how this disgusting spectacle I have just observed could be of benefit to anyone but yourself, sir."

Patrick Ryan's grin faded. He towered over her, a big, bulky man. "Yes. I forget myself, don't I? I am, after all, no more than a Georgia cracker's son, a former overseer, a Confederate soldier whose regiment more or less fell to pieces so that I haven't actually been mustered out, nor yet remain in the service of my country." A hardness came into his voice, kept purposely low. "I may be thanked for saving your daughter from a fate worse than death, isn't that the way you ladies look upon it? The second one of them I've had to rescue in a matter of months, and from the same fate. But I'm not good enough to presume upon that relationship, am I? I'm still poor white trash, to the ladies of Mallows."

Valerie opened her mouth to protest that assessment of himself; though he might have overstepped the bounds of propriety for a few moments, he could not really be said to have forced himself upon her. And a kiss was surely a small reward for what he'd done, not without risk to himself. He was unarmed; any of the soldiers could have decided to kill him, and could have done so with impunity, had he not been clever enough to change their minds about having their sport with her.

He didn't give her the opportunity to defend him, however. He didn't even look at her, speaking only to her mother. "I won't inconvenience you any further, Miss Ellen."

He turned and strode away, and Valerie stifled the urge to cry out after him, knowing that would only make matters worse with her mother.

Ellen was as white as if he'd struck her, as well as defiling her daughter. She accepted Rudy's silent assistance into the buggy and settled against the cushions, her gloved hands knotting in her lap.

"I can't believe it. Wallowing about with a man like that, in public view!"

"Mama, he isn't a *man like that*. If he hadn't come along, I'd have been in the same predicament Julie was, with the deserters, only I wouldn't have escaped. I was terrified, I knew what they intended to do with me! And he was clever, so clever! He pretended that I had diphtheria, and asked them about a doctor, and even wanted them to look at my tongue to see—"

"Stop it. Stop it at once. If he rescued you from the violence of the Yankees, then he's been thanked for that, and we can forget it. I cannot forget, however, the sight of my daughter allowing herself to be . . . to be mauled, and kissed, as if she were a common trollop, right on the street! How much further would you have gone if I hadn't come back when I did?"

"No further at all," Valerie said, controlling her tone with a great effort. "Except that I would have thanked him, quite sincerely, for having the wit I didn't have to extricate me from an explosive situation."

It was as if Ellen's rage had made her deaf. "A man like that, a common overseer! Dear God, it makes me ill to think of him touching you, and you allowed him to do it! You weren't even struggling!"

"Mama, you aren't paying attention. We had convinced the Yankees that I was ill with diphtheria, that he was my husband. He was holding me as a husband might hold a beloved wife who was ill, and we had to go on convincing the soldiers until we could get out of town, or they all wandered away."

"He was holding you, and kissing you," Ellen said with conviction, "the way a man does with a woman he desires. Disgusting, incredible, that you allowed it!"

It was not only that the incident had taken place in public, Valerie thought. It was desire, itself, that was disgusting to her. Her mother could not understand this emotion, this river of ardor that could carry two people away on it, oblivious of everyone and everything else.

Why, she herself had, for a few seconds, responded to it, even with a man she cared nothing about. It was only that she'd known passion, with Jack, and that when a man's mouth covered hers, when his hands touched her, there was an instinctive quickening of the physical senses.

"You do Mr. Ryan a great injustice," Valerie said. "And me, just as great a one. If you think that it would have been preferable for me to have submitted to the maulings of half a dozen Yankees, then you must go on thinking so, but I do not. I am grateful to Mr. Ryan, and I do not care to apologize to you for anything. If we were observed, why, everyone but you saw the necessity for the playacting, and I strongly doubt that anyone else condemns me for it."

Ellen turned toward her, eyes huge in her white face.

"I don't understand you," she said.

"No, that's clear enough." In the release from fear, Valerie felt anger rise within her. "You've preached virtue at me since before I knew the meaning of the word, yet now you sound as if you'd rather I'd been dragged into the alley by those soldiers than to have gone along with Mr. Ryan's improvisations!"

"Don't be a fool! Of course I didn't want you to be raped by the soldiers, or abused by them! I only object to your kissing Patrick Ryan after it was all over with!"

"It was part of the same thing! We had to convince those watching that it was true, that I was ill and that they didn't want to risk contaminating themselves by getting near me!"

"You were kissing him," Ellen said with unassailable certitude, "as if you enjoyed it."

Some of Valerie's anger began to dissipate. "I don't know

332

whether I did or not," she said with a candor that might not do her cause any good. "I certainly didn't find it as repulsive as having my clothes torn off and—"

"Stop it. I cannot believe that you can bring yourself to discuss such an offensive subject."

"What is it you find offensive, Mama? The subject of rape, which would seem to be within the bounds of conversation since the Yankees are bent upon perpetrating it upon any Southern woman they can find? Or being kissed? Is there something essentially revolting about being kissed, Mama? Isn't it a thing two people do, when they care for one another? Didn't you ever enjoy being kissed?"

Ellen turned her head, looking at the old black man's back. Rudy, if he found the conversation intriguing, knew enough to pretend to deafness.

"I don't care to continue this discussion," Ellen said stiffly.

"Don't you? Why not? Why is it beyond the bounds of decency to discuss kissing, or loving? I've grown up knowing that someday I'd meet a man and marry him, and no one ever indicated that that was a wrong thing to do. In fact, it's expected of all of us. That we marry, and perform our wifely duties, isn't that the way it's put? Are we only supposed to submit to a husband's caresses with fear and loathing, or are we permitted to enjoy them, too? No, no, don't look at me that way! We're made men and woman, aren't we, for a purpose? Does it make us disgusting if we fall in love, if we enjoy a relationship with a man?"

"Are you in love with Patrick Ryan?"

"Oh, Mama, of course not! I'm only saying that he's a decent man, who did more for me, and for Julie, than he had any reason to do, except out of the goodness of his heart. If he enjoyed kissing me, after saving me from those men, why, I don't begrudge him that small reward. Especially after the way you talked to him. One would think you'd caught *him* in the act of raping me."

"It isn't Patrick Ryan I'm concerned about," Ellen said. "It's you."

"Because I may have enjoyed being kissed? I'm not sure I did, really; I was still shaking with fright at the narrow escape I'd had. I'm *still* as unsettled in the middle as a bowl of jelly. I'm only saying that I think I *could* enjoy being kissed by a man, a man I loved, I mean. And if you've never enjoyed that, then I'm profoundly sorry for you, Mama."

She was sorry as soon as she'd said that last sentence. Ellen stared straight head, lips compressed. Neither of them said another word, all the way back to Varner Hall.

Della Varner sensed at once that something was wrong. She glanced quickly between her guests, her face anxious. "Are you both all right?"

"Quite all right," Valerie told her after a moment's hesitation showed that Ellen was not going to respond. "There was an unpleasant episode in town, with some Yankee soldiers. Mr. Ryan came along and rescued me, so it came out all right."

"Ah, yes, Mr. Ryan. I remember, your overseer," Della said, relieved. "Very competent young man. Malcolm mentioned he'd met him in town the other day. He's out of the army, I take it. How lucky he was about when you needed him."

"Yes," Valerie agreed. "I'm feeling very dirty. I wonder if it would be possible to bathe before dinner, Mrs. Varner?"

"Certainly! Certainly, my dear! I'll send Astrid up with hot water for both of you. You know the room, on the left at the top of the stairs. We've made it ready for you."

Ellen said nothing as they divested themselves of their travel-stained garments and handed them over to servants to be made ready for the return trip the following day. She continued to maintain silence throughout both their baths and dressing for dinner.

It made Valerie feel quite uncomfortable. She had seldom been in open conflict with her mother, and she didn't want to be now. Yet Ellen was totally unreasonable about the present circumstances, and Valerie could not bring herself to make an apology she resented being pressured to make.

It was not until Ellen sat before the mirrored dressing table, struggling to do the back of her hair, that Valerie was able to take the first step toward a reconciliation.

"Here, let me do that," she said, and took the brush from her mother's inept hand. She swept the thick auburn hair, so like her own except for a few silvery threads, into the familiar chignon. She was not as expert at the task as Lallie, but she did a passable job. Ellen murmured "thank you" when Valerie moved back from the resulting coiffure for a final look at it.

Encouraged by those two syllables, Valerie asked, "Are we

leaving first thing in the morning? Or are there more errands?"

Ellen swallowed, and her fingers trembled visibly as she plucked at the neck of her dress. "We'll go home. My money is no good, you know. They won't take Confederate paper money any more. The war isn't even over, and our own people are refusing Confederate money."

Stunned, Valerie's eyes met her mother's in the mirror and she dropped a hand onto Ellen's shoulder. "What will we do, then?"

"I told them if they would give me credit, I would repay them in a month, when Miss Lacy's house is sold."

"Oh, Mama!" Compassion, and some understanding of what Ellen must have gone through before she came out and found her daughter in a seemingly compromising situation in the buggy, flooded through her; Valerie put her arms around Ellen and hugged her. "I'm sorry! It must have been wretched for you!"

"It was. Though not as wretched as it might have been, if they'd refused me credit. At least I got the supplies. Now we must pray that the house will sell quickly, and for a good price." The quaver in her voice cut through to Valerie's heart.

"It will. Don't worry, Mama, it will," Valerie assured her. "Why should it not? It's a lovely house, and in one of the finest sections of Savannah. Come along, maybe we'll both feel better after we've had something to eat."

Ellen did seem to revive in the company of her old friends; while she could hardly have been called animated, she did relax and converse in a normal fashion, so that Valerie didn't feel compelled to stay with her when her own eyes began to feel heavy.

They scarcely knew she had excused herself, she thought, climbing the stairs. They might well talk half the night, as Della had promised; who knew how long it would be before they had an opportunity to visit again?

For herself, although she was tired, Valerie lay in the unfamiliar bed, sleepless, for a long time.

She had not come as close to being assaulted as Julie had; the men had not actually laid hands upon her. It wasn't hard to imagine what it would be like, though, and it wouldn't be anything like having a man make love to her, gently, tenderly.

335

She thought of Charlotte, torn and bloody, literally driven to madness after the dreadful afternoon when she had been repeatedly raped. Had it not been for Patrick Ryan, it was probably exactly what would have happened to *her,* today.

Someday, perhaps, when the immediate horror of the situation had subsided, she would be fully amused at the way Patrick had rescued her. Had he simply stepped in and tried to challenge the soldiers, they'd have either beaten him up or shot him. As it was, his presentation of her first as a diseased prostitute and then as a wife ailing with a contagious disease had taken them aback. They might, later on, have realized that they'd been tricked; yet their initial reactions had been as Ryan hoped, and they'd backed off.

Whatever one thought of Patrick Ryan, she had to give him credit for an agile mind, and for courage. Interfering in anything the Yankees chose to do was asking for trouble, and he knew it as well as anyone did.

She was sincerely sorry her mother had come upon them in the buggy. Not only because it had upset Ellen so badly, but because if the embrace had continued to its natural conclusion, Valerie might have had time to sort out her thoughts regarding Patrick Ryan.

It troubled her, the way she had begun to respond to his kiss. Was it like that for Blossom, with whatever man she happened to be? Surely it was not normal to be physically stirred by more than one man, to feel that wanton sweet desire; yet had not her mother interrupted them, if, for instance, Valerie had been alone with Patrick Ryan as she had been alone with Jack Ferris that first time, what would have happened? Had she not already tasted the fruits of desire, Ryan might have both frightened and repelled her.

It was not fright, however, nor repugnance, that she had felt in Patrick Ryan's arms. *He was kissing you,* Ellen had said, *the way a man does with a woman he desires.*

Was it, as Ellen stated, disgusting that Valerie had, even momentarily, responded to that animal desire?

Well, whatever it was, it had happened. She was grateful to Ryan, and she knew enough to be wary, now, about any man other than Jack who presumed to touch her. She wouldn't be taken unaware again.

Valerie slid into an uneasy sleep, and did not know when her mother came to bed hours later, nor see the troubled expression on Ellen's face as she gazed down on the sleeping girl. If Valerie had known of her mother's concern, she wouldn't have had any idea what to do about it.

With Valerie and Ellen gone, Blossom moved about the house with a new and exciting freedom. It was easy to imagine herself mistress of the establishment, to look upon Mallows with a proprietary eye.

It was possible, also, to face Evan with a different attitude. His rages did not bother her quite so much; she was thinking beyond them, to the time when she would rightfully have a say about what went on in this place.

In truth, however, Evan's rages did not seem as frequent or as severe, with his mother and one of his sisters out of the house. Julie had been delegated the authority to dole out the prescribed doses of laudanum; otherwise, she left him more or less in Blossom's and Hattie's hands. After a futile attempt to persuade her that his pain was great enough to require more frequent administration of the drug than the one Ellen had specified, Evan gave up on Julie.

"Where does she keep it?" he demanded of Blossom.

"Same place as your mama keeps it. Locked up in that cabinet. And I ain't got the key," Blossom told him bluntly. "All I can do is bring you more whiskey."

He had to settle for that. He drank enough so that even Blossom, who took it for granted that a man, any man, would drink, felt some alarm.

"It ain't good for you, to have so much," she protested, upon learning how quickly he'd gone through the latest bottle.

"Damn it, don't tell me what's good for me, you stupid bitch. I know how much I hurt!"

Blossom stepped back from the bed, out of reach should he decide to take hold of her. For all that he was in a weakened condition, he had a grip like an alligator with those bony fingers. "You going to call me names, Mr. Evan, you can make do with old Hattie lookin' after you. I got feelin's, you know, same as anybody else."

Evan immediately changed tactics. "Yes, of course you have. I'm sorry. It's only that the pain is driving me crazy. I can feel the foot, I keep looking to see if it isn't still there, because I can *feel* it! And it hurts so goddamned much I want to hack it off to keep it from hurting any more, only it's

337

already gone! Blossom, don't leave me alone. You're the only friend I've got in this place."

His lean face was beaded with perspiration, his mouth twisted in suffering that she knew was genuine; Evan was a handsome man, and a beguiling one. Blossom responded at once to his appeal.

"I want to be your friend, Mr. Evan. Long as you treat me nice."

"I will. I will. Blossom, I'm sorry I take things out on you; it isn't that I don't like you, it's that I can't stand the pain! And even when that's dulled by the whiskey, I get so sick of this cold damned room! Isn't there enough wood so I can have a fire in here?"

Blossom moistened her lips. "I got to follow orders, Mr. Evan. Your mama says no fires 'cept in the sitting room. There ain't no man left to chop wood, 'ceptin' them boys, and they're too lazy to get in enough to go around. Your mama says you could sit over there, in the other room, where the fire is."

"And how the hell am I supposed to get there? Crawl on my hands, one knee, and this stump?" The underlying savagery was still there, though somewhat constrained by the need to avoid offending her. "I haven't got enough strength to drag myself out of bed, let alone across the landing."

"We could help you, Hattie and me," Blossom suggested. "Into a chair, and then slide the chair over there. We could do that, Mr. Evan." She waited hopefully.

His initial reaction was rejection, as he rejected virtually everything except drugs and whiskey. Several hours later, however, when the throbbing, burning agony was somewhat eased by alcohol, Evan changed his mind.

"Call Hattie," he told Blossom. "Help me into that damned chair."

The transfer to the sitting room was accomplished, though not without considerable trauma to everyone concerned. Lallie was called in, as well, and it took the three of them to move Evan into the chair, placed on a small rug, which could be slid out of the room and across the landing to the sitting room.

"There, by the French windows," Evan ordered. "So I can see out over the drive."

The exertion was a telling one; he, as well as the women, was drenched in perspiration, and he'd have given his soul for the key to his mother's locked cabinet. If he hadn't known they were capable of stopping him, he'd have taken an ax to it, or whatever else came to hand, to get the drug he craved.

The drug wasn't the only thing Evan had in his mind, however. When they had arranged him as comfortably as they could, and placed a comforter around him, and built up the fire, he spoke without looking at any of them.

"I want to sit here for a while. Leave me alone," he said, his voice muffled.

"I'll wait where I can hear you call," Blossom offered.

"No. No, just leave me for an hour," Evan said. "Come back then."

For long minutes after they'd gone, he stared out at the oyster shell drive, at the familiar live oaks with their hanging moss, to the red clay road in the distance.

I will never ride that road again, he thought. *I will never again sit a horse, or make love to a woman, or dance with one, or fish in the creek on a sunny summer morning. I am dead already, though the pain goes on and on.*

The landscape misted before him, and the suffering in his heart and mind was worse than what he presently felt in his stump. After a time, though, Evan pulled himself together and looked around the familiar room.

There had to be a gun somewhere in the house, he thought. Where would it be? Where would they have hidden it?

Eight

The return journey from Reidsville was accomplished without incident. Whether Ryan was right about the early morning hours being the safest, if the Yankees had moved on, or they were simply lucky, they didn't know. They didn't feel much like talking; they were bringing home the necessities they'd gone for, but that small triumph was overshadowed by the larger picture. Their Confederate money would buy them nothing. The overall economic situation was a grave one, and they had no experience in financial matters beyond what Ellen had learned in the year since Roger's death; during the years that he was away, fighting, he had at least been able to advise her by letter. Now she was on her own.

Malcolm Varner might have been of some assistance, had she been able to bring herself to be frank with him about her situation. Not financially, since it was obvious the Varners were in little better shape than the Stantons, but in the matter of advice about what to do with the plantation and how cash might be raised for the necessary supplies.

Ellen knew that pride was a sin; in the years before her brothers died, when Dolly Mallow still cared about such things, she had taught her daughter from the Bible, that too much pride was a bad thing. Ellen could see how it certainly

340

made matters more difficult, now, yet she could not bring herself to admit to anyone outside her own household just how desperate her situation was. To confess to this would be tantamount to asking for help from people who would not be in a position to assist her, and who would, in turn, be humiliated by having to tell her so.

In addition to sharing her mother's worries about finances, and how to keep Mallows going, Valerie had her own problems. After the episode in Reidsville, Ellen might be more than reluctant to allow her to go with Lacy to Savannah. Valerie was, herself, uneasy about making the trip, since the Yankees were still roaming the countryside unchecked. Yet the lure of Savannah, and Jack Ferris, tugged at her like a powerful magnet.

They arrived home tired and moderately depressed, although both made an effort to appear cheerful when the others came out onto the veranda to welcome them. Sally Ann, looking better than they had yet seen her, carried Hugh Alexander and proudly announced his new accomplishment.

"He can sit up, all by himself!" she said.

The baby cooed and held out his hands, and Valerie took him, burying her face in his now chubby neck. He was so precious, so sweet. One day she would have babies like this, Jack's babies, she promised herself.

Blossom was there, hovering behind Julie and Lacy; Dolly had not come onto the piazza, as was to be expected, but Lallie had, and Pansy.

Ellen sought out Julie first of all. "How's Evan?"

Julie, in turn, referred to Blossom. "Blossom spends the most time with him, she'd know better than I. She got him up, though, into a chair, and over to the sitting room."

"Did she?" In her gratitude for that, Ellen gave Blossom the warmest smile the girl had yet seen from her. "That seems to me an excellent step forward." She turned to touch a gentle finger to the baby's cheek. "I swear, he couldn't have grown in only two days, but it seems that he did."

She chattered on about inconsequential matters until they had assembled around the breakfast room table for a restorative cup of tea, before she gave them the news. What little cash she had was worthless. She had had to ask for credit for the things she was able to bring home, and those were limited to the most essential items.

341

Ellen looked wearily at her mother. "I couldn't bring you any knitting worsted. They wanted sixty cents a skein for it."

They sat, shocked and speechless, all of them but Blossom fully aware of what it must have cost her to beg from common merchants. And even Blossom realized the significance of the news in terms of the future, although she did not feel that it was as catastrophic as the others did. Blossom, after all, had never known luxury or plenty, and therefore had less to lose in her way of life.

"And so," Ellen concluded, looking apologetically at Lacy, "I'm afraid we're in urgent need of whatever can be realized on your Savannah house." Fairness compelled her to add, "If you still are willing to sell it to help us, of course."

"The letters went off, did they not? To the present tenants and to Mr. Tilson, the lawyer? Nothing has changed," Lacy said softly. "I am still too old to return home alone, and there is no money to make such a thing possible with the necessary servants."

"Then I think," Ellen said, "the sooner the better. I wish we had more assurance that it's safe to travel. Valerie nearly came to grief with a wandering band of Yankee soldiers in Reidsville, and apparently there are still plenty of them around. However, I shouldn't think they'd bother to harass or harm an elderly woman."

"She can't travel alone," Valerie said, too quickly, and then bit into her tongue to keep from saying any more.

Ellen glanced at her without any particular evidence of suspicion. "No, of course not. I think perhaps Lallie had better go, too."

Valerie's heart began to beat heavily, quickly. "Won't it be safer if there is a larger party? They seem to prey on women alone, not those traveling in groups. Maybe Julie would like to go, this time." This last was an inspiration; she must persuade Ellen to make a party of the excursion, including herself as one of the members, yet she could not make too much of an issue over the matter of being included. She knew perfectly well that her sister would refuse; there was nothing drawing Julie to Savannah, and she felt more secure at home. Therefore the part of companion should fall to Valerie by default.

"No," Julie said promptly, shaking her head. "I've no desire to go. Don't you think *you* should go, Mama?"

"No." Ellen was just as positive about it. "I can't be away

long enough. It will take you three days each way, and possibly as much as a week or more once you get there, unless Mr. Tilson already has a buyer lined up ahead of time. I'm afraid it will have to be Valerie again, and Lallie, Miss Lacy."

So easily it was done. She had not had to beg to go, she had been assigned to accompany her grandmother. Valerie hugged her elation to herself, scarcely hearing the rest of the plans as they were made.

Ellen sought her mother-in-law out in the privacy of the old lady's room, to thank her again for the sacrifice she was making, and to speak about Valerie.

"I'm concerned about her," Ellen said hesitantly.

"So am I," Lacy agreed, her gaze sharpening.

"You are? Why?"

"Why are you surprised," Lacy asked, "that I, too, am observant? I love the girl; she reminds me of myself, when I was young. The war years have been cruel to us all, and in some ways it's harder on the young ones. They want so much of life, and they're afraid they may not get it. I have had my life, and for me it's only a matter of trying to live out what's left of it in reasonable comfort and security. For Valerie and Julie, they know they should have many years ahead of them, and they long for love and happiness; so far, they've had little reason to think they'll find those things."

Ellen sighed. "God only knows what's in store for any of us. But if the Lord intends them to find love, they will find it. It's a premature infatuation I'm more concerned about, now. I know Valerie was attracted to Captain Ferris."

"I'd have said it was a mutual attraction," Lacy responded, and knew that Ellen was again astonished at her perception of this.

"Yes, well, I thought we were well rid of him, when he left. He's in Savannah, you know, and that's what I wanted to speak to you about. I don't want her to meet him."

"I see." Lacy regarded her with intelligent dark eyes. "And you want me to make sure she doesn't? How, exactly, do you propose that I do that?"

A touch of color warmed Ellen's face. She hadn't expected a response that was almost a challenge. "You'll be together. I'd like you to keep it that way, see to it that she doesn't have a chance to seek him out."

"And if *he* seeks *her* out?"

The color deepened. This was not going the way Ellen had envisioned it. "How could he do that? He won't know *she's* there."

"Won't he?"

Ellen stood very still. "What do you mean by that? How could he? Do you have any reason to think they've been in communication with each other? How could they have been?"

"I don't know that they have been. I only know that they were strongly drawn to each other, and Savannah isn't a large city. If we were there for a week, the odds against running into Captain Ferris are not all that high. And if they are in love, there is little that I, Valerie's old grandmother, could do to frustrate them." Lacy chuckled. "I could certainly have outwitted my grandmother, or my mother, for a romantic interlude. Any girl of spunk would try it, anyway."

"Do I understand, then," Ellen asked, "that you refuse to attempt to play the part of the chaperone, if Valerie goes with you?"

"Not at all. I am quite willing to be a chaperone. That wasn't what you were asking of me, was it? It was to keep her from meeting Captain Ferris at all, which might well be a bad mistake."

Only the recollection of what Lacy was going to Savannah to do kept Ellen's anger and indignation from erupting, enabled her to keep her voice level. "A mistake, to protect my daughter from a Yankee we know almost nothing about?"

"A mistake to forbid her to see him," Lacy suggested. "The forbidden fruit is always sweeter; they've known that for centuries. Valerie is a strong-minded girl, and she's nearly twenty years old, well past the age where she might normally have acquired a husband and learned what loving and living are all about. She longs for those things, like any normal woman. Quite possibly she thinks Captain Ferris is the right man for her. If he isn't, better she discovers it for herself than is expected to take someone else's word for it. Until the decision in that regard is her own, she won't accept it. If she's allowed to see him, openly and with the apparent sanction of her family, she'll find out what sort of man he is. She's bright enough to recognize a rogue for what he is, given the opportunity. And we don't know that Captain Ferris is a rogue, do we?"

"He's a Yankee," Ellen said, her mouth going flat.

"A Yankee. Yes. I've no more reason to love the Yankees than you have, but do we have the right to tell Valerie that she can't consider a Yankee as a husband? When so many Georgians have died, when there are nowhere near enough of them left to provide husbands for the women who remain? The man is well behaved, he obviously comes from a respectable family of some means. Would you have her remain single forever, rather than marry a Yankee?"

"There are worse things than remaining single throughout one's lifetime," Ellen told her, with an intensity that betrayed the depth of her feelings.

"Perhaps, if the choice is one's own. I think you underestimate Valerie's own common sense, my dear. And I will, of course, provide proper chaperonage, in whatever manner you request. I cannot promise, however, to be more clever than two very clever young people, if they would outfox me."

"I will be most appreciative, Miss Lacy, if you will do your best, then, to keep her away from Captain Ferris. Naturally, I will not hold you responsible for any misbehavior on Valerie's part; I only wish that she will have little or no opportunity for any such thing."

"As you like," Lacy said. And once again Ellen knew that the older woman considered her incompetent, a fool.

Ellen, in turn, felt that Lacy was completely mistaken about the situation. One did not tempt a child with something one did not want her to have; a mother protected a daughter in whatever way she could. Though she was not happy about Valerie going to Savannah with her grandmother, Ellen saw no way around it. Sending the old lady with only a pair of servants was out of the question, and Lacy must go there to sign the papers and be paid for her house.

She would speak to Lallie, too, on the subject of Valerie and Captain Ferris. On, not as plainly as she'd spoken to Lacy. But clearly enough so that Lallie would be on the alert to abort any illicit plans of Valerie's.

When she thought about it, it seemed that Lacy was right about one thing. Valerie was ready to fall in love, judging by the way she'd taken to looking up at the Yankee captain through those thick lashes, and the way she'd allowed Patrick Ryan to embrace and kiss her. Ellen had no objection to Valerie finding romance, with a suitable man; it made her stomach churn, however, to think of her daughter being

345

mauled by a common overseer, a man of no station whatever, or by the Yankee physician.

She wondered whether to speak to Valerie herself, as well, or to keep still, thereby avoiding putting any ideas into the girl's head. In the end, she left the situation in Lacy's hands, trusting that the promise to chaperone to the best of her ability would be sufficient to keep Valerie safe.

It took them a week to prepare for the trip to Savannah. New clothes being impossible, they repaired and refurbished their wardrobes as best they could. Valerie gave up, regretfully, the prettiest of her gowns, once intended to be worn to a ball; how she would love to wear it for Jack! Her mother hovered over the trunk as it was being packed, and would have judged it inappropriate for a business trip. It wouldn't do to arouse suspicion.

There were, of course, friends in Savannah, as well as along the way. "Nobody," Ellen said firmly, "will expect extravagance of dress in these times. And you will not be attending any parties."

"No," Valerie agreed with regret. She thought of the apricot-colored velvet, and hoped that Miss Emmonds wouldn't ever sell it to anyone else. If it took a dozen years, Valerie vowed, she would one day have a dress made of it.

The day before they were to go, Gilly and Chad ran away. Old Rudy brought the news. His wife, Sheba, had heard the child crying in the next cabin and had finally gone over to see what was the matter,

"That baby, he soakin' wet and hungry," Rudy reported. "That girl done gone off and left him, Sheba think,"

Ellen stared at him in helpless rage, "Where is the baby?"

"Sheba take him over to Nora. She got plenty milk for two babies."

"And what about Hugh Alexander? Who's supposed to feed *him?*"

It was a rhetorical question, and Rudy made no attempt to answer it. Sure enough, within minutes of the time they learned of Gilly's defection, Sally Ann's son lifted his voice in a wail of protest over his empty stomach.

There were two other women besides Nora nursing infants; Opal, a quiet, plain-faced girl whose own small daughter was obviously doing well on her milk, was called in to attend to Hugh Alexander's needs. Gilly's Rastus was handed

346

over to Nora to rear, and only Ellen cared, one way or the other, that two more people had gone.

The journey to Savannah took three full days. They saw a few soldiers, in both blue and gray uniforms, as well as blacks who were mostly in rags, all of them moving aimlessly about the countryside. Except for the horse and the buggy, there was little about those from Mallows to attract attention, and no one seriously tried to molest them. Valerie, on her grandmother's advice, kept her hair covered with a bonnet that shielded her face, as well. Lacy was an old lady, and looked it; Lallie was clearly a lady's maid, and if Valerie did not appear to be young and attractive, why, all the better.

Both nights on the road, they found refuge with old acquaintances. While no one had much, everyone shared what they did have. They exchanged news, slept in spite of the aches from riding in the hard seats for hours, and set out again at dawn.

By the time the buggy entered the city, Valerie had lost her excitement in discomfort and sheer weariness. There was no question of seeking Jack out yet today; it was late afternoon, and the tenants at Lacy's house had been warned to expect them. With any luck, Lacy said, the people might even have found somewhere else to live, and moved on.

They rolled through the streets, relieved to see the city looking much as it always had. In spite of what they'd heard, both Valerie and Lacy had feared there would be destruction such as had occurred at Atlanta. There was none, however. Savannah was still a beautiful city of park-like squares and flowering trees; live oaks such as had had to be persuaded to grow at Mallows were natives here, their swags of moss moving gently in the breeze from off the ocean.

Lallie had never been here and her dark eyes darted this way and that, assessing this place she had heard so much about. There were a fair number of people on the streets, most of them looking somewhat more prosperous than those they had encountered out in the country; a sizable proportion of them were Negroes. Lallie watched them with interest, wondering if they were slave, or free. To be free, in such a place as this—would that time ever come for her?

Rudy turned the buggy onto Oglethorpe Avenue, named for the general who had been responsible for laying out the city so many years ago. Lallie, who had seen very little be-

347

yond the limits of Mallows, was enthralled by the houses with their lacy wrought-iron lattices in windows, on balconies, and stair-rails, many of them in stucco or red, yellow, gray, or white brick.

Apricot trees blushed with pink blossoms, and both squares and yards were bright with a profusion of flowers and blooming shrubs. Lallie lifted her head and sniffed. "The flowers make the perfume, but what's the other smell?"

"The sea," Valerie told her, smiling. "Fish, and boats, and the marshlands."

Lallie considered carefully before pronouncing her verdict. "I like it," she said.

"I do, too. I've always loved Savannah."

Lacy said nothing. Her eyes were dry, the tears only in her heart. Was this the last time she would ever see these familiar streets, in the city where she had spent a long and happy life?

"Drive through Johnson Square," she said suddenly, and Rudy obediently tugged on the reins. It was slightly out of their way, but she wanted to see it again, the first of Savannah's many squares, a park where she had often walked to services at Christ Church. The imposing Greek Revival building with its tall white columns and wrought-iron railings was just as she remembered it. It was the church where Roger had been christened, where the children she had lost had lain in their tiny coffins while the children's burial service had been read over them before they were put to rest in the cemetery a few blocks away. Their graves were beside Charles Stanton's, and she had fully expected that one day she, too, would lie beside those dear ones.

Now it seemed unlikely to her that she would ever return to Savannah. Once her house was sold, there would be no reason to do so. She would live out the rest of her days at Mallows, and be buried beside Roger, instead of with Charles. Did it matter, where they put her bones when the spark of life was gone?

No, Lacy decided. Dead bones are dead bones, a hole in the ground in one place is much the same as a hole in the ground anywhere else. It was the remaining days that bothered her, the days in Ellen's house and the idea that she would probably never see any of these streets again.

She felt a strong impulse to order Rudy to go on, through Johnson Square with its churches, to drive the length of Bay Street instead of only around the block and back toward her own house; now that she was so close, she could hardly bear the thought of arriving, knowing it was for the last time.

As if catching that thought, Valerie leaned forward. "Before we leave, we must go down to the wharves. I want to see River Street, and the barges. Are they shipping cotton any more, I wonder?"

"It's one thing I must find out about, for your mother," Lacy said. "Look at the azaleas around the Sheridan house, aren't they lovely?"

She did not glance toward her own house until Rudy drew up and stopped before the door. And then it was with a heavy heart that did not lift when she saw that the blinds were drawn, and the place had a deserted air.

"It's empty," Valerie said. "At least I think it is. No one's cut the grass or tended the garden in a long time."

Rudy got down and came back to assist them from the buggy, Lacy first, then Valerie, leaving Lallie to jump down as best she could. Valerie felt Lacy's fingers on her wrist, cool fingers, with a grip that betrayed her in a way her face did not.

"Lallie, run next door and see if they've left the key with the Babcocks. There, the house with the iron dolphins on the drainspouts."

Valerie tried to keep her tone light. "I always loved those dolphins. Particularly when it rained and the water came rushing out their mouths. Look, the griffin is still here, Grandma!"

It was, a grotesque iron creature provided for the scraping of one's boots, looking exactly as it had looked for fifty years, beside the front walk.

The house, however, had a shabby air. The black shutters against the gray brick needed painting, there were rents in the draperies inside the drawing room windows, and a few of the paving stones in the walk had cracked and tilted so that they made walking hazardous.

They waited in silence, looking up at the facade, until Lallie came back with not only the key to the front door, but Shirley Babcock. Mrs. Babcock was close to Lacy's age, and they'd been neighbors for most of their married lives. She threw her arms around Lacy and hugged her, then drew back with a distressed expression. "Dear Lacy, I'm afraid you're going to be shocked at the house. Those Welters were impossible, and when your letter came they simply packed up and left. I sent Amos over to clear away some of the debris, but there was so much I couldn't do anything about."

Though they were forewarned, nothing could have prepared them for the interior of the house. Dirt and debris were things that could be put to rights. Structural damage was something else.

Lacy's dismay was unconcealed as she stood in the broad hallway, staring through the arched doorway into the drawing room on her right, the dining room on her left. It was dirty, yes, but that was the least of it.

Holes were punched through the plaster, as if with a broom handle, and the mirror over the marble fireplace was cracked and splintered. The magnificent bas-relief plaster moldings and ceiling fixtures were chipped and broken, and the chandeliers that had been Lacy's pride and joy were either missing (in the drawing room) or so badly damaged as to be irreparable, even if she'd had the money to do it. She'd had the carpets taken up before she left the house; the hardwood floors so exposed had scarcely a trace of finish left on them, and in one end of the dining room it appeared that there had been a fire, scorching floor, walls, and curtains.

Numbed, Lacy lifted her gaze to the stairway that wound in a tight spiral to the top of the house from the back of the entry hall, and saw more vandalism. Some of the slender posts had been broken free, perhaps for firewood; the remaining posts and railings were scuffed and scarred.

"I'm afraid it's all like this," Shirley Babcock said softly. "Even the trees have been broken in the back garden. There was a fire in the carriage house about a year ago, and it's been gutted. It probably should be knocked down; Amos says it's dangerous the way it is, so don't go into it."

They finished their inspection in silence. Valerie felt tears in her own eyes, remembering how the spacious, airy rooms had looked when her grandparents had lived here. Some of the furniture Lacy had left had disappeared altogether—burned during the coldest part of the winter, no doubt—and the rest was so abused that it might as well have been destroyed, too.

"Come over and spend the night with us," Mrs. Babcock urged. "There's nothing here to make a fire of, and the house has stood empty long enough to be thoroughly chilled. There's nothing to eat, either, and I've a great pot of chowder, plenty to go around."

Lacy's stricken eyes returned to meet her friend's. "We'll thank you for the chowder, Shirley. But I think we'll sleep here. There are still a few of my belongings in the attic, I hope. Lallie and Rudy will bring them down, so we can make up beds. It isn't only a matter of imposing on you, my dear, I truly want to spend these last nights in the place."

Valerie worked beside the others, pulling down feather ticks and quilts and comforters, and made up beds for each of them, in the upstairs bedrooms.

"Do you want to share a bed?" Lacy asked, turning from her inspection of the sheets Lallie had resurrected. "Or would you prefer to have your own?"

Pink tinged Valerie's averted face; she busied herself with tucking a sheet under the mattress on the floor in the corner of the room that had once been an elegant boudoir. She had, temporarily, forgotten Jack Ferris. Now she remembered, and she spoke as casually as she could manage.

"I think I'll make up my own, as long as we have enough ticks and bedclothes to go around. I've had to sleep with Julie for months, now, and I long to be by myself again."

"It looks as if the roof has leaked in the big front bedroom, so maybe you'd better take the middle one, then," Lacy said, and the matter was settled.

They all walked over next door for supper. Mrs. Babcock's chowder was excellent, and a rare treat to those who had not had seafood in such a long time. Their spirits sagged, however, and they had no desire to linger for conversation when the meal was ended.

Tomorrow, Valerie thought, walking back through the twilight to the once beautiful house, tomorrow, maybe she would meet Jack.

Nine

They were up early. Rudy had scavenged enough wood for a fire in the basement kitchen. Lallie made tea from the supplies they had brought with them, and they finished off the cornbread they had carried from Mallows.

"What now?" Valerie asked. "What's on the agenda for this morning?"

Lacy's lips were wooden. "To see Grady Tilson, I suppose. You realize, don't you, that the condition this house is in, its value isn't nearly what I'd hoped it would be."

"It would cost a small fortune," Valerie agreed softly, "to restore it to the way it was. I wonder if anyone has small fortunes, any more."

"Well, we certainly don't. We can clean it up, but that's all. We can't repaint it, or replace those broken windows at the back." Lacy's voice broke. "It was such a beautiful place, once."

Valerie hugged her, feeling her grandmother's fragile bones through the papery old skin and frail flesh. "Do you want me to go with you to Mr. Tilson's office? Or would I be more use here, helping Lallie clean up?"

Lacy pulled herself together. "Better here, I suppose. I won't be much use here, not like you young ones. I knew I was old, Valerie; but not until I saw this house did I know just *how* old."

"Shall I tell Rudy to bring the buggy around?"

"No." Lacy inhaled deeply, expanding her narrow chest. "I believe I will walk. It's a fine morning, and I always enjoyed my city so much, walking through it. I may never, ever do it again, so I shall walk this morning. It isn't that far. Rudy can help you and Lallie. There's plenty to do here, for the three of you."

There certainly was. After Lacy had gone, the others looked to Valerie for instructions on where to start, and she was nearly as lost as they were. Jack Ferris would have to wait; the need here was overwhelming. The house could not possibly be shown to anyone in its present condition.

It was a discouraging business at best. When dirt and the remaining debris were removed, more damage was revealed. Valerie and Lallie worked side by side, washing, scrubbing, sweeping, discarding.

Better no window coverings at all, Valerie decided, than the soiled, torn curtains and draperies that were all that was left of Lacy's elegant furnishings. She told Rudy to pull them down and burn them.

They had been working for more than an hour when there was a sharp rapping on the front door.

Lallie stopped with a rag in her hand and looked directly at Valerie. "Sounds like a man, bangin' so loud. Your mama warned me, Miss Val, she don't want you to see none of them Yankees."

So Ellen had not been as unaware as Valerie had thought. Anger warmed her tone. "And she chose to tell you, instead of me? How gratifying to see how much trust she puts in me." The fact that the lack of trust was entirely justified did not mitigate her anger. "Go see who it is."

"Yes'm," Lallie said, and walked through the corridor to open the front door.

"Hello, Lallie." Jack Ferris stood on the step. "I heard you were in town, and I came around to see if there was anything I could do to be of help."

Lallie stepped backward, propelled by the certainty that he was going to run over her if she didn't move out of his way. "Miss Val!" she called out. "It Captain Ferris!"

She hadn't expected him here, this way, and not so soon. Valerie dropped the cleaning rag and followed Lallie into the front hall, willing herself to control the surge of joy she felt. None of it showed in her voice, for she saw Mrs. Babcock's anxious face through the open doorway behind Jack and spoke loudly enough for the woman to hear her.

"Why, Captain Ferris, what a pleasant surprise. You're just in time to reach up for us and bring down those cobwebs in the corner."

Jack laughed, closing the door behind him. "That wasn't exactly the sort of help I had in mind, but give me a broom."

He had come. Ignoring Lallie's face, uncaring of what report the girl would carry back to her mother, Valerie led the way into the drawing room, pointing out the cobwebs to be brushed down. For the moment, it was enough that Jack was here.

Within an hour, before Lacy returned from the lawyer's office, Jack had sent for help from among his ambulatory patients and off-duty fellow soldiers. They attacked the house as they had once attacked their enemies, with soap and water and elbow grease, doing in a day what would have taken Valerie and Rudy and Lallie all week.

Lacy, more tired than she would have admitted, was amazed to hear male voices as she climbed her own front steps. Shirley Babcock called to her from the adjoining yard, and Lacy paused.

"A Yankee officer came," Mrs. Babcock reported. "And then he sent his aide away, and a whole group of them came. I didn't know what to do."

"Nothing much to be done," Lacy observed. "The Yankees are still in control, aren't they? I'll go in, I guess, and see what they've come for."

The house was in a state of confusion, but already she could see the difference. Captain Ferris stood in the dining room with his back to her, speaking to Valerie. "Repainting inside would do a good deal to restore it to livable condition. Not much to be done about the floors, at least not in a hurry, but even painting the walls would give it back a touch of its old elegance."

"We haven't any money for paint," Valerie said. "And it would take weeks to do the job; we don't have weeks. None of us has ever lifted a paintbrush, either. We might make it worse than it is now. Well, no," she reconsidered, "I guess we could hardly do *that*."

"Be ready for painters in the morning," Jack Ferris told her. He turned then and saw the old lady, coming to greet her with a smile. "Miss Lacy, how nice to see you again. I heard you'd returned to Savannah, and came to find out if I could help. Miss Valerie told me about the house, so I brought in some friends to give you a hand with it."

He was comfortable, open, friendly. Lacy, her mind half on Ferris and half on her house, gave him points for the way he'd approached them. She could hardly refuse his help, Yankee or no, threat to Valerie or no, not when she needed the help so badly.

"I see your friends have accomplished a great deal in a very short time. I am most grateful, Captain Ferris."

"My pleasure. Most of these fellows don't have much of anything to do, anyway. They'll be back tomorrow with paint and brushes, and maybe some of them can clear the garden a bit. I suppose it's the wrong time of the year for pruning, but they can clean out the fish pond and clip back the grass, that sort of thing."

"You're very kind, Captain."

He shrugged off her thanks. "I have to return to duty now, but I'd like to come back, this evening, and take you both out to dinner." He waited expectantly for her acceptance.

Lacy did not miss the happiness in her granddaughter's eyes. Ellen was right about one thing, the girl was mightily taken with the man, and he with her. "I'm sorry, Captain," she said softly, "but much as we'd like to do that, I do not think it would be a wise thing to do."

"Grandma! Why not?" Valerie demanded. "He's been good enough to bring in a whole crew of men, and they've done more in a few hours than we could have done in—"

"I know. And I appreciate every bit of it. But we are Georgians, sir," Lacy reminded him, "and you are a Union soldier. Many of the people in Savannah are my lifelong friends, and even if I never see any of them again after this visit, I wish to retain those friendships. I do not think I would care to create a false impression of too strong a friendship with Georgia's enemies."

"Not enemies, Miss Lacy." He was not angry, only rather resigned. "You and I, and Miss Valerie, will never be enemies, simply because we happen to be on different sides in this conflict. I bow to your decision, however; I do see the merit in it, even if the loss is mine. I hope you will allow me, however, to help with the house. I won't be able to spend much time here personally; though my work load is much lighter than it was, I do still have some necessary duties. I'll do nothing to give your friends a wrong impression, I promise you."

"Thank you, Captain," Lacy told him. "And now, I am very tired, and I would like to sit down and have a cup of tea, if such a thing is to be had."

It was not until Lallie had brought the tea, and Lacy sat in an old rocker still miraculously intact in the basement kitchen, that Valerie finally had a chance to learn how things had gone at the lawyer's office. She had said goodbye to Jack without her grandmother's supervision, a hasty and unsatisfactory goodbye because they had not yet arranged a more private meeting, then hurried downstairs. Concern with her own plans had not made her oblivious of her grandmother's weariness and strain.

"What did Mr. Tilson say? Does he know of any possible buyers?" Valerie accepted the second cup of tea and, in lieu of a chair, perched on the steps that led up to the back door into the walled garden.

Lacy sighed. "He was not as encouraging as I'd hoped he would be."

Alarm flared in Valerie's hazel eyes. "You mean we might not be able to sell it? What will we do, otherwise?"

"He didn't say we wouldn't be able to sell it. He said that buyers are few and far between. Very few people in Savannah have any cash to purchase anything, and then only at the most reasonable of prices. I had assumed that the house was worth what it cost your grandfather to build it, at least—sixteen thousand dollars. Grady Tilson tells me that I'll be lucky to realize a fraction of that, and when he sees what a mess the house is, his estimate will probably go even lower. I had so hoped to take a substantial sum home to your mother, for Mallows."

The concept of going home without the money Ellen needed was frightening, indeed. For a time it overshadowed even her need for Jack. Valerie sat with Lacy until the old lady had drunk her tea, then helped her up the stairs to the feather tick on the floor, for a much needed nap, before she returned to supervise the men with the mops, brushes, and cleaning rags.

Tomorrow, she thought. Tomorrow, they would make their plans, and she and Jack would be together.

The opportunity to see Jack came more quickly, and in a more alarming way, than she'd anticipated.

It was Lallie who heard Lacy cry out, and fall. The girl rushed into the bedroom and found the old lady on the floor, gasping and pressing a hand to her chest. Lallie knelt to touch her briefly, helpless against the suffering she saw, then fled down the spiral staircase, shrieking as she went. "Miss Val, Miss Val, something happen to Miss Lacy! She's in terrible pain!"

One of the men went upstairs with her, taking only a brief look. "Shall I go for Captain Ferris? Or is there another doctor you'd rather have?"

"Yes, yes, send for Captain Ferris! Lallie, run and fetch Mrs. Babcock, she may know something to do!" Frantic, Valerie held Lacy's hand and prayed. *Dear God, don't let her die!*

Except that it did not decrease her own fright, it was almost a relief when her grandmother seemed to sink into a sort of stupor; at least the agony of the pain in her chest had eased, but whether that was good or bad, Valerie did not know.

Mrs. Babcock came at once, her pleasant face twisted with anxiety; she supervised the business of getting her old friend onto the feather tick, mildly scandalized that Lacy Stanton should not have a proper bed to rest upon, but knew nothing to do of a medical nature.

"I think it's her heart, poor thing. She's been under such a strain, and she isn't young enough to cope with such things any more. Go, sit down, my dear, and rest a bit. I'll sit here with her," she offered, and reluctantly Valerie left the upper bedroom to return to the ground floor, to wait for Jack.

He came within the hour, telling her to wait where she was while he examined Lacy. The examination was brief.

"Her heart," he said in answer to Valerie's uplifted face, as they met at the bottom of the stairway. "She's resting more comfortably now. There isn't much to be done, except to see that she rests, and that nothing upsets her. That's probably what caused the seizure in the first place, this business of finding her house in such damaged condition when she needs to get a top price for it."

357

Valerie forced herself to whisper the question. "She isn't going to die, is she?"

Jack didn't offer her any false hopes. "I don't know. Nobody could say for sure. I think not, though; I hope it was a minor seizure and that she'll be all right within a few days. If not, it may cause problems; she can't travel until we're sure."

There were men working in all the rooms around them, none close enough to hear their words. When Jack put his hand over hers atop the post at the foot of the stairs, she reached up with the other one to touch his face.

"Jack, I need you."

"And I need you. I can't stay now, though, I have an irate major who requires that I remove some splinters from his buttock; he was most unhappy with me for leaving before finishing the job, and I may be demoted because of it." He grinned a little. "It might be worth it, at that, if it means spending some time with you. Look, I'll be back around ten. It'll be dark by then, and we can walk in the garden. We can talk then."

Valerie nodded and let him out the front door. Ten o'clock. Hours away. And upstairs poor Grandma Lacy— She'd forgotten she no longer believed in the efficacy of prayer. She stood for some time, leaning her forehead against the closed door, begging Him not to let Lacy die.

It was cold in the garden once dark had fallen. Valerie clutched the shawl about her, listening for Jack's footsteps, then moving quickly forward to unlatch the wrought-iron gate that let him in from the side street. There were gaslights some distance away; none of their illumination penetrated the garden, however, for the brick wall was a high one, and the magnolia tree cut off light from above as well.

He caught her in his arms, hard, and kissed her; a long, deep kiss that proved to her he'd felt as deprived as she had. She clung to him when he finally drew back a little, wanting to laugh and cry at the same time.

"I was afraid you wouldn't come! I thought I'd die if you didn't!"

"All that worrying for nothing," he said, gently teasing, "will put lines in your pretty face. How's your grandmother?"

"Sleeping. Lallie's moved her pallet into the same room, to listen for her at night. It's a good sign, isn't it, that she's fallen into a natural sleep?"

"A very good sign. Valerie, how I've missed you! Every day, and especially every night." He kissed her again, until she was breathless, no longer aware of the chill. "What's out there, that building at the foot of the garden?"

"The carriage house. It's been gutted by fire, though, there's no roof left, and it isn't safe to go into it, they said."

"Looks like we're stuck with the garden then, doesn't it? Where's that fish pond? I don't want to fall into it and break an ankle."

"It's in the center, between the paths. If we stay on the bricks, we're all right." Valerie shivered, and again he drew her close to him, warming her in his embrace. "I've missed you, sweetheart. Say you've missed me, too?"

She reassured him of that, with words as well as desperate kisses. Desperate because, while Lacy's illness might keep her longer in Savannah, it would also hold her there at the house. She couldn't go running off for an exciting rendezvous and leave her grandmother with only the servants.

The chill of the spring night at last grew too much for them; the only place to sit, when they grew weary of walking in the darkness of the overgrown garden, was a stone bench that was both hard and cold.

"There was a fire in the kitchen, earlier," Valerie said at last, when not even Jack's arms around her were enough to alleviate the discomfort. "Maybe we could sit in there; everyone's sleeping two floors above that. It must be warmer than it is out here."

They moved quietly into the house and down the stone steps to the basement, and Valerie felt about for candles. The iron stove gave off a faint warmth, so that they stood for a moment, pressing their hands to it, laughing.

"We're going to have to work out a better place to meet than this," Jack observed, looking around the big room. There was an open fireplace in which no fire had been built for years, from the look of it; and the big table was still there, scrubbed clean so that they could use it for the short time they'd expected to be here. That, and the rocker, were the only furnishings that hadn't been demolished by the tenants, or carried away by them. The walls were stone, as were the floors, and all that stone still held the cold of the winter just passed.

"What else is on this level?" Jack asked.

"The laundry rooms, storage rooms, root cellar, and up

359

front there's a big room that held ice, in the days when we could get it."

"Feels like it's still full of ice. Well, come over here, then. I'll sit in the rocker, and you'll sit in my lap, and we'll pretend there's a cozy fire, and that we're an old married couple, talking for a while, before I carry you upstairs to bed," Jack suggested. "It's a pity we can't really go upstairs to bed, because that's what I want, you know."

Valerie allowed herself to be pulled down on his knees and leaned her head against him, so that their faces touched. "I feel guilty, like this, with Grandma Lacy so sick upstairs."

"You said she was resting, and there's nothing you can do for her at the moment." He nuzzled her neck, sending prickles of pleasure along her nerve ends. "If there's one thing I've learned out of this damnd war, it's that though the dead and the dying may be all around us, the living should continue to go on living. Darling, you don't know how it made me feel when your letter came—delayed only a little while they hunted me up—and knew that we'd be together again for a few days. They're going to pull me out of here, you know. My work load grows lighter every day, and Sherman is—"

Valerie placed her fingertips over his lips, silencing him. "I don't want to know what General Sherman is doing, or where he is, or anything about the war. I want to pretend there is no war, to enjoy being with you for the time we have."

His mouth sought hers, gently at first, and then in a rising passion that might well have led to making love on the stone floor if Jack hadn't heard something. He broke free, listening, and shoved Valerie to her feet only seconds before Lallie, shuffling in her ragged shoes, came down the steps from the main floor.

Valerie was breathing quickly and her hair was disheveled; she struggled for poise, resisting the urge to smooth her hair for fear of calling more attention to her state.

"Lallie, is Grandma Lacy worse? Does she need something?"

"No, ma'am." Lallie was wrapped in an old shawl over a nightdress that had once belonged to Ellen. "She's sleeping fine. Don't seem like she hurts any more. I just woke up hungry and wondered if there was anything left to eat down here. I'm sorry if I botherin' anybody." Her gaze slid toward Jack, then back to Valerie.

"Not at all," Jack said easily, rising from the rocker. "I

360

just dropped by to see how things were going, and Miss Valerie said her grandmother was sleeping. Rest is the best medication for her now, and I didn't want to disturb her. I suppose I'd better be on my way. I'll look in again tomorrow. Goodnight, Lallie. Goodnight, Miss Valerie."

Disappointment was a physical ache. "I'll walk you to the gate, and lock it after you," Valerie offered. "I don't want anyone to wander in from the street."

She didn't think she was fooling Lallie. She'd noted the expression on the girl's face, when she saw them so cozily together in the kitchen, late at night. Did it matter, though, as long as Lallie didn't talk about it?

Jack's voice was amused when he kissed her goodnight at the gate that opened onto Bryan Street. "I think we were lucky, my love, that Lallie came down when she did, and not five minutes later. We'd have been luckier still if she'd chosen to stay in bed, once she got there. Well, it's late, and you're cold. Go to bed, and dream about me, and I'll see you tomorrow."

It was hardly a satisfactory conclusion to their first private meeting. Valerie fastened the gate and stood listening to his footsteps on the brick walk, moving away from her.

He'd be back tomorrow. She fastened her hopes on that. He'd be back tomorrow.

Ten

The men from the hospital were there early with paint and brushes, ready to begin. Valerie saw them started, then took tea upstairs to Lacy.

"Grandma? Are you feeling better," Valerie poked her head around the edge of the door, then entered the room with a smile when Lacy pushed herself into a sitting position.

"I'm only tired. I guess yesterday was too much for me, walking all that distance after discovering what a disaster the house was, and talking to Grady Tilson—what's the noise downstairs?"

"The men Captain Ferris sent over yesterday to clean are back today, to paint. They've even brought the paint with them. Heaven knows where they got it; I thought it better not to ask."

Valerie, highly relieved at Lacy's improvement, knelt to arrange the tea things on the floor. "Mrs. Babcock sent over some lemons, and she said to tell you not to worry about meals; she's going to send them over, for all of us, until you're better. Do you think I should write to Mama and tell her you've had a little spell?"

"No." Lacy accepted the cup and sipped at the steaming beverage. "When we go home, we'll tell her all the bad news at once, when we know what it is. No sense in worrying her by bombarding her with discouraging reports in between."

"Good. I'm glad. I didn't want to write to her, anyway. Would you like an egg for breakfast? Rudy's been out doing his own variety of scavenging, and Lallie will boil us each one."

"A boiled egg. I'd love one," Lacy said with such enthusiasm that Valerie was vastly reassured about the seriousness of her condition. Surely if she were really ill, she wouldn't want to eat.

It did not appear that Lallie had mentioned finding Captain Ferris in the kitchen late last night. Whether it was because she had decided to mind her own business, or simply did not want to upset Miss Lacy, Valerie neither knew nor cared. All that mattered was that nothing be made of the matter.

During the day, various gifts, from food to flowers, arrived for Lacy from old friends who had learned she was in town, and that she'd suffered a physical ailment. Mrs. Babcock came over at noon with another of her nourishing chowders, arriving at virtually the same time as Captain Ferris.

He courteously held the door for her, greeting Valerie in the same tone as he used upon Lallie. "How's my patient this morning?" he wanted to know.

"Feeling much better. Lallie boiled her an egg, and she had tea. That's a good sign, isn't it?"

"Very good," Jack agreed. "I'll run up and take a look at her."

Mrs. Babcock handed over the tureen of soup to Lallie. "Be careful, it's hot. My, how fortunate that you knew one of the Yankee doctors. We hate having anything to do with them, but when it comes to doctoring, better a Yankee than no one at all. So many of our own are either away with the army, or are too old to get about to everyone who needs them, or have died off, like Dr. Chaffee. Your grandmama had Dr. Chaffee for so many years. He passed on last winter, poor soul."

Mrs. Babcock stayed a few minutes chatting, and left Valerie with the feeling that Captain Ferris could now visit the house without causing any undue comment; he came as Lacy's physician.

It was not as a physician that Valerie felt the need of him, however. Now that her worry was reduced over Lacy, she longed to be truly alone with him, as she had been at Patrick Ryan's small house. Where, though? Not here in Lacy's house; last night had been too close a call. Suppose her grandmother came upon her in Jack's arms? For all that she suspected that Lacy would be more tolerant of a passionate kiss than her mother would, Valerie had no desire to test the theory.

It was a large house, yet now full of people, and there was no privacy in it for anyone save her grandmother, who was not disturbed until the men asked if she wanted her room painted, too. At that time, Lacy was moved out onto the second-floor landing while the task was done.

Jack stayed for only a brief time. When he left, he drew Valerie out onto the front porch, where his uniform caught the eye of the passersby. Savannahians, following the lead of those who had decided to welcome General Sherman rather than fight him, now treated the invaders with a wary respect that seldom encompassed friendliness. They stared, covertly, as they passed and Jack maintained a military stance.

"I'm telling you the grave news about your grandmother, so look sober," he admonished. "As long as she's ill, and there's a shortage of civilian doctors, no one will think anything of it if I come here."

"I'm glad you're able to come, for Grandma Lacy's sake. But what about mine? I can't speak to you without being overheard by someone, not for more than a moment."

Jack, back to the street, grinned. "Tomorrow afternoon, I suggest that you get away from the house. Take a stroll down along Factor's Walk, renewing your acquaintanceship with the city. Look in on a few old friends—you know some of them, don't you? The merchants along Bay Street, and the riverfront?"

"My grandfather knew them all. I remember a few of them."

"Good. Look in on them, say hello. Mention that your grandmother's ill and you're hoping to find fresh fruit, something of that sort, to tempt her appetite. And then, down along the Walk take the stairs down to River Street. Late afternoon, around four o'clock. You'll meet an old woman who'll offer to sell you fresh pineapples—just the thing, you'll think, and you'll go with her into her establishment. I'll be in the back room; she has a very cozy apartment there, and her own business will take her back onto the street for a few hours. She's entirely discreet, old Sophie is." His grin widened.

The thrill of excitement was tempered by one of fear. "How can you be sure of that? Grandma's responsible for me, I couldn't do anything that would reflect on her . . ."

"You don't want to come? You don't want to meet me?"

She saw, beyond him across the street, a pair of elderly ladies, who in a well-bred way were assessing the situation; she kept her face carefully blank. She did not try to keep the intensity from her voice, however. "Of course I want to meet you. It's only that it sounds so . . . so sly."

"Would you rather meet me openly, on the street? Or shall I call for you here?"

"No, no, of course not. All right, I'll be there."

"Good." He turned and went down the steps, then paused to say for the benefit of an elderly gentleman making his way toward the square, "If she takes a turn for the worse, don't hesitate to send your man for me. I'll look in on her again tomorrow."

Valerie let herself into the house, both excited and disturbed. It was true, it did smack of indecency, meeting him secretly in the back room of some riverfront shop. Yet what had she expected when she wrote to tell him that she was coming? He had no home of his own to open to her, and had no friends in the city, either, except his fellow officers.

She wanted to meet him, of course she did; her body ached with the need of him. Yet the threat of exposure was terrifying. If anyone knew of the illicit meeting, she would disgrace not only herself but her entire family. It would be wiser not to go, to make up some excuse about why she had not been able to be there as they'd arranged. Yet she knew that she could not deny Jack, nor herself. She would go.

It was astonishing how much a dozen men, even convalescent and handicapped ones, could do in such a short time. A coat of fresh paint made a world of difference in the spacious, sunny rooms. The rugs that had been stored in the attic when Lacy moved to Mallows were unrolled, the tobacco shaken out, and they were put down over the scarred floors. It was a pity there were no curtains and draperies, but as Valerie had realized, the windows looked better bare than with the soiled and tattered window coverings she had torn down.

The garden, too, was greatly improved when the dirt had been cleaned out of the pond and the little fountain reactivated. The grass was clipped, including that which had grown up between the bricks of the walls, and a few of the more aggressive shrubs were cut back.

Lacy, coming downstairs against Valerie's protests that evening, looked around her with misty eyes. "Thank them for me, my dear. They've done wonders. We can't hide the broken windows nor replace the plaster borders and the chandeliers; yet the house is nearly habitable, now. It makes me feel better just to look at it."

There was enough furniture in the attic so that, after they'd arranged it around the drawing room, they could sit down and welcome guests. Not that she was ready for them, yet. Lacy was forced to lie down again after only a short time. But her indisposition, she thought, should not unduly delay them in returning to Mallows, if Mr. Tilson could find a buyer for the house.

He brought the first of the prospects the following day. They were a couple in their early sixties, the man a merchant whose own home outside of the city had been destroyed recently by fire. They walked through the freshly painted rooms, sharp eyes seeing every place there was a missing bit of crystal in the chandelier, a chipped spot in the woodwork, damage done to the plaster rosettes in the dining room, or the gaping holes where the balusters were missing.

Lacy had the misfortune to come downstairs while they were there; she whispered behind her hand to Valerie when they descended into the cellar. "They won't take it; it's no longer fine enough for them."

She was right. They didn't say anything when they returned to the main floor, except to make polite sounds in thanks for being allowed to view the place. The lawyer, a bald gentleman with a surprising girth, lingered behind them with an apologetic smile.

"Had a notion they wouldn't take to a place that's been vandalized, although I must say you've somehow done wonders with it in a short time." He paused hopefully, but when they declined to explain how they had accomplished this miracle, he went on. "I have another fellow coming tomorrow, though; I'll bring him around after lunch. He might well be interested; he has the money to renovate if he likes the basic structure, and that's sound enough."

He had no sooner gone than Lacy requested help in getting back to her bed. "I never minded those stairs when I was living here, all those years," she said, leaning heavily on Valerie's arm. "It kept me young, running up and down. Well, that's all in the past now, isn't it?"

"You'll feel better when this business is settled," Valerie said. "Is there anything you'd like me to do for you now? Read to you, perhaps? I'm sure Mrs. Babcock would loan us something."

She waited, praying that Lacy would say *no*. She must leave the house within half an hour if she were to keep to the schedule Jack Ferris had set.

Lacy sighed, resting a moment between floors. "No, no, child. I think I'll take a nap for an hour or so." Her shrewd old eyes met Valerie's. "You could do with a nap, yourself, I think. You don't look as if you've been sleeping well."

"I haven't," Valerie admitted. "Maybe I will rest, just for a little while. Shall I ask Lallie to sit with you, then?"

"Lallie's about done in, too. We'll all take naps," Lacy decided. "She'll hear me when I wake up, and bring me some tea, and then I'll rest again until it's time for supper. I *am* getting old."

"You're marvelously young for seventy-two," Valerie assured her. She left her in Lallie's hands, retiring to her own room. Very quietly so that the sounds of her preparations would not carry across the landing, she got out the dress she wanted to wear, the light green silk. It would have helped to have Lallie fasten it for her, but she didn't dare put such a request. When she'd managed that, she dressed her hair as best she could without the use of a mirror; for once she was glad that she'd learned to do it herself, or it would have been impossible, this way.

She picked up her slippers, to be put on after she'd reached the main floor; there was no carpeting on the stairs any more, and she couldn't risk being heard. They were the best footwear she owned, of white kid that was not what she would have chosen to wear with this dress; at least the soles weren't flapping, like virtually every other pair she possessed.

Lacy's door was closed, as was Lallie's; no sound came from either room. Valerie closed her own door noiselessly, hoping that they would not think to check on her until she'd had time to come back. Let them think she was exhausted and sleeping; she might even get away with it completely. If not, she would use the story Jack had fabricated for her about visiting old friends.

The day was fine and warm, Savannah at its best. She walked, not too briskly, toward Bay Street, nodding to the people she met. She didn't recognize any of them, although no doubt many of them knew her grandmother. For that reason and because they would know her even if she didn't know who they were, she must be circumspect.

It was with warring emotions that she approached the riverfront. It had always been her favorite part of the city as a child, when she came there holding to Charles Stanton's hand. What time was it? Was she late? No, there was a clock she could see through a window; she had half an hour before she was to meet the pineapple woman, old Sophie. How did Jack know her? How could he be certain she would be discreet? He was paying her, of course, but that didn't always assure trustworthiness. Quite the contrary.

Valerie hesitated, reluctant, now that she was here, to go into any of those brick buildings and introduce herself as Charles Stanton's granddaughter. Charles had been dead for years, his widow gone from the city since the early part of the war, and she didn't really remember any of them.

No, she decided, she would skip that part of the scenario. She moved along to the head of the stairs leading down to the lower levels. The stone steps had been built from ballast carried from the old world, put to good use on the sandy bluff of the river. They were steep, and curved slightly, and it was best to proceed with caution.

The buildings that were two stories high on Bay Street were five stories down along the river, housing the establishments that were at the heart of the cotton business. Valerie had been afraid that a young lady would be conspicuous here, but this was not especially the case; although there were more men there were also women and children out for the sun and the air on a spring day. There were glances in her direction, and whenever she came face to face with anyone of either sex, black or white, a soft Southern voice bid her a good afternoon.

She reached the lower level and stood for a moment, overcome with panic. There was still time to turn around and go home, to forget this madness that might well lead to ruin. What was she thinking of, arranging a meeting like any common trollop? Was she any better, really, than Blossom Curtis,

368

if she met Jack this way? But she and Jack loved each other. Didn't that make a difference? It wasn't an offhand, casual sort of thing. She would never meet any other man, only Jack, because she loved him.

She could not, however, take the necessary steps that would lead her to the old woman selling pineapples. She might have remained rooted there indefinitely, or have turned and fled back up the stone steps, if she had not suddenly seen a familiar flaming red head.

Patrick Ryan, here in Savannah?

Valerie stopped breathing, and her previous panic was nothing compared to what she felt now. Patrick Ryan? Dear God, he must not see her!

He stood on the wharf, talking to a prosperous-appearing man in a business suit and at the moment was not looking in her direction. He might, however, at any moment, and there were not enough people about to conceal herself in a crowd. Her own hair, though not as conspicuous as his, would set her apart from the others, if he caught sight of it. Her straw bonnet covered most of it, yet if they met face to face . . .

Valerie turned, ready to run back the way she'd come, and saw that to do that would almost certainly draw Patrick's attention. Anyone on that high, steep stair would be set off against the gray stone as if she were on a stage; the green silk dress she had donned for Jack's benefit was too fine a gown not to draw the eye of any observer down below, and the climb could not be made in a moment or two.

The other way, then, in the direction Jack had told her to go. Valerie turned her back on Patrick Ryan and moved as quickly as she could without actually running. She knew instinctively that while she might fool some people about the legitimacy of her presence here on the river, she would not fool Patrick Ryan.

"Fresh fruits, miss? I got pineapples, nice juicy pineapples," the voice said.

She might well have passed the woman altogether had not the old crone called out to her. Valerie faltered, looking down into a weathered face with eyes so faded they seemed to be no color at all. The creature was swathed in clothes that seemed as old as herself, in rusty black and gray, and the wisps of hair protruding from beneath the brim of a battered bonnet were thin and as gray as the rest of her.

"Nice sweet pineapples," the woman urged. "Got 'em back

369

in there." She gestured toward the doorway behind her in the face of the brick wall and Valerie turned blindly. "There's a good girl. Go right on through to the back," the woman said. "I'll be with you directly, miss."

She was off the street, thank God for that, and in a tiny cluttered room with scarcely an aisle through it to the curtained doorway at the back. Would there be another way out? Stairs, perhaps, to the upper levels that opened onto Bay Street? Or was she trapped here, where Patrick Ryan might see her if she emerged through the door she had entered?

It was a measure of the agitation she felt that she did not even think about Jack Ferris until she ran, literally, into his arms. The curtains fell into place behind her, and the breath went out of her with the impact.

"Hey! I'm flattered, that you're so anxious to get to me, but slow down, will you? You act as if somebody's chasing you!"

His arms came around her, and he bent his head, but Valerie pushed him away.

"I saw Patrick Ryan out there, on the dock. If he sees me—is there another way out of here?" She glanced around the small room, which obviously served as the old hag's living quarters. It was, somewhat to her surprise, clean and less cluttered than the room in front. There was a wide sofa-bed heaped high with pillows, a fireplace for cooking, several comfortable chairs, and masks of some sort on the walls that looked as if they might have been made in Africa, by witch doctors. There were no other doors, no stairs.

"Way out?" Jack echoed. "You just got here! Who's this Patrick Ryan? Oh, yes, the overseer—well, what difference does it make? He isn't your keeper, is he?"

"He knows a lot of people I know," Valerie said, for once not eager to lose herself in Jack's embrace. "Including my mother and my grandmother."

"So what? You've come down here looking for fruit for your grandmother, remember? A perfectly legitimate errand. Sweetheart, you've let yourself get all upset for nothing. Forget about your overseer, and remember why you've come."

Why had she come? Valerie stood quite still in the center of the small room, shrinking inside. It was wrong, it was stupid. She should never have come, a few minutes' happiness in Jack's arms wasn't worth the possible cost, was it? It wasn't like being in Ryan's small house, at all. Somehow this was

370

cheap, disgusting, not at all as she had imagined it would be, when she'd written the letter.

Jack Ferris read part of that on her face. He made no attempt to hold her against her will. Instead, he smiled and stepped to a low table where there was a bottle and two glasses. "Old Sophie keeps a good wine. Here, have a glass; it will settle your stomach."

She didn't want the wine, yet she remembered how, in moments of shock and stress, the brandy had helped in the past. She allowed him to press the glass into her hand, and sipped at it; she remembered, too, the brandy she'd drunk the night Jack first made love to her. That was different, though; she wouldn't let herself do *that* again, because she wouldn't drink so much, and certainly not on an empty stomach. The wine was sweet and mild. She didn't feel anything from it, not like the apricot brandy.

"Your eyes turn pure green, when you wear that color. Did you know that?" Jack was at ease, smiling. "You must be one of the most beautiful women in the world. No, *the* most beautiful. And for a beautiful lady, a pretty trinket."

He withdrew a small box from his coat pocket and extended it to her. Valerie didn't take it. The wine wasn't helping at all; she still felt trapped, suffocated. She wanted to leave, but Patrick Ryan was probably still out there, and she didn't want to see him.

"You don't want to open it yourself?" Jack sounded mildly disappointed. "I'll do it then. Here, see what I've found for you. As a symbol of the love I feel for you."

Not even the magic of that word—*love*—was enough to banish her doubts and uncertainties. He took the thin gold chain out of the box, letting it slide over his fingers until the medallion lay on his open palm; it was an intricately wrought oval of gold, set with tiny seed pearls.

Valerie stared at it. It was beautiful, yes, it was beautiful. And it had been a long time since anyone had given her a gift of comparable beauty or value. Yet she could not reach out to take it. She was too vividly aware of this room—this place where she did not belong. What had seemed reasonable, so short a time ago, meeting Jack here and no one ever the wiser for it, no longer seemed feasible at all. The risks were too great.

"Let me put it on," Jack said softly. He reached for the ribbons on her bonnet and removed it, setting it aside before

371

he stepped behind her to fasten the chain around her neck. His fingers brushed her nape and she shivered slightly, and then his arms came around her, drawing her against him while he kissed her. A hand cupped her breast, moving, caressing.

"Jack," she began, but he didn't let her speak. He turned her to face him, bending his head to reach her lips. For a moment she resisted, and then the expertise of his mouth and hands kindled the familiar fire; her mind was still there, with its doubts and fears, yet somehow the power of the flesh was stronger.

Had he attempted to woo her with words, she might have held out against him. She was no match, however, for stroking hands, the warm sweetness of his mouth, the lean hard length of his body. When at last his fingers worked with her buttons, she was too far gone in the wondrous lethargy to protest, since his mouth never stopped seeking, giving, taking. When he carried her to the couch bed, Valerie mused in a remote corner of her consciousness that perhaps the wine had been more potent than she'd thought.

It no longer seemed to matter. Nothing mattered but the touch of mouth and fingers and bodies locked together as they were surely intended to be. Valerie gave herself over to ecstasy, sinking into it, drowning in it.

She forgot Patrick Ryan, her family, everything but the sensations that Jack Ferris knew so well how to evoke. The room dissolved around them and Valerie drifted on the magic tide, willing it never to end.

Eleven

It did end, of course. She roused enough to realize that Jack had left her side, that he was nearly dressed while she lay wantonly naked on a strange old woman's bed. She was ashamed, yet too lethargic to cover herself, until he bent over her, laughing, to run a finger over one nipple and brush his mouth across hers.

"Lazy wretch, you'd better get up and get dressed, or it will be dark before you get home. They'll send out the patrol for you."

Her eyes came fully open. "How late is it?"

"Made you forget the time, did I?" he teased. "Here, I'll give you a hand with your stays, or would you rather old Sophie did it?"

She shuddered, sitting up, reaching for the garments that had been tossed thoughtlessly aside. "No, not the old woman." There were no windows back here, she couldn't see anything except by the light of the single candle that had been burning when she came in. How long ago? Surely the candle had burned down a great way?

Alarm made her hurry, and fumble, so that Jack laughed again, assisting her. It occurred to her, then, that he was as expert at getting a female back into her clothes as he'd been

373

at getting her out of them; he'd done this many times, with someone.

Well, what had she expected? A man of thirty, a man with Jack's looks and charm, that he'd remained celibate, waiting for her to come along? His lovemaking alone should have told her that it was not a new thing to him, as it was to her; a man wasn't born knowing all those things, like where to touch, and how, any more than a girl was.

Still, she'd never before given any thought to what other women there might be, or have been, in his life. Did it disturb her to think of other women? Of course, she thought honestly, bracing herself as the strings of her corset were drawn tight. She didn't want to imagine Jack with any other female. Yet the proof of his love was here, wasn't it? It was Valerie he'd made love to.

"There. Maybe you'd better take off the necklace," he suggested, "if you don't want anyone to ask where you came by it. Unless you want to say you found it in one of the local shops."

She had forgotten it. She reached up for the clasp, but Jack was already unfastening it, bending to kiss the back of her neck as he did so. He dropped the chain and medallion into her hand.

"I couldn't say I'd bought it. They know I don't have any money, and if I did, I wouldn't dare spend it on a bauble like this. Not when we all need so many things."

"I wish I could give them all to you, all the things you need." He swung her around to face him, smiling. "This war can't go on much longer. When it's over, we'll be free to do . . . whatever we want. In the meantime, will you meet me again tomorrow?"

The wine-and-love-induced euphoria was past. There was a tremor in her limbs that had nothing to do with either of them. "No, I don't think so. I can't come here again." Aversion to the room rose in her throat like nausea; she couldn't wait to escape it. She reached for her bonnet fingers fumbling with the ribbons under her chin.

"Then I'll come to you," Jack promised. "Every day, for as long as you're in Savannah."

She didn't argue that, indeed, scarcely heard him. All she could think of was getting out of here and home. If they knew she'd been gone for hours, would they press to know where she'd been? Could she convince anyone she'd simply

374

been strolling around Savannah, enjoying the sunshine and the flowers and the fresh air? Would her grandmother know by her face where she'd been, and what she'd been doing?

"You'll have to see that it's safe for me to leave," she said. "See if Patrick Ryan is still out there."

"What's he look like? What difference does it make, anyway? This is a part of town where many people come, simply to stroll and watch the river traffic."

"It matters," Valerie assured him. Her hair must be a mess, she hadn't even had the wit to bring a brush with her; would her bonnet cover it adequately until she could reach her room in Lacy's house? "Step outside and see. He's a big man, very wide shoulders, and he has flaming red hair. He wasn't wearing a hat, that's all I remember, but you'll recognize the hair if he's around."

"All right. I'll look." He withdrew several coins from a pocket and dropped them casually on the table beside the wine bottle and the glasses. "I'll be right back."

He left her there in the room that crowded in upon her. Her eyes were riveted on the coins; he'd paid for the place, paid for the room as if she were a whore he'd taken to one of those places whores went.

What did she know about whores? Didn't they have their own places? Cribs, hadn't she heard Evan speak (when he did not know she was listening) about the cribs, in New Orleans? Well, what had she expected? How else could Jack have obtained privacy for them, except by paying for the privilege?

The logic of it didn't help much. She felt sick, shaken, already forgetting the delights of lying in Jack's arms. She wanted only to get away, to hurry.

"All clear. No redheaded man about that I can see," Jack reported, brushing aisde the curtains and holding them for her. "You go ahead. I'll follow later, when no one can possibly connect us."

The old woman was in the outer room. How long had she been there? Had she heard them, heard Valerie's moans of pleasure, heard the creaking of the bed beneath their bodies? Valerie's face burned; indeed, she felt scalded all over, as if she'd been immersed in a too-hot bath.

"Your pineapples, miss," the old woman said, and pressed them into her hands.

Valerie scarcely knew she had them. She paused in the

375

outer doorway for a quick glance up and down the quay. There were still people about, mostly men, now, and the sun was lower than she'd expected. What would Lacy think, if she knew she'd been gone for hours and hours? There was no sign of Patrick. Besides the color of his hair, he was usually distinguishable because of his height, being head and shoulders above most of the others.

No one looked in her direction. Valerie did not reply to Jack's called-out "See you tomorrow, sweet!" She only just restrained herself from running, which could only further draw attention to herself. She brushed by a peddler with more fruits, scarcely seeing him, headed for the stone steps up the bank to the higher street.

She was able to respond, automatically, to the greetings that still came her way when she met anyone. The pineapples were rough and prickly in her arms, though she scarcely felt them. Please God, don't let them know where I've been, and with whom! she prayed, and then wondered why she had any reason to think that God would be that kind.

A carriage was drawing up in front of the Abercorn Street house when she reached the walk, and she recognized the lawyer, Grady Tilson, when he descended. There was another gentleman with him, older, taller, more distinguished-looking.

Mr. Tilson greeted her with a smile. "Ah, Miss Valerie! I hope it won't be an intrusion, bringing Mr. McGivern around so late in the day. He was to have come tomorrow, but he's most anxious to see the house and make a decision about it; his wife and family are due here within the month, and he must have a place to house them."

She acknowledged the introductions, pulling herself together. At least with these two in the house, there would be no explosion when she walked in. Not a public one. Lacy would never do that to her.

Lallie opened the door; her quick glance told Valerie nothing. "Come in, sir," she invited. "Miss Lacy say she beg your pardon, but she too tired to come downstairs. You feel free to look around by yourself, please."

"Certainly. Mr. McGivern understands that Miss Lacy is ill, and we'll try not to disturb her unduly."

"Here," Valerie said, handing over the pineapples and brushing away the tiny particles that adhered to her bosom. "These are for Grandma Lacy. I'll look in on her, if she's awake."

376

"She only just wake up," Lallie said. "I guess everybody too tired; we sleep most of the afternoon." Was there knowledge in Lallie's eyes, or was that only Valerie's own conscience? "Pineapple. Been a long time since we've seen any pineapple."

Valerie's heart was thudding. Did they think she, too, had slept away the afternoon? Had God heard her, after all? Or perhaps He was simply too busy to bother with one slip of a girl, and she was just lucky. At any rate, she found her grandmother sitting up, looking well rested, and having no questions about Valerie's activities during the afternoon. Valerie had been prudent enough to change back into the gown she'd worn earlier, folding the green silk away so that it would not attract attention if Lacy entered this room; she knew she would not wear it again while she was in Savannah.

She came back downstairs as Grady Tilson and Mr. McGivern were leaving. They thanked her, apologized for disturbing Miss Lacy, and the lawyer assured her that he would be speaking to her grandmother on the following day.

"I think Mr. McGivern likes the house," Valerie reported as they ate the supper Mrs. Babcock had sent over. Backyard gardens, once given over to flowers and decorative trees and shrubs, were now producing lettuce and radishes for salads, a welcome treat after a winter without them, and Mrs. Babcock's cook had sent with the salad a casserole of steamed rice and chicken with leeks to liven it up. With it Lallie served chunks of the ripe pineapple; no mention was made of where it had come from, and Lacy took it for granted that Mrs. Babcock had provided that, too.

"Everyone has been so kind," Lacy said, finishing with a sigh of satisfaction. "Now, if only the house will bring enough to make things worthwhile. I'm ready, I believe, to go home to Mallows."

"You don't want to rest a while longer?" Valerie asked gently. "A three-day trip in the buggy is very tiring. And there are friends you haven't visited yet."

"Give out the word to Shirley Babcock that I am well enough to receive visitors now," Lacy decided. "They will come, those who are still here. A few days will be sufficient to exchange confidences, and then I will be ready to go."

She said it with at least surface calm. Valerie hoped that she had reconciled herself to leaving, for the last time. Perhaps the fact that the house had been vandalized changed

377

things, perhaps it made it easier to leave it forever since it was no longer the same.

They all went early to bed, to save the candles. There had been a time when the house would have been ablaze with light, with little or no consideration of the cost of it. Now they begrudged a single candle.

Valerie lay listening to the murmur of voices across the landing as Lallie helped Lacy prepare for bed. She held the gold and pearl medallion in the darkness, wondering when she would dare to wear it openly, and her emotions were mixed and turbulent. She loved Jack, she had never known anything so stimulating and exciting as his touch; but she would not repeat this afternoon's performance. It had been different than meeting at Ryan's house, in a place where they did not pay for the privilege of those stolen hours. It occurred to her suddenly that Patrick Ryan might very well not feel at all charitable about his bed being used by the lovers, and she wondered if Patrick himself had ever taken a girl into that bed.

Patrick. What was he doing in Savannah? What, for that matter, had he been doing in Reidsville? One would have expected that when his connection with the army was severed, he would have returned home, to plant his own crop, as he had done when he was overseer at Mallows. What was he doing instead?

Her fingers curled around the gift that Jack had given her, Valerie slept.

Grady Tilson arrived at the front door at a quarter past ten. His bald head was tinted pink, as if he'd spent some time in the sun and gotten it mildly burned. He handed his hat to Lallie and stepped into the sparsely furnished drawing room, where Valerie and Lacy waited for him. His smile wavered between them and he accepted the chair opposite them, drumming his fingers on the arms briefly before getting down to business. He cleared his throat, as if preparing for a long summation in court.

"As you may have guessed, Mr. McGivern finds much that is agreeable about your house. He has made an offer, and I told him I would report back to him, directly I had your response to it."

Lacy's hands clasped tightly in her lap. She'd known Grady Tilson for years, and she knew his tone. She did not pray.

378

She knew it was too late for that, and she wasn't convinced that the Lord still listened to Georgians, anyway. Certainly He had appeared to ignore a major share of the petitions they had raised in the past five years; she had no reason to think that He would suddenly concern himself with the price of her house.

Mr. Tilson's gaze shifted to Valerie, who was looking alert and eager. "As I explained to your grandmother, Miss Valerie, houses are not bringing the prices now that they would have done a few years earlier. Even houses in excellent condition, which," he took on an apologetic note, "you know that this one is not. The paint and the general cleaning helped, but not enough to overcome the point that a considerable sum must be spent upon it now to make it habitable."

Some of Valerie's eagerness faded. The news was not going to be good, then. McGivern had made an offer, but not a generous one.

"There are many houses for sale in Savannah. Some of the families can no longer maintain them. Few people can afford servants any more. And in many cases, why, there have been so many deaths in the family that large homes are no longer needed or practical."

Lacy's voice was dry. "You explained all that to me, Grady. Get on with it. What did the man offer for the place?"

"There is so little cash money, you see. Paper money is worthless; those few who put any of it aside now find that it is of no value whatever." It was as if he could not bring himself to put the sum into words. "And there are few buyers. Most of the survivors of the war are in such a condition that they can only dispose of their property, not buy more. Indeed, it is mostly Yankee money being spent, now. Much as we may deplore it, we have little choice but to take it, in gold or silver, when it is offered."

Lacy leaned forward, the blue veins prominent on her papery old hands as they gripped the arm of her chair. "*How much*, Grady?"

The man cleared his throat, swallowed, and spit the words out as if he could not bear the taste of them. "Forty-two hundred dollars."

In the silence, they heard a horse going by in the street, and somewhere below, in the cellar, Lallie dropped something with a small crash.

379

"Forty-two hundred dollars?" Lacy's whisper was a measure of her shocked disbelief. "For a house that's worth sixteen thousand, at least?"

"I know it's worth more, Miss Lacy. Mr. McGivern knows it's worth more. But the fact of the matter is that I don't think you're going to find anyone to pay any more than that. It's a buyer's market, ma'am. There are more houses to sell than there are people to buy them. It's possible that if you hold onto the place, it may eventually bring more. Nobody knows yet what is going to happen, once the war is officially at an end. In a year or two, the house might well go for several thousand more, although nobody can guarantee that. It might not be salable at all. There is simply no way of knowing."

"Forty-two hundred dollars." Lacy stared at him, helpless, hopeless. "It's so little, compared to what we need. And we can't wait a year or two, even if you could guarantee a price. He'd be stealing the house, at that price."

Tilson nodded in commiseration. "That's true. People are stealing things all over the South now, I assure you. That overseer you had at Mallows before the war, what's his name, Ryan? Patrick Ryan? He's a good example. He's buying up real estate for a fraction of its value, because the owners, like yourself, are desperate. One takes what is offered, or goes without. That's what it comes down to."

Patrick, buying up real estate? With what? Valerie wondered, astounded. She couldn't believe he could have saved much, on a three-hundred-dollar-a-year salary.

"Who are you representing, Grady? Mr. McGivern, or me?" Lacy asked.

"Why, you, of course, Miss Lacy!"

"Then ask him for five thousand. He's still stealing it, and if he knows anything about values, he'll see the fairness of that."

"Five thousand." Mr. Tilson cleared his throat again. "Well, he's made an offer, and there's nothing wrong with making a counteroffer. I confess I'm not optimistic, Miss Lacy, because he has a choice of various other houses whose owners are also desperate to sell. However, this one is the lowest price of the lot, and he does have the cash to refurbish it as he likes, so it's the better bargain."

"The better bargain," Valerie echoed bitterly, "and he has cash, but he won't pay a fair price for it."

380

The man looked at her unhappily. "I'm sorry, ma'am. I really am. But that's the way things are."

Lacy visibly pulled herself together. "Try for five thousand, please. We'll have to take what we can get, it seems, but that doesn't mean necessarily accepting the first offer. The location alone is worth what he's offering. Ask for five thousand."

Grady Tilson nodded. "I'll get back to you as soon as I've talked with him."

After he had gone, they sat looking at each other. There was a slight tremor in Lacy's hand as she reached for the teacup Lallie had brought, but she was more controlled than Valerie, more resigned than angry.

"How far will it go, forty-two hundred dollars?" Valerie asked.

"We'll have to pray it will be far enough. Seed for crops, at least. There won't be any slack anywhere, I'm sure. I think what bothers me the most—" Lacy paused and brushed back a wisp of white hair, "is the idea of telling your mother how little it is. She's had so many disappointments and this one may well be the cruelest one of all. Well, that's the way it is. We've tried. We've surely tried. What was all that business about Patrick Ryan, buying up property at reduced prices? I wouldn't have guessed he'd have any cash to work with."

"Nor I," Valerie said, subdued. "How long will it take, do you think, to finish up the paperwork, if Mr. McGivern decides to buy the house?"

"Not more than a few days. I hope." Lacy's gaze raked over her with a sharpness that was more like her usual self. "You're looking rather peaked. Are you feeling all right?"

"Yes," Valerie said, though there was no animation in her voice. "I think I'll look over the rest of the things in the attic and see what you want to take back to Mallows with you. Could we afford to hire a wagon, if you want any of the furniture, or the rugs?"

"Better not, I think. That rose-colored rug that used to be in my bedroom was always a favorite of Shirley Babcock's. We'll give that to her, in thanks for all she's done for us. And I'd like to take that rocker with the cherry-colored velvet cushions; I think Rudy can tie it on the back of the buggy. We'll leave everything else."

How can she be so calm about it? Valerie wondered. *Giving up all that she cared so much about. She was happy in this house with my grandfather and all the memories will be left here for someone else, for a rich man who won't pay what the place is worth because she's so desperate that she'll take anything.*

Lacy had lived for nearly seventy-three years. How many griefs had she known, how many joys, that no one else knew about?

Valerie's speculations shifted to her own future. What did it hold? The next fifty-odd years, until she was Lacy's age? Things were so different, now, from what they'd been in the past. Was there any true happiness in her own future? Marriage to Jack, a family, a gracious life that was, presumably, still attainable in the North? If only he'd ask her in so many words to wait for him, she thought. If only he'd promise to come back for her, when the war was done.

When he arrived, however, to check on Lacy and pronounce himself well satisfied with her improved condition (though he still ordered plenty of rest), Jack said nothing of the future, any further ahead than that afternoon.

"We could just happen to meet, over in the square," he said. "We could sit and talk there, in public, no scandal. Or I could speak to old Sophie about using her back room again."

Valerie suppressed a shiver. "No, not there. All right, I'll take a walk in the square. We can talk, anyway."

"Talking isn't really what I want to do." Jack said, voice heavy with meaning so that Valerie felt the warmth rising in her face. "As long as you're in Savannah, I can't let a day go by without some private time with you. You're the most important thing that's happened to me in my whole life, Valerie. You know that, don't you?"

"Yes," she agreed dutifully.

She watched him go, tall and handsome enough to turn heads even if he was a Yankee, and wished with all her heart that he was hers to love, openly and joyfully. How she longed for that time to come!

Again she waited until Lacy had retired for her afternoon nap before she walked out in Reynolds Square. It was later than she'd hoped, and for a few minutes she thought Jack might already have gone. And then she saw him coming, striding toward her, tall enough so that some of the hanging moss strands brushed his head as he moved beneath the oaks.

He saw her sober face and stopped before the bench where she rested in the shade. "What is it? What's the matter?"

"Mr. Tilson just left the house. Mr. McGivern is buying

the place—for forty-six hundred dollars. That's his final offer. They'll sign the papers day after tomorrow, and we leave for Mallows the following day."

"We've only today, tomorrow, and the next day, then."

Somewhere in the trees overhead, a bird sang a merry, four-noted song. A bank of vivid pink azaleas was a splash of color across the square; Julie's color, she thought, and felt years away from her sister, both in experience and in distance.

Tell me, she begged silently of the man who stood before her. *Tell me again that you love me, that we'll be together after the war is done.*

"We'll have to make the most of the time we have, then," Jack said. "If you won't go to Sophie's again, I'll come to the house. Later, after everyone else is asleep, so we can talk without being overheard."

The need for a commitment on his part, to their future together, was an ache within her, yet she couldn't put it into words, couldn't plead with him to say it. Was she afraid he would say it without meaning it? Or that he would refuse to say it at all? The thought was a stabbing, painful one. Why did it even occur to her? Why couldn't she accept things as they were, wonderful when she and Jack were together?

Because, Valerie thought, *now* wasn't enough. If there was to be no more than the *now*, it was meaningless. It would mean that she was no better—and no better off—than the Blossoms of this world.

Yet she knew that when Jack showed up at the garden gate late tonight, she would be there to open it for him.

Twelve

"What are you looking for?" Blossom asked, stopping in the doorway of Miss Ellen's room, amazed to see that Evan had managed to scoot his chair there all the way from the room next door, where she'd left him.

The exertion of the maneuver had left him soaked in sweat, limbs trembling from the strain, and the pain, the continuous burning pain, never left his stump. He started, staring at the girl with something close to hatred, for having found him here. His mother was out in the quarters, he knew that, and Julie and Sally Ann had taken the baby out on the lawn; he'd seen them there, spreading a blanket for the infant to sit upon.

"I'm looking for something for this goddamned pain," he said through his teeth.

"She don't keep nothin' in those drawers," Blossom told him. "That laudanum is all in the chest, and it's locked. Nobody got the key but your mama."

"Get me the key," Evan said.

Blossom stared at him. "Mr. Evan, I can't get that key! She don't never leave it anywhere I could get it! She carries them keys on her, all day, and I bet she puts 'em under her pillow at night."

384

"I can't stand it," Evan said, and the tremor in his body showed in his voice as well. "Even when I'm drunk, it keeps on hurting. I'm out of whiskey, Blossom. Bring me another bottle, before my mother comes back."

"You had a bottle, last night," she protested. "You couldn't have drunk it already."

"I did. I did, and it still hurts. Go get me a bottle, damn it! Bring me some brandy, instead, maybe that will work better. Go on, get it for me! Blossom——" His tone changed, pleading, beguiling. "Blossom, you're the only one who knows how bad it is. I don't know what I'd do without you. Don't ever go away and leave me, will you?"

She moved into the room, moistening her lips. "I won't leave you if you don't want me to, Mr. Evan. You know I care about you."

"Then get me the brandy. Please, darling, get me the brandy."

Darling. He'd never called her anything like that before. When he stretched out a hand to her, Blossom took it, allowing him to draw her against his chair.

"You're so pretty, and kind. My mother isn't kind, you know. She says she loves me, but she doesn't stop this hurting. She doesn't want me to drink, either. You're the only one who understands what it's like." He lifted her hand and pressed it against his cheek. "Please, Blossom, help me."

She swallowed, "All right. I'll bring the brandy. I don't know as how I can get at that laudanum, though. I try sneakin' into her bedroom at night, and get caught, she'll skin me alive."

"No, she won't. I won't let her. I may be tied to the bed, or this damned chair, but I'm still the master of Mallows. I won't let her do anything to you. I need you."

He released her hand, and Blossom smiled. "All right. I'll try," she said.

Evan waited until her footsteps died off on the stairs, then returned his attention to the chifforobe drawers. He knew the Yankees had confiscated the pistol with which Charlotte had shot the soldier, and also the one she'd used on herself; there had to be others, though, there had been all kinds of guns at Mallows from as far back as he could remember. They would have been hidden, when the family knew the Yankees were coming, but he couldn't believe his mother wouldn't have unearthed a pistol once the enemy had gone. He knew she'd

385

been afraid, in this house, ever since his father had joined the army, and that there were no men on the place she could trust for protection.

He swore under his breath, tossing Ellen's belongings aside in his search. She should have let him die. Even if he hadn't told Valerie, his mother should have known he wouldn't want to live like this. Maybe, he thought, cramming the undergarments back into the drawer in frustrated rage, she thought it would keep him from carousing around, chasing women, raising hell. His father hadn't cared, would have thought him abnormal if he hadn't indulged in a young man's pleasures; his mother had maintained a tight-lipped silence on the subject, when she'd had to know about his actions away from home.

Well, if she thought he was going to get one of those chairs with wheels, which would limit him to the house itself, and just sit around like a breathing turnip, she had another think coming. He was still alive, but he couldn't *live* this way. Be damned if she could make him do that, all for her precious Mallows. It was more important to her than his father had been, or the girls, or himself. She would probably have denied it, if he'd asked her point-blank, but he knew it was true. She lived for Mallows, a house and a few thousand acres. Evan didn't, and they'd taken away any chance he had to live for any other reason.

He slammed one drawer shut and pulled out the one above it, groping where he could not see. Could he pull himself up on the good leg, did he have the strength to stand, could he balance, for a few minutes?

And then he found it. His hand closed over the cold mother-of-pearl handle, and he recognized it at once, even before he withdrew it from beneath the garments in his mother's drawer. It would be loaded; she would keep it ready for action. His mouth twisted wryly. Probably she kept it, to shoot herself or the girls, rather than submitting to rape. She'd figure she'd rather be dead than be subjected to that, although she hadn't allowed him the privilege of deciding to die rather than lose a leg.

He didn't have to think about it. He'd thought about it already, for months, ever since they'd first told him they wanted to take off his mangled foot, and during all the nights of agony since that bastard of a Yankee had sawed off his leg the way a butcher does with a side of beef.

386

Evan put the muzzle of the pistol to his temple and pulled the trigger. All he heard was an empty click.

Not loaded? Where were the goddamned shells, then? Where? Rage gave him the strength to pull himself up onto his good leg, to ignore the pain, to throw things out of the drawer, looking for the ammunition that his mother must have here somewhere if the pistol was to be any good to her.

There was none.

He threw the pistol across the room with all the fury and force that had been building in him for so long. It struck the chest and slid to the floor, useless.

A long splinter had broken loose on the door of the chest, and after a moment Evan's frustration ebbed as the idea came. Behind that door was his mother's supply of drugs and medications. He didn't have the key, but did he need one? It was a flimsy cabinet, and if he could find something to use to remove the hinges—

Ellen's scissors. The handles stuck out of the basket beside her chair.

Sweat stood in globules on his forehead as Evan hunched the chair across the floor; he was unaware of the trembling of his limbs, concentrating everything he had on using those scissors, twisting the screws that held the hinges. It was no use, the scissors blades were too thick. Use them to pry open the door, then, break it off. It had split, or at least splintered, from the force of the thrown pistol. Only his mother would consider such a piece of junk a secure place to lock anything up, he thought, forcing the scissors blade beneath the thin panel. He exerted all the pressure he could muster, and was rewarded by a cracking sound.

He no longer cared if he made any noises. There was only Blossom inside the house, and he could handle Blossom. The door broke, and he jerked the piece off, ignoring the splinter that jammed into his palm, reaching through the opening for what he wanted.

It was there, the new container she'd brought from Reidsville. A whole bottle of the stuff, and she was always so stingy with it. Evan stuck it in the pocket of his robe, suddenly rational again. Make the cabinet look as it had—if his mother didn't come in here until after dark, with only a candle, she might not notice. He poked the pieces back together.

Well, it wouldn't fool anyone who looked at it closely. In a dim light, though, if she didn't go to open it, it might pass until morning. That was all he needed, until morning.

When Blossom came, he was hunching the chair out of the door of Ellen's room, and he asked her, almost politely, to take him back to his own room.

"I'm tired," he said. "I've been up too long. I think I'm even too tired to want to eat supper. Tell them to just let me sleep; if I have the brandy, I'll sleep a long time."

"Your mama won't like it if you don't eat supper," Blossom said dubiously, pushing the chair with all her strength. It made scratches on the floor, but Ellen didn't seem to be making a fuss about it; the floors were all damaged, anyway. "She thinks you're too thin, and you got to eat to get better."

"Right now I'd rather sleep. Just bring up the tray, then, and leave it beside the bed if I'm not awake. Don't tell her."

He allowed Blossom to help him back into bed, wincing and cursing when his stump brushed the arm of the chair. He lay back, exhausted, closing his eyes.

"You want I should help you take off your robe?" Blossom asked. "Your mama says you don't wear that in bed."

"To hell with my mama," Evan said between his teeth. "Just put the bottle there, and leave me alone. Please. Oh, and Blossom, pick up the things I spilled out of her dresser, will you?"

"All right, Mr. Evan. Whatever you say." Blossom moved quietly from the room. What would he be like, she wondered, if he didn't hurt any more, and he didn't drink a bottle of whiskey or brandy in a day's time?

It was Blossom who found him in the morning. The brandy had scarcely been touched, but the smaller bottle beside it was empty.

For a moment the significance of that second bottle didn't register. Blossom had tiptoed toward the bed, noting that he'd never touched the tray she'd brought the previous evening. Evan didn't stir, and she stood looking down on him.

How handsome he was, in his sleep! The lines of pain were gone, and though he didn't smile, there was an expression of satisfaction on his lips, she thought. As if he were at rest, free of pain.

She had his breakfast. Should she wake him up to eat it? She eased the tray onto the table, sliding the supper tray back, and it struck the bottles behind it. Two bottles—where had the second one come from?

And then she realized what it was.

She'd seen Ellen pouring the contents from a similar container into the small vial that she used to dispense the laudanum. Lord God, how had he got hold of that? Miss Ellen surely never would have left the bottle with him . . .

Suspicion exploded into certainty. Blossom knew before she ever touched the hand lying, relaxed as she had seldom seen it, on top of the quilt. The cold hand. He had been dead for hours. Her mouth was dry and she reached out for the back of the nearest chair, for something to hold on, to keep her upright.

That's what he'd been looking for, in Miss Ellen's room. Somehow, he'd gotten into that cabinet. Would they blame her for it? Because she'd been the only one in the house with him?

The book from which she'd been trying to learn to read lay on the floor beside the chair. Blossom looked down on it, thinking that she hadn't ever really wanted to learn to read, anyway.

Much harder to give up was her dream of being mistress of Mallows someday. It would never happen, now.

The evidence was there, plain enough to be read by anyone.

As Evan had expected, Ellen had gone to bed without noticing the broken cabinet. She saw it the following morning only when she returned to her bedroom for a fresh handkerchief, having followed Blossom up the stairs. She had asked the girl to pause, and Ellen dropped a spray of pink apricot blossoms on the corner of the tray; then she smiled and went on to her room.

She stopped on the threshold, staring directly at the cabinet across from the doorway. In daylight it was impossible not to see the wrecked door propped back, not quite in the right place. Her breathing stopped, and then Ellen whirled and moved quickly across the landing to Evan's room. Blossom stood, clinging to a chair back, tears running down her cheeks from stricken blue eyes.

Suddenly perceptive, Ellen saw as well the two trays on the table, both untouched, steam rising from the tea on the nearer one. And the brandy bottle—new since yesterday—and the small colored bottle which had held the laudanum.

And Evan.

Had she known, somewhere in a denied part of her heart, that her son would eventually take this way out of the misery life had inflicted upon him? Ellen didn't remember thinking that, but she was not as surprised as she might have been, either. It wasn't only the pain, though that had been terrible for him to bear; she knew *he* had spent endless hours recounting the things he would never be able to do again. No amount of persuasion could convince him that a man with only one leg was not a total waste, without value in the world. If he'd been a working man, a poor man, who had to have two good legs to earn a living, she might have understood it better, his attitude that every good thing was behind him.

That was not the case with Evan, however. He was the owner of Mallows, a once proud plantation that would rise again to its pre-war wealth and potential. He could have run the place; there was nothing wrong with his mind.

Nothing except that he had wanted to die.

Ellen controlled her grief, as she had had to do so many times before. Like Blossom she felt sick and weak. Unlike Blossom, she pulled herself together and called for help to lift her son's lifeless body, to carry it downstairs, to make a coffin.

The question rose in her throat: Had Blossom helped him do this, or had Evan somehow managed on his own? Ellen looked into the girl's blind, shattered face, and did not ask.

She forced her own mind to remain blank, except for the surface from which she produced the proper orders. She did not ask anyone else to strip the bed in which Evan had died; she did it herself, replacing the sheets with clean ones. She cleared away all evidence that her son had ever lived in this room. If, in those first few terrible moments of realization, she had longed for the oblivion of death for herself, it was a passing thing. Death was for cowards, and she was not a coward.

She thought of concealing the manner of Evan's death. But there was the broken cabinet door, and there was Blossom. She'd always thought the girl stupid, and in many ways she was, but Blossom knew about the laudanum bottle beside his bed. No, better to admit that Evan had been crazed by pain, that he'd broken in to steal the drug, and that he'd taken too much of it. Let those who would, think it had been an accidental overdose, but not try to cover it up. Perhaps, in time, she could convince herself that Evan had wanted only to end the pain, not his life.

Julie did not regard the matter in the same light. She, too, was shocked and ill, but she understood that her brother had chosen the uncertainties of death to the certain terrible reality of living. If those men had succeeded in raping her, she thought she, too, might have chosen not to go on facing life, although she did not think that she would have had the courage that both Charlotte and Evan had demonstrated. It would take far more courage than she had, to lift a weapon to her own head, or to drain a bottle toward the same end.

Poor Evan. And poor Mama, who now had no one but herself to depend upon, in saving Mallows. And there would be Valerie and Grandma Lacy to tell of this latest sorrow. Valerie already felt guilty, for letting them cut off Evan's leg when he'd told her not to. How much responsibility would Valerie feel for this final act of desperation? It seemed that there was no end to the horrors, and Julie prayed fervently that nothing would happen to Ellen. If it did, the rest of them would be lost, she thought. No one else had Ellen's strength.

If she had known how close to failing that strength was, Julie might have been beyond the hope of prayer to remedy the situation.

Thirteen

In the morning, Valerie wanted nothing so much as to get away from this place, to forget about the pathetic sum Lacy had had to accept for it; she had had only half an hour in the garden last night with Jack, and he'd promised that if he could get away from the Federal Hospital he would be back again this afternoon, yet she couldn't wait until then. It would be, she knew, only another brief and unsatisfactory episode, for they could only speak meaningless words if others were present, as they were sure to be. When Valerie had brought up the subject of perhaps walking out with Captain Ferris—since Lacy was not up to walking with her now—to renew her acquaintance with the city she had so loved, Lacy was adamant.

"Much better not, my dear. Your mother wouldn't like it, the Savannahians wouldn't approve, and I wouldn't like it, either. When the war is over, perhaps, we may look upon Northerners as fellow human beings. At the present time, the feeling runs high, and it might even be dangerous for you. The Yankees have not ravaged Savannah, the way they did Atlanta and other places, yet they are the enemy, and the courtesy between us and them is a surface thing, only. It is expedient to maintain it, for our own sakes, yet to go beyond that surface politeness is to ask for trouble. No, do not be seen with Captain Ferris in public, Valerie. Not even in the square, if you meet by accident."

Startled, Valerie glanced at her grandmother, but it did not seem that the old lady *knew;* she was only guessing. She might have been tempted to cheat, except for the fact that Lacy had such an excellent network of spies. Oh, they weren't intentionally spying; but the visitors came in droves, once Mrs. Babcock gave out the word that Lacy wanted to see them.

They came, many bearing small gifts of flowers or food, and they talked. If there was anything going on in Savannah that they didn't tell her about, Valerie couldn't imagine what it was. Except that, as far as she knew, no one reported her excursion to River Street as of any significance.

They mentioned Patrick Ryan, some of them. Everyone knew he'd been overseer at Mallows. He was buying up real estate, they said. Not houses, particularly, although he didn't turn down a piece of land because it had buildings on it. No, he was more interested in large acreages, mostly forested ones. There were two avenues of speculation: Why was he purchasing land that would have to be cleared before it could be cultivated? And where was he getting the funds to buy at all?

Valerie was expected to sit in the drawing room and listen with little or no comment to these conversations. No one stayed long. They all knew that Lacy tired easily, and they were considerate. In truth, Valerie thought the old lady had a tremendous amount of stamina and that she thrived on their visits as little Hugh Alexander had done on Gilly's milk.

It was late afternoon, and Lacy had decided to lie down for a brief rest—"If anyone comes, invite them in and entertain them for a few minutes," she requested of Valerie, putting an end to any idea of a walk in the square—when the doorbell jangled once more.

Valerie braced herself for another old lady or gentleman, whose name and face would blend in her mind with those who'd come earlier, and then she heard Lallie say on a rising note, "Why, Mr. Ryan! Come in, sir, come in!"

Valerie stood up, hands unconsciously knotting into fists. Patrick Ryan was here? Had he seen her, down there on the waterfront? She didn't blush at the thought, she went white and cold. Act, she thought, pretend. He'd told her she wasn't bad at it, the day in Reidsville. Only that day she hadn't been trying to fool *him*.

She turned toward the doorway as Ryan suddenly filled it, his shoulders nearly touching on each side. He wore a dark business suit and a white shirt and a tie; good quality goods, she thought irrelevantly. Even the flamboyant embroidered waistcoat didn't detract from his overall appearance, though the impression she had was *riverboat gambler* rather than *gentleman*.

"Mr. Ryan. What a pleasant surprise," she lied, and indicated the one chair in the room that she thought sturdy enough to support him. "Please sit down. My grandmother will be sorry she's missed you; she's just gone upstairs to rest."

"I'm sorry to hear she hasn't been well. I just found out you were in Savannah, and that she'd had to have a doctor." Patrick spoke easily, taking the seat and crossing one ankle over the opposite knee in a position of comfort.

Valerie waited. Would there be a comment on the doctor?

There was not. "She's feeling somewhat better now, I take it?"

"Yes, she is, although she must rest frequently. I'm afraid I haven't anything to offer you to drink except tea; shall I have Lallie bring some?"

"Tea would be very nice," Patrick agreed, as if he were quite accustomed to sitting in elegant drawing rooms. Well, this one wasn't elegant any more; even the fresh paint and the rug brought down from the attic couldn't disguise the damage that had been done to it. Yet she sensed that it wouldn't have intimidated Patrick Ryan if it had been the most ostentatiously elegant drawing room in the city.

"I'll bring the tea," Lallie said, and ducked back out of sight, leaving Valerie wondering what she was supposed to talk about with *this* visitor. The little old people had bored her; Patrick Ryan frightened her.

"I understand you're in Savannah to sell this house." He glanced around, appraising it.

"Grandma Lacy will sign the papers on it tomorrow. We'll return to Mallows the following day."

Patrick's eyes now appraised *her*, with a shrewdness that was disconcerting. "Did you get enough for it to do what you want to do?"

394

It was none of his business what they'd got for it, yet she heard herself telling him. "Forty-six hundred dollars."

"Disappointing, I'm sure, when the place must have cost fifteen thousand or so to build. Still, that's the way things are these days. Nobody with money, lots of people who want to sell. The seller takes what he can get."

It was said with a lack of any apparent sympathy for those in such a position. She had not intended to mention what they'd recently heard about *his* activities, but she was stung into a biting rejoinder. "Is that the way it is, with the ones you're buying land from?"

"Oh, that news has preceded me, has it?" Patrick grinned, looking unexpectedly boyish. "Well, yes, as a matter of fact, I'm picking up some good land rather cheap."

"And it doesn't bother you? That those who have to sell get so little for it?"

"Why should it bother me? If I don't buy it, they'll sell for the same price, or less, to someone else. Or not sell at all, which is worse, since the land's no good to them without cash and slaves to work it."

"And what do you propose to do with it?" Valerie asked, carried on in spite of herself. "Have you slaves, and cash, Mr. Ryan?"

"No slaves. Nobody's going to have slaves any more. We're going to have to pay them wages. If the income from the land is high enough to cover wages *and* show a profit, that's feasible."

"And the cash? You've managed to come through the war with your army pay intact, have you?"

It was a snide remark. Confederate soldiers made even less than Union ones; even a sergeant probably didn't make over twenty dollars a month.

Patrick took no offense. His grin was still genial. "Oh, yes, I have cash. Not my own, you understand; I'm operating on behalf of a corporation I've formed. They put up the money, I do the work, and we all share the profits. Seems reasonable, doesn't it?"

For a moment Valerie was bewildered. There might be some Southerners who'd come through the war with their fortunes intact; she didn't know of any of them. And then the truth occurred to her, so that she blurted it out.

"Northern money?"

Ryan's grin broadened. "It's the only kind that's any good,

395

Miss Valerie. Anybody who has any Confederate paper might as well warm his hands over it in the fireplace, for the few minutes it will last. Not even the staunchest Confederate supporter will take Jeff Davis's money in trade for anything."

"Northern money. You're acting with Northern money." The idea was still filtering through her mind.

"Yes. You find that shocking? That after fighting them for four years, I'm willing now to work *with* them? Note that word, *with*. Not *for*. It's *my* company; they've invested in it. I learned a lot over the past few years, Miss Val. And one of the things I learned was that there weren't going to be jobs like the one I left at Mallows, for people like me. The whole life-style is going to change in the South, when we can't use slaves any more. And I never intended to remain an overseer all my life, anyway. It's a degrading job, really. Almost as degrading to be an overseer as it is to be a slave. Things will be a struggle, for a few years. The Yankees will want to be sure we've learned our lesson, so they'll crunch us underfoot for a while, until they've made it quite clear that they're the conquerors, we the conquered. But there's a great deal of potential in the South, in Georgia, and I intend to make the most of it. I intend to be one of the top dogs in the New South, Miss Valerie."

Looking at him, too big for the fragile chair, prosperity (even if it was borrowed) emanating from him, Valerie suddenly realized that he just might do as he said.

"With Yankee money." She couldn't stop herself from saying that.

"It's starting with Yankee money. It won't be long before a lot of it, whatever I spend, is my own."

"And that doesn't bother you, to start with Yankee money."

"No. You think it should, don't you? Loyalty to the Confederacy, even to the point of lunacy. The war is as good as over, the slaves aren't the only ones who've been freed. People like me, who hadn't a chance in the world to rise above the station they were born into, are free, too. I always hated the system, but the only way I could see to beat it was to join it. Come up through the proper channels, learn as much as I could from people like your father, and be ready when the opportunity arose. Well, the opportunity is here. And I'm ready."

He was still smiling, but there was a deadly earnestness behind the smile.

"I see." Valerie's response was faint. She did see, in a way, although it would take some adjusting to reconcile this man with the one she'd known all her life. "Well, I'm sure I wish you luck, Mr. Ryan."

The amusement faded, now. "Do you, Miss Val? I'd like to think you mean that."

"Why shouldn't I mean it? We've never been enemies, have we?"

"I hope not. The last thing in the world I want is to make an enemy of you. I'll be returning to my own place within a few weeks; no doubt we'll run into each other then, though I may not be there for long. My new business will require a good deal of traveling, for a while."

"Buying up more land."

"Buying up more land," Ryan agreed.

"I think Mama was halfway hoping," Valerie said, "that you'd return to Mallows, as overseer."

"Before she caught us in the buggy, you mean? Before I insulted her by kissing her daughter?"

"She didn't realize the need for that. I explained it to her; she understands, now."

Patrick laughed shortly. "Does she? Well, you can tell your mama—in case she asks—that the only way I'll ever return to Mallows is as master of it. I'll buy it, if she wants to sell."

Her shock was so great she could not even reply to that at once. Sell Mallows? Ellen would sell her soul first.

He was nodding. "I know. She's scrambling to keep it intact, now. Maybe she'll last a year or two, although the money Miss Lacy got for this house won't do it, alone. Sooner or later, she's going to have to sell it, or lose it. She won't be able to hang on to it."

"You can't know that. My mama is a very determined woman."

"Your mama is a real lady," Ryan acknowledged. "And her stamina and courage are commendable. But she is only one woman, saddled with a job that's way too big for her."

"Evan," Valerie began, but he didn't let her finish.

"Evan never wanted the job of running Mallows. He's not a farmer, and he was never any good at handling slaves. He wouldn't be any better with the blacks now that they're free.

And from what I heard recently, he had a serious injury; they took his leg off."

"Yes, that's true, but—"

"Which means," Ryan continued, "that he's got as good an excuse as he could ever hope to have, for not taking any of the responsibility for Mallows. So sooner or later, and my guess is that it'll be sooner, your mama, gracious and intelligent and determined as she is, is going to have to sell Mallows. When she does, I'd like to make the first offer on it."

Valerie could hardly believe what she was hearing. "Mama would never let any part of Mallows go, unless she's forced to. And when she does—if she ever does—may I offer you some advice, Mr. Ryan, purely in kindness? Don't make this suggestion to her. Maybe you're right, though I hope not, that she won't be able to hang on to everything. Maybe the time will come when she'll sell, to whoever will pay the most. But if you try to tell her that, now—"

"She won't take kindly to such an offer from a former overseer?" Patrick Ryan suggested quietly. "From a Georgia cracker's son? She won't like it that I presume to be good enough to own Mallows?"

Valerie stared at him helplessly. "I didn't mean that to be offensive, Mr. Ryan. I only know Mama rather well, and I don't think she'd take kindly to anyone making her an offer at this time. It would prejudice her against anyone, whether it be you or President Davis."

Did the hard blue eyes soften, or not? "And how would you feel, Miss Valerie? If the place had to be sold, would you be willing to sell it to me?"

"Mallows is not mine to sell. I don't expect that I'll ever have to make that decision."

He laughed, a short burst of sound devoid of mirth. "Well said! I couldn't have evaded better myself. All right, I won't speak to your mama. But remember what I've said. If the time comes that she considers selling, will you let me know? Or is that, too, something you prefer not to say in so many words?"

Valerie's lips parted, although she did not fully know what she intended to say. Before she could speak, however, the doorbell pealed again, with the strident ring that was the result of a too-vigorous twisting of the handle. She turned away from Patrick Ryan, praying that she did not recognize

398

the new caller by his ring. Not now, not when Ryan was here.

And then she heard his voice, clear, easy, too obviously comfortable in this house. "Hello, Lallie. Where is everybody?"

"Miss Lacy resting. Miss Valerie entertaining Mr. Ryan in the drawing room, Captain."

Valerie and Patrick both came to their feet.

"Well, well," Patrick said. "Am I about to meet the Captain Ferris who is caring for Miss Lacy?"

Valerie felt simultaneously hot and cold. Dear God, let him not know about anything other than that, that Jack was Lacy's doctor!

Jack stood in the doorway, not filling it quite so completely as Patrick Ryan had done, attractive in his dark blue uniform with the double row of bright buttons. The two men faced each other, with Valerie midway between them, and she had the horrid feeling that each knew altogether too much about the other. Which was, of course, absurd.

She spoke quickly, before Jack could call her by her first name or in any other way reveal to Patrick Ryan that they meant anything at all to one another. "Good afternoon, Captain Ferris. Grandma Lacy's asleep, I think. Shall I run up and see?"

"No hurry about it, ma'am," Jack said. His dark gaze was fixed on Ryan, so that she had to introduce them.

She did so, formally. Neither man offered to shake hands, although Jack made a rather formal bow; Patrick was content to nod his head.

"Ah, here's Lallie with the tea," Valerie observed. "Won't you join us, Captain?"

"No, I think not. I'll check in on my patient, first. Nice to have met you, Mr. Ryan." As if he'd said, plainly, that he expected Ryan to be gone by the time he came down the stairs.

Patrick made no reply to that, but when she would have poured him tea, he changed his mind. "I think I'll forgo that now, Miss Valerie. Please tell Miss Lacy I'm sorry to have missed her, and that I hope she's feeling better. Obviously she's in good hands, and you, too."

Now what did he mean by that? She was reading double entendres into everything. If only he could not detect anything in her face!

Ryan smiled, and held out a hand which she automatically

399

took, feeling his warm and firm. "It was nice seeing you, Miss Val. Remember me to Miss Julie, and to your mama when you get home. Oh, and that pretty little blond one, what was her name? Blossom? Is she still with you?"

Blossom? Imagine his remembering Blossom, when he'd only met her once. "Yes," Valerie said, "she's still with us. She has, I believe, no family to go to anywhere."

"I'll be seeing you all, before too long," Patrick said. "Be careful going home. There are fewer soldiers about, but plenty of rogues yet. Lallie, could I have my hat, please?"

Valerie was shaking when he left. Several times she'd felt he was playing cat to her mouse. The way he'd looked at Jack Ferris, as if he knew everything about him, including the fact that he'd taken Valerie to bed in Ryan's own house. She drew herself together. He didn't know anything, and what matter if he guessed? So long as he didn't say anything.

She turned eagerly when Jack came down the stairs. Lallie had taken the tea things back to the kitchen, and Valerie felt free to go into his arms when they met for a quick passionate embrace.

"So that was Ryan. What was he doing here?" Jack asked, after he'd kissed her.

"Just looking in on us, the way any neighbor would. I don't want to talk about Ryan."

"Nor I, my sweet. We have only tonight and tomorrow to be together, and as I have a command performance tonight with some of the officers left here in Savannah, that leaves only tomorrow. Listen, love, to what we will be doing, and I didn't even arrange it, I swear! Mrs. Kirkpatrick is giving a musical evening, and she'll be sending invitations around for you and your grandmother to join the party. Miss Lacy will probably be well enough to go, and the house is just off Johnson Square so you can easily walk there. And because I successfully treated her precious daughter for an ailment that shall remain nameless, I and several of my fellow officers have also been invited to attend. In truth, I think it's one of those affairs where she is doing the diplomatic thing by appearing to be civil to the enemy without alienating her own friends. Being a physician has its advantages, since everyone recognizes the need for their services, regardless of politics."

"And what good will it do us," Valerie asked, "to sit on opposite sides of Mrs. Kirkpatrick's music room and listen to some overdeveloped soprano?"

Jack laughed. "I happen to know, from having made a number of house calls, that there are places one may go for privacy. Including a charming summer house in the garden. There'll be enough people there to make it very difficult for anyone to keep track of either of us. And since I'll ostentatiously pay attention to the Kirkpatrick daughter, and make my excuses to leave early after that, we should be clever enough to find a few minutes to ourselves."

The very idea was enough to lift her spirits. She could let him go now without regret, with the promise of that adventure tomorrow evening.

The papers to transfer ownership of the house to Mr. McGivern were signed the following morning. And just as Jack had said would happen, a small black boy delivered an invitation to a musical evening at the Kirkpatricks'.

Lacy read it aloud, and Valerie yawned, patting at her mouth. "Isn't Mrs. Kirkpatrick the one whose sister sings? Badly?"

"Yes. Her sister, however, is in Baltimore, I believe, so won't be singing. I might be up to going, at least for a part of it, if you'd like to go with me. Otherwise, we can stay home and retire early. I've told Lallie and Rudy that we will leave at dawn. The sooner we get home to Mallows, the better."

"Whatever you like," Valerie said casually. And then, observing her grandmother's expression and hoping she hadn't already gone too far in appearing disinterested, "It would be nice for you, Grandma Lacy. No doubt there will be some of your old friends there. Let's go, and if it's a dreadful bore, we can always say you're overtired. No one will think it odd if we leave early, and maybe she'll have something good to eat."

Several hours before they were to leave, however, Valerie made a discovery that caused her to swear aloud, so that Lallie poked her head into the room. "You say something, Miss Val?"

"Sometimes it's damned inconvenient to be a female," she said, removing a bloodied undergarment and inspecting her petticoats to make certain they had not been stained, as well.

Lallie accepted the pantalettes. "Seems to me it's *always* inconvenient to be a female. I have these washed and dried out by morning, when it's time to leave. Shall I tell your grandmama you don't feel too good? You want to stay home tonight and just rest? She ain't so anxious to go, herself."

"No, no. I'll go. It's the last time she'll see most of these people. Oh, Lallie, press out my green silk, will you? It's more crumpled than I thought."

So the evening would not go as Jack had planned, after all. The lovemaking would consist only of kisses and caresses, even if they had the promised summer house to themselves. It was a disappointment, yet at the same time a relief. Because her conscience nipped at her in unexpected moments, and the fear of being discovered had built to major proportions, Valerie realized that she was looking forward to the evening more than before. There was less to be afraid of.

They arrived a bit late, Lacy having had to stop and rest on the way. Mrs. Kirkpatrick greeted them warmly, expressed concern over Lacy's paleness, and urged Valerie to take her into the small study at the front part of the house. "Florabelle's friend, Captain Ferris, is a physician," she said. "I'll send him to you. You really are looking out of sorts, Lacy."

"Captain Ferris has been looking after me," Lacy confessed. "I think you're right. I do feel as if I've overdone."

She was so white, in fact, that Valerie was almost too alarmed to notice Florabelle Kirkpatrick, hovering at Jack's elbow. Almost, not quite. Florabelle was a stunning blond beauty dressed in pale blue gauze over a deeper blue silk.

"I'll see Miss Lacy alone," Jack said, and closed the door in the faces of both girls.

The entry hall was filled with people, most of them middle-aged or older. Valerie saw two other girls, obviously sisters, neither of whom were especially attractive. Florabelle, on the other hand, was well worth a second look.

"Have you known Captain Ferris long?" Valerie asked.

"Ever since he came to Savannah. He's been so helpful." Florabelle smiled radiantly. "Of course, he's a Yankee, but lordy, there aren't any *Southern* men left in this town. Not any *young* ones. He's so busy, but sometimes he has a free evening, and he *adores* Mama's musicales."

"Is that right?" Valerie's lips felt stiff, and she felt old, much older than this fluffy miss who was, probably, no more than seventeen.

"Did I understand Mama to say that Captain Ferris is your grandmama's doctor, too? How did she happen to meet him?"

"He was in charge of a hospital the Yankees established at

402

Mallows," Valerie told her. "They were there in the same house with us for some months."

Florabelle's eyes widened. "Really? How fascinating! Odd that he never mentioned it, knowing you, I mean."

"No, why should he? I mean, we didn't know each other, you and I," Valerie pointed out. She didn't know why, but she had decided she didn't like Florabelle.

Florabelle kept up a line of chatter, occasionally pausing to introduce Valerie to someone, until the door finally opened and Jack emerged. He spoke directly to Valerie.

"Seems she's overdone a bit. I've suggested that she lie back on the sofa in there and rest a bit, perhaps with the door open so that she can hear the music. If she doesn't feel enough better to join the rest of us in half an hour or so, I think we'd better send for Rudy to bring the buggy around to take her home."

"Will she be up to traveling tomorrow? For three days?" Valerie asked anxiously.

"It's impossible to say for certain, but she's determined to go. We'll just have to wait and see. Florabelle," he added, turning aside, "I think I'd better stay within hearing range of Miss Lacy. Why don't you join the others, and I'll come along when I can?"

Suspicion flashed in the blue eyes as Florabelle looked from Jack to Valerie and back to Jack. "I was saving us seats, together. Perhaps Miss Valerie would care to use yours, until you can come along?"

"I think I'll stay within hearing range, too. She was quite ill for a few days," Valerie said quickly. "I wouldn't want her to think I was so unfeeling as to leave her when she might need me."

Florabelle hesitated, and Jack gave her a slight push on the shoulder. "Be a good girl, run along. If I don't make it for all of the concert, we'll at least have supper together."

Florabelle's eyelashes fluttered; she was reassured, and glanced at Valerie as if to make sure the other girl realized the significance of the supper arrangements. "All right. Come as soon as you can, though."

Valerie stared after the departing figure in blue silk and gauze. "Miss Florabelle is quite taken with you."

Jack chuckled. "She's an infant, and as spoiled a one as I've ever seen. Personally, I prefer women." There was no one else in sight at the moment, Mrs. Kirkpatrick having

403

herded her guests into the music room at the rear of the house, and Jack brushed a kiss across her forehead. "Hot-blooded women."

She told him then, blushing, what must cool her ardor for a few days; he swore good-naturedly. "On our last night together. What a rotten bit of luck."

She was aware of her grandmother in the dimly lighted room behind them, and kept her voice low enough so that Lacy could not possibly make out the words. As always, her blood seemed to thicken and at the same time to pulse faster through her veins, when Jack touched her. She could not leave him, *could not*, without some sort of agreement between them. "Not our last night together forever, I trust," Valerie said.

"No, of course not." Jack looked about and then started toward the open doorway of a room opposite, drawing her with him so that they would not be seen unless someone passed directly in front of the doorway. "How am I going to manage without you, Valerie? It may be months before I can get back to Georgia, even after this is all over—there'll be neglected business to take care of at home, and I've no way of knowing what that will stretch out to. No one understands why I wanted to be a physician, a surgeon, when there was a perfectly good business to run." He grimaced. "Business isn't my line, but I'll have to admit it's nice to have a substantial income that enables me to do what I really want to do. Being an army doctor wouldn't keep me in beans and bacon, let alone anything else. So I'll yield to family pressures and stick around long enough to be sure there's a good manager to run things; the one who's doing it in my place now wants to retire as soon as there's someone else to take over, so I'll have to stay home for a while."

In the dim light, she saw his mouth curve in a smile. "First things first, that's the way it'll be. But I'll be back, my love. Back to Georgia, and Mallows, and you."

The sweet warm rush of relief that flooded her carried her into his arms for a long, fervent kiss; it was only the sound of approaching voices that brought them back to their senses.

It no longer mattered that they would not have this evening together. At least, it didn't matter as much.

Because now she knew that Jack would be back for her; she could bear the waiting, however long it took, now that she was safe in her knowledge of that.

Fourteen

The return trip to Mallows took them through a countryside transformed by blooming peach trees, the pale pink blossoms sometimes showering them with delicate drifting petals as they rode. The air was warm and as heady as wine, and drunken bees added their small sounds to the rustling of tender, pale-green leaves. It was a time of year Valerie had always loved, and even the fact that they were returning home with so much less money than they'd hoped for could not dampen her spirits entirely. She would be parted from Jack, yes, but that parting would not last longer than was absolutely necessary; that made all the difference in the world.

Lacy held up as well as anyone could have expected, although she was white and weary when the time came to stop for the night. Valerie urged her to rest as much as she could by lying across the buggy seat with her head in Valerie's lap, which she consented to do from time to time. But Lacy, too, loved the springtime; and unlike her granddaughter, she did not take it for granted that she would see many, many more of them.

To the north of them, in Virginia, the battles went on. A few hardy souls still hoped that the Confederacy might survive; most had long since given up, and many had gone home

405

to their farms and their families, to wait with grim fortitude whatever was to come.

Between Savannah and Mallows, however, there was no sign of war. The grass grew thick and green; fields were being plowed with mules or by hand, precious seed planted and nurtured. It was easy, at least for a short time, to imagine that life was as good as it had ever been.

Pansy heard them coming and set up a screeching they could hear halfway down the line of live oaks. Valerie was glad to be home, yet braced for the impact their news would have on her mother. Forty-six hundred dollars, where Ellen must be hoping for at least two or three times that much.

Rudy brought the buggy to a halt before the front steps. "We home, ladies!" he cried.

And then those in the buggy saw the faces of the women assembled on the piazza to greet them. Valerie's appraisal was rapid; everyone was there, except Evan.

Evan.

She knew, before they told her, that Evan was dead.

Ellen told them quietly, with little visible emotion. "We buried him day before yesterday. I'm sorry we couldn't wait until you got home."

Valerie reached for her mother, hugging her, finding Ellen strangely unyielding; it was as if, Valerie thought, if she bent at all, she would shatter completely.

"How?" she demanded, when she released the rigid figure. "How did he die?"

"Very quietly, in his sleep. Very peacefully."

"But he was healing so well—was there an infection?"

The others stood around them, silent, faces drawn.

"No," Ellen said. "No . . . he had too much laudanum, in trying to kill the pain."

It might have been better to ask the question in private, or of Julie rather than her mother. Yet she had to know, she couldn't wait. "Did he take it on purpose? Did he intend to die?"

Ellen's eyelids flickered and she massaged her temple. "There is no way of knowing for sure, one way or the other. Blossom said he was in terrible pain, and when he got the bottle, he simply—drank it."

Drank it. The entire bottle. Even in his suffering, Valerie thought, he must have known it would be fatal to drink it all. Her own pain was no less for being emotional, rather than physical. It etched lines into her face that made her look much older than her years.

"So I have that to live with, too," she murmured. "That he died without ever forgiving me, for letting them take off his leg. That he was right; that I should have let him die when he wanted to." Her vision blurred, and she could not see more than a featureless oval that was her mother's face. "How do you know what's the right thing to do?"

"You don't," Ellen said. "You only do your best, and learn to live with the mistakes, when you make them."

Valerie groped for a handkerchief, then accepted the one that Julie put into her hand. Some mistakes, which resulted in the needless suffering of someone you love, would be very difficult to learn to live with, she thought.

After the news about Evan, their own disclosure was almost anticlimatic. Ellen accepted the bank draft with a low-voiced "Thank you, Miss Lacy." If she was shocked at the inadequacy of the amount of it, she didn't say so.

Miss Lacy went directly to bed, refusing the bowl of Mamie's soup. Valerie would have liked to do the same thing; she did not, however, but sat at the table to tell the others everything that had happened in Savannah.

Well, not *everything*.

The news reached them less than a week after it occurred, by way of a newspaper from Atlanta left by a traveler who brought, as well, a letter from Henriette.

They read the letter first, and it was a bright, happy one, sounding like the girl they had known all their lives. She and Galen Battersby were engaged to be married; the ceremony would not take place until the fall, because there were so many things to do both on the plantation and in the way of a wardrobe (Henriette had left Mallows with only a few garments spared from Julie's well-worn selection). She wished with all her heart that her beloved friends at Mallows would find it possible to journey to her new home near Milledgeville to share her joyous day.

The other news was not so good. On April 9, at a little town called Appomattox Court House, the Confederates had raised the white flag. General Robert E. Lee surrendered to the superior forces of General Ulysses S. Grant. The Army of Virginia would fight no more. Like the sum of money they had brought home from Savannah, the surrender was anticlimatcic. Everyone had known it would come. And, although they sorrowed over it, it made little immediate impact upon life at Mallows.

Already too much time had been lost. The land must be worked and planted quickly if there was to be any crop this year. The blacks remaining on the place, though numbering no young men older than Thomas, who was now sixteen, must accomplish as much as could be accomplished.

Ellen went, alone with Rudy, to Reidsville. She paid her bills, bought her seed, and hired half a dozen freedmen, who had formerly been slaves. These latter seemed eager for the work, at a promised twelve dollars a month and found; if they thought it was to be easy, working for a thirty-nine-year-old widow, they soon learned the error of their ways.

Slave driver, they called her among themselves, although they were no longer, technically, slaves. Yet if she drove them hard, she drove herself harder. Ellen not only gave orders, she joined the workers in the fields when necessary. Her skin grew burned and then tanned; if her back ached until she wanted to cry, she had no sympathy for those who complained of the pace and wanted to rest.

When the work was done, they could rest.

Sally Ann was put to work tending babies, the black ones as well as Hugh Alexander, so that Nora and the other young mothers could put in their hours in the fields. Lacy and Dolly Mallow were inundated by mending and sewing garments from the coarse, cheap materials Ellen bought to clothe the workers, who had had no new clothes for nearly four years. It was the quality of the material that was cheap, not the price of it. Twelve dollars a yard for calico, one dress apiece for the women, a shirt and a pair of trousers for each man. The old women bent close to their work, putting in small neat stitches; the black women worked until dark and could not see to sew for themselves.

Julie and Valerie were pressed into service with Blossom, Lallie, and Pansy in the fields. For the first time anyone could remember, Ellen forgot about the house. There was no dusting, little sweeping, only Mamie to handle the work in the kitchen. The house came second, after the fields and the gardens were planted. Without the crops, there would be nothing to eat through the next winter.

To begin with, Julie and Valerie swathed themselves in gloves, long sleeves, broad-brimmed hats. They found these
408

difficult to work in, however, and unbearably hot; before long, they gave up on the gloves, reduced the size of their hats, and let sun and nature take their course. Valerie, in a fit of defiance, did away with stays, as well. Ellen did protest that, only to be met with open defiance.

"They kill me. I can't work like that unless I can breathe. Do you want me to hoe cotton, or don't you?"

Jack wouldn't know her when he came for her, Valerie thought, examining her hands. How long, if ever, would it be, before they were white and pretty again?

When the weather turned really hot, Julie moved out of Valerie's bedroom, back into her own. If it bothered her that both her brother and her friend had died in the same room, she didn't talk about it. After all, during the hundred or more years the house had stood, someone had probably died in each of the bedrooms. One could hardly vacate them for that reason.

Valerie would lie at night in the thick dark heat, no breeze stirring the netting that kept out most of the ever present mosquitoes, and think about Jack. Sometimes she would run her hands over her own body, grown thinner and less soft, she feared; mostly she was too tired to do anything except lapse into unconsciousness the moment she touched the pillow.

A few letters came from Jack. Brief, hastily scrawled, nothing in the message that couldn't be shared with the rest of the family. That was only to be expected, she thought, yet she longed for words of love. And she learned that a body once awakened by lovemaking does not forget it; how many mornings she wakened from erotic dreams, with an urge for love so strong that she could have cried with it!

On April 14, 1865, President Abraham Lincoln was assassinated while attending a performance at Ford's Theatre in Washington, D.C. The news stunned the South, as well as the North.

"How stupid," Valerie said, incredulous. "How stupid, to kill him now, when it's all over, when it can only make matters worse for us!"

Worse, they all knew, because upon Lincoln's death, the Vice-President would assume the country's leadership, and Andrew Johnson was far less in sympathy with the plight of the South than his predecessor had been.

Lincoln dead, Johnson burning to punish the secessionists,

409

Jefferson Davis and his Confederate cabinet members fled from Richmond, which had been their capital for four years. They could only wait in dread for whatever was to come next. And while they waited, Ellen saw to it that they worked.

In mid-May came the news that President Jefferson Davis had been captured near Irwinville, in Irwin County to the southwest. With the rest of the South, the women of Mallows prayed that he would not be executed as a traitor, as some bitter souls in the North thought he should be. It was saddening enough that he was to be sentenced to prison for leading his countrymen in honorable secession.

Ellen, stiff-lipped, read out to them a quotation from President Lincoln: *Both read the same Bible and pray to the same God, and each invokes His aid against the other . . . The prayers of both could not be answered; that of neither has been answered fully. The Almighty has His own purposes.* What those purposes might be, none of them could have said. Politics were beyond them; they scratched, literally, for a way to stay alive.

Patrick Ryan returned home, though not for long. He rode up the long oyster shell drive on a handsome stallion very nearly the color of his flaming hair. He was dressed elegantly, and he smoked good cigars, after first asking permission of Miss Ellen.

She had greeted him coolly, though not uncivilly. "May we offer you a cold drink, Mr. Ryan?"

"Thank you. I'd appreciate that." He came into the shadowy house; the drawing rooms had been opened up, the furniture strategically placed to cover the worst of the damage to the carpets. Patrick Ryan was quite at home in a drawing room. He drank lemonade, and asked politely how they were doing.

"As well as can be expected," Ellen said, inclining her head and concealing her hands in the folds of her skirts.

"I'm glad to hear it. If I might make a suggestion, ma'am, about that land you're not working—"

"I'm working all that I have the hands for," Ellen told him. She sat upright, spine stiff.

"Through the summer, yes. In the fall, though, after you've harvested the corn and the cotton. Put your people to work planting trees."

410

"Trees?" Surprise jarred her out of her controlled complacency.

"Pine trees. Trees for lumbering, and for turpentine."

Valerie, who had been leaning one hand on the back of her mother's chair, came to attention. "Are you serious, Mr. Ryan?"

"Never more so. Both products can be harvested with less workers than you'll need for cotton. And there's a growing demand for wood products. Your workers can continue to find something useful to do after your other harvest is in, rather than lying around the quarters having to be fed for nothing."

"Trees," Ellen said again, faintly.

"Thank you for the suggestion," Valerie told him. "We'll look into it."

Ellen glanced at her sharply, saying nothing. The decision was, after all, her own to make. Not Valerie's, nor Patrick Ryan's. Still, maybe he was right. He certainly appeared prosperous enough himself, and it was now common knowledge that he'd bought up thousands of acres of land with nothing but pine trees on it. It was something to be considered later, not now. She was too busy now even to think about the matter.

When the wild strawberries ripened, the small children were put to work picking them for jams and jellies. Even a three-year-old knew he would be punished if he ate of them as he picked; they were needed for the winter. And after the strawberries came the raspberries—once in a while they would have the luxury of eating them with thick cream, for supper; mostly, Ellen insisted that they be preserved against the winter that threatened her, already, in late May.

Three days before Valerie's twentieth birthday on the first of June, the worker who had been sent to Reidsville for the mail and other supplies delivered to her a bundle. It was sizable, and heavy; he carried it to the house and deposited it upon the dining room table. "Said to bring it to Miss Val, at Mallows," he reported.

She had been working all day, picking berries, and her fingers were stained red, though she'd tried to wash them clean; it was impossible to get the juice out from under her fingernails. She stared at the bundle. She was expecting nothing. Yet perhaps—? Jack knew when her birthday was, might he have sent it?

"What is it?" Julie asked, pausing while her mother looked through the small packet of letters.

"I've no idea. Give me the scissors, and I'll cut the string and find out."

She clipped the string, eagerly tearing back the brown paper wrapping, then stopping in stunned amazement.

It was the bolt of apricot velvet she had seen in Reidsville.

The breath went out of her as if she'd been struck in the stomach. Julie, too, exclaimed and moved closer to touch it with reverent fingers, and Ellen forgot her letters.

"What is it? Velvet? An entire bolt of it? Valerie, you didn't . . . ?"

"No, no, of course not. Miss Emmonds said it was worth . . ." She broke off, suddenly realizing what her mother would have to say about sixty-dollars-a-yard fabric, no matter where it had come from.

"Worth what?" Ellen demanded, edging forward to examine it herself.

"A lot," Valerie said in a faint voice. "I don't understand. Where did it come from? Who sent it?"

Julie pushed the velvet aside and groped through the wrappings. "Here, there's a message." She thrust it into her sister's hand.

"It's worth a fortune," Ellen murmured. "It's stunning—absolutely stunning. What does the note say?"

There was nothing she could do except read it aloud, turning to get the late afternoon sun through the side windows. "Miss Valerie: I remembered that you have a birthday soon, and since this had happened to come my way, I thought of you. Respectfully yours, Patrick Ryan."

"Ryan!" Ellen dropped the velvet as if it were hot. "Why on earth would he send you a present of an entire bolt of velvet? Why would he send you any present at all?"

She could not have been any more surprised than Valerie herself was. "I can't imagine. *This happened to come my way.* That must be it. He won it in a card game, or something, and he had no one to give it to, no use for it himself."

"He has a sister," Julie said slowly. She had neither seen nor felt anything so gorgeous in all her recollection, and she saw at once that it was perfect for her sister's coloring.

"Can you imagine Ruth Ryan wearing anything like this? To what, a prayer meeting in New Hope Church?"

"You'll have to send it back to him," Ellen said.

The words dropped into a pool of silence that widened like the ripples from a dropped stone until they reached the shore of Valerie's consciousness.

"No."

Ellen stared at her daughter, seeing the warning signals of heightened color and hands curling into fists. "What do you mean, no?" she asked, ignoring the evidence of a determination that might well be as strong as her own. "You can't accept a gift from a man like Patrick Ryan, and most especially not one as valuable as this! You'll have to send it back."

"I won't send it back. It's the most beautiful thing I've ever seen, and I mean to keep it." Valerie stood as straight as, and taller than, her mother; her color had faded, now, to one as pale as it was possible for her to be, beneath the tan.

"Valerie! No lady accepts gifts, especially expensive ones, from a man to whom she is not married or engaged!"

"Maybe they didn't, in your day, Mama. I think the circumstances have changed. Life is cruel, and hard, and there's scarcely anything worthwhile left, except hope—" Her words caught in her throat and she struggled past the emotion that choked her. "And damned little of that, when it comes down to it. I may never again see anything I want as badly as I want this, and I mean to keep it. I won't give it up for anything as silly as the rules you lived by in an age that's gone forever."

For a moment they faced each other across the table and the expanse of exquisite fabric. Julie watched it, the battle of strong wills, removing her fingers from the velvet as if she might thereby disengage herself from the conflict.

"Valerie, I will not have a daughter of mine behave with so little sense of propriety. We will return the gift to Mr. Ryan."

Valerie scooped up the bolt and held it tight against her breast, which was heaving with intense feeling. "It's my gift and I won't return it. I'm sorry, Mama, but this is one matter on which you're not going to make the decision. *I* am, and I've made it."

She moved around Ellen, brushing aside her mother's outstretched hand, and half-ran out of the room and up the stairs. She stood before the mirror, seeing her own face above the precious fabric; not the pale, pretty face she had seen for years, but a tanned skin almost as apricot-tinted as the velvet.

413

She saw, too, her hands: reddened, roughened, stained with the berries she had been picking.

It started deep within her, and grew into uncontrollable spasms; the shaking, the sobbing. Valerie let the bolt of cloth slide from her hands onto the carpet, and folded over it, on her knees, giving in to the grief and frustration, rage and sorrow, that seemed to have no end.

The velvet remained standing in the wardrobe section of Valerie's chifforobe, untouched. Valerie did not mention it, and neither did Ellen.

Full summer was upon them, and with it the need for dawn-to-dusk labors. The only human beings on the plantation who did not work were the infants, under three years old. All others had their chores, and were expected to be at them for as long each day as there was sufficient light to perform them.

Weeds grew with incredible rapidity, far outdistancing cotton and corn; they must be chopped or pulled out both in the fields and in the household gardens. Anything that could be harvested was eaten fresh or preserved. The women spent long hours cutting, drying, and canning fruits and vegetables. The latter was a particularly onerous chore, because it meant heating the fruits and berries, exposing oneself to the rising steam, then ladling out the boiling contents of the massive kettles into bottles and jars which were once more lowered into boiling water to complete the process. It was hot, dirty, messy, uncomfortable, and made every attempt at keeping one's hair looking respectable no more than a joke. It was also absolutely essential.

Until this year, there had been black women to do these tasks. In the summer of 1865, with the blacks freed and demanding pay for their labors, even an indignant Dolly Mallow was set to shelling peas and cutting green beans until her fingers were sore as boils.

The black women who remained at Mallows were not paid, except in their keep, as they had always been. Yet rumor told them that eventually the authorities would get around to "setting this injustice to rights," and what she would do then, Ellen didn't know. It was all she could do to pay the men she had brought in, men who did not work with any particular goodwill, men who grumbled and complained, and slacked

414

off during the hours when she did not personally supervise their activities.

The heat was sometimes an enemy in itself; to work in the full force of it was to court actual illness, especially for those unaccustomed to physical labor. After a few weeks, however, Valerie felt a strengthening in her body, a new resiliency, that made it, if not easier, at least more bearable.

President Johnson appointed a provisional governor of each of the Southern states, and he issued a statement of his intent toward the defeated Confederates that was hardly reassuring to those below the Mason Dixon line. "The American people must be taught," he said, "to know that treason is a crime. Arson and murder are crimes, the punishment of which is the loss of liberty and life."

Those at Mallows listened to the reading of that statement with outrage. "And what about the crimes of the Yankees?" Valerie cried. "Foraging for food among us might be considered reasonable, at a time when their own supply trains couldn't keep up with them. But what about burning our barns and our crops? What about violating our women? Destroying our homes? What about those crimes? Are they going to be called upon to pay for *that* destruction?"

The newspaper with the so-called amnesty proclamation printed on its front pages did not reach them until mid-June, and again they were stunned.

"This is amnesty?" Ellen asked in horror. "They're not content with killing our menfolk and pounding us to our knees in defeat. Now they insist upon rubbing our noses into the dirt, as well."

Her voice wavered as she read the list of conditions under which the property of Confederates might be returned to them, with the exception of the slaves who were now considered to be freedmen. "The President grants pardon to all who participated in the rebellion, except in cases where legal proceedings had been instituted under the laws of the United States providing for the confiscation of property. From the benefits of this proclamation the following classes were excepted—"

Valerie never remembered all of them, but a certain few were branded on her brain because she knew old friends to whom they applied, people who were apparently to be summarily deprived of whatever property they had managed to retain throughout the long and terrible struggle.

415

"All who are or shall have pretended to be civil or diplomatic officers, or otherwise domestic or foreign agents of the pretended Confederate government. All who left judicial stations under the United States to aid the rebellion. All who shall have been military or naval officers of said pretended Confederate government above the rank of colonel in the army or lieutenant in the navy."

They sat around the familiar table, listening to Ellen's unsteady voice, occasionally murmuring a name of someone that particular statute would affect.

"All who left seats in the Congress of the United States to aid the rebellion. All who resigned or tendered resignations of their commissions in the army or navy to evade duty in resisting the rebellion. All those who have engaged in any way in treating otherwise than lawfully as prisoners of war—" Ellen's voice cracked. "This is only the beginning. Anyone in our own army or navy who was educated at West Point or the Naval Academy. Anyone who held office as a 'pretended' governor of one of the Southern states. Anyone who left their homes in the North to aid the Confederacy. Anyone who engaged in the destruction of commerce of the United States on the high seas. All persons who have voluntarily participated in said rebellion, and the—" She broke off, chest heaving, and pressed a hand to her mouth. Julie, sitting beside her, reached for the paper and found the place, reading out the rest of it.

"—the estimated value of whose taxable property is over twenty thousand dollars."

Her hand trembled on the edge of the newspaper. "That means practically everybody we know, doesn't it? Anyone who has a plantation? And us, here at Mallows?"

Ellen massaged her temple. "The plantation is mine. It belonged to my parents before me, and now it belongs to me. I did not actively take part in the rebellion, so this cannot apply to me, to us."

"But Roger and Evan took part in it," Lacy said softly. "As Roger's widow, won't they . . . ?"

"Mallows is mine," Ellen repeated fiercely. "The only way they'll take it from me is by shooting me, as they shot Roger and Evan."

"There's one more," Julie said, her voice thin and frightened. "All persons who have taken the oath of amnesty as prescribed in the President's proclamation of December 8,

416

A.D. 1863, or an oath of allegiance to the government of the United States, and who have not thenceforward kept and maintained the same inviolate—" She stopped.

That they should have come through so much, and that what remained to them might now be confiscated, was as heavy as a blow could have been.

President Johnson had taken steps to restore customary services in the states now reabsorbed into the United States. There were appointments of tax assessors and collectors of customs and internal revenue; the Postmaster General was instructed to reorganize post offices and post-routes; the Federal courts were to be re-established.

All of these latter things they had taken for granted. It was the matter of the confiscation of property that terrified. Though none of them put it into words, there was not a woman in the house who did not wonder: If Mallows was lost to them, what would they do? Where would they go? How would they survive?

Except for Ellen. She knew only one thing; she would never leave Mallows, for as long as there was a breath of life left in her body. She would die, as Roger had died, in defending it.

Fifteen

June stretched into July; berries gave way to peaches and figs, which only stained one's fingers brown instead of red, Valerie thought wryly. She longed to write to Jack, but his occasional missive gave no return address. She knew he had been mustered out of the army and that he'd gone home to New York City, and that he thought of her constantly. Beyond that, she could only guess.

Why hadn't he given her an address? Just off Central Park, he'd mentioned once, and she tried writing to him with no more than that on the envelope. Whether it reached him or not, she didn't know.

In the small house across the fields, Patrick Ryan came and went at odd intervals. She felt a peculiar ambivalence about Ryan, and his gift to her. She must thank him for it, yet she felt embarrassed and shy about facing him with her thanks. Perhaps, buried down inside herself, she recognized that her mother had a point in saying that a man meant something by his gifts, and that a woman was obligated by accepting them.

She compromised her feelings by writing him a note—brief, grateful, yet not fawning—and giving him nothing on which to base any assumption that her gratitude was any more than that, or that it could lead to anything else. Not that she had any reason to think Patrick Ryan had designs on her. Why he had sent the velvet remained a mystery, unless it was as she had surmised: Patrick had won the bolt of material in a wager, and had nothing else to do with it except give it away.

In July, Gilly came back. Ellen discovered her standing on the edge of the woods just before sunset, her belly bulging with the child she carried. Gilly was barefooted and the dress was the one in which she'd run away, or what was left of it.

Ellen dropped her hoe and walked toward the girl. "Well, Gilly. How are you?"

Gilly looked at her with the whites of her eyes showing prominently. "I hungry, Miss Ellen."

"There's a pot on, at the quarters," Ellen told her quietly. "Beans, rice, and tomatoes."

Gilly's lower lip quivered. "Kin I come back, Miss Ellen? It ain't like they say, out there. Bein' free don't mean nothin', if you don't have no place to sleep and nothin' to eat. I work for you, Miss Ellen."

Like that? Ellen wondered. With her stomach out to there, so she'd have trouble bending over or getting back up, either one? Yet she needed all the help she could get, even a lazy, pregnant little girl.

"I can't pay you anything," Ellen said. "Only in food, and give you a cabin."

A smile lit the round black face. "I work for you, Miss Ellen. I do anythin' you say." She hesitated, then asked, "How Rastus? He growin' all right?"

"You might have thought of Rastus before you ran off with Chad," Ellen suggested, unable to keep a sharper note from her voice. "The baby's fine, Nora nursed him for you. What happened to Chad?"

"I reckon he in jail," Gilly admitted. "He done stole somethin', and they put him in jail. They don't let me talk to him, but I reckon he know where I gone. I ain't got no place else to go."

"I won't have Chad back on this place," Ellen said, even more sharply. "He's no good, Gilly. He's dangerous and undependable."

"Yes'm." There was weary resignation in Gilly's voice. "I kin go eat now, ma'am?"

"Yes. The cabin you had before is still empty. Every hand works in the fields. Be there at dawn. You can use a hoe."

"Yes'm," Gilly agreed.

Ellen watched her go, moving with the awkward balance of the pregnant woman. Would she be of any use at all? Or simply another problem to handle?

Freedmen, she thought, retrieving her hoe. They were free, because someone who knew nothing about Negroes said they were free. But they were children, most of them no more sensible or responsible or better able to look out for themselves than Gilly. And, since the authority of owner had become the diluted authority of employer, it wasn't even possible to control them.

She turned and found that none of them was working; all watched her, and the retreating Gilly. Frustration put a snap in her tone. "There's still half an hour of daylight. Go back to work."

Had she not driven herself as hard as she drove them, there would have been more discontent than there was. Not even the laziest of the men, however, dared to complain that his back ached. Not with this woman working beside him, swinging the hoe in a sort of mechanical determination.

In late July, there was a letter from Jack Ferris. It was brought, with the other mail, by the same man who had carried the gift from Patrick Ryan. This time it was different from the previous letter in that in Jack's bold hand, the word *personal* was scrawled across the end of the envelope.

Ellen, who had accepted the mail, stared at it, a dull flush rising from her neck to flood her face. "Personal? Does he deliberately insult us?"

Valerie had recognized the writing from across the table, upside down, and held out a hand for it. "That's mine, I think? Is there any reason why I should not receive mail intended for me alone?"

For a moment she thought her mother would refuse to hand it over. Ellen might well not have, had she not seen Valerie's unyielding face, the same face she had presented in the matter of the apricot-colored velvet. Ellen handed the letter over, and went through the rest of them. A letter from Henriette, one from a friend in Savannah, one from a distant cousin in New Orleans, from whom they hadn't heard in nearly two years. She opened them and read them all aloud.

Valerie sat listening though only half hearing. Jack's letter crackled in her lap when she moved her hand. She would read it only in private. She carried it upstairs with her when the mail had been dealt with, sinking onto her bed to open the letter with eager fingers.

"My darling Valerie—" it began. She read it quickly the first time, no more than skimming. He loved her, he missed her. And there it was, near the bottom of the third and last page.

"I can't promise at this stage, but it looks as if it might be possible for me to join you in the fall. It may be only a visit—business here continues to press—but if I have to go to Atlanta for the company, I will certainly get to Mallows as well. And then—why, then, beloved, we'll talk of the future."

It was signed in the familiar bold scrawl. "Yours, Jack."

Valerie read it again with rising joy. It was as if a seed, withered inside her, had been watered and now began to expand with renewed life. She read the letter a third time, then put it aside and walked to her chifforobe to open the door.

She took out the bolt of velvet and laid it across the bed. When Jack came, she must have a dress made of it, a dress to make him overlook the tan she had acquired, the sprinkle of freckles that not even a broad-brimmed hat could prevent when she spent so much time in the sun, the condition of her hands.

When Jack came, he must find her beautiful, she thought, and closed her eyes in a thankful prayer. Jack would be here, in the fall.

The summer passed, however, and there were no more communications from Jack. Since they had spent what cash there was, no one went to town for supplies, and what mail they got was delivered by neighbors. Once it came in the saddlebags of Patrick Ryan.

The mail itself, that time, was of no particular interest, consisting only of a reminder Henriette was planning her wedding for September 17, and that she would love to have them at Milledgeville for the event. They all knew there was no possibility of attending; indeed, they wracked their minds for something they could send as a gift, when they had little or nothing to buy one with.

Patrick looked prosperous and at ease in his new role in life. And he brought news.

"We have a new tax collector. The bills will be going out

shortly, I understand, and at rates far beyond the pre-war ones," he told them.

Ellen, torn between the need for news and the faintly unpleasant memories of what she considered Ryan's distasteful behavior on their last meeting, had invited him in and asked Pansy to bring cold drinks. Though he had arrived quietly, unannounced, the word spread rapidly that he was there; within minutes, virtually the entire household, except for Dolly Mallow, had assembled to greet him in the front drawing room.

His mention of tax collections sent a ripple of apprehension around the circle of women.

Ellen could not keep herself from moistening her lips. "How long will we have to pay the taxes, when the bills are presented?"

Patrick shrugged wide shoulders under the black broadcloth. "No one has yet said. But the Yankees have shown themselves vindictive in many ways, and this may well be added to those. Not less than thirty days, certainly. Possibly a few months."

"And what will happen if one is unable to pay in full, and on time?" Ellen was desperately aware of the tiny sum remaining to her, and the inadequacy of her cotton crop.

"I think the idea is to confiscate the property." Ryan was blunt about it. "It can then be sold elsewhere, presumably at a profit for the Federal government. I'm going to be scrambling for the cash to take care of the taxes on the properties I've bought up for Georgia L & T. Luckily, my backers will come up with it, if they have to." He shot a glance at Valerie, then said almost with defiance, "If you've anything you can convert to cash, Miss Ellen, I suggest you consider the best means of doing it. And that brings me to one of the reasons I rode over today, to make you an offer that might help."

Alarm flashed in Valerie's face, plainly written there for anyone to read; Ryan ignored it.

"And what offer is that, Mr. Ryan?" Ellen asked. Her mind seemed as cold and numb as the hands that worked at the skirt over her knees. Anything to convert to cash? Dear God, what was there left? And Lacy's forty-six hundred virtually exhausted already!

"I'd like to buy that four hundred acres that lies directly east of my place," Patrick said. "It's all but useless for crops,

422

but it has a good stand of longleaf pine. Comes to that, that you'd rather sell the timber than the land, I might work out something there, too, though I'd rather have the land and all. Thing is, I couldn't cut the timber before spring, so I couldn't offer much cash on that now. Whereas I could get you cash for the land—"

"Thank you, Mr. Ryan." Ellen's face was wooden, controlled over the deeper panic and anger. Valerie saw the warning signs, even if Ryan didn't. "I have no intention of selling off any part of Mallows."

For a moment he didn't react, and then he shrugged. "Well, ma'am, that's up to you, of course. I'm glad for you if you aren't pressured into such measures, the way most people are. Oh, and there's another thing they're getting particular about. The matter of paying the blacks wages. Unless, of course, they've been charged with vagrancy. Then they can be bound out in service in lieu of a jail sentence."

How easily those words rolled off his tongue, Valerie thought, with a grudging admiration. As if he'd always moved in circles where such words were used. In fact, he was better spoken than many formally educated men, in that he had a large vocabulary and a better grasp of the rules of grammar. When Patrick Ryan said "ain't," it was for purposes of his own, not because he didn't know better.

Julie leaned forward, echoing the word he'd used. "Vagrancy? Doesn't that mean wandering around with no means of support?"

"That's right."

"But they've just freed the Negroes! How can they expect that they will all have work already?"

Patrick grinned. "They don't, I reckon. Most of the Yankees are no nigger lovers. We Southerners care a lot more about the blacks than they do. The *Yankees* don't want to take care of them. So this is their way out. If the freedmen can't find work and be self-supporting, then they're charged with vagrancy, which makes it possible to return them to involuntary servitude for a year at a time. It's a very sensible solution, from the Yankee point of view."

"Then they're really worse off than most of them were before," Julie reasoned.

"Yes," Ryan agreed. "You find that shocking? I would, too, except that I've seen enough things in my thirty-three years to make me harder to shock."

Ellen's words were caustic. "Yet you continue to work with them. To take their money, to use it."

"That rankles with you, doesn't it, ma'am? You think me an opportunist, in the worst sense of that word?" He didn't wait for an answer, taking the affirmative for granted. "Well, in a sense you're right. I don't like the Yankees, especially, but on the other hand, I didn't care a hell of a lot for the Southern aristocracy, either." He didn't apologize for the profanity. "At least the Yankees are willing to take me as the man I am, to allow me to climb above the station I was born into. The old South would never have done that. I can sit in your drawing room, now, smoke the finest cigars, dress as well as any man in the state of Georgia. Have a bank account that surpasses anything in my wildest dreams of a few years ago. The Yankees made that possible. They don't give a damn that I started out as the son of a sharecropper, that I was an overseer, nor even that I fought against them in the war. All they care about is that I know Georgia, and timber, and I'm going to make them some money. If I get rich at the same time, why, that doesn't matter to them one way or the other. It's their own bank accounts they're thinking about. If they, or you, consider that they are using me, why, that's all right. As long as it gets me where I want to go, and it will."

"And where is that, Mr. Ryan?" Julie asked the question without animosity; she, too, had seen what Ellen tried to cover up when he proposed buying a piece of Mallows land, even a relatively insignificant part. She did not want to antagonize Patrick Ryan, and not entirely because she thought he might eventually be of help to them. She rather liked Patrick. "Where do you want to go?"

"Up," Patrick said, and again the grin flashed and he scratched at the corner of the rusty mustache. "All the time I was a kid, growing up eating corn and rice and beans, wearing rags, I knew there was a better way to live." He didn't add that he'd observed that better way, right here on the stage that Mallows provided. "I was a fairly smart boy. I decided a long time ago that it was better to be rich than poor."

Ellen took that to be a facetious remark; she was not as perceptive as both her daughters in seeing that, for all his grin and the lightness of his tone, Ryan was perfectly serious. Her mouth flattened. "And now you're rich, while the rest of us are getting poorer by the moment. That must give you a good deal of satisfaction, Mr. Ryan."

"I'm not rich, yet, ma'am, though I'm going to be. And yes, it gives me satisfaction. Not because anyone else is poorer because of it, though. I hold nothing against anyone at Mallows; Roger Stanton gave me a job that was as good a one as anyone from my station in life could hope for, and he let me learn to read. That was the most valuable thing he did for me. He let me into the world of books, and that expanded my knowledge and my world enough to make possible what I'm doing now, even to learning how to deal with those rich bastards up north who have more money than intelligence. So I'm grateful to Roger Stanton's family, too. I wasn't born into anything worthwhile, the way all of you were. I had to fight and struggle to get away from what I was born to. And if this war, and the coming of the Yankees, makes it easier, why, I'd be a fool not to take advantage of it."

"Even if it means betraying your own countrymen," Ellen said.

"Is that how it strikes you?" He was still smiling, but there was an underlying steeliness now. "I had no status in Georgia before the war. Not with any of the people who counted. Not with the aristocrats, the landowners, the people who had marriageable daughters. Did any of them welcome a common overseer into their homes? Would any of them have consented to my marrying one of their daughters?" He didn't need to have his question answered. "I owe nothing to the South, Miss Ellen. The South, the pre-war South, didn't give me a thing. If the war hadn't come along, probably the best I could have hoped for was to continue as an overseer on someone else's plantation. It didn't matter that I was stronger and smarter and more determined than any of them who had inherited everything I wanted; there was no way I'd ever have gotten any of it."

He leaned back in his chair, touched the cigar protruding from his coat pocket, then thought better of it. "Now it's different. The only thing I owe is to myself. And a debt of gratitude, too, to you people here at Mallows. So if you change your mind about selling that parcel of timber, or if I can help you in any other way, let me know. I hope you won't feel any more degraded by asking and accepting my help than I did, taking Roger Stanton's."

Valerie saw the justice in what he said; she didn't think her mother did, and she hoped he would go before Ellen boiled over in frustration and rage. She'd warned him about making Ellen an offer for the land, and he'd done it, anyway. That he was probably right, and that he did have their good in mind as well as his own, Valerie didn't doubt. Yet that did not weigh very heavily with Ellen. To her, it was an insult, that he should know of her difficulties, that he should dare to assume she would part with even a few acres of Mallows. And the mention of marriageable daughters—had there been something there? Surely he didn't aspire to either of the Stanton girls?

"You are very kind," Ellen told him in a tone that belied the words, "for thinking of us. I do not think, however, that we will be in need of your assistance in any matter, Mr. Ryan." She stood up, and there was nothing he could do except rise with her. He'd crossed the bounds of propriety; he was being asked to leave, and he knew it.

"Oh," Patrick said, "there's one more bit of news. I don't know whether you'll welcome it, or the contrary. The man in charge of collecting the taxes in our area is an acquaintance of yours. A Major Otis Quinn. Of course, he's no longer in the army, but it seems he retains his title."

"Major Quinn?" Ellen was startled out of her mood. Did that offer her some hope, if there was a problem over taxes?

"It seems the Federals are leaving some of their military people here to take over such jobs. We've gained a Federal Court judge who hails from Boston, I believe. It assures fair treatment for all of us, I'm sure."

He could afford to be dryly amused, Valerie thought. But what about the rest of them, those who had no affiliations with the Yankees, no money, nothing but problems? Would a Boston judge deal fairly with them, in matters pertaining to the confiscation of their property by the Federal government, and other such questions?

"Perhaps Blossom will see you out, Mr. Ryan," Ellen told him. "I'm sure you'll excuse the rest of us. We have a good many tasks to see to."

Patrick knew he was being given less than courteous treatment; under ordinary circumstances Ellen would have seen any guest to the door herself. But then, any other guest would not have tried to buy some of Mallows' precious acres.

Blossom, who had sat watching and saying nothing, moved with alacrity. She hadn't cared about half what he talked about; she was more interested in the man himself.

Blossom had been some time without a man. She enjoyed men with a guileless pleasure, and not just in bed, either. She liked an admiring eye, a flattering word, someone to open doors and carry heavy objects and simply provide the masculine aura without which life was, to say the least, incomplete.

And Patrick Ryan was a fine figure of a man. Totally aside from his announced intention to be rich (he was already rich, in Blossom's eyes) was the fact that he was tall and muscular and self-assured. Some might not have thought him handsome, and perhaps the red hair was a warning signal, although Evan had not had red hair and he'd certainly had temper enough. Anyway, Blossom intended to take advantage of the opportunity to speak to their neighbor alone. She walked with him across the entry hall and onto the veranda, working up the courage very quickly to put her question to him.

"Mr. Ryan, you mostly at home, now?"

"Off and on," Ryan said. He smiled at her; men tended to smile at Blossom, especially when she smiled first.

"I was wonderin', would you be in need of a housekeeper? I ain't too bad at that sort of thing, now, I been learnin' since I been here. Miss Ellen, she's more particular than old Mrs. Masterson was, and I learned a lot. I could keep house for a bachelor, real good, I could."

Patrick shook his head, reaching for the reins knotted around the hitching post at the foot of the steps. "I have a nice little black gal, keeping house for me. She does a pretty fair job, Becky does."

Disappointment stabbed at her, but Blossom was not one to give up easily, especially when the prize was a worthwhile one.

"There's things I kin do," she suggested, "that a black gal won't do, not as good."

There was open invitation in the smile that showed the overlapping front teeth.

Patrick's smile softened, as did his voice. "I appreciate that, Miss Blossom. And I'll do you the honor not to play games and pretend I don't understand how generous your offer is. You're welcome in my bed any time. But," before she could seize upon that, "that's all it would ever be. I wouldn't want you to think any such arrangement would ever lead to marriage, because it wouldn't. I got my sights set on one of those society marriages. The aristocracy may not be so partic-

427

ular about joining up with Patrick Ryan, now that he's got money and they haven't."

He swung up into the saddle, looking down on her astonished and disappointed face. "You're a very attractive young lady, Miss Blossom," he told her, and then spun the horse and galloped off between the twin rows of live oaks, the shells spurting up behind the horse's hooves.

She stared after him, chagrined, yet not completely out of temper. Because there was always the chance that he was wrong about the society people wanting the likes of him in their family, if Miss Ellen's reaction to him meant anything. Besides that, there were her own charms. Other men had told her they were considerable.

After a moment, when the receding figure was no more than toy-size in the distance, Blossom smiled again. Maybe she could make him change his mind.

Sixteen

That Ellen regarded Patrick Ryan both as a traitor to the South and to the Stantons was obvious to everyone. "He'll never be any more than he ever was," she stated, "crude, and common."

Both Julie and Valerie felt a tendency to defend him—he had, after all, been of inestimable value to them in the past, and might well be so again, and there was at least some merit in his logic—but they both knew instinctively that to mention him at all would only make matters worse. Ellen was clearly under great strain, and neither of them wanted to add to it.

They did not realize the full extent of the pressures upon her. She had worked herself, and everyone else, into a state of exhaustion, preparing for winter. When the cotton was picked, meager crop that it was, she hoped it would carry them through by paying for the items that were essential and could not be produced on the plantation. She had not, however, given any consideration to greatly increased taxes.

The only way that she could think of to raise money for them—she gave Ryan credit for accurate reporting on the matter—was to sell the silver that she'd managed to retain all through the war. Much of it was buried, the rest hidden; she had it dug up, and set Pansy and Lallie to polishing it.

There was complete table service for fifty, in both the best and the second-best silver. There was a serving set of coffee pot with its own tray and sugar bowl and creamer that had been her mother's wedding silver. There were various fine pieces that had been in the family from as far back as her grandparents' time; and the thought of giving any of it up was an additional ache in her heart. Yet give it up she must. There was no other way to raise cash. Mallows was more important than silver. Silver could eventually be replaced.

Ryan's news about the taxes, and his offer to buy part of her land, had shaken her badly. A similar offer from someone else, someone of her own class (had any of them been in a position to offer her anything), would not have been nearly as humiliating. And his remarks about marrying into the aristocracy left her both angry and resentful. Perhaps the Yankees accepted him; that did not mean that a proud Southern family would ever do so. She thought of the gift he had made to Valerie, and hardened her heart against him. One thing she was certain of, and that was that no man like Patrick Ryan would ever form an alliance with one of *her* daughters. Even one of the Yankees would be more acceptable than that.

Only Lallie, who accompanied her, knew that Ellen took the silver to Reidsville to see what could be realized on it. She would, at the same time, perhaps, consider meeting Major Quinn. She had never especially liked the man, yet he had, in all honesty, left her home in better condition than he might have done. He had shown interest in her belongings, in the paintings and furnishings, and appreciation for them. For all that he was a Yankee, Quinn had some sensitivity, and he was obviously well brought up, insofar as any of the Yankees could be said to be well bred.

She had Rudy and Lallie carry the wrapped silver into Mr. Codder's establishment and deposited on the counter. Her heart was beating so heavily that Ellen felt suffocated, yet she willed a steady voice.

"I would like to have a price on these, sir," she informed him.

Mr. Codder rested his hands on the counter, not touching anything. He cleared his throat, and coughed. "Mrs. Stanton—there is very little demand for silver, these days. People are selling it, not buying it."

430

She stared at him, eyes wide. "It's real silver, Mr. Codder. The finest in Georgia. The coffee set was made by—"

He held up a hand to silence her. "I realize that it's quality merchandise, ma'am. The thing is, nobody can afford to pay for quality materials. The best I could do, say, for the tableware, is ten cents per spoon. I might go fifteen apiece for the forks and knives, but I'd have to ask around, first, see if there's any possibility of a buyer. I couldn't afford to have any money tied up for long—"

"Ten cents per spoon?"

"Mrs. Stanton, would you like to sit down? There's a stool, right there—"

Ellen sank onto it, before her knees gave out. *"Ten cents?"*

"That's only because I know it's good," Mr. Codder said apologetically. "There is one party might be interested in it, but I'd have to ask before I made an offer on the whole set. I have to make a profit, you know, I can't afford not to. Mr. Ryan was asking about—"

Ellen's head snapped back so hard that she put a hand to a painful spot at the back of her neck. "Patrick Ryan?"

"Yes, ma'am. You know Mr. Ryan. One of the few people in Tattnall County has any cash money, these days. I don't know as he'd be interested, for sure, but he was looking at some nice dishes the other day—set of china I took in against an outstanding bill—and maybe he'd want the silver to go with it, you see."

Her chest hurt, her head hurt, her body was one great painful bruise. "I don't think I care to sell to Mr. Ryan," she said, almost inaudibly.

"Well, that's up to you, of course, ma'am. I wouldn't guess as to where else we'd find anybody would pay for them. I might could use one set of the tableware myself—my wife's been wanting something elegant, like this—but for myself I couldn't give you more than a nickel each on the spoons, and say seven cents on the knives and forks. I know it's worth more than that, but the way things are these days—"

She felt sick. All those years, she'd hidden away the silver so that the Yankees wouldn't find it and steal it. And now it wasn't worth anything, unless she let it go for practically nothing to a rogue like Ryan or that dreadful shopkeeper's wife—

"I'll have to think about it," Ellen said. She turned a nearly blind face toward Lallie and Rudy, who waited. "Put it back

431

in the buggy." For a moment she couldn't think what else she'd intended to do. "Oh, the—the tax collection office, where is it?"

"Set up in the building where Linvers used to have the law offices. You know, across the street, down that way." He gestured, and Ellen forced herself off the stool, nodding.

"Thank you."

"You want me to ask Mr. Ryan, next time he comes in?" Mr. Codder called after her; Ellen didn't answer. If Lallie hadn't deposited her bundles in the buggy and turned to assist her, she wasn't sure she could have stayed on her feet.

"Rudy, stay with the buggy," she said, not looking at the old man. "Lallie, come with me."

Lallie felt the tremor in the older woman's arm as they crossed the street. Miss Ellen had been her mistress for a long time, and although she almost never discussed her business or her family problems, Lallie usually knew what they were. She was intelligent and observant, and, for the most part, compassionate. Yet she did not dare offer Miss Ellen any more than her arm to lean upon, as if she were old Miss Dolly.

Major Otis Quinn was in his office and rose to greet them. "Why, Mrs. Stanton! Good afternoon! Come in, come in!" He drew out a chair for her, his glance dismissing Lallie, so that she remained standing just inside the doorway.

"I heard that you were—here," Ellen said. "There is some concern—among my neighbors—about the new taxes we've heard are being levied."

He was smiling, as genial as she had ever seen him. "Ah, yes, the assessor is attending to his business, now, and when he's finished, it will be up to me. I've been meaning to ride out and call upon you, but I've been very busy here, getting organized. And making arrangements for a house for my family, who are moving here within a few weeks to join me."

"Family?" Ellen echoed. "I didn't realize that you had a family, Major Quinn. You never spoke of them."

"My wife is dead, but I have two daughters. One is twelve, the other is nearly fifteen, and a son who is nine. I have been asking about in search of a housekeeper, but so far haven't found one. In the meantime, I stay at the hotel and submit to inferior surroundings and service." His rather wintry smile expanded slightly. "Nothing to compare with what I found at Mallows, of course."

She didn't care about his family. All she cared about was

432

Mallows. Yet she couldn't afford to antagonize him. She murmured something, she didn't know what, making small talk for a few minutes until she could put the question uppermost in her mind.

"The taxes, Major Quinn. Can you give me some idea of what they will be?" It took all her courage to ask; she did not really want to know, because as long as the amount was unknown she could pretend that she could handle the payment of them. Her head was still working, enough, however, so that she realized she could not play ostrich indefinitely. She hoped she was not going to be sick, here in Major Quinn's small, neat office.

"Oh, it's too soon to say about that," the major said. "We have our guidelines, of course, and within a few weeks the assessor will turn over his figures to me, and then I'll be able to give you specific information. In the meantime, I hope that I may invite myself out to Mallows for a visit. I did so enjoy your beautiful home, Mrs. Stanton, and when my children come, I would like them to see the gracious way that you Southerners live. If we are to stay on here in Georgia in this new position, I may well sell our home in the North and try to find something comparable to Mallows for us. My impression is that many Georgians will find it difficult to maintain their properties as they did before the war, and that a good house may be somewhat easily come by."

The office was too warm, too close. Nausea rose in her throat, and Ellen made a small sound of distress. "I'm sorry, I'm not feeling at all well. Some fresh air—"

He rose at once, and threw open the door. "Of course. I quite understand."

"About—about visiting Mallows," Ellen said thickly. "Of course you are welcome to come, at any time."

She managed to get halfway across the street before she threw up.

In August they were still harvesting: pears, grapes, peaches, and quinces. They fed the pigs and the remaining cattle lavishly of the corn, so that they would fatten before butchering time. Though the storerooms grew full, Ellen did not let up in the slightest. They would eat, at least, no matter what else happened. Only in the loneliness of her own room, late at night, did she admit to *what else* might be.

They were all so tired in the evenings that there was little

433

social intercourse much past the supper hour. Valerie, without speaking of it, had cut out the apricot velvet and stitched at it by candlelight, as late as she could manage to stay awake to do it. She waited for more letters from Jack, and found excuses for him when there were none.

Hugh Alexander learned to walk; he was the one bright spot in their lives, making even Dolly smile as he toddled about, charming them all.

Three weeks after Ellen had ridden to Reidsville, Major Otis Quinn sent word that, if it were convenient, he and his family would arrive for a visit the following Saturday afternoon. The messenger, a young black boy, waited expectantly for a return communication, and after a moment, Ellen wrote it out, suggesting that they stay for dinner and spend the night. She did not really want to entertain anyone, but this was too important. She could not afford to antagonize a man who might almost literally wield the power of life and death over those at Mallows.

The others scarcely cared one way or another, except that visitors meant a day off. They couldn't work in the fields or in the kitchen when there were guests. Instead, they were allowed—Valerie and Julie included—to spend the morning hastily dusting and bringing down cobwebs, to tidy up any room that the Quinns might be expected to enter.

Ellen dreaded having to entertain anyone, and especially a Yankee who had so recently been the enemy. When the time came, however, it was not as difficult as she had anticipated. The most unpleasant part of it came in her verbal battle with Mamie, who was "wrung out already," as she put it, from preserving foods against the winter, and who insisted she was too old to cook for a lot of people, particularly Yankees.

"They don't know nothin' about good food," she said, smoldering at remembered insults when the Yankees had shown less than full appreciation of her culinary abilities. "Don't want no okra in nothin', don't like their chicken fried Southern style, want them white potatoes 'stead of yams—why they comin' here, anyhow?"

"It is none of your business why they're coming here. I will work out the menu, and you will prepare the meal, just as you've always done," Ellen said. "I will not listen to arguments, Mamie. You'll obey orders." Why did she have to say everything these days with such emphasis, when it became harder all the time to summon enough strength to do it?

434

Usually Mamie surrendered after a token resistance. This time, she held out a little longer, bringing up a matter that had heretofore been kept below the surface.

"You talkin' to me like I a slave, Miss Ellen. A good-for-nothin' black woman, ain't got no choice. I freed, now. And I s'posed to be gettin' paid. Twelve dollars a month. I ain't seen no twelve dollars yet."

"And you won't, either." Ellen clamped down on the impulse to strike the black woman. "In the first place, it's the men who get twelve dollars a month, not the women. If I paid you at all, I'd say you're worth about seven dollars, maybe eight. Since I cannot pay you anything except in providing you with food, clothes, and a place to sleep, the choice is yours. If you think you can go out and find another position and get paid for it, go ahead. Pack your things and leave today. Or do as you're told, if you intend to stay here. I'll give you half an hour to make up your mind."

Mamie knew when she was outfoxed. Enough stories filtered through to the hands at Mallows to assure them that, unsatisfactory though their situation might be, they were better off than the freedmen roaming the country without roofs over their heads. There were even those who said that being freed was all a hoax, because if they didn't belong on a plantation or a farm, the Yankee liberators would charge them with a crime and apprentice them out, at no pay other than room and board, to anyone who was willing to take them on.

Mamie, and the others, knew perfectly well that though Ellen was a hard taskmaster, she was a decent human being. She never had anyone whipped, and as far back as they could remember, she'd only allowed two slaves (both troublemakers) to be sold from Mallows. She'd never broken up a family. It seemed safer with Miss Ellen than with a stranger who might have no concern for them at all.

Mamie continued to grumble, but she stayed in the kitchen, snapping at Pansy and the two other young girls sent in to help her. Putting on a fancy dinner for that Major Quinn didn't make any sense to her, but nobody'd ever been ashamed of her cooking before, and they wouldn't be, now. If the Yankees were too ignorant to recognize good cooking, why, that was *their* misfortune.

By agreement, a middle ground was chosen in the manner of dress. Part of Lacy's house money had gone for shoes, so that each person had at least one respectable pair of foot-

435

wear. There had been no new garments for the family members; Blossom had been allowed to cut down several frocks of Valerie's. (She was closer to Julie's height, but her buxom figure could never have been compressed into the bodice of one of Julie's gowns.) They would not, of course, wear the simple gingham and calico gowns they wore in the fields; neither would they try to impress Major Quinn and his family with their ornate best clothes.

Second best was the order of the day, and although these dresses were all three or four years old, they were in relatively good condition and made everyone feel, for the first time in many months, rather festive.

Valerie wore her green silk, not because she wanted to (it evoked too many memories that she was not yet prepared to face) but because *not* wearing it would have aroused unwanted curiosity. Julie wore a demurely provocative gown of pink China silk embroidered in white; though modest in style, in that it covered her arms and bosom, it was so molded to her breasts that Valerie had once remarked jokingly, "No one will doubt you're a girl."

Ellen, as befitted a widow, wore black, as did both the old ladies. Sally Ann, though a widow, too, had no black to wear; instead, she was dressed in a severe brown silk that emphasized her carroty hair and milky skin, on which the freckles stood out like spatterings from a child's paintbrush.

Blossom, also, although she was to assist in serving rather than sit at table (to her great disappointment), was nevertheless attired most attractively in light blue poplin. It wasn't an elaborate dress, but when she examined her reflection in the mirror she decided that she was not completely put in the shade by the others. Not even the beautiful Valerie had such a lushly full bosom, and no amount of restraint could conceal *that*.

Major Quinn arrived in a handsome conveyance in mid-afternoon. He introduced them all to his family: Carrie, the oldest daughter, was a petite dark-haired girl with rather frightened dark eyes, very pretty at the age of fifteen; twelve-year-old Isidora was of similar coloring but still so unformed and immature that it was difficult to say whether she would have her sister's prettiness; and the nine-year-old Jay was a normal, lively, undistinguished little boy. All three of Major Quinn's children were obviously in awe of him, and responded at once when he spoke to them. They had been

436

separated from their father for the entire duration of the war, and were seldom relaxed in his presence.

Julie took at once to the girls, and they to her; when she had spirited them away for a tour of the house, they opened up and began to chatter to her like any young girls. Jay trailed along, asking what his sisters considered to be "stupid" questions.

There was a fifth member of the party whom no one had expected.

Major Quinn gestured toward him negligently. "You remember Lieutenant Froedecker, of course. He was good enough to accompany my children here from Boston, where they had been living with their maternal grandfather. The old gentleman did not care to remove himself permanently to Georgia, and so Fritz stepped in. I believe he may be staying on with us for a short time as Jay's tutor."

Fritz Froedecker seemed different, out of uniform. He was still tall and tow-headed, now relaxed and alert at the same time, as his eyes swept over the company, acknowledging the previous acquaintanceship. Only Valerie noticed how his gaze lingered on Julie; Julie herself was oblivious, already engrossed in the youngsters. Fritz trailed after them, ostensibly to keep young Jay in line.

The conversation was kept general; no mention of the war, or of Major Quinn's new position. Quinn requested that he be allowed to walk through the house again, once more asking questions about the paintings and drawing Ellen out on various matters of family history.

In spite of her reluctance to cook for Yankees, Mamie had outdone herself. No great expenditure of cash was required to set a fine table at Mallows in the fall of the year; there was a golden brown roasted turkey, stuffed with wild rice dressing, a ham resplendent in a glaze of honey and mustard and cloves; and every variety of fruit and vegetable from the kitchen garden and the orchards. Certainly the visitors all ate with hearty appetites, right down to the feathery light sponge cake served with sliced fresh peaches for dessert.

Once, we ate like this all the time, Valerie thought. In the candlelight, around the expanded shining table, she could almost imagine that the bad times were over. Well, they would be, for her, when Jack Ferris came.

It was not until the others had gone up to bed that Otis

Quinn and Ellen paused in the soaring entry hall and he looked up at the unlighted chandelier.

"Magnificent," he observed. "I wish I had seen the place as it was, in its full elegance. A pity that so much has worn out, been damaged or destroyed. It will take a considerable sum to restore it, if it ever can be restored."

"When things get back to normal," Ellen said quickly, "and Mallows begins to make money again, I'll see it restored."

"You may well need some help, doing it," Quinn said.

Long after she'd gone to bed, Ellen pondered that remark. He had dropped it at that, not following up in any way, but there had been something intensely personal about his appraisal. Had he, by any remote chance, meant to suggest that *he* might be of some help to her, in restoring Mallows to its former grandeur?

Why should he? Yet any hope of assistance in the matter of survival was one she could not let slide. Perhaps, she thought, Major Otis Quinn would see to it that she did not lose Mallows because of non-payment of taxes. Perhaps he would adjust the assessor's figures, if necessary, so that the taxes were within her means.

She could only continue to pray.

Seventeen

Blossom walked across the fields every day for a week before she caught Patrick Ryan at home. She turned when she heard him coming, holding the basket on her hip, well aware of the picture that she made. The sun glinted on her honey-colored hair, and the lavender and white checked gingham hugged her breasts and waist.

Patrick expressed no surprise at seeing her; he swung down off the big red horse and handed the reins over to the old black man who emerged to take them.

"You done caught me in the act," Blossom said, with only a trace of coyness. "These here grapes are sweeter'n anything at Mallows, and nobody seemed to be doin' anything with 'em. I couldn't bear to see 'em go to waste."

He strode toward her, reaching into the basket for a bunch of the brownish-green scuppernongs, lifting them to his mouth. "Leave them for a week or so more, and they'll be sweeter," he suggested.

She was not in the least disconcerted to see that she hadn't fooled him. On the contrary, she allowed him a tantalizing glimpse of the tip of her tongue, between the crooked teeth. "Well, I didn't know if you'd be here, in a week or two."

Patrick laughed. "I don't know that, myself. Come inside,

it's too hot out here in the sun. Though I shouldn't complain, the leaves are beginning to turn color so it'll be cold, soon enough." He put a hand on her arm and guided her around to the back door, down the steps into the kitchen. "Becky! Where is that black wretch? Becky! We want something cold to drink!"

"The black wretch," Blossom noted when the girl appeared, was more nearly *café au lait* than black. She was also no more than seventeen years old, and had a very pretty face and a figure to match Blossom's. Blossom didn't doubt for a moment that the girl warmed Patrick's bed as well as his supper.

"We're thirsty. We'll have it down here, where it's coolest," Patrick told the girl, and she murmured compliance as she scurried to bring out a bottle of wine and twin glasses. Blossom sat on one of the polished chairs at the table; Patrick took the one opposite her, and poured out the wine.

When she sipped at it, Blossom only just managed not to make a face. It was what they called dry wine, much too sour for her taste. She liked sweet wines. She drank it anyway, looking about with pleasure at the brick-walled kitchen with its gleaming pans and neat curtains.

"This is a mighty nice place," she observed.

"It'll do, for now." Patrick stretched out his long legs, displaying dusty boots.

Without getting up from her chair, Blossom gave the impression of peering into the doors that flanked the stairway. "Two bedrooms down here? And more upstairs?"

Patrick grinned. "Beds all over the place." He raised his voice. "Becky! Go out and work in the garden for a while."

The girl had busied herself in the kitchen; now she cast an enigmatic glance toward Blossom and murmured, "Yas, boss."

The grin erupted into a laugh. "She calls me *boss* when she's mad at me. How are they treating you over there, Blossom?"

"Jus' fine," Blossom said, smoothing her skirt. She didn't ask why the girl was mad, and she didn't say anything more about the bedrooms. She knew Patrick would get to that, in his own good time. She was perfectly content to wait.

The tax bill came at last, when in the flurry surrounding

the major task of fall butchering Ellen had almost put it out of her mind.

Julie brought it into the breakfast room, where they had gathered for their midday meal, and laid it gingerly at her mother's elbow. "This just came, Mama."

Ellen saw at once what it was. She didn't ask who'd delivered it. In fact, her mouth had gone so dry, and her heart was racing so, that she couldn't speak at all. She opened it and stared, all color draining from her face, and then a shudder ran through her, so strongly that everyone around the table was aware of it.

"Mama," Julie said, and put a hand on Ellen's shoulder, then leaned over to look at the figures on the bill. "Sixteen hundred dollars!" The words were only a whisper, yet so silent were the waiting women that every one of them heard it clearly.

Ellen dropped her head forward into her hands and sat that way while they listened to the ticking of the clock. Julie pushed the paper toward Valerie, and they both stared at the staggering sum that was demanded, to be paid within thirty days.

Valerie choked, saying it. "Thirty days! Why, it's nothing more than a legal way to steal the property! The taxes have never been anything like that amount before, have they, Mama?"

Ellen lifted a ravaged face. "No. Thirty days, or six months, what difference does it make? I can't come up with any such sum as that."

Valerie ran her tongue over her lips. "Maybe—maybe Mr. Ryan was right, Mama. Maybe we ought to sell him that stand of trees—"

"No! Don't you understand, what that would mean? If we start selling off bits and pieces of Mallows there won't be any of it left, eventually. We have to keep the place intact!"

Julie's soft voice had a hollow sound. "How?"

The word lingered in the air for several minutes before Ellen pushed back her chair and stood up. "Ask Rudy to bring around the buggy. I'm going to Reidsville. I'll have to try to borrow money against Mallows, as I'd decided to do before Miss Lacy sold her house. It's a valuable property—it must be, to call for sixteen hundred dollars in taxes!—and it ought to be possible to borrow against it."

Valerie shifted uneasily on her chair. "If you borrow, and

441

then have any difficulty in paying back the loan, we could lose the entire place, couldn't we? Whereas if you sell a few acres, there'd be no claim on the rest of the place . . ."

"I'll think of something," Ellen said. "Please, Julie, tell Rudy to bring around the buggy."

They watched her go, none of them hopeful. She would not even allow any of them to go with her, excepting Blossom, who stated an urgent need to make the purchase of some dress goods. Ellen did not ask where she had obtained any cash for such a purchase. The others didn't so much as wonder.

They waited—working while they did so—for Ellen's return. And they prayed.

"You don't seem to understand the current economic picture," the banker said, leaning toward her with an expression of genuine distress. "I would help you if I could, Mrs. Stanton, but my hands are tied. The bank funds are not my *personal* funds, you understand. They belong to our depositors. And, quite frankly, if we had not had an infusion of Yankee money, there wouldn't be much in the coffers at all."

Ellen stared at him, this weary, elderly man, whom she'd known all her life and who looked at least ten years older than she knew he was.

"You're saying there is no possibility of borrowing money against Mallows, then."

"Not the slightest. At least, not through any bank. The thing is, such a loan would not be a good risk. The plantation would be of no value to the bank, if we had to take it in security for a defaulted loan. No one has any money to run plantations these days. There are no slaves to work them. And nobody is buying land, not even small parcels of it; there are hundreds of thousands of acres in the west that are free for the taking, and that's where most people are going. I am truly sorry, Mrs. Stanton, but there is absolutely nothing I can offer you. The only possible alternative, so far as I can see, to having the land sold for non-payment of taxes is to put it up for sale, yourself. There are a few Yankees about with money; both the new tax collector, Quinn, and the assessor, young fellow by the name of Jim Healy, are looking for homes to buy, and they seem to have some funds. Of course, nobody is going to pay you what Mallows was worth, before the war. But you might realize enough to get yourself a small place in town and manage to get by—"

She stood up abruptly, spilling her purse onto the floor, so that Mr. Mandress got down on his knees to pick up the scattered contents.

"There must be some other way," Ellen said. "Rather than giving it away to Yankees."

He rose and handed over the purse. "I hope so, ma'am. I sincerely hope so." But when she had gone, he watched from his office window, shaking his head. The ones who had been the richest, before the war, were now the poorest, and they couldn't understand it or adjust to it, poor things.

Blossom met her in the street, struggling with an enormous parcel of yard goods bought with Patrick Ryan's gold. Nobody could say he wasn't a generous man; all she'd done was mention that she was in desperate straits for clothing, and he'd said genially that no lady should be in such a position, and handed her the gold piece as casually as if it were a penny.

"Did you . . . ?" she began, and then glimpsed Ellen's face, and swallowed the words.

Ellen scarcely saw her; the mist in her eyes would not clear, no matter what she did. "The assessor's office, I think it's in the same building as Major Quinn's. Come along with me," she said.

Blossom, clutching the bundles against her chest, trotted with her across the street. She felt sorry for Miss Ellen, but she was thinking more of the striking cherry-colored foulard silk inside the package, and how she'd finally gained a lifelong goal of owning a red dress. Well, it would be a dress as soon as she could cut it out and sew it up.

The assessor, who was in the process of painting his own name on the door, quickly stepped back and allowed them to enter.

The letters said *James Healy*. Ellen didn't notice. Blossom couldn't read it, but she saw the Yankee, all right. Thirty-five, at a guess. Tall, muscular, fair-haired, and even more attractive than Patrick Ryan.

"Come in, come in," he greeted them. "Here, ma'am, let me take those bundles for you."

He did, depositing them on his desk, then turned with a smile and offered chairs. "What can I do for you, ladies?"

"I'm Mrs. Stanton, from Mallows," Ellen said.

443

Something altered in the young man's face, although Ellen did not see it. "Oh, yes. Beautiful place, Mallows. Probably one of the most beautiful in Tattnall County. Can I offer you a glass of water? You're looking rather pale, ma'am." His gaze slid toward Blossom, who was not pale at all. On the contrary, she was glowing with good health and good spirits, and his attention rested on her a fraction too long for strict good manners. Not that it bothered Blossom.

"Yes, please," Ellen agreed. "I would like a drink."

He brought it, managing to brush against Blossom both coming and going with the dipper to the pail in the corner of the room.

"Now," James Healy said. "How can I be of service?"

Ellen reached into her small bag and brought out the tax statement, to flatten it on the desk top beside her. "I . . . I believe there must be some mistake about the amount of this assessment. It's nearly four times what it has ever been before."

He looked down at the paper. "Why, no, ma'am, there's no mistake. Land values are very high, you know, and as we surely agree, Mallows is one of the more magnificent plantations."

Her throat hurt, and her head, and her fingernails drew blood in her palms where she doubled them inward. "How can that be, sir? That it is suddenly worth four times what it was a few years ago, yet it has no value at all if it comes to a matter of selling it? I've just talked to Mr. Mandress, and he assures me that no one is buying land, that there is no demand for it at all."

"Lack of demand doesn't mean the land itself is worthless," Healy pointed out.

The tightness in her chest increased until she wondered if she could continue to breathe. "But such a sum—there is no way in the world I can raise such a sum! Especially not in a period of thirty days!"

There might have been genuine sympathy on the young man's face. "I'm only the assessor, ma'am. I'm given a set of rules to go by, I don't make them up myself. And according to those rules, this is a fair assessment of your property."

"But what will happen? If I can't pay it?" Desperation had put deep shadows under her eyes, and Ellen was unable to control the trembling of her lips.

"I have nothing to do with that end of it. You'd have to
444

talk to Major Quinn. I believe you're already acquainted with him. He's in his office now, I believe, if you want to go next door. In the meantime, maybe I can help this young lady with her bundles. You have a buggy, I take it?"

Blossom smiled warmly. "That'd be very kind of you, sir. The buggy's over there, in front of the general store."

Ellen rose slowly. There was no help here. She must turn to Major Quinn, then. She moved through the doorway without awareness of the pair behind her, of the growing excitement in both of them as they stared into each other's eyes.

Blossom laughed up into the handsome face. "I guess I just tried to get too much, all at one time. I ain't had much chance to buy anything in a long while, until today. I got me some cherry-colored foulard for a dress," she confided. "I ain't had a brand-new dress in I don't know how long."

"I'm sure you'll be stunning in a cherry-colored foulard," James Healy said, striding across the street with his arms laden with her new acquisitions. "What's a cherry-colored foulard?"

Blossom poked a finger through one of the wrappings. "It's silk, with a pattern in it. See? This one has cherries, just like the color of it!"

"Lovely." Healy ignored the old black man standing near the horse's head. "You're lovely, too. Are you Mrs. Stanton's daughter?"

"Me? Heavens, no! I'm Blossom Curtis. I'm just a stray Miss Ellen took in, because I didn't have nowhere to go. Miss Ellen's a kind lady, mostly. Course, it ain't the same as having a place of my own, you understand. But these days, a person's glad for a roof and somethin' to eat."

He deposited the bundles on the floor of the buggy, making no move to return to his office.

"You're all alone in the world, then? No family?"

"No family. I been a orphan nearly ever since I can remember." She wished she'd worn the better of the two dresses cut down from Valerie's, instead of this one. Still, the way he was looking at her, he didn't find too much lacking. "You think Major Quinn can help Miss Ellen? She's sure enough upset."

Again there was the shifting of expression in Healy's face. "Oh, I think Major Quinn will think of something. He speaks highly of Mrs. Stanton."

"That's good. I hate to see her lose her house. I never had a house, but if I did, I'd hate to lose it."

His gaze had dropped to her bosom, then rose again to her face. "I never had a house, either, until just recently. Bought one here in town. Not a big place, only a dozen rooms. Nothing like Mallows. But the people were willing to sell out, cheap. Going west, they said. Me, I don't hanker to go west and carve out a civilization. I like it where it's civilized already. Funny thing. I'm all alone, too. No family except some aunts back home in Rhode Island."

Blossom wrinkled her nose in thought. "Rhode Island. That's up north, ain't it?"

"Way up north," James Healy agreed. "I'm thinking, Miss Blossom. Seeing you're just visiting, sort of, at Mallows. You can make your own decisions, can't you? I mean, you're not responsible to Mrs. Stanton?"

"Been makin' what decisions there was, long as I can remember," Blossom agreed.

"Well, I've got this house, and no family, and I was looking around for someone to keep house for me. Oh, I got a black girl to do the heavy work, you know. But she doesn't know anything about *running* a household. She's never had a penny to spend in her life, doesn't know how to buy groceries, things like that. So I wonder—would you be interested in taking on the job of housekeeper for me? Perfectly respectable, I assure you. I have a good job, and you wouldn't want for your wages." *Or anything else,* his eyes said.

"Why, I reckon a twelve-room house wouldn't be beyond me," Blossom said, remembering the cramped little house where she lived and worked for the Mastersons. "I'd be right pleased to work for you, Mr. —"

"Healy. Jim Healy. When could you come, Miss Blossom?"

"Why, I got my stuff to pick up at Mallows, or I could come right now, today."

"I tell you what. Day after tomorrow is Sunday, and I could run you out to Mallows, early in the morning, to get your things. Could you get along without them until then?"

"I reckon I could," Blossom allowed. "I got to tell Miss Ellen, though."

"Sure. Only," Jim Healy glanced across the street toward the tax collector's office, "I think we'd better wait here, until they conclude their business." The old bastard, he thought of Quinn. He was determined to get his hands on Mallows.

446

Healy didn't like what he'd been told to do with the Mallows tax statement, but he followed orders if he wanted to keep this job, and he did.

Blossom's heart swelled. A twelve-room house, with a black girl to do the heavy work. And while Jim Healy maybe wasn't as well off as Patrick Ryan, he wasn't fixing to marry some aristocrat society girl, either. And from the look of him, Mr. Healy had a lot of vitality. He was—her mind groped for the word—virile. That was it. Virile.

She stood beside Jim Healy in the autumn sunshine, waiting for Miss Ellen to come back.

"I don't make the rules, Miss Ellen," Quinn told her. "Oh, sometimes I might be able to bend them, a little, but the Federal government hands down the guidelines we have to follow, you know."

Ellen stared at him, helpless, bleeding inside. "But the sum is so enormous! Completely out of reason!"

"Somebody has to pay for the war, you know," Quinn said quietly.

"And it's going to be the Southerners who do it. Major Quinn, there must be something I can do! Mallows has been in my family for—"

He held up a small, well-kept hand. He didn't want her to go through all of *that* again. It would take more than a gesture to halt the flood of words, however, the desperate, anguished words.

"I'll do anything, *anything,* to save Mallows," she told him.

He was more calm in the face of her agony than Mr. Mandress or Mr. Codder had been. "I'll tell you what, Miss Ellen. I'll look into the matter, and then I'll call on you and we'll see what we can work out. It is a large sum, and there's no way I can fail to collect it. If I don't do my duty, they'll replace me with someone who *will* do it. I'll study the situation, and then—oh, say, the middle of next week—I'll ride out to Mallows and tell you what's possible. I don't make any promises, you understand. There is nothing I can do to assure that your estate survives intact. But it should be possible to see that you and your family aren't simply turned out in the cold. Are you planning to stay in town tonight?"

Planning, what had she been planning? She was so numb—how could she be numb and at the same time hurt so badly?—that she couldn't think. She had been, yes, intending

447

to stay the night at the Varners'. She hadn't stopped on the way in, however, because she'd wanted to transact her business before everyone went home for the night. And now, now the thought of exposing her bleeding soul to anyone, even old and good friends, was simply unendurable. This must be how an injured animal felt, when it ran away and hid in a hole to die.

For the first time, Ellen did not immediately repudiate that thought when it came. Maybe Evan had been right, maybe it *was* better to die than to face ongoing torture.

"No," she said, her voice dull. "We'll go on home tonight." It would be very late before she got there, but she had to go home. Home to her beloved Mallows, home to die.

"Good. Well, you'd better get started, then. And I'll let you know when I can, what might be done."

She scarcely remembered getting out of his office, stumbling across the dusty street. Blossom stood beside the buggy with that young man—for a moment Ellen couldn't even remember who he was. Oh, yes, the tax assessor.

He moved to assist her into the vehicle. She heard his voice, yet none of what he said registered. It was only when Blossom reached up and tugged at her skirt that Ellen brought her eyes into focus, and forced herself to listen to the girl's words.

"I ain't goin' back with you, ma'am. I'm mighty grateful for all you done for me, but I got me a position with Mr. Healy, keepin' house for him. We'll come out Sunday and get the rest of my belongin's."

Under normal circumstances, Ellen would have inquired sharply into Healy's background, and made some attempt to determine his intentions. The girl had lived under her roof for almost a year, and she felt more or less responsible for her. As it was, engrossed in her own misery and fear, Ellen was only just aware of Blossom. She nodded, dismissing Blossom, and spoke to Rudy. "Take me home," she said.

It didn't occur to her that they'd had nothing to eat since midday. Rudy didn't complain. He saw that Miss Ellen was in a dreadful state, worse than he'd ever seen her even when Mr. Roger and then Mr. Evan had died.

Rudy had been a slave at Mallows nearly all his life; he'd come there, from a harsh master, at the age of fourteen. He was now, he'd been told, a free man, but what did that mean

448

to him? Where could he go, an old man no longer able to work?

He had watched Miss Ellen grow up from a tiny girl into a lovely woman. She had always been good to him, always fair. He had seen her through happy times, and bad ones. And this time, it was as bad as it could be.

He guided the horse and buggy through the dusk, not looking back, knowing nevertheless that Miss Ellen was hunched in a corner of the seat, unaware of her own physical discomfort as she was unaware of his. Darkness fell. There was no moon, only a few stars. They were enough to enable Rudy to keep to the road, heading for home as quickly as he could get there.

Ellen had sunk almost into a stupor, exhausted, unable to maintain the pitch of panic that had enveloped her at first, when it became clear that her plan to mortgage Mallows was not a possible solution to her problems. Quinn's remembered words hammered at her, wearing down what little courage she had left.

It should be possible to see that you and your family aren't simply turned out in the cold.

Shivering, as the buggy jounced through the night, Ellen easily managed to take that literally. It was fall, and the air was crisp, and it would soon be cold. And if they took Mallows away from her—yes, face it, that might well happen, no matter how hard she resisted the idea—they would literally be out in the cold. Where could they go? What could they do? There was her mother, who was old and perhaps not entirely putting on her air of delicacy, who had not done anything more useful than knit a sock or shell a pan of peas in so many years that she would be totally lost if anything more was expected of her. And Miss Lacy, who seemed to have shrunk since she'd come back from Savannah; Miss Lacy looked her age, and was beginning to act it, as well. She was not as active as she had always been, she had less to say. Had Miss Lacy felt like this, selling her own home? *Dear God*, Ellen thought in a burst of compassion, *why didn't I see how terrible it was for her? It had to be sold, there was nothing I could have done about it, but I could have understood. Would that have helped her at all, if she'd known I understood?*

Two old women, ailing, beyond the years when they could begin again, anywhere, at anything. And Valerie and Julie,

449

and Sally Ann and the baby. They were young, but they didn't know anything to do to keep themselves, to survive. How could they get along, without money? A little house in town? When there were still so many of them, and they hadn't even the few dollars a month to pay rent on the simplest of houses? They'd put in food, at Mallows, but how could they take it with them, if they were forced to leave? Where would they store it?

And what about the Negroes?

They were almost the same as her children. They were a simple, innocent, ignorant people. They had always looked to her to care for them, to see that they were fed and clothed and the roofs patched over their heads. They were less capable of looking after themselves than Valerie and Julie, who had actually been prepared for nothing more than running a household, with plenty of servants, and being wives and mothers. It did not occur to her that she'd not done an adequate job of preparing her daughters for even those things, that her own marriage was scarcely one for them to emulate with enthusiasm.

All those people, all depending upon her. And what could she do? Ellen did not know when the tears began to slide down her cold cheeks, when she finally folded forward and gave in to wracking sobs. She was past prayer. She'd prayed intensely for months, years, and what good had it done her? Now, for a sum that would have been almost paltry before the war, they were going to take Mallows away from her unless Major Quinn could come up with a miracle.

Somehow, Ellen no longer believed in miracles.

"Miss Ellen?"

She blinked, coming out of her half-drowsing state, to see that they were home. Lallie stood on the steps with a lamp in her hand—how had they dared to buy coal oil again, for the lamps, when they couldn't get more than ten cents for a silver spoon?—and Rudy was speaking to her anxiously.

"Home, Miss Ellen. Let me help you down."

She raised her head. She was drained, temporarily incapable of any emotion, even of relief that they were home. She became aware that she was chilled to the bone, and too stiff to move easily when Rudy lifted a hand to assist her.

Lallie cast a quick, shocked look at her. "Lord God, what happened to her?"

450

"Bad day," Rudy said. "I think she need to be in bed."

It was very late. Lallie was in her nightclothes. She held the lamp in her left hand, encircling Ellen's waist with the right arm, leading her inside. Ellen moved as a docile child; she allowed herself to be led up the stairs, and stood without comment or protest when Lallie gently removed her clothes and urged her into bed.

When Lallie finally picked up the lamp to leave her mistress there in the dark, she was frightened. What had happened to Miss Ellen? It must be bad, very bad. Lord God, what would happen to them all if Miss Ellen didn't hold up?

Lallie climbed the second short flight of steps to her room and crept, shivering in the early morning chill, into her own bed.

Eighteen

Valerie drew the story out of her, word by painful word, at the breakfast table. Ellen had recovered enough so that she moved of her own volition; she volunteered nothing, yet seemed willing to reply truthfully when Valerie thought of the right questions to ask.

Ellen expressed no anger, no indignation, and, most unsettling of all, no burning determination such as she had evidenced before. She was withdrawn, resigned, concerned primarily with her own internal suffering. Even Dolly saw it and was alarmed.

"What will we do?" she asked, eyes wide.

"We'll wait until Major Quinn comes and tells us the worst—or the best," Valerie said crisply, knowing that someone must display some control or they would all crumble. "There's no sense worrying about it any more than we already have, until we know what we'll have to do."

For the first time since they could remember, Ellen did not move briskly into the day, organizing, giving orders. She drifted through the house, touching, looking as if she expected never to see any of it again. Julie walked with her, trying to conceal her own distress, wanting only to be there if her mother needed her.

452

Valerie could not bear to watch it. She had to escape, had to find the time and privacy for her own thoughts, hopeful thoughts, whether there was any reason for hope or not. Her own personal future, of course, lay with Jack Ferris. If only he'd come, or at least communicate with her in such a way that she could tell him what was happening! Was there any chance that he could help them, in the matter of the taxes? If they could pay the taxes, Mallows would be safe at least through the winter, or until another tax season came around.

There had been a time—long ago, before she'd been put to work in the fields like a two-thousand-dollar prime buck—when Valerie had enjoyed riding out across the fields and hills. The sudden compulsion to do so again would not be denied, although there was only one horse left on the place, and that more used to pulling the buggy than being ridden.

It was a fine morning, crisp with the hint of the cold weather to come, yet warm in the sunshine. The maples were turning scarlet, the oaks beginning to show gold; it was a time of year Valerie had always loved, and she was young enough and optimistic enough to enjoy it now.

She dressed in the old brown velvet riding habit, suppressed the small twinge of guilt about leaving her mother to Julie, and left the house, calling for one of the boys to saddle the mare.

She rounded a corner of the barn and surprised Gilly, abdomen bulging with the approaching child, in earnest conversation with Thomas. The two jerked apart, although they had not been touching as far as Valerie could see.

"Mornin', Miss Val," Thomas said. "You wantin' a horse?"

"Yes, please." It felt almost like the old days, when the stables were full of sleek, handsome animals, when there were boys who did nothing but care for them, when there had been houseparties and the guests had ridden out on excursions and returned to the house ravenous for the enormous breakfasts that were the mark of hospitality at Mallows.

While Thomas saddled the mare, Valerie stood with Gilly, seeing that there was an upturn to the girl's mouth, a sparkle in her eyes.

"How do you feel, Gilly?"

"I fine, ma'am," Gilly assured her.

"Not missing Chad any more?"

Gilly shrugged. "I reckon I miss him, Miss Val. He good to me, most times. But I think Miss Ellen right; he ain't goin' to do me any good. Not if he wind up in jail. And he got a temper, Chad has."

But he'd been good in bed—or in the hay, wherever they'd met, Valerie thought. Dear God, how well she understood that! She longed for Jack every day—and every night—of her life. Maybe Gilly'd given up on Chad, and was turning her attention to Thomas. Well, far be it from her to interfere. God knew there was little enough pleasure in life these days, for any of them, and probably the affection she won from any young black was the only worthwhile thing in Gilly's young life.

She left them there, still talking, as if they realized that she would not carry tales about them. Valerie forgot them as soon as she felt the horse beneath her; she urged the mare to a canter and then, out on the drive, to a full gallop, bending low over the powerful neck to avoid being slapped in the face by the hanging moss.

It was good, oh, it was wonderful, to speed through her own private world again! Valerie gave herself up to it, not thinking of anything in particular, simply reveling in the sensations of riding once more, soaking in the sunshine.

With no conscious sense of making a decision, she turned to the right at the end of the drive. She passed Patrick Ryan's house, noting the thin ribbon of smoke rising from the chimney, then cut up across the ridge, filled with the sheer exhilaration of escaping, ever so briefly, from the bonds that had constrained her.

She never saw the hole before the mare stumbled, had, indeed, hit the ground and lay there dazed with no sense of transition. The wind had been knocked out of her so that her body ached, and she turned her head, relieved that the horse had already regained her footing. Not a broken leg, thank God, for their sole remaining horse.

"Valerie! You hurt?"

It was Patrick Ryan, coming on the run up the slope.

She pushed herself into a sitting position, pressing a hand to her chest.

"You all right?" He hunkered down beside her, his face close to hers, disconcertingly close.

"I think so." She leaned on one hand, winced, and massaged her wrist. "Nothing broken, any way."

"You ride like a madwoman." There was less than the customary censure in his tone, though.

She breathed through her mouth, feeling the ache of drawing the air into flattened lungs. "I guess so, but it was worth it. I haven't ridden in months, and I needed the exercise."

"Try walking," Patrick suggested. "It's safer. It's also better exercise."

He hadn't moved away. In fact, he dropped into a comfortable position beside her. "You've changed since I've seen you."

"I work in the sun like a slave, if that's what you mean." She regarded her tanned hands with a grimace. "Milky-white skin isn't possible when you have to be out in the sun."

"I didn't mean the tan. Actually," Patrick said, drawing up a knee and clasping his hands around it, "it's rather becoming. I know it isn't supposed to be the standard for Southern women, but on you it's very attractive."

She stared at him in astonishment, too disconcerted by this unexpected compliment to know how to respond.

"What's happening over there?" He glanced toward the brick chimneys to be seen over the tops of the trees. "I got my tax bill, so I assume you have yours, too."

Her full mouth twisted. "I'm sorry you reminded me; it was one of the things I wanted not to think about."

"Bad?"

"Bad," Valerie agreed. She was breathing less painfully now, though the wrist still ached. "Mama went to Reidsville to talk to Major Quinn about it, for all the good it did. Well, maybe they'll be able to work something out. He said he'd think about it and let her know. But they want sixteen hundred dollars!"

Patrick whistled. "What's she planning to do? She can't raise that kind of cash, surely."

"Well, the one thing she refused to consider was selling off part of the land. The part you wanted wouldn't be worth that much, anyway, just for some old pine trees."

"Old pine trees are worth money, but I couldn't offer her that much for them," Patrick agreed. "Not unless she wanted to let more of them go, of course." He reached over and brushed at her cheek. "You have a dirty face."

She didn't move away from that brief touch; she did react to it, however, inwardly. An unsettling, yet not unpleasant, sensation ran through her, making her nerve ends tingle. Not the way they did with Jack, of course. She was beginning to

455

understand, however, the way it had been for the young women before the war, when there had been parties and balls and opportunities to dance with young men, to experiment with romance. To know what it was like to have a man hold your hand, or kiss you. You didn't have to be in love to enjoy things like that, obviously.

"You know," Patrick said, still leaning toward her, the big hand now resting on his thigh, "there might be a solution to your problem. I can't hand over the cash to pay your taxes and keep the place going. But if Mallows were mine, part of the company I've formed, the taxes would be different. Less. And some of my backers are very influential men in the cities up north. Rules and regulations can sometimes be manipulated, if you know the right people."

She knew, seconds before his mouth came down over hers, that he was going to kiss her. She could have stopped him; later, she had no idea why she hadn't.

It was the same as when he'd kissed her in Reidsville, in the buggy, except that this time he wasn't playacting for the benefit of watching Yankee soldiers. And this time Ellen wasn't going to come along and put a stop to it.

Valerie sat, motionless, succumbing to the liquid fire, the melting sensation in her midsection. Not Jack, no, and she didn't love Patrick Ryan. Yet he was a very attractive man, and as expert with his mouth and his hands as Jack had been. She was scarcely aware that he'd moved, put his arms around her; she was drawn into an embrace and a deep kiss that left her tremulous and overheated when he drew away.

"You could marry me," Patrick said. "Your mother could keep Mallows, or at least continue to live there, for the rest of her life. If Mallows was mine."

Her chest was constricted again, as badly as after her fall. She was stunned; she'd never anticipated anything such as this from Patrick.

Her head began to move in negation, ever so slightly. "No—"

He pulled back as if he'd been stung. The wide mouth went flat. "I'm still not good enough for you, am I? I'm still the son of a red dirt Georgia farmer, and all the veneer of clothes and manners and money won't make me good enough for a Stanton, will it?" He rose in a lithe motion, looking down at her with what seemed to be tightly controlled anger.

She scrambled to her feet, too, awkwardly, in time to reach

456

out for his sleeve as he swung away. "Wait, Patrick—it isn't like that!" she protested.

He hesitated. "No? What is it like, then?"

"It has nothing to do with the fact that you . . . that your beginnings are different from mine. Maybe that kind of thing mattered, once, although I'm not sure it did to me. I don't know any more. But now it's we who are the fallen, while you've climbed to the top, or near the top, haven't you? It has nothing to do with that. It's—"

She stared into the hard blue eyes, seeing the nimbus of red hair with glints of gold where the sunlight struck it. For a moment she almost wished it might be different.

"There's someone else," she said softly. "Someone I've fallen in love with—"

"That Yankee captain?" He said it so quickly that she thought he must have already suspected it. "Does *he* love *you?*"

"Yes," Valerie said.

"Are you sure what you feel for him is love?" Patrick demanded. "Not an infatuation, because he was here when you were ready to fall in love with somebody? Plain old animal instincts, of a female who needs a man?"

Heat suffused her face. "I'm a woman, Patrick Ryan, not an animal in heat," Valerie said. "I think I can tell love from *that.*"

"Can you?"

He took the necessary step to reach her, pulling her roughly into his arms. Again his lips claimed her, although this time she was fighting against it, with a brutal urgency. She was no match for him, of course; his strength was far greater than hers, and he'd pinioned her arms at her sides. Don't fight him, then, she thought, let him do it and get it over with, and then he'd see that she meant it. Valerie willed herself to passivity and went limp against him.

Perhaps he took that collapse for the weakness of surrender, for he deepened the kiss and moved his hands on her back, no longer savage but caressing, stroking, in the way she remembered.

Stand still, don't resist, pretend it isn't happening—

The only thing wrong with her theory was that it didn't quite work. In spite of her intention to remain detached from Patrick Ryan's raw emotion, she was caught up in it, as if she'd drunk the wine and waited for her lover, and he was

457

here. The sensations he aroused were violent and frightening, because it would be so easy to succumb to them, to him, utterly, totally.

Some faint vestige of reason remained; with a sudden violence he was no longer prepared for, Valerie shoved him away and stumbled backward several feet, catching her balance against the nearest poplar tree. She was breathing heavily, and her hair had come loose from its combs and pins; a strand of it fell across her forehead and she did not move to brush it away.

Patrick was breathing quickly, too, though he was less agitated than she was. "Say you didn't like that," he challenged. "As much as I did."

"You'd do anything to get Mallows, wouldn't you?" Valerie flung a challenge of her own.

"Damn near anything," Patrick agreed after a moment's silence.

Anger built in her, fueling the necessary resistance. "Including marrying for it."

"Including marrying for it," Patrick confirmed. "You could do worse, girl. That Yankee fop won't save Mallows for you."

"Maybe not," Valerie admitted. "But he's the one I'm going to marry."

For a few seconds she wondered if he were going to reach out for her again. To ravage her, to strike her, she couldn't have said; she only knew the impulse to violent action was there in him. She also knew she wasn't afraid of him, not the way she'd been afraid of those Yankee soldiers in Reidsville.

And then Patrick shrugged, as if it didn't really matter much, one way or the other. "If you change your mind, you can let me know. I won't be at home, I'm closing the house and moving into town for the winter. I'll be traveling between the county seat and Savannah, but I'll maintain an office in Reidsville. You can leave a message if I'm not there."

Fury impelled her to fling a final word after him as he strode away, down the slope of the hill.

"I suggest you don't wait for it, Mr. Ryan!"

Patrick broke the stride and half turned, speaking over his shoulder. "I won't. But if you want me, I'll be around."

She had no response to that. She was shaking so that she could hardly coax her hair into any semblance of order. Part of her anger was directed at the man who had, with no provocation whatever, no encouragement from her, taken such liberties with her person.

Most of the emotional upheaval, however, was because she'd been frightened, was still frightened, of her own involuntary response to Patrick Ryan's kiss. What if he was right? What if she was no different than a cow that needed to be bred, what if she couldn't tell biological need from love? Could he possibly be right about that?

Valerie pushed herself away from the tree, making her way toward the horse that grazed on the dry grass a few yards away. Absurd thought. It was only that he had touched her in much the same ways that Jack had done, and of course she loved Jack, and she *hated* Patrick Ryan . . .

No. She leaned against the mare's warm flank, calming herself before she attempted to mount. No, she didn't hate Patrick. She didn't love him, but she didn't hate him, either.

The day was spoiled. She no longer cared to ride. She led the mare to a fallen log from which she could get an unladylike foot into a stirrup and haul herself into the saddle.

She had no idea why, when the anger had faded, she felt like crying.

Ellen moved, in the following days, like a mechanical toy: stiff, revealing nothing in the way of feeling or emotion. The middle of the week, he'd said. Yet Wednesday came, and Thursday, and Major Quinn had not arrived nor sent any message.

Luckily the season's work had been virtually finished, because she gave no orders, and without orders no one worked. Everyone knew that disaster hovered over Mallows, although in truth not many of the Negroes worried unduly. After all, they had always been taken care of. No doubt they would continue to be looked after; Miss Ellen would think of something.

Miss Ellen did *not* think of anything. She caught herself in the act of draining a glass of Roger's best brandy, and she scarcely felt it. She stared at the glass in horror. No, no, alcohol was not the answer.

There was no answer.

Yet there might be, when Major Quinn came.

She tried to hope, tried to pray, and withered inside a little more with each passing hour.

Lallie was on her way back to the house with an empty slop jar in each hand when she heard the whistle from the stand of pines beyond the outhouse.

She paused, listening, heart suddenly quickening.

"Aaron?"

"Come over here, in the shadows."

She put down the pails and moved toward the trees. "It's all right, nobody around to see you," she said. "Nobody care, any more, the way things are around this place."

Aaron stayed within the shelter of the trees, anyway. He was leaner, she saw at once, tougher-looking. There was a scar on his cheek that hadn't been there a year ago. "Things so bad you got to empty the chamber pots?" he asked.

"Pretty bad," Lallie allowed. "Way things going, Miss Ellen about to lose Mallows."

"You're skinny," Aaron observed. "There's not enough to eat?"

"Plenty to eat. I just run it all off, up and down those stairs. You hungry?"

Aaron's teeth showed white in the black face when he grinned. "A healthy man is always hungry, and never passes up a chance to eat. If there's plenty, I could do with a mouthful."

"All right. I think you could walk into the kitchen and eat it at the table, for all anybody'd care. No slaves any more, we're all free. Where have you been?"

Aaron shrugged. "Up north. Out west. Around. You know something? People don't like niggers, no matter where you go. Don't matter if you know how to read and write, if you're smarter than they are. Well, that *does* matter, they don't like it. And it's cold up north. Winter coming on again, and I've had me enough of northern winters. You think it snows here, a little dusting like the sugar on a cake. Up there, the drifts get up to here, right on the city streets." He gestured at the level of his crotch. "So I thought I'd head back to Georgia, see how little Lallie was getting on. You got skinnier, but you're shaping up in the right places."

He didn't touch her, but she felt as if he had. She wasn't sure if she liked it or not. Aaron was different. He'd gone away a boy, and this was no boy she faced. The old familiarity was missing, yet there was something else, something stronger, maybe. Something exciting.

"Where you headed now? You going to stay around here?"

460

"Don't know yet. Maybe, I can get me some work. They throw niggers in jail that don't work. I got a little money, enough to pay for my eats for a while, if I have to. I won't waste it, though, if you got any meat and corn pone to hand out."

Lallie regarded him with her head tilted to one side, trying to figure out what it was that was different about him, besides the bulge of muscles he hadn't had when working as a house servant. "You talk different."

"I *am* different." Aaron grinned. "Inside, and outside, I'm different. And I practice being what the white folks wants their niggers to be. Don't tread on any toes, unless it's necessary. Out west, they're not so particular as they are in the North, but I don't think that's to my liking, either. I haven't been all the way to California; I may try that out. Right now, though, if nothing turns up fast in Georgia, I'm thinking about New Orleans. Never saw New Orleans, but I know it's a lot warmer than New York City or Chicago in the wintertime. You want to go with me?"

He'd told her he would come back for her. So why was she taken unawares, now that he'd returned?

Lallie hesitated, and he saw it. "You changed your mind? You don't want to go with me?"

"This is a bad time to go," Lallie said slowly. "Miss Ellen needs me right now."

"Miss Ellen always needed you. She'll get along all right, once you're gone."

He didn't understand, and she didn't know how to make him understand. "She's going through a terrible time right now. If she loses Mallows, could be she lose her mind."

Aaron shrugged. "People lose their minds all the time. Everybody got problems. I don't know if I'll ever come back by this way, once I move on. You want to go, it better be soon."

"A few days?" Lallie temporized. "That Major Quinn s'posed to come tell her, any day now, if there's some way she can keep this place. You can hang around for a few days?"

The new strangeness was there again in the dark smiling face. "Depends. You going to make it worth my while to hang around?"

Lallie stood very still. "What you mean, worth your while?"

461

"I mean you got skinny, but you grew into a woman while I gone. I thought about you a lot, Lallie. Saw plenty of women, up there in the North. Never saw one I liked as well as you. A man needs a woman of his own. I thought maybe you'd be the one. Figured if I came back, and you didn't look the way I remembered you, I'd just forget the whole thing. But you're even better now. You got a man, Lallie? You take up with anybody while I was away?"

He moved closer to her, disturbingly close, and yet she was not exactly frightened.

"You know Miss Ellen don't allow any fooling around."

"I wasn't talking about fooling around. A nigger can get married, now, without asking permission from anybody. You know that? Just like white folks. What do you think about getting married?"

Married. The word was almost a foreign one to Lallie, who hadn't thought of it in terms of herself. Excitement trickled through her veins.

"I don't know. Never thought on it."

Aaron spoke very softly. "Think on it."

Lallie licked her lips. "White folks marry when they fall in love with somebody. I don't think I know what that's like. I never felt that way, the way Miss Valerie feels about her captain."

"Maybe you need some help, thinking about it," Aaron suggested. He put out his hands to her upper arms and drew her against him, the new, unfamiliar hardness of his body setting up a tremor that she knew he must be able to detect. His mouth was warm and soft and then, as her own flesh softened, the kiss became harder, building into a passion in him that touched off a like emotion in Lallie.

When he put her aside, they were breathless. "You come back and meet me, after dark," Aaron suggested. "And I'll help you decide whether you want to go with me, or not."

"Lallie?" Pansy's voice rose from somewhere near the summer kitchen. "Miss Ellen wantin' you! Where are you?"

Lallie could scarcely speak for the constriction in her chest. "I'll be back," she told Aaron. "After dark. Right here."

"I'll be waiting," Aaron replied, teeth flashing again. "Right here."

Lallie offered him a smile in return, and then fled. "I'm coming, Pansy! Stop that bellering!"

Aaron watched her from within the hiding place of the trees. He hadn't been sure he should come back; he hadn't been sure Lallie would want him. Confidence grew in him now, however, and he stood there for some minutes, thinking, before he turned and disappeared into the woods.

Major Quinn came on Friday afternoon.

Ellen had almost given up hope. She was sick with apprehension when she led him into the library, and offered him a drink; she wanted a glass of the brandy, herself, and dared not take it. She, who had scorned spirits all her life, now knew how easily one could become dependent upon such a crutch. She thanked God she hadn't known about it earlier; she might by this time be a mindless old woman, though yet shy of forty.

She waited only until he had drained the glass. "Please, sir, I cannot make polite conversation. I must know. What can I do about the taxes?"

Major Quinn stood only a few inches taller than herself. He was no longer in uniform, of course, yet his bearing was military; had his suit had a double row of gleaming buttons, he could have commanded any army. He regarded her dispassionately.

"I have given your predicament considerable thought, Miss Ellen. I see no way around the payment of the taxes, as long as Mallows belongs to one who supported the Confederacy—"

Her stomach twisted and the sickness rose in her throat.

"However, it occurs to me that should it be in the family of a government worker, someone of substance, of course, some arrangements might be made to extend the time of the payments."

What good would that do, to extend the time? She had no prospect of ever seeing sixteen hundred dollars. She had missed a few of his words, and brought herself back to attention.

"—I could personally be of some help. As I'm sure you were aware, I was very much taken by this house. It is a gracious way of living, the way you Southerners do it. And if I am to remain here, as a Federal official, I would like to live in a place like this. Of course I could not live here permanently, since my work must be done in town; and it's too far for riding back and forth on a daily basis. But a marital

463

alliance might well solve your problem, and contribute to my satisfaction."

Marital alliance? What had she missed? Ellen's breath caught uncomfortably in her chest. Her numb lips shaped the word. "Marriage?"

"The idea is not too distasteful, I hope? I do have a family, after all, and they are young enough to need the guidance of a female for some years yet. You said, I believe, that you would do anything to save Mallows. I think such a marriage would be to our mutual advantage, and there would be no need for you to give up your home."

"Marriage." She was so taken aback that she could not think. She had not been a woman who enjoyed marriage; she had, in fact, been more relieved than anything else when there were no more marital bed performances to endure. She had thought such things behind her forever.

Yet to save Mallows? What were the alternatives? She already knew them well; there was no need to enumerate them again in her mind.

He was waiting for her answer. Ellen forced herself to breathe normally, to speak the words she had never dreamed would be asked of her.

"I must admit your proposal takes me completely by surprise," she said. "However—it is true, I am in desperate straits. And I—I would try to be a good mother to your children, sir."

His eyebrows rose fractionally as Otis Quinn surveyed her. A small smile twisted his lips. "You, ma'am? It is not *your* hand I ask. It is your daughter's—the little dark one. Julie. It is Julie I would have for my wife."

A stomach-churning horror washed over her. Julie? *Julie?*

Yet even as the idea fully penetrated her bemused brain, Ellen knew a sort of guilty relief, too. That it was not she herself who would be expected to share Major Quinn's bed.

And then she thought, *Julie, poor Julie.*

Nineteen

"It is agreed, then?" Quinn asked, pouring himself another shot of the brandy as if he were already master of the house. "The marriage will take place a week from tomorrow? That way, we can get everyone settled as quickly as possible. Oh, and I trust there will be somewhere that Fritz can sleep, too? He'll be tutoring Jay, and can perhaps convey something useful to my daughters as well."

"The room that Blossom had, upstairs, is empty," Ellen murmured.

"Very good. Would you like me to break the news to Miss Julie, or would you prefer to do it yourself?"

"I'll do it," Ellen assured him. She dared not have it otherwise, and it would have to be in private, too. God only knew how the child would take it.

"Very good," Quinn said again. "You need have no more worries on the score of the taxes. May I suggest that we arrive, en masse, on Friday night, and that the wedding take place on Saturday afternoon? We will, of course, have no guests. Would I correctly assume that there is no one you, either, will care to invite to the ceremony? In these days, large weddings seem inappropriate, do they not?"

She could hardly have been said to grasp everything he

465

was saying, although she did not disagree with any of it, not aloud. All she wanted was that he should go, so that she could marshal her chaotic thoughts.

And then, when he had gone, panic caught up with her again. For she must break the news to Julie. What a good thing, that it was Julie he'd taken a fancy to, and not Valerie! She knew Valerie; not even for Mallows would she have married a man she hadn't chosen for herself. She had no idea where Valerie had gotten her extreme stubbornness.

Julie was in the upstairs sitting room, working through a basket of stockings to see which of them could be mended, which unraveled to provide the yarn to do it. She looked up, smiling, then saw her mother's face.

"What is it? Has Major Quinn come?" The sock she was holding dropped into her lap, unnoticed.

"He's been, and gone. Darling, I have something to tell you." Ellen's parody of a smile was far from reassuring, and Julie rose in alarm. "No, no, dear, sit down. I'll sit down, too. In truth, I need to; this has all been a—a surprise to me, and while it may surprise you, too, I hope you won't find the idea unpalatable."

Julie could hardly have found this approach reassuring. The tenseness that had begun when she saw her mother's face now solidified at the pit of her stomach. "What are you talking about? Did he say we are going to lose Mallows? Are they going to turn us out?"

"No. No, there is an alternative, and after careful consideration, I've accepted it. I know that you are a sensible girl, and that you'll agree it is the only solution to all our problems."

Uncomprehending, Julie waited. How could *she* play any major part in saving Mallows?

"Major Quinn," Ellen began, "has—has asked for your hand in marriage. The wedding is to take place a week from tomorrow, on Saturday."

For a few seconds Julie didn't react at all. And then the appalling statement worked through her mind, and with it came shock. Petrifying, paralyzing shock. She felt as if someone had struck her a savage blow, knocking all of the wind out of her. Marry Major Quinn?

Taking Julie's inability to speak for tacit consent, Ellen gained courage. "We'll have just family, I think. And I'll bring down the old trunk, and see if my wedding dress can be made to fit—"

Julie broke through the words in desperation. "Mama, you can't be serious!"

"Darling, of course I'm serious. Do you think I would say this if I were not? It's the only way, Julie, the only way! Otherwise, the plantation is lost! We'll be literally set out in the road! With nowhere to go, no money to live on! Julie, listen to me. This is no more than I was called upon to do, many years ago, with your father. And I adapted to the situation very well, you know that. You will, too."

"No," Julie said. Her dark eyes were enormous in a chalky face. "Mama, it's too much to ask of anyone. No, Mama, don't ask me to do this."

"Darling, I don't have any choice! It's you he wants! And he'll take care of everything, we won't lose Mallows, we can all go on living here as we've always done . . ."

"As we've always done?" Julie's voice rose on a note of hysteria as the full impact of the proposal struck her. "Except that I will be married to a man older than my father would be, if he were still alive? I am expected to sleep with him, an old man, a Yankee?"

"Sleeping with a man takes only a small part of one's time," Ellen said, in gross disregard of her own recollection of that side of marriage. "Julie, I know this has come as a surprise, but seriously consider what will happen to us—to all of us—if you don't do it! I've already agreed, and we can't back out now . . ."

"You agreed, without consulting me? Mama, how could you do that? I don't want to marry him, I don't want to marry anybody! The thought of . . . of having to submit to . . . to *that* . . . makes me ill! My flesh crawls! Mama . . ."

Julie saw no yielding in Ellen's face, only quiet resolution. "My own marriage was arranged, without my consent. So was my mother's, and Miss Lacy's. One must defer to the judgment of one's parents in such matters—"

"Your marriage to my father, was it a happy one? Did you love him?" Julie demanded.

"I learned to love him," Ellen said. It was almost the truth. She had, over the years, developed a mild affection for Roger. Especially when he no longer made any sexual demands upon her. "And you'll learn to love . . ." She broke off, for

467

the picture she was painting was ludicrous, even as she said it.

"Grandma Lacy was raped on her wedding night," Julie said.

"What? Julie, for the love of heaven!"

"It's true. She told us. She told us how terrible it was, and how she raged and cried. Mama, don't ask me to go through anything like that!"

"How dared she speak of such matters to young girls! I cannot believe she would have been so ill advised."

"Mama, what difference does it make? What matters is that it was true, even Grandpa Stanton was little more than an animal and you can't have already forgotten what happened to Charlotte. Do you want the same thing to happen to me?"

"Don't be absurd. Charlotte was . . . was attacked by a band of Yankee soldiers, used by them . . . it's not the same as marriage."

"Why isn't it? He's a Yankee, too, isn't he? And he'll expect to . . . to use me, as they used Charlotte. What difference does it make that he's only one, and there were many of them? Does it matter whether it's one man or a dozen, if a woman is taken against her will?"

The discussion went on for some time. On several occasions Julie's voice rose in a hysterical outburst that was heard by other members of the household; they could not make out the words, but certainly recognized the tone of it. They waited, tension building, to learn what had given rise to hysteria.

When Ellen at last left the upstairs sitting room, limbs trembling and bathed in her own sweat, Julie lay sobbing on the sofa behind her. Ellen closed the door so that the sounds of it would not carry throughout the house.

She remembered her own reaction to her father's decision that she should marry Roger. She hadn't wanted to, either, but she'd managed all right. She'd had to, to carry on at Mallows, and Julie would manage, too.

When she emerged onto the second-floor landing, Valerie came out of her own room, her face grave.

"What's happened?"

She thought she was braced for the worst; yet when Ellen told her, she felt as if the floor had shifted beneath her, as if

468

she were falling. She put out a hand to the stair rail to steady herself.

"You can't do it. Not even for Mallows, you can't do it!"

"Valerie, I have told you what is going to happen. I haven't opened up the matter for discussion. It has nothing to do with you, beyond the fact that it guarantees you'll have a roof over your head and food in your mouth. Something none of us was assured of, only a few hours ago. Julie will come around. She'll adjust, as all women adjust. Don't make it worse by trying to start all over again from the beginning."

Valerie stared after her, incredulous, as Ellen went past her and down the stairs. She couldn't be serious, she couldn't treat Julie this way!

She crossed the landing and opened the sitting room door. Julie lay exhausted across the arm of the sofa, and Valerie knelt beside her to wipe her streaming face.

"Help me," Julie pleaded. "Help me change her mind. There must be some other way! I can't marry Major Quinn, Val, I can't!"

"No, of course you can't," Valerie agreed quietly, but her mind raced down a desperate, slippery track, and found no answers.

"I have never interfered in your family affairs," Lacy said, facing her daughter-in-law across the table. "But I am interfering now. You cannot do this to Julie. You'll kill her."

Ellen regarded the older woman with cold dislike. "As you say, Miss Lacy, this is *my* family affair. Not yours."

"She's my granddaughter, as well as your daughter, and I say you'll destroy her." Lacy's voice was raspy. "For the love of God, woman, you lived through a wretched marriage of your own, and now you wish an even worse marriage on your own child! How can you even consider it?"

A corner of Ellen's mind caught on the fact that Lacy had known her marriage to Roger was less than satisfactory; she had not thought that known to anyone but herself. Yet the greater part of her attention remained focused on the primary issue.

"I can consider it because there is no alternative, save being set out into the road. All of us. I assume that you, as well as the rest of us, would prefer to live out the rest of your life in relative comfort."

"Not at the expense of a young girl's life," Lacy told her,

469

dark eyes snapping. "I've always known you for a fool, Ellen, a woman with no juices of her own and little concern for those of anyone else. But not even I could have imagined you could stoop to such a level as this. Let them put us out. People have lost their homes before, and survived. We can take in washings, or make straw bonnets, or hire ourselves out to scrub other people's houses. But for the love of heaven, don't do this to an innocent child!"

Ellen mentally repudiated everything that Lacy said. She had to, for the sake of her own sanity, for the sake of all their lives, their futures. She turned, and walked away, and Lacy stared after her with helpless rage.

"This come for you," Lallie said, handing over the folded paper, sealed with red wax.

Valerie took it, wondering, still so distraught over the situation regarding her sister that it took a conscious effort to wrench her thoughts back to anything else. "Who brought it? Where did it come from?"

"A boy brought it. A black boy. I never saw him before," Lallie said. "He told me to give it directly to Miss Valerie."

Valerie stared at it, at her name printed in small neat letters across the face of the improvised envelope. It was not Jack's bold hand, nor any other that she recognized. "All right. Thank you, Lallie."

She waited until Lallie had gone before she peeled off the wax and spread the paper flat on her bedside table, so that the candlelight fell across it.

The message within was printed in the same small neat fashion, and was brief and to the point.

Jack Ferris is in Savannah. The old French house, on Pulaski Square.

That was all.

She read it again, disbelieving.

Who had sent it, and why?

Jack? He might have disguised his writing, or had someone else address it for him, so that other members of the household would not realize it had come from him. Yet if he'd done that, why would he not have written to her in a more normal way, inside? Especially since his name was spelled out completely, anyway.

She turned the paper over and saw that it had not gone through the mails. Someone had had it hand-delivered, not through the post office. Who? And, if it weren't Jack himself, why?

Immediately upon the heels of that conjecture, she saw a faint ray of hope. If Jack was in Savannah, she could contact him. Maybe he could help, maybe he could stop Julie's forced marriage to save Mallows. Jack had vast business interests; he came from a wealthy family. If he knew how desperate the situation was, would he be able to do something?

Valerie refolded the message, and moved swiftly out of the room. Most of the household had retired for the night, although she thought she heard a door close, somewhere downstairs.

There was a thread of light beneath Lacy's door. Valerie tapped lightly, then opened it without waiting for a reply.

"Grandma? May I talk to you?"

Lacy turned from her dressing table, and Valerie was appalled at her appearance, at the change in only a few hours. Lacy was an old woman. Her eyes were haggard, her skin sagging.

"Come in, child. Undo my buttons, will you? My fingers don't work as well as they used to."

Valerie placed the paper before her grandmother, then obediently began to unfasten the tiny buttons. "I don't know who sent it, but there's no reason to think it isn't true. Jack's in Savannah. I'm going there, Grandma Lacy. To beg him to help us. To stop this monstrous thing Mama is planning. I think she's lost her senses, to inflict such a marriage on Julie, and I can't reason with her."

"Nor I," Lacy said quietly. "I tried. I swear to God, I tried." Her eyes filled with moisture.

"Jack owns a manufacturing plant of some sort, and it makes a lot of money. If he can come up with enough to pay the taxes, Mama won't have any excuse to force Julie into anything. We'll have at least a year, then, before they're due again. In a year, anything can happen."

Lacy looked up at her, aged and tired. "Are you going to tell your mother you're going?"

"No. You'll have to tell her, after I've gone; otherwise, I'll never get away. I won't take the buggy, I can go faster with just the mare. I can get there, see Jack, and be back before next Saturday."

"And if Captain Ferris can't help you?"

"Then we'll be no worse off than we are now, will we? You'll have to tell them something, of course. Just that I've . . . I've had a message from Jack and have gone to meet him. Mama will be upset, if she takes any time to think about it, but I can't help that. Better she should be upset than that Julie should have to marry that odious Major Quinn."

"When are you going to leave?"

Lacy didn't so much as question the necessity for the journey, nor protest her traveling alone. She, too, felt that it had to be done.

"At dawn," Valerie decided. "And Grandma Lacy—if I don't get back on time, try to do something to stop them. If it comes down to the last minute, tell Julie what I'm trying to do; tell her to—to run away, anything, hide in the woods, until I get back."

It sounded so wild, when she said it. Yet Lacy only nodded. "Be careful, my dear. Take no unnecessary risks. And good luck."

"Thank you." Valerie bent to kiss her grandmother on the cheek. "I love you, Grandma."

Lacy squeezed her hand, hard, then let her go. She did not remember when she had been so disturbed, and so impotent to remedy the situation. She rose from the dressing table, removing the dress that Valerie had unbuttoned for her, and prepared for bed. She didn't feel well. It was more than just being tired and worried, she thought. Well, she was seventy-three years old; no doubt it was time she began to feel her years. After all, Dolly Mallow had made a career of being indelicate for the past three decades.

Lacy reached for the post at the foot of her bed, steadying herself. Perhaps she ought to call for Lallie, just in case. She stood for a moment, gathering the energy to walk to the door and call; she felt so strange, so . . .

She gave a small, choked cry. Her fingers loosened their hold on the post, and she slid down it into an undignified heap beside the bed.

Lallie found her there in the morning.

Valerie rose well before dawn; she had slept poorly, and it seemed pointless to try to rest any longer. She might better be on the road.

She had to rouse Thomas to saddle the mare. He was too groggy to evince any curiosity; he had visited Gilly until the

472

late hours, and had not been asleep for more than a short time when Valerie called him out.

She took only a few clothes in the saddlebags, along with a supply of food. It had taken nearly three days to reach Savannah in the buggy; she hoped she could better that time considerably on this trip.

She rode hard, but not so hard as to tire the mare too quickly. Twice she stopped to sleep at the homes of acquaintances. Unlike Thomas, they were curious indeed. They did not pry, however, when she volunteered nothing; everyone had problems, these days, and it wasn't considered peculiar to show a reluctance to discuss them.

She arrived in Savannah at midday on Monday. She was exhausted, and grubby, and longed for a bath, a meal, and a bed. She had taken a few coins from her mother's meager supply, only enough to keep herself fed on the return journey if she could not impose on friends. There were no funds for a hotel.

The French house on Pulaski Square, the note had said. That was some distance from her grandmother's house. She might have passed by it, and gone on to Reynolds Square, to ask Shirley Babcock for shelter before she sought out Jack Ferris. She was strongly reluctant, however, to make contact with any of her grandmother's friends. She would, she decided, go directly to the house and hope that Jack was there.

The Frenches had been contemporaries of her grandfather's; Valerie had visited there as a small girl, and played with a French granddaughter whose name she'd forgotten, now. All she remembered was the hand-painted tea set on which they'd been served cake and "tea," well watered with milk, in a handsome blue and gilt drawing room, while their elders visited at the opposite end of it.

When she reached the square, though, Valerie was suddenly uncertain of the house. It must have been painted, because she remembered it as being pink, and there were no pink houses today. She dismounted and tied the weary mare to the post in front of a tall white house with black shutters and intricate lacy ironwork railings and balconies. Was this it? Didn't she remember that magnolia tree?

She couldn't be sure. All she could do was use the knocker and ask. If Jack wasn't here, but in one of the other houses that faced the square, the resident here would probably know which house was his. Why Jack would be here she didn't know, unless it was on business connected with his manufacturing company. Only now, when she'd ridden all this way, did it occur to her that it might be some sort of monstrous hoax, that Jack might not be here at all. And then what would she do?

A maid in a trim uniform opened the door. Not a black maid, but a white one with a New England accent. "Yes, miss? What can I do for you?"

Valerie saw the perceptive gaze sweep over her, taking in the old riding habit, the dusty skirts, the hair that was losing half its pins.

"I'm looking for Captain—for Dr. Jack Ferris. Do I have the right house?"

The maid didn't open the door any wider in an invitation to enter. Instead, a note of suspicion entered her tone. "May I say who's calling, miss?"

"Valerie Stanton, from Mallows." Her heart rate had accelerated and she was aware of the rise and fall of her bosom under the old brown velvet. "Is Dr. Ferris in?"

"No, miss. He's not. Is it a medical matter, miss?"

Valerie felt the stirrings of annoyance. "No, it's not. He's a personal friend. I'd like to come in and wait for him, if you don't mind."

The maid was disinclined to allow her inside, that much was clear. Yet she was also impressed by the note of authority; for all her shabby garments, this was a lady used to giving orders to servants.

The matter was decided when a feminine voice called from inside the house. "Who is it, Zelda?"

"A Miss Valerie Stanton. Says she's a friend of the doctor's."

"Well, invite her in! Bring her in to me, please!"

Silently, Zelda stepped backward, drawing the door with her, so that Valerie could enter.

It was as she remembered it, although it had certainly been refurbished recently, in the same colors. Zelda led the way to a small sitting room done in pink and green, where a young woman reclined on a pink velvet sofa. She did not rise, but lifted a smiling face.

"Good afternoon. Miss Stanton, did you say? Come in, come over here and sit down by me, please. Jack will be here directly, I think."

Uncertain, Valerie stood in the doorway. The occupant of
474

the sofa was clad, she now saw, in a dressing gown of the same color as the sofa, with wide sleeves dripping lace over fragile wrists. She was pale and, surely, in less than robust health; her fair hair hung loose around her shoulders like a child's, though she was obviously in her middle twenties.

"Perhaps I have the wrong house," Valerie said uncertainly. "I'm looking for Dr. Jack Ferris."

The young woman's smile was wanly sweet in the rather ordinary face. "But of course, this is where he lives. Please sit down. My husband," she said, "should be here anytime."

Twenty

Valerie sank into the chair as her legs literally gave out beneath her. Perhaps she looked as ill as she felt, for the self-proclaimed Mrs. Ferris spoke to the maid.

"Zelda, I think our guest has need of a restorative cup of tea." She, too, appraised the riding costume and the signs of travel. "And perhaps something to eat, as well. Some bread and butter, perhaps, and some of the little cakes? The ones that are too rich for me?"

"No, thank you," Valerie murmured. "Nothing to eat." Dear God, she had somehow stepped into a sort of nightmare, and she couldn't imagine how to extricate herself. Jack's wife? There had to be some mistake, this was impossible. Jack wasn't married, he couldn't be.

Yet the girl smiled at her, and said, "I'm Nola Ferris. Did you know my husband when he was here in Savannah at the end of the war?"

Valerie's gaze wandered to the young woman's hand, where a gold wedding band was a loose fit on her third finger, as if she'd lost weight since first putting it on.

"I'm sorry," Valerie said. "I'm not feeling well, I'm afraid. Do you mind if I put my head down . . . ?"

It was true, she felt faint. There must be some explanation; she couldn't think what it could be, however.

"Oh, you poor thing! Would you like to lie down? There's only one bedroom furnished in the house at this time—we've only been here for two weeks, and we are renting, you see— and that's upstairs. But you're weclome to use it if you wish."

"No, no. I'll be all right." She rested her face briefly against her knees until the worst of the giddiness passed. No doubt it was partly that it had been so long since she'd eaten, but the shock contributed to it, too, the feeling of vertigo and nausea that washed over her.

When Zelda returned with the tea tray, Valerie sat up straight and accepted a steaming cup. Get something into her stomach, and maybe her head would begin to work again, she thought.

She remembered thinking, when Jack had eased her out of her clothes and then helped her back into them, at old Sophie's River Street hole in the wall, that he'd had experience in dressing and undressing women. This woman? This plain but pleasant-faced woman who looked as if she might blow away like a bit of dandelion fluff in the slightest of breezes?

Was Jack actually married to her?

If so, what did that make Valerie?

The tea burned her mouth. She held the cup steadily enough, and Nola Ferris watched her solicitously.

"Do you feel better now, Miss Stanton?"

"Yes," Valerie lied. "Thank you."

"So horrid, feeling sick, isn't it? I've been sick for years," Nola said in a burst of candor. "Isn't it terrible of me to say that, to a perfect stranger? So rude! But I hardly ever have anyone to talk to. Because I almost never leave the house, you see. Jack thought that the climate in Georgia might be better for me than at home. We've rented a house out in the country, but I had a rather distressing trip down here and he thought it might be best to stay in town for a short time. Until I'm stronger again, you see. And you said you're a friend of Jack's—I don't think he's mentioned your name, but then, he knows dozens of people I don't know."

She smoothed the pink dressing gown over her knees. "I knew years ago that I'd never be able to hold him on tight strings. You know, keep him at my side because I was housebound. So I try not to mind when he is out and about, attend-

477

ing social functions and so on, without me. I have to trust him, don't I?"

The smile, the pathetic little smile, was like acid thrown in Valerie's face. Trust him? It was true, she had to accept that it was true: Jack was married to this semi-invalid, and had been for a long time. He'd been married to her all the time he'd been at Mallows, during the days they'd met at Patrick Ryan's house, when they'd been together at old Sophie's place. It was all she could do to keep from throwing up.

Everything he'd said to her had been a lie. No wonder he'd been so cagey about making promises, since he couldn't possibly keep them! No wonder he hadn't asked her to marry him and go with him, no wonder, no wonder so many things!

"Do you live here in Savannah?" Nola was asking, and Valerie tried to pull herself together. She wondered what her hostess would think if she asked for some brandy in her tea.

"No." She couldn't say she'd traveled all the way here just to see Jack, not now. "I live on a plantation in Tattnall County. It's called Mallows," Valerie managed. Mallows, which now was surely lost to them forever. Unless Julie married Otis Quinn. Dear God, what a mess.

Nola sat upright, poking at the pillows that supported her. "Mallows? Why, that's the place Jack is taking me, when he decides it's time for me to travel! He's described it for me, a lovely place, he said!"

Taking her to Mallows? Valerie stared at her, confused, hurt, and angry. How could he be taking his wife to Mallows?

"Well, I guess the little place we've rented isn't Mallows itself, but right next door. The gentleman who owns it has leased it to us for the winter. In the spring, we'll probably go back home, because the Southern summers are probably too hot for me. Anyway, we'll be neighbors, won't we? He didn't tell me there were young people next door!"

I'll just bet he didn't, Valerie thought with some grimness. "You've rented Patrick Ryan's house, then?"

"Yes, that's the name. I met him yesterday, when he came to collect the check. He's a very nice man, isn't he?"

"Oh, very nice." If Nola noted the irony, she did not remark on it. Patrick Ryan. He'd rented out his house, he'd known about Jack, had known he was married.

And he hadn't told her. If he'd told her, she wouldn't have come all this way on a fool's errand, she wouldn't have been
478

faced with this incredible painful situation. Damn Patrick, she thought in rising fury, he'd let her walk right into this with no warning. No, the realization quickly followed, he hadn't *let* her, he'd actually invited her into it! *It had been Patrick who sent her the note,* the message about Jack's whereabouts! How could he? How could he have been so unspeakably cruel?

"Jack showed me Mr. Ryan's Savannah house. On one of these lovely squares—what's it called? There are so many of them I haven't learned all the names yet—it's the next one north of us, Orleans? Is that it?"

"Orleans, yes." It was a miracle that she could speak, and so calmly, on trivial matters, when her head was such a muddle. As her anger grew, however, the righteous indignation pushed aside the physical sickness that she felt. "Mr. Ryan has a house on Orleans Square?"

Nola was clearly happy to have someone to talk with. She was a plain little thing, except for the glorious pale hair, but when she smiled she was almost pretty. "Yes. A very tall house, three stories, of red brick and all that gorgeous ironwork. I've never seen such intricate ironwork, it's like lace on all the houses. I love Savannah, don't you? It's the prettiest town I've ever been in. Of course, I haven't been in very many," she said, her brow furrowing as she tried to be scrupulously honest about it. "We had hoped that we would travel, when we were married, and I would see all sorts of places. London, and Paris, and Rome, you know. Only this thing in my chest happened, and it's kept me more or less in bed for the better part of the six years we've been married. Maybe the climate here will make this winter better, though, as Jack thinks. It's so cold in the winter, at home."

Six years, Valerie noted. Six years, he'd been married to her. God in heaven, how could she have been so stupid? So naive? She hadn't even *asked* if he were married, had simply taken it for granted he was free, as she was. Would he have lied, if she'd asked him?

The answer to that was obvious. Of course, he would lie. A married man who would seduce an innocent girl would hardly balk at a few lies. It was so plain, now, that she *had* been seduced. No matter that she'd been willing, that she'd longed for love and reached out to take what was offered.

Would it ever have happened, that first time, if he hadn't plied her with brandy, which she wasn't used to? Granted

479

that once she'd known the joys of lovemaking she hadn't needed the brandy, but it had certainly helped to break down her inhibitions. And later, at Sophie's—Lord, she could die of the shame of remembering! He'd paid Sophie for the use of her room, he'd had the wine ready there, and softened up her resistance with it, and he'd done it all with the expertise of long practice. How many other women had he taken there, to Sophie's, and to other places?

Nola didn't seem to notice her visitor's agitation. "I'm going to like it in Georgia, and especially when we go out to Mallows," she said. She reminded Valerie of a stray kitten, one that's been found sick and abused and wasted away, cleaned up now, but still a poor little wisp of a thing. "I'm so glad we're going to have close neighbors. I hope you'll visit us often, Miss Stanton. I'll be so eager for company. At home my cousins and their children are in and out, and I'll miss them dreadfully. Josephine has two little boys, and Caroline has three little girls, and they're such darlings. Children liven up a house, don't they? Jack and I had hoped to have children, but after I became ill all the doctors said I should never attempt it. I would have been willing to try, anyway, but Jack said no. He wouldn't let me risk my life. It was enough to be just the two of us, he said."

The two of them, and whatever other hapless female he came upon. Valerie had never felt such rage as she felt at the moment against Jack Ferris. What if *she* had gotten pregnant? What would she have done with the child? Besides disgrace herself and her family, of course. She knew little of such matters, but she didn't think Jack had done anything to prevent a pregnancy. He certainly couldn't have *married* her.

She had drained the teacup, and she put it down carefully in the dainty saucer. "Thank you for the tea. I think—I think I had better go."

She had no idea where she would go. She only knew she could not confront Jack in front of this pallid, trusting woman. Not when she wanted to kill him, to fly at him and tear his eyes out with her fingernails. She had never hated anyone, not even the Yankees who would have raped her, as intensely as she now hated Jack Ferris. The soldiers had at least been honest about their intentions, dishonorable though those had been. While Jack misled her in every conceivable way.

480

She had risen from the chair when she heard the front door open, and knew with soaring panic that it was too late.

He came into the room smiling, calling out a greeting. "Darling, guess what? I found a—"

His smile froze when he saw Valerie. His dark gaze moved to his wife, then back to the slender figure in worn brown velvet, and then the smile came again. Not quite as bright or as deep, but reasonably convincing.

"Valerie! What a surprise! How long have you been here?"

Long enough, Valerie thought. She couldn't believe it, that he looked as he always had: handsome, assured, pleasant. She wouldn't have been taken aback if he'd grown horns since their last meeting.

"Miss Stanton wasn't feeling well, and I offered her a cup of tea," Nola said. She lifted her face, and Jack reached her in three long strides and kissed her on the cheek before turning back to Valerie as if she were any ordinary guest.

"I was just leaving," Valerie said. It was a miracle that she could speak to him in a normal tone of voice, that her fury and frustration and hurt didn't come through in it. "I don't think we have anything to discuss, after all."

"Don't be silly, of course we do. We can go across the hall, into the study. Nola's probably going up for a nap shortly, anyway, aren't you, love? Do you want me to carry you up now?"

She's wild about him, Valerie thought. It shone from her countenance as if she were lit from within. Well, that was understandable. *She'd* been wild about him, too, hadn't she?

"I'll only be a minute," Jack said to Valerie, and then, calling out, "Zelda, will you take Miss Stanton into the study, please? And put out the whiskey!"

"Darling," Nola remonstrated gently. "At this time of day?"

"Only a taste, for medicinal purposes. I think Miss Stanton needs it," Jack said, in a way that made Valerie want to pick up the poker from beside the hearth and strike him with it.

She had no intention of staying, of waiting for him to come back down from the bedroom he shared with his wife. She fully understood at last how it was possible to murder someone. Someone you'd once known and loved. She had no idea where she was going to go. She only knew she had to escape from this house, and from Jack Ferris.

"Miss," Zelda said, alarmed, when she went toward the

front door instead of following the maid into the indicated room. "Miss, the doctor said—"

Valerie ignored her. She went down the front steps and stared out across the square, which formed a garden for all the facing houses. There was a bench, shaded by the moss-swagged oaks, and her first impulse was to sit there for a moment, to gather her resources and decide what to do. It would have been smarter to walk briskly away, but she wasn't sure her legs would carry her.

It was in plain sight of Jack's front door, however. Go somewhere else, and quickly, before he came back downstairs.

It was already too late. She heard his feet on the brick steps behind her, and made a convulsive movement toward the mare, but Jack grasped her arm before she could attempt to mount.

"Valerie, where are you going? Come back inside, we need to talk."

She spun on him then, face contorted with the emotion she felt. "You bastard!" she spat at him. "You rotten bastard!"

"Darling, you're misinterpreting—"

"Am I? I've made a lot of mistakes, but I don't think I'm making one now! You're married to her, aren't you? For six years?"

His fingers tightened and he shook her enough to make her realize that she couldn't leave him until he released her. "Stop it. Yes, I've been married to her for six years. And for five and three quarters of those years she's been an invalid. Three times she's nearly died. She's seriously ill, and she can't live much longer. Probably not through another winter, even a mild one. To be truthful, I didn't expect that she'd still be there when I went home, at the end of the war. Valerie, I love you. I told you that, and I meant it."

"The way you love *her*? When the mood strikes you, and there's a bed handy? When there's no one else about to interfere in your sport?"

He glanced up at the house as if to assure himself that they were not observed from within. "Look, we can't talk here. It's too public, and you're overwrought—"

"Overwrought? You think I shouldn't be?" She'd thought she was gaining control of herself, only a moment ago, and now the hysteria rose again; she would have struck him if he hadn't caught her wrist and held it.

"I know you're upset, and I'm not surprised. I hadn't planned for you to learn about it this way—"

"How had you planned it? Simply to move into Ryan's house, and invite me over for tea, and to meet your wife, and then perhaps for a tumble on the bed, downstairs, while Nola takes her nap up above us?"

"Stop it. I'm going to slap you, hard, if you don't stop it. I mean it, Valerie. Come over here, we'll sit on the bench, and we'll talk like civilized people. You must have come for something, you didn't just stroll in for a casual visit. So calm down and tell me what it was."

She had little choice other than to go with him. At least within the square they were less conspicuous, although she was almost beyond caring about that. She hated him, she wanted never to see him again. Yet he was stronger, and if he chose to restrain her physically, why, the reasonable thing was to give in, at least temporarily. She allowed him to settle her on the bench. He didn't trust her, he kept a hand on her wrist, between them where it wouldn't be noticeable to a casual passerby.

"You've ridden all the way from Mallows, and you didn't know about Nola until just now. Why did you need me?"

It was incredible that she'd ever needed him, physically, the way that she had. Incredible that she'd ever thought she loved him, when he was capable of treating any female in such shabby fashion. Yet she was aware of the leaping pulse beneath his fingers, the purely animal response. Maybe Patrick was right; maybe it was *all* animal response, and nothing to do with love. Could you love someone you didn't even know? Someone totally different from what you'd thought he was? Someone completely lacking in decency and honor?

"What's happened?" Jack asked, and there was a convincing concern in his face. How could he do that, when in that house behind them the fragile Nola was taking a nap, waiting for him to return?

"What's happened." She repeated the words, dully, her agitation subsiding somewhat as sheer depression seeped in. "The taxes on Mallows amount to sixteen hundred dollars, which we can't pay. I was going to ask you for help in taking care of it." Her mouth twisted in a bitter parody of amusement. "Either we pay the taxes, or they take the property away from us. Or Julie has to marry Otis Quinn."

Jack's eyes narrowed. "Otis Quinn!"

"Yes. He's the new tax collector. And it seems he's taken a fancy for Mallows, and for Julie. Mama's willing to allow him to do it, to marry her, but I wasn't. I thought about you, and that manufacturing plant, and I thought maybe you could help us."

She stared at him, so close, as she had viewed him so many times, and thought how she'd loved him, how she'd known every line of jaw and mouth and forehead, how the hairline grew, and the whiskers showed dark by mid-afternoon. She'd known those things, those superficial things. Yet she knew nothing at all of the man inside that frame, behind that face that had so captivated her.

To her surprise, for he hadn't shown any embarrassment up to now, Jack's color heightened. His voice went husky. "My God. I didn't know it was that bad. And Quinn, why the hell does he want to marry Julie? She's only a little older than his own daughters!"

"He wants Mallows, I suppose. For nothing. Maybe Julie is just a bonus. I don't know. I only know she'd rather die than marry him. I'm afraid for her."

"My God," Jack said again. If he wasn't shaken, he was a superb actor. He let go of her wrist and stared off across the square. "Valerie—Valerie, I'd help if I could. If I had the money I'd give it to you. I want you to know that."

She said nothing. By turning her head only slightly, she could see the brick house where he lived. Was that Nola's bedroom—*their* bedroom—on the top floor, where the blinds were drawn? What did it matter, though. She sagged against the bench, her eyes suddenly stinging. Even this pain that she felt through the overpowering anger was nothing, compared to what was happening to Julie.

Jack cleared his throat and spoke without looking at her. "There is money," he said. "Only it isn't—yet—technically mine. You see, the factory belongs to my father-in-law, Nola's father. He's old, and sick, and he hasn't taken an active part in the business in years. He thought I'd do it, run it, I mean. That was one reason he agreed to our marriage. He's put everything in her name; when he dies it will belong to Nola. We have a living allowance, but quite frankly, it takes pretty much all of it to live the way Nola's used to. So I haven't any ready cash of my own. Even the house, at home, is the family one. I can't sell it, not until the old man dies."

484

Valerie stared at him in disbelief. "And you're sitting here, waiting for that? For your *wife* to die?"

"Your tone of voice is out of line, love," Jack told her, and now he did look at her, which made it worse. Because it was the same dear face, and just as attractive as it had ever been, and his voice pleaded for understanding. "I married Nola in good faith, because I fell in love with her. Not for her father's money. I still care for her, because she's a sweet, darling girl. But she's like a sister, not a wife. She's been ill for so long, and all the doctors who were consulted were agreed on one thing, at least. That she cannot possibly have a child. Valerie, I have not touched her, haven't slept with her, in five and a half years. I swear to God."

She was cold, beginning to feel the fine tremors spread through her. "*She's* your wife, not me. You don't have to justify anything to me in that regard."

"Damn it, Valerie, stop it! I have to make you understand, because it's *you* I love! Only I can't leave her! It would be like deserting a child, a sick child! All I can do is wait until it's over, and then I'll be free to marry you, the way I want to do!"

She couldn't believe it. The tremor increased until she could see it in her hands, the hands she knotted together beneath her breasts. "And you want me to wait? Until she dies?"

"It won't be long. Less than a year, maybe only months. Don't look like that! There's nothing I can do about it, nothing anyone can do! She has an incurable illness, and I have the obligation to make her final months as comfortable and as contented as I can make them. I take nothing from Nola; it's out of my hands. But I'd be a fool if I didn't look past the point of her death. Especially since I met you and fell in love with you."

"You never told me about her." She examined the scuffed toe of her boot. "You never told me you were married."

"Valerie." He recaptured her hand. "How could I tell you? What would it have accomplished? For all I knew, I could have been a free man by the time the war was ended. She was deathly ill when I got home, only a few months ago. She recovered against all odds, but the doctors are all convinced that she has little time left. My own professional opinion is the same. Why should that make me a ghoul, if in knowing that she's dying I want to hang on to something wonderful that I found somewhere else?"

"If I'd known you were married," Valerie said, "I would never have—"

She couldn't say the words.

"Do you honestly wish we hadn't had those times together? I don't! They were beautiful to me, and I thought they were to you, too. Listen, Valerie, I know this has all been a shock to you. Don't do anything hasty. Give yourself time to think. Give me time to persuade you—"

She jerked away from his exploring hand on her arm.

"No. No, don't. You've said enough; the picture is clear to me. Only why did you have to come back here? Why didn't you just drop out of my life?"

"Because you're too important in *my* life. Because I love you." It was said with a quiet sincerity that she could not doubt, but she couldn't trust it, either.

Valerie stood up, ignoring her quaking insides. "I have to go now. Goodbye, Jack."

"Wait for me," he said. "Say you'll wait."

She didn't reply to that. She walked quickly across the street, where she blindly unfastened the mare, wanting only to escape. There was nothing to use as a mounting block, so she led the horse. Indeed, she was only vaguely aware of what she did. Eventually, she supposed, she would collapse in hysterical sobs. Right now, she was dry-eyed and numb. For the moment, she didn't even hate Jack any more.

She had walked for some distance before she gradually became aware of her surroundings. Orleans Square, the sign said. Valerie stopped, blinking. This was where Nola Ferris had said Patrick Ryan maintained a house. A red brick house. That one, perhaps, with the ornate railings and grill-work over the ground-floor windows.

Patrick Ryan. He, too, wanted Mallows. He, like Otis Quinn, was willing to marry to get it. As Jack had married a girl whose father owned a manufacturing plant. Were all men alike? More concerned with the financial advantages of a marriage than with love? At least Patrick had been open about it. He'd coveted Mallows since he was a boy, and he still wanted it.

Was there any chance at all that Patrick would help her, with a loan? No, no, what was she thinking? He'd already

486

said he wouldn't do that. The only way he'd save Mallows was for himself, if she married him.

She stood on the edge of the square, staring at the house she thought might belong to Patrick.

Well, she couldn't have Jack. She couldn't picture herself waiting for that poor girl to die, so that she could marry him. The idea of saving Mallows with a dead girl's money turned her stomach, even if Mallows could wait for such a thing to happen.

So why not consider marrying Patrick? If the choice was between that and letting Julie be forced into a marriage with Otis Quinn, which was the lesser of two evils? Patrick wasn't old, he wasn't repulsive. In fact, it had already occurred to her that if it hadn't been that she loved someone else, she might have grown to have some affection for Patrick. The idea of going to bed with him didn't make her want to vomit, as the thought of it with Quinn affected Julie.

Valerie looked at the house, and wondered where the courage would come from, to walk up those steps and ring the bell. She'd shouted after him that he needn't wait for her to come to him, begging, and here she was already.

"Valerie?"

She turned, throat constricting, to see him coming toward her. Walking, bareheaded, striding along the brick walk as if he owned it, and the square, and maybe all of Savannah.

"What's the matter? What are you doing here?"

She swallowed, trying to come up with the right words, failing. He took the reins and secured the horse to his front fence—it had been the right house—and steered her up the steps.

"Come inside. There should be a fire in here—" He opened a door and ushered her into a room that, under normal circumstances, she would have found very comfortable. As it was, she simply sank into a chintz-covered chair near the fireplace and waited while he brought a bottle and a pair of glasses. He didn't ask if she wanted it, he poured and handed her the whiskey. "You look like you need this."

"I guess I do." She swallowed, choked, and sipped again. "Thank you. I've had a dreadful afternoon. Thanks to you, I suppose." He'd taken the chair opposite her, so she didn't have to get a crick in her neck looking up at him. "You sent the note, didn't you? The one telling me where to find Jack?"

487

He answered that obliquely. "I take it you've been to Pulaski Square?"

"Why didn't you tell me he was married? Instead of doing it . . . that way?"

"Would you have believed me? Wouldn't you have had to see for yourself, anyway?"

She sagged into the chair, letting her hands go limp on the polished maple arms of it. "I don't know. Maybe. Did you want to hurt me?"

"I wanted you to see him for what he is. An opportunist son of a bitch." He waited, briefly, to give her an opening to defend Jack. She was too weary to do it. "He married the girl for her money, then found out she wouldn't get it until her father died. Which the old man hasn't quite managed to do, yet, although I'm told he's in poor health. And the girl herself has been on the verge of death for the past five or six years. The situation could go on for five or six more, for all anybody knows. Did he ask you to wait until she dies?"

Valerie didn't answer that. She moved her head against the padded chair back, gathering her courage. "I thought he might be able to help," she said, sounding young and lost. "With the taxes. Because the only alternative to paying them seems to be forcing Julie into marrying Major Quinn."

He sat with little expression on his face, watching her, but that brought him forward. "Julie? And Otis Quinn? And your mother's going along with it?"

She didn't feel up to defending her mother, either. "Yes. The wedding is to be next Saturday."

Into the small silence she exhaled audibly. Apparently he wasn't going to make it easy for her. Or maybe he'd changed his mind, maybe he no longer wanted her, and Mallows.

"And you were coming to me?"

"I don't know. I didn't pay any attention, at least consciously, where I was going when I left Jack's house. I did know where you were, though; Nola told me." Why did she feel she had to be so scrupulously honest, when it felt as if she flayed her own skin from her body? "I hadn't decided, yet, what to do. When you came along."

"And now?"

She made herself say it. "Do you still want me? And Mallows?"

"Yes." It was said dispassionately. "Would you like a formal proposal?"

488

She supposed that, eventually, she would feel relief. Now, she felt nothing. "I'll have to go back to Mallows before Saturday. Convince everyone that there's no need for Julie to marry Quinn. Then——" She hesitated. "We could . . . could be married next month."

For long seconds Patrick Ryan looked at her, and then he shook his head. "No. I'll send the money to Mallows, by messenger, to make sure it gets there safely, to pay the taxes. And we'll be married tomorrow."

She checked the objection that had risen automatically. Tomorrow or a month from now, what difference did it make?

"I'm here on horseback. I have only the change of clothes I brought in the saddlebags."

He shrugged. "We can buy clothes here. There's one thing, Valerie. It's not only Mallows. This has to be a real marriage. None of this separate rooms, marriage-in-name-only business. I expect a wife, a real wife, and a family."

Her face was still, empty. "You aren't going to give an inch, are you?" she asked.

"No," Patrick said. "Are you?"

She remained silent, and after a moment Patrick rose and crossed the room to an oak desk. "I'll write out the check," he said, and Valerie closed her eyes and remained there, listening to the scratch of the pen on the paper, until he had finished.

Twenty-One

Blossom arrived at Mallows on Sunday to find the household in a turmoil. Miss Lacy had apparently suffered a stroke; Lallie had found her, almost lifeless, on the floor of her bedroom. She had been put to bed, and so far had not regained consciousness.

Added to that, Valerie was gone. There was no message of any kind, and they could only guess at her destination and her purpose. Thomas reported that she'd had him saddle the mare; that was all they knew.

Although it was mealtime, Julie had withdrawn to her room and refused to come out or to reply to anyone. Ellen looked like death warmed over, as Blossom noted when she finally managed to corner Pansy.

"What's going on?"

"Miss Ellen say Miss Julie got to marry Major Quinn, or else we goin' to lose Mallows," Pansy reported. "This place sure a mess."

"Oh. Well, I'm sorry," Blossom said. "I have a gentleman waitin' for me. I'll just get my things and go, then."

She had expected that leaving Mallows would be a sad thing, but it wasn't. The house Jim Healy had brought her to was very nice, too, without being intimidating the way a

490

grand house was. And he'd told her she could decorate it any way she wanted to. So far he hadn't done any more than put an arm around her waist and kiss her, and she'd been smart enough to suggest that a ring on her finger would make her more generous with her favors. When she said she wasn't the sort of girl to settle for less than marriage, he'd only laughed. But he respected her. Blossom fully expected that ring long before the winter was out.

If there was a lot of trouble at Mallows, she was just as well out of it, she thought. Her only regret was that she hadn't been able to introduce Mr. Healy to Valerie and Julie.

Lacy, of course, could pass on no message to anyone. When, on Tuesday, she opened her eyes, there was intelligence in them. She could not speak, however. Ellen leaned over the bed, asking, "Do you know where Valerie's gone?" and Lacy could only blink her eyes.

Frustrated, Ellen withdrew. How like Valerie, to go off selfishly on her own errands, at a time like this. (That was totally unfair, but Ellen was too distraught to recognize the fact.) Although perhaps it was just as well, since Valerie'd made it clear she had no intention of trying to persuade Julie to be sensible.

Old Hattie was called in to nurse Lacy, which she undertook with compassion. Hattie didn't mind nursing the sick, especially since the task required that she stay in the house. Between invalids, she had feared they might send her out to the quarters, and this time of year the cold made her bones ache.

Julie, isolated, terrified, rebellious yet without the courage to escape from the torment of living as Charlotte and Evan had escaped, emerged from her room only because Ellen refused to allow anyone to bring her food up to her after that first day.

"This is absurd. You're not the first bride whose marriage was arranged, and you won't be the last. You're certainly going to be a wretched-looking bride, if you don't stop crying all day and all night."

"I feel like crying," Julie said.

One could not, however, cry forever. By Friday, when the wedding party arrived, her face was no longer blotchy and swollen, although her eyes remained slightly puffy. Please God, she prayed, let Valerie have gone for help. Where, and from whom, she couldn't so much as guess.

If the messenger with Patrick's bank draft had ridden straight to Mallows, as instructed, the money would have been handed over to Ellen on Thursday afternoon. He did not, however. In a tavern on the edge of Claxton, on Wednesday evening, he ate a hearty supper and drank even more heartily of an excellent ale. The barmaid was a pretty miss of some fifteen years, whose roguish eyes issued an invitation that Andrew Portsmouth could not resist, and he followed her out into the night when the revelry in the tavern came to an end.

He remembered kissing her, there in the deep shadows at the end of the building. He never knew whether he had been any more successful than that. He didn't remember the blow on the head, although he had a vague recollection of striking out at someone.

When he awoke, it was not only broad daylight, but the shadows across the floor of the unfamiliar room indicated that the afternoon was far gone.

"Ah, it's wakin' up, you are," a woman's voice said. She was fat, and smelled of sweat and kitchen smoke. "There's a good lad, take a sip of this."

He didn't have to ask what had happened. He'd been beaten and robbed. He looked at his trousers across the back of the nearest chair. "Did they get it all?"

"All the money, I'm afraid," the woman said cheerfully. "They didn't bother with this, though. I found it on the ground, and thought maybe it was important."

It was Patrick's bank draft. Crumpled, where someone had walked upon it, but intact. Possibly the thieves hadn't even realized what it was, or maybe they'd known it was made out to someone else and they couldn't transform it into money themselves.

"I got to deliver it right away," Andrew said, and raised up in bed, only to fall back, gasping and holding his head.

The tavern keeper's wife laughed. "Not today, laddy. Maybe tomorrow, if you're lucky. Here, take another sip o' this."

And so it was that the bank draft was delivered a day later than it should have been, and it was not handed into Ellen's hands, at all. She was busy elsewhere when Andrew reached the front door, and Lallie took it. A moment later, Major Quinn saw it in her hand.

"What's that you have there?" he asked.

492

"This come for Miss Ellen." Lallie didn't like the way the man looked at her; it was like having Mr. Roger in the house again, only worse. Her heart bled for poor little Miss Julie. She'd have been afraid for herself, except that she was leaving, with Aaron, as soon as she knew Miss Ellen was all right.

"I'll take it," Quinn said, and removed it from her unresisting fingers. When she had fled, he ripped it open, scanned the check and the brief message that accompanied it, and stood for a moment, a muscle twitching in one cheek. Then he stalked to the study, put the message and check into a drawer, and locked the drawer, pocketing the key.

Interfering bastard, he thought of Patrick, and then forgot about him. Tomorrow was his wedding day, and tonight, why, tonight he'd find diversion elsewhere, to take the edge off his increasing excitement.

Valerie slept her first night in Savannah in a hotel, an experience she had always looked forward to and now cared nothing about. Patrick had taken her there in his own carriage, had requested that she be served by a maid, and had told her he would meet her in the morning for breakfast, at ten.

The way she felt, Valerie reflected, allowing the young black girl to help her undress and get into the tin tub of warm water, she would be unconscious at ten in the morning. She was utterly worn out, and not even the prospect of marrying a man she had no desire to marry was enough to draw her out of the lethargy induced by physical and emotional exhaustion.

The girl brought a meal to her room, and she ate it in bed, nearly falling asleep into the plates. She had no idea, later, what the food had been.

The maid roused her at nine-thirty. "Mornin', miss. The gentleman say make you pretty by ten, 'cause he havin' breakfas' sent up then."

Valerie came reluctantly up through layers of consciousness. "What gentleman?" she asked crossly, and then she remembered.

That brought her into a sitting position, wide awake.

Patrick Ryan. Whom she was supposed to marry today.

To one reared in a society where such things as marriages were often arranged to family advantage, the idea of marrying a man one had not personally chosen, for love, was hardly startling. Contemplating it from the space of only a few hours away was disquieting, however.

Much as she had enjoyed going to bed with Jack Ferris, and already knowing that Patrick's touch was not repugnant to her, Valerie still knew uneasiness. Would he be able to tell that she was not a virgin, for instance? And if he did, how would he feel about it? Even an innocent miss knew that there was a double standard about the matter, although for the life of her she couldn't see why there should be. A man was expected to indulge his sexual needs, indeed was often encouraged to do so, while no decent female succumbed to sexual temptation until after marriage.

No decent female. How righteous she had felt, thinking that Jack would eventually marry her, convincing herself that making love was not really wrong when two people deeply cared for each other! For a moment a resurgence of yesterday's anger nearly choked her.

But there was no sense in thinking about that. Patrick had promised that the bank draft would go off to her mother by messenger this morning, and that should assure that Julie would escape Major Quinn's dastardly plans for her. Valerie had always thought *dastardly* a quaint, old-fashioned, silly sort of word, when she came across it in novels. Today, however, she decided that it fitted Otis Quinn in a way that was far from silly.

And if she could not marry the man she loved—or had thought she loved—what difference did it make, if she must, instead, marry Patrick? While the little black girl helped her to dress—in the simple, rather dowdy light wool gown that was all she had with her, except for the riding habit—Valerie thought about Jack, as inevitably she must.

Did she love him? Patrick had suggested that it was not love at all, but lust, although he hadn't used that crude word. Was he right? She didn't think so. She was angry at Jack, and hurt. She also missed him, or at least the man she'd thought he was. She had a suspicion that she would go on missing him, for a long time.

She looked anything but bride-like when Patrick arrived, along with a waiter bearing a steaming tray. All very proper, with the door left open into the corridor, and the waiter serving scrambled eggs and small sausages and hot biscuits with

494

melting butter and honey, and sliced oranges with sugar on them.

She had not thought herself hungry, yet once the covers were removed from the dishes, Valerie found her appetite readily restored. She very nearly matched Patrick, bite for bite.

"I thought the easiest thing," he told her, when they had finished and the waiter gathered up the dishes to be carried away, "would be to have the shopkeepers come here. You can see what they have, and make your selections in comfort, rather than traipsing all over town. Of course for today you'll have to settle for readymade things. You can order anything you want, however, to be custom-made, for later delivery."

"Anything?" Valerie echoed. "It must be very nice, to have unlimited funds."

"If you think *you* can appreciate that, after only a few years of relatively affluent poverty by the standards of ordinary people," Patrick observed dryly, "then you should look at it from my viewpoint. Of more than thirty years of watching other people enjoy things I didn't have. Yes, you're damned right. It's very nice to have unlimited funds. If they aren't quite unlimited yet, they will be. And there's certainly enough now to clothe my wife appropriately."

Obviously Patrick was not going to be one of those husbands who bothered to apologize for swearing in his wife's presence; watching him now, across the room, as he leaned an elbow on the mantel and lit a cigar, Valerie suspected that he might not apologize for anything, ever.

The dressmakers came, and the milliners, and the man with the boots and evening slippers. Valerie looked at the spread-out wares and gave Patrick an awed grin. "Maybe you'd better tell me when to stop."

He waved a negligent hand. "Go ahead. Pick out what you want."

She did, getting into the spirit of it with reckless abandon when he made it clear that he meant what he said. She thought of the apricot velvet, which was finished and hanging in the chifforobe at home, and knew that none of these could match it for beauty. They ought, all of the dresses, to have been worn with a black armband, at least, in mourning for Evan now that the obligatory year had passed since her father's death. But black for mourning was not a custom strictly adhered to in an era when no one could afford to buy new clothes. One wore what one had, and if there was no black even for a band, why, everyone understood.

She chose half a dozen gowns which could be altered very quickly to fit her, and from the bolts of silks and exquisite woolens, a dozen more, to be made up. It was an exhilarating sensation, enough so that she forgot why she was choosing them, and who would pay for them, until all the samples had been gathered up and carried away.

Patrick was regarding her with wry amusement. "It appears that a female can bear up under any deprivation better than the lack of pretty clothes," he observed.

She remembered the apricot velvet, for which she had thanked him so inadequately with a brief note. "I suppose that's true. We hunger for them, after so long without." She hesitated, then asked impulsively, "Did you know, about the velvet? Or did you simply—win it, in a poker game or something?"

For a moment she thought he would not answer. Then he rose from his chair and reached for his hat on the table beside it. "I was curious to know what had drawn your attention when it was dangerous to be on the streets because of the Yankees. I asked the lady in the shop, and she said you'd been taken with that bolt of material."

So he'd bought it, not won it. Valerie felt a strange uneasiness, one she could not have described and did not understand. "It was the most beautiful stuff I'd ever seen. I thank you for it."

He brushed aside her gratitude as of no consequence. "I'll send the carriage for you at half-past three. I've arranged for Reverend Sweeting to perform the ceremony, in my drawing room, at four. Under the circumstances, I assumed we would invite no one beyond the necessary witnesses. Unless there is someone . . .?"

He waited, and Valerie shook her head.

"I'll see you this afternoon, then," he told her, and took his leave. She leaned against the door after it had closed behind him. Someone? Whom did she know in Savannah, except Jack and now his wife, Nola? Nola might have been her friend, under other circumstances, she thought.

She walked to the window that looked down on the street, watching as Patrick emerged from below and strode away. After a few seconds, her eyes blurred, and she couldn't see him any more.

The ceremony was concluded, and the Reverend Sweeting and his wife had departed. The plain gold band on her finger felt tight and uncomfortable, although it moved easily enough when she twisted it. She had worn the most simple of the newly acquired gowns, a pale yellow silk with a very full skirt (though without hoops) and a plain tight bodice that molded her breasts and modestly covered everything but the base of her throat where she felt the rapid pulsing of her blood. She was obscurely glad that there had been no white dress available.

Now, alone with Patrick, waiting for the girl to serve their supper in the small sitting room he preferred to the drawing room, Valerie was aware of a resurgence of nervousness. She had gone through the wedding itself as if she were wrapped in cotton wool, insulated from everything around her.

Finally, however, that curious detachment that had sustained her through the ceremony was wearing off. Within a few hours she would have to go to bed with Patrick, and the very idea of it made her increasingly disquieted.

Patrick, too, seemed restless and less at ease than he usually was. It made it more obvious that, in general, Patrick Ryan was confident and controlled. He bent over to draw a light for his cigar from the fire on the hearth, and she thought that he had come a long way from a poverty-stricken cracker's son to this assured and competent man in his charming house in Savannah. A grudging admiration arose within her, even as she feared (a little) his new stature. He was no longer cowed by the aristocracy, as why should he be? The aristocracy of the South was no more. General Sherman had vowed to make Georgia squeal, but it seemed to her, now, that it was more like a whimper.

Patrick was watching her, his blue eyes unreadable, as they so often were. And then he grinned.

"Is your stomach fluttering, the way mine is?"

She was astonished that he would be feeling that way, too, and even more amazed that he would admit it. "It's probably only that we're hungry. I couldn't eat any lunch."

He laughed. "I didn't eat any, either. I forgot about it. Well, let's settle things down with a glass of champagne, while we wait for our dinner." He turned away, toward an iced bucket she hadn't noticed on the table in the corner. "I suppose we should have shared it with the Sweetings, but to tell you the truth, I couldn't wait for them to be gone."

497

It wasn't the first bottle of champagne he'd opened and poured, either. Where had he learned things like this, she wondered? You couldn't learn everything from reading books. Could you? What had he done in the years he'd been away, besides fighting the Yankees?

He put the slender stemmed glass into her hand, and Valerie held it until he'd lifted his own. "To us," Patrick said. "To a long and happy marriage."

The toast made her want to cry. Her eyes stung, and she sipped quickly, hoping he would take it for granted that the wine, not the emotions of the moment, was responsible for the moisture in her eyes.

It should have been like this with Jack, she thought. They should have been able to marry, to toast each other in joyful anticipation of their wedding night and all the nights to come. And now there would never be Jack, only Patrick.

Valerie swallowed hard against the surge of longing that swept her, and reminded herself why she had agreed to this. Jack was already married, and he could not claim her. But Julie was saved, Mallows was saved. Like thousands of women before her, Valerie thought, she would survive, too.

It was not Julie, nor Mallows, that Valerie thought about a few hours later when she stood in the bedroom of Patrick Ryan's rented Savannah house.

There had been more champagne after the quiet, elegant supper eaten before the fire. More, but not enough.

She had supposed that Patrick would leave her alone, or to the ministrations of a maid, to prepare for bed. He did not, and so he saw that her fingers trembled over the fastenings, saw her clumsiness, and came to her to help.

Patrick, like Jack Ferris, had also had some experience in the matter of removing female garments, she thought. When, where, and with whom, had he gained this expertise? Not that it mattered; all that was important was that she *think of something*, something other than the hours just ahead of her.

It was not beyond belief that she could have been so mistaken about Jack, for he had presented a certain face to her and she had accepted it for what it appeared to be. Patrick, though, she had been acquainted with Patrick all her life. She had thought she certainly knew the sort of man he was—knowledgeable about estate matters, all business, a man who did his job and kept his place. And now she recognized with

498

a frightening clarity that she didn't know any more about Patrick than she had known about Jack. The man behind that tanned unsmiling face, behind the discerning blue eyes that stripped away her garments even before his hands literally completed the task, was a stranger.

He tossed the clothing carelessly to one side, and stood looking at her in the lamplight. Valerie reached out for the gown that lay across the foot of the bed—a tucked and ruffled and laced lawn shift that Patrick had bought for her only this morning—but he flicked it out of her hand.

"You won't need that for a while," he said.

If he had been nervous, there was no sign of it now. He divested himself of his own garments in a few fluid movements, and the part of her mind that was still functioning noted the broadness of his shoulders, the mat of curling red hair she hadn't expected against the pale skin of his wide chest, the lean waist and flanks. And, of course, the evidence of his rising desire.

She knew, without knowing precisely *how* she knew, that a man could feel physical desire for *any* female; there need be nothing romantic about it, no love, which seemed quite beyond all logic. How much more meaningful it would all be, if love were a prerequisite for it all!

When Patrick spoke, his words were different from what she'd expected too.

"I've waited a long time for this," he told her. "When you were only a little girl, maybe ten or eleven years old, dressed in a pale green gown and looking very much the lady, your father caught me looking at you. Not in any disrespectful way, just looking, the way a hungry child peers into a shop window and tries to quiet the rumbling of his belly on the odors of baking bread. And you know what he said to me?"

Valerie stood, conscious of her nakedness, and of his, unable to move or speak.

"He said, 'If you ever touch one of my daughters, Ryan, I'll have you hung up by your thumbs and beaten to death. And don't you forget that, boy, because I'll wield the whip myself.' I never stopped looking at you, but I managed to be a lot more careful about it from that time on."

He reached for her, then, and carried her to the bed, and her eyes flared in alarm, because he had left the lamp lighted. She could never do this in the lamplight, looking into his face and Patrick gazing into hers; he would see too much, and she would feel too much.

"Please," she murmured. "The lamp."

He hesitated, and she nearly choked on the panicky certainty that he would refuse to put it out. And then he twisted, reached out with one muscular, white-skinned arm that went so oddly with the brown face and hands, and lowered the wick.

In the moments before the small flame was extinguished, she saw his face above hers, and then she closed her eyes and felt his mouth claiming her own.

Pretend, she thought in anguish. *Pretend that it is Jack, before you knew about Nola,* but she could not. Everything about Patrick was different, the taste of him, the smell of him, the texture of his skin and hair. He wasn't Jack, he would never be Jack.

And yet, with his mouth and hands upon her body, Valerie gradually began to respond. She had, after all, been completely carried away in the ecstasy of Jack's lovemaking; could she go for the rest of her lifetime without ever again experiencing that rapturous elation? Might it not be possible to learn to feel it again with someone else?

It was not her own intent to try, however, that aroused her. It was Patrick, who had certainly not spent a celibate thirty or so years, for he knew (even better than Jack) exactly where, and how, to touch her, to bring her, gasping and shuddering, to a powerful climax.

A final cry escaped her lips as Patrick sagged against her, his own passion spent in a last convulsive thrust, and only then—too late—did she remember that *she* was not supposed to be experienced, that she'd intended to *pretend innocence*. If she could not bring her husband virginity, she could at least have salved his pride by making him *think* she was a virgin.

Patrick rolled to one side, leaving an arm across her heaving breasts. "I'm sorry, did I hurt you?"

He had not. He had, indeed, been as gentle as if this *were* her first time, and had been at great pains to see her aroused, too, before taking his own pleasure.

She ought to have assured him of that, but she could not speak. Her throat ached, her eyes stung, and speech was beyond her. Patrick reached up to touch her damp cheeks, and she feared that he would ask for an explanation of those tears

500

which she could not give, for she did not understand them herself.

He made no demands, however. He raised himself on an elbow and kissed her, very gently, on the mouth, then sank back onto the pillow. Within two or three minutes, his breathing took on the regularity of sleep.

Valerie lay awake, fighting the need to cry, cursing the unaccountable impulse, determined not to wake Patrick. Dear God, she thought, feeling the warmth of his body against the length of her own. It was good, as good as it had ever been with Jack, and she didn't even love him! Patrick was right, love had nothing to do with it; it was no more than animal lust, and she was no better than any cheap female who sold herself for a few pennies.

Did it make any difference that the sum was sixteen hundred dollars, and that by submitting, she'd also rescued her sister from Otis Quinn, and thereby assured the rest of the family of a place to live out the balance of their lives? Was that really any different from an arranged marriage, for the mutual benefit of two families, or from what a woman of the streets does in order to survive?

Her sense of values was totally upset, her opinion of her own decency and ethics (which until very recently she had taken for granted) on such trembling ground that she felt as if she were sinking in quicksand.

She could not contain the wracking sob; she turned away, attempting to stifle it, but the movement or the sound brought Patrick awake.

He reached out to her, and she knew that even if she could control her voice and produce speech, she could not explain to him why she had to cry. Patrick did not ask for explanations, however. He simply drew her into his arms and held her, until the inexplicable grief subsided, and at last she slept.

Twenty-Two

Otis Quinn had not touched any of the females at Mallows while he was there on official duty. And on the excursions away from the plantation in search of diversion, he had been discreet. On one occasion in the distant past, he had been involved in a scandal that had been difficult to live down; indeed, had his wife's family been aware of it, they would never have agreed to her marriage to him.

Expediency, and the urgent need for officers during the Civil War, had given him an official standing that Quinn found to his liking. That he climbed to the rank of major had more to do with the vicissitudes of war than with any merit on his part; he was not well liked, and even those who knew nothing of his sexual proclivities suspected there was something unpleasant about him, for all that they could not put a name to it.

Otis Quinn did have one thing in his favor with his superior officers. He was a meticulous man about his person and his work; he seemed to thrive on the wealth of red tape and complicated paper shuffling that most of the others despised, and his attention to detail had on occasion won his superiors commendations of their own, for no more effort than putting up with the superciliousness of the man. Actual

502

promotion to the rank he had attained just before the battle of Atlanta was due to the fact that two good men of corresponding rank had been so severely injured as to put them out of the fight for the remainder of the war. Even so, General William T. Sherman had taken Quinn in dislike and had shunted him off with a hospital command that got him out of Sherman's sight and hearing.

Now, however, Otis Quinn was out of the army. His wife had died during the final few months of the war, and her fortunes were finally his, without strings. In addition to that, he had obtained the coveted position of tax collector, a position in which it was possible to realize a considerable income in addition to the salary. He had met with some small resistance on the part of that young Healy, in the matter of the Mallows taxes, but Quinn was, after all, used to getting his own way and had not balked at the strongest intimidation to bring the young whelp around. Healy was foolishly idealistic but not stupid in the matter of his own future; when he saw that Quinn quite intended to obtain the property, in one way or another, Healy had sense enough to do as he was told and keep his mouth shut.

Quinn feared nothing from Washington. There were too many tax collectors, the Southerners were a beaten and subdued people with no influence in the capital any more, and the government itself proposed that the taxes should be punitive in nature. No, Quinn was not afraid of being reprimanded or replaced. His confidence grew from the time Ellen Stanton first approached him on the matter, and he'd given her plenty of time to stew in her own juices so that she would be sufficiently softened; he had expected her to capitulate to his demands, and she had done so.

He could have had his choice between the Stanton daughters, of course. They were both beautiful. (He did not consider the matter of intelligence; a female's intelligence, or lack of it, was of little consequence in bed.) They were no longer, now that he was out of the army, untouchable. He might have gotten away with something while he was quartered at Mallows, but he had a reasonable amount of control over his bodily demands, and he did not want to risk his command. Sherman had certainly given his men almost *carte blanche* in the matter of Southern women, and rapes were common among the rank and file. But for an officer to molest the women of a great house might well have given way to another scandal, and that Quinn did not want. Besides, even then he had known that he wanted the house, too, that grand and beautiful mansion, and that if he played his hand right he might find a way to have both, one of the women and the plantation.

He never seriously considered Valerie at all. For one thing she was so tall; he didn't like women who were tall. For another thing, that red hair betokened a temper, and he didn't like women with tempers, either. One person in a family with a temper was enough, as long as the temper was his own.

No, quiet little Julie, with those big, dark, frightened eyes, she was the one. His wife had been like that once, shy and timid and pretty, when he married her.

And tomorrow Julie would join him in bed.

The thought aroused him well in advance of the wedding ceremony. He had, in fact, been aroused for a full week, to the point where even the local prostitute could not satisfy him for more than a few hours at a time.

He would, for tonight, take his pleasures elsewhere.

Had Blossom been there, he might well have taken her. Sally Ann did not appeal to him; although she seemed to have little temper to go with her carroty hair, she was too pale and he didn't like freckles. He suspected they were all over her, not just on her face and arms; he couldn't bear breasts that were not clear and smooth and young, and he was sure Sally Ann's would be blemished.

He knew who he wanted. He had watched her all the weeks he was living in this house, seen that she'd avoided him, knew that she still did.

He also knew she was meeting some young buck out there, at dusk, at the edge of the woods. Well, it wouldn't matter to him if the buck had her first. And it would make it easier if Quinn himself also took her outside, away from the house. It would be like the stupid bitch to scream and make an uproar, and he certainly didn't want Ellen Stanton up in arms about a silly thing like a man indulging himself with a nigger wench the evening before the wedding. After the wedding, why, then he'd be in command here, anyway, and Ellen Stanton be damned.

The house settled into silence relatively early that night. Everyone had retired by a little past nine, except Otis Quinn. He waited by the window, where he could see Lallie when she slipped out the back door and disappeared into the shadows.

The excitement grew in him, and he followed her down the back stairs, quietly, and prepared to wait.

"Tomorrow," Aaron said, urgency roughening his voice. "Tomorrow Miss Julie will be married, Miss Ellen will be safe from the tax collector, and tomorrow I am going to leave. There's no jobs in Tattnall County for an educated nigger, but New Orleans is something else. I'm going, Lallie, and you'll have to make up your mind: you coming with me, or not?"

She didn't realize she had made up her mind—at least not entirely made it up—until she answered. "I'm goin'. I know Miss Ellen needs me, but what she's doin' to that poor little Miss Julie, I don't know, it's like Miss Ellen's a different person. Somebody I never saw before. I don't understand her, that's for certain. And I don't want to live in the same house with *him*. The way he looks at me—" Lallie shivered, and moved into Aaron's opened arms. She felt warm there, and safe. "You think I ought to tell her? Miss Ellen? She liable to raise a fit, if I do."

"She can't stop you," Aaron pointed out. "She doesn't own you any more."

"No. But I'd feel bad, if she carried on. I wish Miss Val hadn't run off somewhere. I could talk to *her*. Miss Julie, she's in no state to talk to, and old Miss Lacy still ain't said a word. She just lays there and looks at you when you talk to her. She can't even say if she hurts anyplace."

"Then just come to me, early in the morning," Aaron said. "Bring whatever you can carry, and we'll move on out. I got a ride lined up, feller with a wagon going all the way to Berrien County. Save us a lot of shoe leather." He grinned. "He's deaf, too. Won't hear anything we do at night."

Lallie pushed at him in mock anger. "We ain't doin' anything, until after we married."

"We'll get married. First town we come to has a preacher, we'll get married. Nothing much to it these days, long as you got the money to pay the man and can prove you ain't vagrants. Too bad Miss Ellen can't pay you, like the government says she has to do. We could sure use a little more cash."

"She got about as much cash as I got blond curls," Lallie

505

said, and giggled. Her amusement quickly faded, however. "No, I don't go to make any trouble for Miss Ellen. She been good to me. And I reckon she can't help it, she's hurtin' so bad inside she don't even see what's happenin' to everybody around her. It too bad to leave her that way, but it wouldn't make no difference, anyhow, would it? If I stayed? Miss Julie still have to marry that man, Miss Ellen still be the way she is."

Aaron pulled her down into the snug bower he'd constructed for them against the chill of autumn nights. They could have used one of the empty cabins but he'd chosen this. Since he couldn't talk Lallie out of her clothes, anyway, it didn't matter that they had only pine boughs for shelter.

"Come on. Let's forget about Miss Ellen and Miss Julie and all the rest of those white people. Let's pretend we're married."

He was only teasing, although it would be easy to forget that, and let herself go with Aaron. Still, she knew what white folks thought about such things. Some of them had, for years, bred their blacks like animals. But here at Mallows Miss Ellen had seen to it that matings were properly authorized, and she'd never taken a baby away from its parents, or separated husband and wife. She was a good woman, Miss Ellen was, if only worry and sorrow hadn't practically driven her crazy.

"Hey! You still thinking about white folks?"

"No," Lallie said. "But I ain't pretendin' we married, either." Her voice turned prim. "How about we pretend we engaged?"

From some distance away, Otis Quinn heard their low laugher, and then silence descended. He continued to wait, until he heard Lallie coming through the dry grass that rustled under her feet. The excitement was almost uncontrollable, now, and his mouth was dry, but he hadn't minded the wait, because he knew how much he was going to enjoy what was to come.

Lallie moved with the assurance of one treading a path she had known for years, not needing to see it. She felt warm and happy. She'd never expected to fall in love with Aaron—and here she was, willing to go with him, giving up the idea of going north and passing for white, and having white babies instead of black ones. It was so strange, because she'd never thought of Aaron that way, at all, when he'd been the butler at Mallows.

She sensed movement near the corner of the house and hesitated, not yet frightened.

"Somebody there?" she asked softly.

There was no answer, and after a moment she concluded that she'd either imagined it, or it had been some wild creature that had ventured too far from its lair in search of food. Lallie had her hand on the door when she heard the small sounds, this time recognizable as human breathing and an incautious footstep.

The hand went over her mouth and a familiar voice spoke quietly in her ear.

"Be a good girl, now, and come along without making a fuss."

Sheer terror made her sag against him, and then she struggled, knowing what was in store. She tried to cry out, but the hand covered her nose and mouth, and the other arm was wrapped around her throat so that she feared she might suffocate or die from the pain of it.

Quinn's voice rasped impatiently. "I told you not to make a fuss! I don't want anything from you you didn't give to that buck out there in the woods. You liked what he did, didn't you?"

She was fainting from lack of air. She wanted to fight, but he was hurting her, and she couldn't breathe—for a few minutes she was only semi-conscious, although the pain of the arm around her throat didn't ease.

When he finally released her so that she could breathe, Lallie gasped and folded forward, sucking air into her tortured lungs. She knew where she was. One of the cabins, probably the one at the end nearest the house, which meant there was no one closer than three or four doors away. Even if she screamed, and they heard her, no one would come. Even on a plantation like Mallows, the blacks knew better than to investigate too closely, if there was a white man involved.

"Keep quiet," Quinn told her, "and I won't hurt your face. You've such a pretty face, you don't want it mutilated, do you? It's a pity we can't have a light, I'd like to see you, but it's too big a risk this time."

He gripped the front of her simple cotton garment and stripped it away with a tearing sound. Lallie protested through her bruised throat, and he hit her one sharp, numb-

507

ing blow. He began to speak to her in a voice that was as obscene as the words he used, telling her what he was going to do to her.

Aaron woke and lay relaxed in the bed that he had become used to over the past few days. He had been familiar with slave quarters all his life, though from the time Miss Ellen had chosen him for training he had mostly slept in the big house.

Although he now knew there were worse places, he hated the quarters. The contrast between this and the comfort and elegance of the white folks' house was enough to set a man's teeth on edge. If he'd had to spend his life like this, in a cramped small cabin with a dirt floor, no privacy, no possessions of his own, expected to work as a fieldhand from dawn until dusk, bred to whatever female his owner thought would produce the best child from him, subject to punishment of the most brutal sort for the smallest of transgressions if that should be the master's whim, Aaron thought he would have killed someone. He did not truly understand why more of his fellow Africans had not turned on the whites who owned them, once the Yankees offered them refuge. Of course the refuge was an illusion: the Yankees didn't want to provide for the Negro nor recognize him as a human being. Still, for a time it had seemed that freedom was offered to them in a spirit of genuine compassion.

The truth of the matter was, Aaron felt, that the war had not been about slavery, at all. Instead, the Northern businessmen had somehow benefited from the war, financially, although he didn't understand the ins and outs of it. The issue of slavery was not of primary importance to most Yankees.

He had liked the excitement and color and action in the cities, he felt safer and freer there, although he'd been lonelier, too. Of course, now with Lallie, he wouldn't be lonely any more. And perhaps in New Orleans, a *Southern* city, he would find what he sought: a place in the scheme of things.

He shifted on the corn husk mattress and heard more than the usual rustling sounds. He listened more intently, holding very still, and it came again.

A sort of whimpering, just outside.

Aaron moved with caution, although it was impossible to get off the corn husks in silence. He padded across the dirt floor in his bare feet and stood listening.

508

"Aaron."

It was so low that he wouldn't have heard it, if he hadn't been just on the other side of the door. He flung it open and felt one of Lallie's hands brush his foot—a warm hand, and sticky.

"Lallie?" He knelt to touch her and encountered more blood. He didn't have to see it to know what it was; he could smell it. "Lord God, what's happened?"

She moaned when he picked her up and carried her inside, but he had to do it. He eased her onto the mattress and groped around for a candle. Lallie had brought him matches, so he didn't have to find the remains of a fire to light it.

Disbelief held him rigid when he saw her. Blood trickled from one corner of her mouth and from her nose, and one eyelid was turning blue and swelling shut. But the crimson viscous fluid on her naked belly and thighs told the story most clearly.

"Who did it?" Aaron demanded in a voice that trembled with grief and rage. "Who hurt you this way?"

Lallie opened the good eye and a lone tear squeezed out and ran to mingle with the blood from her nose. "He . . . a bad man," she said, her bruised lips barely moving.

"Quinn? That bastard Yankee?"

Lallie closed her eye to blink away more tears. "Take me away," she begged softly. "Away from this place, forever."

"I'll kill him."

There was cold venom in the words, and Lallie's eye popped open again in alarm. "No! No, Aaron! We just go away! You kill a white man, they kill you! No matter what he does, they kill you!"

For a moment he almost didn't care. He wanted to feel the white man's throat between his hands, wanted to squeeze the life out of it, no matter what the cost.

"Aaron—" Her voice was low and weak. "I hurt bad. I need a woman, someone to help stop the bleedin'. But in a few days I be fine, and we'll go away. Leave him for the white folks to deal with."

He knew she was right. If he killed Quinn, hell, if he killed *any* white man, let alone an important one, they'd execute him. Hang him up and beat him to death, put a rope around his neck and drape it over the nearest tree branch, anything except shoot him so that he got off quick and easy. Still the

509

murderous rage was in him, and he didn't know if he could control it.

"What happen to me," Lallie asked, "you go and get yourself killed?"

In the end that was the argument that won him over, that made him suspend the hating enough to consider the consequences. What would happen to Lallie?

He brought a basin of water and a cloth and tried to sponge away the worst of it himself, but he could see she was right about that, too. The blood continued to seep into the mattress from between her legs, and he didn't know what to do to stop it.

His black hand rested for a few seconds, with tenderness, on her creamy shoulder.

"I'll get some help," he said. "I won't be long."

Lallie lay, soaked in a misery as tangible as the blood, and prayed that he would not encounter Otis Quinn until his anger had had time to subside. If only Miss Ellen could see what the man was! But Miss Ellen, she thought, was lost to her, to all of them. There was no help to be had from her, for Miss Ellen could no longer help even herself.

Lallie lay quietly, and wished with a desperate intensity that she'd gone with Aaron, when he first asked her to, days ago. Before Otis Quinn. Her body, she hoped, would heal. But she wondered if her mind ever would. If she'd ever be able to forget the things Quinn had said and done.

And she wondered, too, if Aaron would ever forget, and how he would feel about her, now.

Twenty-Three

Julie had retired early to her room, but not to sleep. She felt as if she would never sleep again. She had tried, one final time, to reason with her mother. Ellen had put both hands to her temples, as if the pain there was too much to contain unless she pressed it in with her fingers, and spoken in an anguished voice. "Please, Julie, stop it. We've decided what had to be done. Let it rest. I can't think for this throbbing; even the laudanum doesn't help any more. Go to bed and let me do the same."

Julie did not undress. She sat before the small fire—now that Major Quinn was going to save Mallows, they were allowed the luxury of bedroom fires morning and night—and pondered the nightmare of her future. There were only hours, now, before the proposed wedding. If only Valerie would return, if only in some way Valerie could save her! Where had she gone? From whom would she seek help?

Her mother took it for granted that Valerie had run off on some escapade of her own, probably with Jack Ferris. "Selfish," Ellen had muttered under her breath, "she was always a selfish child."

Julie knew different. Her sister had not abandoned her. Valerie was trying in some way to help. Probably, Julie thought,

511

she'd told Grandma Lacy where she was going, what she hoped to do. But Lacy lay in her bed, unable to move or speak.

She had not, as some of the others surmised, lost her senses. Julie was certain of that. Julie had tried to establish some sort of code with her, suggesting that Lacy blink once for *yes* and twice for *no;* the old woman had blinked, at least part of the time, but either she misunderstood, or Julie did not ask the proper questions, or Lacy simply could not control the blinking well enough.

Sometimes tears welled up in the old eyes and ran down the wrinkled cheeks. Julie or Hattie would gently wipe them away. And Julie would retreat to her own room and try to restrain her own weeping, far into the nights.

The tap on the door brought her upright, pulses hammering in her throat.

"Yes? Who is it?"

"Miss Julie? May I come in?"

It was Carrie, Major Quinn's elder daughter. Julie hastily opened the door, wondering what the child was doing moving about the house in the dark after everyone else had gone to bed.

She was a dark, pretty girl, very slight. At least, she had been pretty, until now. Tonight her eyes were reddened and her nose dripped; she wiped at it carelessly with a wisp of handkerchief.

"Come in, come sit by the fire where it's warmer. What's the matter?" Julie asked, with less circuitousness than she would normally have employed. She drew up another chair opposite her own, but Carrie didn't sink into it.

Instead, she twisted the sodden bit of linen in her hands and spoke in a low voice that wavered under emotional strain. "Miss Julie, would you try to help me?"

"How can I do that?" Julie remained standing, too, facing the girl. In spite of her preoccupation with her own sorry predicament, she was brought to sympathy for the woebegone little face a few inches below her own. Her stepdaughter-to-be was, after all, only three years younger than Julie herself.

"Could you . . ." Carrie swallowed hard, and tried for calm. "Could you speak to Papa on my behalf? I know—I know you don't love him, and that your marriage has been arranged, and maybe if you couldn't do anything about your own, you won't be able to do anything about mine, either,

512

but I'll *die*, I swear I'll *die*, if I have to marry that dreadful old man!"

The tears began to flow again; it was not until Julie had produced a supply of linen to sop them up that Carrie was able to tell her story.

"Papa told Fritz, I mean Mr. Froedecker, just this evening, that he'd made the final arrangements. I'm to be married, to a Mr. Goetz, in Reidsville. I wasn't supposed to overhear it, of course, and I wasn't deliberately listening, but they were in the study and I heard Fritz . . ." She paused to mop again at her face. "He was angry. He wasn't raising his voice, but I could tell he was very angry. Not that Papa cares, of course. I had forgotten, during the years he was gone from home during the war, quite how horrid Papa can be. My grandpapa didn't want to send us down here, you know; if Papa hadn't insisted, we could have stayed at home with *him*. He hates Papa, says he was responsible for Mama's death. When the letter came from Papa saying he was sending someone to bring us to Georgia—that was Fritz, of course, and we *adored* Fritz—Grandpapa went into a terrible rage. He's a lovely old man, and he almost never rages, except where Papa is concerned."

The words were spoken so rapidly that they ran together, and Julie felt she was not quite grasping the thread. She put her hands on Carrie's shoulders and pushed her down into the chair.

"Obviously this is going to take a little time. Please, I must sit down, so you sit, too. I don't think my comprehension is quite the thing, tonight. How was your papa responsible for your mama's death? She died while he was still in Georgia, as I understand it?"

"Yes." Carrie blew her nose and tried to be more coherent. "It was so nice while Papa was away. We lived with Grandpapa, in a very nice house, and Mama was much more cheerful than she used to be. Although, to be truthful, she was always very nervous and we had to be careful not to upset her. Well, when Papa wrote to say that he was coming home, why, she became very upset. I heard her tell Grandpapa that she would not ever live with Papa again. She said—she said—" Carrie gulped and blurted out the words as if they were scalding her mouth. "She said that she would rather be dead!"

Julie, who knew precisely how that could be, said nothing,

513

only leaning forward to take the girl's hand in an encouraging way between her own.

"And the next morning, she was. Dead, I mean. They didn't tell us what had happened. They only said she'd died. But I think she killed herself. Rather than live with Papa again when he came home, she killed herself. And that's how I feel about being married to a nasty old man—"

Carrie began to cry again.

The threads of the story were beginning to form a pattern of sorts. Julie had thought herself so immersed in her own private horror that she would not ever fight free of it, and now she was caught up in another, just as bad, with poor Carrie at the center of it.

What could she do? How could she possibly help this fifteen-year-old child when her own case was as bad as Carrie's?

Julie made herself try to think, to reason it out. "Who is this Mr. . . . Goetz? Why does your father want you to marry him?"

Carrie answered the last question first. "I think it's because he's rich. He has a home in Boston, and one, now, in Reidsville, too. He has some government position, I don't know exactly what it is, but Papa said Mr. Goetz can help him, in a business way. Besides that, he's old and he smells funny and I think Papa hopes he'll die and leave what he has to *me*, and then I'll have to let *him* handle it all— Besides," she finished tearfully, "Papa can't abide any of us, and he'll get rid of us however he can!"

She waited, torn between hope and despair, for Julie to react to this. Perhaps, just perhaps, Carrie had misunderstood what she overheard, or there was more to the story and it was not as bad as Carrie feared. However, if she had the right of it, Julie didn't see what on earth she could do about it. Certainly *she* had no influence over Otis Quinn, and she was just as frightened of him as his children were.

She did not even feel capable of murmuring soothing sounds. She stood at last, however, and drew Carrie up with her. "I think we'd both best go to bed now. Perhaps we'll think of something," she said.

God knew what it would be, though, Julie reflected as she finally began to prepare for bed. And God knew why she was retiring, since she'd never be able to sleep. Not with the

514

knowledge that by this time tomorrow she'd be expected to go to bed with Otis Quinn.

Unless Valerie came back. Unless Valerie had persuaded *someone* to help them. Julie clung to that hope, however faint, as she lay alone in the darkness, trying not to cry any more.

It had been over a year since Aaron had been in a white folks' house. Lallie had left the door unlocked, and he eased into the once familiar dimness of the kitchen. The warmth, the odors of cooked food, were all strange, now.

It was light enough to see to make his way across the room. Ordinarily Aaron woke hungry, and he would have been tempted by the aroma of a cake Mamie had baked and iced, or the cold roasted meat left from the previous night's supper.

Now all he thought about was Lallie. Poor battered Lallie, whose lovely face was swollen beyond recognition, and who continued to bleed in spite of the efforts of Rudy's wife, Sheba, and the other woman he had called in to look at her.

He wondered if they still had any guns in the house, or if the Yankees had confiscated everything in the way of a weapon. He wondered, if he killed Otis Quinn, if he had the faintest chance of escaping from Tattnall County, and if the law would come after him, all the way to New Orleans.

A gun, of course, was a white man's weapon. His own mind was a curious blend that did not meld with either white or black. Too educated to be a nigger, too black ever to be considered anything but a menial by the whites. If only there was some way to kill the white Yankee bastard without getting caught. Aaron knew he would do it in a minute. With a gun, a knife, any weapon that came to hand. Including those, he thought, glancing down at his own hands. They were stronger than they had been when he opened doors and carried trays for the Stantons; maybe he could kill Otis with his bare hands. He itched to try.

He made his way through the house hoping that Miss Ellen still had her old room, wondering which door Otis Quinn slept behind. If he knocked on the wrong door, aroused the wrong person—Lord God, Aaron thought, if he was faced with Otis Quinn, could he help himself? Or would he have to try to throttle the man?

The household was sleeping. The first pale rays of sun

came through the windows of the breakfast room when he passed that doorway and went on up the stairs, walking softly. It would be a fine day. A fine day for a wedding, if Quinn lived to see it happen.

Aaron hesitated outside Ellen's door, then decided against knocking. He didn't want to arouse the rest of the household, not yet. First he had to get help for Lallie. He wouldn't have been surprised if they'd put locks or bars on the bedroom doors, but they had not. He eased open the door and stared into the room, then slipped through the opening and approached the bed.

Ellen's appearance in sleep shocked him. She had aged far more than the year or so he'd been gone. There were traces of gray in her once rich auburn hair, and lines in her face that no woman of less than forty years should have displayed.

He put a hand on her shoulder. "Miss Ellen."

She was awake instantly, though her eyes did not focus for a few seconds, and then she sat up in a violent movement that shook his hand aside.

"Aaron! Aaron? Where did you come from?"

"I came back for Lallie. Miss Ellen, you got to come. He hurt her, that Major Quinn, and she's bleeding bad. Sheba can't stop it."

"Who?" Ellen's hair hung loose over her shoulders, a sad reminder of former beauty. "What are you talking about?"

"I'm talking about Lallie. Your Major Quinn raped her and abused her last night. She needs help."

He watched that work its way through her sleep-fogged head. Saw what little color she had seep out of her face until she was as white as her nightdress.

"Where is she?"

He told her.

"I'll be right there. Give me time to get dressed," Ellen said, and a sigh of relief escaped him. After what Lallie'd said about her current mental condition, he wouldn't have been astonished if she'd failed to respond at all.

She came quickly, arriving at the cabin no more than five minutes after Aaron himself had returned. She stood beside the bed, gazing down in disbelief at the girl who had been her trusted maid for so long.

Her lips were so stiff they could hardly make out her word. "Quinn did this?"

"Hurt her bad," old Sheba offered.

516

Ellen glanced at Aaron, then gathered her resources almost visibly. "Leave us alone."

Lallie had sunk more or less into a stupor; she roused slightly when Ellen spoke to her, but neither cooperated nor hindered their efforts on her behalf. Ellen had brought clean linen which she methodically tore into strips for packing the vagina in the hope that the pressure of the absorbent material would help to slow the bleeding. As far as she could tell, there was no damage that should be expected to be life-threatening, although the fact that the girl was still bleeding so long after the assault had taken place was somewhat alarming.

The black women had built up a fire and heated water, and together they bathed Lallie and covered her with the ragged quilt Aaron had been using. Ellen would have liked to move her off the corn husk mattress, into her own room in the house, but she judged that it was too soon for that. Let the girl rest and regain some of her strength, first.

"Find one of the younger women to stay with her," Ellen instructed Sheba, who nodded. But Aaron, from the doorway, spoke with authority that would not be denied.

"I'll stay with her," he said, and Ellen didn't argue.

She returned to the house alone. The sun was well up in the sky; she must have been at the quarters for several hours, although it did not seem that long. She had worked automatically, as she had so often worked with the sick and the injured before, and her mind had not been busy with anything beyond what her hands must do.

Now, however, she began to think again. About what she must do.

Dear God, what was it possible to do? She thought of Otis Quinn with a sickness spreading through her. He had done this to Lallie, and today he was to be married to her own Julie. What could she do? Nothing had changed. There was still the matter of the taxes, the expense of the upkeep of the plantation, and she still had no resources.

Could Julie be right? Could Valerie have gone for help, rather than simply abandoning them to find her own happiness?

"Miss Ellen."

She stared at the sound of the unexpected voice. Fritz Froedecker stood shivering in the early morning chill, and she had enough wit to see that he was pale and grave.

She couldn't manage a conventional good-morning. She simply waited.

"Miss Ellen," Fritz said, holding her gaze with his own intense one. "You can't let him do this. You can't let him marry Miss Julie. You don't know what sort of man he is."

Ellen sighed. "I know," she said.

Anger flared in his face. "Then how can you let him do it? I know about Mallows, your goddamned precious Mallows, but Julie's your *daughter!*"

"I don't know what to do." Her shoulders sagged, her body was as limp as her mind. "I just don't know."

The smell of woodsmoke wafted to them on the breeze. Mamie was beginning breakfast preparations, and getting ready for the wedding. The minister would be here before long; he had to come a long way and had requested (since he was an elderly man) that he be allowed to come for lunch, first, so that he could rest for a time before the ceremony and then the long ride home again. What would she say to the minister?

Did it matter? Did it truly matter, any more, what she said to anyone?

She did not reply to Fritz Froedecker. She went into the house, Fritz following in rising frustration and fury, through the kitchen, where the aroma of frying ham mingled with the fragrance of baking biscuits, and through the dining room and into the study.

"What are you doing? Good God, woman, haven't you heard anything I've said?" Fritz demanded, behind her in the doorway.

Ellen stood before the desk and tugged at the top drawer. It resisted her efforts, and she frowned. "It's stuck."

"What do you want? What's in there?" Fritz stepped to her side and jerked on the brass handle. "It isn't stuck, it's locked. Where's the key?"

Ellen lifted the cover from the humidor where Roger Stanton had kept his cigars. "It's supposed to be in here. It's gone."

"You want me to break it open?" Something about her face defused his anger; he looked about for a prying tool and took up a sturdy paper knife. "It may ruin the drawer."

"Open it," Ellen said.

The wood gave way with a splintering sound, and Fritz

518

jerked the drawer all the way out before he saw what she was after.

In the back corner of the compartment, hidden under an untidy stack of bills, was a pistol.

Ellen started to reach for it, then stared instead down at the envelope with her own name across the front of it. Her own name, in Patrick Ryan's hand; she had seen it often enough, on plantation accounts, to recognize it even after several years.

Her own name, yet it had never been delivered to her; she picked it up, the weapon momentarily forgotten, and read the enclosed note, then began to tremble uncontrollably when she saw the check.

"What is it?" Fritz reached to take the message and bank draft from her hand, his comprehension only a little behind hers. He swore softly and put out a hand to steady the swaying woman beside him.

The miserable, conniving son of a bitch. Not only had Quinn in all probability arranged for the Mallows tax bill to be exorbitant, he had kept Ellen from receiving the check that would have paid it. Of course, because he didn't want it paid. He wanted Mallows, and Julie. God, the thought of Julie and Otis Quinn had been a twisting knife in his guts for the past week.

"What are you doing?"

The sharp voice was full of indignation, as if they'd invaded Major Quinn's private belongings. As, indeed, he considered the desk and the study to be.

He had risen in high good humor after a satisfying night—the girl was sufficiently frightened so that she wouldn't tell anyone what had happened to her—and prepared to accept, at last, his due in life: Mallows, and the girl. He had followed his nose in the direction of the tempting aromas, only to be sidetracked by the sound of voices from the study. Not only did he consider it to be his personal domain, as it had been while he and his men had been quartered here, but he remembered at once what he'd left in the drawer. The key to it was still safely in his pocket, but the drawer stood open. Fritz held the note and the check.

And Ellen held the pistol.

The epithet she hissed at him was one he had never expected to hear from the lips of any female. Indeed, Ellen herself

519

would never have admitted to knowing it, until she made use of it.

She held the pistol quite steady, and it was aimed at a point about six inches above Otis Quinn's navel.

He took a step backward and the color receded from his face. "My dear woman, what are you doing? It's dangerous to handle a gun that way."

Ellen said nothing, only taking a slow step toward him. Quinn looked to Fritz Froedecker and saw nothing there except hatred. No help. No help anywhere.

Quinn took another step backward, into the library, and then turned and moved through that room and into the entry hall. She wouldn't actually shoot that thing, he told himself, surely she wouldn't. Certainly not in front of witnesses, and he heard voices on the stairs.

Sally Ann was there, with Hugh Alexander in her arms, and Pansy.

Quinn felt a surge of relief. A pity she'd found the check, and the more fool he that he hadn't realized she still had a weapon hidden away. But even if she could pay the taxes, and he didn't marry Julie, there would be some other way.

"Major Quinn," Ellen said. The listeners would later remember that her voice had grown clear and strong. "Stand where you are."

He turned, waving a hand at the trio on the stairs, to make sure she knew they were there. "Put it down, Mrs. Stanton. Perhaps we have a few things to talk about, but there is no necessity for doing it at gunpoint."

Julie stood at the top of the stairs, transfixed by the tableau below. Her breath caught in her throat and she pressed a hand to the sudden ache in her chest.

Ellen lifted the pistol in both hands, hands no longer shaking. And then, as Quinn's face shifted, melted, disintegrated with horrified realization, she pulled the trigger.

Twenty-Four

The reverberation echoed in all their ears, and above the spot where Otis Quinn swayed for a matter of seconds, surprise and horror still reflected below the neat hole in the center of his forehead, the crystal prisms of the chandelier tinkled musically.

Julie's fingers curled around the stair railing and she leaned over it, incredulous. She saw Fritz take the weapon from her mother's unresisting hand, heard Pansy's shrill scream, and the baby's frightened whimpering.

From the room behind her, Carrie and Isidora Quinn rushed out, to stand with their hands pressed to their mouths as they stared down.

Fritz looked up and spoke sharply. "Get those children back into their rooms!"

"Go," Julie murmured, and the girls scampered away.

She had killed him. Otis Quinn lay sprawled in the middle of the entry hall, murdered by Ellen Stanton.

It didn't matter *why* she had killed him. Julie let go of the railing and ran down the stairs, brushing past the frozen Sally Ann and Pansy, to reach her mother. What would they do to her? A Yankee, an official, murdered by a Georgian woman?

Julie drew Ellen into her arms, expecting to find her in a

521

state of collapse. Ellen only looked down at her victim, however, with no perturbation whatever, that Julie could see.

Blood was spreading across the floor from beneath the body. Julie stared at it, mesmerized, until Fritz said, "We'll have to tell them I did it. That he provoked a quarrel, something. We'll think of something."

At that moment, Pansy let out another of her blood-curdling screeches. "He's comin'! The preacher's comin'! Oh, Lordy, what'll we do? What'll we *do?*"

Sally Ann was also high enough on the stairs to be able to see out through the fanlight above the door. "He's just turned onto the drive," she confirmed. "Hush, hush!" She rocked the little boy in her arms, glad to have something to hold her attention other than the catastrophic scene below her.

"Will they execute me?" Ellen asked. She sounded so calm that Julie wondered wildly if she'd totally lost her reason.

Fritz stepped back from the body, then looked around and up. A moment later, to the bewilderment of everyone watching, he lunged for the pair of crossed swords placed on the wall near the library door. They had hung there for years, and the blade of the one he chose was not overly sharp; yet he slashed with it at the cord secured a few yards away, the cord that was used to raise and lower the great chandelier for cleaning and affixing of candles.

On the third try, the cord gave way, and the crystal confection, long the pride of Mallows, fell with a thundering crash of breaking glass.

Julie recoiled from the flying shards, drawing Ellen with her. A thin red line etched itself across Ellen's cheek; she did not seem to notice.

Fritz, breathing heavily, replaced the sword with its mate on the wall. "There," he said. "See if they can tell there's a bullet in him, now."

And thus it was that the Reverend Joshua Cutting, arriving in the expectation of a good meal and a comfortable nap before performing a wedding ceremony upon which fee his family would eat for the coming week, walked into an entryway that was a shambles. He found Pansy in hysterics, Ellen Stanton in an apparent state of shock, and the others not much better. All of them except Sally Ann and the baby had at least minor cuts and scratches from the exploding crystal. Fritz Froedecker, ignoring his own lacerations, was applying a handkerchief to the cut on Ellen's cheek.

522

And Otis Quinn, the intended bridegroom, was buried under over eight hundred pounds of crystal that had plummeted from some twenty feet over his head. One booted foot protruded from beneath the sparkling fragments. The rest of him was covered in splintered glass.

Fritz turned away from Ellen, holding the square of linen so that the blood was clearly visible on it. "I don't think there's any chance the major survived; it struck him squarely when it fell."

The Reverend Mr. Cutting was bug-eyed. "Quite right. No one could have survived that. Goodness gracious, what a tragedy! On his wedding day, poor man! And the bride—Miss Julie, is it not? Poor brave young lady, more concerned with her mother than with her own loss! How fortunate that no one else was under it when it fell! I take it the lowering rope simply broke? He had no warning?"

"No warning at all," Fritz assured him. "Mr. Cutting—I know this isn't what you came for, but Major Quinn's children are upstairs. They know something happened, of course, the thing made a great racket when it fell, but they don't know their father's dead. Maybe you could . . . ?"

The minister pulled himself together. "Yes, yes, of course. I'll go up and speak with them. How sad, after they'd come all this way to join their father." He glanced at the foot and the heap of broken glass. "You'll be needing help, to get all that off from him. I'll join you after I've broken the news to his family."

It was impossible to walk without crunching through particles of the smashed crystal. Mr. Cutting made his way around the worst of it and climbed the stairs, pausing to commiserate with Sally Ann. Pansy had, mercifully, more or less recovered from her hysterics, though she continued to wring her hands in agitation.

Fritz glanced up at her. "Come on down, Pansy. Run out to the quarters and round up some help to clean up this mess. You can tell the others that Major Quinn was killed when the chandelier fell on him."

Pansy gaped, not moving, until Fritz amplified this. "You saw it, didn't you? It was an accident; the rope broke and the chandelier fell. He was standing directly beneath it, and he was killed."

Pansy gulped, understanding at last. "Yassir," she agreed.

"That how it happen, all right." She fled past him, not wanting to look when they uncovered Major Quinn's body.

It took them hours to clear the entry hall. Julie had taken Ellen upstairs and put her to bed with a cold cloth over her eyes. Explanations were made to Grandma Dolly, who did not want to come out and view the disaster area, nor to see to her daughter.

The Reverend Mr. Cutting was a slight man, but he worked side by side with the young blacks and Fritz to lift away the twisted metal frame of the chandelier. Death was no stranger to him, yet he did not want to look, beyond the initial inadvertent glance, at the body of Otis Quinn. Indeed, one would have been hard put to identify the man.

Fritz was correct in his assumption that no one could any longer detect a bullet hole in the midst of all those punctures and lacerations. He and Aaron carried the limp figure into the closed-off drawing room and wrapped it in a sheet. Then Fritz immediately sought out the pastor, who was not only hungry and tired, but woefully aware that he would not collect his fee for the wedding.

"If it weren't that we ought to notify the authorities in town and allow them time to examine the body," Fritz said, "we could have you read the burial service over him now, while you're here, sir. But I suppose we have to assume that there will be an official inquiry."

The Reverend Mr. Cutting perked up a little. "Yes, it would be convenient to have the funeral at once, wouldn't it? Save me a trip out here, as you say. As to the inquiry, I hardly think that will be necessary. With all these witnesses to what was clearly an accident, and my own word on that. Perfectly obvious to anyone what happened, and the man is dead. Nothing to be done about that. Do you think, then, a simple funeral, right away?"

"If you think so, sir," Fritz said, as if it had been the minister's suggestion.

"Yes, yes, I think so. And now, while the women are clearing away the rest of the debris, I wonder if I might trouble someone for a cup of tea, and perhaps a bite to eat. If you'll put the boys to work on a coffin, we can proceed after we've all rested for a time?"

Julie, hovering nearby, not because she wanted to see the remains of the man she was to have married, but because she

524

had been terrified that a close examination of Otis Quinn would reveal the real cause of his death, spoke quickly.

"Please, sir, go into the dining room. I'll have something sent to you at once. Pansy, tell Mamie to see that Mr. Cutting has something substantial to eat."

Only after the others had gone, except for the women who were on their hands and knees with cloths to wipe up the very last of the glass particles, did Julie speak quietly to Fritz Froedecker.

"You are very quick-witted, sir."

"Not quick enough, I'm afraid. I should never have let your mother shoot him. I should have done it myself." There was blood on his hands—Quinn's blood—and he wiped at them with what was left of his handkerchief.

The tension was heavy in her voice. "Do you really think we'll get away with it?"

"I think we've already done it." Fritz grinned tiredly. "It's to everyone's advantage that he's dead, including the blacks out there in the quarters. And his children. He was going to marry poor Carrie off to a man more than three times her age, did you know?"

"Yes. She told me."

"Well," he gave up scrubbing at his hands, "as far as the Reverend Mr. Cutting knows, none of us had any reason to wish him dead. He'll bury him today, carry a report to the county seat, and that'll be the end of the matter. We can send the children back to their grandfather in Boston. And you—you're safe from him, now. Forever."

Quite abruptly, Julie realized that that meant something to him, that she was safe. It was written there on his countenance, along with his concern for her. She had not really looked at him until this very moment, had had no idea.

"I'm very glad you didn't marry him, Miss Julie," Fritz said.

"And I," Julie agreed, in what must be the most understated opinion of her entire life. "Only now we're back where we started, aren't we? With an enormous tax bill, and no way to pay it . . ."

"No. Come and see." He touched her elbow, steering her through the library and into the study, putting the note and the bank draft into her hand.

Julie read it in bewilderment, then lifted a protesting face

525

to his. "But this means Valerie has married Patrick Ryan for the money! And she's in love with Jack Ferris!"

"Jack Ferris," Fritz told her gently, "is married. To a young woman who's been an invalid half her life. Most of their married life, anyway."

It took a few seconds for this to penetrate fully. She bit her lip and the tears welled up in her dark eyes. "She did it for me. Poor Val!"

Fritz made no comment on that. He didn't know Ryan, but he knew Ferris. Knew him, and liked him, yet had known all along that his former captain couldn't possibly marry Valerie Stanton.

Julie took a step, blindly, seeking she knew not what. And Fritz was there.

He held her cautiously, allowing her to cry, hoping that the quiet tears would be therapeutic. It was too soon to say anything to her, too soon to be anything more than a friend, a rescuer. Yet electricity was generated within him at the contact, however chaste, with the slim body.

It was the first step, one that had taken far longer than he would have liked. The next one, Fritz vowed silently, would not take nearly so long.

"I don't think I care to go," Ellen said calmly, when Julie told her that Otis Quinn was to be buried a few hours later. And so Julie informed the Reverend Mr. Cutting that her mother did not feel well enough to emerge from her bedroom.

"Perfectly understandable," the minister agreed. "The lady's had a dreadful experience, seeing a man killed that way, right before her eyes."

And so the rest of them stood, briefly, beside the hurriedly dug grave while a few appropriate words were spoken over the remains of Otis Quinn.

By that time, both Julie and Fritz had been apprised of the results of Quinn's nocturnal activity. They had seen Lallie, and listened to Aaron's terse account of the story, as much of it as he knew. Mr. Cutting assumed that Julie's visible tremor was a measure of her own shock at the sudden loss of her bridegroom-to-be. He nodded approvingly at Fritz's solicitous attention to the young woman, and was glad there was at least one man on the place to see to the things that were so difficult for women.

526

As soon as the Reverend Mr. Cutting had departed, after a supper on what had been intended as a wedding feast (with a fee for the funeral paid unobtrusively by Fritz Froedecker), Lallie was moved into her own room in the house. There was no discussion of the matter, but Aaron moved inside, also, arranging a pallet in the attic where the Yankee soldiers had slept.

"He wants to take care of nursing Lallie," Julie told her mother, somewhat troubled. "He says they're going to be married as soon as she's able to travel, and that they're leaving for New Orleans."

Ellen, whose hands were occupied with the mending of a sock, merely nodded. "Hand me that ball of yarn, will you, dear? And the next time anyone travels into town, please bring back some more worsted. We've nearly used up the ravelings from the old stockings."

Julie, on the day that was to have been her wedding day, went to bed alone. She was very tired, and very grateful, and she knelt first to offer her thanks that, at last, one of her prayers had been answered. The bed was chill, and while she lay waiting for it to warm, she thought about Valerie. Valerie and Patrick. Well, Patrick was a far cry from Otis Quinn. She wondered if he'd been in love with Valerie for a long time, and not dared to show it.

And then another face, quite different from Patrick's, rose in her mind's eye. A face capped by a shock of fair hair, with a pair of alert blue eyes that could snap with anger, or soften in compassion. Odd, how she'd never noticed until today what a *nice* person Fritz was.

And clever. Thank God for his cleverness! If he hadn't thought, in split seconds, about cutting down the chandelier, the Reverend Mr. Cutting would have walked in the front door and found Otis Quinn with a bullet hole in the middle of his forehead and Ellen Stanton holding a smoking pistol.

There had been a time—most of her lifetime, in fact—when Julie would have had great difficulty in coping with the idea that her mother had deliberately and in cold blood shot and killed a man. Now, after seeing what Quinn had done to Lallie, knowing how he'd manipulated the tax bill to assure that Ellen would be vulnerable, realizing how close she herself had been to disaster more terrible even than she had imagined, Julie had no trouble at all in accepting the death, and Fritz's concealment of it, as Divine Providence.

Her last conscious thought, as she sank into an exhausted sleep, was of Fritz's guiding hand on her arm, and the solid comfort of his tall body briefly touching hers. There were no nightmares, on the night she had expected to be a living one; Julie slept deeply and peacefully.

And across the landing, Ellen Stanton sat rocking for a long time in the darkness. She did not think about anything in particular. She simply rocked and felt a welcome peace flood through her, and thought that in the morning she would ask Mamie for a coddled egg for breakfast.

Three days after the funeral, Pansy again spotted an approaching visitor.

"A man, riding a black horse, comin' up the drive," she reported.

Ellen did not break the rhythm of her rocking. "Miss Valerie will greet him," she said.

Pansy gave her a startled look. "Mis Val ain't here, Miss Ellen."

"Oh. That's right, I'd forgotten. Well, Miss Julie, then."

Pansy ran her pink tongue over her lips and began to back from the room. "Yas'm," she said, and fled.

The newcomer was of medium height, a compact young man of near thirty years. His clothes were well worn, but of good quality, and he spoke in an educated voice.

"Brian Dallington, ma'am. I've had communication from a lawyer in Valdosta that a distant connection of mine, a Miss Laura Mason, has appointed me to administer her estate. Such as is left of it, after the war. I don't know the particulars, as yet, but believe that the old lady did manage to put away a sum of gold coins which she kept safe from the Yankees. Her heir—there's a small farm, as well as the money—is her great-niece, Sally Ann Cunningham. I'm informed that Mrs. Cunningham was widowed in the last days of the fighting, and that she has a child. Her aunt would like to see her, before she dies. As I have other business in Valdosta also, I decided to travel there now, and offer my services in accompanying Mrs. Cunningham."

Somewhat startled at this disclosure, since Sally Ann had assumed that her great-aunt had died long since, Julie quickly sent for her cousin. Sally Ann appeared, with Hugh Alexander on one hip, to be introduced to this remotely related young man.

They looked at each other, began to talk over the tea that Pansy brought, and within half an hour the toddling child was climbing into his newly discovered relative's lap. By the time Julie came back to see if they were ready for a meal to follow the tea, the signs were recognizable on them both.

Sally Ann had more color than Julie had ever before seen, and she actually laughed aloud when Hugh Alexander tugged at the newcomer's beard and giggled over its texture.

"Mr. Dallington is kind enough to offer to escort me to Aunt Laura's," Sally Ann said. "I've taken the liberty of offering him hospitality until he can find a wagon and a pair of mules, for sale or for hire. For sale would be best, though, as he seems to think I might well want to live in Aunt Laura's house. The farm is small, but can be made to produce a modest living. And," here her rosy flush almost obscured her freckles, "Mr. Dallington is transferring his own business to Valdosta from Augusta—or, rather, opening a new branch there—and will not necessarily be coming back this way for a long time. So we will need a wagon to carry all our belongings. Not that they're great in quantity," she said, reassuring the young man, who was engaged in removing Hugh Alexander's fingers from his ear, "but when you have an infant, there are a good may odds and ends."

Julie regarded her with mixed emotions. "I'm glad for you," she said sincerely. "But we'll miss you. And Hugh Alexander—whatever will we do, without a child in the house? He's been the only sunshine in our lives for so long!"

When they broke the news to Ellen, the reaction was a fond smile. "How very nice for you, dear. I'm sure you'll be very happy in your aunt's house."

It was not until Sally Ann and her son and Mr. Dallington had actually gone that Julie began to feel uneasiness about the new, contented, complacent attitude of her mother. Ellen, who had for years ordered every minute detail of life and activity at Mallows, no longer issued any orders at all. When a question was put to her, her invariable response was, "Ask Miss Julie," or "Whatever you like, dear." When Miss Dolly complained that the last batch of knitting worsted brought out from town was not of the quality that she was accustomed to, Ellen continued to rock without comment. When Mamie came to announce that the last bushel of salt was almost gone, Ellen concentrated on picking up several dropped stitches until the bewildered Mamie withdrew in frustration.

Julie had wondered, with a blush of her own, how her mother would react to the obvious growing attraction between herself and a young man who had no wealth, no distinguished family, and little to recommend him as a suitor beyond the fact that he had a pleasant personality and had been quick-thinking enough to turn a murder into a tragic accident.

Ellen did not react at all. Although she smiled and spoke to them both in calm generalities, she seemed unaware of the warmth that came and went in Julie's face, the moods of abstraction, the smiles and increasingly meaningful glances across a room.

Although Fritz had as yet made no overt move, Julie grew increasingly certain that he would. She was in no hurry, and as long as they had to wait for a reply to the telegram to the Quinn children's grandfather, Fritz had a legitimate excuse for remaining at Mallows.

Julie had been terrified at the attack by the Confederate deserters; her fears had gone beyond terror at the thought of a forced union with Otis Quinn. She had thought the entire idea of a physical relationship with any man so repulsive that she wondered if it would ever be possible to fall in love with someone, as Valerie had done with Jack Ferris. There was nothing repugnant about Fritz, however. On the occasions when he touched her, Julie felt a stirring of something previously not experienced, something exciting and heavy with promise.

If it had not been for Fritz, and the emotion he roused within her, the house at Mallows would have been unbearable in the weeks that followed. With Valerie gone (and the necessity of worrying about her), and Sally Ann and Hugh Alexander no more than ghosts in the shadows where they had moved and played, and Ellen seemingly content simply to sit and knit and rock, Julie wondered if she would have managed to retain her sanity, without Fritz.

She discussed with him her concern over her mother.

"It's almost as if she isn't there, any more," Julie said slowly. "As if she's gone away, and there's only a husk left. She refuses to think about anything more important than whether or not she should finish a sock in gray worsted when she began it in black."

"She's had a very difficult time," Fritz reminded. "She needs a mental, as well as a physical, rest."

530

"Do you think she'll get over it? Come back to normal?"

"In time," Fritz said. "Give her time." Privately, however, he was by no means sure of that.

When Lallie was fully healed—in body, if not in spirit—she packed her few belongings into a bundle and went to Ellen to say goodbye. It was an awkward parting. Ellen almost seemed not to remember what had happened to Lallie, except that she'd been ill. And, contrary to Julie's expectations, she made no objection to Lallie's leaving.

"Goodbye," Ellen said, smiling with an air of abstraction. And it was left to Julie to urge Aaron to write to them, to let them know where he and Lallie went, and how they got on.

The telegram from Otis Quinn's father-in-law was delivered from town by James Healy and Blossom. Julie, newly perceptive about such things, observed the happy, confident air about Blossom. She wore a rather gaudy dress of cherry-colored foulard, and a string of pearls, and a bonnet trimmed with bobbing artificial poppies.

"It was very kind of you to bring this," Julie said, handing the message over to Fritz to read. "I'm happy that their grandfather is going to come for the children; they're looking forward to going back home with him."

James Healy, who was not quite at home in such a drawing room (they had taken him there in spite of the cold, for the house was falling into a state of disrepair and Julie and Pansy could not quite keep up with the dusting, let alone anything else), cleared his throat and produced a second paper from within his coat.

"I had to come out, anyway, to deliver this. There was an error in the first tax bill, and I've brought a refund from the amount you paid. It should have been nine hundred dollars, not sixteen hundred."

No one present gave any indication that they knew Otis Quinn had manipulated the amount of that bill; and, in fact, the additional seven hundred dollars would really have made little difference to Ellen, since she had had neither amount. It had only been done, Fritz reflected, to put Ellen Stanton under the greatest possible pressure, to assure her cooperation in Quinn's vile scheme.

Julie accepted the refund of Patrick's funds, wondering what she ought to do with it. Nothing, probably, until she heard from Patrick and Valerie. So far, there had been no word except the briefest of notes, assuring them that Valerie was well and that she prayed every day for their well-being and security. What Valerie had not said was more disturbing, since Julie could not escape the sense of guilt in knowing that her own freedom had been bought by her sister's bondage.

There was nothing she could do about it, of course. And nothing to be gained by denying the tiny bud of happiness that promised eventually to bloom into full-fledged love. Julie guarded that bud, nurtured it, and waited with as much contentment as she could draw from it for the remaining problems in her life to solve themselves.

Twenty-Five

Marriage to Patrick Ryan was an odd mixture of pleasures and uncertainties.

Even as she felt that there was something vaguely sinful (disloyal to Jack?) about enjoying his lovemaking, there was no denying that she *did* enjoy it. While a part of her recognized that her pleasure was compounded because of Patrick's expertise in knowing exactly what to do and how to do it (and he introduced some startling innovations into lovemaking that had not been included in Jack Ferris's bedroom performances) and she was convinced that she meant no more to him on a personal level than had the females with whom he must have practiced the erotic arts, Valerie found herself responding with an abandon that would have been gratifying had she not felt guilty about it.

It would certainly make life with Patrick more interesting if they were compatible in bed. And she had no reason, other than that she had so recently felt that she loved him, to feel disloyal to Jack. How could she be disloyal to someone who was already married to someone else?

The important thing, of course, was that she'd saved Mallows, and Julie. She had heard nothing from her family, for they did not know where to contact her. She would have given them the address in Orleans Square, except that Patrick had told her he did not know how long they would be there.

Business affairs took up a major share of Patrick's day. He rose early and dressed without disturbing her; it was a rare day when she saw him again before dinner time. Meals and the housekeeping took little or no effort on Valerie's part; Patrick had hired a cook-housekeeper, in addition to the maid, Becky, and there was an elderly black man who tended the yard and the back gardens.

Although Patrick spent money freely enough, it was not long before Valerie comprehended that his fortune was not definitely assured, once and for all. He headed Georgia Lumber and Turpentine, but he was answerable to his investors, many of whom he believed to have more cash than brains. He had a heavy correspondence with those men in the North, most of which he attended to in the study during the evenings, which left little time for a wife, even a new one.

For the first two weeks she spent in the house on Orleans Square, Valerie kept herself busy with fittings and her own sewing of lingerie, which she preferred not to entrust to unknown seamstresses. Once her non-existent wardrobe had been refurbished, however, time began to hang heavily on her hands. The house was only rented, and there was nothing that she needed or cared to do in regard to it.

She did enjoy walking the streets of Savannah. Even in the early winter it was a lovely city, and she began to have a nodding acquaintanceship with her nearer neighbors.

She did not, however, venture down onto River Street, nor risk meeting old Sophie.

When the note arrived from Nola Ferris, Valerie's first inclination was to ignore it, or at the most to send her regrets. She had no wish to further a relationship with Nola.

Patrick read the invitation with an impassive face. "She's very lonely. Why don't you go and see her?"

Valerie stared at him in disbelief. "You can't be serious!"

"Why can't I? You don't have to see Ferris; go when he's away, during the day. Which is more important, your tender sensibilities, or a poor girl who's dying?"

It was, she thought, a grossly unfair way to put it. It also proved to her that Patrick did not care for her as anything but a bed partner and the heiress to Mallows. Otherwise how could he deliberately encourage her in an action that would certainly eventually result in the opportunity to see Jack?

At night, in the dark, Patrick was a considerate and an ardent lover. During the daylight hours, however, he could scarcely have been less like a bridegroom. He made little effort to spend any time with her, pleading the press of business. And when he did talk to her it was likely to be on the subject of buying wooded property and setting up a mill; he rattled off figures that were meaningless to her, described the process by which the trees would be cut, transported, stripped of their bark, and transformed into lumber. He talked about the men who had provided the financing for this venture that was sure to make him rich, until Valerie began to see their faces in her sleep.

He seldom touched her, displayed no affection beyond casually addressing her as "my love," and in general treated her more like a casual friend than a wife. A *male* friend, Valerie thought with a touch of resentment, except after the lamps had been put out.

She did not think she had any intention of visiting the house on Pulaski Square. She tried not to think about Jack at all, though this was impossible of achievement, and resisted Patrick's suggestion that she befriend Nola.

She was, however, bored to the point of distraction. The rented house had no library to speak of; what books were there consisted of volumes Patrick had acquired on such subjects as operating small businesses, operating large businesses, construction of sawmills, and harnessing water power. All these were less than fascinating.

The newspapers carried stories about people she didn't know, and political maneuverings that incensed her to the stage where it was all she could do to read them.

"Have you signed that dreadful oath?" she demanded one evening of Patrick. She began to read it aloud from the newspaper folded in her lap. "I do solemnly swear or affirm, in the presence of Almighty God, that I will henceforth faithfully support, protect, and defend the Constitution of the United States and the union of the states thereunder, and that I will in like manner abide by and faithfully support all laws and proclamations which have been made during the existing rebellion with reference to the emancipation of slaves. So help me God."

"I've signed it," Patrick said, reaching for a cigar. "Anyone who wants to do business with the Yankees had damned well better sign it. It's mandatory for anyone who wants to hold

535

any sort of office. And it doesn't bother me particularly; why should it? The most slaves I ever owned at one time was four, and I gave them their freedom when I joined the army, so the oath hardly deprives me of anything. I signed it because it was expedient, not because I expected to do any boot-licking to Yankee officials. If I do *that*," he added, grinning, "it will be to soften them up for the kill."

Valerie forgot about the newspaper. "You freed your slaves? Three years ago?"

"Three and a half, more like. Yes, certainly."

"Why?"

"Why? Because I knew I was going off to fight in a real war, and I might get killed. I didn't want them to be confiscated by someone who'd mistreat them, if that happened."

"But what about when you came back? You had prime fieldhands!"

Patrick shrugged and put one foot up on the table before him, carefully, so as not to mar its finish. "Worth fifteen hundred or more apiece, yes. But they wouldn't have been worth anything when I came home, as it turned out. Mr. Lincoln emancipated them, remember? So I'm no worse off by having freed them than if I'd kept them. And been responsible for them during the entire war. Why are you all riled up about signing the oath?"

"Because it's intended primarily to put us all in our places. And vindictively so. And that silliness about having to salute the flag every time we pass one, and so they have them flying everywhere. A person could wear his arm out!"

Patrick laughed. "If that makes everyone as angry as it makes you, the Yankees will have achieved their aim, won't they? They beat us on the battlefield, now they have to make sure we're thoroughly crushed and repentant before they'll take their collective boot off our necks."

"Well, I'm not repentant! What do I have to be repentant about? Or you, for that matter!"

"Hell, I'm not repentant, either," Patrick admitted cheerfully. "Only if it makes the bastards happy to think I am, why, I'll salute their flag and take their oath. The happier they are, the quicker they're going to make me rich. And that reminds me. I'm going to have to run up to New York for a few weeks."

Valerie sat quite still. "And I?"

"You, I think, had best return to Mallows. I'll be moving

around too much, living in various hotels and that sort of thing, to make any sort of life for you. I'll come there when I return, so pack up everything from here. We won't be coming back to this house, I think. If Speers and Grassman can be talked out of this latest idiocy of theirs, so that I can go ahead as I'd planned, there should be funds to buy our own Savannah house by spring. A pity it didn't develop sooner; we might have salvaged Miss Lacy's house."

"Yes," Valerie agreed. "A pity."

Her spirits rose at once, at the thought of returning home. She had written to her mother and Julie, but had not had any reply as yet. She hoped the letter hadn't gone astray; the mails were still chaotic and disorganized, and it was said that the new authorities took the liberty of opening the mail of private citizens to "ascertain the sentiments of the people," yet another abomination visited upon the South by the conquering Yankees.

"When will we leave?"

"A week from Tuesday. In the meantime, I strongly suggest that you go and pay a call on Nola Ferris. They are removing to my house on that day, and I've arranged that you accompany them."

Indignation brought her up out of the chair, fists clenched so that the newspaper crumpled into an unreadable mess. "You couldn't have!"

Patrick was unmoved by her consternation. "It's the only sensible thing to do. They're leaving the same time I go north, and I don't want you to travel all that way by yourself. It's foolish, when you have the same destination, not to take advantage of their protection."

"I came here by myself," Valerie pointed out. "And came to no harm. I don't want to travel with—with the Ferrises."

"I've already made the arrangements." His voice was flat, brooking no opposition. "You can visit Nola first, or join her the morning of the journey, but you'll be seeing her, one way or the other."

She was furious with him, livid with rage at this uncalled-for manipulation. She had, she told herself, no intention of following his advice, although she might well have no choice in the matter of returning to Mallows.

It was quite by chance that, the following day, she found herself on the edge of Pulaski Square. She had gotten in the habit of long walks every day, simply to take up the time, and because the exercise made her feel better. She had been through Chippewa Square and had strolled through the Colonial Park Cemetery, renewing her memories of the times she had played there as a child, and had encountered an acquaintance of her grandmother's, a Mrs. Bell. The old lady was tottering along carrying far too many bundles for two arms to manage, and Valerie had offered to help her home with them. The route led from the cemetery south to Charlton Street, where the Bells lived in a charming house just off Lafayette Square.

The old lady, panting her gratitude, had invited her in for a cup of tea. Valerie had no desire for tea, yet sensed that Mrs. Bell was in need of company, and so she accepted, though keeping the visit to a mere twenty minutes or so.

When she came out again into the afternoon sunshine, her intention was to return home by the shortest route. She could have returned by the way she came, of course. But since she'd already seen that part of town once today, Valerie decided instead to follow Charlton Street across to Barnard, which led directly north to Orleans Square and home.

It also led through Pulaski Square.

When she realized where she was, Valerie hesitated, vexed that she had not been paying any attention. She either had to walk entirely around the block, or pass directly in front of the house which Jack Ferris had rented.

If she'd just been starting out on a walk, instead of rather tired from an already long one, she would have walked the extra distance. As it was, she decided that it was silly to make such a fuss about simply walking past a house because a man she had once loved now lived there. Jack probably wasn't at home, anyway.

It was still somewhat uncertain in her mind, how she felt about Jack. She missed him, she admitted that much at least to herself. Yet, at the same time, she despised him, and despised herself as well for missing him. Maybe, she thought in wry amusement, there was something to the notion that some men had about women in general: that they were rather bubble-headed. She was so confused about so many things these days—Patrick, as well as Jack—that she *felt* bubble-headed.

The square lay before her, empty of horsemen or pedestrians. A cat with tawny stripes strolled across the brick walk and disappeared into the shrubbery. Surely she could manage, too, to pass such a short distance, without coming to any harm.

She had not intended to look up at Jack's house at all. In fact, she made it a point to walk on the opposite side of the square, and to move briskly. As if of their own volition, however, her eyes were drawn to the tall white house with the lacework black railings.

And the maid, Zelda. Zelda not only saw her, she waved and came running down the steps and across the square. "Miss Stanton! Please!"

She could not successfully pretend she hadn't heard that voice. Fool, Valerie told herself. Why hadn't she walked that little extra distance, and avoided this?

"Oh, I'm sorry," Zelda said panting. "It's Mrs. Ryan, now, isn't it? Miss Nola told me to run and fetch you in for tea, ma'am. She saw you and hoped at first that you were coming to visit. And then she thought perhaps you'd forgotten which house . . ." She paused, waiting, evaluating Valerie's response.

"So many white ones, and several with a lot of ironwork," Valerie said, hating herself for giving in to that planted way out.

"Yes," Zelda agreed. "Miss Nola will be so glad to see you."

What else could she have done at that point? Valerie followed the maid across the square and into the house.

Nola was again on the pink velvet sofa. Today she was dressed in virginal (bridal?) white, an exquisite creation that was shirred, tucked, and flounced in lace, a garment surely intended for the boudoir. She lifted a wan but smiling face to greet her captured visitor.

"Valerie, how nice of you to come! I may call you Valerie, may I not?" She hardly waited for Valerie's rather wooden acquiescence. "I was so hoping you'd drop by, now that I'm up and about again."

She seemed to take it for granted that Valerie knew of a recent indisposition. While Nola gave orders to the maid, Valerie let her heavy shawl slip off her shoulders and sat in the same chair she'd taken before.

"I'd been so afraid my illness would delay our leaving for Mallows," Nola said, when Zelda had gone. "But Jack has pronounced me fit to travel as scheduled. I'm so glad you're going with us. Jack is marvelous company, but of course since you're a native Georgian, you can tell me a great deal more about this part of the country than he can. But listen to me, running on about myself, when it's you I want to hear about. I didn't realize you were going to marry Mr. Ryan, when we met before."

No more did I, Valerie nearly said. She sat and listened to congratulations, feeling a twinge of regret that her marriage was not as Nola pictured it.

Nola did have a tendency to chatter. It was obvious, however, that she tired very easily. After fifteen minutes, Valerie escaped on the excuse that her hostess was in need of rest.

Well, she thought walking briskly toward the rented house on Orleans Square, at least Jack hadn't showed up this time. But how in God's name was she going to manage, traveling in his company for three days on the trip home?

When it came down to the time, it turned out to be four days rather than three, because they had to stop more often than anticipated so that Nola could rest.

Patrick's leave-taking had been disappointingly casual. When the carriage Jack had hired for the journey drew up in front of the house, Patrick hauled out the part of Valerie's luggage that was to travel with her. (The rest would be sent on by a slower conveyance.) He bent to brush a perfunctory kiss across one cheek, then handed Valerie up into the enclosed vehicle.

"I'll join you at Mallows, probably in a month's time," he told her. If the prospect of being parted from his bride for such a prolonged period was disturbing to him, he managed to conceal it admirably.

Valerie, aware that Nola understood nothing of the marital situation, was embarrassed that Patrick did not at least make some pretense that there was affection between them, for Nola's sake.

Patrick and Jack Ferris exchanged a few brief businesslike words, and the signal was given to the driver, an old black man addressed as Clayton. With a slight lurch, the journey began.

Certainly traveling in an enclosed conveyance had advantages over riding a horse. When it rained, as it did most of their first two days on the road, there was no trickle of icy water down the back of one's neck and soaking into one's clothes. All Valerie had to do was sit back on a comfortably padded seat and endure the trip.

An endurance feat it was. For Nola and Jack sat opposite

540

her, and she must watch them together. For hours every day, minute by minute, as Jack looked after his ailing young wife, Valerie had no choice but to observe.

She hadn't seen or talked to Jack since the first day of her stay in Savannah. She had told herself that she had no desire ever to see him again. She had even, most of the time, convinced herself that he was a complete cad and that she hated him.

Now it was impossible not to be aware of the small services he performed for Nola: seeing that the rugs were tucked around her for warmth, that there were cushions behind her back, that when she needed rest or food a stop was made. He did not do it for show, for her or for anyone else; after only a few hours Valerie reluctantly admitted that Jack was genuinely fond of his wife, and concerned for her.

Like a sister, he'd said. A beloved sister.

Valerie had thought her emotions concerning Jack to be buried; they were now painfully resurrected. She sensed that he was at first self-conscious about Valerie's observance of these intimacies. They were necessary, however, and he was adept at them, and after a time she didn't think it continued to bother him.

It bothered her, however. Watching him with Nola, knowing that she had been his wife all those times Valerie and Jack had been together. She hadn't even had the wit to ask if he were married, had taken it for granted that he was not, and the realization of her own foolishness did nothing to ease her aching heart.

To make matters worse, the maid, Zelda, traveled with them, sitting beside Valerie. She, too, paid almost constant attention to her mistress. If it had not been so obvious that Nola was seriously ill and in need of their ministrations, it might have been possible to resent her. As it was, Valerie could feel nothing but sympathy.

If Zelda read anything on Valerie's face, it was not because Valerie did not battle at all times to conceal her emotions.

When Nola felt well enough to manage it, she kept up a conversation with Valerie regarding the Georgia countryside. The colorful fall foliage had not yet completely vanished, and by the third day, when the sun shone again, the land through which they traveled was appealing enough to draw Nola's admiration time after time.

It was clear, however, that the young woman's strength

was severely taxed by the journey. When they stopped at night at some country inn, Jack Ferris had to lift her out and carry her inside. Valerie, alone in her own unfamiliar bed, would lie awake imagining them together in the adjoining room, wondering what they said and did.

She didn't for a moment consider that they might be making love: Nola was too ill for that, and Valerie believed that what Jack had said was true. He did not sleep with her, did not make love to her. Yet the image would not be put down, of the two of them lying close, naked, in the darkness.

As the miles fell away behind them, Valerie knew an increasing and unwelcome certainty.

She did not hate Jack Ferris, at all.

Had she made a mistake? Marrying Patrick, instead of waiting for Jack, as he'd asked her to do? Neither of them could help what would happen to Nola. There was nothing to be done to prolong her life, and Jack was doing everything any loving husband could do to make her last days easier.

Yet there was Mallows. Jack could not have done anything to help her there, not as long as Nola lived. And if Valerie had not acted to save Mallows, she could not have saved Julie, either.

She was glad when Nola, growing more tired, lapsed into long silences, silences unbroken by the rest of them. And the last day, as the road passed through more familiar territory, Valerie's spirits finally began to rise. They were almost within sight of the chimneys of Mallows. They were almost home.

Twenty-Six

The first thing she noticed, as she stepped through the wide front doorway into the entry hall, was the absence of the chandelier.

Valerie stood looking up at the empty place where the exquisitely beautiful crystal prisms had, for all of her life, reflected the candlelight and sunlight by turn. Incredible, that it was no longer there.

Julie, with a glad cry, rushed into her arms, and they hugged as if they'd been separated for years.

After the first damp-eyed greeting, Valerie lifted her face again to the ceiling. "Where is it?" she demanded.

The happy color receded from Julie's cheeks. "It's a long story. I'll tell you later. Come and see Mama, maybe it will make her better to know you're home."

Julie was tugging her off toward the stairs, but Valerie stopped "Why? Is she ill?"

Julie hesitated. "Not ill, exactly . . ."

"What's that mean? Is she ill, or isn't she?"

"Well, ever since . . . for months, now, or no, I suppose it's only weeks, but it *seems* like months, she hasn't done anything except sit in the upstairs sitting room and rock and knit."

"Mama?" The image of Ellen rocking and knitting refused to form in her mind. "Julie, tell me."

"Come and see her first. Don't be shocked, just . . . just be natural, and see how she takes it. Then I'll have Mamie fix us some tea, and we'll talk. I'll tell you everything. It will take a long time, and it won't be easy."

She had not been inside the house for five minutes, and already Valerie felt the change in its atmosphere. "Where is everybody?"

"Sally Ann and Hugh Alexander have gone to Valdosta, to her Aunt Laura's. We miss the baby terribly. It isn't at all the same without a small child in the house."

"They've gone? Permanently?" This time the image *was* vivid, of the small smiling child who had clung to her, whose hand she had held as he learned to walk, who had sat on her lap and enjoyed being sung to. She felt betrayed, as if it were her own child who had been taken by someone who had no right to him.

"Yes, I expect permanently." Julie decided the details on that could wait, too. "And Blossom is keeping house for a Mr. Healy, in Reidsville; if I read the signs correctly, she'll be Mrs. Healy by spring, or maybe by Christmas."

"Where's Grandma Lacy?" Valerie demanded, then braced herself as her sister moistened her lips before replying.

"She—she had a seizure, the night you left. Lallie found her, and she couldn't speak, or move. She's been that way, ever since."

"Dear God! What have you done for her?"

"There didn't seem to be much that *could* be done."

Julie had put out a hand to Valerie's arm. Valerie brushed it away and moved quickly for the stairs. "Have you had a doctor?"

"There isn't one, excepting old Dr. Church, and he isn't up to such a long ride any more."

Valerie had left her behind, hurrying through the house that seemed to echo with the emptiness. She pushed open Lacy's door and entered the room, striding toward the bed, where the tiny figure lay propped against the pillows.

Hattie turned with a wide smile. "Miss Val! Welcome home!"

Valerie scarcely heard her. "Grandma, it's me, it's Valerie! What's happened to you?"

The papery old eyelids slowly lifted, and Lacy stared at

544

her. The eyes were the same; they were all that was. The old lady had shrunk until she seemed lost in the bed, a child-size creature who looked a hundred years old.

Valerie's heart contracted and her eyes stung. She leaned over the bed, capturing the blue-veined hands in her own. They were cool and lifeless.

"Grandma, do you know me? Valerie?"

Lacy blinked.

"She does know me!" Valerie said, glancing at her sister and the Negro woman behind her. "Has anyone tried to help her? To move, to sit up, to talk?"

"She too sick for that, Miss Val," Hattie affirmed.

"She's not," Valerie said angrily. "She only needs help. I'm here, Grandma Lacy. I'll help you! You'll get better, you'll be able to speak again, and to walk! I know you will!"

Lacy's mouth twisted in a grotesque effort. The sound that she uttered was not intelligible, but Hattie exclaimed in astonishment. "Lord God, she tryin' to talk!"

"She *will* talk." Valerie said it firmly, because she had to believe it. "I have to go and see Mama, now, Grandma Lacy, but I'll be back."

Again Lacy's features contorted with the effort of producing a sound. Valerie squeezed her hands and kissed her. "See, you're already getting better! Stay with her, Hattie." It struck her, then. "Where's Lallie? Isn't she helping with Grandma?"

She was getting used to the way Julie moistened her lips when the news wasn't good. "She and Aaron have gone to New Orleans."

"Aaron!"

"Yes. He came back for her."

"And Lallie just left, with Grandma like this and Mama— however she is?"

"That's a long story, too." Julie had known it would eventually be her lot to explain all these things to Valerie, and now that the time had come she hardly knew how to go about it. There were so many things, and some of them so terrible.

"All right. After I see Mama," Valerie agreed.

Even Julie's warning had not prepared her for her mother. Ellen looked up when Valerie spoke, smiling.

"Hello, Mama. I'm back."

"How nice to see you, darling." Ellen continued to rock, her hands busy with the growing gray worsted stocking.

Ellen looked perfectly all right. Healthy. Normal. Until one looked into her eyes.

Valerie swallowed, appalled. Did Ellen even know she'd been away? Dear God in heaven, what had happened here? She cast a frantic glance toward Julie.

"Did you get my letter, Mama? About marrying Patrick Ryan?"

For an instant there was puzzlement on Ellen's face, and then it cleared. "Oh, yes. I think Julie told me."

She might have just agreed that Valerie had let the cat out. When Julie touched her arm, Valerie withdrew with her from the room, her alarm sending a quavering sensation through her.

"I think you'd better tell me everything," she said.

She managed to sit through most of the recital without undue interruption. Until Julie got to the part where Ellen had shot and killed Otis Quinn.

Valerie's jaw went slack. *"Mama shot him?* I don't believe it!"

"You can't imagine what a nightmare it was." Julie sat with her hands curled around the cup of tea, warming them. "There was a . . . a hole right in the middle of his forehead, and then Pansy started screeching that the minister was coming, and then, thank God for Fritz, he thought of what to do . . ."

Valerie heard her out, incredulous, accepting at last only because of the evidence that remained. At the very end, when Julie lapsed into silence, Valerie struggled to gather her wits. "And what about you? You and Fritz?"

Pink stained Julie's cheeks. "Is it so plain? That I'm in love with him?"

"Yes. I'm glad," Valerie said sincerely. "I was afraid that you'd never fall in love, that you'd think of all men like the animals those soliders were, and Major Quinn . . ."

Julie didn't want to think about that. "Fritz isn't rich or anything, Valerie. Not the sort of man, I suppose, that Mama would have approved, in the old days." There was tacit understanding between them, that what Ellen thought—if, indeed, she thought about anything—no longer mattered. "He wants to go west. He says there are thousands of acres for the taking out there. All a man has to do is claim them. He wants me to go with him."

546

She didn't have to ask. "You're going."

"Yes."

"It will be a hard life, compared to what you've known at Mallows."

"Will it?" For a moment there was a surprising maturity and toughness in Julie's small face, things Valerie had never before seen there. "You mean, like doing my own laundry, and cooking, and things like that? I've told him I'm not very well prepared to be a settler's wife, but I'm willing to learn. Is there any reason why I can't learn to be a woman, the same as thousands of other females have done?"

"No, of course not." Valerie's voice was very soft. "When do you intend to leave?"

Relief shone palpably in Julie's eyes. "Now that you're here, I think we could go anytime. I couldn't leave Mama and Grandma Lacy and Grandma Dolly alone. Would you mind so very much, Val, if I did go, very soon?"

"No, of course not," Valerie assured her.

But later the hurt of it made her ache, the thought of losing Julie. And the thought of those who remained behind, in her charge. Her mother, and her grandmothers. Everyone else gone.

Julie and Fritz were married on the seventeenth of November, 1865, in a simple ceremony in the drawing room at Mallows.

Ellen was there, smiling, accepting kisses from both her daughters and her new son-in-law.

"Wish me happiness, Mama," Julie begged, and Ellen continued to smile.

"Of course I wish you happiness, darling," she said. "I've always wished you happiness."

There was no festive supper, no wedding cake. Mamie had made a cake that other time, for the wedding with Major Quinn. Julie could not bear the thought of another wedding cake.

They had gathered household supplies into the wagon Fritz had bought. This left them little cash, but they were not dismayed by this. No one (except for Patrick Ryan and the Yankees) had any cash, Fritz said.

Jack and Nola came for the ceremony, although Nola tired so easily that they had to return immediately afterward to Patrick Ryan's house. It would have been impossible not to invite them, impossible to snub poor Nola. It meant so much to her to come, for even half an hour.

And then the wagon rolled away, and Valerie fought tears and panic, watching them go.

Dear God, the house was empty!

She tried to talk to Ellen, to bring her out of the trance-like state in which she existed, untouched by anything around her. She spent hours with Lacy, moving her arms and legs, talking to her, and gradually there, at least, she drew some response. Lacy tried to speak, and the day that she actually said "Hungry," Valerie and Hattie broke into cheers.

"She's going to learn to walk again, too," Valerie assured the black woman. "You wait and see."

She had determined, on the journey home, to resist the efforts of Nola Ferris to make of her a confidante. Now, however, Valerie could not remain detached from the residents of Patrick's small house. To begin with, Nola already regarded her as a friend, despite Valerie's attempt at rigidly controlled aloofness on the journey. (The trouble was, Valerie recognized, that she was incapable of maltreating even an animal, and she continued to think of Nola as a small wet kitten.)

The day after their arrival home, a note arrived from Nola, a note of thanks, and a plea that Valerie would visit at any time. She sent back a message with one of the black children to the effect that she'd found things at home in a state of turmoil, and that she must attend to those matters and therefore could not visit. Nola was persistent, however, and Valerie knew with an unhappy certainty that she wouldn't be able to hold out against her forever.

And then there was the matter of her own loneliness. All her life Mallows had been full of people. Now, it echoed with past laughter and voices that one did not quite hear. She found herself pausing, looking about, waiting for Julie, for Henriette, for Sally Ann, and little Hugh Alexander. She missed the baby fiercely, missed the amusement he had brought as he learned to walk and then to speak his first baby words.

She missed, as well, her grandmother and her mother. For though they were there in the house, confined one to a bed and the other self-imprisoned within her own mind, Lacy and Ellen did not seem to be in the house at all. Dolly Mallow was the same as she had always been. Soft-voiced, mildly complaining, uninvolved in the tragedies around her, except insofar as they affected her own comfort.

Valerie began to think rather wistfully of the suppers she and Patrick had shared in the rented house in Savannah. The talk had been on a different level from what she was accustomed to, and she could not honestly claim to be fascinated by the growing of trees and the lumber and turpentine business. Yet Patrick had been young and vital and enthusiastic about those things. He had *talked* to her.

At Mallows, one might go all day without hearing the sound of another voice, these days. It fell to Valerie to decide what work would be done about the place—thank God Patrick would soon arrive to take on *that* chore!—and to arrange for meals. But though there was plenty of food put by to see them through the winter (and she had donated generously of it to Julie and Fritz) there was little pleasure or even practicality in planning elaborate meals when she was the only one in the place who cared one way or another what she ate.

She had more or less ignored the first two notes of invitation that Nola sent. The third one came delivered by Jack Ferris's own hand.

Valerie stopped on the threshold of the library, taken aback at seeing him here. In the very room where they'd first made love. She nearly backed out, involuntarily, but Jack turned from contemplation of the fire and came toward her. If she didn't want to talk to him in Pansy's hearing, she'd have to enter and close the door, which she did.

"I think it would be better," she said, maintaining a façade of calm, "if you didn't come here."

"Valerie, please. Come and see Nola. She's ill, and lonely, and she needs female companionship. Please."

It was disconcerting to be so close to him, to be alone with him. That he still had the power to attract her physically was something she'd learned on the trip out from Savannah. Valerie felt stifled, yet strong in her resolve.

"How can you ask that of me? To go there, to *that* house? After what happened there between us?"

In spite of herself, her breathing had quickened, betrayed by the rise and fall of her breast.

"I don't ask it for me. And I can't even consider your feelings in the matter. Nola's dying, Val. I thought it might help her, to face a less severe winter here, but it's too late.

She's never going to survive to see the spring in Georgia, the beautiful season I wanted so much for her to enjoy. Don't be so cruel as to let her die alone, here far from the rest of her family. She likes you. She needs you. Please come and see her."

There was no mistaking the earnest sincerity of his plea. It *was* Nola he was concerned for. His wife. He saw Valerie's struggle and added the final argument available to him. "I'll stay out of your way. I'll arrange not to be there when you come. You won't have to see me at all."

For a moment more Valerie resisted.

His final soft "please" was, however, too much for her.

"All right," she agreed.

"This afternoon? I'll leave the house at two. I won't come back until I see you leave."

And so she was committed.

It was the first of what were to become almost daily visits to the attractive little house where she had learned the ecstasies of loving. There would never be a moment in that house, Valerie thought, when she didn't remember how she and Jack had made good use of Patrick's bed.

Yet she saw at once the truth of what he said about Nola. The young woman's fair skin grew more transparent hour by hour. She tired so quickly that she no longer even tried to get up for a part of each day, receiving Valerie instead in her bedroom. At least Jack had not installed her in the room where he and Valerie had met; she was grateful, she supposed, for that small blessing.

Still, the house evoked painful memories and Valerie continued to dread going there. After the first visit, she took to carrying with her a book to read aloud to Nola. It saved them both from making conversation, on the excuse that talking was too much of an effort for the sick woman. A novel was out of the question: Valerie feared they would not ever finish it. Instead, she read poetry and short essays.

Nola seemed grateful, and at the end of each reading Valerie would escape with a sense of fleeing a prison. Back to Mallows, which had become a prison of a different sort. Though she almost never saw Jack, except from a distance, there always remained the possibility that she might, and it continued to disturb and upset her even while her gaze raked the top of the ridge, watching for him on his solitary walks.

On the third day of December, a messenger came to call

her to the cabin where Gilly lived with her young son. She had gone into labor.

Valerie remembered vividly the night she had attended Nora and had had to call Jack Ferris in to save her and the baby. How ironic, that the physician could help everyone but his own wife!

There was no need for trepidation this time. Gilly delivered quickly and easily, another fat boy. Valerie left her to the ministrations of the other black women, emerging from the cabin to find Thomas lounging restlessly on the doorstep. He jumped to his feet and conveyed his nervousness by plucking at his clothes and his hair.

"She all right, Miss Val?"

"She's fine. She has another boy."

"Ah, Miss Val. Somethin' I been meanin' to ask you. 'Bout Gilly. I wantin' to marry up with her, Miss Val."

Valerie thought of Gilly's tender years, and dismissed them. Better she should be married than promiscuous. There was, however, Chad.

It was as if the youth read her thoughts. "Chad, he ain't comin' back," Thomas told her.

"No? How do you know that?"

His voice was quiet, so that it would not carry through the open doorway behind her. "He dead. He try to rob a white man, and they done strung him up. I ain't tol' Gilly, yet, but if she have me, I like to marry up with her. I got your permission, Miss Val?"

Her permission. Not her mother's. It was but another mark of the shift in responsibility at Mallows.

"Yes, of course," Valerie said after a moment. "But you'll have to wait a month or two. Until she's recovered from this."

A grin split the black face. "Yes'm. Thank you, Miss Val."

The following morning, when Valerie rose from bed, she was halfway dressed when she was overtaken by nausea. She barely made it to the basin beside the water pitcher.

When she had wiped her mouth, she sank trembling into a chair, drawing a quilt around her against the chill of the room. She was never ill, she thought. Even during the worst deprivation of the war, she had not been ill.

After a few minutes the queasiness subsided. She stood up

and reached for her stockings, and then the realization—or, more truthfully, the suspicion—struck her.

Could she possibly be pregnant?

For only an instant the icy blade of fear flashed through her; all those times she had been with Jack, and nothing had happened. And after only a month with Patrick . . . ?

She had thought her monthly distress simply postponed because of the extreme fatigue induced by four days of travel from Savannah. Now, however, the absence of menses took on a new significance.

A baby? Could she really be going to have a baby?

For a moment she stood in the middle of the cold room, shivering, unaware of the temperature because of the warmth generated within her. A baby of her own, like little Hugh Alexander. Patrick's baby.

Oh, please God, let there be a baby! She wanted to run, to tell someone, but there was, even had she been sure, no one to tell. She doubted that her mother would comprehend the importance of an impending birth. Grandma Lacy could not respond, and Dolly Mallow had no enthusiasm for anything beyond her own comforts.

Still, not being sure was not enough to dampen her own surge of joy. When Hattie had left the room for Lacy's breakfast tray, Valerie leaned over the bed and took both of her grandmother's hands.

"Grandma, do you hear me?"

The dark eyes met hers steadily.

"Grandma, I'm not sure yet, but I think I'm going to have a baby."

Something sparked in the old eyes, surely it did. And then, with little strength but quite definitely, Lacy squeezed Valerie's hands in return.

"You did it! Grandma, you're getting better!" Valerie kissed her, and again she was certain of a returning pressure from the fragile little hands. "I tell you what. I'm going to have Hattie help me get you into a chair, and we're going to take you into the sitting room for a while. Would you like that?"

Once more, that faint, barely perceptible pressure.

Happiness rushed through her veins. Grandma Lacy well enough to get about again, beginning to be able to make her wants known in the garbled speech that took so much effort, and the promise of a baby about the house. Patrick had said he wanted a family, and though she had previously given little thought to it, Valerie knew that she did, too. Mallows would ring again with the sounds of childish merriment; the shadows would be banished. Maybe a child would even bring Ellen out of her placid, vegetative state.

To add to her jubilance, Valerie came downstairs to discover that a neighbor had brought mail: a letter from Julie, and one from Patrick.

She ripped open Julie's first, and scanned the single page. The bliss of a happy newlywed emanated from every word. Fritz, Valerie saw, grinning, was wonderful. He could not be faulted in Julie's eyes. Although they had not traveled much beyond the borders of Georgia at the time the letter was mailed, Julie felt she had learned a good deal about the tasks of a housewife; her only regret was that her hands were not as pretty as they had been, what with washing in cold streams and having nothing in the way of creams to smooth and whiten them. She sent her love to everyone, and would write again at the next opportunity. Fritz said they would undoubtedly be passing through Vicksburg and would they please, please, write to her there, all the news.

For a moment Valerie sat, tears in her eyes, wishing that she could share with her sister in person all that each of them was going through. Julie's obvious delight in her Fritz made Valerie a bit more aware of that lack in her own life, but at least Patrick wasn't an Otis Quinn.

She put Julie's letter aside, to be reread later, and picked up the one from Patrick.

It was briefer than Julie's, and relatively impersonal. He had nearly finished his business in New York, was going on to Washington for a short time, and expected to arrive back at Mallows by mid-December. He hoped that she was well, and signed himself, *Yours, Patrick.*

He would be there at Christmas. Christmas, the holiday which had always had the most meaning for the family, and now seemed so difficult to face. She doubted that anyone other than herself would note the date, or care about it, one way or the other.

Well, *she* cared. And for the sake of the child to come—already, she was assuring herself of the reality of the child—Christmas must continue to be an important event at Mallows.

She spoke to Mamie about the making of cakes and pud-

553

dings, and told her that Mr. Ryan would be arriving before long.

"I think we'll open up the dining room and we'll have dinner there when he comes. Dressed up, and the best china and silver. Like in the old days."

Mamie grinned. "That be fine, havin' a man to cook for again. Women, they don't eat enough to make it worthwhile. You leave it to me, Miss Val. I feed Mr. Ryan like in the old days."

Valerie was walking a week later, with Jack Ferris, when Patrick returned.

Twenty-Seven

She had not meant to talk to Jack, nor he with her. Both had fallen into the habit of long walks; it gave them something to do, and, for Valerie at least, eased the tension of inactivity to some extent.

Physically, she had never felt better in her life. She seemed to exude energy, to the point where her mother remarked mildly, "Darling, do stop moving for a moment. You wear me out to watch you."

The lovemaking between herself and Patrick had reawakened the needs Valerie had tried to suppress. While she continued to feel guilty about those yearnings, Valerie could hardly deny their existence. So many times Patrick's accusation rang in her head: that what she'd felt for Jack was lust, not love. And when she lay restless in bed at night, she could hardly deny, either, that she longed for a man's touch, his mouth, his caress. When she dreamed, it was usually about Jack; but often when she opened her eyes after the lovemaking in the dream, it was not Jack's face she saw above her, but Patrick's.

And whichever it was, the man in her dreams, Valerie could not put aside the guilt.

She had found that if she walked briskly for several hours

a day, she would more easily fall asleep at night. This didn't prevent the dreams; it did, however, eliminate the additional torment of physical longing, of the compulsion to run her own hands over the breasts and the thighs that had known the touch of lover and husband. And while reason told her that it was her own body, and that she had as much right to touch it as any husband, her girlhood training left her ashamed of her failure to resist that temptation.

And so, on a bright and sunny morning when a skim of ice made the puddles crackle underfoot, she was swinging along with an unladylike stride on the main road when she encountered Jack Ferris.

He didn't see her, nor she him, until they were only yards apart. Briefly, Valerie broke stride when Jack appeared around the curve in the road. And then, because it seemed foolish to attach too much importance to a chance meeting, she continued, more slowly.

"Good morning," Jack said when he was within arm's length of her. He smiled. "You have a wonderful glow about you today."

She could hardly say the same for him. He looked tired, and his shoulders sagged, although he was as darkly good-looking as he'd always been.

She sought refuge in a neutral topic.

"How's Nola?"

Jack sighed, thrusting his hands into his pockets and staring moodily at the red dust that covered his boots. "Not well. Neither of us got much sleep last night. It grows harder and harder for her to breathe."

"I'm sorry," Valerie said softly.

He looked up at her, then, with a change of expression that immediately put her guard up. He was going to leave the subject of his wife, and speak on a more personal level, and Valerie knew with a desperate intensity that she did not want him to say it, whatever it was to be.

"Valerie—" he began.

And at that moment they heard the horse coming at a gallop, and they both froze.

They were standing there, a yard apart, when Patrick thundered around the bend in the road and reined in beside them. His hair looked redder than ever in the sun, and he was bigger than ever, too, mounted on the magnificent stallion.

556

"Patrick! You're earlier than we'd expected," Valerie greeted him.

Patrick's eyes flicked at Jack Ferris, then back to her. "So I see."

A dull flush of resentment climbed her throat and flooded her face. "We were both out walking and just happened to meet."

"Of course," Patrick said, carefully noncommittal. "How is your wife, Ferris?"

"Very gravely ill, I'm afraid," Jack told him.

"I'm sorry to hear it." Patrick dismissed the other man without doing anything more than turning his head. "Have you concluded your business so that I may offer you a ride home? Or do you prefer to finish your walk?"

Damnation, Valerie thought. What a miserable foot to get off on, when she had sincerely been looking forward to his return!

"We had no business to conclude," Valerie said, damning Jack Ferris, too, for having been about at precisely the wrong moment.

When Patrick reached down a powerful arm to hoist her up before him, she allowed herself to be swung onto the stallion; they left Jack in the road without a farewell. She was conscious of quickening senses, held against him that way. How much nicer it would have been, had he found her comfortably ensconced at Mallows at some acceptable activity, rather than with Jack!

Patrick urged the horse to a canter, and they moved down the oyster shell drive, between the row of massive oaks with the swags of grayish moss that swayed at their passage.

Once arrived at the front door, Patrick dismounted and lifted her down. His touch was electric, although she knew that he was angry and that probably the sensations he stirred within her were as he'd said: a simple manifestation of the part of a woman who needed a man.

He stepped inside the door and lifted his eyes at once to the ceiling far overhead.

"What the hell happened?"

"It fell." She hadn't even decided whether or not to tell him the circumstances under which the chandelier had been smashed; could she trust him to keep it quiet, if he knew the truth?

557

Patrick, too, was immediately aware of the changed atmosphere. "Where is everybody? This place feels like a tomb."

She told him, succinctly. It *had* been like a tomb, although Patrick Ryan's presence in the entry hall had already subtly altered that.

Pansy came through the doorway from the dining room and gave a whoop of recognition. "Mr. Ryan! Welcome! We been lookin' forward to you comin' here, like Miss Val said!"

"Thank you, Pansy. Do you suppose you could rustle up something for a hungry man to eat? I've been on the road since before daylight."

Her grin widened. "You sit down, Mr. Ryan, and I bring you somethin' as fas' as we can fix it!"

"It doesn't have to be elaborate. Just substantial," Patrick urged. He stood in the doorway of the dining room, seeing Mallows now with a proprietary eye. "I'd forgotten how shabby it's all getting."

Valerie was stung by the implication that they hadn't properly cared for it.

"There hasn't been any money to repair or replace anything for more than four years."

Quite unexpectedly, Patrick grinned. "Well, there is, now. Not as much as there'll be later on, but enough to get started, I think. By this time next year, I want Mallows to look the way it did in the old days, only better. Which room do you want to start on? Aside from replacing the big chandelier?"

Taken off guard, Valerie stammered. "Why, the—the d-drawing rooms are probably in the worst shape. And they used to be so elegant, before they were used as a hospital ward."

"All right. Shall we consult with your mother, about the color scheme?"

She hadn't told him about Ellen. What, after all, was there to tell? That she no longer took any responsibility for anything of greater magnitude than what she should put on in the morning? And that she cared very little about that? Valerie tried to think of a way to prepare him, but she could not. Perhaps it wasn't as bad a situation as it seemed to Valerie; perhaps he would not find Ellen Stanton strange, at all.

Ellen did not rise when they entered the upstairs sitting room; she did smile. "Why, Mr. Ryan. How nice to see you."

Behind him, Valerie tensed. Would her mother even remember that Patrick was now her son-in-law?

558

He bent to kiss her extended hand, as unself-consciously as if he'd been kissing ladies' hands all his life. "Miss Ellen. You're looking very well. How are your headaches?"

"I scarcely ever have one any more," Ellen said. "Please sit down. You, too, darling. It hurts my neck to look up at you great tall things." Her smile softened the mild rebuff.

Patrick sank gingerly onto a fragile enameled and gilded chair. "Miss Ellen, we're going to start refurbishing the house, and Valerie thinks that we should begin in the drawing rooms. Do you have a preference as to colors?"

"The drawing rooms have always been pale yellow," Ellen said, in the tone of one reminding another of some obvious fact. "Trimmed in white, with gold."

Patrick's gaze slid toward Valerie, then returned to her mother.

"Yellow, white, and gold. All right. I'll have the men out here right after the new year to begin on it."

"That will be nice. I hope there won't be too many men, though. Making a lot of noise and mess."

"I don't think they'll bother you unduly," Patrick told her.

It was only when they'd left Ellen that he demanded an explanation. "What's happened to her? It's as if there's no one there any more; as if nothing matters to her any longer."

"Maybe nothing does," Valerie said softly.

"But why? What the hell's the matter with her? Your mother was one of the strongest, most dynamic women I ever met. She didn't just suddenly become like this—a wisp of fluff, uncaring about anything or anybody! Only a few months ago, Mallows was the most important thing in the world to her, more important even than her family. What happened?"

Thus pressed, Valerie told him about Otis Quinn.

"She'd lost my father, she'd lost Evan, she felt more or less responsible for Charlotte, all those people who died—the pressure about money, it was all too much for her. And then, I suppose, when she'd convinced herself that it was right to coerce Julie into a marriage with Major Quinn, and learned at the last minute how he'd raped and abused poor Lallie—" Valerie drew a deep breath. "She had to have known how close she came to subjecting Julie to something like that. A man who'd treat any woman that way, even a slave, would he be any less vicious with his wife? And so she shot him, and killed him."

That Patrick was as stunned as she'd been herself was obvious. For once he didn't try to mask his own emotions.

"Killed him! God Almighty, I'd never have believed it. And then, afterward, she just slipped off into a pleasant world of her own where there are no deaths, no poverty, nothing to be afraid of any more."

Valerie swallowed against the lump in ther throat. "Do you think she'll ever come out of it? Ever be herself again?"

Patrick swore softly. "I don't know. I don't know." He drew himself together, hearing Pansy in the room below. "I think my meal is ready. Will you join me?"

She was relieved that they could return to a more prosaic routine, the simple matter of eating and drinking. While they enjoyed Mamie's hastily produced biscuits and ham and eggs and strawberry jam, washed down with the coffee that had been intended for Otis Quinn, Valerie listened to Patrick's tales about his travels.

He had won his backers over to his own point of view in the matter of setting up their own mills, so that the profits from both forests and mills would come into his own (and his backers') coffers instead of being shared by a middleman. He had orders for the first of the lumber, which was even now being cut and would be delivered, for cash, within thirty days.

There was nothing personal in his conversation at all. Yet Valerie was oddly content to sit across the table from him, listening with half her mind while the other half concerned itself with how to tell him about the approaching baby. She was quite sure now that she was pregnant. The morning sickness was mild, quickly over and done with, and there had been no bloody spotting. By midsummer, she would give birth to Patrick's child.

After he had eaten, he expressed a desire to ride out over the plantation, to assess what needed most to be done. "It looks untended, run-down," he said. He did not ask her to ride with him, which she would have enjoyed doing. Well, it was his first look at Mallows as its owner, she thought. Let him enjoy it however he liked.

Strangely, it did not bother her to think of Patrick Ryan as master at Mallows, as it had when the new master was to have been Otis Quinn. Patrick knew Mallows in a way Quinn never could have. Its future was secure with Patrick.

When he had gone, Valerie stood for a moment at her bedroom window, looking out across the winter landscape. The ice had melted and though the ground was hard, she fancied there was a hint of spring. Already, she derided herself, when it was not yet quite Christmas?

How could it be, that the arrival of one man could make such a difference in the house itself? Although she could hear nothing more than she had been hearing during the day, she knew that behind doors there was a buzz of activity and conversation. The master had arrived; preparations went forth for his comfort. And she looked at the bed in which she had slept for all of her twenty years alone, except for those few months when her sister had shared it, and knew that tonight she would share it with Patrick Ryan.

This evening, which could set the pattern for so many evenings to come, must be as perfect as she could make it. Valerie supervised the setting of the table herself, and although there would be only her mother and her grandmother along with Patrick and Valerie, it was arranged as if for the most important of guests. Which, in a sense, Patrick was. He'd paid for Mallows, after dreaming about it and the life it represented, for years. Now it was only fair that the dream come true for him. Valerie had the chandelier lowered, and the candles all lighted, and wished that the time of year was right so there could have been roses in the silver bowl amidst the sparkle and shine of crystal and silver and fine china.

She paused to speak to Pansy, who ran between kitchen and dining room at Valerie's and Mamie's directions. "I'm going to take a bath now, Pansy. Please come up in half an hour and help me dress, and do my hair."

"Yes'm," Pansy agreed. "Tonight goin' to be special, ain't it?"

"Special, yes," Valerie echoed, and hoped to God that it would be *right*, that it would set the proper tone for the life she hoped would eventually evolve with Patrick Ryan.

The water had already been carried upstairs for her. In the old days, she'd have had a servant to help her undress, to hand her the soap, to scrub her back, and to hand her the towel when she was finished. Perhaps now that Patrick was here, and the money would be available for hiring servants as well as renovating, she could have a maid of her own again. She thought wistfully of Lallie, and wondered where she was and if she was happy with Aaron.

It wasn't, however, that she minded doing for herself. Taking a bath, actually, was pleasanter alone. She sank into the sudsy water and felt the warmth of it like silk upon her skin; when she emerged, rosy pink and feeling luxuriously clean, she wrapped herself in the big towel and stood before the fire to dry.

She would wear the apricot velvet for the first time this evening. She had laid it out herself, along with fresh undergarments. She wished she had perfume to dab behind her ears, and didn't realize that her own clean scent was perfume enough, nor that her own beauty more than made up for the lack of jewels.

If she could make Patrick care for her, Valerie thought, if this could truly be a satisfying marriage for both of them, beyond the fact that they mutually possessed Mallows, why, surely there was the reasonable expectation of contentment. For Patrick as well as for herself.

She didn't step in front of the floor-length mirror until she had put on the gown. Pansy had appeared to help with her stays (she wondered how long it would be before she should discard them, because of the baby) and to do up the back of the dress. Winter had faded some of the tan acquired during the months when she'd chopped with a hoe in the cotton fields like a slave, and her own excitement and anticipation brought becoming color to her face. Pansy was not as good as Lallie had been with a brush and combs, but she'd done a creditable job tonight; Valerie's auburn hair was swept high on her head and waved softly where the combs held it back from her face.

"Lordy, Miss Val, you sure is pretty!" Pansy exclaimed. "That dress *exactly* right for you!"

Valerie thought so, too. She had never looked better. She had a fleeting moment of regret that Jack would probably never see her in this gown, the most beautiful she had ever owned.

There was a tap on the door and Valerie called out, "Come in," without turning from the mirror, taking it for granted that it was one of the women with a message or a request for orders. She heard the door open and said, as much to herself as to Pansy, "I wish I had something to wear with it—my pearls would be nice, if we hadn't had to sell them. I don't even own a trinket."

"Maybe I have something that will do."

She spun, as did Pansy, at the deep male voice.

562

"I picked it up in New York City," Patrick said, crossing the room and bringing a small box out of his pocket. "Turn around, and I'll put it on for you."

Obediently, pulses racing, Valerie turned back to face the mirror. Patrick brought the black velvet ribbon around her throat, and she saw that the brooch fastened to it caught the lamplight with a sparkle and a brilliance beyond that of the finest of Mallows' chandeliers.

Her breath caught in her chest and she put a finger up to touch the bauble. "Diamonds?" she murmured. "Real diamonds?"

"Will it do?" Patrick asked. "Or is it too gaudy?"

"Gaudy!" She echoed the word, her laughter tremulous. "It's the most exquisite thing I've ever seen!"

She swung to face him, her skirts brushing against him, and now it was Patrick who drew in a breath and forgot, for a moment, to release it.

"My God," he said, "but you're beautiful."

"It's the dress," Valerie said, "and the diamonds, of course."

"Good thing you wearin' that dress now," Pansy observed approvingly. "Fit like your own skin, and another month or so and you won't squeeze into it no more . . ."

The servant stopped, clapping a hand over her mouth, as she caught her mistress's expression. "I sorry, Miss Val. I never thought but what you already tol' Mr. Ryan—I couldn't help knowin', what with you throwin' up ever' mornin' for weeks now."

The very promising look that had been upon Patrick's face was gone, wiped as clean as a rag clears a slate. He spoke to Pansy, but continued to look down at Valerie. "You may go, Pansy."

"Yassuh," Pansy said, frightened, and quickly withdrew, closing the door behind her.

Valerie made the effort to continue breathing. Damn the fool girl, anyway! If only she'd broken the news to him herself, on her own!

"Is it true?" Patrick asked, and the animation had gone from him. "Are you carrying a child?"

"Yes."

The word hung between them and then Patrick's words struck her with the violence of a physical blow. Because he

563

looked directly into her eyes and asked, "Is it mine, or Ferris's?"

She could not believe she'd heard him correctly. And then, when the full impact of his question flooded through her—he'd known, all along he'd known about Jack, known she wasn't a virgin when he married her—Valerie slapped him, as hard as she could, across the face. He could have stopped her. He didn't. The imprint of her hand was a red stain on his cheek.

"Mine," Patrick insisted, "or his?"

"I haven't been near Jack Ferris in months," she said, her throat so dry that it was a miracle she could speak at all. "Not since I went to Savannah with Grandma Lacy to sell her house." Perhaps she should not have admitted to anything, but the compulsion was in her to be truthful, entirely truthful. "There is no possibility at all that the baby is anyone's but yours."

He stared at her, a thin white line around his mouth; she could see it even though the mustache covered part of it. A muscle twitched in one cheek, and for a moment she thought he would hit her. He did touch her, but not to strike her. Patrick scooped her up and carried her toward the bed, avoiding the bathtub that still sat in the middle of the floor, and put a hand to the neck of her dress when he had laid her down. Valerie cried out in alarm. "Don't tear my dress! Please, let me take it off!"

For the space of seconds, the fate of the apricot velvet hung in the balance. And then, with a savage movement, Patrick turned her over and undid the tiny buttons, jerking the garment free and tossing it to one side.

Valerie offered no further resistance, except that when his face came down over hers she spoke one more time. "The child is yours, Patrick! I swear it, I swear to God it's yours!"

And then his mouth covered hers and speech was impossible. She had anticipated, from the wild light in his eyes, that Patrick's lovemaking would be brutish, as well. Certainly that first kiss was a searing one, violent enough so that her lips were bruised and her teeth cut into the tender flesh. Instinct told her to give in, to let him have his way with her until the explosion within him had dissipated, until reason returned.

After the first kiss, however, there was no brutality, only passion, in Patrick's touch. And when he had finished, when they both lay spent across the bed, Valerie was the first to re-

564

turn to reality. Her combs and pins had come loose, her hair was all about her face, and she heard the bell signaling that dinner was about to be served.

She sat up and pushed back a strand of hair. "Good grief, what will they think if we don't go down to dinner on time? And how will I get my hair back up?"

To her amazement, Patrick laughed.

"Let them think anything they like. We may miss a few meals altogether once in a while, who knows?"

She sat beside his supine figure, looking into his face. "You do believe me, don't you? About the baby?"

He sobered at once. "Yes. I believe you."

"And you're happy about it? Please, Patrick, want it as much as I do!"

"I want it," Patrick said, and pulled her down for a kiss that burned through her so that she was afraid the entire business would begin all over again, while the others sat in the dining room and wondered what had happened to Valerie and Patrick.

She pulled free with a gasp. "Help me. Help me dress, and do something with my hair."

"It's one thing I never imagined, about living at Mallows," Patrick said, a few minutes later. "That I'd be expected to fill in for lady's maid and hairdresser."

"Hurry," Valerie told him.

Again Patrick laughed, and Valerie suddenly felt as if her spirit soared in an ecstasy as overpowering as the sexual kind, as if all inhibitions were lifted, all fears vanquished.

And all, she thought wonderingly, because of Patrick.

If anyone noticed that they were late for dinner, or that Valerie's coiffure was slightly lopsided, no mention was made of it. Mamie had outdone herself, with baked ham and roasted turkey and all manner of side dishes from the supplies they had worked so hard to preserve. She had even managed a cake, with sugar icing, and Patrick went along to the kitchen after the meal to compliment the cook. Valerie didn't join him, but she heard Mamie's pleased chuckle and Pansy's accompanying giggle.

The amusement died abruptly when there was a rap on the kitchen door. Then Valerie, who had been poking at the pins that threatened to loose a cascade of auburn hair, stepped to the inner doorway, too.

The old man who stood there was the one who had driven Valerie and the Ferrises out from Savannah. Clayton pulled off his cap and stood just inside the door, blinking in the lamplight.

"Yes? What is it?" Patrick asked.

"I brung a message," the man said, twisting the cap. "Dr. Ferris, he say to tell you, Miss Nola done die, an hour ago. She just couldn't breathe no more."

"I see. Does he want some help?" Patrick asked after a pause that lasted a fraction too long.

"No, suh. Don't need no help. He just want you to know."

And Valerie stood with her hands knotted at her breast, and wished with all her heart that the news had not come now, tonight.

Twenty-Eight

That Nola's death had shattered the mood she thought had existed between herself and Patrick, Valerie could not doubt. How much of the dampening of their spirits was because they had both liked the girl, and how much because both were now aware that Jack Ferris was free, she could not judge.

She didn't know, herself, how she felt about Jack. Her initial fury in learning that he had married a girl of wealthy family, that he hoped that Valerie would marry him after that girl had died, had long since evaporated. She believed that he had married Nola in good faith, and that though he had not been faithful to her, he had been kind and loving. And one could consider infidelity a lesser sin than it might have been if Nola had been able to be a real wife to him. God knew that Valerie was aware of how strong that need was, for the physical expression of love.

Patrick said nothing of the matter at all, but although he shared Valerie's bed the night of Nola's death, he made no move to touch her. Nor did he do so in the days immediately following the simple ceremony which they all attended before Jack accompanied his wife's body back to her own family for burial.

While it was true that there was plenty for Patrick to do,

567

both at Mallows and with his lumber interests elsewhere, there would surely have been time, if he'd wanted it, for some private moments with her, Valerie thought. She had hoped that when Jack was gone from Ryan's house, it might make a difference between her and Patrick. That did not seem to be the case.

Georgia Lumber and Turpentine business frequently took Patrick away for a day or two at a time. Again the house was too big, too empty, although in the early weeks of the new year the promised workmen arrived with paint and brushes and everything needed to restore Mallows to its former elegance. Patrick left the decisions on wallpaper and upholstering fabrics mostly to Valerie; they had tried to interest Ellen in helping with the selections, with very little success. Ellen would look at whatever was put before her and say, "That's very pretty, dear," about virtually everything.

Nothing whatever had been said about Jack Ferris returning to Georgia. Valerie did not even know that he had returned to Patrick's house until old Clayton delivered a note, which he specified must be given into her own hand.

She stared down at the paper, feeling almost as if it singed her. What did he want? Why, after she'd begun to forget about him, did Jack Ferris again insinuate himself into her life?

The message was short and simple. *Valerie. Please meet me this afternoon on the path at the far end of the quarters. As always, Jack.*

As always? Disquieted, she read it again, then spoke decisively to the waiting black man.

"Tell Dr. Ferris that I'm sorry, but I can't comply with his request," she said, and withdrew into the house. She should have added, *not this afternoon, or ever,* Valerie thought. She was married to Patrick. She could *like* being married to Patrick, if she could ever again draw him out of that reserve that had rested upon him since the night of Nola's death. There were rare moments when they seemed in complete accord, when they laughed together, when Patrick's lovemaking was almost as unrestrained as it had been the night he'd learned about the baby. Rare moments, but holding the promise that eventually such moments would be the rule, rather than the exception to it.

The following day, Pansy arrived in her bedroom while she

568

was sorting garments to be taken away, to make more room for Patrick's belongings in the chifforobe.

"Yes, what is it, Pansy?"

"Dr. Ferris downstairs," Pansy said. Her face was carefully blank, but her eyes were full of lively curiosity. No doubt the entire lot of them knew she'd been in love with Jack, and had speculated about their relationship. "He say he want to see Miss Val."

"Tell him that I'm indisposed," Valerie stated.

"Yes'm," Pansy said.

"Oh, and Pansy. If he comes again, I will continue to be indisposed. I don't wish to speak to him."

"Yes'm," Pansy agreed.

That ought to have been the end of it. It wasn't.

Patrick had been gone for four days, on business for Georgia L & T, when another message came, hand-delivered, and this time it wasn't a brief note.

Valerie opened it and began to read, then dropped into a chair as her legs became unsteady.

My dearest Valerie:

If you refuse to see me, then at least read this letter. I will be leaving, within a few days, as I've taken care of all the business here, and the rest of Nola's belongings are ready to ship to her family. I will not be returning home myself. I have been offered a business proposition in California, and I intend to take it.

I love you. I have loved you from the moment I first walked into that magnificent entry hall and saw you standing there. I know that you love me, too, or at least that you did once. I know that you married Ryan in order to save Mallows, and because I wasn't free to marry you. The responsibility for Nola is behind me. And I still love you.

Valerie darling, please come with me. If Ryan won't give you a divorce, then we'll simply take new names and a new identity in the west, and no one need be the wiser. Surely two people who love each other as we have done should not be shackled to anyone else for a lifetime. You may have considered me to be weak, to love one woman while legally tied to another. I hope you'll consider that I wasn't weak, but compassionate for a young woman who never hurt me in any way, and that you will believe I can be strong enough for both of us now. Let Ryan have Mallows, if that's what he wants. Don't ruin your life, and mine, by continuing as his

*wife. I'll be praying that you will meet me tonight, at mid-
night, prepared to travel. If you can leave your trunk on the
side veranda, after dark, I'll have it picked up ahead of time.*

It was signed, *Your own loving Jack.*

She felt giddy and half sick. She had taken it for granted
that her marriage to Patrick was irrevocable, and she had
done her best to make it a genuine and worthwhile union.
While Patrick—what did Patrick think about it?

She read the letter through four times before she put it
down on her dressing table. Divorce. Or change their identi-
ties, and go west. West, perhaps, to where Julie and Fritz
were. Leave Mallows forever.

She didn't know how long she stood there, looking down
on the familiar bold scrawl, before she made her decision.

She didn't hear Patrick come home. She didn't hear him
come up the stairs. She had been working with Lacy, who
could now speak clearly enough so that most of what she said
was intelligible, and who could not only sit in a chair but also
take a few steps with assistance. When Lacy had been put
back to bed, Valerie crossed the landing and opened her own
bedroom door, only to stop short on the threshold.

For Patrick was there, in the room they now shared on the
infrequent occasions he was at home at Mallows.

She had not expected him for another four days. He
couldn't possibly have gone to Macon, conducted his
business, and come back in so short a time. Yet here he was,
and she'd stupidly left the letter from Jack lying in plain sight
on the dressing table. Patrick turned from it, his mouth flat
and unyielding.

"Is that what you want? A divorce?"

"Patrick—" Stricken, Valerie tried to marshal her forces.
"I've already—"

"Well, I'll give you the damned divorce," Patrick said in a
voice that chilled her through. "But I won't let you have Mallows. Nor anything else. If you think Jack Ferris is enough,
all by himself, go ahead. Meet him at midnight."

He took several long strides toward her, and she thought
for a moment he meant to strike her.

"Patrick, wait." She put out a hand to catch his sleeve, and
he jerked it away from her, as if her touch was contaminating. "Let me explain—"

70

"I don't want to hear any explanations. Take what you can carry, and get out. Don't wait until midnight, go now."

He brushed past her, nearly knocking her down; she did bump her arm sharply on the edge of the door, and she rubbed at it, moving after him. "Patrick, listen to me! I've written Jack a note telling him—"

It was too late. He was gone, taking the stairs in bounds that, for any man less sure-footed, would have resulted in a broken neck.

Heart hammering painfully, Valerie stood at the top of the stairs, hoping he would pause long enough for her to shout after him. He did not. The front door slammed behind him so hard that she heard one of the panes of glass in the fan-light crack.

She was trembling. She returned to the bedroom and, ignoring the letter from Jack, walked to the desk where she had sat to write her reply. She folded the paper over, lighted the candle, and melted red wax to drip in a blob on the back of it, sealing it. There was an ache in her throat that made it difficult to swallow, and she brushed impatiently at the tears that brimmed over.

Carrying the note, she went down the stairs and out onto the side veranda, looking about for something with which to anchor the message. A large stone, painted white so as to blend with the floor of the porch, sat handy for propping open doors in summer weather. It would serve to keep the letter from blowing away until someone came looking for it.

She had turned, shivering in the chill winter wind, when she heard heavy feet inside, and Patrick came through the doorway to meet her. The wind made his hair stand up in colorful wisps, and his face was grim.

"I've changed my mind," he said.

Unconsciously, Valerie twisted at her wedding band. "Patrick, I have to talk to you."

"It doesn't matter what you say," he told her. "You're my wife. My legal wife, and you're carrying my child. I won't let you go. You don't know what he is, what sort of life he's offering you. You've been sheltered and pampered all your life, and you're a complete innocent about people like Jack Ferris."

She tried to insert a word into the spate of emotion he did not attempt to control. "Patrick, I wrote—"

"Listen to me. Listen." He put his hands on her shoulders

and shook her a little. "I thought maybe I could make you fall in love with me. I knew I didn't have a hell of a lot of chance of it, you being the lady you are and me nothing but a Georgia backwoods overseer, but I've loved you for so long, wanted you for so long— Well, I thought if I saved Mallows for you, maybe I could make you see— I know you think you love Ferris, but for a while, when he was still married to Nola, I thought you were beginning to like me a little. And then when she died, I could see this coming. That he'd want you, and that you'd want to go."

He didn't give her an opportunity to use the breath she'd inhaled.

"Well, I still think I can make you forget him, given a real chance. So I'll tell you what I'll agree to. You stay here with me, until after the baby comes. Say, until it's at least six months old. And by then, if you don't have any contact with Ferris, if you try to make it work out as a marriage and it doesn't, you're convinced that it can't, I'll let you go. Not take the baby, I can't do that, but I'll let you go, if it's hopeless."

Something that had been swelling excruciatingly inside her chest suddenly burst and spread its hot viscous fluid through her.

"Patrick, Patrick, stop talking and listen to me!"

"It doesn't matter what you say. We haven't had a fair chance yet, to make it work—"

"No. No, we haven't." She pulled away from him and snatched up the note with Jack Ferris's name written across it. "Here, read this! Read it!"

Patrick took the paper and broke the seal. He glanced at her suspiciously then read the words aloud, very slowly.

"Jack:

I cannot go away with you. I'm in love with Patrick, and I carry his child. Goodbye."

"I've been in love with you for months," Valerie told him softly, holding her hair with both hands to keep it from whipping across her face: She scarcely felt the cold wind because she was so intent on Patrick. "I didn't realize it myself, for sure, until Jack was free. And then I knew that I could *never* go with him, anywhere, ever. I thought you'd married me only to get Mallows, and I intended to try to make you care for me—"

She broke off, unable to say more.

She moved into his opened arms, and he closed them around her; for a long time they clung together, there on the side veranda of Mallows, with the wind blowing their hair into each other's faces, the red and the auburn.

Valerie closed her eyes and leaned against him, thanking God that the words had finally been spoken, that for once in her life she'd done the right thing.

Maybe her sins had been forgiven. Somebody up there did listen to prayers, after all.

GREAT ROMANTIC NOVELS

SISTERS AND STRANGERS PB 04445 $2.50
by Helen Van Slyke

Three women—three sisters each grown into an independent lifestyle—now are three strangers who reunite to find that their intimate feelings and perilous fates are entwined.

THE SUMMER OF THE SPANISH WOMAN
CB 23809 $2.50
by Catherine Gaskin

A young, fervent Irish beauty is alone. The only man she ever loved is lost as is the ancient family estate. She flees to Spain. There she unexpectedly discovers the simmering secrets of her wretched past . . . meets the Spanish Woman . . . and plots revenge.

THE CURSE OF THE KINGS CB 23284 $1.95
by Victoria Holt

This is Victoria Holt's most exotic novel! It is a story of romance when Judith marries Tybalt, the young archeologist, and they set out to explore the Pharaohs' tombs on their honeymoon. But the tombs are cursed . . . two archeologists have already died mysteriously.

8000

MASTER NOVELISTS

CHESAPEAKE
by James A. Michener

CB 24163 $3.95

An enthralling historical saga. It gives the account of different generations and races of American families who struggled, invented, endured and triumphed on Maryland's Chesapeake Bay. It is the first work of fiction in ten years to be first on *The New York Times Best Seller List.*

THE BEST PLACE TO BE
by Helen Van Slyke

PB 04024 $2.50

Sheila Callaghan's husband suddenly died, her children are grown, independent and troubled, the men she meets expect an easy kind of woman. Is there a place of comfort? a place for strength against an aching void? A novel for every woman who has ever loved.

ONE FEARFUL YELLOW EYE
by John D. MacDonald

GB 14146 $1.95

Dr. Fortner Geis relinquishes $600,000 to someone that no one knows. Who knows his reasons? There is a history of threats which Travis McGee exposes. But why does the full explanation live behind the eerie yellow eye of a mutilated corpse?

8002

JOHN UPDIKE

RABBIT RUN   24031-2 $2.25

TOO FAR TO GO   24002-9 $2.25

THE COUP   24259-5 $2.95

"The best novelist of his generation"—*Harpers*

"No one should need to be told that he has a mastery of language matched in our time only by the finest poets."
—*Granville Hicks, Saturday Review*

8009

of what he does. Quite aside from the fact that poor Charlotte is not responsible, any female should have the right to protect herself against men like that."

No questions were asked. When they assembled in the big room where Sally Ann and Lacy and the baby now slept, Valerie realized at once that everyone took it for granted that she'd been in bed, asleep, when the shooting took place. Hugh Alexander, nuzzling contentedly against his mother's shoulder, for once drew no other attention than that. The women's faces were chalky in the candlelight, and if there was guilt mixed with shock on Valerie's countenance, no one noticed it.

She sat on the little gold brocaded sofa between Lacy and Ellen, contributing nothing to the conversation, picking up details from what the others said. She was as horrified as the rest of them, yet she did not want to talk about Charlotte and the man she had killed. She didn't even want to listen to the rest of them talking about it. She wanted to withdraw to complete privacy and think about herself.

Herself and Jack Ferris.

Henriette turned a tear-stained face toward the trio on the sofa. "What are we going to do? How can we save Charlotte?" she begged.

None of them had any answer to that.

Blossom was the only one who guessed what had actually happened. Had the stupid fool mistaken her directions? Had he gone to that poor crazy girl instead of to *her*? She didn't say anything. This was no time to draw attention to herself; she knew perfectly well that she risked being thrown out in the cold, with nothing but the clothes on her back, if Ellen Stanton knew she had had any assignation in Ellen's own house. There was no risk now, however; if she simply kept her mouth shut, there was no way anyone could know that Private Waynerose had been on his way to Blossom's room and mistaken the way. Yet, she, too, was shaken. She would be more careful in the future, Blossom decided.

While the others sat debating Charlotte's future, planning ways to prevent her being tried and possibly sent to jail, Charlotte took matters into her own hands. When the man appeared in the doorway, she had not hesitated for a moment. And she had had no trouble at all in pulling the trigger to stop him.

She sat, apparently unseeing, as two of the orderlies cleaned up the evidence of the man's death at the foot of her bed. "Looked right at us, she did, but like she was blind, didn't see nothing at all," as one of them later said. "It was creepy as hell." They gathered up their stained rags, and closed the door. There was no way to lock it; a man would have to be left on guard in the hallway outside Charlotte's room.

As soon as the men had gone, Charlotte rose from the bed and padded across the room to the chiffonier. Her groping fingers closed around the mother-of-pearl handle of the dueling pistol Ellen had had hidden in her own belongings, and not yet missed. This time her hands did not shake. There was no need to work up her courage. Charlotte stuck the barrel of the pistol into her mouth and squeezed the trigger.

Twenty-Five

Major Otis Quinn addressed his subalterns in a voice tight with fury. "My official report will state that the woman shot Waynerose, with the pistol that she had managed to conceal in her room, and then *immediately* turned the same weapon upon herself. Captain Ferris, you will add your signature to mine. And if the matter is ever questioned, you will each of you," he raked their faces with the icy glare, "tell the same story. Both of them are dead, and there is nothing to be gained by going into explanations of how one of my officers allowed his weapon to be stolen, and did not report it until it had been used to kill one of my own men. Is everyone clear on this matter?"

It would have taken a brave man to dispute Quinn's version of the affair. Certainly Robert Hoskins had no desire to do so. He felt nothing but relief that he was apparently not going to be court-martialed, although he had no illusions about the major's attitude toward him. Thank God the war was nearly over, and once he'd been mustered out he'd never need to see any of these people again as long as he lived.

Captain Ferris signed his name in a bold hand, testifying to the veracity of the report, with no qualms whatever. There was such a thing as truth, and there was such a thing as stupidity, and when they turned out to be one and the same, why, it was only sensible to prevaricate to whatever degree was necessary to extricate oneself from the mess.

As far as the Yankees were concerned, the matter was closed.

There was guilt, though not as much as she might have expected. When the appalling evening was over, when Henriette had been sedated and put to bed in Blossom's room (much to Blossom's dismay) and all the others had gone to bed as well, Valerie lay in darkness. Julie had elected to sleep up there with Henriette, in case she wakened in spite of the drug Captain Ferris had given her. Blossom had, quite unceremoniously she thought, been told to take a few things over into Lallie's room.

It didn't matter that Lallie's skin was light enough so that a stranger would never have guessed at her Negro blood. Lallie was a slave, and they'd simply taken it for granted that Blossom would move in with her, when the room she had been occupying was needed for someone else. It had been taken for granted that Henriette could not be expected to sleep in the room where her sister and a Yankee soldier had just died. Even Blossom admitted she would not have cared to sleep there, either. Yet why didn't they send Lallie out to the quarters with the rest of the slaves, and let Henriette take *that* room?

Valerie, of them all, was the only one who slept in a room by herself that night. She was grateful for that, because she had a great many things to think about. For a time, when she had put out the candle and lay looking up into blackness, she had, like the others, been overwhelmed by the events of the evening. Two deaths, at a time when they were beginning to believe the deaths were done with, for the most part. Two violent deaths, but they could not completely take away what Valerie had had, for a brief time, down there in the library with Jack Ferris.

Maybe she ought to feel ashamed to be thinking about him, at a time like this. *But I'm alive,* Valerie told herself. *I have waited all my life to be loved by a man, and tonight it happened, and I can't put down the happiness over that. I don't want to put it down; I want to think about loving a man.*

Gradually the horrors of the day faded away, and there return to his wealthy family in New York, and Valerie would get over him.

Ellen did not, however, suspect that the relationship had gone beyond one of languishing looks. Any young woman dreams of romance—herself excepted—and Valerie would naturally be attracted to a good-looking young man, especially one who had tried to do so much for her brother. When Ferris had gone, the matter would be at an end. Valerie was well brought up and intelligent; Ellen totally discounted the hot blood of youth, because she had never felt it and had observed it primarily in the lower classes.

She observed, as well, the way that Lieutenant Froedecker looked at Julie. This was of no concern at all, since Julie was clearly oblivious of it, which was as it should be. Lieutenant Froedecker, also, would soon be gone forever.

Sally Ann received word in early December that her Ward had expired of pneumonia and deprivation in a Yankee prison. She took the news as quietly as she had taken everything else; she was no more than a frail wraith, moving about the house more freely now that some of the enemy soldiers were gone, saying little, eating less. Had it not been for Hugh Alexander, Ellen suspected she would have wasted away to nothing.

As it was, the baby continued to thrive and grow on Gilly's rich milk. He was a happy child, much fussed over by the household of women. One day Blossom brought him in to show him to Evan, who had commented on his crying. Evan, with no hope of ever fathering a child of his own, did not want to look at him, nor talk about him. Blossom did not bring him again.

Lacy continued to share the room with Sally Ann and the baby. It was Dolly who regained the privacy of a separate room when Major Quinn vacated his. And they all regained the upper sitting room; if the remaining officers sometimes joined them there, why, no one was any longer frightened by this. For the most part, Dolly had it to herself, where she sat and rocked and knitted for as long as the worsted held out to work with.

Lallie waited to hear from Aaron. She was worn out from working so hard, and like the other young women, she longed for a better, easier life, and romance. Not the animal coupling of a slave expected to produce another valuable slave, but the affectionate loving that was as possible between a man and a woman of color as between whites. She did not love Aaron, but she depended upon him to get her away from here, to some distant city where she might find love and security and freedom.

Christmas drew near. The holiday had always been a festive one, and even last year, with war raging and nothing to do with, they had managed a celebration of sorts. In December of 1864, they again made an effort. For the baby's sake, they ought to do something, Ellen said. Even if he didn't remember his first Christmas, they should be able to tell him about it.

Gifts were, of necessity, handmade. Embroidered handkerchiefs, stockings, aprons. Small things of no value except for the sentiment behind them. All lavished their maternal instincts upon Hugh Alexander; he was presented with booties and sweaters and a lap robe and bonnets, until Sally Ann had to smile, a little.

Firewood became as precious as food. The snow melted after one day, but the cold remained. The Yankees had made no effort to put in a supply of fuel beyond what would be required for their own needs. Chad and Thomas were set to work felling and chopping trees at the edge of the forest; the pine was quickly burned and did not put out as much heat as hard woods would have done, yet it came more easily to hand.

A few days before Christmas, although the inhabitants of Mallows did not know it, Sherman's forces entered Savannah.

The small Confederate force remaining in the city, under the command of General William J. Hardee, could do nothing to hold the city against the invasion, and prudently withdrew across the Savannah River rather than surrender. This left the city open for the taking.

Its citizens, well aware of the fate of Atlanta, met to consider how they might spare their own city such a holocaust. If Sherman burned the forty thousand bales of cotton sitting in their warehouses, as he could be expected to do, a good part of the rest of the city would go up in flames as well. And so they devised an unorthodox and clever plan. They would greet General Sherman as a guest, offer him Southern hospitality, and make him a gift of the cotton.

What man would burn his own cotton?

The general was offered, as well, the house of Charles
260

Green, on Macon Street, to use as his headquarters for as long as he had need of it. Here, too, the Savannah merchants and cotton factors saved face as well as avoiding inviting the hated officer into their own homes. For although the house was one of the finest in the city, its owner was a British subject, not a Georgian. Mr. Green gave a party for the Federal officers, and with so many of the military present it was not too obvious that few members of local society attended.

Sherman was made welcome, and he would have been a churlish dog, indeed, if he had rewarded Savannah by setting it to the torch. He did not, and the city was one of the few in the South to escape the ravages of war.

The news of the occupation of Savannah did not reach Mallows until New Year's. By then their pitiful celebration was over and forgotten; they had resumed the grim struggle. Only Valerie, of them all, found any reason for happiness, and that was tempered by the knowledge that it must soon end.

The patients in the dwindling infirmary either died or recovered. And the day came at the end of January 1865 when Jack Ferris met Valerie for the final tryst at Ryan's place. He didn't tell her until they lay, warm and sated with their mutual loving, beneath the colorful quilt, late one afternoon. The sunlight streamed through the muslin curtains at the window, and there was the promise of a shared cup of tea from the water simmering over the fire in the kitchen.

Valerie stretched lazily, languorously, turning to him for one last kiss before she left his side to brew the tea, when he drew her close with unexpected violence, burying his face in her auburn hair.

"What is it? Why are you . . . Jack? Jack?"

"We leave tomorrow," he said into her hair. "Fritz is seeing to the loading of the wagons right now. I can't delay any longer, there's no medical reason why the survivors can't travel."

She pushed him away so that she could see his face, momentarily stupefied. "Tomorrow! But you didn't tell me . . ."

"I didn't want to spoil it any sooner than I had to. Darling, you don't think I want to go, do you? I'm a soldier, I have to take orders, and my orders were to follow after Quinn as soon as my patients could be moved. I've already delayed several days longer than I should have, because of you."

Valerie clung to him, willing herself not to cry, not to beg

261

him for some assurance that the parting would be no more than temporary. He had no assurances to give her. The following morning, at dawn, the last of the Yankees rode away from Mallows.